THE DIARY OF
Henry Francis Fynn

Henry Francis Fynn. born 29th March 1803.
Portrait by Charles Bell Esq: Deputy Surveyor General
taken on the 11th October 1844 at the age of 41 years.
Sir Peregrine Maitland departed from Tarka on this day
Lord Mandeville and Capt Maitland Aid de Camps

HENRY FRANCIS FYNN

THE DIARY OF
Henry Francis Fynn

Compiled from original sources

and Edited by

JAMES STUART

formerly Under Secretary for Native Affairs, Natal

and

D. McK. MALCOLM

Lecturer in Zulu, University of Natal

Shuter & Shooter
PIETERMARITZBURG

Shuter & Shooter (Pty) Ltd
Gray's Inn, 230 Church Street
Pietermaritzburg, South Africa 3201

Copyright © Shuter & Shooter (Pty) Ltd 1986

All rights reserved. No part of this publication may be
reproduced or transmitted, in any form or by any means,
without permission of the publishers

First published in hard cover 1951
First edition soft cover 1986

ISBN 0 86985 904 8

Printed by The Natal Witness (Pty) Ltd, Pietermaritzburg
1475L

IZIƁONGO ZIKAMƁUYAZI

UMƁulazi weTheku !
UJoj' ovel' emaMpondweni.
UMahamb' engasayi kugoduka.
UMalamb' adl' iceleƁa lomfula.
(UJojo kathekeli, anjeng' amakhafula)
UMqaqambana ongazulu lidumayo.
Inkonyana yenduna, esisu siƁanzi.
UNsiƁa ziyahluma, ziyavuthuluka.
Umkhathazi wendlovu enohlanya.
Owamith' amazinyana aƁamaningi,
Anda ngemilambolambo,
AƁuy' aƁayizinja, amkhonkotha.
UMashingila ongashoƁa lenyamazana.
Umwancula owasila lubelo,
NgokuƁaleka kwaZulu, wajuƁalaza.
Mhlan' unameva njengemamba,
UƁuhle Ɓangizindlazi zaseManteku,
Zona zimpofazana ngamaphiko.
UMhlophe wakithi, ondleƁe zikhany' ilanga.

THE PRAISES OF MBUYAZI*

Prince of the Bay !
Finch that came from Pondoland.
Traveller who will never go home.
Ahungered, he eats the spinach of the river.
(Finch who does not beg like the Kafirs)
Throbbing as if it were the heavens thundering.
Bull calf with the broad body.
Feathers, now growing, now falling out.
Tamer of the evil-tempered elephant.
Who was pregnant with many young ones,
Who increased river by river,
And then became dogs, and barked at him.
Suddenly turning like the tail of an antelope.
Loosely hung and with tail bobbing,
Retreating from Zululand, he sprinted ahead.
Back which has thorns like the black snake,
Beautiful as the mouse-birds of the Bay,
Which are yellowish on the wings.
Our whiteman, through whose ears the sun shines.

*Fynn's Zulu name.

CONTENTS

PREFACE BY SECOND EDITOR ix

PREFACE BY FIRST EDITOR xi

PREFACE BY THE AUTHOR xv

HISTORICAL INTRODUCTION BY THE AUTHOR . . 1

THE DIARY 35

EPILOGUE 220

ADDITIONAL NOTES ON HISTORY AND CUSTOMS BY
    THE AUTHOR 267

INDEX 327

PREFACE

To add yet another preface to the two already written seems almost unpardonable, but a few words of explanation are necessary. Capt. James Stuart, who began the work of editing the Fynn papers, was after all not able to finish his task, and I was prevailed upon by his relatives to complete it. The bulk of the work had already been accomplished, and every effort has been made to keep intact, as far as possible, Capt. Stuart's work. It seemed, however, that a rearrangement of the chapters was required, and also the inclusion of additional material from the original papers, which I am sure Capt. Stuart would have incorporated had he reached finality. There are also deletions and alterations which I felt compelled to make and for which I accept full responsibility.

The book falls into four parts. Firstly, a short history of events leading up to the period covered by the Diary; secondly, and most important of all, the Diary itself, the most of which was written shortly after the events described therein had taken place; thirdly, an Epilogue, being a brief résumé of events which carries on the account of Natal history up to the arrival of the Voortrekkers; and fourthly, additional notes on the customs and social life of the Zulus as observed by the author during his sojourn amongst them, and written down by him some time later. This latter portion will be of great interest to ethnologists for purposes of comparison with the situation today.

Zulu names have been given in the spelling accepted by present authority, except where the name itself could not be traced, in which case the author's version has been retained.

An extract from a letter written by Mrs. James Stuart, wife of the first editor, is of interest :—

"The following are some of the reasons for the long delay in preparing the Fynn Diary for publication: the fragmentary nature of the Diary; the need for extensive and difficult research work to fill up large gaps in the narrative; the Diary's very poor legibility; Mr. Stuart's occupation with other essential matters and studies, including service in three wars, and then his death on March 8, 1942, followed by the risk of transport to South Africa in war time.

"Very valuable help has been given by the late Col. Denys Reitz, Mrs. Reitz, Mr. Justin C. Stuart, Major R. G. Robertson and Senator the Hon. W. Heaton Nicholls; also the Governor-General the Rt. Hon. G. Brand van Zyl, who brought the manuscripts safely to South Africa in his private aeroplane at the close of 1945. To these and many others the Executors acknowledge a deep debt of gratitude and express very sincere thanks."

I wish to record my deep gratitude to Miss Killie Campbell, who provided for all the necessary typing, gave much encouragement and valuable suggestion, and placed her incomparable library of Africana at my disposal.

D. McK. MALCOLM.

Durban, Natal.
July, 1948.

PREFACE

THE AUTHOR OF THIS BOOK, before and after writing his accompanying preface, passed his life under exceptionally strenuous and precarious conditions, especially during the two decades that followed his arrival in South Africa in 1818, that being the period to which most of his writings refer.

Although many of his experiences are unquestionably of unique interest, although he repeatedly enjoyed unrivalled opportunities of acquiring authentic information, much of it unobtainable by the other Europeans then in the country, difficulty in expressing himself on paper, added to living in abnormal and unsettled times, resulted in such records as he was able to make being for the most part compressed and disconnected. Feeling unable to put together the type of book his travels and adventures obviously called for, he, on various occasions in later years, invited and received the literary assistance of others, notably in the years 1832–34 and 1859–61. But although four or five hands, apart from his own, are observable in his record and although, probably in 1834, a few chapters were composed under his immediate supervision, and others sketched in part, a great part of the material accumulated, especially in later years, was not worked into the single continuous narrative he had it in mind to put forth.

The whole of the extant papers of Henry Francis Fynn were entrusted to me by his late son Henry Francis Fynn, Junior, of Natal, himself an acknowledged authority on native affairs and able to draw on outstanding experiences of his own in the public services of Natal and Zululand. I had, moreover, the benefit of many intimate conversations with the latter about the papers. In addition, he took exceptional pains in affording all the information he could about his father, especially in regard to the later years of his life; of this the fullest use has been made. Moreover, he concurred with me in thinking that every effort, within reason, should be made to piece together all that is of value in the MSS. on the foundation laid down by his father.

Almost everything relating to Natal and Zululand in the years 1824–1836, when all was fresh and beginning slowly to assume its destined shape, is worth preserving, especially when recorded by a man like Fynn—a man who, whilst being a close and competent observer, had rapidly acquired a perfect knowledge of Zulu and cognate dialects, had travelled and lived among natives more than any of his companions, and was by far the best informed as to the conditions of the country and its inhabitants. That this pre-eminence is not being conferred by me alone is plain from such facts as: (*a*) in his well-known and authoritative compilation Bird has accorded Fynn's testimony precedence over that of all other persons who lived in or through the period in question; (*b*) before the first Natal Native Affairs Commission of 1852–3, our author's evidence was adduced at much greater length, and more meticulously recorded than in regard to any other witnesses; (*c*) in *Natal Papers* (pub. 1834)— an authoritative work—its compiler, J. C. Chase, says of one of his (Fynn's) papers,. " the history of the tribes found by Farewell and his party in possession of the country of and around Natal, derived from Mr. H. Fynn . . . can be depended on"; (*d*) Fynn's friend, N. Isaacs, author of the well-known work, *Travels and Adventures in Eastern Africa*, in a letter to Fynn of December, 1832, says: " I am most anxious, my dear fellow, to see your work out. When do you intend to publish ? "

The fact is that Fynn stood and still stands in a category of his own, and it is this freely and unanimously accorded precedence which straightway invests almost everything from him about the earliest days of Natal and Zululand with a distinction and quality of its own.

On his arrival in Natal in 1824 Fynn commenced taking notes, and continued doing so until 1834, for a future history of Natal (evidence, *Native Affairs Commission* 1852–3, Part V, 44). The earliest notes I find are but few, also scanty and disconnected. In or about 1830, however, he set about recording his experiences in the form of a continuous, closely written narrative in a note-book of upwards of 144 pages, the size of the pages being $9\frac{9}{10} \times 6\frac{2}{10}$ inches. But, as I ascertained from the late William Bazley of Umzimkhulu, who was an intimate friend of the author, the above note book is not the original narrative, for that was buried in Fynn's younger brother Frank's grave ! Only natives were present when Frank died, hence, acting strictly in accordance with their national custom, they placed deceased as well as all his personal effects, including

Henry's precious MS. (believing it to belong to Frank) in the same grave. On hearing what had happened Henry felt there was nothing to be done but to re-write the whole of the contents from memory as well as he could. To have opened his brother's grave to recover the MS. would have been a most heinous and unpardonable offence, the act of a sorcerer or murderer, in the eyes of the natives of those days; an unthinkable proceeding. Fynn, as Bazley and Fynn's own son informed me, used to wrap his manuscripts in the ear of an elephant he had himself shot, place the parcel in a sack and on occasion carry it on the heads of natives or pack oxen. It is therefore not to be surprised at that the later note-book, as well as some of the existing papers, should have become damaged and, in places, wellnigh indecipherable—the faintness of the writing here and there may also (apart from its age) be due to the fact that, according to Bazley, when Fynn ran short of ink he was obliged to " use a certain white flower which, when bruised, turned black."

With the idea of publication always in mind, Fynn, in later years, especially in later years after he returned to live in Natal (1859–1861), continued to amplify his material as well as try to make good what he had lost. What in his earlier writings has been but briefly noted he now expanded into full and detailed descriptions. For instance, he dealt in this way with his visit to and experiences in and about Delagoa Bay in 1823; with what occurred when he landed at Port Natal, notably when he journeyed north-eastwards to open up communications with Shaka, i.e. prior to Farewell's joining him with the rest of the party; with what took place at the Royal kraal when Shaka's mother, Nandi, died. All this and other matter which falls within Shaka's reign and that of Dingane was evidently intended to be incorporated and worked into the book he contemplated bringing out, not a series of separate and largely redundant fragments. His experience has been exceptionally widespread, full and privileged, hence called for an extensive, continuous and authentic work. The opportunity for finally arranging and composing that book never arrived, for death carried him off suddenly at a comparatively early age.

If it so be that, after the lapse of a century and more, any new light is thrown by this publication on the early days of Natal, particularly on her admittedly " dark period " (June, 1832–June, 1834), I shall feel the part I have been privileged to perform has not been altogether in vain. The torch was kindled and borne by Fynn; all I have done was to receive it from him, through his son, and bring it to the homes of those for whom it was originally intended. I have even attempted to do more, viz. to " bring back his spirit," as the Zulus would say, to his own kith and kin, he of whom the natives of Zululand, Natal, Pondoland and Kaffraria were proud to apostrophize as:

Jojo, wokhalo, owavel' emaMpondweni
Wahamba angathi kasayi kugoduka.

JAMES STUART.

216 Anerley Road,
Anerley, London, S.E.20.

PREFACE

[Written about 1833.—*Editor.*]

IN SUBMITTING this work to the public the author has been actuated solely by a wish to afford information respecting a very highly favoured portion of the globe, which has hitherto been unknown or neglected. What little has been published respecting Natal is confused or contradictory because hastily written; moreover, it was afforded by visitors whose stay was short, their time occupied by commercial pursuits, whilst ignorance of the language precluded them from obtaining accurate information. However imperfect the present work may be considered to be, the author has none of these excuses to plead in his defence. A ceaseless intercourse with the natives for nine years, possessing the esteem of their king Shaka, the acquirement of their language shortly after his arrival and that matured by subsequent study, combined with his method of committing to paper events at the time they occurred, enable him to hope that his labour will not prove unacceptable to the enquiring public.

Unlike the works of some travellers, it is not heightened by perilous escapes from " flood and field "; it is not interspersed with occasional rencontres with wild beasts or venomous reptiles, but it has been the writer's wish to convey to his readers a faithful, circumstantial and unvarnished detail of incidents as they met his eyes.

A long residence, the author is not ashamed to confess, has endeared the people to him, but he has adhered strictly to plain matter of fact in describing their persons, manners and customs and feels conscious every particular will be fully corroborated by those whose publications may follow his. He sincerely deplores the horrid despotism by which they are governed, to this he imputes the majority of their vices, and ventures to predict when such despotism yields, as it will soon do, to the progress of opinion and civilization, and benefited by an intercourse with Europeans, they will ascend to the rank of a high spirited, brave, ingenious, and civilized people.

The author laments, as sincerely as his readers will conceivably do, his inability to take advantage of the innumerable specimens of mineralogical and botanical research which everywhere present themselves, but trusts the period is not far distant when the productions of Port Natal and the surrounding country will be presented to their view by a scientific hand.

HISTORICAL INTRODUCTION

[When Fynn began to get his writings into order with a view to publication, he felt the need for a brief account of the events in Zulu history immediately preceding and leading up to those in which he was personally concerned, and which are recorded in the Diary itself. He did so in the words of the following pages.—*Editor.*]

Chapter I

IN the year 1824, on my arrival at Port Natal, Shaka was chief of the Zulu country. From his statements, corroborated from other sources, I received the information in reference to events which appear to refer to the year 1750 or thereabouts. It may be necessary to remark that a custom prevails among the tribes which enables the year in which any remarkable event occurred to be traced with some probability of correctness. An annual feast is observed, when the chief eats of the first fruits of the season, prior to which ceremony not even a fallen grain may be eaten under penalty of death.

The country between Delagoa Bay and the Thukela had for many years been a scene of commotion. At the time here referred to it was occupied by various tribes, the two most important being the Ngwane and the Mthethwa, the latter having Joɓe for its chief. The first account given of this chief in any way connected with subsequent occurrences is that, before he had selected from his wives the one who was to be the mother of his successor, he had several sons, of whom it is only necessary to mention two, Godongwana, the eldest, and Mawewe, whose mothers were of different tribes. The friends of Mawewe, with the view of establishing him as the successor to his father, circulated a rumour that Godongwana intended to assassinate his father Joɓe, then an old man. The chief, on being informed of this by the mother of Mawewe, believing the rumour, ordered a party to destroy Godongwana and his adherents. In the attack made on Godongwana's kraal the latter escaped to a neighbouring forest, though severely wounded with an assegai, in the side. He was closely pursued, but one of his pursuers, seeing him concealed beneath a fallen tree, pointed him out to a man close by who, probably wishing him well, requested the other not to speak of it, and immediately called out to those in the rear that further pursuit was useless as no trace could be seen of the fugitive. These then relinquished the search and returned to the chief to report, adding, however, that his son must certainly die of the dangerous wound he had received.

Godongwana, however, lived. He made his way to a distant tribe where his mother's relatives resided. These cured him of his wounds and supplied his wants. Joбe, having heard of his recovery, sent presents of cattle and quantities of brass to the chief of the tribe, requesting him to put the lad to death. Godongwana got to hear of this from his relations and at once made off to the Qwaбe tribe. To that tribe again similar presents were sent by Joбe, which resulted in Godongwana again effecting his escape, this time to the Langeni tribe. He, however, remained there only a short time, for the vengeance of his father still pursued him. Joбe, as on the previous occasion, presented the chief of that tribe with oxen, begging that his son might be put to death.

The chief refused to kill him, fearing it might be made a pretext for a war at some future date, though he consented to allow the Mthethewa tribe itself to surround the hut in which Godongwana was wont to sleep, and to despatch him themselves. Having obtained information as to the hut he usually occupied, a day was appointed for his destruction.

On the evening preceding the appointed day there was a dance. At this Godongwana was present. He was dressed in a fine black kaross, whilst his attendant had on an inferior red one. While at the dance, he was secretly informed of the plot. He replied, "I'll run away no more; I am tired of being hunted like a wild animal." He retired to his hut at the usual sleeping time, and desired his servant to sleep where his, Godongwana's, mat was ordinarily spread, as he himself wanted to ramble with some girls. As it was cold he proposed an exchange of karosses.

When this had been done, he seated himself at a distance and awaited the arrival of the party ordained to kill him. These soon made their appearance and promptly killed, not him, but his unfortunate servant. Being now satisfied that his death was seriously contemplated, which it would seem he had before somewhat doubted, he fled once more; this time to the Mlotha tribe. From there again he went on to that of the Mthimkhulu. Among these latter people he was " picked up " or sheltered by an old woman, who, however, gave him so much work to do in the way of collecting firewood and other domestic duties that he, not again trusting to his good fortune, ran off to a tribe living under the chief Bungane.[1]

It so happened that several head of cattle belonging to a member of the tribe had just been struck by lightning, in consequence of which the herd they belonged to was kraaled at some distance from the owner's residence.[2] Godongwana was employed by the owner, who had naturally small regard for the life of a stranger, to milk those cattle, which he did.

When returning with the milk he was met by the chief Bungane himself, who, after asking and being told from whence he had come, and seeing he was in no dread of lightning, decided to take him under his personal protection as well as into his own service. Godongwana's general smartness, activity and courage, induced Bungane to inquire more particularly into his origin, being convinced he must be superior to the other wanderers they had from time to time come by and sheltered in these parts. After some hesitation he stated who he was. After hearing the story of his various hair-breadth escapes, Bungane, suspecting that he was the son of a chief, consoled him with sincere promises to protect him in the future.

He had not been here long before an opportunity presented itself of his meriting the admiration of all around him. One day he went out with the tribe headed by Bungane and mustered for the destruction of a lioness that had recently made some havoc among their cattle. They were following its spoor with the intention of attacking it. Godongwana asked to be allowed to engage single handed with the animal. The

---

[1] MS. has Pangane.
[2] The segregation of cattle under such circumstances no doubt took place in accordance with native custom.—*Editor*.

offer was at first rejected but his frequent entreaties overcame the objections. The chief promised that if successful he would be rewarded with a kraal full of people and cattle.

On his arrival at the den of the lioness he found two cubs, but she herself was absent, evidently in search of food. Following the track of the mother, he soon met her returning. At this moment he was still well within view of Bungane and his men. He forthwith resolutely attacked and slew the lioness, and afterwards returned with her two cubs.

His astonishing bravery convinced Bungane he was fitted for the management of greater things, and, in consequence of what he had done, he prophesied that he would one day become a great king. When he got back to the kraal at which he had been staying he was given a large present of cattle and made chief of a portion of the tribe.

After a time it was reported that Joбe was dead, and that Mawewe had succeeded him. While this was no more than a doubtful rumour, the attention of the various tribes was excited by the appearance of an *umlungu*, or white man, said to have come from the west and to be endeavouring to reach the sea. This strange phenomenon was represented by those who had seen it as having a human aspect; equipped as Europeans generally are, it was regarded as a marvel; his garment, though so small as to be held in the grasp of his hand, when slipped over his head, covered his body; his hat, which he removed at pleasure, was conceived to be part of his head; his shoes made it appear that he was devoid of toes, and his footprints showing no traces of them confirmed this idea; his heel was so long as to penetrate the ground; he was mounted on an animal of great speed, and carried a pole in his hands which spat fire and thunder, and killed all wild animals he looked at; he was represented as the chief of the diviners, from whom they all derived their powers.

At his presence the natives fled, after killing an ox to be consumed by him, and whenever he entered a kraal beads and brass and other trinkets were left behind where he had been sitting, and found by the natives on their return, he then being at a distance.

Others supposed him to be some superior kind of doctor, possessed of all the magic powers requisite for causing or presenting rain and thunder, lightning and other celestial disturbances. Bungane, more daring than his neighbours, awaited his arrival. During his stay with the chief, the white man actually performed a surgical operation on Bungane's knee, which had for some years been affected in some painful way, but whether he was cupped, lanced or otherwise I could not discover. Whatever the reason may have been for the operation, Bungane appears to have submitted thereto for the purpose of fortifying his army, it being the custom for chiefs to have incisions made in whatever parts of the body that had been recommended by his doctors.

The European of whom this description is given was probably Dr. Cowan, who travelled from Cape Town in a north-easterly direction in the year 1806. This traveller endeavoured for some time, in vain, to procure guides to direct him to the sea coast, then distant nearly 300 miles; and at length was accompanied by Godongwana, who with his followers proceeded to his country with the object of dethroning Mawewe and establishing himself in his stead. Godongwana went in company with the European till they arrived in sight of the sea near the Thukela or Fisher's River.

Arriving in the neighbourhood of the coast, the stranger separated from Godongwana, the latter having his own affairs to attend to, and proceeded towards the sea. He entered a tract under the rule of Phakathwayo, chief of the Qwaβe tribe, who had him seized and put to death, conceiving him to be some unnatural animal.

A belief was prevalent among the tribes on the coast that white men were not human beings but a production of the sea, which they traversed in large shells, coming near the shores in stormy weather, their food being the tusks of elephants, which they would take from the beach if laid there for them, and placing beads in their room, which they obtained from the bottom of the sea.

Godongwana temporarily took up his abode near his own district, when tidings of his arrival began to be rumoured about. It was reported he had brought a large force and was riding on an *injomane*, i.e. the name which had now been given to horses. A song was later on sung by the Qwaβes relative to the European who had come on horseback. News of this presently reached the Mthethwa people, causing them to believe it alluded to Godongwana himself, for, of course, they had not at that time heard of the European traveller. The song, with its literal translation, runs as follows:

> *Ithe catha, catha, wemuka,*
>   *Wemuka naye ;*
> *Wemuka nenjomane.*

> Clatter, clatter, away he goes,
>   He goes with him;
> He is going off with a horse.

The idea of Godongwana riding on a strange animal like a horse, as well as being in possession of a weapon of thunder (a gun), both of which were said to have been brought by him from some distant country, caused a feeling in the minds of the Mthethwa people similar to that which had pervaded the different tribes through which the European had passed. They imagined that Godongwana had, by some magic power, gained an ascendancy over the guardian spirit of his brother Mawewe, and only their assistance was wanting for its complete establishment. Several chiefs visited Godongwana, with Mawewe's consent, to ascertain the truth. They were favourably inclined to Godongwana and, during their visit, formed a scheme for ousting his brother. Mawewe accordingly sent an army, but the chiefs who were acting in the interests of Godongwana purposely kept their forces in the rear of those that were friends of Mawewe. The latter, on coming up to Godongwana and such men as were with him, were at once attacked front and rear, i.e. in front by his own immediate following, and in the rear by many of Mawewe's tribe who had espoused Godongwana's cause. On these two bodies falling on Mawewe's men they simultaneously shouted out Godongwana's war cry. Thus surprised they were soon utterly routed.

On the news reaching Mawewe, he fled forthwith, whereupon Godongwana, without further opposition, became chief of the tribe. His first act was to forbid the name of Godongwana being any longer applied to him, saying that although his father had driven him to undergo the various hardships he had experienced, when he, Joβe, had become a spirit he favoured his cause. His name would therefore have no reference to the distress to which his father had subjected him. And so he ever afterwards went by the name of Dingiswayo—" one in distress," in allusion to having been an outcast.

Mawewe found protection among the Qwaɓe tribe. Dingiswayo demanded that he should be given up but, although frequent applications were made, the chief refused to do so. Dingiswayo now collected several Delagonians who were in the habit of bringing small quantities of beads and barter among his and neighbouring tribes. Such bartering he now claimed as a personal privilege. He rewarded them well for their beads and sent chiefs with presents of oxen and ivory to the Portuguese and to a native chief in their neighbourhood called Makhasane, requesting the former to let him have a company of soldiers to assist him in attacking his neighbour Phakathwayo. He promised Makhasane that, having become the sole merchant, he would trade only with him. He accordingly ordered those of his own subjects who dared to engage in barter to be put to death.

This prospect of opening up a trade with the Zulus, by means of which the Portuguese would be enabled to procure supplies of ivory, became a sufficient inducement to the latter to furnish the military assistance asked for.

Previous to the arrival of these troops, several skirmishes of a trifling nature had taken place between the Mthethwas and Qwaɓes, the latter being resolute in refusing to give up Mawewe. The arrival of the soldiers, however, induced Dingiswayo to use them in making a combined attack, when the Qwaɓes were defeated and driven to the Entumeni forest on the Mhlathuze River. The using of musketry caused widespread terror, as his friends believed that these were the guns Dingiswayo was reported to have brought with him from the west, and which he had only kept back because of having no need for them in his contest with Mawewe. After successive attacks, they were driven to the Thukela River, which, owing to recent rains, was not fordable. Many were drowned in attempting to cross. Phakathwayo himself drove some oxen into the river, and, holding on to the tail of one of them, managed to reach the opposite bank in safety. The chiefs left in command, seeing the danger in which they stood, and being close pressed, condemned Phakathwayo's folly in losing so many lives merely to protect Mawewe. They determined on giving him up to the Mthethwa tribe and did so.

Mawewe was then taken by the Mthethwas into Dingiswayo's presence, who no sooner set eyes upon him than he ordered him to be put to death. Several chiefs who were Dingiswayo's relations pleaded hard for his life, requesting that the chief should treat him in the future as his dog, but Dingiswayo was obdurate and, turning his face to one side, ordered his brother to be taken off and killed.

Dingiswayo began his reign about 1795, being then about 25 years of age. The hardships he had undergone afforded much of that experience by which he endeavoured to profit during the remainder of his life. By means of the strong natural capabilities of which he was possessed, he succeeded in raising himself and his people above all other tribes along the coast, while his ingenuity as a mechanic and the mildness of his rule, although a despotic chief, the ability displayed in the military system he introduced, as well as his universal kindness, so endeared him with the people, that he will be revered by them as long as the Zulu nation exists.

The surprising strides he made in improving the form of government, in war, and in the encouragement of ingenuity led to the supposition that he must have derived knowledge from some other source than intercourse with native tribes; and there is a probability that during the time he was with Dr. Cowan he acquired much information from him, and that on this he founded his plans for the future.

Previous to his reign it had been the custom among all tribes east of Natal, extending as far as Delagoa, to attack and defeat their enemies at night by surprise. They adopted the tactics of closing the doors of the huts, which are very small, burning all the inmates and looting their cattle. When quitting a kraal they would take a child belonging to the party attacked and, thrusting it on a pointed stake set up at the gate of the kraal, leave it as a sad and conspicuous memorial of their victory.

Dingiswayo had not long exercised supreme authority before he suppressed this cruel system, substituting one of his own, which after his decease was acted on by Shaka. This, combined with the latter's vigorous despotism and total disregard for the lives of his fellow creatures, had led to the destruction of thousands and the present desolate state of the surrounding country.

The first act of Dingiswayo was to form his people into regiments and to subdivide these into companies. The regiments were each distinguished by a name, and by the colour of the shields carried by the men. Over regiments and companies he placed captains, the principals being called captains of regiments, the inferior ones captains of companies. He had other regulations which will be mentioned when describing the Zulu forces. He introduced war-dresses of a most imposing appearance to be worn by the chief men and warriors as if he would claim for them rather the respect of their enemies than to terrify them by that appearance of fury which would be supposed to be the vice of the savage. He had no sooner organised this system than he began attacking all the surrounding tribes.

The wars which Dingiswayo began with this neighbours were not at first on a great scale. But they were successful, and spurred him on to more important movements. He assumed a despotic power hitherto unknown. In declaring war, being the first of the native chiefs in that part of South Africa that entered upon hostilities with other tribes in a regular warlike manner, he assigned as his reason that he wished to do away with the incessant quarrels that occurred amongst the tribes, because no supreme head was over them to say who was right and who was wrong; a state of things that could not have been the design of Mveli, the first of the human race.

Dingiswayo's proceedings sufficiently testify that these were really the views that actuated him. The first tribe he conquered were the Qadi. He directed their cattle to be brought to his place of residence and there to be assorted. The oxen were distributed among his warriors, but he restored the cows to the defeated tribe, from whom he exacted submission to his authority. On this principle he continued his conquests. The most important of the conquered tribes were the Qwaбe, Langeni, Qadi, Zulu, Ntshali, Buthelezi, Kuyiwane, Thembu, Swazi and the Xhosa. The only chief he had not subdued, i.e. up to the coming of Shaka, was Zwide, chief of the Ndwandwe tribe.

He gave his commanders strict orders not to allow the whole of the tribe's property to be plundered, and to destroy no more people than was absolutely necessary. His superior discipline, to which neighbouring tribes were unaccustomed, insured his success. After the whole of any tribe's cattle had been taken, the oxen only were retained by Dingiswayo, whilst the cows were returned with an assurance of the victor's desire being to live on amicable terms. He, moreover, requested his people to promote intermarriages with the vanquished and so bring about a general union. He went on to express the opinion that it was not the intention of those who first came into the world that there should be several kings equal in power, but that there should be one great king to exercise control over the little ones. In one instance, they had attacked a tribe which was not prepared to submit without stubborn resistance. During the contest, the Mthethwas destroyed their cooking utensils and broke the stones used for grinding corn. This so exasperated Dingiswayo that, on their return, his warriors were refused admission into his presence, and he went crying about his kraal: " Why have my people broken the pots of the Khondlo ? " By such mild means he conciliated his enemies, upon which several tribes voluntarily became tributary to him and assisted him in his battles. Before long he so enlarged and improved his army as to make himself respected by his friends and feared by his foes.

In the first year of his chieftainship he opened a trade with Delagoa Bay, by sending 100 oxen and a quantity of elephants' tusks to exchange for beads and blankets. Prior to this a small supply of these articles had been brought to that country from Delagoa Bay by the natives. The trade thus opened by Dingiswayo was afterwards carried on, on an extensive scale, though the Portuguese never in person entered his country. The encouragement held out to ingenuity brought numbers around him, liberal rewards being given to any of his followers who devised things new and ornamental. His mechanical ingenuity was displayed in the carving of wood. He taught this art to several of his people.

Milk dishes, pillows, ladles of cane or wood, and snuff spoons were also produced. (Many curious specimens of excessively neat workmanship are still made in the Zulu country.) A kaross manufactory was also established, a hundred men being generally employed in that work. From the presents received from Delagoa Bay he selected some for imitation; and a handsome reward was offered for the production of a chair, a table and milk tureens. All these were made for him and highly ornamented.

The chair was cut from a solid block of wood, and was by no means disgraced by the presence of its model of European workmanship. The chiefs of the Zulus still have chairs made for their use by their own subjects. An umbrella could not be imitated, but the idea of its use was supplied and a shield was substituted for it, and continues to be used by the Zulu chiefs. It is held over them by their servants, and is more suitable and characteristic than an umbrella could be, which must be held by the person using it.

But like other celebrated chieftains, Dingiswayo, after reigning a few years, was destined to experience a sad reverse of fortune. After he had made a series of successful attacks on the tribes surrounding him, there remained the Ndwandwes, a powerful people living to the north-west of him, whom he had not been able to defeat. With the object of vanquishing this tribe, he concentrated the whole of his forces and marched in person at their head. The Ndwandwes, headed by their chief, Zwide, were prepared for the attack. After a very severe engagement, Dingiswayo was taken prisoner and brought before Zwide, who showed every desire to save his life, on condition of his becoming a tributary chief. Such a proposal Dingiswayo rejected with indignation and used such insulting language that Zwide saw no other hope of obtaining a cessation of hostilities than by putting him to death. He was immediately killed. His bowels were opened, his gall was taken and drunk by the Ndwandwe chieftain—a custom which is always adhered to when the bodies of those called kings fall into the hands of their enemies; the idea being that such an observance confers on the successful chief all the virtues and courage of his less fortunate rival. The body was then boiled down and the fat preserved, in conformity with a custom which is said to exist among the chiefs north of Delagoa.

Chapter II

BEFORE proceeding further with the acts of Dingiswayo, it becomes necessary to take some notice of the Zulu tribe under Senzangakhona, one of those subdued by Dingiswayo. At that time the tribe numbered only 2,000 men. Before the date of Dingiswayo's conquests, the custom of circumcision had been general among all Kaffir natives: but he ordered the rite to be deferred until he should have brought under his dominion all within his reach. Owing to this circumstance, circumcision fell into disuse among all the eastern tribes, and the omission of the ceremony extended to all who acknowledged his authority. Among these was Senzangakhona: the rite was postponed in his case. But by long usage it was unlawful that, though a chief might set aside a number of women for a seraglio, he should, until after circumcision, have any intercourse with them for the propagation of his race. Among the females thus set apart by Senzangakhona was Nandi, of whose death an account is given later. She was of the Langeni tribe. She had not been more than six months in the seraglio before she appeared to be enceinte. This caused so much speculation and conversation among the other women that they publicly charged her with having illicit intercourse. On this reaching the ears of Senzangakhona, his conscience told him it was brought about by his favours. To avoid the disgrace attendant on such a proceeding, from his not having been circumcised—which would have disgraced him in the estimation of his neighbours—he assured the other women that Nandi was not pregnant, but suffered from a complaint called *itshaka* or looseness of the intestines, which was the cause of the swelling. This set the matter at rest and seemed to the women to be conclusive. Senzangakhona was now circumcised and Nandi in time produced a son, who, owing to the circumstance just mentioned, was called Shaka, in imitation of the word *itshaka*. Nandi was of a violent, passionate disposition and during her residence with Senzangakhona she frequently got into fits of outrageous violence. In consequence of this, she was on the point of being killed, but escaped with severe threats. This, however, seems to have produced little or no effect, as, one day, in the presence of Senzangakhona, she struck one of his leading men a severe blow over the head with a knobstick, when Senzangakhona, still disposed to save her, ordered her from his presence, never to return. He shortly afterwards married several other wives, some from the seraglio, others from his neighbours. He appointed Bibi[1] his queen, who bore him a son, Sigujana.[2] By the other wives he had numbers of sons and daughters, among them Mhlangane, Dingane and Mpande.

On leaving Senzangakhona, Nandi went to her father, Makedama.[3] She was not there long before she married a commoner of the Langeni[4] tribe named Gendeyana (sometimes called Ngendeyana), by whom she had a son called Ngwadi.

When Dingiswayo heard of Shaka he invited him to come under his protection, saying that, as he had been driven from his father, and had become an outcast wherever he went, Shaka should be under his especial care. Shaka accordingly went, when he was put under the care of Ngomane,[5] commander-in-chief of Dingiswayo's army.

He distinguished himself at an early age, by his courage and self-command, being always the first in attack, and courting every danger. He was known by the name of Sikiti, also by that of *Sidlodlo sekhanda* (the honour of the heads of regiments). Various were the acts by which he signalized himself in action, much against the express wish of Dingiswayo, who objected to his taking an active part in battle, considering it unnecessary for a prince to expose himself to that extent. On such occasions, in consequence of his keenness to fight, Dingiswayo would order his shield to be taken from him. Shaka, however, always managed to steal another from one of his companions. He soon became known among the neighbouring tribes as " Dingiswayo's hero." With Dingiswayo he remained until the year 1816, when his father Senzangakhona died. Sigujana, the rightful heir,[6] was now about to become

---

[1]Bibi, daughter of Nkoɓe (alias Sompisi), chief of the Ntuli tribe (section of the Bele tribe).—*Editor.*
[2]MS. has Isecogaan.
[3]A mistake—should be Mbengi ; Makedama was son of Mgabi, Nandi's eldest brother.—*Editor.*
[4]Gendeyana was of the Qwaɓe tribe.—*Editor.*
[5]Son of Mqomboli.
[6]Another MS. gives Mfokazi as the name of the heir.

the chief of the Zulu tribe. However, Shaka besought Dingiswayo to establish him in the Zulu chieftainship. This Dingiswayo refused to do, stating that the Zulu tribe was under his authority, and that Sigujana, as heir apparent, had a prior right. As, however, there appeared to Dingiswayo nothing to prevent Shaka assuming that position, he advised and induced him, by promises of assistance, to put Sigujana to death himself and, if necessary, to take the Zulu chieftainship by force. But before Dingiswayo could, with any propriety, interfere on his protege's behalf Sigujana must be got out of the way. Shaka thereupon employed his half-brother Ngwadi to dispatch his rival. In this Ngwadi was successful, killing not only Sigujana, when bathing in the river, but a brother of his who happened to be with him at that time. It was at this stage that Dingiswayo assisted Shaka with a military force. Placing himself at the head thereof Shaka now entered the Zulu territory and proceeded at once to his father's kraal. As he entered the kraal, dressed in war attire, his men sang the following song, composed by him for the occasion:

>Ohah! O-o-hah!
>   Who is it that opposes us?
>When we stab we proceed forward,
>   While there are some who retreat,
>The aged must be separated and placed in the rear.
>   Do you not see they impede the King's army?
>They were men formerly,
>   But now our mother's mothers.
>We must find petticoats to wear.[1]
>   See, they go out of three roads:
>As it comes they are seen
>   Painful is it to be said I am a commoner.
>I am at a loss for a pit to run away
>   In front and rear there are all enemies.

The force which accompanied Shaka, and the proffered assistance of uMacingwane, a powerful neighbouring tribe, caused the Zulus to make up their minds in favour of Shaka and forthwith cordially to receive him as their chief.

---

[1] Shaka compelled all the old men to wear petticoats of monkey skins for war-dresses, shaped like those of women.—*Editor*.

During the first year of his chieftainship, Shaka continued tributary to Dingiswayo, which prevented him from displaying his abilities or following his own inclinations. The experience he had gained during his attendance on Dingiswayo, and his own ambitious views, could not find scope for action so long as his protector was alive. Shaka took the earliest opportunity of ridding himself of such an obstacle. About 12 months after Shaka succeeded his father, Dingiswayo went out to attack the chief Zwide. Shaka accompanied Dingiswayo, commanding one division of the force. Knowing the spot where Dingiswayo would post himself to observe the battle, Shaka secretly communicated this knowledge to the enemy, who sent a force and took him prisoner. He was kept bound for three days and then put to death. The Mthethwa tribe, their chief being a prisoner, was defeated. Some joined the ranks of the victors, while the remainder returned to their country, acknowledging as their chief, Mondisa, Dingiswayo's brother. The various tribes who had been conquered and formed part of the Mthethwa tribe refused to acknowledge Mondisa, and took the opportunity of claiming their independence. Shaka was now at liberty to exercise his full power and indulge his leading passion.

He soon found a pretext for attacking Mondisa and that part of the Mthethwa tribe that had remained with him. The tribe was still in confusion from the loss of its chieftain, and in fear of retaliation from the tribes which, having been conquered by Dingiswayo, were now left at liberty. With only a comparatively small force, Shaka succeeded in conquering them, killing half of those left and inducing the remainder to place themselves under his authority. They had no sooner done this than he put to death their chief, Mondisa, brother of Dingiswayo, appointing one of his own choice in his place.

With this additional strength he meditated greater conquests, and fought over again Dingiswayo's battles, but now they were attended with greater slaughter.

To give an adequate idea of Shaka's proceedings from the death of Dingiswayo to the time when he, Shaka, was assassinated by his brother Dingane would require an extensive work, while the object of what is here recorded regarding him is chiefly to give an insight into the revolutions the various tribes have undergone and the rise and progress of the Zulu nation, to elucidate which it has been necessary to give a more minute account respecting Dingiswayo and the tribes antecedent to their being under the domination of Shaka. Hence the little mentioned regarding Shaka can give but an indifferent idea of the character of that chief.

It was pointed out above that Shaka's conquests were attended with greater slaughter than those of Dingiswayo's. The main reason for this was that he disapproved of the old custom of carrying many assegais and throwing them at the enemy. To substitute a different mode of attack Shaka assembled two of his regiments. The men were then ordered to supply themselves with a reed each from the river bank, that he might be convinced of the effect which only one weapon would produce when used at close quarters. The two regiments thus weaponed were ordered to oppose each other, the one throwing the weapon, the other rushing on and stabbing their opponents at close quarters. The result of this collision was momentous and met with Shaka's entire satisfaction, few having escaped being wounded and several being killed.

Shaka then ordered six oxen to be slaughtered in his presence, and collecting the assegais of his followers with the exception of one left to each, he ordered the shafts to be broken and used as firewood in cooking the meat, of which the prime parts, after being soaked in cold water, were given to those who had been seen to shrink in the combat. This originated the use of the single assegai by eastern tribes. He also took the opportunity of commanding the word *itshaka* never more to be used ; *tshuda* was to be substituted therefor.

Dingane was at this time in disgrace in consequence of an amour with a girl. He was on the point of being killed when he effected his escape to the Qwaƃe tribe. It was at about the same time that Shaka prohibited his soldiers from marrying wives or engaging in amours of any kind.

Having received a quantity of beads from Delagoa Bay, a market he kept open after the death of Dingiswayo, he sent a present of some of them to Phakathwayo, chief of the Qwaƃe tribe. Phakathwayo, however, immediately returned them, saying they had been bewitched by Shaka, who wanted to put him to death. This accusation Shaka made a pretext for immediate hostilities. He attacked Phakathwayo in two different directions. Phakathwayo, on being closely pursued, fell dead from fright, whilst his tribe, after a short conflict, fled to the Entumeni forest near by. On the news of Phakathwayo's death being reported to Shaka, he pretended to be very sorry at what had happened. He sent two oxen as an offering to his (Phakathwayo's) family spirits, with prayers to bring about his resurrection. He, moreover, assured the Qwaɓe tribe of his regret, adding that his intention in coming at all was merely to demand an apology for the way in which Phakathwayo had insulted him. As, however, their king was dead, for the spirits did not seem inclined to raise him up, they would now stand in need of a protector; and seeing that Phakathwayo had no heir, and his brother Nqetho was too young, they had better put themselves under his protection. This they agreed to do, which considerably increased the size of Shaka's army, making it quite formidable. Dingane, by making an abject submission, was allowed to return to the Zulu tribe.

Shaka next attacked Mahlungwana,[1] the chief that had promised to assist him on the death of his father. He defeated him, upon which many of the tribe gave their allegiance to Shaka.

The next to join him were the Langeni tribe. These freely submitted in the expectation of receiving favourable treatment. Shaka's mother, Nandi, was a member of this tribe. It was at this time that she took charge of Shaka's household, all the small tribes in the neighbourhood having by then joined him.

Another chief he attacked was Matiwane, chief of the amaNgwane tribe. After a slight contest, this tribe retreated to the northward.

Zwide, chief of the Ndwandwe tribe, witnessing Shaka's daily increase of power, the inevitable result of which he had anticipated, suddenly and unexpectedly invaded the Zulu country. Shaka, who was unprepared, hastily collected his forces and pretended to retreat from the attacking army. He kept on retiring more and more into the heart of his country for two days, taking the precaution of everywhere burying all the corn along his route. This so harassed and distressed the invaders that, exhausted by hunger and fatigue, they were compelled to retrace their steps, during which they were

---

[1] MS. has Amaclungwani.

constantly attacked by Shaka. He followed them to their own country, destroying great numbers.

Shaka continued his attacks on the surrounding tribes, always observing the strictest discipline among his troops and dealing out cattle with a liberal hand, until his army increased to such a size as realized his wishes.

He now started a desolating and destructive war on all around, and directed that no quarter was to be given. He ravaged and depopulated the country to a distance of 300 miles to the westward, 200 miles to the northward and 500 miles to the southward. In this vast area only two tribes, the Ngwane under Matiwane, and the Nhlungwini under Madikane, escaped his destructive powers, and that only by their becoming roving marauders.

His next attack was on his old foe, the Ndwandwe tribe, then under Sikhunyana. These people he completely defeated. Previously to this expedition he had behaved with a degree of humanity and mildness as compared with his subsequent conduct.

His inclinations, until the defeat of the Ndwandwes, had been restrained by fear lest his subjects should detach themselves from him. Having, at length, defeated the only remaining formidable enemy, with nothing to fear from any other quarter, and when he imagined that his extensive power placed him in a state of perfect security, his real character began to develop itself. Up to this time he had, in great measure, acted in accordance with the system of his late protector, Dingiswayo, but, owing to his increased sense of security, his former tactics began to be blended with a more rigid despotism. He kept his subjects in perpetual awe and continual astonishment from the variety of his exploits and brilliancy of his achievements. But after the annihilation of the Ndwandwe people a reign of terror commenced, when his excessive cruelties overleaped all bounds. Unfortunately for his subjects, he must have imbibed the idea that the minds of such a heterogeneous mass of people, made up of many varying tribes, ought to be continually agitated, and that daily examples of his might and ferocity were necessary to keep them in a state of awe. Notwithstanding such a policy the people, throughout the whole country, gave themselves up to constantly reciting his eulogies and extolling his heroic deeds. Thus it was that his name was everywhere dreaded and seldom made use of except in the taking of oaths, when what was said and so sealed might strictly be relied as being the truth.

Shaka having, after much opposition, overcome the neighbouring tribes, in order to prevent a repetition of revolt, put to death the chiefs and principal families of the conquered, selecting, however, the younger men, whom he attached to his regiments, forming together a body of 50,000 effective followers: these he governed with despotic severity. Having, with the exception of Matiwane, who fled to the north-west, brought under his dominion all chiefs and tribes between Delagoa Bay and uMzimvuɓu, he determined to continue his wars, so long as any body of people could be found to stand in opposition to his force. To fight or die was his maxim, and certain was the death of any man or body of men who retreated before the enemy. The countries to the north-east, as also the coast southward, were separately invaded. Those who attempted to withstand him were overpowered by numbers, and ultimately exterminated, neither sex nor age being spared. Many were burned to death, their huts being fired at night; while the barbarous cruelties he practised struck terror into many who had never seen his force and fled at his name.

The recital of his cruelties, though horrid, is necessary, for the omission might leave him entitled to be regarded only as a savage. One instance is related by his followers and participators in the deed as having occurred in the commencement of a battle with Zwide. Some aged women having been taken in the outskirts of their country were seized and brought into Shaka's presence. After eliciting from them the information he required, he ordered them to be bound with straw and matting, which being set on fire, the tortured victims were driven towards the enemy amidst the acclamations of Shaka and of the furious demons attending him. Whilst those opposed to him were subjected to such cruelties, his own followers were not exempt. The instances are numerous in which, though not a semblance of crime was imputed to them, he has had men seized and their eyes taken out of their sockets; and then they were allowed to move about and be ridiculed by all who met them. It is needless to dwell on the enormity of his cruelty. It required some offset to gloss over this, his predominant feature. He seemed to possess qualities that might do so, and these, though only assumed, were sufficient for the ends he had in view. When the feelings of his heart were appealed to, he was by no means deficient in kind expression, and tears appeared to be always ready at his command. Excessive liberality gained for him that ascendancy for which he was esteemed above all before him. His despotism made the lives and property of all his followers exclusively his own. Hence his treasury, though exhausted by liberal gifts, required but the death of two or three wealthy owners of cattle to replenish it. The successes that had always attended him in his numerous wars, and his own pretensions to superiority, led his followers to believe that he was more than human: and in this light he was ever adored by his subjects. He succeeded in overrunning the whole country from Delagoa Bay to the St. John's River; and if death had not put a stop to his ambitious career, or had he not been deterred by the probability of a collision with the Cape Colonists, he would assuredly, ere this,[1] have exterminated every tribe of Kaffirs up to the Colonial border. The numbers whose death he occasioned have been left to conjecture, but exceed a million. Of the tribes yet extant who escaped subjection by Dingiswayo the first was that of the chief Zikode, who occupied the tract from St. Lucia to Delagoa Bay. He fled beyond that port inland, and his is now the only tribe north of Delagoa speaking the Kaffir language. At the death of this chief he was succeeded by his son Soshangana, who was three times attacked by Shaka. On the last occasion Shaka's army, before making their intended attack, was surprised in the night by Soshangana and his followers, who were led to make this movement by a deserter, one of Shaka's chiefs. Little is known of Soshangana or his people, though they cannot be much less numerous than Shaka's adherents.

The next tribe of importance, in point of numbers, is that under the chief Mzilikazi, misnamed by the colonists Motsilikatzi, an error arising from the adoption by the tribe of the name of their head, and so calling themselves Amaziligazi.

Previous reference has been made to Zwide's invasion of Zulu territories. It remains to be noted that when Zwide was forced to retire three of his petty chiefs were left behind, two

---
[1] About 1842.—*Editor.*

of whom, Beje and Mlotshwa, joined Shaka, by whom they were afterwards put to death.

The third, Mzilikazi, with 300 followers, became a freebooter. He began his aggressions by setting fire to the huts of petty tribes by night. His men, scattered abroad for the purpose, gained advantage without difficulty, receiving into their ranks such as escaped the flames. The tribe of Mzilikazi rose into notice, but was never considered important until the year 1830, when he was attacked by Dingane. The extensive increase of the adherents of Mzilikazi was caused by the accession to their number of the refugees driven out by Shaka, especially when Zwide was defeated in 1826.

The mode of government to which the eastern tribes have been accustomed has been despotic, though it was not till after the chieftainship of Shaka that it can be said to have attained a very arbitrary character. The advantages resulting from that mode of government and the success of the new mode of warfare induced the natives to imitate the example of Dingiswayo and Shaka; but the different degrees of power assumed by the rulers admit of a softer designation than despotism; for such tyranny as Shaka's could not be adopted by them with any probability of success, for their retainers would certainly, in such case, have attached themselves to Shaka, whose continued fortune offered a strong inducement. By his tyranny and barbarous acts, Shaka secured the most abject submission to his will, and restrained his subjects from the most trivial offences. If we keep out of sight Shaka's barbarities, the Zulus were a superior people, distinguished for good order and discipline. The region devastated by the marauding chiefs exceeds the Cape Colony in extent. It is, for the greater part quite void of inhabitants. Many of the inhabitants who escaped from the spear were left to perish by starvation. Their cattle having been taken and their grain destroyed, thousands were left for years to linger on the slender sustenance of roots—some even of a poisonous kind. One species could not be safely eaten until it had been boiled repeatedly for 24 hours ; and, if the cravings of starvation led to a disregard of caution, they knew the fate that awaited them. Insanity was the invariable consequence. In this state they cast themselves down from mountain cliffs or became helplessly the prey of wolves or tigers.[1] In my first journey from Natal to the Mtata in 1824, I witnessed very awful scenes. Six thousand unhappy beings, having scarcely a human appearance, were scattered over this country, feeding on every description of animal, and driven by their hungry craving in many instances to devour their fellows. The excessive liberality of Shaka in his gifts of cattle to the European party enabled them to do much in alleviating the distress which they witnessed around them; the first attempt, however, in affording relief was attended with obstacles. The safety of the party would be endangered by Shaka's displeasure, and, moreover, as Europeans had never before been seen in the country, the motives of their offers of help were misconstrued by these victims of misery, who fled from them as from destruction. The treatment experienced by the first of the natives who accepted relief soon brought the remainder to Port Natal—above 4,000 of both sexes were saved in this way—and Shaka, hitherto implacable in their regard, became softened and, feeling a deep interest in forwarding the views of the Europeans, he encouraged rather than discountenanced the protection afforded to the distressed, and he spared the lives of those of his subjects who, having been sentenced to death, had made their escape and fled to Port Natal. Their arrival among the Europeans being reported to Shaka, he replied: " They have gone to my friends and not to my enemies: take care of them as of your own." To these circumstances it is due that a body of natives under the control of the European party was collected at the port. The fate of the natives became identified with our own, and could scarcely be separated. While their recent destruction in the attack on the Zulu nation is much to be deplored, they have proved themselves deserving of the protection that has been afforded them by dying in the cause of their protectors, and in the same field. Their general good conduct has led to the belief that under an established government the natives would prove to be good subjects and exemplary soldiers.

This body of people was small in proportion to the numbers who had fled from the country in fear of Shaka and took refuge among the western tribes of Kaffraria. From these they received the name of Mfengu, from the word *fenguza*, which is

---

[1]Leopards.—*Editor.*

expressive of want. The first of these refugees expressed their need of sustenance by saying *fenguza*, " we want." Hence all who followed them at different periods, though belonging to various classes, were called Mfengu. The position of these peoples in their state of servitude under their Kaffir masters was one of restlessness. Being generally industrious, they aimed at the acquisition of cattle. Once in possession of such property, they evinced a disposition to be free from bondage. A custom prevails in all Kaffir races in regard to cattle acquired by a dependant. They are considered to be his property only so long as he remains in his subordinate condition, or by permission of his master builds a separate kraal, in which case he is still looked on as an adherent; but if he join another chief or withdraw from the authority of his master his property is subject to seizure. In their anxiety to be no longer menial servants, the Fengus have taken every opportunity to escape with their property. The first that occurred was when an attack was made by Ncaphayi on the Tambookies. Some of the Fengus joined Ncaphayi, and the Tambookies, in a spirit of revenge, persecuted those who had not joined the ranks of the invaders, and had remained with their masters. The rumours as to the conduct of the Fengus who had escaped reaching the other tribes, the persecution became general. The next instance occurred in 1834, in the last Kaffir war, when they embraced the opportunity, and became British subjects. In the confusion caused by the war some had lost their cattle, while others had brought away those of their late masters, with which they had no sooner escaped than they extensively increased their stock by plundering the cattle taken by the Colonial forces from the Kaffir tribes. The Fengus, like the natives at Port Natal, belonged to fragments of every tribe defeated by Shaka; those at Natal, however, had advantages that materially influenced their character—for they lived in a rich and extensive country and being supplied with cattle and grain, had no inducement to roam. Under the government of their own chiefs and laws, they had always been under sufficient restraint and were an orderly people. The Fengus, on the contrary, have for years been without any settled abode, divided from their chiefs, having nothing but the name of Fengus to connect them with their fellows, and roving from place to place. They have fallen materially in character, and bear little resemblance to those of their countrymen who have not been exposed to the hardships endured by the Fengus.

The Kaffir tribes may be considered to be almost exclusively a pastoral people, and wholly so as regards the tribes near the Cape Colony, since the quantity of grain produced among any portion of them wi l barely suffice for their consumption for three months in the year. The amaMpondo, before their defeat by Shaka, in 1824, were a pastoral people. Having then lost much of their stock, they became agricultural and pastoral. The Natal refugees also became agriculturalists, loss of cattle having in most cases been the only stimulus to tillage. To this rule the Zulus are an exception, being at once agricultural and pastoral. An excessive fondness for cattle is exemplified in all the Kaffir tribes. Those of the eastern tribes who have been restricted by the penalty of death from committing theft have substituted in its room open war on all who possess them. This predominant feature has been the foundation of the numerous wars and commotions which have ever kept the country in constant agitation. During the life of Dingiswayo thefts of cattle from one another were not infrequent. Under Shaka no penalty less than death was inflicted for the offence, and this at once put a stop to that description of plunder. During the 12 years of my residence in the Zulu country not a single instance occurred of cattle stealing.

Chapter III

BUT Shaka's innovations were not confined to the expansion, organization, discipline and efficiency of his army, vast, complex and mobile as it was, nor was his time and attention wholly occupied by the campaigns or deeds of his warriors and the numerous direct and indirect consequences thereof. He was shrewd enough to see that the success of his system, as a whole, and the many far-flung and exacting operations he was always engaged in depended, to no small degree, on the way in which the relations between the sexes were controlled. Among his extraordinary developments in this connection were the royal *izigodlo* or seraglios, and, once organized and developed by Shaka, they were maintained by later kings, very much on similar lines, though not on so large a scale.

Zulu Kraal on the Umngeni, with Cattle and Sheep
From the painting by George French Angus in *Kaffirs Illustrated*

The seraglio of the Zulu king[1] consists of the upper part of the royal kraal, and measures about 300 yards in length by 200 in breadth. It is separated from the main or lower portion of the kraal by a neat fence of closely plaited brushwood, five feet in height. The area cut off by the fence is subdivided by similar fences into compartments for the different divisions of the household, and these subdivisions are such as to give the whole appearance of being an intricate labyrinth. In each compartment there are neatly finished huts, the insides being of the neatest workmanship. The sticks are worked so closely together as to be of themselves nearly watertight. The spaces between the huts are levelled and kept constantly clean. Each compartment is named according to its use, or the division of the household who occupy it.

The seraglios of Shaka contained not less than 5,000 girls. When he wished to add to their numbers, the girls throughout the country would be assembled and made to dance before him. He would then select those he admired and allocate them according to age or beauty to such divisions as seemed to him fitting. The whole of these girls were divided into regiments, one of these being attached to the *isigodlo* (seraglio) of each regiment of soldiers. The soldiers were prohibited, under penalty of death, from entering a seraglio. These establishments are regulated and controlled by adopted mothers or queens. It has been no uncommon occurrence for a regiment of soldiers and another of girls to be surrounded and slain on the slightest suspicion of intercourse; in which case sometimes not less than 3,000 people would suffer, whereas, in fact, only a very few, and possibly none at all, were guilty. As Shaka seldom visited a regiment to whose barracks a regiment of girls was attached, such being only inferior regiments, many of the girls saw him only once in three years, whilst numbers did so only when he originally selected them. Those who resided with him at the principal royal kraal, not being more than three or four hundred, exclusive of his real and adopted relations, were not allowed to marry and were, with the others, kept in a state of most abject submission. They were supplied with provisions by cattle being killed solely for their use. The

---

[1] There were 10, 15 or more such establishments, being attached to each royal kraal, the largest, of course, at the principal royal residence.—*Editor*.

cattle slaughtered for them were called *umlomo* cattle, i.e cattle of the mouth, or mouth cattle. Such cattle were not allowed to be touched by the other people. As soon as the meat had been cooked, it was taken to the King, and, after being assorted by him, it was carried in baskets to the various establishments. Shaka sometimes sent cattle for the use of those residing at a distance. At the conclusion of every meal, thanks were returned, being chanted in set phrases, of which the following are illustrations:

" Wen' ongangeZulu ! "   " Wen' ongangezwe ! "   " Wen' ongangezintaɓa ! "   " Wen' omnyama ! "   " Wen' ongangolwandle ! "   " Wen' owakhula siliɓele ! "

Of which the following is a literal translation:

" Thou that art as great as the sky ! Thou that art as great as the earth ! Thou that art as great as the mountains ! Thou that art black ! Thou that art as vast as the sea ! Thou who growest while others are otherwise occupied ! "

The whole time of the inmates of the main seraglio is taken up in decorating themselves according to the King's fanciful taste and attending on him. There were generally 400 or 500 who attended on him, though this number was often augmented by 600-700 by drafts from several of the other seraglios. Shaka usually passed his evenings with these girls, often by joining in the dances and himself dancing in the centre of those performing. They dressed in accordance with the modes in vogue at the respective seraglios they had come from. Such costumes were superb and far beyond anything the reader would imagine after taking into consideration the apparent absence of articles which would seem to be necessary for creating grand effects. New songs were composed in sets, year by year, and sung in rotation. The music and dancing that accompanied each song was varied in such a way that one half of the circle would sing the men's part, whilst the rest of the circle would sing the women's. In all these performances the greatest order and precision was invariably observed.

It frequently happens that they fall into disgrace with the King. In such cases, the male relatives of the girl are obliged to forfeit cattle, whereas the only return derived by a father or relative is the honour of his daughter, sister, etc., having been selected by the King for admission into the seraglio. As a matter of fact, in no palace in Europe is greater decorum, order and etiquette observed than in these seraglios and their various compartments.

Shaka had various huts reserved for his own private use. There was one in which he had his meals, another to dress in, another to sleep in, and another for giving audiences. Other huts again were used for storing his provisions. Only one or two of his old chiefs were admitted into his apartments, and then only by invitation. A free admittance, however, was allowed to Europeans, in whose company he was always happy. He regarded them as his real friends, and made them partakers of his meals—this being considered by him to be a high honour. His meals generally consisted of stewed beef or mutton, *amazambane* (potatoes), beans, a pudding made of Guinea corn flour, mixed with rich soup, beer, plantains, and sugar cane, when in season. All the food was cleanly cooked by his female attendants, and served up in wooden dishes of curious workmanship.

The mode of life was extremely regular. Rising early, he would leave his hut and sit at the upper end of the cattle kraal under a euphorbia tree. He sat either on a mat or a chair—carved out of a solid block of wood in imitation of a chair which had been brought by the Portuguese from Delagoa Bay. There would be a servant at his side holding a shield over him by a long handle to protect him from the rays of the sun. His hairdresser would stand to shave him or dress his ring, and whilst so engaged would keep as respectful a distance as the nature of the profession would allow. While undergoing this operation, Shaka kept on talking in a careless way, apparently indifferent to the operation, and yet a single incision on the head of majesty would have been fatal to the surgeon-barber, who was, in consequence, obliged to watch for his opportunities and when they occurred hastily spring forward and detach the hair required, or give the ring a polishing touch.

The chiefs and regiments belonging to the kraal, as well as those coming on and going off duty, no sooner heard of his rising than they collected and approached him. When they got within 30 yards of him they would salute with respectful fear by saying: "*Bayede!*" a salutation due only to kings. They would then seat themselves on the ground before him in silence and proceed to listen with great attention and anxiety. They caught with great eagerness every word that escaped him in course of conversation and answered him only with acclamations of praise or by expressing astonishment at his talents. They quitted his presence on his rising to bathe in an apartment he used for that purpose. He would be attended by two servants carrying water and a decanter of oil, also his doctors. The latter were employed on such occasions to strengthen him with magical arts, and decoctions of various vegetables prepared for the purpose. Whilst being doctored in this way, all persons who had lost their relatives by death were obliged to purify themselves before they could be admitted into his presence. Purification took place in this way. The mourner would have to take the gall from the side of a living calf, then sprinkle it at the entrance of the bathing enclosure. In the case of poor people, a brass ball would be thrown on to a few beads, all of which thereafter became perquisites of the servants waiting on the King.

After bathing he breakfasted and frequently slept for an hour or two, when he would again appear before his people, who had eagerly awaited his return. If a regiment was called, the little boys were always on the alert to make the hindermost hurry up by striking them severe blows on the head which they dare not resent. The same was done by the men to the boys on the latter being summoned.

Cattle and war formed the whole subject of his conversations; and during his sitting, while in the act of taking a pinch of snuff, or when engaged in the deepest conversation, he would by a movement of his finger, perceivable only by his attendants, point out one of the gathering sitting round him, upon which, to the surprise of strangers, the man would be carried off and killed. This was a daily occurrence. On one occasion I witnessed 60 boys under 12 years of age dispatched before he had breakfasted. No sooner is the signal given, and the object pointed out, than those sitting round him scramble to kill him, although they have good reason to expect the next moment the same fate themselves, but such apprehensions are far from their thoughts; the will of the King being uppermost.

I have seen instances where they have had opportunities of speaking while being carried off, but which they always employed in enthusiastically praising the heroic deeds of their King. No sooner is the signal given, and the condemned individual taken hold of, than one, while the others are dragging him away, seizes the head and by a sudden jerk and twist, dislocates the neck joint, the others in the meantime beating him with knobsticks. As soon as they arrive at the *Golgotha*, about a mile from the kraal, where all these executed are placed, then they thrust a stake through the body. There the vultures sit in flocks waiting for their daily prey, whilst the surrounding bush abounds with wolves which, by their cries at intervals during the day, proclaim their anxiety for the approach of night.

The following instances will enable the reader to form some idea of his atrocities. His objection to being imagined a father will be evident from the following fact. Nandi, his mother, governed his concubines. She produced an infant with its mother to Shaka, observing that, from the likeness she could trace in the child, it was his. The mother had resided in her, Nandi's, kraal before and since becoming enceinte, and could only have been visited by him. He immediately seized the little innocent, and, throwing it up into the air, it was killed by the fall; the mother was instantly ordered to be put to death, whilst Shaka so severely beat his mother, Nandi, with a stick, for presuming to accuse him of being the father that she was lame for three months. When she recovered, she had the ten concubines put to death who had agreed with her proposal to show Shaka the infant.

A man named Mpisana,[1] who had been accused by the doctors (*izinyanga*) of witchcraft, was ordered to be dragged alive by a cord fastened to his ankles down a steep hill leading to the Mhlathuze river. He was then suspended to a mimosa tree by his heels and burned to death, by a fire made under him.

Mantshongwe[2] and Msoka, two chiefs charged with a similar crime, had their eyes taken out. They were then allowed to live if they could while being tormented by people sent for that

---
[1] MS. has Impesan.
[2] MS. has Machongwa.

purpose. As both assistance and food were refused them, they soon died.

Shaka's servant, Ngozingozi,[1] i.e. wound and wound, a name acquired from the numerous wounds that had been inflicted on him by Shaka, was on one occasion, obliged to go on reciting the King's eulogies and declaring, upon oath, that he was never hurt by Shaka, during the whole time that the latter was in the act of burning him on the neck with a firebrand.

The principal residence of Shaka, before he defeated the Ndwandwes, was called Giɓixhegu[2]—turn out the old men. The Ndwandwes were no sooner defeated than he collected all the aged men in the country and had them killed. A special song was composed on that occasion, the words of which were: Produce the cowards, etc. Each regiment produced its own, when they were at once carried off and killed. The name of the royal kraal was changed to Ɓulawayo[3] and by that it was thenceforth known.

During his midday council persons under different denominations were constantly proclaiming his achievements and innumerable titles. Some of these were decorated with horns on their heads; others in leopard skins; some made themselves resemble dogs, others dressed like women. Others again, by their foolish antics and attitudes, did everything in their power to keep the King amused.

Among the peculiarities, shortly after our arrival in the country he formed a regiment of women, attaching to each division thereof female officers, the whole being called after us, *uNkisimana*—Englishman. These were employed more for his amusement than for any other purpose.

Another singularity was that Dingiswayo and, after him, Shaka each pretended to be afflicted with certain evacuations in the way that women are, though not at regular periods. On these occasions numerous cattle were slaughtered and many people killed.

As an instance of Shaka's vanity and desire to be thought wonderful the following may be mentioned. While crossing the Mhlathuze River with his army, he placed his soldiers in

---

[1]MS. has Gose um Gose.
[2]MS. has Gebecaigu.
[3]MS. has Umbulawio.

various positions to try if he could dam up the river. Whether he succeeded in raising the water any height I don't know, but he has the credit of having stopped it entirely.

In the afternoons cattle were issued by the King for slaughter to the regiments on duty and should a European or a visitor from any other tribe arrive, though only a single individual, an ox or cow is given him, with beer, etc. Anyone daring to offer the King provisions for sale would have been killed.

Shaka was given to dreams and necromancy. Moreover, he uttered prophecies, one at least of these being remarkable and very well known by the natives of Zululand and Natal, no doubt because it came true within but ten years of his death. [As the author does not give details of it we venture to give it here. When Shaka was assassinated, a comparatively young man, he was still at the height of his power. Not 50 Europeans had up to that time visited the country (we mean of course during his own reign) and not ten of those had lived there for a year and upwards. There was therefore every probability, from the ordinary native's point of view, not only that Shaka would continue to reign for at least another dozen years but that after him the wonderful Zulu power and autonomy would be maintained unimpaired for a much longer period. Shaka, however, was not an ordinary Zulu. He could see far ahead. He saw clearly that as soon as he died the country would be overrun, i.e. conquered by the white man—the makers of muskets, gunpowder and ships. This then was the substance of his prophecy: "As soon as I go, this country of ours will be overrun in every direction by the white man. Mark my words." He spoke in metaphorical terms, but the above is the sense of the prophecy, being completely verified on the 16th December, 1838, when the Boers utterly defeated Dingane at Blood River, forcing him to vacate and set fire to his own capital. —*Editor*.]

As to necromancy, the two following anecdotes may serve to indicate something of Shaka's attitude and relation thereto:

When he was living in the Mthethwa tribe under Dingiswayo he made the acquaintance of a certain Zulu chief called Mmbiya. The two soon became so intimate that, later on, when Shaka ruled over the Zulus in conjunction with that of the Mthethwa, Mmbiya was taken into great favour. He died in 1826, much to Shaka's regret. A few months afterwards a report was current that the spirit of Mmbiya, in the form of a homeless snake, known as *idlozi*, had appeared at his own kraal, and intended to visit Shaka. In consequence of this, Shaka sent chiefs and sent them repeatedly to see it. On each occasion they took oxen which were duly sacrificed to the spirit. That this spirit was really that of Mmbiya was confirmed by all who went to the place. With such persons Mmbiya is supposed to have entered into conversation and this on topics of a political nature. On every occasion it extolled Shaka, referring to him as a superior power, and at the same time assured those present that he, Shaka, was in very great favour with the spirits. Finally it declared that it had come by direction of the spirits to make this announcement. The chiefs did not neglect to ask for snuff, upon which the spirit directed them to proceed to a particular spot where the snuff box would be found. So satisfied were they that the spirit was indeed that of Mmbiya that they induced Shaka to believe it too. The latter now appointed a day on which the spirit was to appear before him. In the meantime he caused a handsome kaross with which the spirit was to be clad to be sent to it.

On the day appointed Shaka and his chiefs were in readiness to receive the much revered visitant, when, to the astonishment of all, an old woman, pretending to be the spirit in question, began delivering her message. Shaka soon put a stop to this by declaring her to be an impostor and ordering her to go away. At the same time he expressed the opinion that she had undoubtedly been directed by Mmbiya to do as she had done, owing to his not wishing, for some reason or other, to appear himself.

The other anecdote is as follows: During the latter part of Shaka's reign there was a man called Bandla, a member of the Cele tribe, who was attacked by illness in the same way as neophytes are, and was thus supposed by his friends to be called by the spirits previous to his becoming a necromancer. One day, when he was extremely ill, and apparently at death's door, he suddenly disappeared. Whilst there was no doubt but that he was dead, his disappearance remained a mystery. The usual ceremonies of mourning were observed and after a time he was forgotten. But greatly to the surprise of both relations and friends he reappeared in the act of carrying a goat into his hut.

His friends immediately flocked round to know from whence he came and how he had disappeared. He thereupon accounted for his absence and reappearance in the following manner:

As he lay in the last agonies of death, a lion, he said, had entered the hut and carried him gently away. It frequently put him down and blew on him. This appeared to invigorate his whole frame. When his pains had been relieved, he was carried by the lion through an opening in the earth, which led far underground to a world of spirits. The spirits asked him from whence he came, at the same time telling him, in order that he might convince his countrymen on the earth he had come from, that death was only a sleep from which they again rise to live in happiness. The immense numbers that had now collected round him proceeded to sing the following song:

> *Eih, eih, eih,*
>   *O ! waduka,*
> *Washon' ezizweni, eah.*

Oh he went astray
He made his way into strange countries.

He was shown all the former kings living in amity, also all his relations and their children. Each individual was occupying the same position which he filled before death. Moreover, they retained the same age and vigour as before death, having plenty of corn and cattle, and amusing themselves with dancing and singing.

He was taken to those of his wives that had died, when he found they had been kept as they were in all cases till the death of the husband.

Having remained several days in this world of happiness, one of his relations scratched the pupil of his eye by way of making a mark whereby people of the world would be convinced of the truth of his story. They then ordered him back to the world till he should obtain an heir to his property, when they would tell him to come to them by the way of death. They, moreover, said that on approaching his kraal he was to go to a certain bush where he would find a goat entangled; this he was then to carry home, kill as an offering to them (the spirits) and sprinkle its gall over his body. He was now conducted back to earth, where he found the very goat that was now before them. As for the mark in his eye he exhibited it too.

This account soon reached the ears of the neighbouring tribes, his repeated declarations as to its being true and the evidence of his neighbours, as far as they could confirm it, being proved, made him a favourite of his chief, Magaye, and afterwards of Shaka.

This man was later on accidentally killed by some Zulus when chasing stolen cattle in 1828. His manners were peculiar as was his dress. His character being undoubted, his account of the world below is still believed by his countrymen as an undoubted truth.

THE DIARY

Chapter I

I LEFT England and arrived at the Cape of Good Hope in the year 1818. In December of the same year I left Cape Town in H.M. brig *Leveret*, for Algoa Bay, en route for the "Somerset Farm."[1]

Owing to recent inroads by the Kaffirs on the Colony, prior to their attack on Grahamstown, it was necessary for all Government waggons to be accompanied by military escorts when travelling through the country. Such escorts were not discontinued until after the arrival of the Albany settlers in 1820. In 1822 I left the Somerset Farm and walked from Grahamstown to Cape Town. One of the first persons I met at Cape Town was Mr. Henry Nourse, whom I had known

---

[1]As Fynn spent three years at this place, it will be well to append some account thereof.

The farm was started by Lord Charles Somerset, Governor of the Cape Colony in 1814. It proved a success, especially after one Robert Hart took over the management in January, 1817.

"The Somerset Farm," says G. Thompson, who visited it in 1823, i.e. the year after Fynn left there, " lay at the foot of the Boschberg ridge of mountains . . . about fifteen miles from the course of the Giant Fish River. It is watered by the stream called the Little Fish River.

Somerset Farm . . . [in 1823] was an extensive Government establishment under the superintendence of Mr. Hart, formerly adjutant of the old Cape Corps. The agricultural part of the concern was by no means the principal department. The supply of rations to the British settlers for two years after their arrival, and the provisioning of the troops on the Frontier for several years past, was committed to this establishment. It was, in fact, rather a commissariat depot than a farm ; and the purchasing of cattle, sheep and corn from the Boers, and forwarding them as required to the various military posts, constantly occupied a great number of Hottentot herdsmen and waggon drivers. Five or six English ploughmen and three or four mechanics, with a clerk or storekeeper, were the whole of the British population of the place, exclusive of the three superintendents and their families. The greatest activity and bustle appeared to pervade every part of the establishment ; and even the languid Hottentots seemed here to emulate the ardour of Englishmen, as if they had caught a portion of the activity and enterprise for which the indefatigable Mr. Hart has long been distinguished."

—Thompson, G., *Travels and Adventures in Southern Africa*, vol. I, 54-57.

It was in April, 1824, that the establishment was broken up and the now well-known town of Somerset East laid off on the land.—*Editor*.

slightly on the Frontier. I informed him I was in search of occupation, upon which he promised to keep a look out for me.

At that time my brother William was in the employ of John Murray, a ship chandler in Cape Town. I went to stay with him. After three weeks I began to despair of obtaining a position, not for want of openings, but because I was too diffident to ask. Under this feeling of despair, I decided to return to England, but was without the means of doing so.

On going one day to the office of Messrs. H. Nourse and Co., merchants, I found that two vessels, the brig *Mary*, and the sloop *Jane*, were about to be sent to Delagoa Bay on a trading expedition. Henry Maynard, a nephew of H. Nourse, was appointed supercargo of the former, whilst I was offered, and accepted, a like post on the *Jane*. I joined my ship at Simon's Bay. Ten days were spent there in getting ready for the voyage. Commodore Nourse,[1] brother of the merchant and uncle of Maynard, was, at that time, in command of that naval station.

Whilst Nourse and Co.'s preparations were in progress, Lieutenant George Francis Farewell, R.N., who will frequently be referred to later, was, in conjunction with Lieutenant James Saunders King, R.N., making arrangements for a voyage, also of a commercial venture, to St. Lucia Bay.[2]

The *Jane*[3] left Simon's Bay before the *Mary*. Authority had been given me, should the conduct of the captain require it, to remove him from his position, a precaution deemed necessary owing to his constantly becoming intoxicated. One William Collins, coxswain to the Commodore, and from whose vessel he had just been discharged, was appointed mate, on the understanding that, if the captain were suspended, he must act as substitute. To what extent the owners were justified in delegating this authority, or what would have been the result had any case of suspension been referred to a court of law, was fortunately not put to the test.

Our voyage to Delagoa took 12 days. With the exception of a little severe weather and the captain being frequently intoxicated, nothing unusual occurred, except the finding

---

[1] Joseph Nourse. cf. Theal, *Beginning of South African History*, 439.
[2] This venture and the important outcome thereof will be dealt with in a subsequent chapter.—*Editor*.
[3] She left about the middle of June, 1823.—*Editor*.

ourselves surrounded, when off St. Lucia, by five water spouts. Two of these approached us so fast that we expected to be engulfed. A small cannon we had on board was heavily charged and fired at the two spouts, whereupon they disappeared.

On entering Delagoa Bay the captain was again so intoxicated as actually to endanger the safety of the vessel; in defiance of the mate's opinion as to the course it should follow, he ran her stern on to the bank of Elephant Island, whereupon she went over on her beam ends. This led me to desire Collins, the mate, at once to take command. The captain, Fotheringham, willingly relinquished his command. In a few days he transhipped to a whaler, the *Saucy Jack*, a type of vessel well known to British men-of-war. She had formerly been an American privateer. Owing to her splendid sailing qualities she had invariably escaped when chased, even over long distances, by our vessels. She was ultimately captured by a man-of-war boat, though only when lying at anchor.

On our vessel being thrown on her beam ends, the cargo got shifted and several of the crew fell overboard. As the tide was then receding, the water was shallow, hence those who had fallen overboard, as well as the rest of the crew, took up a sitting position on the keel until the return of the tide, when, with the assistance of the boats of the *Saucy Jack*, she righted on being got off shore. Next day we anchored on the right bank of the St. George's River,[1] opposite the Portuguese fort. The Portuguese settlement is on the left bank of the St. George's River and falls within country known as Mattoll. The country on the right bank is called Tembe, and at the time was under chief Mayetha. The Maphutha River forms the south-eastern boundary of this district, beyond which is the amaThonga tribe, under chief Makhasana.

On landing, the manifest of our cargo was submitted to the Governor. A strong desire was shown to purchase the cargo wholesale. To dispose of the goods in that way, however, was not the intention of the owners. I accordingly awaited the arrival of Mr. Maynard, by whom the manner of traffic to be carried upon would be decided. The *Mary* arrived a few days later, when the *Leven*, a sloop of war, with her consort, the *Barracouta*, anchored in the mouth of the St. George's River

---

[1] Known to the natives as Imbuluze ; also called English River in early publications.—*Editor*.

and soon began surveying the rivers and coast round Delagoa Bay.[1]

The *Leven* and the *Barracouta* formed part of the southeast surveying squadron, which consisted of the *Leven*, *Barracouta* (Captain Vidal), and *Cockburn* (Lieutenant R. Owen), with Captain W. F. W. Owen, R.N., in supreme command. I had already seen the Captain at Simon's Bay, also many other naval commanders, but, from the first time I met him to the last, I was constantly struck by his appearance and general character as resembling what I had read of the great Admiral Drake. From what I saw of the terror in which he kept the Portuguese at Delagoa Bay, and (as I afterwards heard) at Sofala and Quilimane as well, I felt convinced that if a European war broke out in those days, a second Drake would easily have been found.

As I was supercargo on a merchantman, it was not likely I should become acquainted with the precise services on which Captain Owen was employed by the British Government. I have, however, much reason to believe that, in addition to his more prominent duty of surveying the south-east coast of Africa, he was authorized, in the course of his voyages, to take formal possession of such countries as might be taken over with advantage by the British Crown.

I cannot pass over a trifling incident at which I was present, which occurred prior to the squadron proceeding to Delagoa. The principal frigate at the Cape station, the *Andromache*, was commanded by Commodore Nourse, whose vessel and crew were the perfection of cleanliness or, as the sailor terms it, " fit as a fiddle." The *Leven* and her crew were precisely the reverse, resembling a whaler more than a British man-of-war; in all other respects there was perfect order among the officers and crew. Their general appearance, however, was most unsailor-like. Officers and men were decorated with immense beards, in the growing of which they were encouraged by their Commodore, the object being to save that portion of their faces from those terrible foes in tropical climates, mosquitoes, which, though they may not be the cause of fevers in swampy countries, are, by disturbing rest and sleep, irritators of persons suffering from fever.

---

[1] It was in September, 1822, that the *Leven* and *Barracouta* first arrived at Delagoa Bay to undertake the survey.—*Editor*.

I was standing with two officers of the *Andromache* on the beach of Simon's Bay when Commodore Nourse came to where we were just as Lieutenant Owen arrived with a message for the former. At the time considerable ill-will existed between the two commanders. On Commodore Nourse replying to Captain Owen's message, he added an invitation to Lieutenant Owen to dine with him that evening, on condition that he first shaved off his beard and moustache. Lieutenant Owen replied that he would report the invitation to his commanding officer. His chair at the Commodore's table that evening was vacant.

The fort already alluded to as being at Delagoa had walls that were made of mud. The eight or ten pieces of cannon within it were so rusty that Collins said if they were fired off he would rather be in front than at the back. Within the fort, we were shown the chapel, viz., a room about 12 feet square. The padre, who had just closed the service, accompanied us to the cells, where we saw about 80 slaves in irons. They had been captured in fights between neighbouring tribes, and had recently been purchased.

The fort and settlement of Delagoa were as contemptible as can well be imagined, though they had been occupied for a period of perhaps 60 years. The inhabitants consisted of the Governor, four or five sub-officers, a priest, five or six licensed traders, who, with the exception of a couple of sergeants, were Portuguese from Europe. The soldiers were all dark coloured natives; they had been collected on the spot and drilled on military lines. The officers, especially the Governor, wore dashing uniforms on gala days; the clothing of the native soldiers, however, was incomplete, many of them being without jackets or shoes, while a number of their muskets were fastened with rope yarn to their stocks; and other makeshifts were resorted to so as to bring them under the name of " guns."

The principal provisions of the settlement consisted of fowls, pigs, eggs and rice, all of which were abundant; the rice was grown locally in large quantities by the natives. For the most part the soldiers reared their own provisions. Each private received, as pay, two yards of blue calico per month, and about a quarter of a pound of beads. Fish, too, was abundant, caught by the natives by means of reed fences fastened to poles and placed in the river so as to serve as a standing net; from such enclosures the fish was collected at low tide. The articles procurable by barter at the settlement were sea-cow and elephant ivory, also ostrich feathers. The principal objects for sale, however, were slaves.

The rule for trade at Delagoa, which I believe is followed also at Sofala and Quilimane, is that all produce for shipment is weighed under the superintendence of an officer appointed for that duty. All articles, for instance elephant tusks, above 50 pounds in weight, may be purchased only in the name of the Governor on behalf of the Government of Brazil. The Governor may purchase for himself tusks above 40 and below 50 pounds in weight, whilst each sub-officer and the licensed traders were allotted other weight limits within which they might purchase. This principal applies, at the Portuguese settlement of Sofala, to the purchase of gold dust, where, instead of weights, sieves are used. All grains that do not pass through the largest sieve are purchased for the Government. Sieves of a smaller scale are allotted to the different ranks of officers and licensed traders, while in the case of slaves choice is regulated in accordance with the rank of the purchaser.

Several days passed in attempting to dispose of our cargoes to the Governor. Although really desirous of obtaining hippopotamus ivory, we depreciated its value by professing a wish to purchase elephant tusks. We did not, however, succeed to any considerable extent in our speculation with the Government, and, indeed, had little desire to have much to do with it, as we preferred to deal with natives at a distance, as far as we could manage to get in among them. With that object in view therefore it was arranged I should proceed in the *Mary* up the Maphutha River.

Among those who accompanied me was the Rev. William Threlfall.[1] As we were crossing the bay a hippopotamus rose out of the water near us. It was no sooner seen by men of the *Leven* than several of them took boat and harpoons and went in pursuit. The animal eluded them for a considerable time. Then, while they were looking out on one side of the boat, it

---

[1] On a previous visit to Delagoa Bay Capt. Owen contemplated the cession of the Tembe country to Great Britain. He accordingly brought the Rev. William Threlfall, of the Cape, with the intention of settling him as a missionary in that country. This expedition referred to seems to have started on or about 1st September, 1823. cf. Cheeseman, *Story of William Threlfall*, Cape Town, 1910.—*Editor.*

came up on the other and, gripping the gunwale with its jaws, tore out one side of the boat. The sailors then had to swim for it. As we were nearest them, we picked them up, put them on board their own ship, and again set sail for the Maphutha.

Our entrance into this fine river was considerably delayed by taking soundings. We amused ourselves by firing our small cannon into the midst of hundreds of sea-cows, basking at midday on the open sandbanks, but we were not successful in hitting any of them.

It took us three days to go 40 miles up the river. The banks were densely covered with beautiful forest timber. We continually met natives sailing in boats closely resembling those known in India as massuly boats. At intervals we saw native kraals in the background; near these we landed, when we found we could not proceed further up the river. The kraal on the right bank of the Maphutha belonged to one Mɓongi, a counsellor of chief Makhasana, whose territory we were then in. We at once informed him that the object of our visit was to trade, and at the same time sent a present to his chief, as is customary in transactions with tribes on this coast. After waiting two days, Makhasana himself arrived on board with a present in return, viz., two elephant tusks. The trade having been thus opened by the chief, his followers came with elephant and sea-cow tusks. Our trade then went on pretty briskly, but this was not allowed to last long. Two Portuguese boats, with two sergeants and armed soldiers, came and located themselves close beside us, with their Portuguese flag hoisted in defiance. This led us to hoist our piece of bunting, and we soon found ourselves contending to ruin each other's prospects, or, to take another view of the case, giving the highest marketable price to the natives for their ivory. They must have had many transactions with whalers or other ships from the depth of cunning they showed in all their transactions, and they turned the rivalry between us to their advantage. The chief said to me that if I would make them a large present of blankets, brass and beads he would not only give us the preference over the Portuguese but send me ten tusks of his best ivory. This I was simple enough to accede to, and, after several days delay, obtained nothing but excuses and a certainty of getting nothing in return for our present. I at once decided on what action to take. When Mɓongi and the chief's son came on board we made them prisoners, though allowing their followers to inform their chief that we would detain them until he fulfilled what he had undertaken to do. Numbers of natives collected on the bank and the Portuguese showed every disposition to join them in frightening and compelling us to give up the prisoners. We, however, stood firm. We kept watch day and night for two days, when their chief sent the ivory he had promised to give. I could not but think I had acted rashly or at least very simply in having brought matters to such a pass. To amend the past I sent the chief another present to conciliate him.

An accident that occurred to one of the Portuguese boats caused them to return to their settlement. Trade then went on again satisfactorily, especially in sea-cow tusks, which, as I said, we were the more desirous of obtaining.

Wishing to see as much of the country as possible and to see more of certain other strange natives, locally known as Orontonts, who, as I had observed, differed considerably from those of Delagoa and lived to the south thereof, I made friends with and accompanied them to their kraals, a distance of about 50 miles along the coast southwards.

I had already noticed that the natives of Delagoa appeared to be in great dread of the Orontonts. I found out that these people, the Orontonts or Hottentots, belonged to the Zulu tribe, under Shaka, and were a very powerful nation. Among the natives of Delagoa there were many who could speak English. A party of these, accompanying me to a Zulu kraal, enabled me to hold a conversation. I discovered that their chief, Shaka, resided at too great a distance from there for me to reach him. Apart from this I became considerably indisposed, hence went back to where our vessel was, upon which I was immediately laid up with a severe attack of fever.

During my absence, Maynard had sent for the schooner, hence I found myself left with only the sailor who had been with me the whole time. I obtained possession of a hut like those at Delagoa and there I lay for several days. I must have become delirious, for the first thing I remember was being taken from the hut by a native doctor and several women. On coming to an open space, they lifted me up and placed me in a pit they had dug and in which they had been making a large fire; grass and weeds had been placed therein to prevent my feet from being burnt. They put me in a standing position, then filled the pit with earth up to my neck. The women held a mat round my head. In this position they might have kept me for about half an hour. They then carried me back to the hut and gave me native medicine. I felt I was recovering. On the third day, I was able to communicate with the vessel.

Prior to receiving an answer, the Rev. Threlfall, who had made an excursion along the left bank of the river, with the object of selecting, within the Tembe country, a station at which he could carry on mission work, was also attacked by fever. He was brought to the hut where I was. I got native women to adopt the same procedure towards him as I had myself gone through, which had the desired effect, though he did not recover his strength. We then proceeded down the Maphutha to the shipping, where, to the disgrace of those who had it in their power to help, he was refused admittance and left to be humanely received by the Portuguese, who were not his countrymen.

When I arrived at the shipping I was still weak. On being invited to do so by the Portuguese Governor, I stayed with him on shore for several days. From him I learnt that a tradition existed as to a white man called John having reached Delagoa with a coloured woman many years previously. They had come across country from the Cape of Good Hope, their companions having died or been killed on the journey. The Governor, however, could not say what had become of John and the woman.

The various tribes in the vicinity of Delagoa, like all other native tribes of Africa, are constantly engaged in petty warfare, and, wherever there is a Portuguese settlement, these contests are encouraged, and, not infrequently, one or other of the rival parties is aided by Portuguese soldiers. The prisoners taken by each tribe are purchased by the Portuguese to become slaves. Mayetha, chief of the Tembe country at the time of my visit, had recently been defeated and many of his subjects sold into slavery. It was, therefore, natural that Mayetha, from seeing the terror of the Portuguese in the presence of a British man-of-war, should rejoice at the opportunity of ceding his country to the British Crown, in prospect of protection for himself and the remnants of his tribe. A treaty of amity, protection, and cession was therefore drawn up, without the knowledge of the

Portuguese authorities, and the country of Tembe ceded to the British Crown. The British flag was hoisted in the presence of the officers and all British subjects then at Delagoa Bay and the country officially taken possession of on the authority that had previously been delegated to Captain Owen.

To afford encouragement and some shadow of protection while the cession of the country was being submitted to England for approval, it was necessary that an agent be pointed out to Mayetha, as one to whom he might refer for advice when in difficulty. A ready agent was soon found in the person of Lieutenant Decher, second in command at the Delagoa settlement. This man was disgusted with the Governor and proffered his services to Owen, whereupon he was appointed British Consul for the country of Tembe. The proceedings, up to the date of Owen's departure, were supposed to be known to but few people.

A few days after the appointment came the birthday of the Empress of Brazil. A grand fete was arranged for the occasion. The Governor and his suite paraded in much gold and tinsel, whilst the infantry did likewise in their best uniforms. About 40 men drawn up in two lines of which those in front wore two shoes and stockings apiece, while those in the rear one shoe and stocking apiece, just as I had seen done when Portuguese troops paraded in St. Jago.[1] Next came a dinner at the Governor's house to which were invited the captains of the three vessels then at Delagoa; I too came as supercargo. I sat to the right of the Governor. All went satisfactorily until Lieutenant Decher, who was sitting on my right, requested the pleasure of taking wine with His Excellency. The glasses had been filled and brought to the salute, when the Governor threw the contents of his glass in Decher's face, addressing him as he did so as British Consul. Decher was immediately put under arrest and our dinner came to an end.

Later on a salute was fired from the fort as well as by the shipping. Whilst re-loading a cannon one William Kelly, mate on our ship, had his arm blown off, owing to the vent not having been stopped up.

I may state here that Mr. Threlfall obtained a passage to the Cape in the *Saucy Jack*, though he was a considerable time

---

[1]Santiago ? No visit to Santiago or St. Jago is elsewhere referred to in the author's MSS.

there before he recovered his strength. He gave up all idea of returning to Delagoa and, instead, contemplated establishing a mission among the Hottentot-Bushman tribe in Namaqualand. He travelled thither on foot, accompanied by a Bushman as guide. This man, however, murdered him on the journey for the sake of the beads and trinkets he had with him for purchasing food.

The distance from St. Lucia to Delagoa may be about 250 miles. Marshy country extends along the coast; it is the malaria from this which produces the fever so prevalent at Delagoa Bay and in that part of the Zulu country nearest these extensive swamps. This is proved by the fact of the fever prevailing in both these localities owing to the south-west and north-east winds which pass over them.

Captain Owen completed his survey of the south-eastern Africa coast, and I have heard it said by nautical men that it was a very correct one. That he allowed no difficulties to stand in the way of his executing his commission was pretty clearly proved by the exertions he made to survey every river and inlet. In the course of this work he lost two, if not three crews, and I have heard it stated, though do not know if it be a fact, that this neglect of his men's lives met with much displeasure from the Home authorities, so that he felt obliged to absent himself from home shortly after his return. During his absence on the survey changes had taken place in the Ministry, hence those who had confided in him and entrusted him with his duties were no longer in power.

I was at Delagoa Bay for six months.[1] During this time I visited the inland chiefs and their people,[2] and had various interviews with the Portuguese of that settlement. Two officers of the *Leven* had already preceded me by a few months in going up the Maphutha, but both of them contracted fever and died.[3]

---

[1] From about June to December, 1823.—*Editor*.
[2] In August and September.—*Editor*.
[3] This evidently refers to the party under Lieut. R. Owen who had been directed " to complete the survey of the great bay (Delagoa) and of the river Maputa." This expedition, extending over three weeks, took place in January, 1823. Hoad and Tudor, with several others, when some miles up the Maphutha, went off on an embassy to Makhasane. After seeing the chief, they continued to follow the course of the river, but as some of the party were simultaneously striken with fever, one or two of them dying, Owen hurriedly returned to his base on the 28th of the same month. cf. Owen, *Narratives of Voyages to Explore Shores of Africa, Arabia and Madagascar*, 1833, vol. I, 212-225.—*Editor*.

Chapter II

AS I had gone to Delagoa as supercargo of a merchantman, I felt no interest in making myself acquainted with the history of the tribes in those parts; hence it is only by comparing what I have since acquired about Kaffir tribes in other parts of South Africa that I can form any opinion as to the past or present state of those round about Delagoa.

There seemed to be several tribes between Delagoa Bay and Sofala, the next Portuguese settlement to the north-east. They are distinct in language, manners and customs from the Kaffirs and Zulus, though differing little in colour. Their mode of government is somewhat similar to that of the Kaffirs. Evidently for at least a hundred years they have been oppressed by their neighbours the Zulus, and similar large tribes occupying country inland of them. Such tribes never allowed them to possess cattle in sufficient numbers for their own support. They are far more industrious than the Kaffirs, far more ingenious and have a better kind of dwelling house; they make their own boats and are expert huntsmen and swimmers. These are the people I should recommend as being at once procurable and adaptable to the labour requirements of Natal sugar planters. Their country is within a few days sailing of this port, and the same conditions could be carried out as in regard to the Coolies,[1] whilst they would be found fully as serviceable in every particular.

The natives of Delagoa and the surrounding country are called Amanhlwenga by the Zulus, and differ from the latter in manners and language, and are generally similar to those inhabiting the country between Delagoa and Sofala. The principal chief is Makhasane, who lives in the country west of the Maphutha River.

The country of the Tembes, east of the Maphutha and divided from the Portuguese fort by the English River, was occupied by chief Myetha, who had been in a state of constant warfare with Makhasane. The advantages derivable from these

---

[1] These words prove that this paragraph was written in Durban in or about 1860, since the Coolies (Indians) did not begin to arrive in Natal until 1859.—*Editor*.

conflicts were beneficial to the Portuguese, for they purchased the prisoners captured by the rival parties and made slaves of them.

Those who were made prisoners were sold, whilst those who escaped were caught in the woods in a famished state, owing to their corn having been destroyed. Hence nearly the whole of the tribe was sold into slavery, the country west of English River being subject to Makhasane. The land near the coast is low and swampy. It is generally of a sandy nature, but in some places there is rich and very fertile mould.

During the " healthy season " the climate is salubrious. The sickly or " unhealthy season "[1] begins in the latter part of October, including November and December, when fevers and ague prevail owing to the humidity of the air, the wind bringing with it noxious vapours rising from the extensive swamps. During the unhealthy season, the Portuguese encourage ulcers as much as possible; these they keep open to prevent their being attacked by other complaints.

The natives are generally industrious in the field, and always have enough for their own consumption as well as some for sale. They grow Indian corn, millet (*luphoko*), Guinea corn, beans of various kinds and red rice. Quantities of the latter are sold to the factory[2] as also to vessels visiting the Bay. It is generally sold in paddy, that being the state in which they keep it for use. Poultry is plentiful.

The situation of the tribes for trade purposes is very advantageous, for they have the Zulus on one side and the Portuguese on the other, and formerly the Ndwandwes to the north.

During the chieftainship of Joɓe, father of Dingiswayo [chief of the Mthethwa tribe], the natives of Delagoa trafficked very little with them, but Dingiswayo monopolised the whole market until he was killed by Zwide [chief of the Ndwandwe tribe], which induced the Delagonians to open up a trade with the latter. They continued [after Dingiswayo's death] to trade with Shaka, by whom they were looked on as being the only people who possessed beads and brass [copper]. The former article gave rise to many conjectures.

---

[1] The unhealthy season in recent years has been regarded as extending over January, February and March as well.—*Editor.*
[2] At the fort.

Some supposed them to be found on the sea coast of Delagoa at low water; others, that they grew in bunches on trees, which ideas still exist here and there among the Zulus. As these people were looked on as being the sole merchants, they were left unmolested by both the powerful chiefs referred to, to both of whose markets they carried monkey and genet skins procured by hunting and catching them in traps. For the beads, brass and blue cloth (dungaree) that were brought they received in return elephant and sea-cow ivory, iron and tobacco.

Trade with the Portuguese factory, on the east side of the English River, was equally beneficial. The ivory procured from the Zulus and Ndwandwes together with the prisoners taken in their wars (which they sold as slaves) they bartered with the Portuguese for beads and brass. Ambergris is also sometimes found on the coast, and used to barter with. The death of Myetha, however, has set aside all the competition which formerly existed between the two chiefs, the trade being now monopolised by the factory which prohibits the ships of other Powers from trafficking with the natives.

From a long intercourse with Europeans, which has introduced many necessaries of life of which they formerly were ignorant, one would expect the natives of Delagoa to be more civilized than the Zulus, subject to a despotic form of government. This, however, is not the case, for the Zulus are a mildly disposed people and of clear intellect, whereas the Delagonians are dependent solely on intercourse with Europeans for improvement in their productions. Compared with the Zulus, they are a stupid, ignorant people, filthy in their persons and disgusting in their manners, although cleanly in regard to their food, always washing their hands when engaged in cooking it. The walls of their round huts are built of reeds with slanting roofs projecting beyond the walls. The reed walls are neatly built, and the houses kept very clean. Generally, each hut contains four or five large baskets, four or five feet in height; in these they keep their corn. The doors, as a rule made of wood, are generally four or five feet in height and each with a lock and key on lines similar to those of the poor Cape Boer. Sometimes they are neatly carved. They have also baskets and mats of neat workmanship. Many possess boats which at least show that much patience has been exercised in their construction especially when account is taken of the difficulties under which the work had to be done.

Trees that can readily be split are cut down and split into planks, even though they are as much as 18 inches thick. One tree therefore will seldom yield more than three planks, these are dubbed down and fitted to a keel. Holes are bored on both edges, and dry rushes placed over the seam. It is then sewn together with rope made from the bark of trees. Sometimes mats are used as sails, at other times paddles. These boats are 12 to 18 feet in length, with a carved head at the bow, so roughly executed, however, as scarcely to be known as such.

The chiefs and principal people wear a profusion of beads, with heavy brass bangles from the wrist to the elbow; sometimes a covering of blue cloth is worn.

The head is shaved, leaving part of the hair on top in a conical shape, four inches in length and three in breadth. It rises from a point in front to about three inches on the crown, where it is combed and plaited with a thorn.

On a certain part of their persons, they wear a tube of finely plaited sennit of neat workmanship, sometimes exceeding two feet in length.

Married women wear a blue linen petticoat; their hair is kept short. The girls might be said to be naked, as they only wear a cloth but a few inches square in front; round the waist is a leather thong, from which hangs, behind the person, a double string of brass balls, weighing in all from five to seven pounds; in addition they are decorated with beads and brass bangles, the latter being worn round the arms. Their musical instruments are of two kinds. One is a bow forming half a square, having two holes within four inches of each end. A thin piece of wood, two inches broad, is wedged in the holes, and extends from one hole to the other. This has in it 14 holes of one inch in diameter, to which are attached gourds of the *indondondo* plant; these are attached to the poles. The larger gourds are placed at the end and decrease regularly in size towards the other end. The skin of a bullock's heart is laid on each gourd and fastened down with wax. Above each of these is a thin piece of wood eight inches long; this is strung by a leather thong from one end of the bow to the other. These pieces of wood are beaten with two sticks headed with fungus. The instrument is musical, and any tune may be played on it.

The other kind of instrument consists of a piece of wood a foot square and two inches thick, hollowed from one end to the other. A number of thin iron prongs of various lengths, without any regularity in arrangement, are fastened at one end by a small iron bar, the other end being bent up. The music is produced by these prongs being pressed down with the fingers.

Dancing is their principal amusement; during it they make the most indecent gestures; the songs, too, which accompany the dancing are of the most indecent kind.

Of fruits they have the pineapple, cocoanut, and banana, each in great quantities. Saffron grows wild; it is used in their food. Fungus is procured by the natives, who, in order to obtain it, bleed the trees, when a thick white substance runs down into baskets and pots, placed under the incisions to receive it.

A Lieutenant-Colonel of the Sofala Militia, a coloured man, who had been wrecked at Natal, informed us of a powerful chief living to the northward of Sofala, who governs with despotic sway. It is the custom there for the chief, after reigning a short time, to select a woman from the many in his seraglio. He appoints her queen, but co-habits with her only on the first night after marriage. She then goes off to the eastern portion of his territory which she governs in accordance with his commands, conveyed to her by emissaries. He never sees her again after the marriage. At his death she resigns the government. The chief's body is placed on a bier. His sons or brothers, if there be more than one of them, fight among themselves for the bones or seize them by some stratagem; he who obtains the greatest share succeeds to the command of the nation.

In this territory are extensive gold mines which have been worked for ages back, as far as can be remembered. The natives, however, are unacquainted with the proper method of mining. They have dug without any precautions for safety, with the result that many, while mining, have been buried in the earth. Of late years, the mines have again been opened, when the bones of those entombed were found filled with gold. The mining law is that all nuggets of the size of a pea and over are the property of the king, but all smaller sizes belong to partners in the undertaking. The gold collected for the king is converted into bangles for the use of the nation, but much of what goes to the others is bartered at the Portuguese factory. No Europeans are allowed to enter the territory.

What amount of truth there is in this account I must leave to Mr. C.[1] to determine.

Chapter III

THE writer of incidents in the early history of Natal has not the means, even if it were necessary, to give the biography of Lieutenant Francis George Farewell, who first projected a British settlement at Port Natal. He was the son of the Rev. G. Farewell, of Clifton, Bristol. He became a midshipman in the Navy at an early age, and subsequently served with Captain Hoste, under the command of Admiral Hood, in the Mediterranean. He distinguished himself in several actions.[2] But, although mentioned for gallant conduct in the *Naval Chronicle*, and promoted to the rank of Lieutenant, he was obliged, on an early conclusion of peace, to retire on half pay.

Having private means, and being of a venturesome disposition, he purchased the *Princess Charlotte*, of 400 tons, and decided to engage in mercantile " speculations," by carrying, in whole or part, cargoes of merchandise to sundry ports. On freighting his vessel he sailed first to Calcutta, then to Rio Janeiro [Buenos Aires] and the Isle of France [Mauritius]. At the last named place, he obtained a fresh cargo, which he conveyed to the Cape, and then returned to Rio. His vessel was wrecked, when he lost nearly all he possessed.

He returned from Janeiro to Cape Town and took up his abode for several months in the house of a Mr. Petersen, proprietor of a boarding house. This led to his marrying that gentleman's daughter. With what had remained of his capital he chartered the brig *Salisbury*, commanded by Lieutenant James Saunders King, who, shortly before, had, like Farewell, been obliged to leave the Navy; King then became part owner with his mother in several ships engaged at that time in the

---

[1]The reference here is probably to J. C. Chase, the well-known compiler of *Natal Papers*, to whom Fynn occasionally afforded information about Natal.—*Editor*.

[2] "Whilst serving in the Navy, he received several wounds, and at a very early age was entrusted by Sir William Hoste with the charge of the Island of Lipa, at that time a place of importance in the Adriatic."—Farewell, in a letter to Lord Charles Somerset, Bird's *Annals of Natal*, I, 191.

West Indian trade. The *Salisbury* proceeded to Rio Janeiro, Isle of France and St. Helena. On these voyages Farewell, who was accompanied by his wife, got to know King so well that a close intimacy sprang up between them.

In the meantime, the brig *Orange Grove*, belonging to H. Nourse and Co., also of Cape Town, which had been sent up the south-east coast, had returned with a cargo of ivory, wax [ambergris], etc., part of it obtained at Delagoa Bay. This led to Farewell and King, during their voyage to St. Helena, considering the advantages of a mercantile trip to St. Lucia Bay, near which a large part of the Zulu nation lived under their great chief Shaka. Farewell's view was that the whole of the ivory and the gold dust obtained by the Portuguese at Delagoa Bay was derived from this powerful chief's territory.

On his return to Cape Town, Farewell succeeded in persuading several merchants to join him in a speculation to St. Lucia, on the coast of Zululand. He once more chartered the *Salisbury*, also a smaller vessel, the sloop *Julia*, freighting both with a cargo designed for native traffic. In this venture he was associated with King as well as with A. Thompson and Co.

When Farewell put in at Algoa Bay, about the end of June, 1823, he found there Captain W. F. W. Owen, R.N., who had just arrived from Delagoa Bay, where he had been engaged in surveying that port on behalf of the Admiralty. Farewell went on board Owen's vessel, the *Leven*, and obtained such information as he required in regard to the coast, also two native interpreters, Fire and Jacob. Of the latter, who subsequently played an important part in connection with the British settlement at Port Natal, a somewhat extended account will be given later.

On reaching St. Lucia, Farewell and King made several attempts to land the cargo and open a communication with Shaka, who resided about 50 miles inland of that bay.

[In regard to this minor though notable exploratory voyage, King wrote two accounts,[1] one in a letter to Earl Bathurst,[2] dated at London, 10th July, 1824; the other, July, 1826. In his second account, King says: " In the latter part of 1823,

---

[1]Theal, *Records of Cape Colony*, 58, 122.
[2]Henry, third Earl Bathurst. He was Secretary for War and the Colonies under the Earl of Liverpool, continuing in such capacity until Liverpool resigned in April, 1827.—*Editor.*

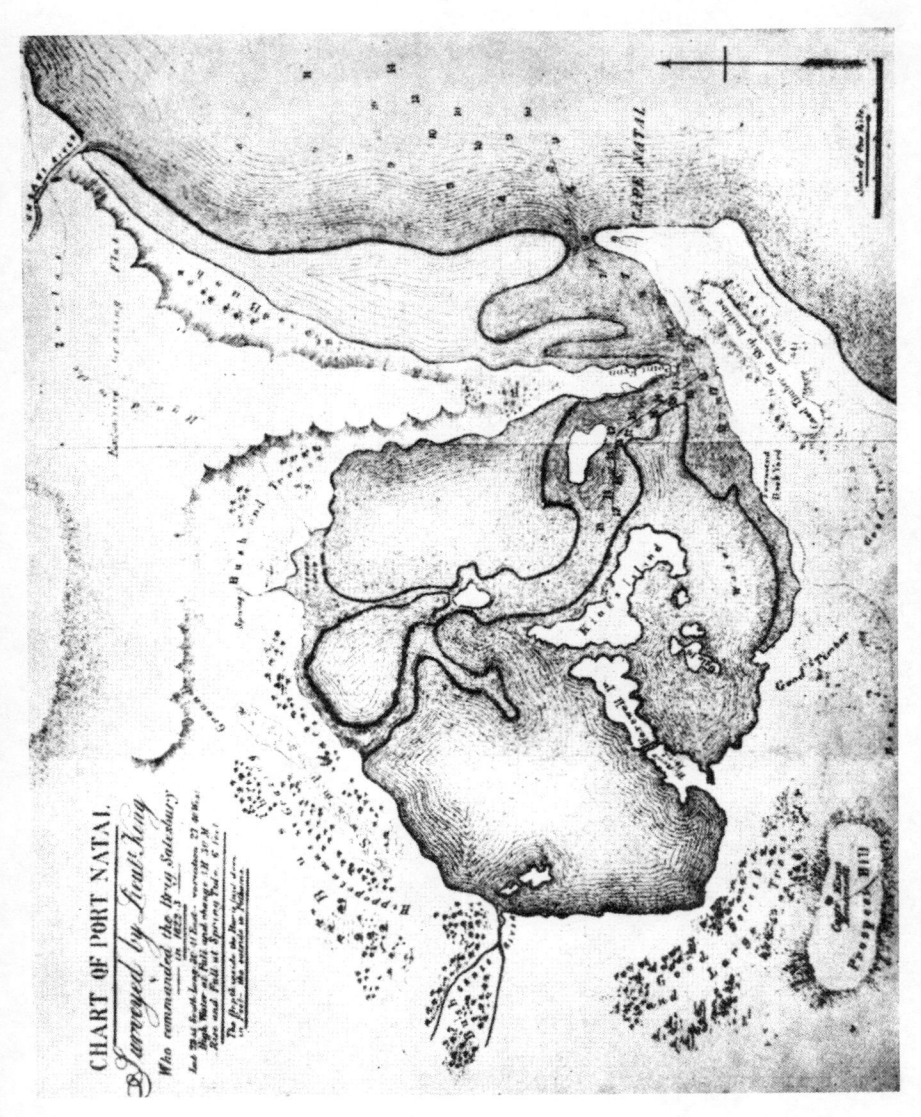

CHART OF PORT NATAL.
Surveyed by Lieutenant King. From *History of Old Durban*, by George Russell.

Lieutenant Farewell and Mr. Alex. Thompson accompanied me in the *Salisbury*, on a voyage to the East Coast of Africa. Having arrived in the neighbourhood, where we intended to commence trading, we attempted at several ports, but it appeared impossible to land. The boats were then sent on shore at St. Lucia, on the coast of Fumos. Mr. Farewell's upset, but, although considerably bruised, he providentially escaped being drowned. Several days after, Mr. Thompson met with a similar accident, his boat being overwhelmed when nearly a mile from the beach; they all gained the shore by swimming, except three poor fellows, who perished in the attempt. We now determined on abandoning the spot, our views being chiefly directed to another quarter. Several weeks elapsed, when we ran into Port Natal, but the voyage proving unsuccessful, altogether, we returned to the Cape of Good Hope. The *Salisbury*, and the *Julia*, our tender, were the first vessels that had entered that port during the lifetime of the oldest inhabitants."[1]]

[The following comments, by Fynn, are in connection with the same occasion.]: The vessel (*Salisbury*) was frequently driven from the outer anchorage, and the attempts to land resulted in loss of boats and cargo. In the last attempt, when the three sailors were drowned, the Kaffir interpreter Jacob, who was also in the boat, managed to swim ashore along with several white men including Thompson. When the *Salisbury* and the *Julia* put out to sea, on account of boisterous weather, Farewell was obliged to leave the sailors and Jacob on shore. Five weeks elapsed before the sailors could be recovered ... but during that time they were well treated by the natives. The *Salisbury* then put back to Algoa Bay for supplies, after which she once more proceeded up the coast.

Farewell and King now attempted to enter the Port of Natal and open up a communication with the chief Shaka by an overland, north-eastern route of 150 miles. The *Julia*, commanded by Armstrong, entered the port, the *Mary*[2] remaining at the outer anchorage.

---
[1]Thompson, G., *Travels and Adventures in Southern Africa*, II, 406. Before it appeared, in a somewhat abbreviated form, in Thompson's work, King's account had been published in the *S.A. Commercial Advertiser*, July 11th, 1826.—*Editor*.
[2]A slip of the pen; it was the *Salisbury*. It was in 1825 that the *Mary* came to Port Natal and was wrecked 30th September.—*Editor*.

Armstrong, though a heavy and most unfitted man for such an enterprise, was selected to open up a communication with the natives. He walked north-east to the Umngeni River in search of natives and, meeting none on that side of the port,[1] he passed over to the south of the Bay, where a few had been seen. These, however, fled at his approach. All prospects of establishing communication were now abandoned and the two vessels returned to the Cape.

[The following further extract from King's letter to Earl Bathurst in connection with his and Farewell's first visit to and entrance of Port Natal, made public only in comparatively recent years, is of exceptional interest:[2] " Having been so unsuccessful in not gaining a port [i.e. at St. Lucia Bay], we proceeded to the southward and passed several rivers, apparently very spacious inward. But the bars having little water on them were not capable of admitting a boat going over. Having an idea that gold might be procured about these rivers, and having experienced many privations, we determined on returning to Port Elizabeth to replenish and prepare accordingly, at which time several of the settlers volunteered to go with us. After being some considerable time on the coast, it came to blow very hard. Being then on a lee shore, and very near the entrance of a river, I determined on attempting the bar, consequently we cut our cable and ran in, where we fortunately arrived safe. This, my Lord, is the spot which I think would prove of the utmost advantage to Government.[3] The particulars and benefits to be derived I will endeavour to point out.

The harbour, though small (being the only one on this extensive coast) is very easy of access for vessels of a certain draft. It abounds with hippopotamus and fish of various sorts and the soil in its vicinity, in my opinion, is particularly productive. At present, Indian corn is the only produce grown, which is large and in great abundance. The plains are very extensive, and the pasture for their cattle rich. Near the anchorage is excellent timber for ship building. It resembles

---

[1]Also because: " deterred from proceeding further by the interpreter who assured them the natives were contemplating their destruction."—Author's MS.
[2]Moreover it is fuller and more instructive than the letter from Farewell to Lord Charles Somerset written about the same time.—Bird, *Annals of Natal*, I, 71.
[3]The reference here is, of course, to Port Natal.—*Editor*.

the cedar. Also at the head of the harbour are fine tall spars, fit for masts, etc. This country, as far as I can venture to speak of, say a distance of about 40 miles, is beautiful and blest with a salubrious air, and a productive soil. Likewise, within that short distance, are several extensive, winding rivers, which adds greatly to its importance. Our first interview with the natives at this place appeared rather hostile on their part, they being armed with their assagai and shield. But when we became better acquainted, they were extremely well disposed and expressed a particular desire for us to remain among them. I should not, my Lord, have ventured to offer an opinion of the capability of the soil of this country, but having several very clever men who appeared perfectly acquainted with agricultural pursuits, and who were unanimous in declaring that, if Government were acquainted with its advantages, they would not hesitate to remove the unfortunate settlers thither.[1] Here they would in all probability succeed in their crops, and have a harbour which would enable them to export their produce to other countries. In addition to this is a very spacious bay, which would afford shelter for such vessels as could not venture over the bar, with north and westerly winds. A chart of which, and several sketches, together with a few of their weapons, I am in possession of; and will, if your Lordship pleases, forward for your Lordship's inspection. . . . I trust your Lordship will not think me presumptive to state that I have served as a midshipman in His Majesty's navy upwards of ten years and can produce the most satisfactory testimonials of my character from the different captains I have had the honour to serve under, one of which, Lord James Townshend—who has examined the different surveys of the East Coast, and has ascertained that the Admiralty are not in possession of any plans of this harbour. . . ."]

The *Salisbury* and the *Julia* reached Cape Town on the 3rd December.

Although, owing to Natal being almost without inhabitants, there were no better opportunities of trading there than at St. Lucia, Farewell was of opinion that if a settlement were established at Port Natal, and the Zulu nation, upon which

---

[1]Theal, *History of South Africa*, 1834–54, 117.

the Delagoa Bay market seemed to depend, were induced to trade at the port, the project might yet prove a success. As this view was shared by King, the two agreed to enter into partnership and endeavour to carry out the idea. To this end, King was to proceed to England to make the necessary arrangements, whilst Farewell was to do likewise in Cape Town.

The *Mary* and the *Jane* (on which I was employed as supercargo) returned to Cape Town within a day of each other. We found that the *Salisbury* and the *Julia* with Farewell and King had arrived a few days before us from St. Lucia. We had made a satisfactory trip, while they had sustained nothing but losses. This, however, in no way damped Farewell's hopes, for he was already contemplating another trial at Port Natal.[1]

Before he had been a month in Cape Town, he had so represented the great advantages to be derived from a trade in ivory by way of the port, obtainable from the chief Shaka, that he induced his father-in-law, Mr. Petersen, and another Dutch gentleman of the name of Hoffman to join him in partnership. He convinced them that all the ivory procured at Delagoa Bay by the Portuguese was obtained from Shaka, the Zulu chief, whose cattle kraals were entirely made of elephant tusks. I cannot allow myself to make a statement against the veracity of this gentleman without expressing the opinion that he was either told or given to understand this by some native who intended merely to imply that the elephant tusks were placed *around* the cattle kraal.

Farewell at this time made proposals to me about joining his party, representing, as he had done to his partners, the immense profits which would be derived from the speculation. He proposed that I should have the entire management of the trading transactions. Instead of allowing me salary, I should receive a handsome percentage to be decided upon after being one month in port. I at once consented, as it was understood the speculation would be completed within six months. Travelling and new scenes were to me a greater object than any pecuniary advantage. It then fell to my lot, during the

---

[1] When Farewell learnt (in Capetown) that our voyage to Delagoa Bay had been successful he formed the opinion that the Delagonians procured their ivory from a people more powerful than themselves and concluded, from what he had seen and heard at Port Natal, it must be the Zooloes. He inferred from this that a settlement founded at Port Natal would succeed in drawing the ivory intended for the Delagoa market.—Author's MS.

period of preparation, to make purchases of the articles required for native trade. Farewell, from the opinion he had formed of Shaka's greatness, purchased a far greater variety than I should have done, in consequence of my experience of the petty chiefs at Delagoa Bay.

I found the party was to consist of from 30 to 40 individuals, and such a variety of material was provided that if I had been capable of bestowing a second thought on the matter I would at once have become convinced it was never intended that six months should terminate the speculation. But a few days in connection with Farewell, Petersen and Hoffman were enough to convince me that the necessary confidence which should exist in such an undertaking did not prevail.

In beating up for volunteers, Farewell used all his diligence to induce as many Englishmen as he could to join the party, while Petersen and Hoffman used their efforts to enrol Dutchmen. This created daily soreness, and I began to doubt if the expedition would ever leave the Cape. I also observed that Hoffman was obtaining from some of the junior clerks in the Colonial Office information from the records in reference to a party of the Dutch East India Company who had occupied the Port of Natal when the Company was in possession of the Cape of Good Hope.[1]

---

[1] Mr. Farewell engaged the brig *Antelope* and the sloop *Julia*, and he obtained permission of the Colonial Government to form a settlement at Port Natal, although the people (engaged by him) were led to believe that the stay would be only from three to six months.—Author's MS.

Chapter IV

WHILE matters appeared to be in a very unsatisfactory state between the co-partners, it was arranged that I should proceed in advance, and endeavour to effect a communication with the chief, Shaka. I accordingly sailed in the *Julia*, a small sloop of between 20 and 30 tons, having with me stores and three mechanics, Ogle, an Englishman, a Prussian, and a Frenchman, also Michael, a Hottentot servant, and Frederick, a Kaffir interpreter, from the Cape frontier.[1] Nothing worthy of notice occurred on the voyage, except that it was tedious and unpleasant owing to the smallness of the vessel and its crowded state, with 26 persons, besides cargo on board. Our little craft crossed the bar at half tide and we anchored early in the morning of the 10th March, 1824,[2] opposite to where the present Custom House stands, that is, about a quarter of a mile within the northern point of the port. The bay appeared to be surrounded by bush in every direction; the only spot that was somewhat open was the locality now known as Khangela.

About three o'clock I proceeded to this spot in a boat, accompanied by three mechanics. On landing there with provisions and bedding, I sent the boat back to the vessel and strolled about the Khangela flat on the chance of finding some natives. We strolled both to the right and left of Khangela to select a spot for building, until sunset, but met with no trace of any inhabitants being in the country. Traces of sea-cows everywhere abounded. We selected a hollow or dip under rising ground to protect us from the winds, and then began to prepare for the night, cooking food and arranging beds.

---

[1] The plan was that the mechanics should get on with the buildings, etc., pending the arrival of Farewell, Petersen, Hoffman and the rest of the party. —*Editor*.

[2] This is evidently a mistake and one which has led authorities like Bird and even the Native Affairs Commission of 1852–3 astray. The MS. in which the above occurs appears to have been written at the author's dictation about 1854. In a more deliberate one of about 1834, however, the date of his arrival in the *Julia* is given as May, 1824. Other considerations, too lengthy to go into here, seem to us clearly to point to May as correct, for instance : (*a*) Farewell, who is known to have arrived at Port Natal about six weeks after Fynn, got there in the *Antelope* in July ; (*b*) Theal (*Hist. of S. Africa*, 1824–54, 118) proves by the *Cape Gazette* that the *Julia* reached Table Bay from Saldanha Bay with a cargo of grain on the 27th March.—*Editor*.

Moderately tired after our walk, we soon went to sleep. We had, however, not been long in that condition when, about midnight, a storm broke over us. Not only we, but our bedding, became thoroughly drenched, and a stream of water which rushed through the hollow forced us to move to higher ground. Fortunately, we had collected a large quantity of fuel, and having some large logs on fire we removed them and the fuel to higher ground. Sleep was impossible. We employed ourselves in making a blazing fire and wrapping ourselves in our wet blankets. While thus occupied we were surprised by the howling of troops of wolves, which were coming from different directions, to where we had located ourselves. We increased our fire as far as the rain would permit us, in the hope that the wolves would be kept at a distance, but, in defiance of the fire and our yells, they approached and stood before us. To see them was impossible. We had not brought firearms with us, and as the wolves approached nearer and nearer, we had no better mode of defence than by standing back-to-back with firebrands in our hands. Several came so close as to snap at us, and we were able to strike them with firebrands.

In rushing to our standing position, we had separated from our bedding. One of the wolves seized therefrom the leather trousers belonging to Ogle, in which he had a Dutch 60-dollar note. This he was determined to defend. He rushed forward, caught hold of the band of the trousers as the wolf was dragging them, and succeeded in recovering them with the loss of only one of the legs. Although all of us had rushed to his assistance in the dark we succeeded only in beating the wind with our firebrands, though that had the effect of scaring the wolves away.

The Prussian, anxious to secure his bedding, was on all fours rolling it up when a wolf came and caught him by the foot. He screamed out most vociferously: " My toag! my toag! " meaning his toe. This caused a roar of laughter, as we were now less fearful, finding we were not likely to be rushed upon en masse. A firebrand thrown at the wolves released him from his predicament. The troops of wolves had regularly besieged our position, and we momentarily expected to be torn to pieces. We then all stooped down together to extend the fire round our position. In this we only partially succeeded, owing to the scarcity of the fuel, while the smoke almost blinded us. To obviate this, still back-to-back, we took up a sitting posture; we talked to one another and Ogle sang songs at intervals. We continued in this way, momentarily expecting the wolves would rush upon us, until day had fully dawned, when we put up a signal for the boat. On its arrival we returned to the vessel. After having breakfasted and recounted our night's disaster, we proceeded to what is now known as Cato's Creek, another open space larger than that at Khangela. The Town Hall of Durban now stands on that spot.

I now, however, selected a spot opposite the present church of St. Paul's in Durban, where the present railway station stands. To guard ourselves from another and similar disturbance by the wolves, we had taken with us a mainsail. Of this we formed a tent. We chopped down bushes and fortified ourselves with a strong fence. We heard the wolves during the night, but, conscious of our security, slept at intervals, though disturbed every now and then by the howling.

On the following morning the mechanics, assisted by the crew of the vessel, were set to work to cut timber and build a 12 foot square house of wattle and daub.

Taking my Kaffir interpreter, Frederick, with me, I walked round to the head of the bay in search of inhabitants; we came across none, though we found several footprints. On the following day, two or three natives were seen from the vessel running about in the water at low tide, on the Bluff beach. I immediately proceeded thither with Griffith in the boat, in the hope of communicating with them. But as we approached they fled to their dense fastnesses on the Bluff.[1] We, however, ran down one of them and having shown him we were well disposed towards him, by holding up a few beads, he accompanied us in the boat to our vessel, then on to our camp. His name was Mahamba. He and my interpreter understood very little of each other's dialect, though speaking in the same language. My enquiries as to where Shaka resided were unsatisfactorily replied to. All I could learn was that their nation had been destroyed by Shaka and that he was a powerful chief living to the northward, and that I would have to travel 30 days before I reached him. I was sure this was incorrect

---

[1] We found at Natal about 60 persons, remnant of a tribe recently destroyed by Shaka, living on the westerly point of the bay in a most distressful and famished condition.—Author's note.

as I had seen kraals only 30 miles north of the port, when our vessel had been driven past it. But such was their fear of him that they durst not accompany us or leave the bush at low tide to get fish, their only sustenance.

I immediately decided on commencing my journey and travelling along the coast north-eastwards, in search of Shaka's residence. Prior to leaving, I marked out the house that was to be begun in my absence on a spot which is now within the market place of Durban and about 200 yards in front of the door of St. Paul's Church. After seeing the house commenced and, through the assistance of Mahamba, brought about a friendly feeling with the few natives who with him occupied the fastnesses of the Bluff, also after opening up a trade with them to supply the workmen with fish, the only food these people had to subsist on, I started on my journey to the northward. I expected to be away for two or three days, imagining I should reach Shaka's tribe within a distance of ten or 12 miles. I left on the 15th with the object of visiting Shaka. I took with me Frederick, my Kaffir interpreter, Jantyi Michael, my Hottentot servant and Mahamba.

After travelling about three miles we crossed the Umngeni River. Mahamba showed great fear of the crocodiles and sea-cows which were in great numbers. We, however, passed by without harm. As there were no footpaths or human foot-prints, only elephant and sea-cow tracks being observable, I decided on keeping to the beach. When about 12 miles from the port I found myself so completely tired out that I sat down and ordered coffee. Mahamba produced fire from the friction of two sticks. While the kettle was being brought to the boil, I sat on the beach and as I was looking across the sea, then at low tide, I saw on my right a dense mass of people coming fast from the direction I had come. My view extended over several miles of the beach, but I could not see the rear of this immense black and continuous mass of natives, all armed and in their war-dresses. Our surprise was great and had I known the character of these people and the danger I was in, as I now know it, it is a question if I would have stood my ground, though an attempt to run away would not have saved me.

I immediately concluded they had come in pursuit of me after having already destroyed the party I had left building. The bush along the beach was dense and, as I was sure they had seen me, flight appeared inadvisable, though strongly urged by Jantyi and Frederick. Mahamba at once disappeared. On the approach of the head of the column I was struck with astonishment at their appearance, for it was sufficient to terrify. Evidently they were equally surprised at mine, and looked at me with a kind of horror. I stood up on their coming close towards me in the hope of communicating with their commanders through my interpreter and telling the object of my being in their country. When I was telling the interpreter what to say, viz: that I had come across the sea and was desirous of seeing Shaka, one of the foremost men made a sign by spanning his hand round the front of his neck and pointing to some beads round the neck of another native, evidently asking for beads. This sign was no sooner observed than Jantyi fled precipitately into the bush, and Frederick immediately followed his example, leaving me alone to my dumb show efforts at communication, and, no doubt, with misunderstanding on both sides. The signs consisted in pointing in the direction from whence I had come, and in that in which I wished to go; moreover I frequently repeated the name of Shaka. The leaders talked much among themselves, but at length passed on along the beach. This dense mass of natives continued to pass by me until sunset, all staring at me with amazement, none interfering with me.

I have since been of the opinion that my coolness, for I certainly felt no fear, saved me from instant destruction. In the passing of this force I could not but remark that they moved in divisions, the leader of each showing me the immense control they had over their followers; they frequently struck at them at the slightest appearance of disorder.

My bodyguard, Frederick and Jantyi now appeared with Mahamba. They were surprised to find me not dead. Jantyi exculpated himself by declaring that the signs the man made by spanning round his neck signified nothing less than an intention to hang us, whereas all the man meant to convey was a request for beads to put round his own neck. That this view is correct was shown by what we afterwards heard had occurred at the port, namely, that one of the native fishermen had beads, which he had procured from us, taken from him by one of these men.

I had not the slightest fear in the presence of this dense mass of armed natives, not less than 20,000 strong. That my life was in imminent danger I can now be in no doubt, for, if the leading chiefs had felt a disposition to take my life, they would have met with approval from Shaka on reporting that they had killed a white animal out of the sea. My life evidently was saved on this occasion by that wonderful talisman of this country, the name of Shaka.

We remained at this spot for the night, during which Mahamba deserted and went back to the Bluff. On the following morning we proceeded along the well-beaten track of the army until we reached the Thongati River, some 25 miles from the port, where we found a native kraal of seven huts. The surprise of men and women at seeing a white man created a general fear. The children screamed as the mothers took them up, while the men could only with difficulty be persuaded to come near us. At length by throwing bunches of beads to them they were led into converse with us and afterwards to communicate freely with us and bring their women back from the bushes to which they had fled. Siyingila, the owner of the kraal, presented me with a cow for slaughter. He had but two. We learned that the army, which had passed the day before, had proceeded northwards.

Whilst my communication with these people was going on, another dense column of the same kind of armed warriors came from the direction of the port. I at once became convinced that Shaka's nation was a powerful one.

On their reaching the kraal where I was, the women again fled with their children and great dread was perceptible in Siyingila and his men at the presence of this force. The cow, which had by this time been skinned, was soon surrounded, its slaughterers, Frederick and Jantyi having fled. The chief commanding this force held an excited conversation with Siyingila, Shaka and myself evidently being the subject thereof. The former then sent some of his followers to drive away the men who had surrounded the cow. I then requested the chief to help himself to a portion of the meat, upon which he appointed several men to cut it up. When this had been done, instead of helping himself as desired to do, he insisted on my giving him what I thought fit. I gave him half, and one quarter to Siyingila. They expressed their thanks, then moved quietly on. However, there still appeared to be no end to those following them. By this time I had learned they were Shaka's army returning after having attacked chief Faku, who was said to live a great distance to the southward.

I had taken possession of a hut which had been given me to sleep in when the screams of the women and children became violent. They fled from the kraal in fear of the Zulu forces which still continued to pass, while Siyingila and his men, who remained in the kraal, communicated near the hut in which I was with each party that passed about Shaka and myself. None of the armed forces attempted to approach, but every other hut was pillaged.[1] The women saved only what they were able to carry away with their children. We slept undisturbed until the dawn of the following day when we were awakened by the cries of the women and including those of the surrounding kraals, who, having all fled at the approach of Shaka's force, had, towards daylight, been scattered by packs of wolves; five of the children had been snatched from their mothers' arms and devoured.[2]

I was requested by Siyingila not to proceed further until Shaka had sent to express his wishes, seeing that he (Siyingila) had sent messengers to report my arrival. To this I assented. After waiting three days, a party of about 30 natives, accompanying their chief, Mbikwana, arrived from his kraal about ten miles to the north.[3] On approaching me, with four large oxen being driven before him, Mbikwana made a long speech

---

[1] "A great number of the Zulu army lingered on their march in this locality, having travelled from the seat of war a distance of 225 miles through a country having no inhabitants. This locality was the first where they could procure grain and it being on the outskirts of their own country, the inhabitants being tributaries, they pillaged their fields and cellars and most of the inhabitants fled from fear. Numbers of the Zulu stragglers came to the kraal, where I was, demanding grain. But the headman placed himself at the gate using my presence as a shield, telling them no one must enter the kraal where the King's white man was resting. This saved him from being molested, while it aided, without any intention on my part to do so, to dignify my position."—From another MS. by the author.

[2] "I returned to the port, where I found all our people exerting themselves for our future comfort. After remaining five days at Natal, I again attempted a journey to the King. I passed the first river, the Umngeni, at 8 o'clock, where I found the calf of a hippopotamus lying dead. This the Kaffirs who were with me quickly devoured. There were only eight of them and the animal weighed at least 200 lbs. This enormous breakfast incapacitated them from travelling. I arrived at Siyingila's kraal, whom we found nearly famished from the depredations which had been committed by the Zulu warriors."—Author's MS.

[3] It seems, from another MS., that immediately before Mbikwana's visit six messengers came from him " to enquire the object of my visit, presenting me with two oxen. I informed them we had come to purchase ivory and were desirous of seeing the King with that object."

in honour of Shaka, his nephew; he related his greatness and his valiant deeds as a warrior, and added that he, Mbikwana, acting on behalf of Shaka, who had not yet heard of my arrival in his country, presented me with four oxen that I might not starve in the country of so great a king.[1] That I must at once remove from the kraal of so insignificant a people I was then with to his, Mbikwana's, kraal, nearer and in the direction of Shaka's country.

Mbikwana appeared to be about 60 years of age. He was active and intelligent. His followers and all who approached him paid him the most servile attention. He made the most extensive enquiries as to the object of my visit. He not only assented to my sending three of the oxen to my party at the port, but provided people to take them there. The fourth was slaughtered on the spot, the meat being freely distributed to all the neighbouring kraals. I accompanied him to his own kraal, where we met two messengers with two more oxen as a present to me from Shaka; he wished, moreover, to know the object of my visit. On the following day Mbikwana pointed out to me a petty chief named Mhlophe whom he appointed to be my *induna* (captain); he had five followers. Their duty was to be constantly about my person and to supply my wants. Mbikwana said it would be necessary for me to remain in the locality until Shaka communicated to me his further wishes.[2] I remained in this locality 14 days, on each of which I was presented with an ox. I distributed the meat to the immense numbers that came to see me. The idea of selling the cattle was not entertained by me.

My pack, at first carried by Mahamba, and afterwards by Jantyi, consisted of two blankets, a feather pillow, a coffee-kettle, some sea biscuits, rice, and a box of scales belonging to a

---

[1] In the course of his speech, Mbikwana " complimented me on my greatness, my valour in crossing the seas to visit his king, and all the country possessed was from thence at my command. This was a far higher position than I had ever contemplated holding in any country and I looked on his words as so much froth. The dignity of carriage of this old chief, the submission and respect shown to him by his followers, much surprised me, giving me at once an idea that the frontier Kaffir tribes, also the tribes of Delagoa, could be in no way compared to the superior standing of the Zulu nation."—Author's MS.

[2] I ascertained " it was the King's wish that I should remain with his uncle Mbikwana until his army, just returned from the war, had been collected, so that he could receive me with proper dignity."

medicine chest containing a lancet and a few small packets of medicine.[1]

On the third day at Mbikwana's I found out that one of the women of the kraal was in a violent fever. My interpreter told me that the women of the kraal were talking of removing her to die in the field. I immediately requested Mbikwana to permit me to attempt to cure her. He not only ridiculed this, but asked why I should befoul my hands with a dog like her. I persisted in my request and, her husband favouring it, Mbikwana permitted me to proceed. I observed that my feeling her pulse and looking at her tongue was much ridiculed. On the third day, however, as she had evidently much recovered, great astonishment was expressed. In six days the woman had entirely recovered. I was then surprised to learn that rumour had given me the credit of having raised this woman to life after having been already dead. When I took her in hand, crowds of applicants came to request me to cure them of diseases, although many of them appeared to be in perfect health. Those whom I could not supply continued from day to day to put forward their applications.[2]

A party of about 30 natives, in charge of a chief, now arrived from Shaka. This man's speech, as in the case of Mbikwana, was in honour of Shaka, his greatness, his deeds as a warrior, etc. This chief had brought to me from Shaka a present of 40 head of cattle, oxen and milch cows, that my people might not starve, also seven large elephant tusks, with the assurance that Shaka was much pleased at my coming to his

---

[1] " In my biography [I have failed to find this.—*Editor*.] I have shown how I became ' loblolly boy ' at Christ's Hospital (London) when I obtained the smallest particle of knowledge of medicine. From my experience in connection with fever when I was at Delagoa (in 1823) I had resolved, on coming to Natal, to carry with me a small medicine chest, hence had one with me on the present occasion."—Author's MS.

[2] Another account of this incident is : The most exaggerated reports were circulated as to my ability as a doctor. The woman was said to be positively dead when restored by me to life. This rumour soon reached Shaka. During the time that I remained at Mbikwana's numerous were the applications made to me for medicine, some by messengers from minor chiefs who did not appear. The greater number complained of pains in the loins, shoulders, etc., evidently from rheumatism. I observed that all the applicants had been under the hand of their native doctors, who had scarified the parts and inserted some powder or drug which left marks darker than the natural colour of the skin ; from the applications being numerous it was plain the native remedy was not, in all cases, to be depended on. By some of Mhlophe's followers, I sent the ivory and cattle I had received, to the port, to await the arrival of Lieut. Farewell from the Cape, or my return.—Author's MS.

country, but that he would not be prepared to see me until after his army had rested after their return from their recent war with Faku, and that I might not, in the meantime, want for anything he had sent me an induna with ten followers to be my guard and attend to all my wants. His name was Msika. There was something so frightfully forbidding in this man's countenance that, in addition to the conviction that one of his duties was to spy and report on my every action, I felt he looked as much like a murderer as it was possible to infer from his countenance. After expressing my thanks for Shaka's liberality, I said that in appointing this man he had done more than I required, for I already had Mhlophe, with whom I was satisfied, whereas this man showed in his countenance and manner a disposition for murder though I had no doubt, from the convincing proofs of Shaka's feeling towards me, that I was mistaken. Several hundred natives were present during this harangue. During the whole of that day my observation as to the murderous disposition of this man afforded a very great deal of amusement.[1]

Two of the native fishermen from the port now brought a letter from the captain of the sloop informing me of the arrival of Lieutenant Farewell and his party. I thereupon returned to the port with my cattle and ivory, after telling Mbikwana that I would await at the port Shaka's further communication.[2]

---

[1] Another description of this incident runs thus : Another messenger with twenty attendants came from Shaka. He informed me he too had been sent to be my attendant and was superior in rank to the former captain Mhlophe. A more villainous and murderer-like face I had never seen. I hesitated some time as to how I should reply. At length, in the presence of 100 natives who were present with Mbikwana, the King's uncle, I plainly told him that I did not like his looks and that murder was imprinted on his face. My candour might have proved to be anything but wisdom. It however, produced a simultaneous roar of laughter, and, though Mbikwana enjoyed it as much as the rest, many ran away roaring with laughter. Believing that I had at least acted unwisely, I soon got into familiar conversation with my new friend, telling him I was fond of a joke and that no wise king would kill his subjects for their looks. I found this captain, Msigali, too glad of being on a friendly footing with me to take offence at my indiscretion.—Author's MS.

[2] The messengers I had sent to the port with the cattle and ivory now returned with a letter from Lieut. Farewell informing me of the safe arrival of himself and party in the *Ellen* [A slip—it was the *Antelope* according to a much earlier MS.—*Editor.*] and wishing my early return. The *Ellen* [*Antelope*] being a chartered vessel, had to sail again for the Cape, whereas the *Julia* (in which Fynn had previously arrived) had been purchased by Farewell to lie at Natal for future communication with the Cape. I communicated that arrival of the party by messengers to Shaka and at once returned to the port and joined the party there. They were highly gratified at my success in having opened up communication with Shaka and also procured cattle for the immediate needs of the party. Moreover they were much interested in the description I gave them of my trip.—Author's MS.

Chapter V

LIEUTENANT Farewell and his party consisted of 30 persons. We were thus 35 in number with those who came with me. Most of them were Dutch, three Germans, two Frenchmen and one Dane. Farewell, Ogle and I were the only Englishmen; strange to relate there was no Scotsman in the party.

Farewell, Petersen and Hoffman shared in superintending the men employed on the temporary buildings and in securing the cattle and the 11 horses which had arrived in the *Antelope* from the wolves that prowled about night after night. They had already taken three calves. Leopard spoors were also found daily in the neighbourhood, hence night watches were appointed for the security of the place.

A day was now set apart as a holiday, when the British ensign was hoisted. Two cannon which we had brought with us were fired, also small arms. Formal possession was taken of the Port of Natal with its surrounding unoccupied country. Though we did not then know its extent, we soon learned that it reached from north-east to the port, to St. John's River on the south, and from the sea to the Drakensberg on the west.

Shaka's uncle, Mbikwana, with about 100 followers, came to the port by Shaka's direction to say the King was now prepared to receive us. We accordingly made arrangements that Hoffman should remain at the port to superintend the buildings, while Farewell, Petersen and I, Frederick, the interpreter, and three Hottentots were to proceed to Shaka. We went off accompanied by Mbikwana and his followers, all the latter being employed in carrying the presents intended for Shaka, also our bedding, clothing, etc.[1]

We took the route I had previously travelled. On arriving at the Umngeni, much time was lost by Farewell persisting in our searching for gold in the river. What were deemed to be indications of gold proved to be nothing but mica.

A sea-cow path had to be followed through the bush to take us on to the beach. I may here state that Petersen was

---

[1] We started with 13 Europeans, 8 horses, 4 Hottentots and 30 natives,—Author's note.

SHAKA, KING OF THE ZULUS
From Nathaniel Isaacs' *Travels and Adventures in Eastern Africa*, vol. I

63 years of age, corpulent and subject to ill health, not of the sweetest temper, and seldom spoke without swearing. The delay at the river in searching for gold had by no means sweetened his temper. While going along the sea-cow track, one of his legs became entangled, as well as his neck, in the monkey ropes which, in this country, abound in bushy parts. He now broke out into a violent temper, swearing: " God verdam, dat is geen paad voor een man van dree en sestig jaren." The whole body of the natives looked with astonishment on what had produced such passion. Farewell burst into a fit of laughter and I could not help doing likewise. This considerably increased the difficulty of our position, for Petersen at once insisted on going back to the port and returning to the Cape. However unfitted he was for such excursion, he had so far involved himself in the undertaking that his sole motive for undertaking this journey was evidently to get an ocular demonstration of the cattle kraals alleged to be formed out of elephant tusks. He therefore required very little soothing. We went forward and continued the journey beyond the Thongati River without any difficulty. We had, however, no sooner crossed the river than our path led us through a swamp, with here and there clumps of earth sufficiently solid to enable a pedestrian to step without difficulty from one to the other. I took the lead and crossed without mishap. Petersen, to ensure a safe passage, ordered the Hottentot John to cross before him and attempted to follow his route. His horse, however, brought him into a deep part of the bog, and poor Mr. Petersen and his horse rolled over. Here was a new scene of difficulty—changing of clothes, and making of coffee, interlarded with strings of Dutch oaths. It got dark before we had reached Siyingila's kraal, where it had been arranged we should sleep.[1] Two oxen were presented to us for slaughter and we commenced making our preparations for the night, several hours of which were taken up with crimination and recrimination between father-in-law and son-in-law, the former accusing the latter of intending to kill him by bringing him to this barbarous country. I, fortunately being innocent in this matter, was able to step in as a mediator and, at length, I succeeded in getting such amount of sleep as the noise and

---

[1] We, therefore, were obliged to camp for the night on the beach about half-way to Siyingila's kraal.—Author's note.

tumult of a hundred beef-eating Zulus—not disposed to leave off till morning appeared—would permit.[1]

I may at once state that the distance from the port to Shaka's residence was 200 miles. Our progress was exceedingly slow, each day's journey being arranged by Mbikwana. We afterwards found out that he had not taken us by a direct route, but to kraals of minor chiefs and some of the barracks of Shaka's regiments. Cattle-slaughtering occurred sometimes twice and thrice a day. Numbers of Zulus joined our column in order to relieve Mbikwana's people of their burdens. We were struck with astonishment at the order and discipline maintained in the country through which we travelled. The regimental kraals, especially the upper parts thereof, also the kraals of chiefs, showed that cleanliness was a prevailing custom and this not only inside their huts, but outside, for there were considerable spaces where neither dirt nor ashes were to be seen.[2]

Frequently on the journey we saw large parties seated with grotesquely dressed men apparently lecturing in their midst, and on several occasions saw individuals seized and carried off and instantly put to death. The grotesque characters we learned were " witch finders " whilst those singled out and put to death were said to be " evil doers."[3]

---

[1] Next day we passed Siyingila's kraal and arrived at that of Mbikwana. Here we rested two days on account of the exhausted state of the horses, which had just come off a voyage. We then travelled a further 20 miles, when Mr. Petersen being taken ill again delayed us a day. We had now passed the Cele territory under Magaye who had recently been defeated by Shaka, to whom they were now tributary. This accounts for the advantage taken of them by the Zulu warriors when passing through their district.—Author's MS.

[2] One afternoon seeing a flock of vultures near us, I shot one and on going to pick it up found they were devouring dead bodies, of which there were five. They appeared to have been killed the day before.—Author's MS.

One day we arrived at a large kraal containing 190 huts, the barracks of one of Shaka's regiments. We had not been there many minutes before our attention was drawn to a party of 150 natives sitting in a circle with a man opposite them, apparently interrogating them. In reply, they each beat the ground with a stick and said, He-sa-gee ! [*Yizwa Zhi !—Editor.*] After they had been answering with the same word about an hour, three of them were pointed out and killed on the spot. This man, whom they called an *inyanga*, or as we should say a necromancer, was dressed in an ape skin cap ; a number of pieces of different roots were tied round his neck ; and a small shield and assegai were in one hand, and the tail of a cow in the other. He was an interpreter of dreams and thought capable of telling what has happened in any other part of the country, also if one has injured another by poison or otherwise. His decision is fatal to the unfortunate individuals pointed out by him.—Author's MS.

Messengers passed three or four times a day between Shaka and Mbikwana, the former enquiring about our progress and doubtless directing how we should proceed so as to fall in with his own preparations for our reception. We had thus dallied 13 days on the road in travelling 200 miles, when the locality of Shaka's residence was pointed out to us about 15 miles off. While encamped that night we saw much commotion going on in our neighbourhood. Troops of cattle were being driven in advance; regiments were passing near by and on distant hills, interspersed with regiments of girls, decorated in beads and brass with regimental uniformity, carrying on their heads large pitchers of native beer, milk and cooked food. The approaching scene we anticipated witnessing cheered us considerably that evening. Farewell and Petersen expressed extreme affection and attachment for one another, with mutual apologies for past small differences.

It was not until ten o'clock the following morning that a proposal was made about advancing. In about two hours we arrived at a ridge from which we beheld an extensive and very picturesque basin before us, with a river running through it, called the Umfolozi.[1]

We were requested to make a stand under a large euphorbia tree, from whence, about a mile before us, we saw the residence of Shaka, viz: a native kraal nearly two miles in circumference.

While in this position, messengers went backwards and forwards between Mbikwana and Shaka. At length one came and desired Mr. Farewell and myself to advance, leaving Mr. Petersen and our servants and native followers, who were carrying Shaka's present, at the euphorbia tree. Mbikwana and about 20 of his followers accompanied us.

On entering the great cattle kraal we found drawn up within it about 80,000 natives in their war attire.[2] Mbikwana requested me to gallop within the circle, and immediately on my starting to do so one general shout broke forth from the whole mass, all pointing at me with their sticks. I was asked to gallop round the circle two or three times in the midst of

---

[1] Evidently the Umhlathuze is meant, for the Umfolozi cannot be seen from the position the travellers had now got to.—*Editor*.

[2] "On entering its gates we perceived about 12,000 men in their war attire, drawn up in a circle to receive us." The author here refers to warriors only, whereas in the text he includes regiments of girls, women, servants, etc., as well.—*Editor*.

tremendous shouting of the words, "*UJojo wokhalo!*" (the sharp or active finch of the ridge).[1] Mr. Farewell and I were then led by Mbikwana to the head of the kraal, where the masses of the people were considerably denser than elsewhere. The whole force remained stationary, as, indeed, it had been since the commencement of the reception.

Mbikwana, standing in our midst, addressed some unseen individual in a long speech, in the course of which we were frequently called upon by him to answer "*Yebo*," that is to affirm as being true all he was saying, though perfectly ignorant of what was being said.[2]

While the speech was being made I caught sight of an individual in the background whom I concluded to be Shaka, and, turning to Farewell, pointed out and said: "Farewell, there is Shaka." This was sufficiently audible for him to hear and perceive that I had recognised him. He immediately held up his hand, shaking his finger at me approvingly. Farewell, being near-sighted and using an eye-glass, could not distinguish him.[3]

Elephant tusks were then brought forward. One was laid before Farewell and another before me.[4] Shaka then raised the stick in his hand and after striking with it right and left,[5] the whole mass broke from their position and formed up into regiments. Portions of each of these rushed to the river and

---

[1] Literally the words mean : Long tailed Finch of the Ridge, which implies that the person to whom the words are applied is quick and brave in attacking and overcoming his enemy.—*Editor*.

It is customary for the principal warriors of each regiment, in their war dances, to dance forwards [i.e. each dances a pas-seul by rushing forwards, gesticulating as he does so with the shield and weapons he is carrying.—*Editor*.], when they are applauded by their own heroic names. They, therefore, on the occasion in question, considered I was adopting their own practice, hence cheered me by a phrase or name commonly found among their own heroes. On entering the kraal's gates . . . we were desired to gallop two or three times round, then twice more ; then to return and bring the remainder of the party with us. We were desired to gallop four times more round the kraal and then stand all together about 20 yards from a large tree at the head of the kraal.—Author's note.

The probabilities are that Fynn began galloping alone, hence he was acclaimed, his prowess as a pioneer doctor having already become known, as stated in the text, and that in the succeeding gallops he was accompanied by Farewell.—*Editor*.

[2] Evidently the King, but Shaka was so surrounded by his chiefs that we could not see him.—Author's note.

[3] A speech in answer to Mbikwana's was then made by a chief opposite. —Author's note.

[4] Mbikwana now made another speech.—Author's MS.

[5] "and springing out from amidst the chiefs."—Author's MS.

the surrounding hills, while the remainder, forming themselves into a circle, commenced dancing with Shaka in their midst.[1]

It was a most exciting scene, surprising to us, who could not have imagined that a nation termed " savages" could be so disciplined and kept in order.

Regiments of girls, headed by officers of their own sex, then entered the centre of the arena to the number of 8,000-10,000, each holding a slight staff in her hand. They joined in the dance, which continued for about two hours.

Shaka now came towards us, evidently to seek our applause. [The following from Bird's *Annals of Natal*, contributed by the author, describes the scene. " The King came up to us and told us not to be afraid of his people, who were now coming up to us in small divisions, each division driving cattle before it. The men were singing and dancing and whilst so doing advancing and receding even as one sees the surf do on a seashore. The whole country, as far as our sight could reach, was covered with numbers of people and droves of cattle. The cattle had been assorted according to their colour. . . . After exhibiting their cattle for two hours, they drew together in a circle, and sang and danced to their war song. Then the people returned to the cattle, again exhibiting them as before, and, at intervals, dancing and singing. The women now entered the kraal, each having a long thin stick in the right hand, and moving it in time to the song. They had not been dancing many minutes, when they had to make way for the ladies of the seraglio, besides about 150 others, who were called sisters. These danced in parties of eight, arranged in fours, each party wearing different coloured beads, which were crossed from the shoulders to the knees. Each wore a head-dress of black feathers, and four brass collars, fitting closely to the neck. When the King

---

[1] In another MS. Fynn has : The whole body then ran to the lower end of the kraal, leaving us alone, with the exception of one man who had been hidden in the crowd. This man proved to be a native of the Cape Frontier, who had been taken prisoner in a war between the Colonists and Kaffirs and set to Robben Island. Captain Owen of the *Leven* had taken him as an interpreter to attend him during his survey of the Eastern coast. Afterwards the interpreter had been given over to Farewell on his voyage to St. Lucia Bay. There he ran off and sought protection with Shaka, who gave him the name of Hlambamanzi, denoting one who had crossed (swum) the water. Among the colonists he had been known by the name of Jacob Sumbiti. He spoke good Dutch.

Further particulars about this man will be found in Isaacs, *Travels and Adventures in Eastern Africa*, II, 251-58, 264-69 ; Owen, *Narratives of Voyages to Euplore Shores of Africa, Arabia and Madagascar*, I, 59, II, 222.—Editor.

joined in the dance, he was accompanied by the men. This dance lasted half an hour. The order observed and the precision of every movement was interpreted to us by his interpreter, Hlambamanzi. He desired to know from us if ever we had seen such order in any other state, assured us that he was the greatest king in existence, that his people were as numerous as the stars, and that his cattle were innumerable. The people now dispersed, and he directed a chief to lead us to a kraal where we could pitch our tents. He sent us a sheep, a basket of corn, an ox, and a pot of beer, about three gallons. At seven o'clock, we sent up four rockets and fired off eight guns. He sent people to look at these, but from fear did not show himself out of his hut. The following morning we were requested to mount our horses and proceed to the King's quarters. We found him sitting under a tree at the upper end of the kraal decorating himself and surrounded by about 200 people. A servant was kneeling by his side holding a shield above him to keep off the glare of the sun. Round his forehead he wore a turban[1] of otter skin with a feather of a crane erect in front, fully two feet long, and a wreath of scarlet feathers, formerly worn, only, by men of high rank. Ear ornaments made from dried sugar cane, carved round the edge, with white ends, and an inch in diameter, were let into the lobes of the ears, which had been cut to admit them. From shoulder to shoulder, he wore bunches, five inches in length, of the skins of monkeys and genets, twisted like the tails of these animals. These hung half down the body. Round the ring on the head,[2] were a dozen tastefully arranged bunches of the loury feathers, neatly tied to thorns which were stuck into the hair. Round his arms were white ox-tail tufts, cut down the middle so as to allow the hair to hang about the arm, to the number of four for each arm. Round the waist, there was a kilt or petticoat, made of skins of monkeys and genets, and twisted as before described, having

---

[1] This word, often applied to Zulu head-dresses and especially Shaka's, seems to us inaccurate. Zulus do not wear turbans. They wear headbands or circlets cut out or made of various skins or other substances.—*Editor.*

[2] This clearly proves that Shaka wore a head-ring (*isicoco*). We have sometimes heard doubts expressed on this point by Europeans. Well-informed natives, however, believe the King to have worn a ring, without, in these latter days, being able to prove it. The only portrait of Shaka we know of which can claim to be authentic (that in Isaacs' *Travels and Adventures in Eastern Africa*, I, 58) leaves one in doubt, for the band there shown round the head may well be the circlet or headband known as *umqhele*.—*Editor.*

small tassels round the top. The kilt reached to the knees, below which were white ox-tails fitted to the legs so as to hang down to the ankles. He had a white shield with a single black spot,[1] and one assegai. When thus equipped he certainly presented a fine and most martial appearance.

While he was dressing himself, his people proceeded, as on the day before, to show droves of cattle, which were still flocking in, repeatedly varying the scene with singing and dancing. In the meantime, we observed Shaka gave orders for a man standing close to us to be killed, for what crime we could not learn, but we soon found this to be a very common occurrence."[2]

Mr. Petersen, unfortunately, at this moment placed a musical box on the ground, and, striking it with a switch, moved the stop. Shaka heard the music. It seemed to produce in him a superstitious feeling. He turned away with evident displeasure and went back immediately to the dance.

Those portions of regiments which had separated prior to the dance now returned from the river and from behind the adjoining hills, driving before them immense herds of cattle. A grand cattle show was now being arranged. Each regiment drove towards us thousands of cattle that had been allotted to their respective barracks, the colour of each regiment's cattle corresponding with that of the shield the men carried, which, in turn, served to distinguish one regiment from another. No cattle of differing colour from those allotted to a given regiment were allowed to intermix. There were many droves without horns, others with pendulous projections, four or six inches long, which covered a considerable portion of the animal. The cattle of the other droves had four, six, and eight horns apiece. This show of cattle continued till sunset, with dancing at intervals, when we proposed to pitch the tents we had brought with us. A man was ordered to point out a spot for the purpose. Greatly to Farewell's astonishment, this man proved to be Jacob, his interpreter, who had landed at St. Lucia the year previous when he, Farewell, lost his boats and the sailors therein were drowned. Jacob had been taken to

---

[1] Somewhat oval in shape (seven inches by five inches) about the size of a man's open hand. It was midway down the shield and on the right-hand edge thereof.—*Editor.*

[2] Bird, *Annals of Natal*, I, 77.

Shaka, who immediately appointed him one of the sentries for guarding his establishment.

Two oxen were slaughtered for us. After dinner we prepared to retire, but messengers from Shaka requested us to go to him, with Jacob the interpreter.[1] I was then led into the seraglio, where I found him seated in a carved wooden chair and surrounded by about 400 girls, two or three chiefs and two servants in attendance.

My name Fynn had been converted into Sofili by the people in general; by this, after desiring me to sit in front of him, he several times accosted me in the course of the following dialogue:

"I hear you have come from umGeorge, is it so? Is he as great a king as I am?"

Fynn: "Yes; King George is one of the greatest kings in the world."

Shaka: "I am very angry with you," said while putting on a severe countenance. "I shall send a messenger to umGeorge and request him to kill you. He sent you to me not to give medicine to my dogs." All present immediately applauded what Shaka had said. "Why did you give my dogs medicine?" (in allusion to the woman I was said to have brought back to life after death).

Fynn: "It is a practice of our country to help those who are in need, if able to do so."

Shaka: "Are you then the doctor of dogs? You were sent here to be my doctor."

---

[1] The first meeting of Shaka with Farewell, Fynn, and the rest of the party was manifestly a unique and memorable occasion. Instead of the formal, stiff and constrained ceremonial customary at such a moment, Shaka, whose heart had been mysteriously touched by the advent of British settlers to his shores, converted the occasion into a grand and dramatically planned festival. We cannot but think these warm-hearted exhibitions of regard should be attributed in the main to two influences seemingly trivial in themselves: (a) Jacob's previous lengthy contact with worthy officers of the Royal British Navy; (b) Fynn's discreet, courageous and humane bearing during the weeks he was striving to open up communication with Shaka. His spontaneous humanity straightway disarmed all suspicion and even caused him to be taken as typical of the race he belonged to. Thus, through the agency of Fynn and Jacob, the British people henceforth began to stand in a favourable light. Shaka, despot though he was, one of the greatest the world has ever known, took them to his heart and, as will be seen, never failed to treat them as friends. More than this, the conviction then arrived at as to their friendliness has, after many sad and trying vicissitudes of later years, been honoured down to the present time.—*Editor*.

Fynn: "I am not a doctor and not considered by my countrymen to be one."

Shaka: "Have you medicine by you?"

Fynn: "Yes."

Shaka: "Then cure me, or I will have you sent to umGeorge to have you killed."

Fynn: "What is the matter with you?"

Shaka: "That is your business to find out."

Fynn: "Stand up and let me see your person."

Shaka: "Why should I stand up?"

Fynn: "That I may see if I can find out what ails you."

Shaka stood up but evidently disliked my approaching him closely. A number of girls held up lighted torches. I looked about his person and, after reflecting on the great activity he had shown during the day, was satisfied he had not much the matter with him. I, however, observed numerous black marks on his loins where native doctors had scarified him, and at once said he had pains in his loins. He held his hand before his mouth in astonishment, upon which my wisdom was applauded by all present. Shaka then strictly charged me not to give medicine to his dogs, and, after a few commonplace questions in which he showed good humour, I was permitted to retire for the night.[1]

Very few, if any, of the Zulu army had any sleep that night. Cattle were slaughtered in great numbers, and all the country round about was illuminated by the fires, around which the people sat in groups.

The following day had been appointed by Shaka for receiving our present, which, fortunately, had been well chosen by Farewell for presentation to so superior a chief as Shaka. It consisted of every description of beads at that time procurable in Cape Town, and far superior to those Shaka had previously obtained from the Portuguese at Delagoa. There was a great variety of woollen blankets, a large quantity of brass bars, turned and lacquered, and sheets of copper, also pigeons, a pig, cats and dogs. There was, moreover, a full-dress military coat, with epaulettes covered with gold lace. Though Shaka showed no open gratitude, we saw clearly that he was satisfied. He

---

[1] I remained till ten o'clock when I left him with a promise that, agreeable to his request, I would remain with him a month after the departure of Messrs. Farewell and Petersen.—Author's MS.

was very interested in the live animals, especially the pig, until it got into his milk stores where it committed great havoc, and set all the women in the seraglio screaming for assistance. All this ended in the pig being killed.[1]

The showing of cattle and dancing continued during the day, whilst other regiments, which had come from a great distance, arrived and took part in the festivities. Among the articles we had brought were some Congreve rockets. These we kept back. On returning to our camp, as the evening was dark, we fired them off, having first informed Shaka, and asked him to order his people to look upwards. Their surprise was great; I, however, question if the showing of such wonders to ignorant natives is advisable after so short an acquaintance between white and black as ours had been. In conversation on our object in coming to Natal, this part of South Africa, Shaka showed great desire that we should live at the port. Each evening he sent for me and conversed with me through the Kaffir Jacob, the interpreter, for three or four hours.

On the first day of our visit we had seen no less than ten men carried off to death. On a mere sign by Shaka, viz: the pointing of his finger, the victim would be seized by his nearest neighbours; his neck would be twisted, and his head and body beaten with sticks, the nobs of some of these being as large as a man's fist. On each succeeding day, too, numbers of others were killed; their bodies would then be carried to an adjoining hill and there impaled. We visited this spot on the fourth day. It was truly a Golgotha, swarming with hundreds of vultures. The effects of this together with the scenes of death made Mr. Petersen decide at once to dissolve the partnership and leave for the Cape.

In the afternoon of the fifth day Shaka sent for me and requested me to proceed with some of his servants to a distant kraal where the chief uMpangazitha was very ill. I went and found him in high fever. I bled him, gave him medicine and caused him to be brought to a full perspiration. At midday on the following day he was able to report himself comparatively

---

[1]The bringing of the live animals to Shaka was due to a suggestion by Shaka's uncle Mbikwana, who had returned with me to Natal to accompany us all to Shaka's residence. He asked us not to omit to take one of each species of domestic animals we had brought with us, among which was a pig. All were taken to the *isigodlo*, a seraglio, for the amusement of the women.—Author's MS.

well.[1] As this captain was a great favourite with Shaka, my success gave him much pleasure.

Mr. Petersen could not but observe the high estimation in which I was held from my success as a doctor. He produced a box of pills which he assured Shaka were good for all diseases; he urged him to take two as a trial. Shaka told Mr. Petersen to take two himself, which he did. Showing no disposition to take them, and on being further urged to do so, Shaka told Mr. Petersen to give two to each of several of his captains who, swallowing the medicine as directed, said they had no taste. Mr. Petersen still urged, when Shaka insisted, before he himself did so, that the former should swallow two more, desiring the captains to watch him as he had not seen him swallow the two first. This Mr. Petersen for a considerable time refused to do, until Shaka and his people said he wished them to take medicine which he would not do himself. Fear then overtook him and he swallowed two more.[2]

In the afternoon I walked to the riverside to observe the droves of sea-cows which there abounded. On returning to dine at the tents, I could not but observe the gloomy silence of Farewell and Petersen. The cause of this they did not communicate until after dinner, when I learned from them that, on informing Shaka, during my absence at the river, of our wish on the following day to return to the port, he had at once assented, though only on condition that I should remain with him—in this he persisted in defiance of their objections. As the King's word was the only law in the land, they became uneasy until they found I was not only willing but desirous of seeing as much as possible of this new country. It was therefore

---

[1] Five days afterwards I heard of his final recovery.—Author's note.

[2] Another MS. has these additional details : During my absence Mbikwana informed Shaka that Mr. Petersen also had medicine. Mr. Petersen was requested to produce it and state its virtues. He produced a box of pills which he said were good for all diseases and strongly advised Shaka to take two. The King took four and giving one each to four chiefs, made them swallow them. Mr. Petersen was also desired to take four. Mr. Petersen after vainly endeavouring to convince the King that four were too much for one person was reluctantly compelled to swallow the four. Shaka asked the chiefs how they tasted ; they replied : ' Not at all,' they having swallowed them as directed. The King now swallowed two and ordered Mr. Petersen to keep him company. This Mr. Petersen peremptorily refused to do, but the King insisting, and the chiefs adding the pressure of the argument that one who recommended medicines should not refuse to take them himself, Mr. Petersen was compelled to swallow two more, that is, six in all. The consequences of this to a person of 63 does not require to be explained in detail.

decided that I should remain, with the Kaffir Frederick as my interpreter, and the Hottentot Michael as my servant.[1]

On taking leave of the King on the following morning, Shaka presented Farewell and myself with five elephant tusks each and 40 head of cattle, and promised he would send out his soldiers to kill elephants for us. I accompanied Messrs. Farewell and Petersen a few miles, returned to Shaka by sunset and sat with him two or three hours in the evening.

Chapter VI

AT noon on the day Farewell and party left for Natal Shaka presented me with 15 oxen, and in the evening left for another kraal 15 miles away. He sent the next day requesting me to follow him.

On my arrival he desired me to look at and then to count a large drove of oxen I had not before seen. I did so, making the number 5,654. When I announced the result the crowd that was present burst out laughing, asking how it was possible for me to count so many, seeing I had not once counted up to ten on my fingers. They at once concluded I had not counted them at all, and the interpreter could not convince Shaka of the possibility of counting without the use of the fingers. Their

---

[1] On the following day, Shaka, having understood that Farewell and Petersen intended to return to Natal the next morning, collected all such of his forces as were in the neighbourhood, male and female, numbering about 25,000. At about 10 o'clock, they began, as on the first day, to dance, and at intervals, to display their cattle. They had marked their faces with clay of various colours, white, red and black, and other shades. When these amusements had been continued till 4 o'clock, the King desired his people to look at us and behold a wonder—white people! Hence only to consider his greatness, he who was able to tell all future descendants of his nation that he was the first of their kings to be visited by Europeans, and at the same time consider how proud he was to say they were subjects of King umGeorge. His own forefathers as well as their own were cowards who did not dare admit a white man into their presence. He went on to relate the case of a white man who had escaped from a wreck, only three years before and had been put to death by his neighbour, Phakathwayo, King of the Qwaβes (i.e. the Qwaβe tribe), supposing him to be a monster that had sprung out of the sea. He would expect his nation to look on us as kings, hence pay us the respect due to kings, not consider us as being their equals. After this speech had been delivered, in a firm and eloquent manner, we retired to our tent. The next morning I accompanied Messrs. Farewell and Petersen to take leave of Shaka. After receiving presents of cattle, etc., they departed, while, according to promise, I remained, as did also a Hottentot servant.—Author's MS.

way of counting is to begin with the little finger of the left hand, the thumb of the right hand being six, and so in rotation to ten, which is the little finger of the right hand, 20 being two tens, 30 three tens, until they come to ten tens, or a hundred, which they call a great ten. There are some who have an idea of a thousand, which they call a great *ingwane* (*Inkulungwane*).[1]

Shaka went on to speak of the gifts of nature, or, as they term it, *uMvelinqangi*.[2] He said that the first forefathers of the Europeans had bestowed on us many gifts by giving us all the knowledge of arts and manufactures, yet they had kept from us the greatest of all gifts, such as a good black skin, for this does not necessitate the wearing of clothes to hide the white skin, which was not pleasant to the eye. He well knew that for a black skin we would give all we were worth in the way of our arts and manufactures. He then asked what use was made of the hides of cattle slaughtered in our country. When I told him they were made into shoes and other articles, which, however, I could not explain so as to make him understand, he exclaimed that that was another proof of the unkindness of our forefathers, for they had obliged us to make use of hides to protect our feet, but as such protection was unnecessary in their case their forefathers revealed to them that hides should be used for making more handsome and serviceable articles, namely shields. This changed the conversation to the superiority of their arms; these he endeavoured to show in various ways were more advantageous than our muskets. The shield, he argued, if dipped into water previous to an attack, would be sufficient to ward off the effect of a ball fired when they were at a distance, and in the interval of reloading they

[1] Inguarn (ingwane) does not stand as a separate word in Zulu though it may well do so in some cognate dialect. Dohne says natives use inkulungwane when they have hundreds for all ten fingers, the fingers then being all bent together and so representing a thousand.—*Zulu-Kafir Dictionary* under *Inkulungwane*.

[2] This Zulu word means literally The First Appearer, The First to Emerge, The First to Exist, hence The Creator. It is associated with another word, *uNkulunkulu*, signifying the First Ancestor or Father. Both these terms have, in subsequent years, been thoroughly inquired into by such missionaries as Gardiner, Grout, Schroeder, Colenso and Callaway. What is, however, specially notable is that Shaka himself used the word *uMvelinqangi* in conversation with Fynn some 11 years before the earliest missionary set foot in either Natal or Zululand, whilst the mention of it in the MS. we are using is possibly the first occasion on which it was committed to paper.—*Editor*.

would come to close quarters, when we, having no shield, would drop our guns and attempt to run, but, as we are unable to run as fast as his soldiers, we must all inevitably fall into their hands.

I found it impossible to confute his arguments, as I was unacquainted with his language, and his interpreter on whom I had to depend would not have dared to use strong arguments in opposition to the King. I was obliged, therefore, to accept all his conclusions, for there was not the least hope of proving myself capable of arguing in a way he could be made really to understand.

Next day, when out walking in the hope of shooting a sea-cow, I met him on the road going towards his kraal. When he heard I was going out shooting, he ordered a man to fetch a fat ox which he said I was to take with me for food on the way. When I told him I was returning the same day he still insisted on my taking it. Only with great difficulty could I show how unnecessary it was, for only my Hottentot servant was with me.

When I returned in the evening, he asked me to give him an emetic. This he took in the way I desired him to do, but immediately afterwards he thrust his two forefingers deep down his throat as possible, remarking that that was their custom and therefore must be better than ours. I remained till late in the evening, conversing on different matters relating to England. Whilst in the presence of his people he placed the worst construction on everything, ridiculing all our manners and customs, though in perfect good humour. When none of his subjects were present he would listen with the greatest attention and could not help acknowledging our superiority. He, however, took exception to our method of imprisoning criminals, regarding it as the most horrid pain that man could endure. If one were guilty why not punish the deed with death? If suspicion only attached to the individual allow him to go free; his having been put under arrest would be sufficient warning for the future. This argument had arisen from the fact of his interpreter having been taken prisoner and sent to Robben Island. Through him, therefore, it was out of my power to explain how wishful we are to save the lives of the innocent, and in how few instances life was despised by its possessor. I had therefore to give way as before.

The following day was spent in dancing and this was kept up till the evening.[1] Having spent the whole afternoon in reading, I was induced to take another peep at the dancers. As it was dark when I entered the kraal where the dancing was going on, the King ordered a number of people to hold up lighted bundles of dried reeds to give light to the scene; these bundles, however, called for great attention as they frequently went out. I had not been there many minutes when I heard a shriek and the lights were immediately extinguished. Then followed a general bustle and crying. Having left Jacob, as I shall henceforth call the interpreter, and Michael, the Hottentot, in the hut, I endeavoured to ask of everyone who would stand to listen what the occasion was of this extraordinary commotion. At length I found out that Shaka, while dancing, had been stabbed. I immediately turned away to call Michael. I found him on the top of the wall[2] shouting and giving the hurrah, mistaking the commotion for some merriment. I immediately told him what I had heard and sent him to prepare a lamp, and to bring linen and some camomile tea, which was the only medicine I had by me. I also desired him to send the interpreter to me. All this time the bustle and confusion were very great.

When Jacob and Michael arrived we proceeded to Shaka's hut in the palace,[3] where we supposed him to be. Here there was a very great noise going on, and the crowd so dense that it was almost impossible to move. Jacob joined in the general uproar, following the example of many others. He fell down in a fit, so that I could now neither ask questions nor come by any information as to where Shaka was.

I attempted to gain admittance into his hut. There was a great crowd round it. My lamp was put out. The women of the seraglio pulled me, some one way, some another; all were in a state of madness. The crowds still increasing and the uproar becoming more dreadful, in consequence of the shrieking and crying, made my situation very awkward as well as extremely unpleasant.

---

[1] As it was August, the sun set about 5.30 p.m.—*Editor*.
[2] No doubt the wooden fence of the cattle kraal, where the dancing had just been going on.—*Editor*.
[3] That is, in the seraglio or harem, at the uppermost part of the kraal.—*Editor*.

Just as I was making another attempt to enter the hut, where I still supposed the King to be, a man, who was carrying some lighted reeds, attempted to drag me away. I refused to go with him, for I did not know what his intentions were nor why the King had been stabbed so shortly after our arrival; at the moment I suspected it was on account of his having allowed us to appear among them without being acquainted with their political affairs. The man made a second effort to pull me along, and was then assisted by another. I then thought it best to see the result and, if anything were intended against myself, to make the best of it. I accordingly walked along with them for about 40 minutes, and my fears and suspicions were relieved on seeing the King in a kraal close by.

I immediately washed the wound with camomile tea and bound it up with linen. He had been stabbed with an assegai through the left arm, and the blade had passed through the ribs under the left breast. It had made the King spit blood. I could not account for the assegai not entering the lungs; it must have been due to mere accident; I was for some time in doubt. His own doctor, who seemed to have a good knowledge of that nature, also attended him. He gave the King a vomit and afterwards administered purges and continually washed the wound with decoctions of cooling roots. He also probed the wound to ascertain if any poison had been used on the assegai.

Shaka cried nearly the whole night, expecting that only fatal consequences would ensue. The crowd had now increased so much that the noise of their shrieks became unbearable, and this noise continued throughout the night. Morning showed a horrid sight in a clear light. I am satisfied I cannot describe the horrid scene in language powerful enough to enable the reader, who has never been similarly situated, to appreciate it aright. The immense crowds of people that arrived hour after hour from every direction began their shouting on coming in sight of the kraal, running and exerting their utmost powers of voice as they entered it and joined those who had got there before them. They then pulled one another about, men and women throwing themselves down in every direction without taking care how they fell. Great numbers fainted from over exertion and excessive heat. The females of the seraglio, more particularly, were in very great distress, having overtaxed themselves during the night. They suffered from the excessive heat and from want of nourishment, which no one dared to touch, whilst the four brass collars each had, fitting so tightly round the neck as to make it impossible for the wearer to turn her head, nearly suffocated them. Several of them died. Finding their situation so distressing, and there being no one to afford them relief, I poured a quantity of water and threw it over them as they fell; this went on till I was myself so tired as to be obliged to desist. They then made some attempt to help one another.

All this time I had been so busily employed as not to see the most sickening part of this tragical scene. They had now begun to kill one another. Some were put to death because they did not cry, others for putting spittle into their eyes,[1] others for sitting down to cry, although strength and tears, after such continuous mourning and exertion, were quite exhausted. No such limits were taken into account.

We then understood that six men had been wounded by the assassins who wounded Shaka. From the road they took, it was supposed that they had been sent by Zwide, King of the Ndwandwes (Ndwandwe tribe), who was Shaka's only powerful enemy. Two regiments were accordingly sent off at once in search of the aggressors.

In the meantime the medicines which, on his leaving, Mr. Farewell had promised to send were received. They came very opportunely, and Shaka was much gratified. I now washed his wounds frequently, and gave him mild purgatives. I, moreover, dressed his wounds with ointment. The King was in a hopeless condition for four days. During all that time people were continuing to flock in from the outskirts of his country and joining in the general tumult. It was not till the fourth day that cattle were killed for the sustenance of the multitude. Many had died in the interval, and many had been killed for not mourning, or for having gone to their kraals for food.

On the fifth day there were symptoms of improvement in the King's condition; these favourable indications were also noticeable on the day following.

At noon on that day the party sent out in search of the would-be murderers returned, bringing with them the dead

---

[1] And so to pretend it was tears.—*Editor.*

bodies of three men whom they had killed in the bush (jungle). These were the supposed assassins. The bodies, having been carried off, were laid on the ground in a roadway about a mile from the kraal. Their right ears were then cut off and the two pursuing regiments sat down on either side of the road, while the whole of the people, men and women, who had assembled at the kraal, probably exceeding 30,000, passed up the road crying and yelling. Each one, on coming up to the bodies, struck them several blows with a stick, which was then left on the spot, so that nothing more of these was to be seen; only an immense pile of sticks remained, but the formal ceremony still went on. The whole body now collecting, and three men walking in advance with sticks on which were the ears of the dead and now shattered bodies, the procession moved to Shaka's kraal. The King now made his appearance. The national mourning song was chanted. After this a fire was made in the centre of the cattle kraal when the ears were burnt to ashes.

From the moment that Shaka had been stabbed the wearing of ornaments was prohibited, nor was anyone permitted to wash, or to shave his or her head,[1] moreover, no man whose wife was pregnant was allowed to come into the King's presence. Every transgression of these regulations was punishable by death; several cases occurred of persons being put to death on these grounds.

There now being every appearance of Shaka's complete recovery, the chiefs and principal men of the nation brought cattle to the King as offerings of thanksgiving; and on the next day the principal women of the nation did the same. Shaka then offered sacrifices to the spirit of his deceased father.

The restoration of the King to health began to bring about great changes. The tumult gradually ceased.

Mr. Farewell and Mr. Davis,[2] having received a letter from me stating particulars of the recent occurrences, now arrived on a visit to Shaka. They had not been seated many minutes when a man, who in ignorance or neglect of the prohibition

---

[1] There was, in those days, no shaving of faces among the Zulus. Women, as well as men, however, often shaved the upper parts and sides of the head.—*Editor.*

[2] Bird, *Annals of Natal*, I, 84, has " Mr. Isaacs " here, which, of course, is an oversight. The text refers to July, 1824—Isaacs did not arrive in Natal until September of the following year.—*Editor.*

had shaved his head, was put to death. After this the privilege of shaving was again conceded.

A present to the King from Mr. Farewell had been brought to the kraal during the King's illness, and he had on that account been unable to receive it. It was now called for. Shaka now made a grant of land to Mr. Farewell, who drew up a document in connection therewith. The grant extended 50 miles inland and 25 miles along the coast, and included the harbour of Natal.

The following is a copy of the grant in question:

I, Inguos Shaka, King of the Zulus and of the country of Natal, as well as the whole of the land from Natal to Delagoa Bay, which I have inherited from my father, for myself and heirs, do hereby, on the seventh day of August in the year of our Lord eighteen hundred and twenty four, and in the presence of my chiefs and of my own free will, and in consideration of divers goods received—grant, make over and sell unto F. G. Farewell and Company, the entire and full possession in perpetuity to themselves, heirs and executors, of the Port or Harbour of Natal, known by the name of "Bubolongo," together with the Islands therein and surrounding country, as herein described, viz: The whole of the neck of land or peninsula in the south-west entrance, and all the country ten miles to the southern side of Port Natal, as pointed out, and extending along the sea coast to the northward and eastward as far as the river known by the native name "Gumgelote," and now called "Farewell's River," being about twenty-five miles of sea coast to the north-east of Port Natal, together with all the country inland as far as the nation called by the Zulus "Gowagnewkos," extending about one hundred miles backward from the sea shore, with all rights to the rivers, woods, mines, and articles of all denominations contained therein, the said land and appurtenances to be from this date for the sole use of said Farewell and Company, their heirs and executors, and to be by them disposed of in any manner they think best calculated for their interests, free from any molestation or hindrance from myself or subjects. In witness whereof, I have placed my hand, being fully aware that the so doing is intended to bind me to all the articles and conditions that I, of my own free will and consent, do hereby in the presence of the undermentioned witnesses, acknowledge to have fully consented and agreed to on behalf of F. G. Farewell as aforesaid, and perfectly understand all the purport of this document, the same having been carefully explained to me by my interpreter, Clambamaruze, and in the presence of two interpreters, Coliat and Frederick, before the said F. G. Farewell, whom I hereby acknowledge as the Chief of the said country, with full power and authority over such natives that like to remain there after this public grant, promising to supply him with cattle and corn, when required, sufficient for his consumption, as a reward for his kind attention to me in my illness from a wound.

SHAKA, his X mark.
King of the Zulus.

Native witnesses:
Umbequaru (Shaka's uncle), his X mark.[1]
Umsega, his X mark.[2]
Cuntelope, his X mark.[3]
Clambamaruze (King's interpreter), his X mark.[4]

Two certificates (the one signed, the other witnessed by the author of the present work) are attached to the grant referring to its having been correctly interpreted to Shaka, etc., which, however, there is no special reason for including here.[5]

When Shaka had quite recovered from his wound he quitted the kraal in which he had been stabbed and removed to the one at which we had first visited him.[6] Farewell, Davis and I accompanied him, the natives singing the whole way. On the day after our arrival a force of 4,000 men was sent inland, with orders to conceal themselves in ambush, until they should be joined by another detachment, which was to march next day.

[1]Correct spelling Mbikwana—the man who has already been frequently mentioned in these pages.—*Editor*.
[2]Probably intended for uMsika.—*Editor*.
[3]Evidently Mhlophe.—*Editor*.
[4]This, of course, is Hlambamanzi, alias Jacob.—*Editor*.
[5]The above is taken from Bird, *Annals of Natal*, published 1888, vol. I, 193. A copy of this grant was duly transmitted by Farewell on 27th August, 1824, for the information of the Governor of the Cape of Good Hope —*Editor*.
[6]That is at Bulawayo, known as Gibixhegu.—*Editor*.

These, about 3,000 in number, were mustered in the kraal, and being ordered to march out of the kraal, they ran in four divisions to the spot at which they were directed to halt, and there formed three sides of a square. A fire was made in the middle, and a pot containing a mixture of roots, plants and water was kept boiling. An *inyanga*[1] (doctor), in his ceremonial dress, kept dipping an ox-tail frequently into the decoction. The men placed themselves in turn with their backs towards him, when he sprinkled them with the mixture, which was supposed to have the effect of giving them strength in war, and ensuring a good result.

A speech was made by Mbikwana in which he showed what the aggravating cause was that called for revenge, namely, the attempt on the life of their King. The order to march was given, and they were directed to spare neither man, woman, child nor dog. They were to burn their huts, to break the stones on which their corn was ground, and so prove their attachment to their King. The command was given to Benziwa, an elderly chief.

The force moved off in the following order:

The first division wore a turban of otter skin round the forehead, with a crane's feather, two feet long, erect on the forehead; ox-tails round the arms; a dress of ox-tails hanging over the shoulders and chest; a petticoat (kilt) of monkey and genet skins made to resemble the tails of those animals; and ox-tails round the legs. They carried white shields chequered at the centre with black patches. Each shield was held by sticks attached to it, and at the top of each stick was a genet's tail. They each carried a single assegai and a knobbed stick.

The second division wore turbans of otter skin, at the upper edge of which were two bits of hide resembling horns; from these hung black cow-tails. The dress round the chest and shoulders resembled that of the first division, a piece of hide cut so as to resemble three tails hanging at the back. They carried red-spotted shields.

The third division wore a very large bunch of eagle feathers on the head, fastened only by a string that passed under the chin, trappings of ox-tails over the chest and shoulders, and, as the second division, a piece of hide resembling three tails.

---

[1] Here war-doctor.—*Editor*.

Their shields were grey. Each man carried an assegai and knobbed stick.

The fourth division wore trappings of ox-tails over the chest and shoulders, a band of ox-hide with white cow-tails round the head, and their shields were black.

The force descended the hill in the direction of the enemy's country. They held their shields down at the left side—and, at a distance, very much resembled a body of cavalry. The first and third divisions marched off making a shrill noise, while the second and fourth made a dreadful howl.

During Shaka's illness a carpenter in the employ of Mr. Farewell arrived at his residence. He had been sent to build for Shaka a house like those used by Europeans. He brought with him a saw, a hammer, a gimlet, and an adze, also some nails. Shaka wished to know the uses of these things, except the hammer, for he knew that a tool of that description was used by Zulu blacksmiths. After the uses of the gimlet and nails had been explained, he sent for a piece of the hardest wood grown in his country, namely, a species of ironwood. He desired that the gimlet should be tried on that. It snapped at once. Then he said the nails must be used without the gimlet. These, on being hammered, bent into all kinds of shapes. Much pleased with his own cunning, he declined to have the house built, directing the carpenter to build them in England where the wood was softer than the iron and not attempt to build in Zululand where our iron was softer than his wood. After this, he frequently talked of sending six of his men to build a house for King George in the Zulu style, for, though assured that King George's houses were much larger than his, he would not be convinced that they were as neatly constructed. Mr. Farewell and Mr. Davis as well as I, having expressed our gratification at the King's complete recovery, parted with him on the following day, and in six days arrived at Port Natal, the distance between there and Shaka's residence being 125 miles.

VIEW OF PORT NATAL
From Captain Allen F. Gardiner's *Narrative of a Journey to the Zoolu Country*

Chapter VII

ON our arrival at Port Natal we found that Petersen and the Afrikanders, who comprised nearly the whole of our party, intended to return to the Cape. The sloop *Julia* was accordingly prepared to convey them but this could only be done by her making two voyages, she being too small to take them all at one time.

On the following day possession was taken, in the name of His Britannic Majesty King George IV, of the land at Port Natal and inland thereof that had been granted by Shaka to Mr. Farewell, four six-pounder rounds of ammunition and 20 of musketry being fired to celebrate the event.

Next day I again set out to visit Shaka, taking with me a present from the party. I remained three days with the King. During this time the army that had been sent out against Zwide returned, bringing with it several droves of cattle. It had, moreover, destroyed a number of kraals. I delivered the present, and, being assured of Shaka's satisfaction therewith, returned to Natal.

Not many days after this I resolved to visit a people we had heard of as living to the westward of Natal, called the amaMpondo; the distance of their country from Natal, and the situation thereof being quite unknown to me accounts for my having taken provisions for only four days. Finding it impossible, without an order from Shaka to procure guides, and conceiving it not likely to obtain that favour, I started with merely an interpreter and four Hottentots.

On the first day we travelled about 20 miles to a place we afterwards called Joɓe's Rocks—deriving the name from a man called Joɓe, chief of a party of bush Kaffirs we found there. On seeing us they left their dwellings and ran into the bushes. Not until an hour or two had passed in making signs as well as running after them could we manage to induce them to return, and this was effected only by catching one of them and giving him some beef and a few beads. When he saw we had no shields or assegais he called out to inform his companions of the fact. This allayed their fears, for until then they supposed we had come with no other intention than to destroy them. They lived in hovels and subsisted on fish, shell-fish and wild roots, the roots, however, requiring great preparation before they could become fit to eat.

I enquired of the man we had caught the distance to the amaMpondo, but could get no satisfactory information. He told me I should be three months on the road; that I must pass through a desert and, on the journey, meet with only a few stragglers obliged, like himself, to live on roots. I, however, could not but think this was only a device to make me return and so prevent such tracks as there were from being turned into a general thoroughfare.

After resting the night, I proceeded in the morning along the beach. I frequently climbed the hills to obtain a view of the surrounding country, more especially to see if there were any signs of its having been burnt or if any smoke could be seen rising from bushes in which fires had been lit. In this, however, I was unsuccessful. After I had travelled until sunset, in a winding direction, we encamped in the bush without having come across a single individual during the day or advanced more than ten miles in a direct line from where we had started in the morning.

Owing to the height of the grass and intertwining briars and bushes, we found it impracticable to do otherwise than keep along the beach, repeatedly examining the country as we had done the day before. In the evening, whilst searching for water and a place to bivouac in, we came across a man, woman and child. We caught the man and the child, but the woman escaped into the bush and all our efforts to find her proved futile. I asked the man the distance to the amaMpondo and the time it would take to reach their country, but we got no better information than Joβe had given. I therefore resolved to go on travelling until noon the next day, when, if unable to obtain more definite particulars, I would abandon the journey for the time being and return to the port.

We made our companions in hunger partakers of such food as we had left and passed the night in their hut. This place we called Klaas's Flat from the fact of one of the Hottentots having spoken of the bush Kaffir as Klaas. On the following morning we travelled until noon without any better result. As our provisions were now exhausted we returned to sleep at Klaas's Flat. There we, fortunately, found two fish on the beach.

After having divided them between us, we went back to Natal, reaching there the next day.

We learned that during our absence Messrs. Petersen and Hoffman, with some of their party, had sailed in the *Julia*; also that Shaka had sent a message to Natal requesting me to pay him another visit. I accordingly proceeded to his residence, where I found that a number of natives of Delagoa Bay had recently arrived with tribute for the King. It turned out that one of them knew me very well, having seen me at Delagoa in 1823.

The King, having heard in my absence that I had gone off on a journey to the westward, asked me to give him particulars thereof. He laughed heartily on hearing the account. Moreover, he wanted to know how I could expect to travel through those parts without his assistance, for obviously my troubles had all arisen out of his having killed off the inhabitants of the surrounding countries. I had, therefore, got only what I deserved for attempting to travel among people from whom it was impossible to reap any kind of benefit; indeed, I could only expect to be either murdered by them or poisoned by bush Kaffirs.

I endeavoured to explain the reasons for the attempt I had made by saying it was customary with my countrymen to try and become acquainted with the manners and customs of other natives with a view to self improvement, and, in return, to strive to benefit those with whom they come in contact by teaching them something of British manners and customs. If we had not been habitually actuated by such impulses, and put them into practice, we would not have had the pleasure of making his own acquaintance or of receiving from him those marks of kindness and attention he had already shown us. But I might have saved my breath on this occasion as well as on many others, for I found I had to deal with a king who had no idea of any limit to his powers, and who was confident his commands were both lawful and strictly reasonable. To this I made no reply, considering that doing the deed, although forbidden, would be less likely to irritate than attempting to justify it in words at that moment. He treated me kindly during the remaining part of my visit, which lasted only two days. I then returned to Natal.

When I got back, within four days of my departure, I found that Mr. Davis had returned with the *Julia* from Algoa Bay. On hearing that I intended once more to return to the amaMpondo and meant to be better prepared for the journey than on the former occasion, he volunteered to accompany me thither, that is, during such time as the sloop was being cleaned and put in order for her next voyage with the remainder of the party—the first portion having already gone off with Mr. Petersen.

On this the second journey to the westward, after the necessary preparations had been made, I was accompanied by Mr. W. H. Davis, Joe (one of Mr. Farewell's servants) and two Hottentots. But when just about to start we found the loads rather too heavy for the two horses we were taking, so we were obliged temporarily to increase our party by three women obtained from the bush,[1] to help carry the things. We, moreover, had with us two cows, a few salt fish, 12 pounds of rice, 15 pounds of biscuits, also some tea and sugar.

The first day's travelling brought us to Joɓe's Rocks. Joɓe, as had happened before, ran away as we approached, but returned on hearing that I was with the party. We slept at his place, and, resuming our former route the next morning, passed the night in the same bush as we had slept in on the preceding journey. The next day we reached Klaas's Flat, where we killed one of our cows. We rested in the hut we had formerly occupied, namely that in which we discovered Klaas and his family, but the woman and child had now deserted it. On moving forward the next morning, accompanied by Klaas, we came across two half-starved boys in the bush. We soon found ourselves surrounded on all sides by matungulu bushes, laden with fruit. This induced us to take advantage of the opportunity by resting and refreshing the horses.

After spending about two hours in collecting a plentiful supply of fruit to take with us, we journeyed on till the evening, when we bivouacked for the night close to a small stream. When preparing supper we discovered, to our great surprise, that there were no more biscuits, and on making a close enquiry among our people we learned to our great regret that while a

---

[1]The word bush here, and in some other places, means the sylvan mode of existence to which they had been reduced as the result of Shaka's wars.—*Editor.*

ZULU KRAAL NEAR UMLAZI, NATAL

From the painting by George French Angus in *Kaffirs Illustrated*

number of us were engaged in picking fruit the others had eaten up the biscuits, some ten pounds in weight. The one who had been carrying the bundle at first declared that in the hurry of starting it had been left behind. The meat of the beast killed the day before had become putrid owing to having been tied up in leaves and carried on the peoples' heads on an excessively hot day. We, therefore, had to be very careful of what remained of our beef and rice, for previous to the killing of the cow we had been partaking only of fish and biscuits.

On going forward the next morning we were joined by another woman carrier. In order to reduce the weight of the loads carried by the others, which included our clothes and bedding, we gave her the rice, tea and sugar to carry. My horse, which on the preceding day had become very fatigued, was now so exhausted that I was obliged to get off and lead him. After proceeding some distance, we came upon traces of cattle. On following the hoof marks we were soon brought in sight of the kraal the cattle belonged to; no sooner did we get there than we came face to face with several men armed with shields and assegais and ready to attack us.

Aware that our having come from Shaka would be dangerous to us if known, I simply told them that we were from a European settlement, subjects of King George, and anxious to reach the amaMpondo. On finding us amicably disposed, they took us into their kraal. There was but one cow in the kraal; it belonged to the headman, whose name was Mzoɓoshi. As he and his adherents were living entirely on roots, there was no possibility of procuring from them provisions of any kind for our journey, and they said the distance still to be covered was very considerable. Mzoɓoshi informed us that his chief resided about 20 miles from there, and that it would be necessary for us to visit him before we could proceed any further. We gladly took advantage of the opportunity of going there as it might afford us a chance of purchasing the provisions we needed for the rest of our journey.

In the evening we were visited by Mbalijala and his followers; this man's kraal was but a short distance from that of Mzoɓoshi. He was pointed out to me as being the brother of their chief Mangcuku. After he sat for a few minutes in conversation with Mzoɓoshi, the two parties combined and struck up a dance in honour of the occasion. They felt sure that some great change in the country was imminent, seeing that white people had now appeared among them. Up to that moment, they said, they had only *heard* of the existence of such animals. Their forefathers had told them that if the vessels that conveyed us across the sea were to put any of us ashore it was to be looked on as a sign that peace would be established throughout the land. They remained until after sunset. That night we once more reposed in a hut.

When we awoke the next morning we found the people already prepared to accompany us to their chief. After an early breakfast we left with Mzoboshi, Mbalijala and the majority of their followers; they conducted us by a stony and bushy route, which caused a lot of pain owing to my shoes being in bad order. The sun had already set when we arrived. Much to our regret there was no better prospect of obtaining provisions here than at Mzoboshi's, for the people had very few cattle.

Mangcuku, the chief, apparently about 25 years of age, made his appearance in the midst of his followers, all being clad in their war-dresses. He paid us the compliment of having their war song sung. When this had come to an end, he promised to renew his visit in the morning to talk over details in connection with the remainder of our journey. On applying to Mangcuku and on paying therefor[1] we were able to obtain a little sweet milk. This milk proved to be a great luxury. We decided to rest two days at this kraal.

Whilst at the kraal, a messenger was sent to warn us to fasten securely at night the door of our hut, as on the preceding night leopards, which in that part of the country were very ferocious, had carried off two women from a hut adjoining ours. We accordingly took the precaution, and lucky it was we did do, for not more than half an hour afterwards we heard a leopard prowling about the hut we were in; finding all secure, he contented himself that night with seizing a calf. It was too dark when we heard the calf bellow to attack the leopard with any prospect of success, though we looked forward to having our revenge on the following morning. As soon as it became daylight we followed the leopard's track, and found him not more than two hundred yards from the kraal. The interpreter,

---

[1] Not in money, but probably by bartering with beads.—*Editor.*

Fire, shot it, the ball passing through the two shoulders; a second ball from me sealed its fate. When quite satisfied it was dead, the natives danced about in ecstasy of delight. They ran their assegais through and through the corpse to avenge the death of their companions. They then lifted the body on to their shoulders and carried it off; afterwards they danced round the criminal as he lay on the ground. The animal was then skinned and his hide placed on the cattle kraal fence and there allowed to rot. Such procedure took place in accordance with custom, for the hide was deemed to be unfit for use owing to the animal having devoured human flesh. To signify his pleasure at the death of the leopard, Mangcuku presented me with a cow and, as he clearly realised the superiority of our arms over theirs, he promised to reward me handsomely with cattle if I would join in an attack he proposed making on people living to the westward. Although I positively refused to comply, he would not be persuaded but that I refrained only because, by holding out, I anticipated the promise of a greater reward.

As there appeared no hope of increasing our stock of provisions we now made arrangements for continuing our journey. I went into the cattle kraal to obtain milk I had already purchased by Mangcuku's orders, and for which I had already paid him. Finding the man who was there disinclined to give it, I took it by force. He immediately flew to his assegais, whereupon Mangcuku ran up, intervened and took him aside, away from where our interpreter was standing.

From what the interpreter reported, I concluded that they were not well disposed towards us for having persisted in refusing to join them in the intended attack. I thereupon endeavoured to convince them of the impropriety of our fighting people whom we did not even know, and who had not injured us in any way, adding that were we to take part in any such proceeding it would be at the risk of incurring our own King's serious displeasure.

On leaving them, we took the cow Mangcuku had given me and returned to Mzoɓoshi's kraal, where we slept. The cow was now slaughtered and part of its meat dried for use on the journey, the distance to be travelled being still unknown to us. We felt that the people we had just visited were not our best friends, and perceiving some difference between them and

Mzoɓoshi, who, however, possessed nothing he could give us, we determined to leave with him the only cow we had by way of making sure of having some food available on our return.

We concluded that the people Mangcuku contemplated attacking were the amaMpondo, hence they could not be far off. Our dried meat, rice, tea and sugar would therefore last until we got to them, when there would be a better chance of replenishing our stores for the return journey. Even to the last moment I could obtain no information as to where the amaMpondo lived. As often as I questioned these people, they replied simply by pointing to the other side of the river. This caused me to be somewhat suspicious as to their intentions. As I could not depend on my horse for even a day's journey, I left it behind, and went forward on foot, though only after coming to an understanding with my companion, Mr. Davis, known as " ride and tarry."[1] On getting to the Umzimkhulu or Bloody River, however, Mr. Davis when crossing a gully so hurt his foot that, unable to walk, he was obliged to ride, hence he did the riding and I the tarrying, seeing the third horse was unable to do more than carry our bedding.

We had just crossed the river when the interpreter informed us that the woman the last to be engaged was missing, together with the bundle she was carrying containing the whole of our rice, sugar and tea, that is, all we had taken the precaution of keeping in reserve in case of failure to procure supplies on ahead. We stopped and searched about for her for some time, but without result. We then went on with our dried beef, but had not gone far before the boy who was carrying it also disappeared. Owing to his knowledge of the bush being better than our own he easily escaped. This further misfortune now left us entirely without provisions.

In the course of our search for the boy, we found three men by the side of a river; they were living on roots and honey. They brought us three large pots of this food and we sat down and partook of it. We then held a consultation as to what course to pursue, seeing we were now without means or hope of subsistence. The question now was whether to return to Natal, without having accomplished the object of the expedition, and in doing that, risk being cut off by the people we had just left,

---

[1] Whereby one rides for a time, whilst his companion walks, then vice versa.—*Editor.*

for we felt satisfied it was they who had induced our carriers to run off with the provisions, or to proceed on our journey. We thought it wiser to send Klaas back to fetch the cow we had left at Mzoɓoshi's and await his return on the following day. This he faithfully promised to do. In the meantime we continued to live on the honey. But, owing to eating too heartily of it, we found ourselves in a manner stupified by it. We stayed where we were until the evening of the next day, without seeing any sign of Klaas. Next morning we discovered that our only remaining boy had absconded.

After waiting till noon, without seeing anything of Klaas, we removed to the hut occupied by the men who were with us. We found it occupied by a large family. The headman was an elderly man apparently about 80 years of age. All the inmates were subsisting almost entirely on honey and roots, occasionally catching birds and scaring buck. In front of the principal hut was a patch of Indian corn not ten yards square. As they feared that, in our hungry state, we would be unable to resist the temptation of stealing, we were intreated not to touch the corn as the lives of the whole family depended thereon, for, should it be eaten by them or by others, Mbalijala, who had heard of its existence, and had ordered it to be reserved for his own use, would put all of them to death. I assured Songomela that it would not be touched by us.

Finding him to be a man of intelligence, I enquired as to the present state of the tribe and how it had been brought about.

He informed me of the wreck of the *Grosvenor* and indicated where I could see its remains. He said he had heard from people who were present that the vessel had, for several hours, been drifting about in the neighbourhood before coming ashore. On the occasion on which he saw her, however, all the passengers, crew, etc., had left, except the blacksmith, who remained at the spot making assegais and copper rings for wearing round the neck. Some time afterwards Europeans arrived with waggons d awn by oxen, and proceeded as far as the Bloody River (Umzimkhulu). What seems to have attracted his attention most was the whip with which the bullocks were beaten, of this he gave a detailed description. They gave away blankets and beads to the natives, but he was unable to ascertain the real object of their visit. After stopping a few days at the Bloody River, they returned westward by the route they had come by.

Night came on, and yet no Klaas and no cow, so that we gave him up for dead. As only two of the women we had brought from Natal remained, and these were unable, for want of food, to carry our baggage, we decided to leave them at Songomela's to continue living on roots as they had been in the habit of doing. We, however, found it impossible to subsist on roots, hence, next morning we pursued a course along the beach in the endeavour to live, if possible, on mussels. Of these, on that day, we made a meal. We arrived at the habitation of Songomela's eldest son, Osiyana, where we obtained some honey. We continued our journey on the following morning.

When about five miles from Osiyana's huts, and while breakfasting on a bed of oysters, Osiyana himself, with a party, overtook us, his intention being to accompany us to the amaMpondo, where, if they could see any hope of peace, they proposed to live. We had not gone far before all but four of them were obliged to return on account of fatigue. They were nothing but skeletons.

In the course of this day's tedious march we met several droves of elephants. We reached the Umthentu River, where we observed among the rocks something resembling the trunks of old trees; these had apparently become jammed in the crevices of the rocks. On examining them, we found them to be the trunks of trees which had petrified and become as hard as the solid rock by which they were held. We counted six of these trees. One or two had retained several of their largest branches, and showed the marks of such as had decayed. The knots and grain of the wood were still perfect. In breaking several pieces off by means of large stones, as much fire was produced as if the hardest flint had been struck. This induced us to look along the shore to see if these characteristics were general but found them in no other place than between the Umthamvuna and Umthentu Rivers and there only between the high and low water mark.

At Umthentu we fed on mussels and slept in a cave among the rocks. By this time we all felt weak for want of better food, hence, on the following day, travelled about six miles, where we again fed on mussels. We slept at the Umsikaba River. On leaving there in the morning we soon arrived where the wreck of the *Grosvenor* Indiaman had occurred. This we found was about one mile off St. Stephen's Point, and where it forms a very shallow bay. There were immense rocky precipices along the whole of the shore, in this part of the country, and, in the steepest portions thereof, the remains of the wreck were still to be seen. We waited there till low water, when we counted five of her guns of large calibre (32–36-pounders) and 86 pigs of iron ballast, scattered here and there about the rocks. Many of the pigs of ballast had so jammed in the crevices of the rocks as if designed to link them together, and this to a height of 30 to 40 feet above sea level. I suppose they must have been carried or floated there with parts of the wreck. On further search we came across a flat-topped knoll covered with ballast laid on the ground with great regularity; this had evidently been placed there on purpose. In the belief that something had been buried on the spot, we removed the iron and began, weak as we were, to dig. After digging for some way down Osiyana told us the Indiaman's blacksmith had set up and worked at a forge on the spot. This made me desist from searching any more. I now proceeded to a river close by where I found the remains of an Indian bamboo chair, but, judging from its appearance, I was not satisfied that it had belonged to the wreck in question.

As we travelled along we found an abundant supply of water from waterfalls. From knowledge of that part of the country, which I subsequently obtained, I was led to believe that the passengers and crew of the *Grosvenor*, who complained so much of the want of water, must have travelled close to the sea from a fear of being seen by the natives. In that case they would have come across very little water as many of the streams do not flow into the sea, but simply ooze into it through the sand, and those that do flow in are salt for a considerable way inland.

After the searching we had done on this day we were greatly fatigued and our horses completely knocked up; moreover, our feet and legs were swollen in consequence of our shoes having quite worn out. On the following day, therefore, we could proceed only at a very slow rate. We made our breakfast off oysters. Osiyana informed us that we could not then be very far from the amaMpondo, but he was not at all sure of the distance.

At night we got to a waterfall, where we rested. Finding ourselves next morning unable to proceed on account of weakness, we decided to remain where we were for the whole of that day. On going to the rocks to get shell fish, we saw a man at a distance. He ran away, as indeed did all strangers, owing to not being accustomed to see " white animals " like us. We saw that, physically speaking, we were not worse off than he was. Indeed, he even was more like a skeleton than we were. We caught him and enquired how much further we had to go to reach the amaMpondo. To our intense satisfaction, he said that by travelling at a moderate pace we would reach them by midday. This intelligence revived our spirits, and made us not feel so weak or suffer so much pain in our feet. After breakfasting on such food as was available, we pushed on and passed a cave of sufficient capacity to shelter 50 men, with water, moreover, close by. About a mile beyond the cave, we found a long spar which, owing to its distance from where the wreck had taken place, we doubted if it had belonged to that vessel. The distance from there to the site of the wreck would have been about 25 miles. I noticed that the spar had been burnt through the middle in order to remove the iron; otherwise the timber was still quite good.

We found the country about here to be different from that we had travelled over since leaving Natal. In and about Natal were to be found extensive flats, with bushes scattered about them. The country we were now in, however, was very hilly with immense forests, and containing the finest timber I had seen in that part of South Africa.

About four o'clock, I picked up a piece of honey that had been thrown away by an amaMpondo. This I devoured with greater relish than anything I had ever eaten before. A few minutes afterwards, we came upon some cattle tracks and cow-dung. This delighted us all. Following these tracks we came in sight of three kraals, which appeared to be but a short distance from us. To guard against causing too great a surprise to the people on entering their kraal, for we were declared to be the first Europeans who had paid them a visit, I desired two of the four natives that then remained with us to go to the kraal in advance and prepare the inmates for our approach. We waited till they had sufficient time to get there, then we followed. To our great surprise, after we had passed through the intervening bush, longer than we had expected, we found our messengers sitting at the edge of it and close to the kraal. On asking why they had not gone forward, they replied they were afraid because of their having brought us with them. As there was no time to lose, we entered the kraal and found a number of boys and girls engaged in dancing. On seeing us they immediately fled into the bush, whilst the men ran to get their shields. On looking round for Fire, our interpreter, he was missing, and as I was unable to inform them from whence I had come, or of the object of our visit, and as, moreover, I wanted to show that I was well disposed towards them, I gave several of the elder men some beads, and then asked for food. They brought me a pot of milk and asked me various questions, which, I understood plainly enough, had reference to Shaka. As I was aware that they had recently been defeated by Shaka, I thought it wise to appear to know nothing about him, for had I admitted knowing their great enemy nothing I could afterwards say in self defence would have convinced them I was not one of his spies. On their frequently mentioning the name of Shaka, therefore, I pretended not to know what it was they referred to, merely pointing to my stomach and myself and repeating the word Shaka, as if I understood it to mean hunger. This device proved so successful that I was not again troubled with his name until the middle of the night when the interpreter arrived on the scene, the explanation as to his not having come sooner being it was on account of fatigue. The people of the kraal came with him to my hut, when I at once took the opportunity of telling the former that the object of our coming was to open a trade in ivory with their people; that we had come from the Colony by sea,[1] and that having been in distress for want of provisions, had been a long time in search of their kraals. They appeared to be inclined to talk all night but I begged them to defer all further enquiry until the morning as we were then so tired. They therefore left us to take the rest we so badly needed.

My first step was to send messengers to their king, Faku, who lived 30 miles further on, to inform him of the object

---

[1]That is, the Cape Colony. During the earlier part of the nineteenth century it was customary in other parts of South Africa to refer, in ordinary conversation, to the Cape Colony as simply the Colony or the Old Colony. —*Editor.*

of our visit, and of my intention of returning to Natal before I could pay him a visit.

After the messenger had been dispatched, I was presented with a cow by the chief of the amaNtusi tribe, Manyaɓa. This tribe was part of the amaMpondo nation. The cow was killed and the day was spent with our amaMpondo visitors in making various mutual inquiries. On the following morning we were awakened by the noise of the inmates of the kraal. They were getting ready to hunt some elephants that were near at hand. We accompanied the party. Each man carried as many as six or 12 assegais. Presently, they and their dogs approached the elephants. The dogs, by constantly barking, so attracted the elephants' attention as to afford the hunters an opportunity of coming close enough to throw their assegais. The first that was flung struck one of the animals' left shoulder. This hit, in accordance with custom, entitled the thrower to claim the tusks. The rest of the party then threw a shower of assegais. This process was repeated until the elephant became so exhausted as to become an easier target to its assailants, who, creeping closer, whilst the dogs continued to keep the animal at bay, threw their assegais at it with greater force than before. When, at length, the elephant's strength failed he fell, crushing the bushes under him, and then died in a few minutes. The hunters now withdrew their assegais, almost as numerous as the quills of a porcupine. Another elephant was then attacked and dispatched in like manner, except that it did not suffer its fate quite so tamely, for it twice chased the hunters during the assault. On seeing the second one fall, with no others near at hand, we returned to the kraal, leaving the hunters engaged in cutting their game in pieces. The three men who were with me, as well as Osiyana, when it was time to go, were not at all inclined to move from the elephant.

Osiyana now said he was determined not to throw in his lot with the amaMpondo as he had intended to do, but to return to his home and await my return from Natal (as I had already led him to believe I would do), when he would go and reside with me. After having done some business during the day, I told Manyaɓa I proposed to return to Natal on the following day, provided the messengers from Faku arrived in time. They did not, however, do so until the morning after, bringing with them a cow as a present from the king, coupled with a request that I would soon return to his country.

I purchased a calf, which was all that could be got for food on the road. This was killed before I left, but owing to their continual encroachments I was able to reserve very little. I therefore had to depend on the cow from Faku which I reckoned would be sufficient to keep us in provisions until we reached the Umzimkhulu.

Having now completed our forward journey,[1] which at the outset we imagined would take only three or four days, we resolved to start at once on the return journey to Natal. We managed to pass the first night in a cave near the River Umsikaba, after partaking of the head of the calf, which was all that remained of the animal. As we intended to kill the cow at noon on the following day, we got away early in the morning of that day. On passing the mouth of a small stream, we saw a hippopotamus walking about on the beach. We off-saddled the two horses to give them a rest, then attempted to prevent the hippopotamus from getting to the sea, and so make it possible to stab him with our assegais. After half an hour's chase, however, we failed to do this, so returned to where we had left the horses. During our absence, it seems that one of them neighed and so frightened the cow that it ran off and got out of sight of its driver, Osiyana. We remained there all day searching about for what was our sole means of subsistence. But all our efforts proved futile, as the animal had evidently made off in an inland direction, where it was impossible to follow its spoor. We were, therefore, once more in the predicament of having to depend entirely on mussels. We decided to travel as far as we could during the night, and got as far as the Umthentu River, where we took an hour's rest. Mr. Davis now proposed that each of us should exert himself to the utmost to reach the Umzimkhulu, and that, in case anyone was unable to keep up through weakness or other cause, the rest of the party should not wait but go on without him. As the object of the proposal was to stimulate everyone to do his best, it was agreed to.

---

[1] Apparently the author did not reach the Umtata River, as in his evidence before the Native Affairs Commission 1852–3 he says he did do. There is, however, no doubt that he did reach it when he made his second journey. —*Editor.*

When we had walked about 15 miles, I saw some bush Kaffirs near our route. I went up to them—Mr. Davis and Joe, however, passed them and continued to go ahead. I found the head of one of them covered with wounds recently inflicted. This led to my asking how they had been caused. He said he had been at Umzimkhulu and been beaten by Umbalijala, brother of Mangcuku, for having, as they presumed, shown us the way to the amaMpondo. I was sorry it was not in my power to compensate for the injuries that had been done him on our account. Those with him had already washed the wounds with herbs. I told them I would be coming back again when I would remove him from his present position. During the half-hour I was with them I overlooked the arrangement come to in the morning. As soon as it occurred to me, I marched on quickly. Fire and Osiyana remained to beg for tobacco and I expected they would soon follow. After going some distance without seeing either Mr. Davis or Joe, I. quickened my pace; following the horses' track, until I came to the River Umphenjathi. But this river, between the time at which Davis and Joe had crossed it and my reaching it, had swollen so much on account of the tide as to be impassable. As there were no signs of Fire and Osiyana coming on, and being alone, I concluded they had most likely gone to Osiyana's kraal, which, I recollected, must now be close at hand. I went n search of it but, through its being in the centre of the bush, I could not find it. I met a girl of about 8, and called to her, feeling sure she belonged to Osiyana's kraal. But, through fear of conversing with a human being other than those she lived with in the bushes, she ran away, whilst I remained for a time, without hope of seeing anyone. This continued until I had crossed the river, after which I proceeded along Mr. Davis's track as fast as the famished state in which I was could allow. After walking about 20 miles, I overtook them at the Imbizane River. They were having a strong argument as to which road was the best to go by. Joe, an old sailor, refused to go anywhere else than along the beach, which he was confident would, some time or other, bring him to the Umzimkhulu, where he would find Mzoɓoshi's kraal. Mr. Davis and I recognised, on the other side of the river, the route we had before used, hence we walked through the bush until we came to our old track. There we found a man lying asleep. I caught hold of him. On waking, he was greatly surprised, and, making sure he would be put to death, he attempted to run. We pacified him and showed him some beads. After a great deal of trouble, owing to the absence of our interpreter we managed to make him understand we wanted to find the way to Songomela's kraal, adding that if he would conduct us there he should have the beads we had shown him. He then went along with us. It was after sunset when we arrived at Songomela's kraal. We found the two women we had left there on our forward journey. These now rejoined the party. We pushed on in the evening towards Mbalijala's, at the risk of obtaining there only the scantiest supply of food, rather than eat the intoxicating roots which were all Songomela had to offer; that is unless we took their small piece of corn, with the esult that, after our departure, and when we were unable to protect them. they would be immediately put to death by Mbalijala. Having tightened our stomach bands, to prevent feeling extreme pangs of hunger, and after drinking water at every brook we came to, we arrived at Mbalijala's kraal. Had this kraal been but a short distance on, it would have been impossible for us to reach it. As it was, we had travelled from about five in the morning to twelve at night, covering a distance of not less than 70 miles. Such a feat could not possibly have been achieved if we had had food to subsist on. It was hunger and hope that drove us on.

We waited some time before the gate was opened for us by an elderly man. He gave us a hut to sleep in whilst I went to that of Mbalijala's mother. Mbalijala himself was away on war service against a tribe inland of the amaMpondo. On attempting to enter the hut to procure some milk, the door was shut in my face, and I was ordered to remain outside. No entreaties would induce them to let me in. I then took off a handkerchief that was tied round my neck and gave it to the old man who had opened the gate, begging him to let me have some milk. I also gave him a snuff-box (worked over with beads), being all I had, upon which they gave me some milk in a pot-cover, which held no more than a pint. As I saw no hope of getting more, Mr. Davis and I drank it, which however, left us as badly off as if we had had none at all.

Our bedding had remained behind with Fire, and as we were unable to obtain a mat at the kraal, we lay down on the bare floor, with some firewood as a pillow. Hard though our circumstances were, we managed to sleep soundly until eight o'clock, when we determined at all risks to seize their milk as soon as the cows had been milked. We waited till eleven o'clock to carry out the intention, only to discover that the cattle had been taken into the bush and there milked—on purpose to prevent our seizing it—just as if they had been aware of our intentions. I then entered a hut where I saw two calabashes of milk. On going for a pot to put it in, I left Mr. Davis to keep watch at the door and prevent it being removed. On returning, however, I found the calabashes had already been passed out of the hut—through an opening at the back of it.[1] All our attempts to obtain milk having thus been frustrated, we went across the Umzimkhulu feeling as faint as we could without actually falling. Nor was there any ground for hoping we should receive more favourable treatment at Mzoɓoshi's kraal, as we suspected that long before then the boy Klaas, whom we had sent for the cow we had left at that kraal, had been killed by the inmates. As Mzoɓoshi's was only about two miles off, we got there in about an hour's time. Mzoɓoshi, too, we were informed, was away fighting. We asked the mistress of the kraal for milk. She gave us two large pots of it and produced also the cow we had left with them, as well as my horse. And so we became much more hopeful.

We enquired about the boy Klaas. They said he had been killed by them, but had not asked for the cow. He had been caught in the bush below the kraal, after stealing some assegais and curiosities I had left at Mzoɓoshi's. As we knew nothing more about him than his having travelled with us part of the way, we could not do otherwise than accept what they told us as being correct. We then killed the cow, and satisfied our hunger. The only anxiety that now remained was in regard to our absent followers.

After inquiry, we ascertained that as soon as we had left that part of the country (on our forward journey) the tribe, under Mangcuku, called the amaNdulo had immediately gone inland to attack the amaMpondo, which accounted for Mbalijala's and Mzoɓoshi's present absence.

We rested the night at the kraal, then resolved to wait for those we had left behind, and at the same time dry some beef

---

[1] Under normal conditions Zulu huts have no opening at the back.—*Editor*.

for the journey. In the meantime, towards evening, Fire made his appearance in company with the two women who had rejoined us at Songomela's kraal, whilst Joe arrived about the middle of the night. Both were too weak to go in the morning. Nevertheless, we proposed to start, and as my horse was fresh, Mr. Davis and I arranged to "ride and tarry," leaving Joe, Fire and the two women to come on with the dried beef as well as they could. We made an early start, taking with us only as much beef as was sufficient for the remainder of the journey. But we had not gone far before we lost it all, together with my hat and green hide shoes, while crossing at high tide.

We now felt that such a disaster as losing our provisions could not be repeated, for, between there and Port Natal, no supplies of any kind were procurable. We therefore pushed on as fast as possible. Late in the evening the darkness compelled us to put up for the night just where we were, but we had not been asleep for more than two hours when we were awakened by wolves attacking my one-eyed horse on his blind side. I gave Mr. Davis two brass arm rings to jingle together and, with the help of firebrands and a sword, we at length managed to drive them away. This caused us to get on the move. We afterwards called the hill we had slept at "Wolf's Head." When we left there it was with the intention of not again resting until we had reached the port, that is with the exception of halting to obtain mussels. These, indeed, we were able to get in the middle of the day, but so poor as to be fit only for the consumption of hungry travellers like ourselves. When we had somewhat refreshed ourselves we walked on until we got to Joɓe's hut. Of him we hired a man to carry our blankets, for the doing of which I gave him two brass rings I had brought from Mzoɓoshi's kraal. The roots the natives lived on were so bad that we could not manage to eat them. We were now obliged to proceed on foot as the horse was much too tired to go on. We continued to travel until darkness prevented our going any further, but we rested on a hill which brought us within view of Natal. From there we intended to proceed when the moon rose. I woke just at that time and roused Mr. Davis, also the man I had got from Joɓe. The latter, however, proposed sleeping a little longer, that is, until the moon had got well up. Still feeling the want of sleep, we again lay down and fell into a deep slumber, from which we did not wake till daylight. We then found the carrier's reason for wishing us to lie down again was simply to afford him an opportunity of escaping, owing to the fear of the Zulus, who, as he knew, lived with us at Port Natal. We resumed the journey in an extremely weak and famished condition, and in addition had to carry the blankets ourselves. We were, however, soon obliged to throw the blankets away. The immense quantities of water we drank had the effect of so exhausting us as to prevent our arriving at Mr. Farewell's house until late in the day and, as may be conjectured, in a most miserable condition. He was absent. It seems that, having taken provisions with him in the boat, he had gone down the Bay in the hope of meeting us, as he had heard of our approach from natives that had seen us that morning.

All were greatly surprised on seeing us again as they had long given us up for dead. Joe, Fire and the women arrived safely two days later.

Chapter VIII

AFTER resting a few days at Natal, I went off again on a visit to Shaka, who, as before, was angry at my proceedings, assuring me that the visiting of strange nations would ultimately ruin me. Business being my object, in a few days I returned to Natal, and from thence went off again to the amaMpondo, for the purpose of forming a trading establishment there. Having taken every precaution, in the way of provisions and other respects, before starting as well as *en route*, to obviate the dangers and distress I had experienced on the former expedition, I reached my destination in due course without difficulty or happening upon anything worth relating, except the having come upon and rescued a number of people when almost at the point of death, through having tried to appease their hunger by consuming injurious poisonous roots. I stayed only two days with the amaNtusi tribe, an advanced division of the amaMpondo, then proceeded on to King Faku's kraal.

After having waited two hours for an interview, exposed to an oppressive sun, I was directed to a hut; an ox was presently brought there for our consumption.

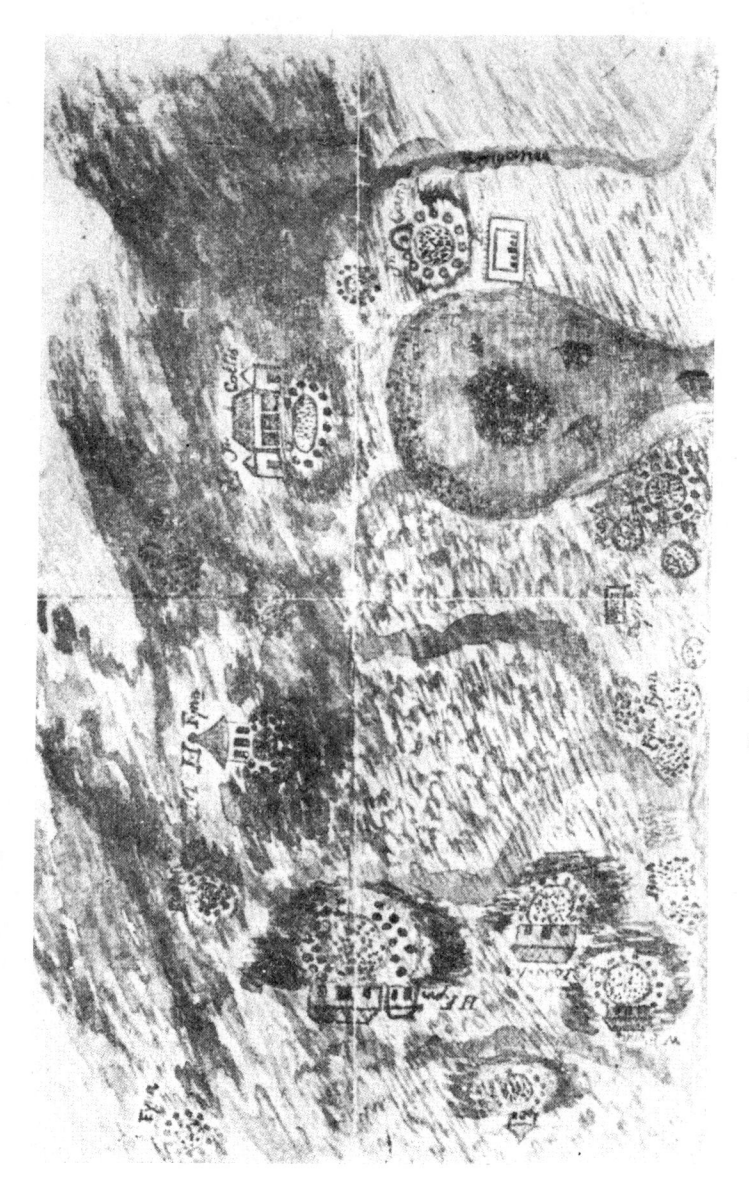

The Settlement at D'Urban
From a drawing by Henry Francis Fynn

In the morning the representatives of the nation kept on assembling until about eleven. I was then requested to attend and did so, only to realise that I was to be put on trial under what appeared to me difficult and dangerous circumstances. I was accused of being employed by Shaka as a spy. The proofs adduced against me were three. First, that I could not have come from the eastwards without having been sent by Shaka, it being asserted that there were no Europeans in that direction; secondly, they had seen me use salt, which they had never heard of as being found anywhere except near the River Thukela, which is in the very heart of Shaka's country; thirdly, Shaka was said to be of white extraction, therefore I was probably one of his relations.

I made the best possible defence I could, placed, as I was, under the most awkward circumstances. I assured them I had come from the Colony in a vessel and expressed my deepest indignation at being suspected of being engaged in the contemptible office of a spy. Nevertheless, during such time as the trial lasted, I expected to be condemned. As each of those present had the right of interrogating me, the case was not concluded until four o'clock. I had no sooner replied to one man than another stood up and repeated the same questions. At length, the charges were dropped and, after Faku had received from me a present of beads, I proceeded to the particular business I had come upon. After this visit to Faku, which lasted two days, I returned to the amaNtusi tribe to set up there a trading station for the purchase of ivory.

When this had been arranged, I made an excursion along the coast, crossing the Umzimvuɓu or St. John's River at its mouth. Leaving Faku's kraal inland about 15 miles, I crossed the Umgazi River, where I heard of another man called Faku, who was said to be of European extraction. I sent for him and remained until his arrival at the kraal of Mbalawa, a petty chief of the Red Kaffir (Bomvana) tribe. This man was said to have recently killed a European whose name, however, I was unable to ascertain. On the expiration of two days Faku arrived, when I found him to be the son of the blacksmith of the *Grosvenor*, a man whom the natives called uMɓethi.[1]

---

[1] The author writes Umbate, but the last letter is evidently meant for i as indeed often the case when he writes other words ending in i, e.g. *izinkabi*, spelt by him incarbe.—*Editor*.

He informed me that several descendants of Europeans lived near him. This induced me to accompany him to his home. The first kraal that called for notice was that of Majuɓana, a man fully 50 years of age, tall and of a copper colour. His father, Ndapha,[1] lived a mile away. Owing to the fact that he, too, had European blood in him, I decided to proceed to Faku's kraal and bring them all together in order to obtain all the information I could. The number of people in whom I traced European descent was ———.[2]

Ndapha, the chief of that part of the country, was the son of an English lady, whom they called Dawa and said to have been remarkably handsome. I could obtain no further information than that she had come from the eastward and would not consent to live with her husband if he retained the women he had already married. He consented to put them aside. She had but one son, Ndapha, now the father of a large family; she used to dress in native costume, twisting or plaiting her hair into cords which extended to her waist, and covered, or rubbed over with red clay. It was on account of her extreme beauty that, even to this day, the people when reciting her eulogies use the expression, "*Izinkaɓi zikaDawa*," i.e. the oxen of the white lady.

My present host, Faku, was the son of Mɓethi, the blacksmith of the *Grosvenor*, who, after the passengers and crew had gone off in different directions in the hope of reaching some European settlement, remained in the vicinity of the wreck and employed himself in making assegais and brass rings for the natives. By these means he accumulated a few head of cattle, when he took a native woman to wife. By her he had one daughter and one son, namely, Faku. It, however, so happened that Faku's mother, when pregnant, was carried off by a wandering tribe that had come from the east. She was taken to the Umtata River, where the Faku in question was born.

From other sources I ascertained that the father was in despair on account of the loss of his wife. He resided for a time among the amaXolo[3] tribe, near the Umzimkhulu, with his daughter, and built a canoe for exploring the river. He,

---

[1]Spelt Umdaper in MS.
[2]Left blank in MS.
[3]MS. has Amacholues.

however, failed to proceed far up because of the beds of rocks that extend across it. Leaving his daughter (who was afterwards married to a native blacksmith), he went off in an inland direction, from whence, soon afterwards, news was received of his death by the amaXolo. His daughter was killed in 1823 in the general slaughter of the surrounding peaceful nations by Shaka. Faku is still living, he has a large family and possesses a few cattle.

The next to arrive was Mornegal, the eldest of four brothers; he is the son of Kapa.[1] Kapa was a cooper who made tubs, tables and stools for his own use, also trousers and hats of hide. He told his son Mornegal that his (Kapa's) father was called Jeffrey. Kapa had died but five months previous to my arrival. It would appear, from the account given to Mornegal by his father, that the latter, at one time, must have been a slave of European extraction; for he informed his son he was sitting on the rocks picking shell-fish when he was seized by some sailors, put on board a vessel and " fastened," then taken off to where the ship was wrecked.[2] Mornegal, though black, has a countenance strongly resembling that of a European.

The next to arrive—from the eastward—was Peter, evidently of Malabar caste. He was a man of about 80 and spoke good Dutch. He pretended to have been wrecked on the coast some years back. At first he concluded I was going to take him to the Colony, where he would become a slave, but after his fears had been dispelled, through our getting to know one another better, he confessed he was a run-away slave of the Cape Colony, where he must have lived for about 20 years. He had a son of about that number of years and a daughter of 18, with several other children. He said his master at the Cape was Hendrick Fleck.

The next was also a slave from the Colony, Jantze Lapoot, whose master had been Baas Konier. He had run away from Uitenhage, to Kaffirland, but was retaken. He made a second and more successful attempt to escape, when he came on to this place. Biales, of whom I have only hearsay knowledge,

---

[1]MS. has Capa.
[2]That is, in that part of the Cape Colony the author was now visiting. —*Editor.*

was a European. He had died some time back, leaving a son named Jukujela,[1] whom I did not see.

After compensating these people for their trouble, I left with the intention of paying Hintza,[2] chief of the next tribe, a visit. Peter had already invited me to put up at his kraal, where he said he would provide me with bread, which at that time was very scarce. I promised, in the presence of Faku, to visit him, for his kraal was on my way. Peter had not been gone many minutes before Faku warned me to be particularly careful as to what I ate, as there were people in that part of the country who used poison, but would not explain from whom or where I was likely to experience such treatment.

Faku accompanied us on the following morning to Peter's kraal. Fourteen loaves, which corresponded exactly with the number of our party, were put before me. One of these, larger than the rest, was pointed out by Peter as intended for me as the principal, the smaller ones were for the other members of the party. Faku immediately helped himself to one of the smaller ones. This induced me to follow his example. Peter, observing that I had taken one of the smaller ones, made some remark about having taken some trouble to please me; but I, however, pacified him by alluding to the necessity of having a loaf to eat on the journey, adding that I intended reserving the larger one for that purpose. I accordingly ordered it to be packed up, but, not having an opportunity of examining it, threw it into the first river we came to. I now passed on with Faku to the Umtata River,[3] where I visited a petty chief called Ngathane,[4] who was preparing for an attack on a neighbouring kraal. He presented me with an ox, but as Faku again urged me to be cautious as to what I ate, without giving any idea as to where I should suspect foul play, I concluded he was aware of some design on my life. In these circumstances, I decided to return to the amaNtusi tribe.[5] Faku accompanied me. I rewarded him for his attentions.

On returning to the amaNtusi, and during my somewhat lengthy stay there, I had an opportunity of observing the

---

[1]MS. has Jugugaler.
[2]MS. has Einza.
[3]MS. has Umtarte River.
[4]MS. has Ingatarne.
[5]MS. has Amantucens.

custom of circumcision. Boys of 13 and upwards who have not been circumcised are annually collected in each neighbourhood. The man whose business it is to perform the operation lives apart from everyone else, his hut being generally a short distance from those of the rest. He uses for the purpose an assegai which he sharpens on a rough stone. This is done that the blade may become more like a saw than otherwise, its roughness being supposed to accelerate the cure. After each boy has undergone the operation, the parts are washed with an infusion of roots of a cooling nature. Each now puts on a dress specially prepared for the occasion and occupies a hut in which he and the others live apart from all relations and friends. In such locality the neophytes live from one to six months, food being brought them during that time from their respective homes. The dress is made of a kind of flaggy grass,[1] tied in bunches and is intended to cover nearly the whole body, the face being painted with clay.

The lads amuse themselves principally with dancing. At the end of their period of segregation they are deemed to have arrived at the state of manhood, hence entitled to engage in courtship, become married, etc.

[We propose to introduce here the following incident which no doubt occurred in connection with the present journey (forward or return) and inadvertently omitted by the author from his MS.—*Editor.*

Captain J. S. King, in his "Account of Mr. Farewell's Settlement at Port Natal and of a visit to Shaka,"[2], after referring to the author (H. F. Fynn) as having undauntedly penetrated forests, passed through nations, and frequently with no other than black companions, proceeds: " Several attempts have been made on this gentleman's life, one of which is worthy of remark. Being a few miles distant from a tribe, he sent a messenger to say he was friendly, and would advance. No sooner had they received this intelligence than people were dispatched to kill him while asleep. However, the chief who had this task to perform, finding to his surprise that he only differed in colour from themselves, said: ' I am commanded by my chief to put an end to you, as no *white creatures*

---

[1] A grass with sword-shaped leaves, usually growing in moist situations.—*Editor.*
[2] *South African Commercial Advertiser*, 11th July, 1826.

are allowed to enter his territory. But I see you are equal to us,[1] therefore feel yourself secure, at least from the weapon which is in my hand.' Regardless of the remonstrances of the savage, Mr. Fynn insisted on making his way to the nation, which he accomplished, and was tolerably well received. He naturally felt much attached to those who thus spared his life, and they are now living under Mr. Farewell."]

After I had resided with the amaNtusi tribe for about four months, whilst on one of the excursions I made from there to the Umzimvuɓu River, I heard of a European who passed among the natives under the name of Calamaish. I tried to ascertain his whereabouts but found he had returned to the Colony from whence he had come. He afterwards proved to be a Mr. Thackwray, a Kaffir trader. During the various excursions I made in this part of the country I visited most of the tribes living eastward of the Umtata.

Nine months had now elapsed since I left Natal. During the last four, having worn out every article of European manufacture, and no others being procurable, I was reduced to the necessity of wearing skins. A report was now in circulation among the natives that spies had been seen inland of the amaMpondo, supposed to have come from Madikane, a marauding tribe. A few days afterwards a letter arrived from Mr. Farewell to inform me that Shaka's spies were in my neighbourhood, that Shaka had frequently inquired after me, and that he intended to attack the amaMpondo. This, therefore, would make it necessary for me to remove my establishment, goods, etc., and to pay him a visit. This was all the more necessary as the correspondence which was taking place between Mr. Farewell and myself was causing great suspicion in the minds of the amaMpondo; they imagined it related to them and Shaka. I therefore, returned to Natal for the purpose of paying Shaka a visit.

[This volume is not so well provided with illustrations that we can afford to omit a vivid pen sketch of the author from the hand of his friend and partner, Nathaniel Isaacs. He is before us at the very moment of return to Natal, itself then, by the way, in a nascent and very humble state of civilization, after one of his memorable journeys to Pondoland. If ever

---

[1] That is like us in all respects except colour, for by that time he was able to converse in their language.—*Editor*.

South Africa could boast of a Robinson Crusoe of her own, as affable, shrewd, politically sagacious, courageous and large-hearted as Defoe's, here is one to life :

" In the afternoon [15th October, 1825], Mr. Fynn arrived from the country of the Amampontoes [amaMpondo], a tribe inhabiting the banks of the St. John's River, a distance of about 200 miles from Natal. This gentleman had been trading with the natives and had collected a great quantity of ivory. For eight months he had separated himself from his solitary companion, Mr. Farewell, and had associated solely with the people with whom he sojourned. We sat attentively to hear him detail his adventures—the many vicissitudes he had endured, and the obstacles with which he had contended, not only in having been often without food, and ignorant where to seek it, but in daily terror of being destroyed by wild animals, or massacred by savage natives. He had from necessity assumed the costume of the latter while with them, but resumed his own on his return to his habitation. It is almost impossible to convey a correct idea of the singular appearance of this individual when he first presented himself. Mr. Fynn is in stature somewhat tall, with a prepossessing countenance. From necessity his face was disfigured with hair, not having an opportunity of shaving himself for a considerable time. His head was partly covered with a crownless straw hat; and a tattered blanket, fastened round his neck by means of strips of hide, served to cover his body, while his hands performed the office of keeping it round his ' nether man '; his shoes he had discarded for some months, whilst every other habitment had imperceptibly worn away, so that there was nothing of a piece about him. He was highly beloved by the natives, who looked up to him with more than ordinary veneration, for he had often been instrumental in saving their lives, and in months of pain and sickness had administered to their relief. About a hundred had attached themselves to him, so much so that they were inseparable."[1]

---

[1] Isaacs, *Travels and Adventures in Eastern Africa*, I, 39. Of this work and the extract above Mendelssohn, *South African Bibliography*, I, p. lxii, writes : " What a romance, to be sure, is the first settlement of Natal. To me at least the Travels of Nathaniel Isaacs is as fascinating as Robinson Crusoe. . . . Even Defoe imagined nothing more wholly satisfying to the adventurous mind than Fynn. . . .

Let us now stand aside for Fynn himself to go on with his narrative.]

During my absence from Port Natal, I ound that two vessels had touched there, the *Salisbury*, brig, on a trading voyage to the southward and eastward, and the tender of the *Leven*, commanded by Lieutenant Hawes, attached to the surveying squadron of Captain Owen, then engaged in surveying the African coast.

After remaining a few days at Natal in order to rest, I again visited Shaka. I was much gratified at the kind manner in which he received me. Nothing of importance had happened in Shaka's country during my absence, except the death of Zwide, King of the Ndwandwes—Shaka's principal enemy; his son, Sikhunyana, had succeeded him.

When Shaka heard that the ivory I had purchased among the amaMpondo had been left there, he accommodated me with 60 men to bring it to Natal, a distance of more than 200 miles. It was, of course, understood that I myself would accompany the carriers, but as these people were so entirely unacquainted with carrying loads of this description I succeeded in getting only part of the ivory to Natal. It was owing to the presumed loss of the *Julia*—nothing having been heard of her for 11 months, that is, since she sailed from Natal—that it became necessary to transport the ivory by carriers to Natal. The arrangement previously arrived at had been that, on her voyage back from Algoa Bay, the *Julia* would touch at the amaMpondo for the ivory and afterwards convey it to the Colony. In consequence of her being unavailable, and of my having, therefore, to depend on carriers, several journeys were necessary before the whole of the ivory could be removed.

While I was conducting the remaining portion of the ivory to Natal I heard of the wreck of the brig *Mary*.[1] Lieutenant King,[2] who had been told by Lieutenant Hawes of our being greatly in need of a vessel, volunteered to come to our assistance, but owing to the foregoing tragic occurrence he was only partially able to assist us, that is from supplies recovered by him from the wreck.

---
[1] On the outer northern beach at Port Natal, 1st October, 1825.—*Editor.*
[2] Owner of the *Mary*.—*Editor.*

Lieutenant King, though owner of the *Mary* had come as a passenger. The sailing master, was a Mr. Hutton, formerly a ship-builder. As he had brought all the tools necessary for ship-building in the *Mary*, King decided on building a vessel at Port Natal. Some of the crew, however, with the mate, were determined to return to Port Elizabeth in one of the boats. As they showed every disposition to mutiny, King provided them with a boat and provisions and allowed them to go.

On the mate entering the boat, with those of the crew who were leaving with him, he asked them who was to take command of the boat. The unanimous answer was that he should do so. He replied: " Then let my first order be obeyed. Let all spirits be thrown overboard." This was immediately done, whereupon the boat crossed the bar, and after landing at three different places along the coast, reached Port Elizabeth safely on the fifth day.

As I was watching the boat go over the bar, I picked up from the wreck a pamphlet which I eagerly read as it contained a description of an elephant that had been shot at Exeter Change by a regiment of Horse Guards. The large number of balls fired before it fell was also given. The description rather damped my expectations, for, of course, one of our principal objects in coming to Natal was to procure ivory by shooting elephants.

On hearing of the wreck of the *Mary*, Shaka requested the whole European party to pay him a visit, Farewell, King, Isaacs, King's friend, and I, together with the ten remaining men of the crew.[1] We accordingly proceeded to Shaka's kraal, some 140 miles from Port Natal.[2] Shaka sent a four-horned bullock to meet us. He received us in a most affable manner and gave us two oxen to slaughter. We managed to pitch our marquee and tents by sunset. Shaka then sent for me. I was taken into his seraglio. This was now his regular practice whenever I visited him, and he rarely ever allowed me to leave before twelve or one o'clock, owing to the intense interest he took in the different subjects he questioned me

---

[1] Isaacs did not visit Shaka on this occasion ; he remained behind to take charge of Farewell's establishment.—Isaacs, *Travels and Adventures in Eastern Africa*, I, 50.

[2] The journey began on 26th October, 1825.—*Editor*.

about. On the evening in question he amused himself by treating with ridicule the power of European firearms, urging that native assegais were far superior. I contended that, with our guns, we could kill elephant, sea-cow, buffalo and all other kinds of game, as well as the birds of the air, and do so at a distance their assegais could not reach. He, however, persisted in his argument until I retired to rest. Dancing and feasting occupied the morning of the following day; at midday we retired to our marquee. About an hour later a messenger appeared to say that Shaka required our immediate presence with our guns, as a troop of elephants was close at hand. I immediately went to the King and begged him not to require us to shoot the animals as the guns we had were fit only for killing birds and small game. I told him that the one used for shooting elephants was of a larger kind. I merely got laughed at for my pains and on being reminded of the conversation of the previous evening, found there was no alternative but to comply. He insisted on our going, so off we went. Our army was eight to ten strong. We had among us only three fowling pieces, two blunderbusses and four muskets. I must say it was fully in expectation of being afterwards laughed at by everyone that we reluctantly set forth on this venture. We arranged among ourselves to approach to within 40 yards of the animals, then to fire a volley with no other hopes than that the elephants would turn and make off. It was evident, as we proceeded in the direction of the elephants, that the several Zulu regiments that accompanied us depended solely on our efforts, or, at least, were determined not to use their own weapons until we had failed. We had travelled about half an hour when we suddenly came upon a troop of 16 elephants. We marched slowly and cautiously towards them, but as we were manoeuvring to get within the distance we had decided upon one of the sailors suddenly fired at the nearest bull. To the astonishment of the Zulus and our own far greater astonishment, the elephant dropped dead. It was some time before we could satisfy ourselves of the fact as to how such a thing could have occurred, for in those days it was considered almost impossible to kill with leaden balls. Shaka's consternation was great, and he admitted that our weapons were superior to his own.

 On examining the elephant, we found the bullet had penetrated the ear. It was a mere chance shot. The sailor was certainly not accustomed to using a gun, he had no more knowledge of shooting than sailors usually possess, nor had he ever seen an elephant before.

In the evening, when again conversing with Shaka, in the seraglio, he asked me who had the right to the elephant tusks. Owing to the knowledge I had by that time acquired of his character, I foresaw the object of the question and replied that while we had shot the elephant, we could not forget that we had done so at his residence, as his guests. The tusks were, therefore, at his disposal. This answer gave him great pleasure, whereupon he immediately said we could take them.

The day after this occurrence Shaka requested me to attend his grandmother, who was dangerously ill with dysentery and fever. I accordingly went to see her. As her age was about 80, I saw no hope of recovery, and candidly told the King my fears. He requested me to put a white shirt on her. I did so. He then began to cry bitterly. Jacob, the interpreter, told me of Shaka's great affection for his grandmother. When she happened to visit him he frequently washed her eyes and ears which were in a sad state because of her age; he also pared her nails and otherwise treated her as a father might his child. We could hardly believe that a man of an apparent unfeeling disposition could be possessed of such affection and consideration for others. Further observation, however, convinced us that this was indeed the case.

The following evening, while we were sitting with him, he was informed that she was dead. He remained for some moments in deep contemplation. His feelings then seemed to overpower him. He burst out crying and did so aloud. This set the whole of the people in a state of uproar, which continued for about an hour. The great Zulu song was then chanted. The immense number that took part in the singing, the lateness of the evening, and the mournful solemnity of the tune, were sufficient to depress the spirits of the stoutest hearts. After the singing had gone on for about an hour, the crying was repeated and kept up all night; it continued also on the following day. The inmates of the surrounding kraals arrived in hundreds to join with the others in expressing their common sorrow. The mourning came to an end at sunset. When things appeared to be tranquil again, we returned to Natal, only for me, however, in a few days to undertake yet another journey to the south-west.

During my absence in the Pondo country the brig of war, *Helicon*, arrived. Mr. King took the opportunity of returning in her to the Cape. I heard this while still on my journey.

Chapter IX

WHEN I next returned to Shaka's kraal, May, 1826, I saw Somaphunga,[1] brother of Sikhunyana,[2] then king of the Ndwandwe tribe. Somaphunga, afraid of being put to death by his brother, had escaped and come to tender his allegiance to Shaka. He, moreover, gave such information to the King as could not possibly have been obtained by means of spies.

I had not been at the port many days before messengers arrived from Shaka to call all hands, white as well as black, to resist an attack which was momentarily expected on Shaka's kraal.[3] This placed us in an awkward position, as we were far from being fit for active service. Powder was scarce, and our arms out of repair. Moreover, we were aware that, by complying, we should be violating the laws of our country, and embarking on a course which could in no way prove beneficial to us. On the other hand, we dreaded the consequences that might ensue from refusing to obey the order. After a general consultation, we decided to proceed to Shaka's residence. On arriving there, we found everything quiet and peaceful. A day or two after our arrival, however, the whole nation had been called to arms.

Shaka acquainted us with his intentions, and spoke of the necessity of our accompanying him, it being the custom, when the King proceeded in person to war, for every able-bodied man to accompany him. Attempts to explain the nature of the laws of our country and the duties they imposed on us, especially in regard to attacks on other nations, caused him to make some very unpleasant observations. We realised that the

---

[1]MS. has Umpoonya.
[2]MS. has Iseconyarna, son of Zuede.
[3]The summons arrived at the port on or about the 12th of June, 1826.—Isaacs, *Travels and Adventures in Eastern Africa*, I, 128.

SOLDIERS OF THE ZULU KING'S ARMY
From the painting by George French Angus in *Kaffirs Illustrated*

more we showed ourselves ready to accompany him, the better it would be for us. He showed us how dependent we were on him. He also pointed out that vessels seldom, or never, visited Natal; that he could destroy every one of us in such a way that there would be no one left to tell the tale; and that, if the English should seek to avenge our being massacred, they would be terror-struck at the magnitude of his army. On Mr. Farewell refusing to lend Jacob a musket, one was taken from us by force. After these arguments, we proposed to retire to rest, seeing it was late. Shaka then remarked that there would be no necessity for our taking part in the actual fighting; all he wanted us to do was to accompany him, i.e. give him our moral support.

On the following morning we found out to our surprise that the whole army had already moved off during the night; two chiefs only being left to accompany us. We made all possible haste to overtake them, but were unable to do so until we had reached Noɓamba, the residence of Shaka's father, Senzangakhona, a distance of 60 miles from where we started. Noɓamba was now the general rendezvous of the forces. Thence the army was to proceed in separate divisions and by different routes. Here we rested two days, the divisions having been dispatched each with its orders and spies sent on ahead of the remaining forces (each regiment being headed by its chiefs), with heralds, in the meantime, loudly and repeatedly reciting the numerous heroic achievements and altogether wonderful characteristics of their sovereign. The day was exceedingly hot. Every man was ordered to roll up his shield and carry it on his back—a custom observed only when the enemy is known to be at a considerable distance. In the rear of the regiments were the baggage boys, few above the age of 12, and some not more than 6. These boys were attached to the chiefs and principal men, carrying their mats, headrests, tobacco, etc., and driving cattle required for the army's consumption. Some of the chiefs, moreover, were accompanied by girls carrying beer, corn and milk; and when their supply had been exhausted these carriers returned to their homes.

The whole body of men, boys and women amounted, as nearly as we could reckon, to 50,000. All proceeded in close formation, and when looked at from a distance nothing could be seen but a cloud of dust. We had not rested from the time we started, and were parched and almost perishing from thirst, when, coming to a marshy stream, about sunset, the craving to obtain water caused a general and excessive confusion. After the first regiment had passed, the whole of the swamp became nothing but mud, yet this mud was eaten and swallowed with avidity by the following regiments. Several men and boys were trampled to death; and although there was a cry of " shame " raised by many, and a call to help the victims, everyone was too much occupied to attempt to extricate them.

We travelled on until about nine at night, when we arrived at some kraals belonging to a once-powerful nation, the Iziyendane,[1] of whom no more than 150 or 200 souls now remained. They were a different people from any we had yet seen. They were of a strong muscular build, more active than the Zulus, and not having their heads shaved, but wearing their hair about six or eight inches long and twisted in strings of the thickness of whip-cord. As these people had a perfect knowledge of the country, Shaka engaged them as guides and spies.

Next morning we proceeded at daylight, marching over extensive plains of hard and stony ground. At eleven we rested and Shaka employed the Hottentots in making sandals[2] for himself. Cattle were killed for the use of the army. We ate the same food that Shaka did. Each day cattle were dealt out for the use of our Hottentots and natives. We had not been sitting more than an hour when Mr. Farewell was attacked by an ox and so severely injured as to be unable to proceed any further. The King left him in the care of the chiefs who had been directed to remain there, with a part of the seraglio women, until his return.

At one o'clock we proceeded on our march. The whole army was then made to form a single line across the plain, when we drove before us hartebeest, rhinoceros, pheasant and partridge in great numbers. We encamped at the end of the plain under stunted bushes that were dotted about here and there. The army rested here for two days. During the halt a force was detached and sent on ahead.

---

[1] A Bechuana tribe.—Author's MS. Also Shaka's name for the regiment composed of members of the Hluɓi tribe. Their patroness was Shaka's mother, Nandi. The word is derived from *yenda*, meaning to waver, as corn or branches in the wind.—*Editor*.
[2] Of ox hide.—*Editor*.

On resuming our march, Shaka requested me to join the detachment that had already gone on. He did this merely to please his own fancy. I accordingly went on. The frost of the preceding night had been so severe that many of the detachment, from the excessive cold, had slept, to wake no more. During the whole of this day's march not a tree or bush of any kind was to be seen; we were, therefore, obliged to roast our meat with dry grass. We encamped where we found the detachment, namely, in a cave of a mountain. This cave was shaped so as to form three sides of a square. It was known by the name of Inqaba ka Hawana—Hawana's Fastness—from a chief of that name who, some years back, had revolted and defended himself successfully by taking refuge there.[1]

The following day Shaka arrived with the remainder of the forces and next morning we proceeded in one body to a forest, where we rested for two days, awaiting the return of the spies. Several regiments were sent to kraals deserted by the hostile nation, the people having betaken themselves to a general rendezvous. They returned on the evening of the following day loaded with corn, a great luxury to us who had had nothing but meat for several days, and that extremely poor. To us, who were not used to such kind of living, it caused such pain in our teeth as prevented us from chewing.

When the spies returned, the army moved forward early in the morning and bivouacked at the foot of an immense forest, from which the enemy was not far distant. We had generally marched ahead to relieve ourselves from dust, and we had done so this morning till we came within sight of the enemy, when we thought that we ought to join Shaka, expecting him to be close at hand. We found that he was on the opposite mountain, and seeing a regiment carrying white shields, I diverted my course to it at once.

Michael, the Hottentot, and Frederick were induced by Jacob to join a division that had been ordered to move round the mountain to the rear of the enemy, under the belief that a force would be sent that way by the enemy to attack ours in the rear. When I had reached the bottom of the mountain and was ascending the opposite one, expecting to find Shaka

---

[1]This place figured prominently in the Zulu War of 1879. It is about 20 miles to the east of Utrecht, and a mile or two from Kambula, where Col. Evelyn Wood's well-known battle was fought.—*Editor*.

there, I met one of his servants, who informed me that the King had remained at the forest, and advised me to go back, as, the ascent being difficult, the regiment would leave me a long way behind. Being a stranger to their mode of attack I determined to ascend the mountain and be a spectator of passing events.

The hill from which we had first seen the enemy presented to our view an extensive valley to the left of which was a hill separated by another valley from an immense mountain. On the upper part of this there was a rocky eminence, near the summit of which the enemy had collected all his forces, surrounding their cattle, and above them the women and children of the nation in a body. They were sitting down, awaiting the attack.

Shaka's forces marched slowly and with much caution, in regiments, each regiment divided into companies, till within 20 yards of the enemy, when they made a halt. Although Shaka's troops had taken up a position so near, the enemy seemed disinclined to move, till Jacob had fired at them three times. The first and second shots seemed to make no impression on them, for they only hissed and cried in reply: "That is a dog." At the third shot, both parties, with a tumultuous yell, clashed together, and continued stabbing each other for about three minutes, when both fell back a few paces.

Seeing their losses were about equal, both enemies raised a cry and this was followed by another rush, and they continued closely engaged about twice as long as in the first onset, when both parties again drew off. But the enemy's loss had now been the more severe. This urged the Zulus to a final charge. The shrieks now became terrific. The remnants of the enemy's army sought shelter in an adjoining wood, out of which they were soon driven. Then began a slaughter of the women and children. They were all put to death. The cattle being taken by the different regiments were driven to the kraal lately occupied by Sikhunyana. The battle, from the commencement to the close, did not last more than an hour and a half. The numbers of the hostile tribe, including women and children, could not have been less than 40,000. The number of cattle taken was estimated at 60,000. The sun having set while the cattle were being captured, the whole valley during the night was a scene of confusion. Parties of three, four, and five men each went about killing cattle and cutting off the tails of others to form part of their war dress. Many of Shaka's wounded managed to crawl on hands and knees in the hope of getting assistance, but for the enemy's wounded there was no hope.

Early next morning Shaka arrived, and each regiment, previous to its inspection by him, had picked out its cowards and put them to death. Many of these, no doubt, forfeited their lives only because their chiefs were in fear that, if they did not condemn some as being guilty, they would be suspected of seeking a pretext to save them and would incur the resentment of Shaka.[1]

No man who had been actually engaged in the fight[2] was allowed to appear in the King's presence until a purification by the doctor had been undergone. This doctor gave each warrior certain roots to eat, and to everyone who had actually killed one of the enemy an additional number. To make their bravery as public as possible, bits of wood are worn round the neck, each bit being supposed to reckon for an enemy slain. To the end of this necklace are attached bits of the root received from the doctor, part of which has been eaten. They then proceed to some river to wash their persons and, until this had been done, they may not eat any food, except the meat of cattle killed on the day of battle. Having washed, they appear before the King, when thanks or praise are the last thing they have to expect; censure being loudly expressed on account of something that had not been done as it should have

---

[1] The following incident in connection with this very battle was told me many years ago by a son of the hero therein mentioned. "Among the regiments directed to attack Sikhunyana's army, when concealed in the forest, was one called Izimpohlo, of which my father, Nohadu, was a member. As it charged, Sikhunyana's forces appeared at the edge of the forest drawn up in wall-like formation. As the Izimpohlo got close up, the enemy flung a shelf of assegais at them. (The assegais coming simultaneously and horizontally from so many looked like a shelf.) One of these struck Nohadu in the ankle. His assailant turned quickly (like the others) to retreat into the forest, but only as quickly to become entangled in monkey ropes at the edge of the forest. Seeing this, Nohadu, instead of stopping to withdraw the assegai, rushed, assegai and all, after his foe and forthwith stabbed him to death. Shaka happened to see all this, also the colour of Nohadu's shield, from the hill where he was watching the battle. When all was over, discussing the various incidents, Shaka remarked, ' Whose was that *hemu* (dark and light shield) I saw at the edge of the forest ? ' Nohadu being present, claimed it as his. This proved to be indeed the case. Shaka, thereupon, directed his war doctor to look for a suitable beast for his hero to kill and so conform to yet another Zulu custom known as *ukuncinda*."—*Editor.*

[2] This means : No one who had actually killed any of the enemy.—*Editor.*

been, and they get off well if one or two chiefs and a few dozen soldiers are not struck off the army list by being put to death.

During the afternoon a woman and child of the defeated tribe, the latter aged about 10 years, were brought before the King, and he made every enquiry respecting Sikhunyana; what had been his plans when he heard of the intended attack, and what was the general feeling as to its result. To induce her to set aside all fear, he gave her some beer and a dish of beef, which she ate, while giving all the information she was possessed of. When her recital was finished, both mother and child were sentenced to instant death. Being present, I begged the life of the child, that it might become my servant. An application to save the life of both was little likely to succeed. From her information, Shaka found that Sikhunyana, with a few men, had escaped. A regiment was ordered to pursue them, whilst another was detached to kill the wounded of the enemy. I now took the opportunity of writing Mr. Farewell an account of all that had taken place. The army, after clearing up, commenced its return home.

When we had been three days on the march orders were given for the army to be divided into three corps; one of which was to accompany Shaka; the other two were to attack two tribes under Mlotshwa[1] and Beje.[2] These chiefs had formerly been under Zwide, the late king of the defeated enemy. In an unsuccessful attack on Shaka these two tribes had been cut off from the main body and were induced to join Shaka. Believing that they had joined him only from motives of policy he dealt kindly with them at first, but the moment their former king had been subdued, and they could have no opportunity of revenge, they were attacked.

Mlotshwa took up his position on the Phondwane[3] mountain, where his father had several times successfully defended himself. This was in the centre of a plain, and could only be ascended by two different passes guarded by men who hurled down masses of rock on their assailants. The women kept up the supply of these boulders for the men. This mountain hold was usually well stored with provisions. His provisions

---

[1]MS. has Umloacha.
[2]MS. has Bacha.
[3]MS. has Umpondwarna.

being exhausted, Mlotshwa submitted himself to Shaka and was again received into favour.

Beje's capabilities of defence were equally good. He, too, had a strong position among the rocks, and succeeded in cutting to pieces one of Shaka's regiments, raised only two months previously, and numbering two thousand men. This regiment had the name of the regiment of " Warmth," or in the Zulu " Motha." A few escaped and came to the army, now on its return homeward; but orders were given to put them to death at once, as men who had dared to fly.

Shaka now started on his return journey, leaving the regiments to attack the above-named chiefs. We accompanied him. When we had almost reached the place where we had left Mr. Farewell, news arrived of a vessel having anchored at Port Natal. We accordingly left Shaka and went to Natal, where the vessel that had arrived on 6th October, 1826, from Algoa Bay, proved to be the schooner *Anne*, with Mr. King and Mrs. Farewell on board.[1]

About this time, Michael and John, two of the Hottentots in the service of Mr. Farewell, were sent by him elephant and sea-cow shooting. They had not been long absent when we heard that they had committed a crime likely to endanger the whole of our pa ty. The laws of the Zulus are so severe against the crimes of adultery and rape that, up to this period, we had not heard of a single violation of them. These Hottentots had seized and ravished by force the daughter of a Zulu chief, who, dreading the result of connection with a European—all persons wearing clothes (as our Hottentots did) were deemed by the Zulus to be Europeans, for as yet our race was not regarded as earth-born, but as animals that had sprung out of the sea—reported the crime to Shaka. This incensed him

---

[1] The following extract from Reminiscences of F. M. Wolhuter published in the *Times of Natal*, 14th December, 1892, is of interest. "A lady once escaped from the Zulus in men's clothes. It was Mrs. Farewell. Lt. Farewell was married at Capetown about 1824 to Miss Elizabeth Smidt. Her parents lived at No. 1 Burg St., now called St. George's St. Her mother and my father were brother and sister. She was the first lady Chaka ever saw and he determined to seize her and make her his wife. Fortunately, Lt. Farewell heard of this and in the dead of night Mrs. Farewell dressed in men's clothes and under a sufficient escort rode away from the laager as hard as possible to a place of safety. When Mrs. Wolhuter was in Capetown in 1842 the two ladies used often to chat about their experiences in Natal. Mrs. Farewell had no children by her first husband, but had some by Mr. Gustaaf Aspeling, whom she married after Lt. Farewell was murdered."

against the whole of our race, and Mr. King, who arrived at this critical moment, was placed in an extremely awkward position. After Shaka had vented his rage on him, he demanded satisfaction, as the culprits belonged to us. Had his own people been the offenders they would have suffered death the instant the deed was done.

Mr. King acknowledged there was sufficient cause for his anger, assuring him that such crime was also punishable by death under the laws of our country. This had such an effect on Shaka's mind as completely to avert what he intended in the event of Mr. King attempting to palliate their crime. He then demanded that the whole European party, then at Natal, should join him in an attack on Beje, whom he was unable, without the assistance of our muskets, to drive out of his stronghold, except by sustaining great losses. Mr. King saw the necessity of acceding to his wishes to prevent his avenging himself on the whole of us. After some deliberation, Messrs. Cane and Isaacs, together with part of the crew of the *Mary*, also two Hottentots, and several natives (with guns) volunteered to go. They succeeded in completely defeating Beje's tribe and killing the chief himself.[1] On our side, Mr. Isaacs was severely wounded. Shaka did not as much as thank them for their services; on the contrary, he took every opportunity of depreciating what they had done and minimising the value of fire-arms in the estimation of his people.

I now proceeded to the Umzimkhulu River[2] with a party of natives, who had learned the use of fire-arms in our service, for the purpose of elephant hunting. I had not long been established there before natives from the surrounding country, because of their distressed and famished state, flocked to me for protection from that death which those who had joined me in my former expeditions had escaped. It was not long before the remains of four tribes, with their chiefs—amounting to more than 2,000 of both sexes—came to live under me. Many of them were people who had made their escape when at the point of being put to death by the Zulus. By merely notifying such arrivals to Shaka, the refugees were allowed to reside with us, a favour contrary to all former custom.

---

[1]This took place at the Ingome forest, in the north-west of Zululand, February, 1827.—Isaacs, *Travels and Adventures in Eastern Africa*, I, 197, 210 and 211.

[2]MS. has Imsumculu.

Messrs. Farewell, King, Isaacs, Cane and Ogle, as well as myself, have in this manner been the means of saving the lives of hundreds of people. The country for 25 miles round Natal was uninhabited except by the few previously mentioned. There are now more than 4,000 inhabitants under our protection, and our departure from the country would be the signal for their immediate destruction.[1]

Chapter X

AFTER the defeat of Beje, the Zulu *impi* returned to Zululand, and Isaacs with it. He found Shaka at his Dukuza kraal [where the town of Stanger now stands] on 18th March, 1827. On reaching Port Natal in the following month, the state of affairs there in connection with the ship in the course of construction—afterwards named the *Elizabeth Susan*[2]— was so unsatisfactory that King resolved to proceed to Delagoa Bay by land and obtain a passage to the Cape of Good Hope, where he would engage a vessel to go to Natal. This proposal, however, on the situation improving, was modified, it being decided that instead of himself a youth, John Ross, of about 15 years of age should make the journey for the purpose of obtaining medicine of which they stood in much need. To enable the lad to do this it was necessary for Isaacs to appeal to Shaka for an escort to protect Ross as well as provide him with food on his 300-mile journey there and back. Shaka supplied the escort and after a few weeks Ross returned safely. In July King, accompanied by Isaacs, proceeded to survey the mouths of the Rivers Umhlathuze and Umlalazi. Later in the same month they visited Shaka at his Bulawayo and Dibinhlangu residences.

Shaka now, for the first time [the author's MS. proceeds], having begun to hunt elephants with his whole force,[3] Mr. King, myself, and several other Europeans, being out on an excursion,

---

[1] This was probably written in or about 1832 or 1833 or even in 1831 when Fynn was on the Cape Frontier. Two of the sheets of the revised version of these notes bear on them the watermark of 1827.—*Editor.*

[2] To replace the *Mary*, which, as will be remembered, was wrecked at Port Natal on 1st October, 1825.—*Editor.*

[3] With the object of procuring ivory to be exchanged for Macassar oil. —*Editor.*

met him on his return from one of these hunts. Shaka, travelling slowly, induced Mr. King and party to return to Natal, but Shaka insisted that I should accompany him to the kraal where he was going to reside.

After travelling slowly for two days, we passed his usual residence, Bulawayo, closely adjoining which was the kraal of Nandi, his mother, and, proceeding forward, arrived about nine at night, at the place Shaka intended to fix his residence, that is, the one he had come purposely to rebuild. This work was begun on the following morning. Messengers now arrived to announce that Nandi was very unwell. Doctors were immediately dispatched, and also some European medicines which Shaka had been made a present of, and had by him, having first asked their uses. As messengers continued to arrive with accounts of the invalid getting worse, Shaka decided to return to her kraal[1] accompanied by his forces.

We started at nine o'clock at night and arrived at Bulawayo about three in the morning. Shaka now requested me to visit his mother.[2] I went, attended by an old chief, and found the hut filled with native doctors and nurses, and such clouds of smoke that I was obliged to bid them all retire, to enable me to breathe within it.[3] Her complaint was dysentery, and I reported at once to Shaka that her case was hopeless and that I did not expect that she would live through the day.[4]

The regiments, which were then sitting in a semicircle around him, were ordered to their barracks, while Shaka himself sat for about two hours in a contemplative mood, without a word escaping his lips, several of the elder chiefs sitting also before him. When the tidings were brought that she had

---

[1] A distance of 80 miles from the hunting ground; which distance was travelled during the latter part of the day and the night.—*Editor.*

[2] Fynn had then been with Shaka some time and, from various cases wherein he had been successful in restoring health to sick natives and once healing Shaka when severely wounded, implicit confidence was placed in his abilities.—*Editor.*

[3] Another MS. has: "On my arrival at her hut, which was crowded to excess with native doctors, several of whom had to move out before I could enter it. Being an exceedingly hot day, sufficient to sicken one of the strongest constitutions, I recommended at least half her medical attendants and nurses to make room for a little air. When this had been done, an opportunity was afforded me of seeing my patient."

[4] He requested me to go back again to observe if there was any change, which I did.—Author's MS.

expired[1] Shaka immediately arose and entered his dwelling, and, having ordered the principal chiefs to put on their war-dresses, he, in a few minutes, appeared in his.[2]

As soon as the death was publicly announced, the women and all the men who were present tore instantly from their persons every description of ornament. Shaka now appeared before the hut in which the body lay, surrounded by his principal chiefs in their war attire. For about 20 minutes he stood in a silent mournful attitude, with his head bowed upon his shield, and on which I saw large tears fall.[3] After two or three deep sighs, his feelings becoming ungovernable, he broke out into frantic yells, which fearfully contrasted with the silence that had hitherto prevailed.[4] This signal was enough. The chiefs and people, to the number of about 15,000, commenced the most dismal and horrid lamentations.

I expected, on seeing the old woman in her last agonies, that I should again witness a scene like to those at which I had been present on two similar former occasions. Not for a moment did I anticipate the extent to which the proceedings were now to be carried. The people from the neighbouring kraals, male and female, came pouring in, each body, as they came in sight, at the distance of half a mile, joining to swell this terrible cry.

Through the whole night it continued, none daring to take rest, or to refresh themselves with water, while at short intervals fresh bursts were heard, as more regiments approached.

The morning dawned without any relaxation, and before noon the number had increased to about 60,000. The cries

---

[1]Everyone now left the hut and began to strip off their beads and other ornaments. The females from the seraglio approached the hut, and a general shouting commenced.—Author's MS.

[2]His face painted with substances of various colours, prepared for the purpose.—Author's MS.

[3]Occasionally wiping them away with his right hand. He presented the appearance of a brave warrior in extreme distress, sufficient to extort pity and commiseration from the hardest of hearts.—Author's MS. Another MS. has : " Shaka shortly made his appearance dressed in his war dress, his face besmeared with preparations of different colours and which had been made up for the purpose. He was attended by his chiefs and stood several minutes in a most mournful attitude. His face lay carelessly over his shield on which his tears dropped, and as they fell he used his right hand to wipe them away."

[4]" *Maye ngo Mama !* " (Alas, my mother). These are the words he is said to have uttered. Such ejaculation is common among Zulus on various occasions of bereavement.—*Editor.*

now became indescribably horrid. Hundreds were lying faint, from excessive fatigue and want of nourishment; while the carcasses of 40 oxen lay in a heap, which had been slaughtered as an offering to the guardian spirits of the tribe.[1] At noon the whole force formed a circle with Shaka in their centre, and sang the war song, which afforded them some relaxation during its continuance. At the close of it, Shaka ordered several men to be executed on the spot, and the cries became, if possible, more violent than ever. No further orders were needed. But, as if bent on convincing their chief of their extreme grief, the multitude commenced a general massacre. Many of them received the blow of death, while inflicting it on others, each taking the opportunity of revenging their injuries, real or imaginary. Those who could not force more tears from their eyes—those who were found near the river panting for water—were beaten to death by others who were mad with excitement.[2] Toward the afternoon I calculated that not fewer than 7,000 people had fallen in this frightful indiscriminate massacre. The adjacent stream, to which many had fled exhausted, to wet their parched tongues, became impassable from the number of dead corpses which lay on each side of it; while the kraal in which the scene took place was flowing with blood.

---

[1] From thirty to forty cattle were killed, not as the reader might suppose, to be eaten by the mourners, but to be devoured by dogs, flies and birds of prey; no food of any kind was to be eaten during the day. Having eaten nothing since starting on the journey the evening before, I was at a loss how to act. Application to Shaka, situated as he was, would have been both improper and useless. On searching for a hut to sleep in, I fortunately observed two calabashes of beer belonging to a chief who dared not use it. I conferred on myself the privilege of doing so. I slept as well as the horrid cries during the night would allow. Shaka appeared early in the morning dressed as before, and immediately ordered one of his aunts, who had been on bad terms with his mother, with the whole of her attendants (some 12 or 14 girls), to instant death.—Author's MS.

[2] Every man's hand seemed remorselessly turned against his fellow creatures, and this scene, heightened by the deafening cries of victor and victim, from the body of more than 30,000 people, renders any language of mine inadequate to convey to the reader this never-to-be-forgotten scene. Those who had quarrelled in the past; the stronger took the opportunity of avenging themselves on the weaker, and those most intent on rioting and bloodshed appeared to be the only ones to escape. A petty king being asked for after the tumult had somewhat subsided, was said to have gone to the river to drink, when he was instantly ordered to be killed. Whilst masses were thus employing themselves, Shaka and his chiefs, the latter surrounding him, were tumbling and throwing themselves about, each trying to excel in their demonstrations of grief by alternate fits of howling.—Author's MS.

Amidst this scene I stood unharmed, contemplating the horrors around me; and felt as if the whole universe was at that moment coming to an end. I stood there alone, a privileged being, not compelled to take part in this frantic scene; and I felt truly thankful, not only that I was a British subject, but that I had so far gained the respect of this tyrant as to hope for escape even from this horrible place of blood. While standing thus, motionless, a regiment of young Zulus passed by me, when two of them with their uplifted knobkerries (heavy headed sticks, or life preservers) rushed towards me, the leader demanding fiercely why I stood there without a tear. I made no reply, but gazed upon them sternly and steadily. They moved on shouting vengeance.

The sun again set, and Shaka now put a stop to this ungoverned general massacre.[1] The cries, however, continued during the whole of the next night, and until ten the following morning, when the chief became somewhat pacified and his subjects were permitted to take some refreshment.

The ceremonies of his mother's burial were the subject of much deliberation between Shaka and his favourite counsellors. On the second day after her death the body was placed in a grave, in a sitting posture, near the spot where she died.[2] At this part of the ceremony I was not allowed to be present, and, if what was related to me at the time by several of the attendants be true (and I believe it to be true, knowing to what extent superstition will carry this people), it was fortunate for me that I was not present, to witness the horrid spectacle of

---

[1] Late in the evening, on being informed of the dreadful loss of souls that had taken place, Shaka put a stop to the outrage, it only requiring a single word from him to do this. The crying, however, continued all night, every now and then becoming more violent from fresh arrivals. The scene of horror continued on the third day though attended with about only 12 or 14 murders. On the fourth day tranquillity was restored and Shaka for the first time since the beginning of the convulsive obsequies seated himself before his people. The chiefs, however, to express their sorrow, busily employed themselves by sending parties throughout the country to destroy every soul that had not attended to express their sorrow for the old witch, so that, while tranquillity prevailed here, remorseless murder was stalking through the land.—Author's MS.

[2] A grave was dug in the hut where she died; in this she was placed, on a mat, in a sitting posture. She was then covered with another mat, and her hut let fall upon the spot. Branches of the milk tree were planted on the site, to form a grove.—Author's MS.

ten of the best-looking girls of the kraal being buried with her, alive.[1]

All who were present at this dreadful scene, to the number of 12,000, drafted from the whole army, were formed into a regiment[2] to guard the grave for the next 12 months, and during that time were prohibited from all intercourse with the tribe or any of their nearest relatives. About 15,000 head of cattle were set apart for their use, which were contributed by all the cattle holders of the country, as offerings to the spirits of the departed queen and her ill-fated attendants. Had I been present on this occasion I should have had to keep guard with the rest.

Hitherto, the proceedings had been local. But now the chiefs, anxious to show further proof of their attachment, proposed that further sacrifices should be made. And Ngomane,[3] Shaka's principal favourite, made a speech proposing the following resolution:

" That, as the great female elephant with small breasts, the over-ruling spirit of vegetation, had died,[4] and as it was probable that the heavens and the earth would unite in bewailing her death, the sacrifice should be a great one; no cultivation should be allowed during the following year; no milk should be used, but, as drawn from the cow, it should be poured upon the earth; and all women, who should be found with child during the year, should with their husbands be put to death."[5]

---

[1] Among other enquiries I made sometime after, I was informed by three persons at different times that Nandi was buried with ten maids placed alive in the grave. Others I have asked denied this, probably wishing it to be kept a secret. How far this is true or false, I leave the reader to judge, after forming an estimate of Shaka's character. For my own part I do not think it improbable, knowing the extent of Shaka's pride and cruelty. On the hill where the barracks were built and where the body lay, no person dare put the point of his stick on the ground, but was obliged to carry it in his hand.—Author's MS.

[2] Larger than any other in the army.—*Editor*.

[3] Principal chief, confidant and adopted father. When Shaka went, as a young man, to offer his allegiance to Dingiswayo, the latter put him under the care and protection of Ngomane.—*Editor*.

[4] As the result of her death, the word *nandi*, which means anything nice or sweet, should never more be used; instead of *nandi*, the word *mtoti* must be adopted; as she was the mother of an elephant, mother of a lion, of a leopard, and of wild beasts—in allusion to the titles of Shaka.—*Editor*.

[5] Nothing now surrounded them but death and destruction; locusts would cover the earth and no man should live. All this was unanimously agreed to. —Author's MS.

At the close of this speech, which was received with acclamation, regiments of soldiers were dispersed throughout the country, who massacred everyone they could find that had not been present at the general wailing.

During the next three months the first two of Ngomane's propositions were strictly carried out; at the end of which time these orders were redeemed, by large offerings of oxen being made to Shaka from all the chiefs. But the third condition was strictly enforced throughout the year, during which also lamentations on a smaller scale took place from time to time at Shaka's residence, when I was not present.[1]

At the end of the year Shaka left this kraal, where his mother died, and came with his whole nation and cattle to Dukuza, a kraal he had recently constructed on the Umvoti River, and the place where he was subsequently assassinated. Having heard of his approach, so near to the Bay, I started to pay him a visit, and met him on his march a few miles south of the Thukela. He appeared rejoiced to see me, and would not allow me to separate from him, carrying on a lively and pleasant conversation during the march. While passing a large pool of water, one of the chiefs remarked that alligators abounded there; upon which Shaka asked me if I had the courage to swim across the pool—promising me five head of oxen if I did. It was an awkward question, but I was determined not to show any signs of fear, and at once took off my trousers and in my shirt swam across the stream. He applauded my courage and then asked if I expected the oxen. I said " No ! " which produced a hearty laugh from himself and his counsellors.

We proceeded on the road until we came in sight of Dukuza, when he separated from his chiefs and followers, and took me with him under a large euphorbia tree and, while putting on his war-dress, told me that another lamentation was then to take

---

[1] Whenever Shaka shed a tear, which he often did, the howlings were renewed. This, I think, he often did from political motives. After mature reflection, I think I may safely assert that the whole thing was nothing more than a political scheme.—Author's MS. Another MS. has : " The whole scene was a political scheme in furtherance of Shaka's vain imaginations and to keep the minds of his people filled with wonder. During the twelve months following the death of the female elephant the whole tribe were three times called together to repeat their lamentations. On the last occasion, the cattle of the whole tribe were collected, the bellowings of which was to be figurative of their lamentations."

place at Dukuza. I begged him to grant me one request. He smiled and asked what it could possibly be. I entreated him for his own sake, as well as mine, not to allow on this occasion any of his people to be put to death. He at once called for Ngomane and, laughing at the strangeness of my petition, that I should plead for the life of dogs, gave orders to him to see that none were put to death. He then told me to separate from the mass, stand on a hill, and quietly observe the ceremony of this, the last, lamentation, by which he was to be purified from his uncleanness.

He now advanced, with his chiefs, in their full war-dress. Presently Dukuza, lying, as it were, in a basin, came in full sight; and the outrunners, shouting out the praises of Shaka, announced his approach. Upon this he began to sigh and sob badly, pretending to falter and stumble in his steps, and then commenced crying aloud. The whole of the able-bodied population of the country, each regiment by itself, came all in sight, as it were, in a moment, standing upon the edge of the hills which surrounded Dukuza. They took up, as before, the frantic cry of their chief; but now with the general yelling was mingled the bellowing of about 100,000 oxen, brought from the remotest parts of the country expressly for this occasion. I stood at the distance of half a mile, near enough to see that no lives were sacrificed; and was glad to find that at sunset the lamentations, which began late in the afternoon, were brought to an end,[1] the regiments being ordered to rest, and to slaughter cattle for the evening meal.[2] I retired to my hut, but to sleep was out of the question, from the bellowing of the oxen and the dinning sound of the multitude.

The next morning the purification took place. Every cattle-owner had brought calves for this purpose, each of which was ripped open on its right side, the owner taking out the gall of the living animal, which was then left to die in its agony, and not allowed to be eaten. Each regiment in succession then presented itself before Shaka, and as it passed in a circle round him, each individual, holding the gall-bladder in his hand,

---

[1] Without much disturbance. A chief was struck a violent blow, the intention being evidently to kill him. Shaka saw this and immediately interfered. Such action put a stop to all further bloodshed on that occasion. —Author's MS.

[2] At nine o'clock, the crying came to an end, and 65 head of grown cattle were slaughtered.—Author's MS.

sprinkled the gall over him. After this proceeding, Ngomane made another speech:

"The tribe had now lamented for a year the death of her, who had now become a spirit, and who would continue to watch over Shaka's welfare. But there were nations of men, inhabiting distant countries, who, because they had not yet been conquered, supposed that they never should be. This was plain from the fact of their not having come forward to lament the death of the Great Mother of Earth and Corn. And, as tears could not be forced from these distant nations, war should be made against them, and the cattle taken should be the tears shed upon her grave."[1]

The war-dance was now performed; several droves of oxen were slaughtered; and Shaka was finally washed with certain decoctions, prepared by native doctors. And thus this memorable lamentation ended—in which, however, I cannot help suspecting that reasons of state policy had as much to do as any feeling of regret for his dead mother; and that he wished his people to infer, if such a sacrifice was necessary upon the occasion of her departure, how frightfully terrific would be that required at his own. Such considerations as these might possibly tend to prolong the life even of such a tyrant. And yet he fell at last at the hand of an assassin.

Nandi was the daughter of a chief of the Langeni tribe,[2] which lived between the Zulus and the Mthethwa tribes on the River Umhlathuze.[3] She was betrothed by her father to Senzangakhona,[4] chief of the Zulus before they became a nation, and father of Shaka. In those days it was the custom for chiefs not to co-habit with their wives, only *soma*[5] with

---

[1] Another MS. has : "As tears could not be forced from foreigners, an attack should be made on the Frontier tribes, whose cattle should be considered as tears shed for Shaka's dead mother." A further MS. has : "All that now remained to complete the ceremonies of Nandi's death was a declaration of war against some nation or tribe in which the Mkhindini [MS. Umquindein] that had been guarding the burial ground was to be the first to attack the enemy, the cattle captured by it to be considered as being tears shed for her by foreign nations."

[2] MS. has Amalangeines.

[3] MS. has Umclatuse.

[4] MS. has Sensagacone.

[5] It is a common custom among the Zulus for a betrothed pair to indulge in frequent surreptitious though unconsummated intercourse. The practice, though technically unlawful, is nevertheless universally connived at, even by the girl's parents ; but it is only tolerated between a couple who have been properly affianced in accordance with native custom.—Bryant, *Zulu-English Dictionary* ; cf. Colenso, *Zulu-English Dictionary*.

them—a practice which was supposed to be followed until the chief had undergone the rite of circumcision. But chiefs were generally backward in being circumcised—never till they were 30 or 40 years old—and apparently under the idea that they would be deemed to be younger than they really were.

Nandi, however, had been but a short time betrothed to Senzangakhona when she became enceinte. This was generally reported to be not the case, but only one known as *itshaka*, signifying a looseness of the bowels. In the course of time, however, Nandi gave birth to a son, when, instead of being called *itshaka*, the appellation was softened to Shaka. He was Senzangakhona's eldest son, though not his heir, seeing that Nandi, the mother, was not the *inkosikazi* or queen. The real queen shortly afterwards bore the heir to the Zulu throne, namely, uMfokazi, elder brother of Dingane (who later became king) by the same mother.

By the time Shaka reached the age of 5 Nandi had frequently been in disgrace on account of her violent temper. At about this time she was expelled from the seraglio for having struck one of Senzangakhona's chiefs a severe blow on the head. She accordingly returned to the Langeni tribe, where she married a commoner named Ngendeyana,[1] by whom she had a son, Ngwadi.[2] After Ngwadi's birth, Shaka left her and placed himself under the protection of Dingiswayo,[3] king of the Mthethwas. Dingiswayo gave him in charge of Ngomane,[4] his fighting commander, i.e. he who delivered the oration in connection with Nandi's obsequies.

Nandi remained with her husband and son Ngwadi, until Shaka came to the throne. By that time her husband was dead. She now joined Shaka as superintendent of his seraglio. During her residence with him her temper knew no bounds in her thirsting for bloodshed. She let but few opportunities escape her vengeance, and this both in the absence and frequently in the presence of Shaka. She would have men and women put to death before her eyes with no less compunction than in eating her dinner. Their heads would be broken, their necks twisted, and a stick thrust up the fundament and through the body, in her presence.

---

[1] MS. has Ungideann.
[2] MS. has Enguade.
[3] MS. has Tingiswao.
[4] MS. has Gomanney.

Chapter XI

DURING his four years' knowledge of us, Shaka, from the incessant enquiries made of his interpreter, Jacob, and of myself who had by this time acquired a knowledge of the Zulu language), received so much information respecting Europe and our sovereign (whom he called umGeorge) that he expressed a desire to send chiefs to visit both the Colony and England. He proposed also to send six young girls as a present to his brothe King. He accordingly requested Mr. King to conduct them thither and conferred on him the captainship of the regiment Dukuza, as, unless he accepted such appointment in his army, he was not likely to study Shaka's interest, at least not so much as if he belonged to the Zulus. In order to satisfy the King, Mr. King accepted the office, though merely nominal. Upon this, the King gave him a head-dress of black feathers, the ensign or badge of that regiment. He appointed Sotoбe, Mbozamboza and Jacob, with Sotoбe's and Jacob's wives to accompany them, in order that their native costume might be seen by the Europeans. At the same time Shaka gave Mr. King 86 elephant tusks, and one or two large ones which, he said, were to be his mouth[1] to King George.

The vessel was launched, and the party sailed forth on their mission. The idea was that Sotoбe and Jacob were to proceed to England with Mr. King, while Mbozamboza was to return from the Colony as Mr. King might arrange. As some doubt arose in Shaka's mind as to their safety, I voluntarily became a hostage for their safe return.

I must now allude to an incident which, though trifling in itself, f om a European's point of view, nearly brought serious disaste on our party at Port Natal.

One day, after the defeat of Sikhunyana, Shaka saw me writing a letter to Mr. Farewell.[2] He asked me if the ink would wash off the paper. On my replying in the negative, he asked if it would stain a shield. I told him it would not, but the hair and the skin might appear slightly tinged. He thereupon

---

[1] Or introduction.—*Editor*.
[2] He stood over me and watched me very attentively.—Author's note.

threw a bottle of ink over a white shield to observe its effect. . . .
In the evening he asked how it was that Europeans had different
colou ed hair, and if there were no preparations to change
its colour.[1]

I told him Macassar oil was said to produce that effect.
On arriving where we had left Mr. Farewell,[2] he asked Mr.
Farewell the same question and received the same reply. When
Messrs. King and Isaacs arrived they were asked, and understanding what we had said, agreed with us. Shaka, finding us
all agreed as to its virtues, called us into his hut and, ordering
all his attendants to go out, made us swear by him that we would
not mention what had taken place concerning the oil, and went
on to say he would collect ivory in great quantities and give the
tusks to whatever person produced the oil. He said he wanted
it for his mother- and father-in-law, who were grey-headed,
which did not look well in such great personages. We, however,
saw that he wanted it for himself, having a few grey hairs
on his chin.

We now endeavoured to assure him of our having great
doubts as to its powers, fearing should it not prove what we
had led him to believe it was he would be displeased; but the
more we attempted to deprecate it, the more he thought of its

---

[1] . . . according to one's choice. I replied in the negative; at the same time, not for a moment supposing anything would come of what I said, I added that there was a substance, called Macassar oil, which was said to darken the hair. At this he was highly gratified, but said no more on the subject till some weeks later, when Messrs. Farewell, King, Isaacs and I were at his residence [24th July, 1827]. He expressed doubt as to whether anyone in England dared use the oil but umGeorge, supposing the latter to hold his subjects under the same restraint as he did his. On being assured the oil was easily procurable, he expressed the greatest satisfaction. . . . To defray all expenses he said he would commence hunting elephants, whose ivory should belong to Mr. King, seeing he had a vessel and would therefore be able to supply the oil. It was not long before he went to hunt elephants with the whole of his tribe. During that hunt 48 elephants were killed. He gave the tusks to Mr. King. This took place in the presence of his people, when he assured the chiefs that, for the ivory which was being given Mr. King he, in return, would bring cloth, beads, etc., for their use; but when speaking to Mr. King in private he said he wanted nothing of the kind for such dogs as his people were. —Author's MS.
The hunting here referred to probably took place late in 1827 or early in 1828, for that of 27th August was suspended on account of Nandi's illness. The *Elizabeth and Susan*, with Lieut. King and Shaka's ambassadors left for Algoa Bay in March, 1828.—*Editor.*

[2] Probably at Di6inhlangu (near Bulawayo). On only one occasion in the author's MSS. have we seen Farewell referred to as having been left behind, viz: during the expedition to Sikhunyana (August-October, 1826), consequently the above conversation would have occurred in or about October, 1826.—*Editor.*

value. He said he could plainly see it was an oil used by umGeorge and that none of his people were allowed to touch it. Seeing the improbability of our procuring any in the immediate present, we attempted, though in vain, to lessen it in his esteem. He had, however, set his mind on this invaluable oil. It was his constant theme and induced him to take the whole of his force elephant hunting, which hunting, as has been seen, was suspended owing to the death of his mother, Nandi.

When he presented Mr. King with the 86 tusks, on the latter's departure for the Colony,[1] he told his people that he, Mr. King, would bring back immense quantities of such things as they required. Afterwards, however, in his hut, he told Mr. King to bring nothing but Macassar oil. His people were dogs, he would give them nothing. All he wanted was Macassar oil and medicine.

Only three days after the vessel's departure, messengers arrived from Shaka to Mr. Farewell and myself, requesting that all blacks in our respective services be sent the following morning to follow up a party that had stolen some cattle. As the situation we were in compelled our compliance, they went. I proceeded to my residence at the Umzimkhulu, a distance of 80 miles from the port. I had, however, been there only two days when I was surprised to hear that Shaka was near at hand on his way to attack the amaMpondo. As I received this intelligence from a chief on whom I could depend and who, moreover, had been sent ahead for the purpose of reconnoitring, I no longer doubted its truth, and, for the first time, saw into Shaka's scheme for obtaining our natives and Hottentots, for we had frequently told him we would not let our people assist him in attacking the amaMpondo.

I went to meet him. I found him about 40 miles from my place; he was resting there for the night, having left the whole of his forces about five miles in the rear. We went forward next morning and, in the afternoon, arrived at one of my kraals, where I had about 100 muids of Indian corn. On his asking therefor, I gave him the whole of it for the use of his army.

On the following day we arrived at my residence (at the Umzimkhulu). Knowing it to be the custom for me as host to

---

[1]In the *Elizabeth and Susan* in March, 1828.—*Editor.*

present the King with a bullock, I produced my herd and requested him to make himself welcome to as many as he thought fit. He selected 17 and thereupon made my place his headquarters. The army, after resting three days, marched towards their destination, some 120 miles further on to the south-westward. Shaka himself remained behind with only a small division, to act as circumstances might dictate.

By this time I had acquired a thorough knowledge of the Zulu language, manners and customs, hence was able to spend my time pleasantly with Shaka; he always demanded my attendance during his leisure moments. All this, moreover, gave me an opportunity of minutely ascertaining the basis on which he acted.

On the day of the army's departure the regiments assembled to the left of my place, drawing up in such a way as to form three sides of a square. The doctors having performed the usual ceremonies of strengthening them for the attack, Shaka came into their midst, and, in a speech, began to explain to them that the necessity of the expedition was to erase his wounded feeling for the mother he had lost. To make the loss more memorable, it was necessary that regret should be felt by other tribes in addition to his own. They must, therefore, exterminate the whole of the tribes between him and the Colony. He wished, he said, to open a road, and, for that purpose, had already sent chiefs in order that he might be on good terms with the white people.

When he had finished speaking he ordered the Mkhindi (short-skirt) regiment to take the lead. The army then divided into two divisions, which thereupon took different routes. Each of these divisions was subdivided into different regiments and companies, these, again, being headed by their respective chiefs. Mdlaka was in supreme command. The forces were directed to form a junction at the Umsikaba River, within the territory of the enemy.

The chiefs, after starting, were called back and ordered not to proceed further than Hintza's people. Shaka's cousin, Maphitha,[1] was detained and given secret orders by Shaka to find some plausible excuse for returning should the army happen to fall in with any white people.

---

[1]MS. has Amapeta.

Eight days after the departure of the army messengers arrived to say that it was about to enter the tribe when the messengers left. Daily intelligence now arrived of its repeated successes, and of its having crossed the Umtata River.

During the absence of the army I was constantly with Shaka and frequently had warm arguments with him. In these we used to differ much in opinion. One arose from his repeatedly calling his commander-in-chief, Mdlaka, a fool. I pointed out, why not take away the command. For his public abuse would prevent the army from obeying such orders as were given by him. He argued that they were all fools, but, being his people, no one would abuse them. To prove the truth of this assertion, he called on several chiefs to acknowledge themselves fools. This they did, saying I was one too, as well as the rest of the white people. No sooner, however, had they left his presence than Shaka offered me a pancake as apology for what he had said, which, he remarked, he knew to be wrong, but it would not do for his people to know that.

On arriving at my place, he had sent to Natal for a new frying-pan. I attempted, at his request, to show his maid-servants how to fry beaf-steak and pancakes. The latter were made of green Indian corn and water and fried in soup fat, for by Zulu custom neither sweet milk[1] nor butter might be used.

Another argument arose in connection with the present campaign. We differed as usual in our opinions. I told him it was my opinion that if he wished to be on amicable terms with the Colonists a war with the Frontier tribes, as then going on on their borders, could not convince them of his being peacefully disposed. He, on the other hand, maintained they were not, as I held, allies, but enemies, and that we white people were merely playing with them. Black people who had committed an offence should not be talked to but killed, i.e. dealt with as he did. They would not then offend any more. " How is it," he observed, " they attempt to play on your superiority of force and arms ? You know they steal your cattle and kill your countrymen. By destroying a tribe entirely, killing the surviving chiefs, the people would be glad to join you on your own terms. You could then seize all

---

[1]That is, of a kraal in which one does not live.—*Editor*.

the ivory and horns[1] without paying for them, and give me the beads."

A rather curious incident occurred whilst Shaka was still at my place. I was surprised one morning to see one of my servants, a most faithful fellow, crying in my hut, evidently in great distress. He had already been four years in my employ. On inquiring into the cause of his grief, he said he had dreamt that he saw me being killed by Shaka's order at the back of my own garden. So great was his distress that I was quite unable to pacify him. At breakfast I mentioned the matter to Shaka. He said the proper thing to do was to consult an *inyanga* or diviner. This I then did for amusement. After the necessary ceremonies had been gone through, the diviner replied that Shaka had appeared in the dream merely because of his greatness. Nothing would induce him to kill me. The man went on to interpret the dream as meaning that one of my greatest and nearest relations, on the other side of the sea, was dead. With this explanation the servant was satisfied. Strangely enough, not many weeks later, after I had gone back to Natal, a vessel brought a letter announcing the death of my mother. She had died a little before the servant had his dream. Later on, when I had quite forgotten the matter, the same servant alluded to it in the course of an argument in support of his belief in *izinyanga* (diviners). Against such belief I often attempted to argue, though with little effect, for all that natives would allow was that diviners of the present-day, perhaps on account of their being more enlightened, were not as competent as those of former days.

Owing to the knowledge I had of Faku, Shaka asked me one morning if I thought, were he to withdraw his army, Faku would consent to becoming his tributary. I replied in the affirmative and recommended, as an inducement, the return of the girls who had been captured and sent to him by the army, and refraining from destroying more corn. To this he assented. He accordingly sent messengers to Faku with proposals for peace, at the same time returning the females as proof of his bona fides; he, moreover, directed his army to withdraw and to stop destroying the corn. Several chiefs of petty tribes in Faku's neighbourhood, with messengers from Faku, returned

---

[1] This refers to tusks, usually called by Zulus *izimpondo zezindlovu*—horns of elephants.—*Editor.*

with the army to thank him for his liberality in thus sparing their lives. They were rewarded with presents of cattle, selected from those that had been taken from them.

Messengers now arrived to inform Shaka of the near approach of the army; they were severely beaten with sticks for bringing such information. Shaka wanted to know why they had not reached the Colony and defeated the tribes according to his orders. In consequence of this the army could not approach him; they, therefore, remained three days on a plain four miles away, in a starving state, although amidst droves of cattle they had taken, to the amount of 30,000.

On the evening of the third day Shaka requested me to collect the people and deliver an order from him for them to scour the surrounding country in search of buck and bring the skins to him. I would be able, he said, to point out the bushes that most abounded in game. He desired Ngomane to go with me and inform them that during their absence certain chiefs to the eastward of the Zulus had been co-habiting with their women and were wearing beads and brass, forgetting the death of such an important personage as his mother. For having done this, they had insulted the Zulus beyond hope of forgiveness. He, however, did not wish them to be attacked that year as the army was still tired, nor did he wish his men to know of the insults that had been received. Ngomane, on coming before the army, was to pretend he had only accidentally met me on the road, then say he took that opportunity of informing them of the insult, and it was his opinion that, if they had the hearts of Zulus to insist, the King would afford them an opportunity of immediately avenging the wrongs they had been subjected to. He was, moreover, to give them 50 head of cattle, as from himself (Ngomane), such, however, to be reported to Shaka as having died from fatigue. I went on, anxious to witness the result of this scheme.

When the army had assembled, I delivered Shaka's order. After this, Ngomane, standing in the centre of the assembly, introduced himself and set forth everything as he had been desired to do. He begged that, if they had any regard for him, an old chief, they would not let Shaka know that he had acquainted them with what he had been saying, as should they presume to do that it would result in orders being issued for his death. He again assured them that Shaka was ignorant of the proposals he had made.

He had no sooner sat down than several chiefs rose to acquiesce in his opinion. One in particular said that the whole army, during such time as they had served under Shaka, every time a war was proposed had expected to be defeated, but, under his command, they had become so used to conquering and to seeing the enemy entirely defeated on every occasion, that they were now ready to face whatever enemy might offer, and that as soon as possible. The general acclamations of applause that followed this speech convinced Ngomane of their willingness to carry out what he had proposed. We returned to Shaka after Ngomane had given the cattle referred to, which, he said, were to be reported on the following day as having died.

When Ngomane acquainted the King with what had taken place, Shaka told him he had omitted a very necessary point in not requesting the troops to send chiefs to him to request and insist on the King giving his consent. These, however, soon appeared, when Shaka argued with them and appeared determined not to consent. Only after much entreaty did he do so. When people arrived to report the death of the cattle they were severely beaten and threatened with death for not having taken better care of them, as Shaka pretended to suspect that they themselves had killed them.

It is necessary here to observe that Matiwane's tribe was located some way up the Umtata River before the Zulus appeared in that country. The great consternation the frontier tribes were thrown into, in consequence of Shaka's invasion, gave Matiwane an opportunity of attacking them and capturing their cattle.

This man's forces, in consequence of reports being circulated in the Colony of an intended invasion by the Zulus, with me at their head, were supposed to be a division of Shaka's army. Reports such as these induced the Colonial Command of 1828 to advance against this supposed formidable enemy. The Zulus had, by that time, returned to their own country, but the Colonial forces, misled by their interpreters, were brought into conflict with Matiwane, who was, indeed, an *uMfecani* or marauder, though erroneously supposed at the time to be part of Shaka's forces.

It was a very shrewd political move on the part of the Frontier tribes to direct the British forces against Matiwane, as it prevented this chief from taking advantage of their distressed state. Had Matiwane not been conquered, he would most likely have proved a very great annoyance to the Colony. The thorough manner in which they were defeated will ever be remembered by those who were present. Although many in the Colony condemned the proceedings as improper, they did not have the opportunity of witnessing the dread caused by that marauder's depredations, the accounts of which, exaggerated to the utmost by those who escaped, ran through the country like wildfire. There can be no doubt but that this action prevented, and will prevent, the loss of many more thousands than were slain on that day, namely by keeping ambitious or ignorant people from attempting what they might otherwise have ventured upon.

The day after Ngomane addressed the army Shaka permitted it to appear in his presence. He examined the cattle which had been captured, and had them sorted according to their colours. Those which had been seized by the Mkhindi regiment were kept apart, but to them were added some of the cattle captured by natives in our service, viz: three small droves. When the latter cattle were seized one of the amaMpondo people had been shot.

After the cattle had been sorted, the army formed up in the centre of a plain, where it went through the usual ceremonies at the hands of the doctors. The whole of it then proceeded by order of the King to wash in the sea. When the troops returned from the sea a song, which had been composed by Shaka during their absence, was sung. Roughly, it was as follows:

> Zhi, zhi, zhi, zhi, zhi, zhi, zhi, zhi,
>   We never heard of wars like those of the Bathwas
>   and the Jayis,
> Also that of Mlotshwa, son of Vezi,
>   All enemies indeed,
> They ran off with Phunga's cattle,
>   And threw in their lot with the Swazis;
> So too, Mlotshwa, who likewise stole from Ntombazi;
>   Though we at first were his protectors

> And put ourselves betwixt him and the foe.
> > We removed Mlotshwa from the stump behind which
> > > men are wont to hide,
> Oh, Swazis and Mthethwas, how have we offended you?
>
> Give ear, oh people!
> > The honey's been eaten by the ratel
> The bees have flown and quite deserted you.
> > You turned from the path without even trying it.
> Not by word of mouth are arguments decided,
> > But by facts being put to the practical test.
> You drove them away there, o'er Nhlokonhloko hills,
> > Raising great dust in the land,
> Who dare now take and slaughter them.

The following is an explanation of the foregoing: The interjections Zhi, zhi, zhi . . . are exclamations of triumph.

The Bathwas and amaJayi were two tribes; Umlotshwa the chief of yet another. These three tribes were continually at war with Shaka, though at length he defeated them. At first he had invited them to become his subjects, but they declined. Mlotshwa subsequently stole a lot of cattle belonging to Shaka (inherited by the latter from his great grandfather, Phunga), joined the Swazis (other enemies of Shaka), and then took refuge in their caves. After this he joined Shaka's most formidable foe, the Ndwandwe tribe, only, however, to be put to death by Ntombazi, Zwide's principal wife. It is this that makes Shaka say that he was, at first, Mlotshwa's protector and offered him peace. For the Zulu army, when attacking Zwide, at the time hostile to Mlotshwa, passed by Mlotshwa, i.e. beyond where he was living. It is the same incident which makes him say further that he put him (Mlotshwa) in the rear, i.e. set the Zulu army between him and his enemy.

The association of the names Swazis and Mthethwas is deliberate. The latter, of course, were, by this time, Shaka's subjects, but, owing to having recently offended him, he here uses their name in conjunction with that of the former to show his great displeasure at their conduct.

The latter portion of the song beginning " Give ear, oh people!" alludes to the Zulu army's dilatoriness in attacking the Pondos so much as to afford the latter an opportunity of running off with the greater part of their cattle. This made it possible for any other tribe but the Zulus to capture them. The word honey means cattle, and being eaten by the ratel refers to those who might have seized them as the Pondos were making off with them helter-skelter. Ratel is the Cape ratel, an animal very fond of honey. The two lines about arguments means that all the Zulu army says in defence of their conduct is of little avail, as, after consideration of the actual circumstances Shaka is convinced of their being unsound.

The driving them over the hills of Nhlokonhloko merely refers to the cattle fleeing over the hills with their owners, the Pondos. There is no such hill as Nhlokonhloko in those parts. The word Nhlokonhloko is a fictitious term used in derision of the Pondos, who are accustomed to wear their hair extraordinarily long (*inhloko* means a head). The plural *inhlokonhloko* might be said to mean a mass of heads or many head-dresses. Raising a great dust refers to the clouds of dust caused by so many cattle fleeing in all directions. The last line, " Who dare now take and slaughter them," means that, having succeeded in escaping him (Shaka), what other person could possibly capture and enjoy them.

After the singing, the thought of his mother produced a tear from Shaka, which instantly affected the whole army, and a general uproar commenced, but it lasted only half an hour.

The next day Shaka commenced his return and insisted upon my accompanying him, the captured cattle being stationed in different parts of the country.

On our crossing the Umzimkhulu, where the tide was high, many little boys would have been carried down with the stream. Shaka, foreseeing this, plunged into the river, with only his head-dress on, and remained one and a half hours in the water, giving the boys to the care of the men, who otherwise would have left them to their fate, and collecting the calves, which were nearly drowned, ordering fires to be made to assist in their recovery.

In the evening he slept at the kraal where I had given him the corn. Here he put to death one of his sisters for having taken a pinch of snuff out of his snuff-box. Such opposed kinds of conduct in one person appeared to me to be strange, but I afterwards became convinced that both the contradictory dispositions, delicate feeling and extreme brutality, were intimately blended in him.

We proceeded on our journey, and in three days arrived at Port Natal. On the fifth day Shaka rose very early. I overtook him when he was ascending a hill, on the side of which, at the bottom, the Mbelebele[1] regiment happened to have bivouacked. When he, Shaka, perceived that the regiment was not yet moving he ordered his servants to run and stab a few of them. They did so and killed five. The regiment then ran on ahead with all possible speed to lead the way and clear it of thorns, the omission to do which, in accordance with the usual practice, they supposed was the reason why the servants were killing them. In their haste a group of men passed within five yards of Shaka, not having noticed him till they got within that distance. He looked at them so fiercely as to make them run back, whereupon he vociferated his usual oath, *"Mnkabayi,"*[2] in so violent a manner as to bring them to a momentary stand. He then ordered an attendant to single out a man and stab him. They sat down, about 80 in number, when the attendant for some moments looked about for a bad-looking man; he found one, then stabbed him in the left breast and, by Shaka's order, left the assegai in the body that it might be seen by passers-by. The moment the assegai pierced the body Shaka averted his head, his countenance betraying something like a feeling of horror, but we had not proceeded more than a mile when two other unfortunates experienced the same fate.

As soon as we came in sight of Dukuza we rested near a drove of cattle. He called the boys employed in herding them and asked them if they sucked the cows that had small calves. They denied having done that, upon which he directed them to take the usual oath. This they refused to do, knowing they were guilty. He then told them to go to the army about a mile distant, and say he had ordered them to be put to death. They did what he told them to do and were instantly killed.

When, in the evening, we arrived at Dukuza Shaka was received with shoutings and acclamations of praise, celebrating his repeated successes. After the war-song had been sung the people retired to rest. On the following day I left for Natal.

---

[1]MS. has Umbalabala.
[2]MS. has Umcarbe, Shaka's elder sister.

I had gone only two days when the army was sent off to attack Nkantolo and Sindane, two tributary chiefs, for having dared to disobey the orders before mentioned, and from thence to proceed to Soshangane's, 80 miles to the north-east, beyond Delagoa Bay and near 500 miles from Dukuza. They had been gone scarcely two days when Shaka found that, from the strictness with which his orders had been enforced, scarcely an able-bodied man had been left at home with him and sent to the army for the return of all the baggage boys, compelling the soldiers to carry their own baggage. With these he formed a regiment which he called Nyosi, i.e. Bees.

In a few days all communications were cut off from the army by Sobuza, chief of a tribe which had several times joined the Zulus and as often revolted, intercepting all messengers and killing them, protecting himself from the Zulus by the capabilities the caverns of that country afforded him. He kept the road constantly patrolled, so that information was only received of the defeat of the two tribes which had insulted the memory of Nandi.

About this time Shaka composed the following song:

SONG OF SHAKA

Abambulali ngani njengoyise ?
Abambulali ngani njengoyise ?
    Bayamzonda.
Inkonyana yozondwayo njengoyise.
Inkonyana yozondwayo njengoyise.
    Bayamzonda.

Translation:

Why do they not kill him as they did his father ?
Why do they not kill him as they did his father ?
    They hate him.

The calf of the hated one, like his father,
The calf of the hated one, like his father,
    They hate him.

Uyise meaning his father, who he wished to be believed was murdered, the calf of the murdered one is himself, intimating that he preferred death to constant trouble.

About this time he dreamt he had seen the vessel in which his chiefs had embarked, and the mast was broken. With this he informed Mr. Farewell, concluding that something serious had befallen his mission and he sent an ox to be killed at Sotoɓe's kraal to intercede with his spirits for his welfare. This had not happened many days before the vessel arrived with Sotoɓe, Mɓozamɓoza, Jacob and Mr. King, accompanied by the *Helicon*, brig of war.

Mr. King was in a state of serious illness occasioned by the many mortifications he had experienced. Mr. King, on leaving Natal, had arranged his affairs, expecting to proceed with the chiefs entrusted to his care to England, but on arriving at Algoa Bay Major Cloete was sent from the Cape to take charge of the chiefs and act as the Colonial Government should direct. This Mr. King could not consent to, they having been given into his charge, and my remaining a hostage in Shaka's hands for their kind treatment and return.

The consequence was a misunderstanding, which was secretly fomented by Jacob, always anxious to injure the whites, between Major Cloete and Mr. King, the chiefs becoming the sufferers, being frequently examined and interrogated in a way they did not understand and had not been led to expect. The advance of the Zulus towards the frontiers made matters still worse. They were suspected as spies and interrogated on a subject they could not possibly know anything of. Fearing the result, should they be taken from Mr. King's care, one of them attempted to run away in the night to reach the Zulus, and although the Government were not sparing in their expense for all their wants, and Mr. King's friends behaved in the kindest manner to the visitors, yet they were disgusted with the place and glad to return on any conditions.

Expecting to see castles, cities, soldiers and ships, they saw only a village and oxen which they were in the habit of seeing in their own country. The place could not impress them with any idea of British greatness, but materially served to eradicate those ideas of Britain's grandeur and power we had all striven to inculcate.

Owing to Mr. King's state of health he was unable to accompany the chiefs to the King's presence on their return, and Mr. Isaacs proceeded with them, taking a present from the Colonial Government and one from Mr. King. The description given by the chiefs of their reception differed very much from what Shaka had expected, and they represented everything to the greatest disadvantage to escape being punished by death for not proceeding to England. This, with the deficiency of the so much expected Macassar oil, enraged Shaka against the whole of us, his passion for the present venting itself on Mr. Isaacs, whom he endeavoured in every way to insult, accusing Mr. King of having plundered his property and bestowing abusive epithets on the whole of us—and, from some motive or other, he determined on sending Mr. Cane overland to the Colonial Government to complain of the treatment he had received, giving him orders to demand all the ivory from the frontier chiefs and give it to the Colonial Government, though he must have known such orders were useless.

Mr. Cane had not left many days when Mr. King expired, his complaint being irritated by his disappointment at the failure of this mission. Shaka was, however, glad to be able to say that an *umnumzane*, i.e. gentleman, had died a natural death and not by the hands of his people or himself which was more than his forefathers or neighbours could boast of.

After sprinkling the gall of a calf round Shaka to purify him after the death of Mr. King, we returned to Natal.

A few days only elapsed when Mr. Hutton, commander of the *Elizabeth and Susan*, formerly of the *Mary*, was taken ill and died. The command of the vessel then fell on Mr. Isaacs, who, after arranging Mr. King's affairs, sailed for Algoa Bay, when Mr. Farewell took a passage for the Colony.

From the time the army had left, the active mind of Shaka could not be quiet or free from bloodshed. He had, six months before, publicly asserted his skill as a necromancer and now, for want of other active employment, began to exercise his new profession. For that purpose he collected the women of each kraal round his neighbourhood, separately, to find out those possessed of magic arts, going over the forms usual on such occasions. They were interrogated as to their having magical powers or not. Finding the answer in the negative had no effect, some had the boldness to avow their being acquainted with them, but either answer produced the same result. Dead bodies were to be seen in every direction, not less than 400 or 500 being killed during the absence of their husbands at war.

During the life of Shaka his despotic sway was so feared that his name was seldom mentioned but as the form of an oath, and much more dangerous was the attempt to trace in any way the particulars of his family, who were not permitted publicly to be known as his relatives. His brothers, though numerous, were not allowed to call themselves so, except Ngwadi, brother on his mother's side. Dingane and Mhlangana were only partially known, the former much resembling Shaka in person. Their apparent fondness was so great that one was seldom seen without the other. In the same house lived Mɓopha, son of Sithayi, a Zulu chief and principal servant of Shaka. These were the three conspirators who put Shaka to death.

There is little doubt that the intention of killing Shaka had been long in contemplation. As I have since understood, it was intended to have taken place at my residence during the attack on the amaMpondos, at which time both brothers remained behind with Shaka feigning sickness, when an opportunity was wanting to effect their purpose.

On the 24th September, 1828, Shaka, while taking his usual sleep at midday, dreamt he was killed and Mɓopha's sister, one of the seraglio, knowing the result would be likely to prove her brother's death, told him what had transpired, to give him an opportunity of killing a cow as soon as possible, to invoke his spirit. This information induced Mɓopha to urge his accomplices. Some Bechuanas arriving with crane feathers, which Shaka had long expected, these people were brought to him, he being in a small kraal he had built about 50 yards from Dukuza, calling it Nyakomuɓi or Ugly Year. There he went to receive them. The two brothers, being informed of it by Mɓopha, took a circuitous route to come in at the back of the kraal, having concealed assegais under their karosses, and sat behind the fence. Shaka asked the Bechuanas what had detained them so long, in a harsh tone. Mɓopha immediately threw a stick at them. They ran away instantly, supposing it the signal for their death, which had been given to Mɓopha by Shaka unperceived by them, as was his custom in those cases. Shaka asking why he had struck them, Mhlangana embraced the opportunity and, from behind the fence, stabbed at the back of his left shoulder. Shaka had only time to look round and, seeing the two brothers, exclaim : " What is the matter, children of my father ? " when Dingane stabbed him. He then threw the blanket from him and, taking the assegai from his side with which Dingane had stabbed him, fell dead near the kraal gate. Ingnasconca, uncle to Nandi, and Nomxamama, two chiefs coming up with Ngomane, the two former were instantly killed and the latter wounded, but allowed to live should he recover from his wounds. The few people in the neighbourhood had run to the bushes for fear and were with great difficulty, using threats and hopes, induced to assemble and sing the war-whoop song, the females of the seraglio joining, some crying, others singing. The war-whoop having been sung, an ox was killed as a thank offering to the spirits, which was no sooner done than a dispute arose between the two brothers who should first use the gall, which, in these occasions, is partly drunk and the remainder sprinkled over their bodies and the bladder worn round the arm, each insisting on his superior right. They were, however, pacified by the interference of Mбopha, who was proclaimed in the presence of the few people collected as being invested with sovereign power, till the return of the army, when they should act as they might think proper.

During the night the news spread over the country, and messengers were sent to inform the Europeans at Natal of the event that had taken place, assuring us, as well as all they were sent to, that Shaka had intended our deaths, but which they had been fortunate enough to frustrate.

The body of Shaka had remained all night on the spot where he fell. When Sotoбe and several others proposed his having the rites of burial, to which, his having been so great a king, he was entitled, let faults have been what they might, the brothers asked Sotoбe by what means they could repress Shaka's anger so that when he became a spirit he might assist them in their endeavours, he recommended that a piece of *umutsha*, or dress worn behind, to be cut off and put into his mouth, which would have the desired effect. This being done, the assegai was taken from his hand, his personal property was all collected, amounting to several tons of beads, brass and various other articles. A grave was dug, his mat laid down, his head placed on his pillow, his blanket placed over him, and his property placed by his side. The earth was then thrown in and a hut built over it. The people employed at the burial were posted as guard over him, having cattle and corn given them for their subsistence. They were now isolated from their countrymen, not being allowed to associate with anyone or go out of the place, and everyone entering the kraal was subject to the same restrictions on pain of death.

Chapter XII

UNTIL the return of the people, by whom the claim to the succession to the kingdom could be discussed, Mɓopha assumed the direction of affairs, and set on foot an expedition against Ngwadi,[1] another of Nandi's sons by Ngendeyana,[2] who no doubt would have aspired to succeed Shaka. It was not likely that he would succeed in that object, but the attempt might have caused much unnecessary bloodshed.

The first thing Mɓopha[3] did was to have all the cattle that had been taken from the amaMpondo[4] collected and brought to him. These cattle had been left along the route the army had taken through the uninhabited country between the Umzimkhulu and Port Natal, with only a few people to herd them, and might have been retaken by the amaMpondo without more trouble than that of driving them. It was nothing else but the dread of Shaka which prevented their being retaken.

Mr. King's vessel the *Shaka*,[5] commanded by Mr. Isaacs owing to the death of Mr. Hutton shortly after that of Mr. King, had in the meantime sailed for the Colony.

Whilst the cattle were being collected, many slight quarrels occurred between Dingane and Mhlangana, on subjects of apparently the most trifling description, and scarcely a day passed without something of the kind. Once a dispute about

---

[1]MS. has Engwade.
[2]MS. has Ingindearn ; also pronounced Gendeyana by Zulus.
[3]MS. has Umbopo.
[4]MS. has Armumpondoes.
[5]Went also by the name of *Elizabeth and Susan*.—Editor.

two sticks rose to a very high pitch, and showed evidently that these disagreements were only occasioned by their broodings on the subject of the grand point which each was wishing to attain. However, their better sense induced them to set such feelings aside, and prepare to attack Ngwadi. Both saw the urgent necessity of destroying him, as, if this were not done, opposition might be anticipated on the return of the army.

They started from Dukuza[1] under the command of Mбopha, in two divisions, one being the regiment of Nyosi, or Bees, that had been raised by Shaka, and the other consisting of all the stragglers that had remained at home from sickness or other causes. At the time of Shaka's death[2] the Bees were away destroying certain kraals to the eastward. Ngwadi, during Shaka's reign, had been much in his favour and regarded as a king over his own kraals in a very independent way, not conforming to Shaka's orders unless they related to him personally.

When the nation was ordered to the north-eastward Ngwadi had remained at home with his own division. This force being so greatly superior to that under Mбopha, the greatest secrecy was required on the part of his assailants, in order that he might be cut off before the kraals in his neighbourhood should know of the impending attack; and in this Mбopha succeeded so far as to be able to make the attack at break of day.

It being the custom among warriors to assume names of distinction, by which they are subsequently known in the regiments to which they belong, Ngwadi had chosen that of our sovereign George, adding to it the prefix *um*, for the Zulus do not use any word of one syllable.[3]

The inhabitants of his kraal no sooner set their eyes on their foes than they flew from their huts to attack, swearing (like Britons), as they did so, to die " by George " for their king. Although their numbers were small compared with that of their aggressors, not one attempted to escape. This unparalleled little action was most desperately and heroically fought by Ngwadi's men, only as warriors of Shaka could do. All flashed their assegais to the end, killing more than their own

---

[1]MS. has Tugusar.
[2]*Circa* 29th October, 1828.—*Editor.*
[3]Except for interjections.—*Editor.*

number before they themselves were completely annihilated by the few left surviving of Mбopha's army.

Not more than 20 of Mбopha's force were left alive out of 300; of Ngwadi's party not a solitary one—they had fought literally to the last man. Ngwadi alone made eight lick the dust before he fell, stabbed in the back by a boy during the battle.

This obstacle to their designs being removed, Mбopha and his associates returned to Siphezi,[1] one of Shaka's kraals, to await the homeward march of the great army, when a king would be elected. The one brother was now only an obstacle in the way of the other. Mhlangana could not endure long suspense, being under the impression that there was more hope for his brother than for himself. Of the two Dingane appeared to have the greater influence. One day Dingane saw him sharpening an assegai, and because on being observed Mhlangana became agitated, the former suspected that it was intended to take his life. He informed Mбopha of the circumstance and of his suspicions, and requested him to sound his brother as to his intentions, so that he (Dingane) might know how to act.

Mбopha accordingly went to Mhlangana, apparently in the most friendly manner, and, speaking in a careless way about Dingane, ridiculed the idea of his sharpening an assegai for his brother, since the murder would not attain his object without the approbation of the army. He persuaded Mhlangana not to think of committing any more outrages, as, in the absence of the army, they had perhaps already gone too far. Mhlangana replied that he would not wait long and see such a fool as Dingane with pretensions which the least of his brothers would be more capable of realizing; Mбopha expressed his concurrence in this, assuring Mhlangana that the act he was meditating was unnecessary, as he, Mбopha, intended from the first to do all in his power for him, and only awaited the return of the army to convince him of his good wishes; but he strongly recommended him to set aside his present intentions, as the whole of the community was still in terror from what had already occurred. This to some extent succeeded in pacifying Mhlangana and gave Mбopha time to tell Dingane the result of his visit. The latter had no sooner heard this than he collected a

---

[1] MS. has Isepase.

few people on the spot, with the assistance of Mɓopha, and made them surround the hut, from which Mhlangana was then dragged forth and summarily put to death.[1]

This effectually removed every obstacle that stood between Dingane and his assumption of sovereign power, that is, until the return of the army, which occurred about 14 days later.[2]

The troops on their arrival were in a miserable plight. They had passed by Delagoa Bay into the interior, and had marched as far as Inhambane, frequently losing their way before they fell in with Soshangane. This chief they proposed attacking the next day, but being surprised during the night by Soshangane's army—when one regiment was entirely destroyed —their plans of further acting on the aggressive were frustrated. Soshangane had been urged to attack them by a Zulu chief who had deserted from the Zulu army. Owing to their famished condition the Zulus were unable to renew the attack. On the way back the army completely lost their way, imagining that they had got to the east of the sun. They had suffered severely from sickness and hunger. In the regions beyond Delagoa Bay they, for the first time, met with locusts, which rose in clouds from the eastward. These insects were, for many days, almost the only food the army had to subsist on. Large numbers died of sickness, whilst fully half of the force remained behind, enfeebled or prostrate through illness, and were unable to reach Zululand until two or three months after the return of the main body.

Shaka did not live to witness the miserable spectacle they presented on their return, as, unaccustomed to such a reverse of fortune, he would probably have resorted to such acts of cruelty as might have had serious results. Nothing of the kind had occurred during his reign. To return without the defeat of the enemy, without even a trophy of cattle, would have aroused his severest anger; his independence of all self control would have hurried him to such acts as would have compelled the nation to revolt and destroy him, or suffer in some terrible way.

---

[1]This occurred *circa* November, 1828. This is not the account of Mhlangana's death usually accepted by the Zulus. cf. Dhlomo, R. R. R., *uDingane* chapters IV and V. See also *Olden Times in Zululand and Natal*, by A. T. Bryant, p. 669, where another account is given.

[2]The army began to return gradually by degrees after Ngwadi and Mhlangana had been put to death, probably during November, 1828.—*Editor.*

On the other hand had they been successful, there is no doubt they would have been driven to excesses and not borne the murder of Shaka as quietly as they did. Their fatigued and famished state required that rest for their weary limbs which the flattering promises of Dingane had induced them to look for.

In the circumstances there were few who did not bless the spirits of their forefathers for allowing them to enter their huts and rest themselves, few who did not contemplate their late sad position and compare it with the present and that which the promises made them led them to expect. For Dingane not only behaved towards them in their distressed state with liberality and kindness, but promised to set the minds of his people at ease in the future by not imitating the conduct of Shaka, in such matters as he considered to be hurtful to them.

He composed or caused to be composed national songs, containing denunciations against the former state of things; his general conversation was, moreover, directed against the severe character of Shaka's government. He adopted mild measures, and thought that he was establishing himself firmly, when obstacles occurred which showed him the true state of things, and the motives that had driven his predecessor to such extreme lengths of severity and cruelty. I shall not be in the least surprised to see repeated by Dingane the very acts for which he and his confederates assassinated Shaka.

The deep impression Shaka had made on his subjects, as well as the numerous cunning devices he had from time to time resorted to, caused many to suspect that he, Shaka, was still alive and that, in order to be quite satisfied as to their loyalty, he had conspired with Dingane to the effect that the latter should temporarily pose as king. Dingane knew of these prevailing suspicions, also that a large section of the nation deeply deplored the death of Shaka. He consequently decided to allow Shaka's favourites to retain their respective positions for the time being, a policy which seemed to hold out prospects of a better future. The favourites, however, remained in office only until he had firmly secured the sovereign power, when he found an excuse for putting to death Mdlaka, Shaka's commander-in-chief, a man who had held that position from the commencement of Shaka's reign, had had the entire management of the army and who had rigorously and successfully fought his many and famous battles, conquering every nation or tribe he attacked. He had given great satisfaction to Shaka, though it was never acknowledged. But as his protector was no longer living his days were numbered. Such a man had to be removed if room was to be found for creatures of Dingane's own choice, by means of whom he could then inaugurate his own despotic career.

The person appointed to take Mdlaka's position was Ndlela, a man who, as it happened, was greatly respected by the people. The remainder of Shaka's favourites were removed one by one from their positions, and a body of chiefs selected by Dingane himself were appointed in their place. On such chiefs, therefore, was laid full responsibility for dealing with and settling all the disputes of the people. It appeared at first as if Dingane did not and would not interfere with this tribunal, so much so, that persons accused of having committed crimes might expect to be tried fairly, instead of their fate depending, as had formerly been the case, merely on the King's own decision. This, however, proved to be only a show of justice, for all cases, prior to any proceedings in connection therewith, were reported to him. If trivial he disposed of them himself; if important they were referred to the chiefs for adjudication, steps, however, being taken in each instance to acquaint the judges beforehand with the King's private opinion. And so it happened that all these decisions were invariably biased to the extent of being made to conform to the King's will, pleasure or personal caprice.

Not three months after the return of the army from Soshangane's, the people became convinced that Dingane's promises were nothing but words. Numbers were put to death for the most trivial offences, and many for having expressed disappointment at non-fulfilment of the promises he had made. Then did the destruction of human beings begin to go on as a matter of daily routine, as it had done in Shaka's day, and many of the former objectionable customs were retained, contrary to the expectation of the people in general.

It is true that the people at large under Dingane were released from the state of perpetual terror they had experienced during the reign of his predecessor. At the same time there appears to be a want of that affection and respect which Shaka always engendered or commanded. The manners of the people appear under Dingane to have undergone a considerable change. There is more ease and freedom in conduct—this being especially noticeable in their dancing. Instead of the energy and fieriness of disposition that used to be observed in the dancing and singing there is now a coolness, sedateness and formal regularity. In other words, the personal dispositions of the kings themselves are reflected in the very styles in which their subjects are wont to dance and sing.

The immense number of girls who were collected during Shaka's reign were, in that of Dingane, released from his seraglios and permitted to marry among the chiefs and elders. Dingane retained only about 300. The order these are kept in as well as the extreme neatness and grandeur of their costumes, far surpassing what one would expect to be possible when obliged to make use of only beads and brass, is enough to convince one that Dingane is at once resourceful and endowed with superior taste.

During his visit to the Zulus in 1832 Dr. Andrew Smith could scarcely believe that such grandeur as he beheld, on being invited one evening to come into Dingane's seraglio, could be found among the native tribes of Kaffraria or indeed anywhere else.

The Zulu nation is composed of a multitude of tribes. These were combined by Shaka into a single nation, a nation which he alone had the ability to control. Under Dingane a number of the tribes became insubordinate, he being regarded by the tribes that had been annexed as having no claim on their allegiance.

Among the songs composed by him reflecting on the conduct of Shaka was one exposing the folly of depriving people of the right or liberty of marrying, though this was not to be understood as consenting to them marrying, as will appear from what took place in the following notable instance. Now it so happens that the case about to be quoted, although aptly illustrating the foregoing statement, became the starting point of a whole series of other events which, being important, I propose forthwith to enter upon, particularly as the whole fall within the earlier years of Dingane's reign.

Nqetho,[1] heir apparent to the chieftainship of the Qwabe[2] tribe, had just married two wives. One of these was the widow of his deceased brother, but in accordance with custom automatically became his, Nqetho's, wife. Since Nqetho's brother's[3] death she had lived in Shaka's seraglio, but as that vast establishment had now almost entirely broken up, to make room for the smaller one of Dingane, she claimed Nqetho as her husband. In consequence of this he sent to Dingane that only one woman had come to him to be married, alluding only to the other girl. But Dingane, having heard of the other (i.e. the spinster), handed Nqetho's messenger over to the chiefs, by whom he was to be tried for attempting to impose on the King.

The chiefs decided in favour of Nqetho, giving it as their opinion that he was not obliged to report his having taken to wife a woman who was already married to him by an ancient custom. Dingane was of a different opinion, pointing out that his orders were that no marriage of any kind was to be entered into. When Nqetho received this information, he concluded that his life was in danger, real and immediate.

He forthwith collected a few of his tribe and revolted.[4] He made his way into the centre of the tribal area by night, using the general cry of rebels. He proclaimed liberty to the oppressed, was lavish of promises of good, and quickly appointed people in different parts to call the Qwabes[5] together. In three days he had managed to collect a large body without interference of any kind by the Zulus. The outrages committed by this tribe, and the cattle they seized in various directions, induced many to believe that Dingane's not acting promptly in repressing the lawlessness arose from a sheer sense of fear, brought on by the suddenness and energy of the rising, which resulted in many more joining Nqetho than would otherwise have been the case.

A few days later a skirmish took place with a small part of Dingane's forces, the latter being compelled to retreat with loss. This incident gave still further confidence to Nqetho's

---

[1]MS. has Catu.
[2]MS. has Quarbe.
[3]Phakathwayo is the man referred to. He was chief of the Qwaɓe when it was conquered by Shaka early in his reign. He died a day or two afterwards, not of wounds, for he was not physically injured, but of grief, humiliation and despair.—*Editor*.
[4]This occurred about March, 1829.—*Editor*.
[5]MS. has Quarbes.

army, which was fast increasing in numbers. Nqetho now took up a position in the centre of Magaye's[1] tribe, a small tribe tributary to the Zulus and living 25 miles east of Port Natal, and at the same time furtherest westward of the tribes that had attached themselves to the Zulus. Nqetho required Magaye, the head of the tribe, to join him. Magaye was irresolute, not knowing how to act. He was anxious to join Nqetho but feared the Zulus. Several days passed in doubt as to whether Magaye would join Nqetho or not, but after the whole of the former's corn had been consumed by Nqetho's people he determined to remain loyal to Dingane.

In consequence of this Nqetho attacked Magaye the following morning. The latter retreated, suffering his cattle to be taken with a loss of only one man. Nqetho then moved to the uninhabited country in the south-west.

Three days only had elapsed when Zulu emissaries came to Magaye to request him to send spies to Nqetho; these spies, they suggested, should be directed to put forward as their excuse for making the visit that they had come from Magaye to beseech Nqetho, on account of their relationship in marriage and for " auld acquaintance " sake, to return just a few of the many cattle that had been taken from him.

When the messengers reached Nqetho, instead of their plausible request being granted, they were promptly suspected of being what in fact, they were, and forthwith put to death. The captured cattle were now divided into two large droves, one of which remained with Nqetho and his army, whilst the other lot, treated as a reserve, was driven off in an inland direction.

Pushing on, the Zulus overtook the Qwaƃes about 25 miles from the sea, on the River Embokodweni,[2] which enters the sea about 15 miles from the port. The Qwaƃes boldly stood their ground in anticipation of attack. As soon, however, as the Zulu force came up, although each army got ready for action, neither side felt disposed to attack the other; the Zulus then contented themselves with capturing such cattle as they found in Nqetho's immediate possession, without being interfered with in any way by Nqetho, and then withdrew.

---

[1]MS. has Margi.
[2]Now wrongly called Mbogintwini.—*Editor*.

Owing to no communication having passed between the armies, and to the fact that when seizing the cattle only a few men that happened to be in the way were killed, one might have supposed that what occurred was in accordance with some preconcerted arrangement, and not in accordance with Dingane's specific instructions, as was no doubt really the case.

While passing through Magaye's country, on their return homewards, the Zulus invited the chief to point out any of his cattle which he could find among the droves taken from Nqetho, saying that such would be given up on his entering the cattle kraal and personally indicating them. Whilst engaged on this he was treacherously put to death on the ground that he had held communication with Nqetho after the latter had revolted.

On hearing that Magaye had been assassinated Dingane pretended much to regret his death, declaring his innocence of the order, and offering a reward of a hundred head of cattle to anyone who would point out the murderer, who as a matter of fact was well known to him as to everyone else in the country.

By this time the Qwaϐes, having continued to move westward, had temporarily established themselves on the Umzimkhulu River. The land they settled on had been in the occupation of a few natives who, on hearing of Nqetho's approach, had hastily abandoned their kraals and made off eastwards. The Qwaϐes remained here only until they had consumed such food, stored in pits or otherwise available, as they could find. When the grain had been consumed, Nqetho moved further to the south-west, where he attacked a tribe called amaGushara, which were living inland of the amaMpondo. These people escaped only with their lives. As a result of these and subsequent frequent encounters with the occupants of various kraals, in which the latter were always defeated, the Qwaϐes soon became a terror to all tribes residing on the eastern border of the Colony. When Nqetho first appeared among them, a Dutchman, Klaas Hochenberg, who had for a long time resided among the frontier tribes, joined one of these tribes, the amaXesiϐe, in attacking and repelling the invaders. In the action that followed Hochenberg and a Hottentot were killed.[1]

As Nqetho had no intention of attacking the amaMpondo, he expressed a desire to their chief Faku of entering into terms

---

[1] Nqetho was himself wounded in the thigh.—Author's MS.

of friendship with him, although cognisant of the fact that a spy had been sent to Faku by Dingane to watch his, Nqetho's, movements.

Lieutenant Farewell happened at this time to come overland on his return to Natal, having visited the Colony shortly after the death of Shaka, to arrange his affairs. He had with him several waggons laden with goods and was accompanied by Thackwray, Walker and Cane, also some Hottentots and native servants. There was no necessity for him to traverse the area then in occupation of the rebels from Zululand. The knowledge he had of Nqetho was slight, obtained from the visits he had from time to time made to Shaka, when he had casually seen, though not actually communicated with, the man, but the good treatment he had uniformly met with among the Zulus may have induced him to expect the same from Nqetho, without, however, considering what motives the latter might have had for destroying him as being a friend of Dingane.

Want of oxen for the waggon as well as provisions caused him to pay Nqetho a visit in the hope of obtaining assistance. He accordingly left his waggons and other property among the amaMpondo and set out for Nqetho's kraal. In addition to Thackwray and Walker, Hottentots and native servants, Farewell took with him a certain native boy, son of a Zulu spy. This spy, who was travelling in disguise, had been sent to keep an eye on Nqetho's movements. Farewell happened to meet him on his journey through the amaMpondo country. On Farewell proposing a visit to Nqetho, the spy asked if his son might accompany him. The request was granted, although contrary to the advice of Cane. The fact that Farewell was being accompanied by such a person, if it came to light, though only of a political nature, was no doubt itself sufficient to incite Nqetho to put Farewell to death.

Over and beyond this, from Nqetho's point of view, a number of practical advantages would at once accrue from his murdering Farewell's party. They had no sooner arrived at Nqetho's kraal than the identity of the boy was discovered, when the people began murmuring amongst themselves. Nqetho was, of course, fully alive to the fact that Farewell would give Dingane all the information he could about him, his place of refuge, military strength, property, etc., whilst the very merchandise, or at least the principal portion thereof, that Farewell was then in the act of transporting from the Colony he knew was intended for Dingane. Unless, therefore, he destroyed the owners, his object of considerably annoying and destroying his enemy could not be achieved.

It appears from the only information we received, namely through John Cane, a carpenter in Farewell's employ, who had remained in charge of the waggons, that on Farewell's arrival, after the usual formalities consequent upon such meeting had been completed, an ox was presented to him for immediate use. He was then conducted to an outer kraal, a short distance from that of Nqetho, as affording more suitable ground for pitching the tent he had with him. There being nothing to cause suspicion of any kind, they retired to the tent and went to sleep.

The following morning[1] guns were heard by the people in the kraal occupied by Nqetho, upon which Nqetho cried out: " They have entered ! " implying that the enemy had arrived on the spot. The people, supposing him to mean they were being attacked by the European, were much surprised to learn the real cause later on from others. The regiment known as Umzimvuɓu, which had been raised by Nqetho since his arrival from scattered remnants of Matiwane's tribe, had attacked Farewell and party by surrounding the tent and, after cutting the ropes, had proceeded to stab Farewell, Thackwray and Walker through the canvas after the tent had collapsed. A gun was discharged whilst this was taking place, but it must always remain unknown whether it was fired deliberately (if so, by whom ?) or whether it went off by accident. Two small native boys, servants of Farewell, who were also in the hut, escaped being killed; this, as report says, they managed to do by each taking hold of a piece of meat as the tent was in the act of falling and running out with it in the dark. They had the presence of mind to say they belonged to the same tribe as that of the revolters, and had gone into the tent merely to steal meat. One of these, an old servant of Farewell's, having worked for him almost from his first arrival at Port Natal, happened to be a member of the Qwaɓe tribe. When it was daylight he was taken to Nqetho, who engaged him as his body servant. This boy after the defeat of Nqetho, an account of which will be given later, went to the Cape

---

[1]*Circa* 29th September, 1829.—*Editor.*

Colony. Three Hottentots had slept in a hut near the tent. One of these escaped after fighting his way through and killing two or three Qwaɓes in the act of doing so, but the other two, owing to their not making any resistance, were killed on the spot.

A strong force was dispatched, without any loss of time, to loot the waggons which, as already remarked, were in charge of John Cane and others. In the meantime, however, Cane had been informed by the Hottentot who escaped of what had happened.

When Cane saw approaching a force much greater than his own, and as the Hottentots who were with him refused to fight, he decided that, as there was no means of protecting the waggons, the only course left was to abandon them. This he accordingly did. The raiding party thereupon took from the waggons whatever could be carried, that is, much property of considerable value, and drove off the oxen as well.

Nqetho endeavoured to persuade his people that he was in no way responsible for these atrocious murders. He declared he knew nothing of the matter until everything was over. It had been committed by the captains of the Umzimvuɓu[1] regiment, who were in consequence, for a time, disgraced. Nqetho expressed his regret at what had happened, remarking how unfortunate it was for him that a white man (presumably Dr. Cowan) had been killed by his brother[2] only a short time before their tribe was overwhelmed by Shaka. Nqetho suspected that the murder of Farewell and party would be productive of similar disasters to himself. Such premonition appears strange, and probably truly reflects his feelings after the deed had been committed. The captains were in private conversation the whole evening after Mr. Farewell's and party's arrival. But, whatever arguments Nqetho made use of to convince his people of his innocence, the latter well knew the improbability of the murders having been committed otherwise than by their chief's orders.

Any other Europeans would probably not have met the melancholy fate that Mr. Farewell and his party did. In this particular instance the provocations and temptations were too great for the assassins to withstand. Nqetho well knew, from

---

[1] MS. has Umsimfubu.
[2] Phakathwayo.—*Editor*.

the knowledge he had of our practice, that Dingane would come by the whole stock Farewell was conveying to Natal. Dingane, moreover, would learn from the spy the exact position and state of Nqetho's army. By destroying Farewell and party, therefore, Nqetho concluded he would be injuring his enemy, and in addition to being a material gainer he would become more dreaded by his enemies in the immediate surrounding districts on account of the outrage.

A day or two only had elapsed when they experienced an unusually heavy downpour of rain, which lasted for four days. Moreover, two of the oxen taken from Farewell died. Such facts, considered in connection with the abnormal rain, were attributed to the spirits being angry on account of the murders. The tribe in general began to fear that a curse had come upon them for taking the lives of white people, lives that had been held sacred by Shaka, whose greatness in achievement as well as in *savoir-faire* could not be surpassed.

Faku, king of the amaMpondo, whose nation occupied country below that of the Qwaɓes, had so far remained unmolested by Nqetho. He had even acknowledged Nqetho as his superior. However, whilst ostensibly subject to Nqetho, Faku had been holding communications with Dingane and was daily in expectation of the latter launching an attack on Nqetho. Nqetho, however, aware all the time that Faku was behaving with duplicity, directed his army to move off and attack him. Of this design Faku received timely and sufficient warning. He directed his army to take up a position on the bank of the St. John's River, where for several days it awaited the attack. Nqetho's forces had, in the meantime, proceeded along the banks of the Umzimvuɓu, where, it seems, they were detained for several days by the manoeuvres of Faku's army. During this time a messenger was sent by Nqetho to his army with orders to return on the ground that, in a dream he had just had, Shaka had appeared to him and inquired why Faku, who, subsequently to Shaka's last Mpondo war, had given his allegiance to the Zulus, was now being attacked. The army, however, not being in the habit of turning their backs on the enemy when so close at hand, paid no attention whatever to the command. That very day they went off and attacked Faku. But Faku, as it turned out, had been carefully manoeuvring for position. He at length succeeded in getting the Qwaɓes into a bend of the river, where, owing to his own superiority of numbers and a more advantageous position (a position that permitted only one regiment to attack at any given moment), he completely defeated his rival. In addition to those killed in battle, many of Nqetho's men, unable to resist the pressure of their assailants, threw themselves into the river and were drowned in attempting to make their escape over to the other side; many others again were torn to pieces by the hippopotami that abounded in that part of the river. The few that escaped, together with one or two regiments that had been kept at home in reserve, became now fully convinced that ruin had overtaken them solely because of having murdered Farewell and his party, seeing that previous to that fatal occurrence they had prospered in every attack they had made.

But although they arrived at this conviction, there was now no opportunity of retreating with such men and property as still remained to some inhabited territory. In these circumstances Nqetho, reduced now to a mere handful of men, though still in possession of large droves of cattle, and numbers of women and children, resolved to attack Ncaphayi,[1] chief of a marauding tribe living a little inland of him, and to do so immediately. Ncaphayi had for some time been living in the neighbourhood, keeping himself out of Nqetho's reach until a favourable opportunity presented itself.

The amaMpondo were not inclined to follow up their victory, dreading that if they took the cattle the Zulus would claim them as theirs, and in that way, having no doubt incurred Dingane's displeasure, they might bring on themselves another and far more serious attack by the terrible Zulu power.

Nqetho planned his attack on Ncaphayi to take place in five days time; it was his intention then to remove to the eastward with his cattle and women, and laden with the beads and other plunder taken from Farewell's party. During the interval, however, Faku dispatched a messenger to Ncaphayi to apprise him of the heavy loss that had been sustained by Nqetho and to suggest his attacking the small force that remained. This Ncaphayi speedily did, that is, on the very day as that on which Nqetho had resolved to deliver his own attack on Ncaphayi.

---

[1] MS. has Ignapie.

The kraals of Nqetho's people were surrounded and the huts set on fire, whilst the whole of their ill-gotten spoils, including their very numerous cattle, were captured.[1]

Some of the Qwaɓes were killed, some were taken prisoner, whilst others escaped. Amongst those who got away was Nqetho himself, reduced now to a state of destitution. He, with a few of his people, took an inland course which led past the Zulu country, the object being apparently to join Mzilikazi, a chief who lived north of the Zulus, but in traversing the intervening country he was taken and killed.

The remainder of the ill-fated Qwaɓes returned by the sea coast in the hope of finding homes among the Zulus, but all were ordered to be put to death, together with those who had attempted in any way to harbour them. Thus ended the once formidable tribe of the Qwaɓes. Their destruction is still regarded by surrounding tribes as having resulted directly from the murder of Farewell, Thackwray and Walker.

In conclusion it may be remarked that during a visit paid by Mr. Isaacs to Dingane the latter ordered him to bring his gun.[2] On this being produced Dingane ordered him to shoot two of Nqetho's wives who happened to be sitting down at a short distance in front of the King. This Isaacs positively refused to do. He was then severely reprimanded by all present. Dingane argued that Isaacs, as well as all Europeans, held mistaken views regarding humanity, the present being a case in point. How could we, he urged, have any proper feelings if Isaacs refrained from killing the two women whose husband had murdered Mr. Farewell ? Mr. Isaacs' attempts to argue proved useless, for Dingane ordered the gun to be taken by his, Isaacs', Zulu servant Noziphongo[3] The latter dreading a second order, and Isaacs knowing that the women would not escape death by his refusing to execute them, then allowed Noziphongo to do so. The one was instantly shot, but the second, while the gun was being reloaded, held her mat up before her; she was attempting to run away when another shot also brought her down.

---

[1] It is important to note that the cattle, or many of them, belonged to the Zulu King, consequently we shall find them becoming the principal cause of warlike expeditions against Ncaphayi, by the Zulus in the near future.—*Editor*.

[2] This occurred on 5th July, 1830.—*Editor*.

[3] MS. has Nosepongo.

"These unfortunate women," says Isaacs, "had returned to their friends after the revolt of that chief, as had many more whom Dingane ordered to be sacrificed. This he had done to everyone who had revolted with his enemy, except about one hundred who had sought refuge with Mr. Fynn; those had obtained their pardon and were living under my friend's protection."[1] Others again, it seems, went to live under Ogle and other British settlers.[2]

Chapter XIII

DINGANE'S pretext for putting Shaka to death was the latter's having unnecessarily kept the nation in a state of perpetual warfare, hence, when the former became King, he promised that shields and assegais should be laid aside and the dancing stick used in their stead. When Nqetho's revolt took place it was indeed necessary for shields and assegais to be used to some extent in self defence, but after that other occasions for resorting to such weapons were not wanting. For instance, the chief Ncaphayi, who captured cattle from Nqetho, at that time practically in a defenceless condition, cattle which Dingane regarded as belonging to himself, was followed up, but the Zulu forces turned back after coming in sight of the raiders and without molesting them in any way. Several attacks have since then been made on various other tribes living both far off and near by, the last being against Mzilikazi, but in each case without any success. Within the limits of his own dominions he has not spared the lives of his subjects. He has massacred numbers with the same unsparing hand as his predecessors, though in a more treacherous and crafty manner.

Few of the many tribes tributary to the Zulus during the reign of Shaka, who was always more partial to foreigners than to his own countrymen, were spared by Dingane, who had no difficulty in inventing reasons for destroying them one by one, so that he might derive from the conquest of people already

---
[1] *Travels and Adventures in Eastern Africa*, II, 45.
[2] Bird, *Annals of Natal*, I, 150.

his subjects that glory which he was incapable of winning in wars against admittedly hostile neighbours—incapable because of the Zulus having, when under his control, lost that daring and prestige for which they had been so conspicuous in the reign of Shaka.

Instances of Dingane's artful and underhand methods of surprising his subjects and then doing them to death have already been given; others will be found further on, e.g. the massacre of Mkhonto and his tribe.

After Lieut. King's death and Lieut. Farewell's departure for Cape Town, subsequent to Shaka's assassination, Dingane carried on no trade other than with natives from the neighbourhood of Delagoa Bay, nor did he receive presents of European goods, except such as were sent by the Portuguese by means of native carriers, until Mr. N. Isaacs arrived at Port Natal in an American brig commanded by Captain Page. Owing to the intimacy that had already grown up between Mr. Isaacs and myself, we entered into partnership with every prospect of our commercial ventures proving successful. And these favourable expectations would probably have been realised had it not been for the extraordinary circumstances that arose in consequence of certain false and vindictive reports made by Jacob. These reports being of importance have to be dealt with at some length in the following chapter.

In February, 1829, i.e. shortly before the revolt of Nqetho, I received a letter from Messrs. Cowie and Green informing me of their arrival at a kraal on the Umzimkhulu River belonging to natives in my employ. Hearing they were short of provisions, I sent them one or two head of cattle. Four days later I met them ten miles from my place, reaching it the same night. They stayed with me seven days. As they expressed anxiety in regard to the remainder of their journey, I decided to accompany them as far as the Zulus.

It had been their intention on leaving the Colony to have travelled across the sub-continent. This idea was, however, abandoned on reaching Faku's tribe. They left waggons there with the intention of returning to that district after proceeding as far as Natal, they being at that time under the impression that the Zulu king lived in the neighbourhood of Port Natal. After much trouble with the waggons, although only one was actually upset, we at length arrived at Dingane's kraal. The

King expected a present in accordance with the usual practice, but there was none to give. I therefore suggested that it would be in their interest, in the circumstances, to present an ox. When that had been done, I explained to the King the object of the journey.

An ox was given us by the King daily for food all the time we were there. On obtaining from me a description of the country ahead, they resolved to continue their journey to Delagoa Bay. They expressed a wish that I would accompany them; with this proposal, however, I could not agree, as, having been there before, there was no personal curiosity to satisfy.

At their request I managed to persuade Jacob to accompany them, also lent them one of my servants, and, on account of the representations I made to the King on their behalf, he directed certain natives of Delagoa Bay, who happened to be on the spot, to accompany them as guides. Dingane, moreover, supplied them with sufficient cattle for consumption on the way, besides authorising them to help themselves to food at any kraals they came to on the return journey. The Hottentots were to have brought the waggon back with me, but this plan could not be carried out as the oxen were taken sick before they could leave.

We accordingly left them at the royal kraal. I escorted the travellers some little way. They told me they were in hopes of selling one of their horses to the Portuguese, which would enable them to make some return for the kindness Dingane had shown them. I returned to Natal with the Hottentots, intending to come back later for the waggon, but the revolt of Nqetho, which broke out just about that time, prevented it. I began to get anxious when I found the time at which the travellers were due to return had gone by.

My servant, the one referred to above, then arrived with a report to the effect that Messrs. Cowie and Green had both succumbed to malarial fever. He also brought a book and sundry other articles that had belonged to the deceased. I sent the book as also Dr. Cowie's will to Mr. Munroe, under cover of a letter from myself, giving all the particulars I could. This parcel was, I suspect, opened and detained by someone *en route*, as I have had no acknowledgment of the receipt thereof. The way in which my name has been mentioned in connection with the affair, as also the allegation that the deceased's property was left with me, coupled with the failure to acknowledge receipt of the parcel I sent forward, convinces me that my suspicions were well founded.

It is unnecessary to re-write what is already common knowledge in regard to the ill-fated expedition. I shall, therefore, confine my observations to the least known parts that were traversed. The Maphutha River is about eight miles from English River, to the east of which is the Portuguese fort. The Maphutha is the largest river on that part of the coast, its breadth ranging from 500 yards near the mouth to 50 higher up. As far as 30 miles it has water for vessels of 60 tons burthen. It is, however, not known how far boats can be got to go up; but when I was with Mr. Threlfall in 1823 we succeeded in going a distance of 50 miles. There is beautiful scenery along its banks, each for about 40 miles being overhung with forest trees of good timber, and so close to the water's edge that it would be possible whilst vessels were moving up the river to break-off projecting branches here and there. Further up the river the country is not clothed with forest. It then begins to rise gradually towards the mountains that are visible from Delagoa Bay. This higher ground is free from the marshes so frequently to be met with in the neighbourhood of the Bay, and in which the inhabitants cultivate rice.

The natives have boats composed of roughly made planks, sewn or held together by means of rushes. These boats are generally to be found at the ships' landing place, for the purpose of conveying passengers on payment of corn, beads, assegais, etc.

Messrs. Cowie and Green crossed well above the landing stage. Mr. Green swam over. The doctor and the others with him got over with the assistance of native swimmers. The party then passed through a piece of country called Tembe, which lies between the Maphutha and English Rivers. They here separated from Jacob owing to the latter's suspicions that the Portuguese would either make a slave of him, or poison the the party. The travellers then passed on towards the fort, making a crossing in the Governor's boat.

In regard to the other details, I can only go by what was told me by my servant, who, of course, knows no more than he actually saw. He said that Messrs. Cowie and Green were supplied with tea, rice, sugar and biscuits. As to the circumstances under which they came by their death, the account he gave corresponds with what has already been published.

A Portuguese sloop called the *African Adventure*, of about 120 tons burthen, was wrecked at Port Natal in January, 1830. " It appears that this vessel had sailed last from Sofala, laden with slaves, and bound for Mozambique. The weather had been hazy, and an adverse current had occasioned their losing course. The first land they descried was that in the vicinity of Natal. As the passage from Sofala to Mozambique is only two days, and they had been out nearly three weeks at sea, they were entirely out of provisions, and had been eight days without water. A number of slaves had died, and a great many had been thrown overboard, to shorten that term of misery to which they were doomed. Out of 160 slaves, with whom they left Sofala, only 30 landed at Natal. . . . The few who had escaped the dreadful suffering of starvation were in such a state of exhaustion that, although the boat was sent over the bar for water, they ran the vessel on shore, without waiting to see what the boat could obtain.

There were several passengers on board, amongst whom was the wife of the commandant. She was a very delicate woman. The Portuguese left her to herself, and even deprived her of a few trinkets with which she wanted to purchase a few necessaries. Mr. Fynn, however, with his accustomed hospitality and generous sympathy, provided for the passengers and crew during their stay at Natal (upwards of a month) and then supplied the lady with a pack bullock, and the party with an escort to Dingane's kraal, to which his brother was sent to accompany them. Dingane consulted Mr. Fynn how he should act towards them, observing that they were not King George's people, but he was told they were the same, and that King George would be glad to learn he had treated them well. " Oh," said the King, " then I will do with them as you please," and at once gave them an escort to the Portuguese settlement at Delagòa Bay, at the same time presenting to them several head of cattle. The Portuguese, to show their gratitude, had all their baggage brought before him and desired him to take what he pleased; but the monarch, with a feeling that did honour to human nature, said: " No, your vessel is lost, and you have been unfortunate, I cannot think of taking anything from you."

[The foregoing is from Isaacs' work, II, 12-14. The information was, however, originally supplied by the author himself, for Isaacs himself was not in Natal when the incident occurred. Among Fynn's MSS. we have found a note in which he says the Zulus could not be hoodwinked as to what had occurred and regarded the conduct of the Portuguese, in making slaves of the natives, as disgraceful.—*Editor*. Isaacs' account goes on:] "Although all Europeans had been treated with every mark of respect," says Mr. Fynn, " and assistance afforded them when in need, it was with the greatest difficulty my brother could persuade them to admit these Portuguese into their kraals and supply them with food, even though they offered to pay for it. On arrival at Dingane's kraal an ox was given for their consumption—it indeed being customary to treat all visitors in that way. Next day, when accounting for their presence in Zululand, it was necessary to refer to the slaves they had had on board, which had the effect of convincing Dingane that they must be identical with the Portuguese at Delagoa Bay, of whom accounts had come to his notice of their making slaves of the people, placing them in irons, etc. After their interview they were directed to sleep at another kraal. Owing to this, and to the way in which they were looked down upon, they were afraid lest they should be put to death. My brother had much trouble in convincing them to the contrary. He begged Dingane hard to give them assistance. With a liberality that Zulus can display once their feelings are aroused, the King not only presented them with seven oxen, but made certain natives of Delagoa, then on a visit to his kraal, depart sooner than they had intended in order that they might accompany the travellers to their destination. On the return of these natives we learned that the Portuguese had got safely to the end of their journey. The Lieut.-Colonel and a Chinaman who were also of the party left for the same place four months later."

Chapter XIV

REFERENCE was made in the preceding chapter to certain reports by Jacob as bringing about an extraordinary situation, rendered extraordinary by the nature of the action that Dingane saw fit to take, involving no less than the total destruction of the residence of one of the English settlers in addition to seizure of such part of his property as happened not to have been removed in time, an incident that so alarmed the rest of the settlers as to cause them all to fly for safety in different directions, three by going overland to the Cape Colony with their adherents and belongings, one by embarking on a ship that fortunately happened to be at Port Natal and bound for Cape Town, and the others by concealing themselves in the bushes. Thus, for the moment, the settlement seemed to have been broken up completely at a stroke. Nothing of the kind had ever occurred to any of Farewell's party, who, on account of the peculiarly privileged position they all stood in ever since arrival, were familiarly known as the King's white people and therefore universally regarded as being constantly under the monarch's special protection.

The matter being important as well as unprecedented, and, at the same time, somewhat involved, it will be as well to preface the narrative with some detailed account of the antecedents of the man who instigated these inquisitions and revolutionary proceedings, viz. Jacob, a native of the Cape Colony, a man of considerable influence and notoriety, whose name has already frequently come up in the foregoing pages.

Jacob originally belonged to a tribe under the chief Ndlambe that occupied land on what was once the borders of Cape Colony. At an early age he was captured by Dutch farmers during one of the numerous incursions they were at that time making among the tribes with the object of recovering stolen cattle. He was named Soembitchi by his master and remained in his service long enough to acquire a fair knowledge of the Dutch language.

He then ran off to his own country, being thereafter frequently employed to interpret for his countrymen in their dealings with the Dutch. When, later on, the former organised parties for stealing cattle in the Colony, he used to accompany them as guide. In one of these raids, after capturing a drove of cattle in the neighbourhood of Bushman's River, the party he was with entered a bush and killed an ox. While busy skinning it they suddenly heard the trampling of horses, and Dutchmen crying out " Vang hom! Vang hom!" i.e. Catch him, catch him. When the natives emerged from the bush and looked to see what number of Boers were coming after them, they were observed, then closely pursued, which ended in Jacob and two others being arrested.

Some argument ensued as to whether the prisoners were or were not to be shot. One was actually set up as a mark, and several shots fired at him before he was killed. The other, however, and Jacob, owing to their knowledge of Dutch, were spared. They were each then tied to a horse and the horses made to canter to a Dutchman's farm, whilst a Hottentot riding behind flogged them with a sjambok as often as they failed to keep up. Owing to the severe sjamboking they received, Jacob's companion died. Shortly after this Jacob managed to escape, once more running back to his own country.

He was now taken by Major Frazer, commandant of the Frontier, and used as an interpreter. Jacob, however, remained only a short time, when he again returned to his country. At that time a law was in force prohibiting Kaffirs from crossing the Fish River boundary. In company with several others, Jacob one day conveyed an elephant's tusk to the missionary station at Theopolis with the view of selling it. After finding a purchaser, a Hottentot, and after concluding a bargain with him, the latter called Jacob's attention to the existing law, and recommended him to make off as soon as he could, at the same time refusing to pay what he had promised to do. Jacob was determined to recompense himself in some way, so on the way back he stole and made off with a number of cattle. He was pursued and arrested. He was then sent under escort to Grahamstown, where, as it happened, the notorious Kaffir chief Lynx was in custody. The two were then transported to Cape Town and directed to undergo their sentences on Robben Island.[1]

When in 1822 Captain W. F. W. Owen, R.N., arrived at Table Bay with his squadron, for the purpose of surveying the south-east coast of Africa, Jacob was placed on board his ship, *H.M.S. Leven*, by direction of the Governor, and told he would have

---

[1] " He was sent to Algoa Bay, and from thence to Cape Town, by the brig *Salisbury*, which vessel had been engaged to convey troops. The voyage was a boisterous one and occupied forty days. As Jacob suffered severely from the inclemency of the weather the commander of the vessel, Lieut. King, knocked off the irons with which he was manacled, gave him clothes, and otherwise occasionally indulged him with an allowance of grog. The feeling thus shown towards him was not ill bestowed ; for, although he was literally nothing more than a savage, he took the earliest opportunity with which he was favoured of showing his gratitude."—Isaacs, *Travels and Adventures in Eastern Africa*, II, 225

to act as interpreter.¹ It so happened that his services were not required in that capacity, the reason being that Capt. Owen did not visit any country south-west of Delagoa Bay, where the man's services might have been useful, but only places beyond or northward of that bay, where the native dialects differ widely from the Kaffir language.

Owen extended his voyage to several ports in that part of Africa, e.g. Madagascar, Mozambique and the Isle of France (Mauritius), after which he returned to Algoa Bay. It so happened that Farewell and Thompson had already reached Algoa Bay with two chartered vessels, the *Salisbury*, Capt. King, and the *Julia*, and were making final preparations for a voyage to St. Lucia. Jacob asked Capt. Owen to allow him to join Farewell's vessel as interpreter. Owen agreed and after paying him such wages as were due to him and making such arrangements as were necessary in regard to his services in the future he passed him over to Farewell on loan, upon which the latter sailed off to St. Lucia.²

---

¹Owen, being bound for the south east coast of Africa, applied to the Governor for interpreters. Jacob and six others, at that time Robben Island convicts, were handed over to him in the belief that they would prove of assistance. The following particulars are taken from Owen, *Narrative of Voyages—Africa, Arabia and Madagascar*, I, 59, 82, and Boteler, *Narrative of Voyage of Discovery to Africa and Arabia*, I, 14, 15, 36, 37. " Jacob was known to Owen by the name of Jackot. Jackot was very handsome, strong and tall and possessed of a commanding figure. He quitted the shore with a heavy heart for Kafirs have an unaccountable dread of water. He and his companions were for a time placed in different messes for the purpose of making them learn English. Jackot had been a chief in his own country and famed for deeds of arms. He and his companion Fire became quite accustomed to the ship and appeared anxious to accommodate themselves entirely to our manners. They favoured us at times with an exhibition of the Kafir war exercise. They appeared to have the most thorough contempt for the Delagonians. . . . Jackot, who was on shore one day, persuaded one of them to try his assegay at a mark ; he complied, and although he was near, missed it by a considerable distance. Jackot took up the weapon and with the usual prelude of vibratory motion, launched it with such force and accuracy, that it pierced the body of the object, a slender tree, at the distance of sixty yards, and deeply fixing itself in the wood quivered with the force of the blow. The natives who were present were astonished, and Jackot apparently exulting in the consciousness of his own superiority walked away with a stately step." Jackot and Fire, however, as also the others, are said to have entirely failed as interpreters, though in other respects, " excellent and trustworthy men."
—*Editor*.

²" They (Farewell and Thompson) applied for interpreters to Captain Owen who very readily agreed to furnish them, provided the people consented to accompany them. Accordingly, Lieut. King went on board with Mr. Farewell to engage these people. At first, they refused to go and expressed a wish to return to their own country, but Jacob, on seeing Lieut. King, without the least hesitation, consented to join him."—Isaacs, *Travels and Adventures in Eastern Africa*, II, 252–5.

Owing to the coast about St. Lucia Bay being dangerous, great difficulty was experienced in landing. In one case the boat was upset, when two sailors lost their lives.[1] Jacob, who happened to be in the same boat, managed to save himself by swimming to shore. Shortly afterwards he was punished by Thompson for some offence, upon which he ran away. As no more was heard of him, Farewell concluded he had been killed, and continued to be under that impression until our arrival at Shaka's residence.

It appears that, when he deserted, he was taken to Shaka, who, from the fact of his having escaped drowning by swimming, nicknamed him Hlambamanzi.[2] Shaka, with his accustomed liberality, then gave him ten head of cattle and placed him under the protection of a chief to find him a wife. In view of the statements he no doubt made to Shaka about the conduct of Europeans in general towards him, it is remarkable that Shaka was not unfavourably disposed towards us, though it is evident Thompson himself would not have met with a pleasant reception had he been of our party.

Our arrival on the scene in 1824 brought Jacob's qualifications as interpreter into request. Shaka took him into favour, and, that he might always be near at hand, appointed him one of the night guards of the *isigodlo* (royal harem). Owing to the general information acquired in the Colony as well as among the Dutch in his various disasters, owing also to what he had learned during his voyages with Capt. Owen, when the scenes were so often and greatly varied, all this, added to a naturally observant and intelligent disposition, also to his extreme craftiness and capacity for deception, made Jacob particularly acceptable to Shaka in the execution of his various purposes.

When I had been about 12 months in the country, most of which time I had had but little opportunity of conversing with Europeans, the knowledge I gained of the Zulu language enabled me to follow his interpretations closely, and to check him in the false renderings which he had long been in the habit of giving without danger of refutation. Owing to his docile

---

[1] Farewell in his letter of 1st May, 1824, to the Governor of the Cape Colony says that four men were drowned attempting to land.—Bird's *Annals of Natal*, I, 72.

[2] MS. has Clamber amanse. *Hlamba* is a verb—to swim, and *manzi*—water. Thus *Hlambamanzi* is water swimmer.—*Editor.*

manner, he always remained in favour with Shaka. In his conversations with the King he used to praise or disparage our country and manners so long as Shaka was inclined to listen to him.

In consequence of the gifts of cattle repeatedly made to him by Shaka, he became a man of some importance; he was the owner of several kraals,[1] and a number of followers, whose lives he used not to spare when he wished to kill any of them. Among his followers was one who was constantly in attendance on him, called Hlomula. This youth's manners had so captivated several Europeans that they, in turn, tried to persuade Jacob to give them the lad, but without effect. One night Jacob fell asleep, though at the time on duty guarding the King. Shaka happened to wake, called Jacob, and finding him asleep ordered Hlomula to beat him. Jacob woke on being called and then apologised to Shaka. Shaka asked Jacob if he had heard the boy refuse to beat him as directed. He admitted having done so, whereupon Shaka exclaimed " Kill the boy at once, he fears you more than he does me ! " The boy was seized by Jacob and there and then put to death.

When the mission consisting of Sotoбe and Mbozamboza was sent by Shaka under care of Lieut. King to the Colony (June-September, 1828) to negotiate a friendly alliance with King George, whom he said he esteemed as a brother, Jacob was one of the party.[2]

During the interviews that took place between King and Major Cloete[3] a misunderstanding arose between them. Jacob played his usual role of deceiver, which had the effect of heightening the misunderstanding between the parties. Moreover, on his return to Natal he lost no opportunity of

---

[1] One of these was established on the right bank of the Thongathi River.—Author's MS.

[2] Whilst Shaka was making these arrangements Jacob appears in some way to have misconducted himself, for Shaka, as Isaacs says, intimated " it was his wish Lieut. King should kill Jacob . . . as he Shaka was afraid that this person would incense the Governor of the Cape ; but to such a course Lieut. King seriously and immediately objected and thus Jacob's life was spared."—Isaacs, *Travels and Adventures in Eastern Africa*, I, 256. This incident deserves to be borne in mind in view of what subsequently occurred.—*Editor*.

[3] An officer who was directed by the Governor to ascertain the object of the mission. The way in which he did this has already been commented on.—*Editor*.

assuring Shaka that his (Shaka's) emissaries had had the worst of treatment meted out to them at Algoa Bay.

[As both Fynn and his friend Isaacs were intimately acquainted with Jacob the accounts given by each, and by them alone (if we exclude the slight notices from which extracts have already been given), of a man much less known to the public than he ought to be, become naturally complementary to one another. We therefore have no hesitation in introducing a further extract from Isaacs' work, which, though well known, has for many years been out of print and nowadays rarely to be met with.—*Editor.*]

" After Jacob joined the *Salisbury* at Algoa Bay in June, 1823, he and his companion Fire sailed for the River St. Lucia, where, after encountering many difficulties, the party landed. Previously, however, one of the boats under the charge of Mr. Farewell foundered in the surf, when Jacob distinguished himself as an expert swimmer, and not only saved his own life, but that of Mr. Farewell also. From this event he was called by the natives Hlambamanzi. Here it appears the party commenced trading; but Mr. Thompson, one of the supercargoes, having struck Jacob, the latter, fearing a repetition should they return to the vessel, sought rather a living on shore, than a return to the vessel. He accordingly shaped his course inland, in a north-westerly direction, travelled about 50 miles and reached Noбamba, the principal kraal or village of Shaka, the then King of the Zulus. At this time, it may be remarked, Shaka had been successful in subduing all the surrounding tribes; by which means he had acquired considerable forces and made the Zulus the most powerful nation on the south-east coast. Through their own manoeuvres, they suspected all strangers as spies; and in consequence of this suspicion Jacob was nearly losing his life, and was kept in apprehension for a considerable time. From his natural shrewdness, he at length, however, found out Shaka's weak side, saw his disposition, and how to flatter his desires. He devised many plans which pleased the despot exceedingly, by which he was elevated above the ordinary warriors.

The manner in which he first brought himself into notice was as follows: Finding Shaka very suspicious of his subjects conniving at his destruction, he related to him many stories of the white people; first how the king was guarded by sentinels;

then that he (Jacob) had been made a sentinel, and while on board of a king's ship the *Leven*, had paraded before the captain's door, in the dead of night, while he was sleeping; the reason the captain assigned for choosing him was that he, Jacob, being a stranger, would be vigilant, as his life depended on that of the captain. To verify these things in Shaka's mind, he asked ' what would become of him now, if the King did not protect him—would not the King's subjects destroy him, on suspicion of his being a spy ? ' Shaka felt the force and plausibility of his story, immediately raised a party of sentinels and placed them under the command of Jacob, at the same time taking him by the ear (a custom they have of impressing anything on the mind) saying ' Recollect, if anything happens to me to-day my people will kill you for being in my favour; your prospects depend upon my safety.' Shaka then told one of his ministers Mbikwana to take care of him, and furnish him with three wives and some cattle. Hlambamanzi had now frequent opportunities of conversing with his sovereign, and relating stories concerning the *abelungu*, or white people. The King found him an amusing fellow with whom to pass an hour or two at night, when all his attendants had retired. Shaka, ignorant of Europeans, and never before having had intercourse with anyone who had known them, found what Hlambamanzi related exceedingly interesting; particularly as their manners and appearance were so different to anything the savage mind could fancy. The King had always thought there was no other land but that which himself and his people inhabited, and that he was the only great king in the world.

He caused Hlambamanzi to build himself a kraal that he might be nearer to him; he increased his cattle and wives, the latter to the number of ten, which ranked him as a minor chief. Having now ingratiated himself in the favour of the King, Hlambamanzi became popular among the chiefs, and from the opportunity he had of conversing with the Zulu monarch he acquired considerable influence with the government, so that at the period of Messrs. Farewell and Fynn's arrival he had it in his power to serve them, which he did by recommending the white people to the consideration and respect of the King, who, from the information thus communicated respecting them, excited in Shaka no ordinary anxiety and solicitude to see them. The arrival of the white people, therefore, in 1824, was conceived to be a good omen.

Mr. Fynn was the first who penetrated into the interior; he was treated well, but ordered to return until the pleasure of the King was known. Shaka sent his principal chief, Mbikwana to see him, who made a favourable report; and the whites were permitted to accompany him to Giбixhegu. On their arrival they were received by the sovereign with an air of surprise and amazement, but with a civility which they little contemplated, and which they attributed to Hlambamanzi.

His career, from the time of the white people settling amongst them, became evidently more useful and important to the King, to whom he not only acted as chief sentinel, but became also interpreter to His Majesty on all occasions in his interviews with the white people; and the latter had great reason to be satisfied with him, as he evinced a desire to promote the object of their visit to Natal. He now had address enough to prevail on Shaka to induce Mr. Farewell to give him a musket, which gave him an opportunity of not only proving his own value, but of course showing the deadly weapons with which the white people fought, and which exalted us as warriors in the Zulu monarch's estimation.

Jacob had now become a great man; he had arrived at the acme of influence with the savage monarch, and on the arrival of Lieut. King and myself in 1825 he came to Natal on purpose to greet his old master, Lieut. King, as a manifestation of his gratitude for having been released by him from transportation. It is not easy to describe the joy he evinced on seeing us, and of the care and anxiety he displayed on hearing of our disaster of being shipwrecked. He sought to aid us in every way. He sent us a bullock for food, offered to Lieut. King a quantity of ivory, and accosted him as father and protector, compelling his wives as well as his people to do the same.

Both Lieut. King and myself had no reason to be displeased with the conduct of Jacob until the return of the first mission to the Cape (on which he acted as interpreter), when he plotted with the Zulu chiefs, Sotoбe and Mbozamboza, to give Shaka an unfavourable opinion of the Cape authorities, and to bring the failure of that mission on Lieut. King and myself. From that period Jacob created in us a suspicion that he was a dissembler, and that it would be dangerous to repose any confidence in him in future; and after events proved that our inferences were not erroneous. He became the perfidious and designing villain which we had predicted."

[After Shaka's assassination Jacob transferred his residence to Port Natal. When Dingane directed Cane to make a visit (his second) to the Colony Jacob was ordered to accompany him. Jacob, however, went only as far as the amaMpondo, when, under the pretence of being afraid of proceeding further, he parted company with Cane. In consequence of this Cane was obliged to go on alone.

On his return to Zululand he reported to Dingane the loss and inconvenience he had been put to on account of Jacob's desertion, whereupon Jacob was ordered to forfeit ten head of cattle. This he refused to do. However, two cattle were surrendered, though much against his will. After this he was again ordered to proceed with Cane to the Colony. It was only the fear of being put to death that made him obey; he went off breathing vengeance against Cane for forcing him to go against his will.

This time he went the whole way. On his return to Natal with Cane, the two remained some time in the vicinity of the port on account of the rivers being swollen. Whilst waiting, one of Dingane's messengers happened to arrive at Natal, when Jacob took the opportunity of whispering to him, for the information and warning of the King, that the Europeans of the Cape Colony, on the advice of Cane, were about to attack the Zulus.

When this report reached Dingane it was already clear that Cane had been unnecessarily dilatory about continuing his journey to its natural end in Zululand, and instead of going himself with the goods purchased or otherwise procured for the King in the Colony he had contented himself with forwarding them by irresponsible native carriers.

In these circumstances Dingane got exceedingly angry and in a few days dispatched a force to attack and destroy Cane and the whole of his people. Fortunately for Cane, he got word of the intended attack on the evening preceding the morning on which it actually occurred.[1] He at once made off. As soon

---

[1]The attack actually took place on or about 18th April, 1831. Zulu kaNogandaya, a famous hero, was in command of the Zulu force.—Isaacs, *Travels and Adventures in Eastern Africa*, II, 218–227.

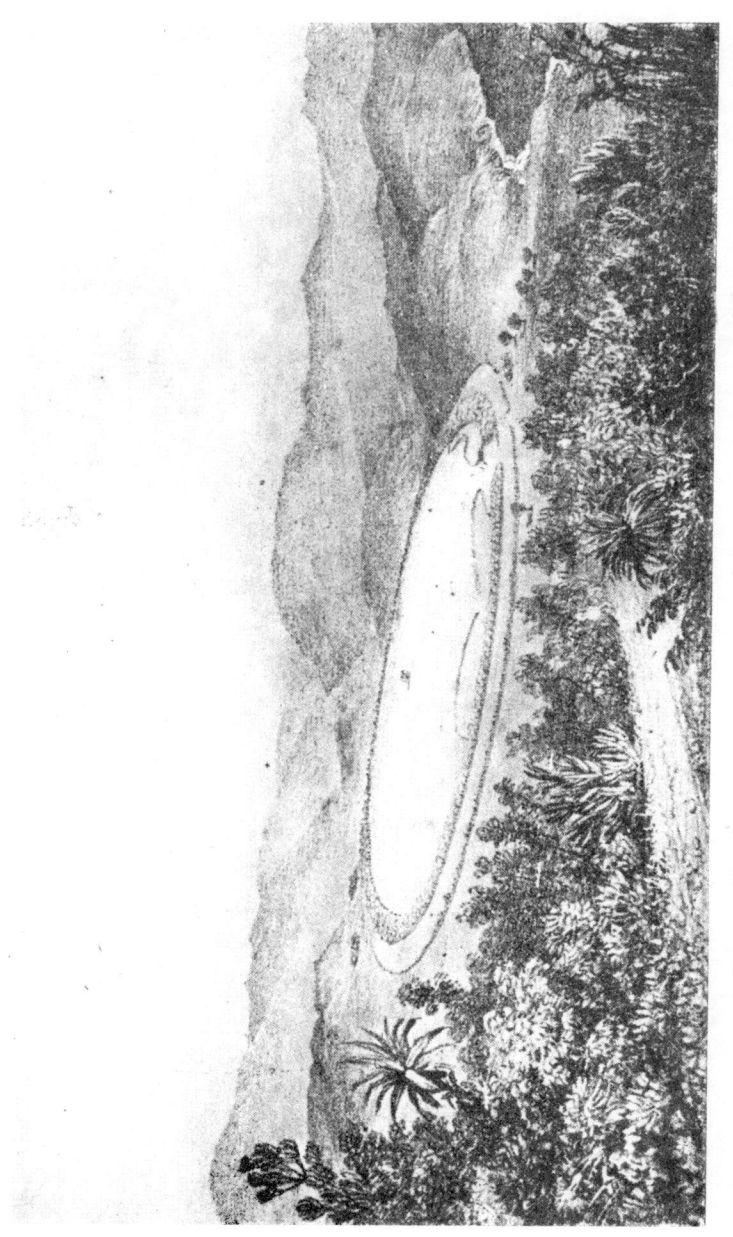

VIEW OF UMGUNGUNDLOVU (taken from the road leading to the Thukela)
From *Narrative of a Journey to the Zoolu Country*, by Captain Allen F. Gardiner

as the force arrived they surrounded the premises. Finding them deserted, they proceeded to destroy all the immovable property and to seize a portion of the cattle that had not been removed in time. As a result of these violent and unprecedented proceedings, Cane nearly lost the whole of his property. —*Editor.*]

Chapter XV

THE false information maliciously communicated by Jacob to Dingane produced a remarkable change in the King's attitude towards the European settlers. At first it appeared as if only Cane was the person affected, it being generally known that Jacob had openly quarrelled with him only. But whilst having every reason to be dissatisfied and angry with Cane, who had certainly been negligent and dilatory in the execution of his duties, the nature of the rumours was such as to make Dingane suspect not only Cane but every other white man in the country of being actively disloyal towards him.

He felt he could trust none of them, not even Fynn. Indeed, just because Fynn at this time was the most prominent among them, he probably, in Dingane's estimation, was more to be feared than the others, particularly as he had been a close friend and favourite of Shaka. In short, it was believed that the Zulu nation had all along been harbouring " snakes," which, finding themselves at length in a position to do so, were now about to turn and attack their protectors.

The position, to an intensely ignorant and suspicious mind like that of Dingane, was peculiarly disturbing and alarming. Whilst he secretly suspected every white man of being disloyal, he was wise enough to know that with only Jacob's uncorroborated testimony to rely on he could not be openly distrustful. What he did was to set about manoeuvring in various ways, and this went on for so considerable a period as to render fundamentally insecure the position of the settlers at the port. In such circumstances it became practically impossible any longer to carry on trade in the country.

As Dingane owed Fynn and Isaacs, then in partnership with one another, 50 elephant tusks it was agreed that Isaacs, accompanied by the former's brother, W. Fynn, should proceed to the King and endeavour to get the ivory sent to the port, so as to be in readiness for a vessel expected soon to arrive. Isaacs and W. Fynn, leaving Port Natal on the 9th April, reached Mgungundlovu on the 17th, only to find that orders had already been issued for the seizure of Cane's cattle.

Dingane, however, said that he had directed that warning was to be given to Fynn beforehand, to enable him to acquaint the other settlers and so prevent their becoming alarmed. Isaacs took the opportunity of discussing the false reports Jacob had made. He pointed out to the King how absurd it was to suppose that any attack on him by troops of the Cape Colony was in contemplation, incidentally suggesting that Jacob's malicious utterances had probably been made in consequence of a long-standing quarrel between him and his fellow ambassador, Cane.

Before Isaacs and W. Fynn could get back to the port the attack on Cane had already taken place, viz. before dawn on or about April 18th, 1831. But luckily for Cane, he received warning beforehand, hence the Zulu force was not able to do more than capture a few cattle belonging to his companion Halstead, besides burning Cane's house to the ground and otherwise completely wrecking the place.

Fynn soon got to hear that a force was on its way to attack Cane and official warning was sent to him beforehand (as Dingane assured Isaacs would be done). He naturally concluded that the despot's intention was not only to destroy Cane, but every other settler at or near the port as well. Fynn accordingly hastily made preparations to fly south-west with his people, taking care to advise such other settlers as happened to be at or near the port of his plans.

As soon as one comes to the conclusion that a Zulu attack on him is imminent, the wisest course is to move forthwith and do so swiftly, i.e. where from want of guns and men, as in this case, it is quite impossible to hold one's ground. Only civilized nations know how to dilly dally about attacking or pursuing the enemy—not Zulus. The reason why Fynn was not advised of the impending attack was, as the commander of the forces informed Isaacs, because there was no opportunity of doing so. He also said his orders were not only to take Cane's cattle, and wreck his homestead, but to put him to death; and this certainly would have been done had he been caught.

Fynn withdrew, probably on the very evening preceding the attack on Cane. At this moment Isaacs and W. Fynn were still at Mgungundlovu. Naturally Fynn, not knowing exactly where they were, was most anxious about them. After retiring to a district occupied by Mzoɓoshi on the Ilovu River, a dozen or so miles from the sea shore and about 20 miles from Port Natal, he halted and wrote the following letter, which, as it fully relates the circumstances, at an interesting and little-known period in the history of Natal, and has never been published, we do not hesitate to insert here. It is undated, but the contents are such as to enable us to fix on the 21st of April as its approximate date.—*Editor.*]

My dear Isaacs and William,

The having some faint hopes that you are still alive is what induces me to write and inform you of our situation, and the circumstances under which we came to retreat. You are aware of the report brought by Khokhela,[1] viz. that the King would send for all the Europeans and then attack the blacks. After you left, the rumour was exaggerated by people in this direction. Mtoɓela then arrived with two oxen and your notes. I forwarded one of the latter to John (Cane) and read the other. I next drew Mtoɓela's attention to the rumours in circulation, at the same time informing him that in two days time I would myself go to the King, though leave the guns behind as to bring them was likely to involve us in serious trouble with our Government. He then requested me to let him know when I could start and so enable him to send a messenger in advance of us. When I informed our principal people of this, they expressed doubts as to our safety, having regard to the nature of the reports in circulation; I, however, still determined on going to you. Early next morning John arrived. He informed me he had just heard of two regiments having crossed the Thukela, and had, in consequence, already sent his people and cattle to the Bluff Point. On hearing this our people advised that we should get ready to retreat. I, however, refused to move; at the same time I sent out spies and

---

[1] This may be Khokhela (son of Ncumbatha), a man of high rank and associated with Mtoɓela and Zulu, the man in command when Cane's house was wrecked. His kraal was near Mhlali (right bank).—Isaacs, *Travels and Adventures in Eastern Africa*, II, 144.

directed two smart lads to take a letter to you. The letter,
I said, must go as speedily as possible so that even though
it arrived after we had been attacked, you, with your horses,
might have some chance of escape. I was fully persuaded
that the King was keeping you in the dark and that, until
he had heard of our actually being put to death, he would
treat you well. If, on the other hand, he learned that we
had escaped, he would, just because he had been treating
you well, have no difficulty in persuading you that we had
foolishly run away in consequence of idle reports, in which
case you would, of course, induce us to return. My letter
had not been gone ten minutes when Mbangwa sent to say
that, while one of the boys was cleaning his gun, Mtoɓela
exclaimed: "*Iya Iya!* we know what those'll do!"—
which appeared strange, as he had been sent by the King
to fetch those very guns. Soon after this we were surprised
to see the two men I had sent with the letter for you
return with a stranger, the latter completely out of breath.
The perspiration was pouring off him; indeed it was several
minutes before we could get him to speak. He said he belonged to Njanduna, though of the Hlongwa tribe, and had
come to inform us that Hlomendlini and Njanduna were on
the point of moving off to attack us. The attack, he said,
would be sure to take place the next day at daylight. It
occurred to me that the treatment you had received from
Khokhela[1] was strange in the light of this news. Lukilimba
advised me on no account to enter the Fengu area, but
go with him to a certain naturally protected rock, where the
whole Zulu army could not defeat us. He said that if we
went to Fengu we would be parted from our corn, our
cattle would starve, and the impi would find there such an
abundance of corn that fresh regiments would come and
eventually starve us out. It appeared therefore reasonable
that escape in that direction was impossible. First of all I
went to your kraal, where I took flints, beads, and writing
desk. I shared Du(?) with the people, all of whom I saw
out of the kraal. I next sent for Mtoɓela, who was at Frank's[2]
kraal and told him all we had heard, and what the reports

---
[1]MS. has Cocaler.
[2]Frank is Francis, a younger brother of the author. His Zulu name is Poɓana.—*Editor*.

appeared to point to. Not a single word could he utter to show that our suspicions were ill formed. When the people found out that Luho[1] was missing, they asked where he was and, as no satisfactory explanation could be given, they concluded he had run away.

Mtoбela now asked what I should do if the impi did not arrive on the following morning. I replied that that would prove that I had been misled, an answer that I thought would induce him to delay the attack until we had got well out of the way. I now took all the cloth, some powder, lead, and a little spirits, expecting to arrive early the following morning at the rendezvous we had agreed on, but, owing to there being no road—nothing but the most troublesome bushes, rocky country and thick grass—we couldn't get far. Early next morning we proceeded on our way. After hearing from such of our people as had remained behind to act as spies, that no impi had arrived up to the moment of their departure, we killed two cows and bivouacked for the night. Next morning we made special arrangements to pass over some nasty-looking country near the River Ilovu, for by this time our people were quite knocked up. Just then intelligence reached us that two regiments having passed inland of us with the intention of encircling us, and, as by this time we had heard of John's kraal having been surrounded, there seemed to be no doubt but that that would also be our fate. Our case, therefore, seemed desperate. Under these circumstances I gave you up for gone. I threw away my medicine chest, writing box, your desk and all the cloth, keeping only such papers as, in a dim night light, I judged had writing on them. These documents I intended forwarding to your friends. About an hour later, we happened to think of William's Spanish dollars. These were specially sent for during the night, for by that time we were determined to make off to the Colony without further delay. On the day preceding the night in question messengers were sent back home to conceal all our elephant tusks. Early next morning, before daylight, we all went forward in such a way as to baulk any who were or might be follow-

---

[1] Possibly some notable refugee who had come to live with the settlers for protection.—*Editor.*

ing in our track, i.e. if they managed to get as far as that. At midday yesterday we were informed that only one regiment had been to attack John, and that a vessel or two had arrived in port. I am waiting, a short distance above Mzoɓoshi's district, to hear the truth of the reports as well as send this to you, to find out if we can look forward to the pleasure of meeting you at a place where, I can assure you, we concluded we could never hope to see you again.

Don't delay in sending me your ideas on the subject, and if any doubt as to your safety occurred while you were at the King's kraal. Hoping you are in . . .

[In a day or two after sending this letter, on hearing that the Zulu force had withdrawn, that Isaacs and W. Fynn were safe and were on their way back to the port, Fynn also returned, reaching there on the 24th of April, viz. on the same day that his brother and Isaacs got there.

Fynn now fully discussed the situation with Isaacs, Cane and his brothers William and Frank, the conclusion come to being that there was nothing else to do but withdraw for a time from Natal. As, however, owing to the nature of the trade they had been carrying on, their property was in a very scattered condition, time was necessary for collecting it and generally winding up their businesses, every advantage, of course, being taken of the moral and practical support afforded by the brig *St. Michael* being at the port, she having opportunely arrived two months sooner than it was anticipated she would do. In these circumstances it was decided by way of gaining time to send a message to Dingane boldly informing him of the vessel being in port, and of their intention to leave the country as they felt they could no longer confide in him or his people.

A few days later, messengers arrived from Dingane to say how sorry he was for the trouble that had been caused to Fynn, who was to be invited to return and told to be under no apprehension for his safety in the future. As, however, Fynn had already returned, he was notified of the King's desire that he should send such black men as were trained to arms, with their muskets, "to assist His Majesty in his attempt to dislodge

Mzoɓoshi[1] from the position he had taken up in the rocks," seeing that Ogle had already agreed to accompany them. Ogle's tactless consent greatly compromised the settlers, Fynn in particular, for Ogle was a member of the very first party that came to Natal with Farewell and Fynn in 1824. In the circumstances, as Ogle had already pledged himself, the settlers thought it advisable to accede to the King's wishes. Dingane was accordingly informed that he might expect them. On the 14th May Fynn and his brother William left for Dingane's kraal accompanied by about 80 native carriers laden with presents for the King.—*Editor.*]

Chapter XVI

[THE reader will now be in a position to appreciate the following account by Fynn himself of his visit to Dingane, a visit fraught with such grave and unprecedented consequences.[2]—*Editor.*]

" On my arrival the King greeted me kindly and was much pleased with the presents. All the people were surprised, and observed they had never seen such a present before. It consisted of beads of various descriptions, brass bugles and other ornaments, snuff boxes, iron pots and kettles, rugs, blankets, printed cottons, white and blue calico, Scotch plaid, and woollen clothes to the value of 2,000 dollars. The King was rather angry at not getting more than 11 muskets, as I told him that 15 boys

---

[1]MS. has Umseboacher. The man here referred to is very probably identical with the person of that name alluded to in the author's letter above quoted. Of this man, Isaacs (*Travels and Adventures in Eastern Africa*, II, 129) says : " He was a chief who had about 200 natives under his command, and sought leave to live among us ; but as Shaka had lent him fifty cows, the Zoolas were entitled to his services. Dingane, however, gave us both the cattle and the services of the tribe. ' I consider him and his people,' said the King in December, 1830, ' to belong to you ; your claim is perfectly correct and I now concede to you the cattle which Shaka lent him ; but he is still under my government and I have the privilege of killing him if he offends me, because he is of my country and you are our friends.' "

Mzoɓoshi was at this time living on the coast near Ilovu River (cf. Isaacs, *Travels and Adventures in Eastern Africa*, II, 86–7). More will be heard of him later on.—*Editor.*

[2]See Isaacs, *Travels and Adventures in Eastern Africa*, II, 264. But this has been amplified slightly here and there by the light of an earlier report by Isaacs to be found in *South African Commercial Advertiser* No. 548, of 12th September, 1832.

were coming; but when I stated the cause he seemed pleased. He only gave me about 2,600[1] pounds of ivory and 20 head of cattle. I remonstrated with him, and used every argument to show the impossibility of the vessel returning as he wished unless he was more generous. He then said: ' I do not want the vessel to return. You are never satisfied. Last year the vessel went away dissatisfied. Now I am convinced that you white people are tired of me. I shall therefore not expect a vessel in future, but depend entirely on any trifle that you may pick up.'

Jacob had reported to the King that as he was going to the Colony he had met a Frontier Kaffir, who told him he wanted to find a home with the Zulus, as there was no living so near the white people; that at first the white people came and took a part of their land, then they encroached[2] and drove them further back, and have repeatedly taken more land as well as cattle. They then built houses (i.e. missionary establishments) among them, for the purpose of subduing them by witchcraft; that at the present time there was an *umlungu*—and a white man's house, or missionary in every tribe; that they had even got as far as the amaMpondo (St. John's Cave); that lately no less than four kings[3] had died, and their deaths were attributed to the witchcraft of the *abelungu*, as all the *izinyanga* (doctors) or prophets had predicted it; that during his stay at Grahamstown the soldiers frequently asked what sort of a country the Zulus had; if the roads were good for horses; if they had plenty of cattle; and had said ' we shall soon be after you '; that he had heard a few white people had intended to come first and get a grant of land as I, Farewell, King and Dambuza[4] had done; they would then build a fort, when more would come, and demand land, who would also build houses and subdue the Zulus, and keep driving them farther back, as they had driven the Frontier tribes. That when they left Grahamstown to return here John[5] told him that Mr. Collis and a number of people were coming to settle at Natal, because the country was much better than their own; that Colonel

---

[1] In *South African Commercial Advertiser* No. 548, of September, 1832, Isaacs (reporting what the author had told him) has 1,600 lb.
[2] Isaacs in *South African Commercial Advertiser* as above.
[3] Paramount chiefs.—*Editor*.
[4] Isaacs' Zulu nickname.—*Editor*.
[5] John Cane, Jacob's fellow ambassador.—*Editor*.

Somerset, who is the terror of the Frontier tribes, was about to advance with some soldiers to see Dingane, because of having heard so much about the Zulus and he thought John had remained at home to guide them.

After hearing this statement, I sent to inform His Majesty that Jacob was a consummate villain and an atrocious character, and that His Majesty would find him a dissimulating wretch, who would lead him to do great wrong to the white people. The King sent to desire me to talk over the matter with the chiefs. Accordingly the chiefs, Jacob and I assembled at the river, the usual place of debate, when Jacob related his story (as above detailed) and called his servant and Ogle's man to confirm it.

I declared the whole to be a tissue of falsehoods invented by the interpreter himself, in order to be revenged on John Cane; and that time would prove the villain had long contemplated to induce His Majesty to injure us; that he had neither regard for the King nor regard for the Zulu nation, but would, whilst it suited his purpose, betray the King as willingly as he had attempted to destroy us. I then gave them instances of Jacob's treachery and enormities, and called on Lukilimba and others to prove his worthlessness and his crimes.

The chiefs, however, observed that they had heard enough, and were perfectly satisfied; but I felt differently, for I could plainly perceive they were prejudiced from the effect of Jacob's report, and implicitly believed all he had asserted, in spite of all that I had said. The chiefs returned to the King, I following them; when we reached the royal apartments, I was directed to sit outside with Mtoбela, while the others went in to converse with His Majesty. I sat waiting for some time, but, finding they did not come out, I retired to my hut.

When I got an opportunity of speaking to the King I assured him that Jacob's assertions were all utterly false. I requested him to say what, in his opinion, could have induced the Colonial Government to think of attacking him; what was the motive; if cattle were wanted why had the numerous herds on the frontiers remained so long unmolested; if land, why had the vast territory between the frontier and the Zulu country remained for years uninhabited; lastly was there anything, any wrong or crime the Zulus had committed, which the Government wished to avenge ? The fact was that the

Government had hitherto molested no one, nor wrongly deprived any man of his property. Dingane fully agreed with me, but insisted on my saying no more about the matter as he had quite made up his mind to put Jacob to death.

On the following day our elephant party,[1] 12 in number, arrived and the same evening, to our utter astonishment, a company of soldiers also arrived from the Portuguese settlement at Delagoa Bay, the latter having been compelled by Dingane to come to his assistance. This showed clearly how serious the consequences might have been had we refused to bring our men and muskets. The next day the army set forth on its expedition, Ogle and Jacob being included as members of our party.

In the evening I heard of Lukilimba having been summoned to the palace (seraglio). An hour afterwards he came into my hut to say the King had asked him why he had not collected such of his followers as had dispersed to various kraals in the preceding year on the occasion of his being attacked. As he spoke, I noticed he was trembling; however, I made no inquiry as to why he was agitated.

Next morning I went along with him to take leave of Dingane. I was amazed then to hear Lukilimba bluntly requesting the King to remove him from my protection and control, and putting forward many arguments to induce Dingane to do so. I may as well point out at once that this man Lukilimba was a Zulu chief who had revolted during Shaka's reign and subsequently returned to the Zulus. After this, in Dingane's reign, he was ordered to be put to death, but on my specially interceding on his behalf his life was spared. He was then placed under my charge and protection. Whilst with me I made him presents both of cattle and corn.

As soon as the King heard Lukilimba's application he pretended to be opposed to granting it, asking what made him wish to be removed from me, who had exerted himself so much on his behalf, and when everyone else wished him to be put to death I had in fact saved his life. Lukilimba, however, continued to beg and implore the King to remove him, if only to Mzakali's kraal, which was in our neighbourhood.

---

[1] That is, our coloured servants, trained to arms, whom I had been directed to bring.—Author's note.

To this I strongly demurred, begging that, if he must be removed, then let it be to a greater distance. I went on to say that I had objections to the application being granted under any conditions whatsoever, for, in the then doubtful and unsettled state of affairs in Natal, everyone would begin wondering what it was Lukilimba foresaw which made him so anxious to move, particularly at a time when so many strange reports were in circulation.

After I had said this, Dingane immediately consented to his removal and, as he did so, remarked to me, ' Let us fall in with his request, then see where and when he will find a protector such as you have been. The fact of your being present when he makes the application will at once put an end to any doubts in the minds of the people in Natal, for you personally know that Lukilimba proposed being removed, not I, who am his King. Had it originated with me suspicions might well have arisen in the minds of others.'

So far I was satisfied with the King, but could not conceive what had induced Lukilimba to leave me, until that moment, completely in the dark as to his intentions. That day we started off on our journey back to Natal, my brother William, however, remaining behind to take note of any movements in connection with ourselves.

During the first day of the journey I did not speak to Lukilimba, but, on the second, he sent two boys to request me to grant him a hearing. On his coming up, I told him it would be little use, seeing he had deceived me by not informing me of his intentions when in my hut on the night preceding his interview with Dingane. I said that under the circumstances I did not know how I could believe him, even if he were to speak the truth or put forward an apparently reasonable excuse for what he had done.

Mtoɓela, the chief who had been deputed to accompany me home, was at the moment some distance from us. Lukilimba, seeing this, told me of a plot that had been entered into to take our lives as soon as the vessel sailed from Natal; that nothing but the greatest fear of death had kept him silent on the night in question; that during that night he had been summoned to the King, who was attended by four chiefs, one of whom being Mtoɓela; that the King had then started by saying: ' Lukilimba, when you come tomorrow morning with

Mr. Fynn to take leave of me, request me to remove you from his protection. This I shall at first object to doing. You will then more strongly insist upon it, and, after some time, I'll give my consent. Tell me, whatever it is that induces you to live with those wild beasts ? Am I not able to give you cattle ? It was the voice of my people, not my wish, that you should be put to death. I was and am still partial to you, and wish to make you a captain.'

When the King had finished, one of the chiefs pulled him (Lukilimba) by the ear, saying: ' Rascal, do you hear ? You dog that is admitted into the King's presence and honoured by the King's voice ? I can see right into your heart. Dare, rascal, to divulge the King's secret; if you do, you'll not see the setting sun. White people don't keep these things secret; They confront us with everything they hear as having emanated from us. If, therefore, Mr. Fynn be told this secret, told by you, we'll see by his eyes that you have done so.'

Lukilimba then assured them that he would keep absolutely secret what had been communicated to him by the King. He next asked Mtoбela what he was to say to me, for, of course, I was aware that the King had called him. Lukilimba was then advised to say just what he did say to me, viz. about collecting his people. ' I therefore warn you to be careful,' continued Lukilimba, ' if you remain at Natal. The moment the vessel leaves I'll make off to some distant country. Should you decide to leave Natal, I shall accompany you and die where you do. Rather than deceive you I would eat the bones of my long-deceased father.' "

[The author gave his partner Isaacs a full account of what happened on this memorable occasion. Isaacs made a record thereof in his Journal, copious extracts from which were published in the *South African Commercial Advertiser*, June-Oct., 1832, as far as one can judge before the author had made his own record of what took place. The following taken from that Journal (No. 556), and not to be found in Isaacs' well-known book, will, although somewhat recapitulatory, serve to throw additional light on an interesting and important situation, as well as on Zulu psychology—the kind of psychology which, *inter alia*, underlay the massacre of Piet Retief and party.—*Editor.*]

"Kelimba gave a long account of his life from the time that he first ran away from the Zoolas, to the present time, and then asked Dingana to point him out a place to live, as he was tired of living with white people, and that he wanted to get clear of them, and, upon the whole, spoke in a most disrespectful manner of the Europeans. Dingane put himself in an artificial pet, and said: Can you have a better place than you now have with Mr. Fynn? Kelimba insisted upon being removed, and said that if the King would not point out a place he would go and live with Umsega. Mr. Fynn then observed that he could not allow him to live so near him after such base conduct, he having saved his life, and supported him at the time the King was going to kill him, and took his cattle away, and has ever since treated him like a chief; therefore he (Mr. Fynn) could not account for such conduct, particularly as they travelled here[1] together and not a syllable was mentioned prior to this about leaving, or respecting ill-treatment; and, in fact, his principal object in coming was to prove that Jacob was treacherous to the white people; and the scale to be so reversed, in the space of a night, was a mystery to Mr. Fynn. Dingane agreed with all that Mr. Fynn said, and continued to say to Kelimba: 'Who is Umsega? Look, there he sits, he is nothing but dirt, do you see his little black eyes? He is not a person to take care of you!' Kelimba replied: 'Oh father, what am I to eat? I have no cattle, and my people will not consent to leave their corn.' The chief Intobaler (Mtoɓela) interrupted him and said: 'What, do you suppose anyone would say no, if the King told you to remove, and would he not provide for you?' Mr. Fynn had been made acquainted that Kelimba wanted to hunt the civet cat for Dingane, and knew that it could not be done without cattle; therefore he (Mr. Fynn) thought that his object was to procure cattle for the purpose, and said: 'Why, Kelimba, don't you tell the King what you mean; that is, you are going to hunt the insimbees, but have not the means of supporting your people?' To which Dingane quickly replied: 'No, no; if you go to hunt you'll go far away from Mr. Fynn, and who will protect you? You will do wrong to leave such a friend as he has proved to you. But, however, if you persist in leaving the

---

[1] i.e., Dingane's kraal, Mgungundlovu.—*Editor*.

white people, you can join Umsega, as you object to come to this side of the river.'

Mr. Fynn observed that he did not want Kelimba, neither would he allow him to enter his kraals again; but the white people at Natal would think it very strange that he left, particularly as they were all partial to him, and felt for his recent situation; and what had just passed would only tend to confirm the report in circulation, respecting Slome-en-lene (Hlomendlini). Dingane, in an angry tone, said: ' How can that be, when you are present to hear that it is his own wish to leave you, and I want him to remain with you ? ' ' Yes,' said Mr. Fynn, ' that's very true, but they'll think that Kelimba sees or knows something more than we do, and for that reason wants to remove from us.'

Thus saying, Mr. Fynn got up, and bid the King adieu, and Kelimba accompanied him, when Mr. Fynn abused him for his treachery; and the former said: ' Why did you not abuse me before the King, and perhaps more would have come out ? ' They travelled homeward, and Mr. Fynn treated him with great coolness, and would not allow him to eat with him as before. This appeared to hurt his feelings, and he tried several times to speak with Mr. Fynn privately . . . . (When later on, Mr. Fynn consented to hear him) he told him, in a pathetic and tearful tone, ' that the King's servant came one night and desired me to follow him; he took me to Boper's hut; he told me to go inside and disappeared himself. The chiefs Intobaler [Mtoбela] and Tomboosa [Dambuza][1] were sitting therein waiting for me. They took hold of me and pulled my ears, and said, we are sent by the King to inform you that he is very partial to you, and wishes to create you a chief again; pulling my ears, they continued to say, we are now going to confide in you; what we are going to mention is from the King's breast, and if you speak a word to anyone you are a dead man. ' This,' says he, ' so frightened me that I said: ' Oh Father, oh friends, whatever you advise me I'll do; if it is at the expense of my life.' ' Well,' said they, ' when Mr. Fynn " wallaleesers " or takes leave of the King, you must make a speech and bring out in a decent manner that you

---

[1]The Induna who was declared by Mpande to have advised Dingane to put to death Piet Retief and party as well as the Boers at Weenen.—*Editor*.

have been a long time from your tribe (the Zoolas) and that you want to leave the white people and return; speak ill of them when you can. The King will appear to know nothing of it, and perhaps abuse you, for the purpose of deceiving Mr. Fynn. Nevertheless, you must persist in leaving the white people, as the King's intention is to lead Mr. Fynn and the white people astray; therefore you must act as we tell you; and we trust you because you are a Zoola, and we know it is the King's intention to make you one of us; but on no account speak with the white people of what has passed this evening ... (In a later conversation, during the dead of night, Kelimba said) he thought Dingane intended to destroy the malonges as soon as the vessel left, under the impression that an army was coming from the Colony, and that we should serve them as spies —knowing, as we did, every path about the Zoola's territories; and, to accomplish his aim, he wants to separate us, as he has heard that I showed you the path when you fled before, at the time John's place was attacked, and from me being a Zoola, he knows that I am aware of all their schemes, and of course thinks that I am in your interest, and will tell you all I learn; therefore he wishes to separate us; but, I can assure you, I'll never see the Zoolas again. Tell me your intentions, and I'll stick by you, and if you do not leave Natal when the vessel goes, I shall run to the bush. They say the King wants to make a captain of me, but I know them too well to be caught a second time. I advise you to leave, Mr. Fynn, but I think there is no danger while the vessel remains here, as they want to manage it so as to kill all, and not leave one to tell the story, as you know the Zoolas are afraid of the Governor, and think that your countrymen would come and revenge themselves; therefore you may be sending corn ahead."

I remained some minutes in silent agitation, then told him that, for the present, we must to all appearances continue to be on the worst of terms, which would afford me an opportunity of considering with my friend Mr. Isaacs and the rest of my countrymen what had best be done.

I now pushed on to overtake Mtoбela. On coming up to him, he asked where I had left Lukilimba. I said I wanted to say nothing to so ungrateful a vagabond, and hoped it would not be long before he left my place. On hearing this Mtoбela was very pleased. He recommended me to drive him away as soon as I got back to Natal.

That night, after settling down to rest and sleep, Lukilimba came stealthily to me to say he would appear to be on the most friendly footing with Mtoɓela, and not come near me. Next morning I sent a note to my brother William begging him to follow on as speedily as possible, as I saw no prospect of our remaining any longer at Natal. I also wrote to Isaacs. [The note, in pencil, ran thus:

Dear Isaacs,

Please come and meet me as soon as possible. I am waiting for you at the Mdlothi River. Come immediately. I shall not start before I see you. I can't say any more just now, only that there is nothing to fear, neither must you let anyone know that there is news of consequence. Don't be the least flurried, nor cause anyone else to be so. It's only news I've heard.

The above had no signature or date. (Isaacs in *South African Commercial Advertiser* No. 584, 12th September, 1852.) —*Editor.*]

My brothers William and Francis left Natal with part of the men and women. I followed next day with Lukilimba. When I left, Cane's people were already on their way from his place.

On hearing that Lukilimba's family had gone by an upper and different route, I asked him the reason, when he said he would overtake the people in the evening. I had gone only five miles when a girl came running after me to say she had been sent by a woman (whose husband had recently died) to request me to wait for her, as the woman travelling with her had run away. I rode back. On coming up to her I noticed she was trembling and that Sobageli, Lukilimba's brother, was behind her. She told me that her reason for sending after me was to request me to let some man conduct her to our people's wives, who were some way on ahead. I immediately concluded that she wanted to avoid being courted by Sobageli, who, prior to her late marriage, had been her lover. I directed Andries, a Hottentot, to take her where the other women were, whilst I myself pushed on to Mzoɓoshi's kraal, where I intended to sleep.

DINGANE
From Captain Allen F. Gardiner's *Narrative of a Journey to the Zoolu Country*

On arriving there I heard that several boys had run off with 20 of my cattle. The circumstances being what they were, it was, of course, useless to follow them. My brothers had passed early in the morning. That evening one of my people informed me that Lukilimba did not intend coming along with me; that it was he who had instigated the boys to run off with my cattle; also that news had just been received that other boys engaged in carrying on our remaining property had also vanished on the same man's advice.

Lukilimba and his brother had in fact, throughout the day, been endeavouring to persuade everyone to desert us, assuring them that he knew we would all be killed, including all those who happened to be in our company. I immediately called the woman whom I had seen trembling when Sobageli was with her in the morning. She then explained that her reason for sending after me was because she found herself alone with Sobageli. When others were present he had not dared to try and persuade her to desert us, but when he found her alone he tried to force her to stay behind, swearing by his King that he knew of a plot from which none of us, or anyone with us, could escape.

I remained for some minutes contemplating all the mysterious incidents that had come to my notice, and then sent for Lukilimba. I asked him if he would continue to go along with us. He said " No," giving as the reason for changing his mind that he saw everyone deserting me, either through fear of being starved on the way or being killed by the amaMpondo. He consequently had begun to think as they did, so proposed turning back the next morning. I was on the point of taking hold of my pistol to shoot him, when a second thought induced me to look into the matter a little further.

Not being able to sleep, I arose before daylight and consulted with several of our people as to his conduct, after which I resolved to shoot him, which I did half an hour afterwards. I then continued on my journey. On arriving at the kraal to which I had sent forward my cattle and corn, I found it deserted, and my cattle nowhere to be seen. My brother William proposed going on ahead of us to the amaMpondo to prevent their supposing that our people were part of Dingane's army.

On the seventh day after leaving Port Natal we slept in a bush on the Mbilanhlola River, little expecting that the Zulus would follow us. We were, however, alarmed next morning before daybreak on hearing a violent noise and commotion, which proved to be the Zulus stabbing our people while we were all still asleep. The cries of those being murdered woke all the native chiefs, and in a few minutes all had scattered and made off to various parts of the bush. Several muskets were fired in succession. Those of us who had guns, viz. nine in all, though in very bad order, for our best guns were with Dingane's army, soon got together.

Among the nine was my brother Francis, who, in the dark, had been actually trampled on by the Zulus, but got off without any other mishap. They managed to capture and drive off our cattle; this was done at the very outset of the attack.

In proceeding from a rock to where the rest of our party were I passed close to the impi, which thereupon broke into three sections. These sections intended in this way to surround me—one by advancing towards the sea shore from an inland direction; another by proceeding along the beach; and another by keeping their ground and crying out "There he is! There he is! Stab him!" The inland party was prevented by a steep precipice from executing their movement, whilst that which had proceeded along the beach was checked by our guns.

On coming up to my people they showed me the folly of remaining where we were, as, should the enemy see that I was not moving on, they would not quit the spot until they had succeeded in killing me, which would have prevented our assisting the wounded in any way. I accordingly left the place. The enemy then soon disappeared, when we ascertained that our losses were five men, 20 women, 15 children, and 17 wounded. The Zulus lost 13 men. In addition to the foregoing casualties, 150 head of our cattle were captured, also two horses, together with cloth, beads and medicine. Everything else, including paper of every description, was destroyed on the spot. All that we succeeded in recovering was two books.

We now pushed on towards the amaMpondo country (chief Faku) as rapidly as we could. When we got there we were in a state of starvation, which continued until we reached Bunting, a mission station near Faku's chief kraal, where we were treated in the most humane and hospitable manner.

[Fynn and party, which then numbered about 70, including women and children, reached the Umzimvuɓu early in July, after a wearisome journey of 25 days.

Their arrival was at once reported to the Pondo chief, Faku. The latter, being at a loss as to how to treat them, consulted Mr. Boyce, the missionary in charge at Bunting, who replied in these terms: " They are my countrymen and in distress, therefore I should help them as much as I could; for it was not our custom, when people were in trouble, to talk to them about their faults, but to assist them. Faku must take care they are not injured while living under his protection." Mr. Boyce not only assisted the refugees to the utmost of his power, but strongly advised Faku to do likewise.

The result was that Fynn and his dependants were soon rehabilitated and in a position to think about returning to Natal. The opportunity of doing this occurred in a few weeks' time; viz. in August, when Collis arrived at Bunting en route to Natal. This enterprising colonist had two waggons with him, also a small party of Englishmen and Hottentots. A short time before he had paid Natal a visit, and was now returning to settle down there permanently.

Whilst Collis was at Bunting, Boyce received a letter from Cane, then in Natal, in the following terms:

" We are well in this quarter, after three months living in the bush, daily expecting the Zulus to attack us. It all turns out, however, to be an alarm of our own. Had Mr. Fynn only stayed a few days more, he would not have been assegaied. His departing in the manner he did gave Sotoɓe, a chief of this quarter, and with whom he was not on the best of terms, an opportunity of following him, to retake the King's cattle as he termed it. His Majesty (Dingane) has sent to me to send after him, to inform him, should he be inclined to return, he may; and I could please myself to send or not. His people refusing and mine being too busy, was the reason no person came after him. Since the above report reached me from the King (Dingane) I hear he has sent to Faku respecting the people that came from this part, not to harbour them, if Caffres. Any of the white people can depart by informing him and obtaining his leave ...[1] "

---

[1] *South African Commercial Advertiser* No. 443, 10th September, 1831, p. 2, col. 3.

From this we see that when Fynn fled from Natal, Cane instead of taking his people off towards the Colony, as he had at first proposed doing, went and hid in the bushes near the port. A considerable time passed before he could get an opportunity of seeing Dingane and personally assuring him that Jacob's alarming allegations were all utterly false. When at length the interview occurred Dingane pointed out that Jacob's assertions seemed at the time they were made so reasonable that he, Dingane, could not have acted otherwise than he had done, but added that if within six months of their conversation no European army arrived he would have Jacob put to death. The time stipulated by the King had passed by. In the meantime, Jacob was found to have stolen some of the King's cattle which had been placed in his charge. For such offence he could not possibly have escaped being killed, and it was probably this, and not his wanton false and mischievous reports which finally induced Dingane to order Cane to kill him.

Had the issuing of such an order depended merely on the falsity of the reports it is probable that it would have been deferred indefinitely. As Cane was anxious, in carrying out this order, to prevent the destruction of the whole of Jacob's people along with himself, as would have been but in accordance with the usual Zulu practice in such circumstances, instead of resorting to such action he offered a reward of five head of cattle to anyone who should kill him and him only. Ogle undertook to do this. He accordingly invited Jacob over to his place on the pretext of having business to discuss. Jacob fell into the trap, when Ogle's people dispatched him quickly.[1] The whole of his cattle[2] were then taken and, by direction of Dingane, handed over to Cane by way of compensating him for those previously taken from him under a misunderstanding. —*Editor*].

---

[1]This happened at the latter end of January, 1832, a date fixed by the author in a letter to the *Grahamstown Journal*, 30th March, 1832.—*Editor*.
[2]Seventy head.—*Editor*.

Chapter XVII

[FYNN, as we have seen, left Bunting in company with J. Collis and others in August, 1831. He and they reached Port Natal during the following months. Among the more notable incidents that had occurred during his three months absence was one in connection with the Cele tribe.

During the reign of Shaka the chief of this tribe was Magaye. After this man had been assassinated, by order of Dingane, about February, 1829, under the circumstances already detailed, his son Mkhonto[1] was appointed chief in his stead. —*Editor*.]

He, however, held the position for only 12 months [writes the author, in a letter dated 30th September, 1832, to the *Grahamstown Journal* of 29th November, 1832]. During my absence in Pondoland in 1831 the whole tribe were ordered to collect together at one of Dingane's kraals, for the purpose of fencing it after a plan which only members of this tribe were competent to execute. The fence being completed, they only remained for orders to return to their homes, when a Zulu entered the kraal in haste and reported to Sotoɓe, the chief of that kraal, that a lion was devouring an ox belonging to Dingane. Sotoɓe placed himself at the head of four regiments and, disposing the Celes in the centre, proceeded a short distance, under the pretence of attacking the lion, when the signal was given for their indiscriminate massacre and Mkhonto and his tribe were thus treacherously killed.

Owing to my return to Port Natal[2] after paying Dingane a visit, those who had escaped or had avoided death by having remained at their homes sick arrived at Natal and placed themselves under the protection of Messrs. Collis and Ogle, whilst six brothers of Magaye put themselves under my care.[3] Only a short time had elapsed when a messenger from Dingane came to Collis, Ogle and me, with orders to " pull our ears," as the phrase went, meaning to draw our attention to the order

---
[1]MS. has Mconto.
[2]September, 1831.—*Editor*.
[3]This would have occurred without delay, probably in September or October.—*Editor*.

and desire that we should give up the Cele refugees. We immediately ordered the messenger to return, saying we doubted his authority, although we were sufficiently satisfied of his being sent by Dingane, but we treated lightly the risk of offending by the argument I was able to hold in defence of our conduct. I accordingly proceeded to Dingane to account for our having doubted the authority of his messenger; I stated that from the manner they had been deceived in the affair of the lion, his now ordering " our ears to be pulled " in so public a manner was sufficient to cause them to run away, and he would accuse us of having induced them to do so. In reply, he said he only wanted to kill the brothers of Magaye, upon which a long argument ensued between us, from my requesting, if it were his determination to destroy them, that he would find some plan by which they might be executed by his own people. Finding me urgent and seeing no likelihood of their being effectually destroyed, he at length gave them to me. On my return to Natal I found those people had, during my absence, proposed running away, under an apprehension that I should return with positive orders for their destruction, but, many of their wives objecting, they had remained, and their husbands' intention became publicly known. Eight months now elapsed[1] and they as well as I were entertaining hopes of their lives being spared. At this time I proceeded with Dr. A. Smith to the Zulus.[2] From the repeated demands I had made for the restoration of my cattle, Dingane made an enquiry into the case, and ordered the cattle to be brought to him by the chiefs who had reported only 30 (which he had given them) instead of the 300 that had actually been taken from me. He desired me to return to receive them. Dr. Smith left in the morning, but I remained with Mr. Collis to overtake him in the afternoon. On taking leave of Dingane he asked me how many chiefs of the Celes were with me in Natal. I replied six, when he ordered me to proceed home and kill them, alleging that, while under my protection, they had been guilty of witchcraft in one of his kraals, some 70 miles from Port Natal, from whence I knew they had not gone beyond a distance of 20 miles. A severe argument ensued in consequence of my refusing to

---

[1] i.e., September, 1831—April, 1832.—*Editor.*

[2] Dr. Smith's visit to Dingane, in company with the author, as guide, took place about April, 1832.—*Editor.*

kill them, till at length the outrageous passion he evinced compelled me, for my own welfare, to submit and undertake to have them killed. On his becoming milder, I again urged him to send his people for the purpose. This he refused to do, on the plea that they would run away at the sight of them, and I left them with the hope that I might plan their escape and deceive him by reporting their deaths. I saw plainly the plausibility of his scheme. In the first place, the cattle, he concluded, would be a sufficient inducement for me to take their lives, and if I did not obey his peremptory order he would then have sufficient excuse for not returning my cattle. Their escape would be another excuse for him, as it would furnish him with a good reason for accusing me of being the cause, but should I have them killed, the loss of the cattle to him would be overbalanced by the grand point he would gain in making the natives believe there remained no more hope of protection by the Europeans at Natal, from his destructive murders. I had, on my journey to Port Natal, deluded myself with the hope of disposing of the chiefs, without murdering them, proposing instead to supply them with corn, and to send them to live in the vacant country lying to the south-west, but on a more due consideration of the improbabilities of their leaving their families, and the publicity of their former intentions, in consequence of their wives refusing to go with them, I felt I was hazarding a risk dangerous to myself, and determined to confer with the other Europeans at Port Natal. For that purpose, I sent circulars requesting them to meet and discuss the question. I also forwarded a messenger to Dingane, excusing myself for the present from making my appearance on the ground of being delayed in consequence of his order. As, however, there were but three Europeans at the port, Collis, Cane and Ogle being absent, I deferred the question till more persons should be present, when the reports before mentioned sickened me, with the little chance of my again being on a friendly footing with Dingane.

Many instances of a similar nature were frequent in Natal, and have been the cause of much trouble to us in consequence. The dread we were held in by the natives on our first arrival soon vanished by the kind manner with which the half-starved stragglers, who at that time were on the point of death owing to Shaka's destructive attacks on the tribes which he laid waste, were treated by every European then at Natal. This induced many people who escaped at the point of death by Shaka's rigid government to fly to us for protection, which we as repeatedly reported to Shaka, whose more noble spirit spared their lives, saying as they had flown to us, who were his " relations," they were safe. The number, in consequence, has well exceeded our expectations, there being not less than three or four thousand men, women and children under protection of the Europeans in Natal, who would be a most useful people should there be a settlement, but at present[1] they are trammelled by the Europeans, because obliged to submit to the Zulu King's despotism.

Although the present doubtful state of Natal is attributed to the falsehoods of Jacob, I am satisfied that the principal cause is the jealousy occasioned from so many natives being with us, and although it may not be Dingane's intention to murder all the whites at Natal, I have no doubt he is at the bottom of the reports, and many instances might be adduced which would show how he was interested by them.

[The above letter deals only with Cele tribal affairs and important issues that sprang therefrom. The following one, though of a slightly earlier date (August, 1832), published in the *Grahamstown Journal* of 21st September, 1832, throws further light on the situation in Natal at that particular moment. Whatever in those days Fynn saw fit to communicate to the Press regarding Natal affairs invariably commanded attention. In directing the attention of his readers to this very letter, this is what the well-known and capable editor finds himself justified in saying: " We have good reason for believing that this writer is better acquainted with the crooked policy of the Zulu chief than any person who had ever visited that country. His opportunities of gaining information have been more frequent and of longer periods than those afforded to any other person, and his intimate knowledge of the language and customs of that people give him a decided advantage. We, therefore, cannot believe, as has been asserted, that he abandoned Port Natal without very sufficient reasons for doing so."—*Editor.*]

---

[1] This was written September, 1832.—*Editor.*

Faco's Tribe.[1]

Dear Sir,

It will no doubt appear unaccountable to you after the return of Dr. Smith from Natal, with such apparent fair prospects of our residing there, according to the promise made to Dingane, how many disturbances should arise to cause any doubt as to our safety, but, shortly after his departure, Mr. Collis left, then followed Mr. Cane who, with his party of Hottentots, went out elephant hunting. The Messrs. Cawood and Ogle were also from home on their several occupations and this at a time when the tribes and neighbours north, east, and west of the Zulus are in motion, being sure that someone or other of them will be destroyed— as a winter was never known to pass, since Shaka became chief of the Zulus, without some tribe or other being destroyed. No sooner had the persons mentioned left Natal, than reports of an intended attack on us were in circulation, the truth thereof being so little doubted as to make us determined to sleep in the wood. Spies had been seen among us. This we at first doubted, but were at length sufficiently convinced that that was the object of their coming. In this state, we remained several days in the woods, there being at that moment but three guns at Natal. I, at length, determined on leaving, and profiting by my last year's experience by not delaying on the road. Mr. Cawood arrived from the Zulus, the day I left. He informed us that the Zulus were about to attack Mzilikazi, who lives to the north-east of their country. As, therefore, the reports in circulation appeared to them groundless, the Messrs. Cawood preferred awaiting the chance of a vessel they daily expected, rather than, by going overland, run the risk of narrowly escaping as I did last June. Had Messrs. Cane and Ogle, and every other resident of Natal been present, I would not have left, as we, no doubt, would have agreed to act on one plan. As, however, the above two persons were absent, they, with myself, being the only persons that have been sufficiently long with the Zulus to enable them to judge of their movements, I decided to leave, for, having lost all I had last year, I saw plainly

---

[1]This means that he is writing from near the St. John's or Umzimvuɓu River.—*Editor.*

that there were no hopes of retrieving my cattle without losing more than their worth.

A servant of Mr. Cane's arrived yesterday. He says he left more than nine days after us. Nothing further had transpired, and, in consequence of my leaving, I think that Dingane will, if possible, pacify those remaining and wait for an opportunity when they are unprepared. Lieut. Edie's feather, which is in Dingane's possession, is supposed to be bewitched, and dreams are said to be the cause of the attack.[1] We have just heard that Mpande, heir apparent to the Zulu chieftainship, has been driven off to the bushes and his cattle seized. Two other brothers were killed before Mr. Collis left. As he set such an excellent example in killing his brother Shaka, no doubt someone will follow it, when perhaps there will be peace again at Natal, as there was during Shaka's life. At present it would be folly for anyone to attempt a residence, the security of property being so doubtful. Port Natal has for this nine years past been open, and has not been wanting in persons capable of opening a trade with the Zulus to advantage, had there been a government protection, without which no persons, with the least prospect, can with spirit enter into business of any kind under so despotic a government, the like of which I don't believe exists on this earth. Only imagine to yourself a few Europeans, each guided by his own interest, and the little chance of success will be at once evident. Only read over the letter in the *Grahamstown Journal* of 3rd August,[2] where it says: " I left and no one knows for what." When the fact is I nearly lost my life and, in the end, quite all my cattle. Do you think, if there had been no cause, my cattle would not have been returned ? As to the letter of Mr. Collis it would be impolitic of him to allow I had cause for leaving, as it would deter other persons from settling at Natal. We differ in opinion as to the place being settled by people without a government, but suppose the traders will be all employed in their separate pursuits, and no disturbances amongst themselves, when could they meet together to defend themselves against the superstitious

---

[1]This probably refers to the attack Dingane was at that time presumably intending to make on the Europeans to whom Edie belonged.—*Editor*.

[2]The reference is a letter by James Cawood, dated 3rd July, 1832.—*Editor*.

suspicions of the Zulus. Their suspicions of our bewitching hides and horns that their cattle may die, has prevented that trade being opened years back. The late Mr. Farewell attempted it, and collected several hundred horns, but was not allowed to remove them. Mr. Isaacs and myself succeeded in purchasing about 80 hides from Dingane, as also others from the natives—in fact, several attempts have been made before the arrival of the Messrs. Cawood, and only relinquished in consequence of the doubtful state we have been living in for the last three years, which must continue to remain so till some great change takes place in the Zulu government; but time will, no doubt, produce a profitable market at Natal, and that as soon as the despotic government is suppressed.

[In December, 1831, the Government arranged with Dr. Andrew Smith, medical officer of the Cape Town garrison, to pay a visit to Natal, as well as to Dingane, with the view to obtaining reliable information as to the local state of affairs, the capabilities of Natal, etc. Smith was accompanied by Lieut. Edie, and had waggons with him. He left Grahamstown in January, 1832. Proceeding overland, he reached Fynn's residence, near Port Natal, on the 25th March. After resting a few days, he and Fynn went on to Zululand. Smith had several conversations with the King, saw something of the remarkable native life at the royal kraal, returned with Fynn to Natal, and from thence went back by the same route to the Cape Colony, reaching Grahamstown early in June.

He published a full and useful itinerary of his journey in the *Grahamstown Journal* of 24th August, 1832. The forward journey alone extended over ten weeks. " Persons who may be about to visit Natal," he says, " will see that they must not trust for every article of diet to the Caffres; that they must be particular in the selection of articles for traffic; and that though in the land of savages, they have ample opportunities of having injuries avenged whenever such are properly represented. They will, moreover, perceive that the utmost caution is necessary to guard against thefts, and that a watch during the night is of the greatest importance. They will find that the road between the Umzimvooboo and Natal offers much at any time to try the patience, but that it is particularly harassing if travelled during the rainy season, namely between September and April."

Smith refers here to much the same route that the author travelled over to and fro, though under more exacting conditions, seven years before; again in 1831; and yet again in 1832, to say nothing of later occasions. Indeed Fynn was the first European to traverse the country in question, since its depopulation by Shaka's devastating wars, a depopulation which, becoming practically complete in or about 1820, converted the whole of a most fertile and extensive area into a howling wilderness.

The information obtained by Smith was soon to prove of great value to the Government, viz. on the occasion of 190 " merchants and others, inhabitants of the Cape of Good Hope," petitioning King William IV " to take measures for the occupation of Port Natal, and the depopulated country in its vicinity, which extends about 200 miles along the coast to the westward, reaching to the country of the Amapondos, and inland about 100 miles," included in the historical précis[1] officially drawn up by him, May, 1834, in that connection.

In January, 1832, the number of British settlers at Natal was slightly augmented by the arrival of the Cawoods (James and Joseph S.) together with their wives and families. They had come with the object of establishing a system of commerce. They brought with them six waggons laden with merchandise suitable for the kind of trade they proposed to carry on. Settling themselves at the head of the Bay, they proceeded to collect, as Fynn, Isaacs, Collis and others had for years been doing, ivory, hides, horns, etc.[2]

We have seen that Fynn got back to Natal in September, 1831. The following letter by him, dated 21st February, 1832, and published in the *Grahamstown Journal* of 30th March, 1832, throws light on the six months immediately preceding. As there is nothing in the Fynn manuscripts that deals specifically with this particular period, we give it *in extenso.—Editor.*]

" On my return to Natal, Dingane ordered to death those persons whom we had cause to complain of, reserving Jacob a longer time, to be better satisfied as to the truth or falsehood

---

[1]Steedman, *Wanderings and Adventures in the Interior of Southern Africa*, II, 289.
[2]See Bird's *Annals of Natal*, I, 255-269.

of his statement, and at the latter end of last month ordered John Cane to have him killed, giving Cane Jacob's cattle in place of those that Cane had lost. In consequence of Jacob's rascally affair, the only hope I have of retrieving my property is a trial which is to take place, in which three chiefs are the defendants, they having taken 300 head from me, and reported only 30 head to Dingane. This so enraged him as to leave little doubt but that they will suffer for it. Although Dingane has punished with death all those whom we had cause to complain of, yet we are not on that firm footing that we were before these events took place, and for some time not likely to be, as every trifling movement of ours, in the minds of these superstitious people, is construed as something foreign from its intent, which before was never thought of. For instance, the Messrs. Cawood praying on the flat, when their waggons were outspanned, and publicly in their houses—the one prays, the congregation is silently attentive, and a hymn is sung. How must this appear to the Zulus, when on going to war, they invoke their spirits, a chief stands in the midst of the people, appealing to the spirits for assistance in the intended attack, the people all mute and silent until he has finished, when the warwhoop is sung in a most solemn manner. This will at once prove the necessity of a missionary among them, these uncivilized beings. Reports assure us of traders coming here. It is my opinion, in our present situation, that there ought only to be three or four families at Natal; if much above that number, the Zulus will and must look on us with suspicion, unless some authority is sent from the Colony to bring our Government and the Zulu Chief to some settled understanding. Dingane has been told these five years, that an authority was coming to him from Government. It, however, does not appear likely that Government will trouble their heads with this place till they find that it ultimately must be so, when perhaps not with the same advantage as at present. The capabilities of the port are superior to any on the coast, the vacant country, climate and soil being so much superior, with a surety of crops, which the Cape Colony does not afford, will induce everyone who visits this place to be in its favour; and although it will take time and proof to persuade those who know nothing of the place to believe in its capabilities, yet I do not hesitate to say it will not be long before this will be a settlement of importance.

It is now only 14 days since we heard of an attack made on Mzilikazi (known in the Colony as Umsilikaats) by the Bastards, who took all their cattle; but they were retaken during the night. The white people have the credit of this. All we can say will not persuade them to the contrary. They naturally ask why Matiwane was destroyed ? What had he done ? We lived here on the most peaceful terms with Shaka, and it is only Jacob that has made this difference with Dingane; but Jacob is no more. Mr. Collis will leave here in another month's time, and I doubt not but that Messrs. Collis and Cawood, or any other visitors, will on their arrival convince Government of the necessity of some person of authority visiting, and in fact residing here. The Zulus will attack Ncaphayi[1] who lives inland of the amaMpondo in March. Mzilikazi's captain or fighting general, who came here to Dingane for protection, has since run away. They now consider him to be a spy. He was disgraced for not having followed up the Bastards, when they retook their cattle. Since my return, the King has made me several presents of fine cattle, and promises me a great deal more."

[" A winter was never known to pass, since Shaka became chief of the Zulus, without some tribe or other being destroyed." So wrote Fynn in August, 1832. His opinion on fleeing from Natal early in the preceding June was that either the British settlers at Port Natal, the amaMpondo, or Mzilikazi were about to be attacked. It is quite possible that the first named would have been selected had they not all either made off in good time or taken refuge in the bushes. However, what actually happened was that an army was sent against Mzilikazi. It left Zululand at the latter end of June or beginning of July and did not return until the end of August.

At this time Mzilikazi was settled near the Oliphants River in what is now the Transvaal. The campaign appears to have failed. The army returned with 140 oxen,[2] having had nearly three regiments destroyed . . . . Dingane demanded of the

---

[1]MS. has Ingnapie.
[2]A later report per Joseph Cawood says that " large herds of cattle have been brought in from Mzilikazi's territory."—*Grahamstown Journal*, January 24th, 1833.

regiments not engaged, a cow from each man, or his sister to dispose of for one. Those who had neither cow nor sister were sent, *à la* Zulu, to inform Shaka. Several of the chiefs have returned wounded. It is supposed that they did not encounter the main army of Mzilikazi, as those they met with asked " why they did not come on and meet the fighting men who were coming up."[1] One of the Cawoods adds[2] that the report of three regiments having been killed is contradicted. " We have also heard that Dingane has killed some of his chief captains for running away. It appears it was not his wish for them to go on this expedition; and he has therefore put those to death who returned without fighting."

Early in November we find Fynn writing as follows to the Rev. W. B. Boyce at Buntingville: " In one of my former letters[3] I informed you of Dingane's severity to his defeated soldiers, since which one of his regiments has left and is supposed to have joined Mzilikazi. I have just heard that two divisions of Zulus, with cattle, are on the Msikaba River[4] on this side of Natal, and are coming in this direction. I suppose there are others that have since left. I have sent to see who they are, and shall acquaint you when I hear."

Nothing more seems to have been heard in the Cape Colony about this movement.—*Editor.*]

---

[1] From a letter by C. P. Pickman to B. Norden in which he is repeating intelligence communicated to him by James Cawood then at Port Natal. The letter is dated amaPondoland, September 19, 1832.—*Grahamstown Journal*, 12th October, 1832.

[2] Letter dated 10th September, 1832 (see *Grahamstown Journal*, 22nd November, 1832). At this moment the Cawoods happened to be almost the only Europeans at Port Natal, Collis, Ogle and Cane having temporarily gone. —*Editor.*

[3] I have been unable to find this.—*Editor.*

[4] Some 35 miles to the eastward of St. John's (Umzimvubu) River.—*Editor.*

EPILOGUE

Chapter I

THE state of affairs at Natal was fast becoming impossible. Indeed, in January, 1833, the whole of the Cawood party, who, as we have seen, reached Natal exactly 12 months before in hope of establishing a system of commerce, already had serious intentions of withdrawing themselves from that promising field. . . . It appears that Dingane's principal chief had established a fixed value for hides and other produce, and that the rate was so high as to render it useless to continue the traffic; they were, in consequence, removing their property to the nearest missionary station, under the Rev. Mr. Boyce in the amaMpondo country, " and it is their present determination to return to the Colony as soon as they shall have accomplished this part of their undertaking."[1] But, prior to their abandonment of the station, various events occurred to which the reader's attention is now invited.

For long past, ever since the murder of Farewell, Thackwray and Walker by Nqetho in September, 1829, Dingane had intended to attack him. It will be remembered that, though the Pondo chief Faku soon signally defeated Nqetho it fell to another chief Ncaphayi, himself a refugee from Natal, to complete the rout, and, what in a Zulu's eyes is of the utmost importance, succeeded in capturing the whole of the numerous cattle and other property in possession of the Qwaƃes. All the property he forthwith appropriated, including what had been looted from Farewell's waggons.

Now, as we saw in a previous chapter, when Nqetho revolted, he drove off a vast number of cattle belonging to the Zulus as well as to chief Magaye, then tributary to the Zulus. A large portion of these were recovered, but Nqetho managed to escape with the balance to Pondoland, a circumstance that, of course, soon came to Dingane's notice. Had not Nqetho been defeated a few months later by Faku, and routed by Ncaphayi, it is

---

[1] *Grahamstown Journal*, 24th January, 1833, its informant being Joseph Cawood.—*Editor*.

certain Dingane would have attacked him, if only to recover the cattle he had wrongly made off with.

When Ncaphayi possessed himself of Nqetho's cattle, in fair warfare though it might have been, he did so with the full knowledge that the Zulus would thenceforth regard him as their foe, and as one to be attacked, defeated, and dispossessed at the earliest opportunity. Faku saw clearly that such cattle were a snare, as something that would inevitably excite Zulu ire against him, consequently when the chance of capturing them arose he left them severely alone.

Ever since Shaka's assassination Dingane had been busy exterminating Shaka's various favourites, of whom Nqetho himself was one. Ngwadi, Shaka's stepbrother, Zihlandlo, Magaye, Mdlaka, Shaka's famous commander-in-chief, and others, moreover, Mhlangana and other members of the royal house, had by this time all been " removed," and in each case by resorting to swift and treacherous measures.

In due course, then, we find Dingane seriously contemplating an attack on Ncaphayi. The usual precaution of sending spies in advance to the country it was proposed to raid, to ascertain, *inter alia*, if the inhabitants had cattle, was duly taken by Dingane, the men sent being Mgoduka, Mhlangana and Mphezulu. These, on their return, reported favourably, a report, however, that was soon to bring misfortune upon them.

But as Faku, a far more important chief, lived in the same quarter as Ncaphayi, it was commonly supposed, especially by those at a distance from Zululand, that the object of attack by the army dispatched in April, 1833, was Faku and no one else. Being apprehensive that the traders at Port Natal would, from motives of policy, oppose this ambitious project, he, Dingane, determined to mask his intentions and, by making an extensive detour, to fall upon the devoted amaMpondos at a point altogether unexpected. In the prosecution of this plan, a large force was marched to the northward with instructions to reach a certain point, when they were to turn to the westward, and to proceed until they were able to attack the amaMpondos in the rear, where they were least prepared to make resistance.[1] In the execution of these orders, they advanced so

---

[1] The army seems for a considerable distance to have marched along the range of the Drakensberg mountains.—*Editor*. See Holden, *History of the Kafir Races*, 50.

far into the interior, and into a country which had been entirely depopulated, that at length they became bewildered; their supplies failed, misunderstanding arose; famine began to be felt to such a degree that their shields were consumed for food, and thousands of them perished in the trackless wilderness in which they found themselves entangled. Some were slain in personal feuds, but the greater part died from the effects of famine. The survivors wandered from place to place, subsisting in the most precarious manner, and it was at this time that a small party of the wretched fugitives fell in with a few Hottentots who happened to be engaged in elephant hunting on the Umzimkhulu River.[1]

The Hottentots were inhabitants of the Kat River settlement. It seems that, about the beginning of the same month as that in which Dingane's army left Zululand, a party of Hottentots proceeded from the Kat River on a hunting excursion.

In this pursuit they successively crossed the Zwart and Witte Rivers, the Umthatha, the Umzimvuбu and the Umzimkhulu Rivers. Having outspanned at the latter, which they reached on or about 10th May, the party proceeded out in different directions in quest of game. "Two were shot," says Piet Kieviet, a young member of the party. "The next morning early five of the party proceeded to the river to hunt sea-cows, leaving me, Goliath and Stoffel to take care of the waggon. In the afternoon of that day a large party of Zulus, armed with assegais, knobkerries and shields, came to the waggon and sat down close to us. They asked for meat, saying they were very hungry. Goliath and Stoffel gave them part of the flesh of the elands. They then asked for a pot, which was also given them; and having boiled and eaten a quantity of meat, they composed themselves to sleep. Our oxen had been grazing near the waggon all day. In the evening we tied them to the waggon. The following morning early the Zulus asked for more meat, which was immediately given them. About nine o'clock three of the persons that had been absent at the river returned to the waggon, each having a musket with him. The remaining two had proceeded up the river to look for tobacco. We sat round the fire, and the three men placed their guns behind them,

---

[1] *Grahamstown Journal*, 25th July, 1833.

close to the bush. In the afternoon the Zulus asked for more meat, but refused to take any part of the carcase, saying they wanted the breast of the elands. We gave them what they wanted, which they also boiled as before. After having eaten it, they came and sat down near us at the fire. A few minutes afterwards, Kieviet Kleinbooy happened to turn his head round to look at something behind him, when one of the Zulus stabbed him in the neck with an assegai. He got up and ran a short distance but fell dead in the river. Andries Kobus and Smit Nel (my brother) were stabbed at the same moment. Before the Zulus came to the fire where we sat Stoffel and Goliath had gone to put the remaining meat of the elands, etc., into the waggon preparatory to our departure, and when they saw Kieviet Kleinbooy stabbed they ran off. They were, however, soon overtaken and murdered by two of the Zulus. I also attempted to escape into a bush, but was pursued, overtaken and brought back to the waggon. After they had murdered my companions, they broke the muskets to pieces, and took the waggon chain from under the waggon, which they put into a bag. They also took out of the waggon some meat and a spade, together with some of the clothes and the blankets of the murdered men. With this booty they went off, taking me and the oxen with them, and making me carry the waggon chain on my head. After travelling about a month we arrived at Jandoona, a place two days' journey on the other side of Port Natal, from whence four messengers were dispatched to Dingane, ten days' journey distant. The messengers returned saying that the King wished me, with the ten oxen belonging to our waggon, to be taken to Port Natal to the white people, and I and the ten oxen were accordingly conveyed to that place by five Zulus. When we reached Port Natal, we found it nearly deserted, there being only some Zulus under Messrs. Cane, Ogle, Fynn and Collis. I was taken back to Jandoona. The messengers were again dispatched to the King, who returned with orders to take me to Amapondoland. I was accordingly conveyed towards that place by nine Zulus, but on the road we fell in with Mr. Ogle, to whom I was given in charge by the Zulus. We returned to Port Natal together, and from thence the Zulus went to Jandoona and brought nine oxen to Port Natal, one having died in the interim."[1]

[1] *Grahamstown Journal*, 10th October, 1833.

After the murder of the Hottentots the Zulu army made its way slowly towards the coast. At length some of the men reached a small kraal of the amaMpondo, the people at which, having gained information that, in the course of their wanderings, they had met with and killed a party of " white men "—as they termed the Hottentots from their European dress, and comparatively light complexion—and, not knowing of any white people except the Cawoods, who about this time were employed in the removal of the produce collected by them at Natal to Faku's country, it was at once concluded that they were the victims of their cruelty,[1] and that this was but the commencement of a general attack in contemplation upon the settlement.[2]

The extraordinary situation that now arose is set forth in a statement[3] by Ogle, who was an eyewitness:

" Shortly after the murder of the Hottentots . . . . I was informed by one of my people that a great multitude of Zulus had just arrived at Natal, being the remains of a large commando which had been ordered some time before by Dingane to proceed into the interior. My informant stated that one of these marauders had got, amongst other things, a spade, and he suspected from the circumstances that they must have fallen in with and plundered some Europeans. On hearing this, I immediately proceeded to the spot and observed, as had been stated, the handle of a spade projecting from amongst other lumber with which a pack-ox was laden. I instantly cut off the lashing which secured the pack and drew out the spade, upon which one of my people immediately declared he knew it as having belonged to the Cawoods. The Zulus declared they had found it on their march, but there was so much prevarication in their story that no credit was given to it. Believing that the Cawoods had been their victims, I immediately dispatched a message to J. Cane, acquainting him with my suspicions. At this time the place was filled with the Zulus. I should think there could be no less than 40,000, being about half the force originally composing the commando; but they were in the most wretched, dispirited and disorganized state.

---

[1] *Grahamstown Journal*, 25th July, 1833.
[2] Gardiner, A. F., *Journey to the Zoolu Country*, 289, no doubt from information given him by H. Ogle ; cf. Bird, *Annals of Natal*, I, 125.
[3] *Grahamstown Journal*, 10th October, 1833.

My message to Cane occasioned great excitement amongst his people. They flew to their arms and, at the onset, one of Dingane's powerful chiefs was shot dead.[1]

This led to further excesses and, as the Zulus made no resistance whatever, a dreadful slaughter took place. I should think that 200 must have been killed. Many more shields and assegais than this number were brought in, but some, in all probability, were thrown away to facilitate escape.

To account for this strange conduct on the part of the inhabitants of Natal, it must be remarked that the natives who are living under the protection of the traders are persons who have been dispossessed of their property and driven from their country by the Zulu chief, and who have the most inveterate hatred for him and the people under his subjection. This feeling, heightened as it was by the supposition that the Cawoods had just been murdered by them, rendered their rage ungovernable; and the condition of the Zulu army offered so favourable an opportunity for retaliation that it could not be resisted.[2]

On the day following this affair the traders, who included J. Collis, had time to reflect on its probable result, and, it being the unanimous opinion that Dingane would pour down upon them with an overwhelming force, it was deemed prudent to abandon the station.

The whole of the inhabitants are now living in that country to the eastward of the amaMpondo, which having been formerly depopulated by the Zulu tyrant was, until their arrival, entirely uninhabited. I have since been to Natal and, from the messages I have received from Dingane I have no scruple in saying that the traders may with safety return to their former station."[3]

Ogle in this statement makes no reference to the boy Piet Kieviet, the oxen, etc. This omission is, however, made good in a letter by Fynn:[1] " Mr. Ogle has returned with the oxen

---

[1] He was shot dead by a Hottentot in the service of the traders.—*Editor*.

[2] Another reason was that on reaching the port they proceeded to take a number of settlers' cattle; not an unnatural thing perhaps for a starving Zulu army to do. But within their own country.—Holden's *History of the Kafir Races*, 50.

[3] Collis, who as already remarked, was present and had an opportunity of knowing what had transpired on this occasion, seems to have differed on many points in Ogle's story, " but still the main particulars are fully corroborated."—*Grahamstown Journal*, 21st November, 1833.

[4] *Grahamstown Journal*, 26th September, 1833.

and leader[1] of the party (of Hottentots) destroyed by the Zulus. He was met on his road by Zulus sent in search of the Europeans. He went with them to Natal, and received six head of cattle and the leader. He then remained till the messengers went to the King and came back. Dingane denies all knowledge of the affair and says he does not swear by his father, but by God—the Englishman's King—that he will never destroy a European. They are welcome to return to Natal if they think proper. But he does not wish them to return, as something appears to obstruct the friendship between them. Mr. Ogle requested him to remunerate, as far as he was able, the friends of those murdered. His reply was: 'Who would remunerate for the lives of the many people destroyed by the Europeans, with their shields and war dresses?' The same messenger assured Mr. Ogle that the spies had all been killed, they being the only persons concerned in the destruction of the Hottentots. The captain in command of the spies was a captain who left Mzilikazi 18 months back. Dingane said he did not like to kill him as he was a foreigner, but to prevent him killing another white man he ordered his eyes to be picked out. The following day he sent to him to know how he was able, without eyes, to distinguish day from night. His answer was, his ears allowed him to listen to the birds; when they sang it was daylight, and when they did not sing it was dark. Now, all I have to remark is that, if the above report is true (which Mr. Ogle obtained only from the messengers sent to him by Dingane, and who are the only people who have crossed the Thukela since the uproar at Natal) Dingane is innocent without a doubt. But then, I would say what a contrast there is between Shaka's government and his. If he, Dingane, has the same power as Shaka had, it is evident the people would respect Europeans more than has of late been evinced, if his conduct towards them did not give scope for such outrageous conduct, taking away their lives and property."

Gardiner says, "No sooner was the affair related to Dingane, than he ordered all his people then inhabiting the district between the port and the Thukela to withdraw; and, notwithstanding two entire regiments were stationed there, the whole moved off, and have never since occupied any portion of the

---

[1] i.e., voorlooper.—*Editor*.

country to the southward of that river, which is now considered as their boundary in that direction."[1]

The army had more to report than that they had for a long time been in a state of starvation and had even been shot down in hundreds by British settlers[2] and their followers, on passing by the port. They had been sent expressly to recover Zulu cattle taken by Nqetho in 1829, cattle which, as we have seen, were subsequently captured from him by Ncaphayi. But before their arrival in Ncaphayi's district the people and the cattle had completely disappeared, having probably had either timely notice or having probably good grounds to suspect what was coming.

As for Ncaphayi, what manner of man was he? He at this time was " slight and active, of middle stature; the scorching quickness of his eye; the point of his questions, and the extreme caution of his replies, stamping him at once as a man capable of ruling the wild and sanguinary spirits by which he was surrounded."[3]

His people were " peculiarly wary in their attacks generally in the night . . . . they had long been the terror of this part of the country."[4]

It was, of course, this circumstance (failure to find and recover cattle) which had reduced the warriors to a state of starvation, for Zulu armies never take a commissariat when on campaign. In looking about them for someone on whom to fix the blame for the disaster, Dingane remembered that his spies had previously reported quite favourably, that is, declared they had seen sufficient cattle to justify his organising a raid. Mgoduka and his colleagues, on being found guilty of negligence, were " sentenced to lose their eyes, as they (the eyes) had brought a false report." They had seen what in fact did not exist. " An Englishman pleaded for them and one was spared; but nothing could arrest the sentence of the other two—the eyes must tell lies no more."[5]

---
[1] Gardiner, *Journey to the Zoolu Country*, 289. Gardiner is here relating what Ogle had most probably told him.—*Editor*.
[2] As a matter of fact, the chief blame does not rest on the European traders.—*Editor*.
" On the contrary, it appears . . . that they exerted themselves to stop the carnage which ensued and . . . were actually instrumental in saving many lives."—*Grahamstown Journal*, 10th October, 1833.
[3] Gardiner, *Journey to the Zoolu Country*, 281.
[4] Ibid., 277.
[5] Holden, *History of the Kafir Races*, 50.

One cannot but be struck by the manner in which Dingane treated the boy, Piet Kieviet, who had been taken captive. " The promptitude with which he dispatched him to a point from whence he could be taken to the Colony, the particular care taken of the oxen stolen from the murdered Hottentots, and the severe punishment inflicted on the leader of the party who committed the atrocity—all these indicate so clearly a sincere desire to continue on good terms with the Colony, that there is still a prospect of the friendly intercourse so long subsisting being ere long renewed."[1] A surmise that was soon to prove true, though on a basis as radically insecure as any in the preceding years of this despot's reign.

This attack by the traders and their adherents on Dingane's army has always been regarded as something mysterious, apparently because no adequate explanation thereof seems ever to have been published. And yet, looked at in the light of the intimate knowledge and experience of Dingane's character and policy set forth by Fynn in the preceding pages, there is nothing whatever mysterious. At this time about 3,000 refugees from Shaka and Dingane are computed to have been living under the settlers. All these knew well that Dingane had begun to resent intensely their being where they were, constituting, in his estimation, practically an *imperium in imperio*, and, therefore, regarded not only as a standing but a constantly growing menace to his authority.

At the same time, the Europeans had with them a number of Hottentots, and all in possession of arms and ammunition. There had been many signs that Dingane was not only suspicious of the settlement, but was openly and covertly striving, generally by foul means, to render it so weak and insecure that its members would find it more to their interest to return to him than to continue under a patently precarious and feeble authority. That was his game, which we believe will be clear to anyone who has carefully gone through the cumulative evidence already recorded.

The intelligence that the Zulu army had in April, 1833, left for an unknown destination was as quickly known by the natives at Port Natal as if it had been telegraphed, it being literally their business in those troublous times ever to keep

---

[1] *Grahamstown Journal*, 10th October, 1833.

a finger on the Zulu pulse. Fynn, of course, gathered his generally wonderfully accurate information from these very natives at the Bay.

He and they knew of Ncaphayi being a likely objective, and when word reached Natal that the Zulu army was at the Umzimkhulu on its way back, and had actually killed some " white people " there, presumably the Cawoods, though actually the Hottentot hunters, it was concluded that having dealt with Ncaphayi or Faku, as the case might be, their intention was obviously to deal next with the settlement, the Cawoods, of course, being members thereof.

When the starving army reached Port Natal and, just because they were starving, proceeded to help themselves to some of the cattle they found there, the natives would naturally have assumed that the previously anticipated attack on themselves had already begun. That we believe is the reason why, under the bona fide impression that the army was hostile, they proceeded to defend themselves by boldly launching an attack, though, as it proved, against a force incapable of aggression or resistance.

Thus, though it might well have been Dingane's intention to exterminate the settlers, the moment for doing so had clearly not then arrived. In any case, the army had become so enfeebled by starvation that it was in no fit state for fighting. Thus the attack took place under a misapprehension, and it was because this was clearly established that Dingane condoned the offence.

Chapter II

SINCE the affair with the Zulu army in June, 1833, Ogle seems to have been the first of the settlers to venture back, viz. in August of the same year, only to learn that Dingane had never intended to do them any harm, and that they were welcome to return, if they wished to do so.

In consequence of these seemingly satisfactory assurances of the Zulu King, about 30 persons, supported by some of the most respectable merchants of Grahamstown, left there in

April, 1834, with the intention of forming a permanent establishment in the vicinity of Port Natal.[1]

Cane, who had latterly been living near the Umzimkhulu River, was entrusted by Dingane, in May, with a letter to the Governor in which Dingane declared he earnestly desired " to continue on friendly terms with the white people." On reaching the Colony, Cane reported that the natives of Natal and Zululand " are already glutted with beads which they procure from the Portuguese settlement at Delagoa Bay at a much cheaper rate than they can be purchased at Grahamstown." He also stated that ivory is extremely scarce, most of the Bushmen who formerly followed elephant hunting as an occupation having given it up for the more certain and less harassing pursuits of tillage.

In the meantime, interesting though secret developments had been taking place among the Boers in the Cape Colony. Though accounts of Natal had from time to time been brought to the Colony by Farewell, King, Fynn and others, it was not until that of Dr. Andrew Smith was published that the attention of the Dutch farmers was really attracted to the district with a view to their occupying it. " They quietly collected 14 waggons," says Cloete,[2] and a party headed by Piet Uys, Colens Uys, Hans de Lange, Stephanus Maritz and Gert Rudolph[3] started from Uitenhage in the beginning of the year 1834, taking the lower route along the eastern slopes of the Khahlamba or Drakensberg range, following nearly the same track by which Dr. Smith and his party had explored this district. Their arrival agreeably surprised the small party of English who had settled themselves down at the Bay, where Messrs. Ogle, Toohey[4] and King .... gave them a hearty reception, from whose accounts, and from their own exploration of the country, they soon came to the conclusion that this would be a country in every way suited to them and their countrymen;

---

[1] Bird, *Annals of Natal*, I, 261.

[2] *History of the Great Boer Trek* (published by John Murray, 1900), p. 72.

[3] *Grahamstown Journal*, 5th June, 1834.

The Narrative of W. J. Pretorious in Bird's *Annals of Natal*, I, 231, says, " The men of principal note were Stephanus Maritz, Jacobus Uys, Karl Landman, Johannes de Lange and Jacobus Moolman." See also Mackeurtan, *Cradle Days of Natal*, p. 169.

[4] Cloete is mistaken as to Toohey (D. C.) for he did not arrive in Natal until early in 1835. Then again he might also have mentioned J. Collis, John Cane and others, who had by then returned.—*Editor*.

they loitered here some time, shooting and examining the country, and would have pursued their explorations still further if they had not been suddenly startled by the astounding intelligence that the Kaffirs had made a sudden general irruption into the eastern province,[1] and thus provoked a third Kaffir war. This compelled them to beat a hasty retreat, and they most providentially succeeded in returning unattacked through the whole of Kaffirland, while the Kaffirs, having deserted their own country, appeared wholly intent upon laying waste the eastern districts of the colony.[2]

Fynn, too, made his way back once more to Natal. The following piece, dated Umzimvuɓu, 27th June, is connected with that visit: "During my visit to Dingane," he says, "I had some conversation with two Portuguese soldiers from Delagoa Bay. I was much surprised to hear from them that their Governor Deneis(?) was put to death on May last by a Commando from the Zulu chief, and their present Governor was Newburg. After hearing the whole of the circumstances, I determined on questioning Dingane, having doubts as to the possibility of his putting to death a governor who had a fort and soldiers under his command, and concluding, if true, how improbable it appeared that another governor so directly after the occurence should be on such amicable terms with Dingane as to send him presents of brass and beads, for which purpose the soldiers had come. On my questioning Dingane, he showed evident symptoms of surprise, and asked who were my informants; and when I acquainted him appeared much to regret I had gained the intelligence. After a few moments consideration, he told me, almost in the same words as the two soldiers, that he had sent to the Governor to demand a quantity of brass, which was refused him, under an appearance of his having none. Dingane knowing he had brass, sent a force to

---

[1]This occurred on 21st December, 1834.—*Editor.*

[2]These farmers were on their return to the Colony as Gardiner was travelling overland towards Port Natal, January, 1835.—Gardiner, *Journey to the Zoolu Country*, p. 89. Of this exploring party, Gardiner says: "They had heard much of the soil and capabilities of Port Natal for agricultural purposes, and, resolving to decide for themselves on the accuracy of the reports they formed a large party, and, with ten or twelve wagons proceeded at once to this place. After advancing towards the Tugela and thoroughly examining the whole district, they not only acknowledged that the accounts they had heard had not been exaggerated, but set out on their return for their several families, with a full determination to locate them in this neighbourhood—a resolution which the sudden breaking out of the Kafir War has alone prevented."

put him to death. But the Governor, having previously heard of the force coming, proposed giving 100 large bangles to pacify his anger. The force returned with the brass, but on their arrival at Dingane's he ordered them immediately to return and fulfil his former orders, when they succeeded in putting him to death."[1]

J. Collis must have visited Dingane either in company with Fynn or about the same time, for, in the letter from Port Natal, 3rd September, 1834, he says: "During my visit to the King, one of his regiments ran away to Natal. Three others were sent after them, but with orders not to cross the Thukela River. He informed me that he would not pursue them further; for if his soldiers came to Natal, there would be people killed; this would alarm the whites and perhaps cause them to leave."

From this, it seems the King felt he was unable to restrain his army once it had arrived at its destination. Implicit in any order to proceed to a given place, e.g. to seize or recover cattle, was that, in the execution thereof men, women and children would be destroyed. Even if the King had expressly directed that no one should be killed, mere execution of that type of order carried with it, from the soldiers' point of view, destruction of those in possession, including dependants.

Of course, massacres were more terrible and widespread where chiefs or indunas were, rightly or wrongly, believed to have committed specific offences, e.g. practising witchcraft, poisoning others, appropriating royal cattle, disobeying royal orders, e.g. in connection with marriage, first fruits, etc. (A case of this kind will be found a little further on in this narrative).

Criminals of this class were looked upon as enemies of the State, so, as in war, not only such persons but all related or connected with them in any way must be put to death, to prevent anyone coming forward to avenge the death of their chief or head. The theory is that even infants are potential enemies, and the safest thing is to remove them forthwith. Among many cases of the kind that in Gardiner (*Journey to Zoolu Country*, pp. 44-47) might be cited as an example.

---

[1]*Grahamstown Journal*, 7th August, 1834.
   In the same paper of October, 1834, J. Collis writes, " The Governor (Dennis) a Swiss has been assassinated by the captain, second in command." He discredited the rumour that Dingane had put him to death.—*Editor*.

At the same time we can see how it was fast becoming more and more impossible for a despotically governed people to live alongside one governed on civilized lines without clashing. Open rupture may be deferred for years, but it is bound to come sooner or later. In the case of Dingane, it was deliberately precipitated by himself within about three years of the time in question. That was indeed the climax which already for years Fynn had seen and declared to be inevitable.

The desirability and even necessity of the settlement at Port Natal being formally recognised by the Home Government had for long been agitated by letter, by petition, as well as in the local press. As far back as September, 1824, Farewell, in a letter to the Governor of the Cape of Good Hope, referring to the extensive grant of land in the neighbourhood of Port Natal that Shaka had just made him, said: " I took possession of the country . . . . hoisted the English colours and fired a salute in the presence of Shaka's chiefs, which proceedings, I trust, will meet with your Lordship's approbation and sanction as well as that of the English Government."[1]

The Government would not, however, consent to identify themselves in any way with the settlement. In 1828, Shaka dispatched two ambassadors in charge of Capt. King to King George, " to negotiate a friendly alliance " between the two nations (English and Zulu). This mission, as we have seen, resulted in a fiasco. Yet a further mission was sent by Shaka the same year to the Governor. This time the Governor arranged for an officer to pay the Zulu King a visit, but before he could start, intelligence arrived of Shaka having been assassinated, when the proposed visit fell through.

Although Dingane was of a very different disposition to Shaka, he early saw the necessity of being on good terms with the British Government. He too, sent embassies for the purpose of cultivating friendly relations. One of these reached Grahamstown in November, 1830. In reporting on it, the Governor expressed a wish to send, with the sanction of the Secretary of State, " some person in whose judgement I can place full confidence . . . . to ascertain the real wishes of Dingane, the Zulu Chief, as well as the nature and capabilities of the country."

---

[1] Bird, *Annals of Natal*, I, 192.

Whether or no this wish was acceded to we know not. Anyhow, Dr. Andrew Smith, an officer of the Government, paid a visit early in 1832 to Natal as well as to Dingane, subsequently reporting, *inter alia*, that he firmly believed Dingane " would be ready and willing to enter into an alliance with the Colony."[1] In the meantime Mr. Saxe Bannister had been pressing the settlement on the notice of the Home Government. The same theme, from 1832 onwards, was repeatedly agitated in the *Grahamstown Journal* as well as in the *Cape Town Commercial Advertiser*.

To such an extent had public interest in Natal been aroused by January, 1834, that the resolutions passed at a meeting convened in Cape Town on the 20th of the month were embodied in a petition signed by 192 merchants and others.[2] This prayer, although accompanied by all the information Smith had been able to elicit on the spot, was refused by His Majesty's Government, on the ground that " in the present state of the finances of the Cape any additional expense for the establishment of a new settlement would be highly inconvenient, and could not with propriety be incurred."[3]

It was in September, 1834, that Fynn definitely severed his connection, for the time being, with Natal. He and his brother, William, thereupon took service under the Cape Government, then on the eve of the sixth Kaffir war. By this time his residence in Natal had extended over a period of ten and a half years. He was literally the first British settler in Natal, for he preceded even Farewell and Cane, also King, Hutton and Isaacs. More than this, his knowledge of the Zulu language; of native history, habits and customs; of Shaka in especial, of Dingane and Mpande; of countless other Zulu notabilities— princes, indunas, councillors, heroes, heads of kraals—in both reigns; to say nothing of the geography, fauna and flora of the country and adjoining territories, was unique and unrivalled.

His intimacy with the Zulu language, his travels on foot amongst the native people, his warm-hearted disposition, his unfailing humanity to those in distress, and in those hard times they were very numerous and everywhere in hiding, especially in Natal, were such that even in these days, even a century

---
[1] Bird, *Annals of Natal*, I, 263.
[2] Ibid., I, 253.
[3] Ibid., I, 273.

later, his name is held in honour throughout the length and breadth of the land. In these things he always was first.

A portion, and unfortunately only a comparatively small portion, of his experiences are set forth in the foregoing pages. But, though temporarily severing his connection with Natal—we say temporarily, for 17 years later he returned once more to the Garden Colony to pass the concluding ten years of his hard, strenuous, brave, honest, loyal and humane life—he continued to reside in parts of the old Colony near enough to maintain touch with the affairs of Zululand and Natal, i.e. a country he hoped one day to return to and die in.

If he was far removed in a physical sense, he was yet able to employ agencies most of us know little about to place and keep him in vital, continuous and effective contact with the general course of events. It is for this reason, whilst noting Fynn's departure from the scene of his earliest and most exciting adventures and adversities, that we feel justified in carrying on further our chronicle, so as at any rate to cover the next three important and little-known years, that is until we reach a time when the Emigrant Boers, under Retief, having arrived on the scenes, events began to occur in rapid succession, on a vaster and more significant scale, a more spectacular manner, and on a radically differing political basis.

Fynn became Headquarters Interpreter (i.e. to the Governor Sir Benjamin D'Urban) on the outbreak of hostilities. These had begun with a vast raid on Sunday, 21st December, 1834, when some 12,000 to 15,000 men, under Makome, Tyali, Mhala and other Xhosa chiefs, made their way across the Colonial border along its whole length from the Winterberg to the sea.

Without going into the wholesale and indiscriminate ravages committed by those hordes, and the military operations directed successfully against them by the Government, down to the conclusion of peace in May, it may be mentioned, incidentally, that in March, 1835, when war was at its height, Fynn proceeded by sea from Algoa Bay to Port Natal, by direction of the Governor, thence overland to the Umzimvuɓu, for the purpose of opening up communications with the Thembu and Mpondo paramount chiefs, whose people lived to the east of the Xhosas, and securing their neutrality, and, if possible, active assistance against the belligerents. Faku agreed to remain neutral but undertook to do no more than prevent the Xhosas from taking refuge in his district, and to seize any cattle that might be driven within his borders.

As for the Thembu chief, Vadana, he declared he was ready to give all the assistance in his power, and would place his warriors at the disposal of a British officer if the Governor chose to send one.[1] It is quite clear these negotiations owed their success largely to the assurances Fynn was able to give that neither Mpondos nor Thembus would be attacked by the Zulus. In other words his intimate knowledge of the situation in Zululand, and the messages he had, when passing through Natal, sent to Dingane acquainting him of the state of affairs, backed by great personal prestige among the natives along 300 or 400 miles of the south-east district, as well as his previous acquaintance with Faku, proved of substantial practical value at a critical moment. Gardiner, who paid Faku a visit at the end of July, wrote: " There is every reason to believe that had not Mr. Tainton, a local missionary, remained and Mr. Fynn arrived (with assurances from the Governor) he would have removed to the opposite side of the Umzimvuбu, under the apprehension that he was considered as an accomplice and should share the fate of the hostile amaXhosa."[2]

When Fynn and his brother withdrew from Natal (September, 1834) very few settlers remained, among them Cane, Ogle, Halstead, Collis and possibly F. Fynn, one of the author's younger brothers. There were, moreover, others (late arrivals), e.g. Richard Wood (in the employ of J. Collis), C. Blanckenberg, C. J. Pickman, Chas. Adams and J. Francis.

Dingane continued to employ appallingly harsh methods in ruling his people. For instance, during the same month, " it appears that one of his captains or chiefs had given him some umbrage, and the sequel was that, on the very common plea of having been detected in an illicit amour with one of his wives, he and all the persons composing his kraal or village were ordered to be put to death. Under this barbarous mandate, it is said between 3,000 and 4,000 souls were inhumanly massacred."[3]

---

[1]Theal, *History of South Africa*, 1834-54, 21.
[2]Gardiner, *Journey to the Zoolu Country*, 242.
[3]*Grahamstown Journal*, 30th October, 1834.
We have been unable to ascertain the name of this Induna or chief. Possibly Duбe of the Nyuswa (amaQadi) tribe is referred to.—*Editor*.

EPILOGUE

We have now reached a stage at which definite Christian influence began, for the first time, to bear on Dingane and his people. The conditions under which missionary work was attempted could hardly have been more difficult.

Unpropitious and discouraging as it was, that it came to be undertaken at all, under the auspices of the Church Missionary Society, was due primarily to the extraordinary enthusiasm, pertinacity and persuasiveness of an officer of the Royal Navy, Captain Allen Francis Gardiner.

Gardiner was born on the 28th June, 1794, and was the fifth son of Samuel Gardiner of Coombe Lodge in the county of Oxford. He entered the Naval College at Portsmouth in February, 1808. After a varied naval career, we find him visiting the Cape of Good Hope as a Lieutenant in the *Gannymede* in 1815, and yet again in the *Dauntless* in August, 1822. He was promoted to the rank of Commander in 1826, but opportunities for further employment in the service did not occur after this date.

" As a work into which he might throw his whole energy. . . . he chose that of a missionary pioneer." With this in view, he went to South Africa, reaching Cape Town in November, 1834. " He looked at the state of the Cape Colony, and saw it threatened by invasion from the Kaffirs. He knew that beyond these were the Zulus . . . . still unvisited by the messengers of the gospel. And there he resolved to go."[1]

On leaving Cape Town he proceeded overland to Grahamstown, reaching there on the 4th December. It was here that he made the acquaintance of Fynn, i.e. shortly before the latter's own voyage by sea to Natal, in connection with the Kaffir war, and from thence went overland to Faku, the Pondo chief. Gardiner reached Natal in January, 1835.

His first interview with Dingane took place in the following month. Of the presents he made to the King in accordance with local custom, that which was most prized was a red cloak.

" For the selection of this article, which was composed of red baize, with a long silky nap . . . . I am indebted to Mr. Fynn, who recommended it to me in Grahamstown, as a description of cloth in colour and texture more likely to please his Zulu Majesty than any other that could be procured, and

---
[1]Marsh, J. W., *Memoir of Allen F. Gardiner*, 49.

certainly no advice could have been more correctly given. No sooner was it opened than it was displayed in every possible manner; first on the King's shoulders, then on one of his servants, who was ordered to turn and twist about in all directions, that its every bearing and fold might be shown off to the best advantage; it was stretched to its widest extent and two men, holding it up at arm's length, were directed to run at full speed backwards and forwards, that he might witness its appearance while flowing in the air. At length for some minutes it was hung upon the fence opposite his own house, that the curiosity of the people who were viewing it from a distance might be satisfied. Strange to say, after all this display, he never wore it, but has had it carefully preserved ever since for the Grand National Assembly at the Feast of the First Fruits, which takes place annually about the first week in January. In the evening I received the important information, by special messenger, that it was neither too long nor too short, but exactly suited."[1]

Nearly a month elapsed without any progress being made in what Gardiner had so much at heart, viz. the religious instruction of the people, although he assured the King that " any intention to interfere with either their laws or their customs was the farthest removed from his thoughts."[2] At last, on 7th March, Dingane's induna, Dambuza, stated definitely that they did not wish for teaching, that they could never learn, and that such words as he (Gardiner) had spoken they were sure they could not understand. If, however, he would instruct them in the use of the musket he might stay. Ndlela, the principal induna, supported his colleague, whereupon Dingane, upon being appealed to by both indunas to decide, said simply: " I will not overrule the decision of my indunas,"[3] and there, for the time being, the matter ended.

On his getting back to the port, the settlers, whilst regretting Gardiner's unfavourable reception, assured him that " the presence of a missionary establishment at Natal would meet with all the support in their power." Gardiner thereupon selected a site, on high ground overlooking the Bay, for a missionary station which he named Berea, " since notwith-

---
[1]Gardiner, *Journey to the Zoolu Country*, 67.
[2]Ibid., 68.
[3]Ibid., 68.

standing my ill-success with Dingane the Word has been gladly received."[1] About this time it was rumoured that the Zulus were meditating an attack on the settlement. A public meeting of the settlers was convened, when it was decided to defend instead of temporarily abandoning the place. A stockade was accordingly erected round a wattled house, for the protection of the settlement. In consequence of the many Zulu men, women and children who, at different times, had taken refuge at the port, and the frequent threats of reprisal by Dingane, which had recently become more alarming, a meeting of the European inhabitants was held on 25th April " to devise some plan for our mutual security."[2] It was unanimously resolved that, " as this appeared to be a favourable opportunity, a treaty based on the following terms should, if possible, be entered into with Dingane, viz. provided he will guarantee the lives and property of every individual, white and black, now residing at Port Natal, we on our part, engage to repel with all our power, and never more to receive any deserter from his dominions; and immediately to acquaint him of the circumstance, should any of his people elude our vigilance."[3] It was at the same time agreed that no deserters should be given up until some arrangement of this nature had met with his sanction. Gardiner was requested to negotiate this treaty. Leaving on the 28th, he reached Khangela, the kraal at which the King was then living, on 4th May. Dingane at once entered into the plan. He undertook " never to molest any of his subjects now at Natal for past offences; said he should keep his word, but knew the white people would be the first to break the treaty."[4] In short, he eagerly and whole-heartedly accepted the proposed treaty, which was thereupon reduced to writing and duly signed on both sides. Dambuza now explained that " the reason we did not let you remain before was because we did not know you—we wished you to go back and bring such ' a word ' as you have now done. That news has made our hearts glad (alluding to the terms of the treaty); now we wish

---

[1] Gardiner, *Journey to the Zoolu Country*, 80.
[2] Ibid., 108.
[3] Ibid., *Journey to the Zoolu Country*, 108.
[4] Ibid., 127.

you to stay; and where you are to teach is in the Hlomendlini (district)[1]. . . . you may teach in all the towns there."

Dingane inquired the object of Fynn's visit to Faku, upon which Gardiner explained the position. A few days later the King asked him to transmit the following message to the Governor of the Cape Colony: " Mr. Fynn sent me the news about the amaXhosa. I am grieved to think they should act so against the white people—those people whom I love. I have long let the amaXhosas alone. It is a pity the white people trouble themselves with them—they should leave them to me. I hope they will not destroy them all; if they do there will be only a desert left."[2] Fynn, no doubt, had wisely taken the opportunity of sending the above message when passing through Natal en route to Pondoland.

Dingane placed on Gardiner the responsibility of seeing that the white settlers observed the treaty. Gardiner on his way back to Natal learned that two women, one man and three children had recently deserted and probably gone off to Natal. He, moreover, had already agreed to surrender to Dingane a man who shortly before had fled to Natal. After some trouble all these deserters were secured and subsequently conveyed to Dingane by Gardiner in person. Dingane was naturally delighted. " Now," he exclaimed, " we see that you (Gardiner) belong to the Zulus." " Now," he went on, " his people would love him, whereas before they had hated him, because he refused to permit an army to go down to Port Natal: that for two years the chiefs had been urging him to destroy all the black people there, but that he had withheld his consent . . . . Now he was convinced that the white people at Port Natal wished to do him good."[3] The next evening the principal indunas came to inform Gardiner that the King had made him a present of 12 head of oxen, to be considered as a token of his gratitude, for having concluded a treaty with him; that, as such a " fast word " had passed between them, it was right that there should be something to show, as a proof that it had been accepted on both sides. Gardiner would that day be " received into the

---

[1]This district, spoken of as Hlomendlini, including uHlomendlin'omhlophe and uHlomendlin'omnyama, fell within the Thukela and Amatigulu Rivers and extended some 35 miles up the left bank.—*Editor.*

[2]Gardiner, *Journey to the Zoolu Country*, 139.

[3]Ibid., 162.

country and the oxen would be token to all of what Dingane had done; that he was not yet tired, but would do more hereafter. . . . It was not the King only who thanked him that day; it was the whole Zulu nation."[1] It is quite clear that, by proposing and, later on, faithfully observing the provisions of the treaty, Gardiner found the real and readiest way to Dingane's heart. This question of desertion, ignored by Shaka, had by this time begun to assume formidable proportions. Indeed it was of paramount importance. Drastic action of some kind was fast becoming imperative, for the despot's authority was obviously being undermined, which, of course, Dingane was certain to resist to the utmost of his power. What despot ever beheld the sapping of the foundations of his position without striking a blow in self-defence? Of course there had been numerous desertions in Dingane's reign, far more than in Shaka's, chiefly as a result of his ruthless policy of exterminating Shaka's favourites in the fond belief that a perfectly happy and peaceful reign would be the result. Ngwadi, Nqetho, Zihlandlo, Magaye, and Mdlaka were among those favourites.

In addition to this he actually made a point of putting nearly all his brothers to death, one by one. Gardiner tells us of one of these very executions, viz. a man known personally to himself, whom he calls Goujana, though probably meant for Ngqojana. In all these cases, notably Zihlandlo and Magaye, there were survivors, who, if they did not make off to the Colony or Mzilikazi or elsewhere, promptly placed themselves under the protection of one or other of the settlers in Natal. Thus, unless Dingane was able to massacre not only a chief but every one of his dependants, the survivors, by joining the British settlers, must be regarded as inimical and therefore as determined on revenging the death of their relations at the first favourable opportunity. Thus the European settlement, in the eyes of Dingane, was objectionable, not only because an *imperium in imperio* but because it harboured many that could confidently be assumed to have vowed everlasting vengeance against himself and as constantly plotting to bring about his downfall. Hitherto the only course that seemed to offer a possible solution was the fatal one of using force, i.e. taking the bull by the horns, and attempt to massacre every soul in the

---

[1]Gardiner, *Journey to the Zoolu Country*, 171-2.

settlement, white and black. That this was actually contemplated on at least three occasions has already appeared. The principal difficulty in the way of destroying the settlement was, however, that at least all the white men and all their Hottentots were in possession of muskets, a difficulty that tended to become more and more insuperable as time went on. Besides this it was always possible for people to take refuge in the surrounding dense bush at a moment's notice. Thus Gardiner's proposal was at once propitious and providential; it was exactly what Dingane wanted. He therefore jumped at it, but, as the despot himself correctly surmised, " the white people would be the first to break the treaty," thereby rendering it nugatory. It was indeed broken and surprisingly soon. How this came about will presently appear.

On the 23rd June, a meeting attended by 16 of the settlers was held for the purpose of selecting the site of the town. The site was decided on the same day. It lay between the so-called River Avon on the west and Buffalo Spring on the east. The Avon is no doubt the Umbilo River, whilst Buffalo Spring, near the landing place in Lieut. J. S. King's chart of Port Natal to be found in Isaacs, is where ships formerly drew fresh water.

The name D'Urban (after the Governor of the Cape of Good Hope) was given to the town. A list of subscriptions, " for the purpose of clearing the bush, and other necessary improvements to the town and township of D'Urban," was opened, a suitable set of regulations drawn up, and a Town Committee of householders (not exceeding 13 in number nor less than five) and other officers were appointed to see that the regulations were duly conformed to. The town lands were to extend for four miles inland and include Salisbury Island; each of the then inhabitants of Natal was entitled to a building plot; every person taking an allotment undertook to erect a house of specified dimentions within 18 months; no Kaffir hut or straw building was to be erected in the township, except for the temporary use of labourers engaged in building; every holder, on taking possession, to pay a sum of 7s. 6d. to the Treasurer; 3,000 acres on the River Avon (Umbilo) were reserved for the endowment of a clergyman of the Church of England, and a separate subscription list opened to collect funds up to £500 for the erection of a church, Sir B. D'Urban and Captain Gardiner heading the list with £50 each. A lot was reserved for a school, with 2,000 acres at Umlazi River for its support; provision was also made for a hospital, cemetery, etc.

The members of the first Town Council were Captain A. F. Gardiner, J. Collis, F. Berkin, J. Cane and H. Ogle. A petition signed by 30 residents was at the same time transmitted to the Governor of the Cape Colony, praying that it might please His Majesty to recognise the country between the Umzimkhulu and Thukela Rivers, "which we have named Victoria in honour of our august Princess," as a colony of the British Empire and to appoint a Governor and Council, etc. It was pointed out that the number of natives at the settlement at that time could not be less than 3,000. Though Fynn was now living in the Cape Colony, he subscribed liberally to both the Church and the Town funds.

The first complaint as to infringement of the treaty arose within a bare two months of its being entered into, in connection with two European traders, Halstead and Snelder, who, whilst trading in Zululand, misconducted themselves, e.g. by persuading Zulus, particularly young women, to desert, which they did by concealing themselves in the waggons, thereafter being conveyed by stealth to Port Natal. Dingane naturally became highly incensed. He peremptorily ordered one of these men to leave the country; at the same time he prohibited all further trade with Natal, and directed that, with the exception of Gardiner and his interpreter, no white person was in future to cross the Thukela.[1]

When the offenders reported to Gardiner what had occurred, the latter felt it his duty personally to ascertain as soon as possible the position from Dingane himself. He therefore proceeded once more to Zululand, when Dingane declared that Snelder[2] had induced two young Zulus to accompany him to Natal; that Halstead had falsely informed the induna of the Zulu kraal at which he had been trading that his disposing of his cattle to him (the induna) was being done with the King's permission and that the traders generally were inducing his people to desert; indeed, he felt he could not depend on them, because they had so often deceived him.

---

[1]Gardiner, *Journey to the Zoolu Country*, 192.
[2]According to G. Cyrus, Gardiner's interpreter, David Stiller (Steller) was the man charged with this offence.—*Editor*.

Dingane then said he would from henceforth look on Gardiner as chief of the white people, and therefore personally responsible for the due observance of the treaty. Gardiner pointed out he had no power. " You must have power," said the King, " I give you all the country called Siбuбulungu. You must be chief over all the people there." Gardiner saw that, under the circumstances, nothing could be done without the active support of the Governor, to gain which it became necessary for him to visit the Colony. An officer, he felt, with adequate power and authority should be appointed on the spot to enforce the treaty and generally regulate and control the the affairs of the settlement.

Though he reached Durban on the 17th July we find him on the 20th starting off on horseback on an overland journey to Cape Town some 800 miles away. And so the granting of an application to establish mission stations in Zululand was made by Dingane to depend on the not unreasonable condition that the British settlement at Natal be duly organized and efficiently controlled. That is, Dingane saw that the time had arrived for creating a British Colony in Natal and actually gave Gardiner authority to do so.

The next stage, of course, was to induce the British Government to accept the responsibility and take steps accordingly, tasks which, curiously, Gardiner found it impossible to carry out, notwithstanding that both the United States and the Emigrant Boers of the Cape had already in view the possibility of converting these regions, the most favoured in South Africa, into a country of their own.

Now, as we have seen, war had broken out between the Xhosas under Hintsa and the Cape Colony in December, 1834. These people and their allies occupied territory between the Fish River and the Bashee River. Peace was concluded with Hintsa's son and successor Krcli (Sarili) on the 19th May, but for several months after this parts of this extensive district remained so unsettled, notwithstanding the peace with the Xhosas, that small European parties travelling through the country were liable to be attacked and destroyed; indeed, more than one was destroyed. Such, briefly, was the state of affairs when Gardiner reached Buntingville, a Methodist mission station planted between the Umthatha and the Umzimvuбu (St. John's) Rivers. He made every effort to proceed, even proposing to Faku that his army (which Gardiner was prepared to accompany) should make " a sudden and rapid march to the Kei, without turning to the right hand or to the left. . . . On reaching the English troops they would meet with the most friendly reception."

As, however, Faku had other ideas, the suggestion fell through. He then visited Ncaphayi, in the hope of procuring guides to conduct him by an inland route. Ncaphayi is, it will be remembered, the chief who, early in 1830, succeeded in finally routing Nqetho and taking possession of his cattle. Here again, Gardiner met with disappointment. The chief declined to provide guides, " as should anything happen, the blame would probably be attributed to him."

In these circumstances, all that remained was to return to Natal, and this Gardiner did, reaching there during September. " On the arrival of my waggon " (on the 15th), he says, " preparations were commenced for a journey across the Khahlamba[1] mountains, it being now my intention to endeavour to reach the Colony by that route, every other being completely closed; and, after communicating with His Excellency, to proceed directly to England, in the hope of procuring missionaries to occupy the stations now formed."[2]

He left the port on the 24th of the same month, with two waggons, accompanied by Ogle, his interpreter George Cyrus, his driver Dick King[3] and one other European Wyngart. He reached the Drakensberg by a route that passed near where the towns of Richmond and Bulwer were subsequently built, and on 10th October, being unable to discover a practicable pass for waggons through the mountains, moved downwards towards the mouth of the Umzimvuбu, only to make his way once more to Buntingville, the place he had left in August to get back to Natal. This time, however, he succeeded in getting through to Cape Town and, sailing from there in the *Liverpool* on 19th December, reached England in February, 1836.

But other people besides Gardiner were beginning to be interested in sending forth missionaries to the Zulus. The attention of the American Board of Commissioners for Foreign

---

[1] Drakensberg.—*Editor.*
[2] Gardiner, *Journey to the Zoolu Country*, 302.
[3] Who subsequently became famous because of his great ride from Durban to Grahamstown.—*Editor.*

Missions, for instance, had been drawn to the matter, probably by the Rev. Dr. Philip, superintendent of the London Society's Missions in South Africa, with the result that six men were sent out, three to Zululand and Natal, and the rest to Mzilikazi's territory. All reached Cape Town in February, 1835. Those destined for Natal, viz. Messrs. Alden Grout, George Champion and Dr. Newton Adams, M.D., were obliged to wait for some months in Cape Town and later at Algoa Bay, as the overland route via Grahamstown and Bunting could not be used on account of the Kaffir war.

They eventually reached Natal in the *Dove* in December, 1835. Arrangements were then made for visiting Dingane to obtain permission to settle and carry on mission work in the country. They reached Mgungundlovu on the 16th January, 1836.[1] As in the case of Gardiner, the application was referred by Dingane to his indunas. The latter " feared evils from the introduction of white men into their country, and wished the line of the whites to be beyond the Thukela." However, the end of the matter was that permission was granted; they were told they might begin in the Hlomendlini district (i.e. the area within which Gardiner's Culula station had already been established). This district took its name from two large military barracks of that name, built by Dingane within 15 miles of one another. One of these, the more important, was called White Hlomendlini (omhlophe) and the other Black Hlomendlini (ommyama). The word itself means " arm oneself indoors."

" And then," said the King, " if you succeed I will bring the school right into the heart of my dominions. I will learn myself, and set an example to my people."[2] The station established in the Hlomendlini district was called Nginani (I am with you). It was eight miles north of the Thukela River, about the same distance from the sea, and on a small river called Msunduze. Mr. Champion, who was first designated to this place, began work there on 26th September, 1836.[3]

In view of the fact that this was the first American mission station established in Zululand, the following account of its inception will be perused with more than ordinary interest.

---

[1]Bird, *Annals of Natal*, I, 201.
[2]Ibid., *Annals of Natal*, I, 207.
[3]Ibid., 209.

"When we arrived," says Champion, who was accompanied by his wife, " on 21st April, 1837, we immediately commenced some rude dwellings of stone and mud, the only materials easily obtained, meanwhile abiding in tents. . . . Two or three months even elapsed before these were completed, so little assistance could we derive from the unskilled natives, and so many were our other avocations, such as journeyings to the King, etc. And then our houses—with not a board or a straight piece of timber in them, 30 feet by ten, with earth floors, naked walls and grass roofs, and doors and windows of weeds and grass (resembling perhaps more a stable at home than a dwelling house)—would doubtless be objects of wonder to new-comers from civilized lands; but they were to us, compared with the dirty native huts around us, truly places of comfort. . . . Meanwhile a cattle fold and calf house must be constructed; a smith's shop was in progress, and various other things were done, necessary to our beginning to live among this people."[1]

Obviously it was Gardiner's energetic and persistent pioneering work that had prepared the way for this remarkably favourable reception.[2] Without that assistance the Americans would no doubt have met with a rebuff at the outset, just as Gardiner himself had done, whilst the thorny question of deserters from Zululand, unless tackled in the resolute way Gardiner had done, would have stood indefinitely in the way of their application being granted. It is easy to decry or belittle what Gardiner did, but it is equally easy to realise that, but for him, the American Mission would not have been allowed to start when it did; if allowed indeed, at that time, in the country at all. The poison injected by Jacob into Dingane's mind had by no means worked itself out. It was because Dingane regarded those missionaries, in common with all other white people at Natal as under Gardiner, and amenable to his control, that he was prepared to treat them in so liberal a spirit. What assurance, for instance, had he, apart from Gardiner's own promise, that a treaty of such vital importance to his position would be carried out ?

---

[1] *Missionary Herald* (American Board of Commissioners for Foreign Missions) for the year 1838, p. 31.
[2] It was in consequence of the agreement between Captain Gardiner and Dingane that they were permitted to enter.—Marsh, J. W., *Memoir of Allen F. Gardiner*, p. 98.

It is true that Gardiner went away just at this moment and for no less than 19 months, but Dingane was quite prepared to let matters remain in abeyance until his return, particularly, as will presently be seen, as the Governor of the Cape Colony informed Dingane he not only approved of the treaty but would send an officer to Durban as *locum tenens*, during Gardiner's absence.

In a general letter by Champion, Grout and Adams, dated August, 1836, published in their mission periodical, the missionaries express themselves thus: "The Chief (i.e. Dingane) no doubt has erroneous ideas in regard to our work, but we believe him to be a reasonable man in many respects. *We believe that if flourishing schools were formed in this country, they would give us at once access to his confidence, and access to the whole country with the words of salvation.* Without the approval of the King, nothing can be done; with his word, everything—according to Zulu notions. Thus you see that much, perhaps all, of our future success may depend upon a right beginning. The King is aware that ours is a work of time, but still he will be looking for immediate fruit."

The words we have italicised are, we venture to think, of paramount importance when dealing with uncivilised people like the Zulus. It is the visible, homely or concrete, not the invisible, alien, or abstract that appeals at once to their intellect and imagination. The fact that 99% of their everyday conversations, as also of their nursery tales, proverbs, metaphors, songs, oratory, eulogies, prayers to departed spirits and so forth are concrete in form and phraseology surely gives us the right clue for gaining access to their minds with ideas familiar enough to ourselves but utterly foreign to their nature; surely, then, the true starting point in the work of converting the people must be with what appeals to the eye and the other senses rather than to other merely embryonic and undeveloped faculties or instincts that are or may be within them. Until, therefore, we become as little Zulu children themselves, we shall find it impossible to lead them into the Kingdom of Heaven.

Bishop Gray, who visited Natal in 1850, and Bishop Colenso, who arrived a few years later, realised the value of this mode of procedure, for, in February, 1856, we find that with the strong influence and assistance of Mr. Shepstone, Secretary of

Native Affairs, "nineteen young Kaffir children were brought by their friends to Ekukhanyeni, and delivered formally up into the hands of the Bishop (Colenso) for education, by the chiefs Ngoza and Zatshuke. By April, 1857, the number had grown to 33, all but two of whom were sons of chiefs or captains, the headmen of their tribes."[1]

It so happened that the other three American missionaries, Messrs. D. Lindley, H. J. Venable and A. E. Wilson, who proceeded to Mzilikazi's country from Cape Town were unable to establish themselves at Mzilikazi's kraal in Mosiga valley on account of hostilities that had broken out between him and a division of the Emigrant Boers. The Boers, under Maritz and Potgieter, attacked Mosiga on the 17th January, 1837, killing 400 of the Matabele, without loss to themselves, besides recovering waggons and about 6,000 cattle that had recently been seized from their murdered compatriots. The missionaries and their families then retired with the Boers, only, however, to make their way via Cape Town to join their comrades in Natal, reaching there at the end of July.

In addition to the station Nginani in the Hlomendlini district, permission was subsequently given for another, some five or six miles from the military barracks Dlangezwa, on high ground on the left-hand side and overlooking the Mhlathuze River. It was at this post, called Themba (trust), that Venable and Wilson then began to be employed.

An army comprising all the strength of the country was sent by Dingane in June, 1836, to attack Sobuza, King of the Swazis,[2] whose country lay some 150 miles to the north-east of Mgungundlovu. It was in connection with this campaign that Gardiner afterwards (June, 1837) wrote thus: "the whole of the British inhabitants with three or four exceptions have voluntarily joined the Zulu army and by means of their firearms killed and wounded numbers of his enemies, for which they have been handsomely rewarded with the cattle they have captured."[3]

The following account is by William Wood, an eyewitness, soon to be heard of in another connection: "Dingane's principal messenger acquainted us that it was the King's order

---
[1] Grout, *Zululand*, 280-1.
[2] Bird, *Annals of Natal*, I, 210, 378.
[3] Ibid., 320.

that the English at Natal should arm themselves and come to him at Mgungundlovu, as he wished to send them against an enemy who had robbed him, and who had placed himself in such a position that the King's troops were of no avail in capturing him, and firearms alone could be effectual. . . .

When the residents at Port Natal were acquainted with Dingane's order they made preparations for fulfilling them; and when they had mustered as many as they could bring together, their strength consisted of about 30 English residents, amongst whom were John Cane (who commanded the party), Thomas Halstead, Richard Wood (my father) Richard King, Robert Russel, Thomas Carden, Richard Lovedale and William Kew; also about 40 Zulus, all of whom were armed with guns. Having arrived at a small hill which rises at the back of Dingane's kraal, they fired a salute, upon which the King was greatly alarmed, and sent a messenger to ask them what they meant by firing. They said it was customary for all kings and great men to receive such tokens of respect from those who carried arms. This answer dissipated the King's fears, and he sent them an invitation to come into his kraal and refresh themselves, which they did. Next day they started in search of the enemy, reinforced by a large body of Dingane's troops, commanded by Ndlela. Having travelled some days they arrived in the vicinity of the Phongolo mountains, where a party of Sobuza's people were posted, and, lest these should discover that Ndlela had Europeans with him, they covered the English with their shields while ascending the mountain. Sobuza's people had taken up a very good position on the top of a hill, immediately over, and commanding the entrance to, a natural cavern in which they placed the cattle they had captured from Dingane. By rolling down large stones, they had for some days prevented the approach of a party of Dingane's troops who had before attempted to recapture the cattle.

The nearest approach which could be made with safety was by ascending a small hill opposite. This the party did, and found themselves separated from Sobuza's people by a deep gulph (gulley ?) at the bottom of which ran the Phongolo River. As they were within speaking distance, John Cane, who commanded the Europeans, told them to deliver up the cattle which they had taken from the King, or he would fire upon them, adding that it was useless of them to resist, for as

Dingane himself had taken the trouble to come so far to get his cattle, he was determined to have them.

On hearing this, Sobuza's people made no reply, but turned their backs on them in token of contempt. John Cane's party then fired a volley over their heads and he again begged them to agree to his demand, and told them that if they delivered up the cattle he would allow them and their wives and children, who were still with them, to depart unharmed. They still returned no answer, and he then fired at them and shot three or four. Cane repeated his demand, but they treated them in the same manner, upon which his party again fired and shot some more of them. A Zulu woman[1] was then seen to approach the brink of the precipice leading a boy of about 12 or 13 years of age by the hand, and having an infant fastened at her back. Looking towards the Europeans, she cried out: ' I will not be killed by thunder, but will kill myself,' saying which, she pushed the boy over the precipice and jumped in herself after him.

The firing continued until the party cried out for mercy, and promised to give up the cattle, which John Cane sent a number of men round to receive. He then distributed a few head amongst them, and commenced his journey to Mgungundlovu."[2]

As soon as Gardiner got to England he arranged for the publication of a highly interesting journal he had been in the habit of keeping whilst in South Africa. The work, entitled *Narrative of a Journey to the Zoolu Country in South Africa*, appeared in or about September, 1836. It was well received by the Press; the *Christian Observer*, however, took strong exception to the treaty, copy of which, as well as a detailed account of the surrender by Gardiner of the refugees, already referred to herein, having been inserted in the work. "A British Officer," said the *Observer*, "should not have acknowledged his (Dingane's) tyrannical right to prevent any of his subjects emigrating from his dominions, and still less have agreed to capture them, and send them back to torture and death. It is a picture so sickening and revolting that we lay the book down with pain and regret. . . . It is a treaty of blood, and

---

[1] The writer probably means a Swazi woman, against whom the expedition had been sent, for Sobuza was King of Swaziland.—*Editor*.
[2] Wood, William, statements respecting *Dingaan, King of the Zulus*, etc., in part reprinted in Bird's *Annals of Natal*, I, 376, 387.

blood has already cemented it. . . . Captain Gardiner, it is understood, intends on his return to uphold and enforce this abominable treaty—a treaty with a tiger ! Why had he not rather said to Dingane: ' Cut off my head and attack, burn and destroy our settlement, if indeed you dare to do so in the face of British retributive justice, and what is more, of the anger of God, rather than I will be the individual to lead fugitive children and unoffending men and women to be slaughtered in your execrable den. The Lord of Hosts is with us; the God of Jacob is our refuge.' "[1]

Gardiner, of course, replied to this hysterical criticism[2] pointing out that " the whole gist of the argument hinges upon the gratuitous supposition that the Europeans at Port Natal were independent of the Zulu King at the period when the treaty in question was agreed upon. Far otherwise was the case. The simple circumstances were these: 30 European adventurers voluntarily locate themselves within the territory and jurisdiction of the Zoolu King. In the course of time many of his refractory subjects (from whatever cause it matters not) find their way to this settlement, and place themselves under the protection of the foreigners. Jealousy and dissatisfaction naturally spring up between the two parties—the Zoolu King soon becomes irritated, and his chiefs, clamorous for revenge, demands and threats alternate, till, foiled in the accomplishment of their purpose, the insult can no longer be borne; retribution is demanded, and the summary extirpation of the whole native population, amounting to no less than 3,000, is determined. Such a crisis had occurred, and was actually impending, when the treaty in question was framed, and that with the sole object of averting the attack. . . . Had we been independent of Dingane, had there been at that time any recognised authority at Port Natal, the case would have been wholly altered, and the condition of restoring deserters would never have been contemplated. Situated as we were, his demand was just and our compliance equally obligatory, unless we were willing either to join the rebels or to abandon the remaining 3,000 to their merciless, but no less rightful sovereign, and his exterminating soldiers. . . . I have already received

---

[1] *South African Commercial Advertiser*, 22nd March, 1837.
[2] His letter addressed to the Editor of *The Record* was dated, Hampstead, 4th October, 1836.—*Editor*.

the thanks of many, both black and white, who, shielded by this much maligned treaty, have escaped the midnight flames and the Zoolu spear. . . ." Among those knowing the state of affairs in Natal better than the Editor of the *Christian Observer*, and approved the treaty, was no other than Sir Benjamin D'Urban, Governor of the Cape of Good Hope. In a communication His Excellency transmitted to Dingane in December, 1835, he said: " I rejoice to hear of the good word which has passed between the Chief and Captain Gardiner and of the treaty concluded between them for the town and people of Port Natal." The Governor went on to intimate that a British Officer " would speedily be sent to Port Natal to be in authority there in the place of Captain Gardiner, until his return, and to communicate with the Chief, Dingane, upon all matters concerning the people of Natal."[1]

Apart from soliciting the British Government to take possession of and annex Natal, Gardiner, when in England, got in touch with the Church Missionary Society with a view to their undertaking a mission to the Zulus. Now, before leaving England in 1834, he had already made known his object to the Committee of the Church Missionary Society, and expressed his desire that they should undertake a mission to the aborigines of South Africa. Though the Committee did not feel at liberty to hold out any prospect of their complying with his wish, they expressed their readiness to receive any information he might be able to communicate to them.[2] On getting back to England, then, he wrote to the Society on 1st March, 1836. He says, *inter alia* : " It has pleased God to open a way whereby the Gospel of Christ may obtain an effectual entrance among the Zulus. . . . A whole province has at length been thrown open, and the instruction of children in every part of the district. Both in this province, called Hlomendlini, and at Port Natal, a missionary station has been formed, and buildings erected for the purpose; and from the impossibility of procuring a missionary, I have been engaged for some time in instructing the natives, who attend with great intelligence, and even send their children to the school without solicitation or prejudice. . . . Permission was first granted to

---

[1] Gardiner, *Journey to the Zoolu Country*, 394.
[2] *Church Missionary Record for* 1836, VII, 68.

teach in the Hlomendlini province on the 10th of May, 1835, and the mission was opened on the 24th . . . To occupy the ground already open, not less than six missionaries are absolutely necessary, viz. one at Port Natal, three in the Zulu country, and two among the Inhlangwini (tribe) amounting altogether to about 8,000.

Some progress has already been made in translating the New Testament into the Zulu tongue. Mr. Fynn,[1] the only competent person in South Africa, having kindly undertaken that work; and I trust there will soon be a considerable portion prepared for publication. . . .

The proposition which I would make to your committee is that you would accept the land and buildings at Berea and Culula as they now stand, and take the whole management of the missions into your own hands. Berea, consisting at present of a school-house, dwelling house, and four large huts, stands upon a plot of ground of at least two square miles in extent, fertile in every part, and guaranteed in perpetuity, as the exclusive property of the missionary establishment.

At Culula, three huts only have as yet been erected; and the whole hill, with fine stream of water at its base, and as much more land as may be necessary for cultivation, has been given over to the station by Dingane himself."

In consequence of these representations, the Church Missionary Society designated the Rev. Francis Owen to Mgungundlovu, the instructions of the Committee being delivered to him on the 8th November, 1836. Shortly after this a second missionary was sent to Zululand, viz. the Rev. H. Hewetson. Owen, with Mrs. Owen and his sister, sailed for South Africa in the *Palmyra* on 24th December, 1836. Gardiner accompanied the party, which reached Cape Town on 2nd March. Gardiner arrived in Natal on 24th May, whilst Owen, travelling overland by waggon from Algoa Bay, did not do so until the beginning of August.

During Gardiner's protracted absence, apart from the advent of the American missionaries in December, 1835, and other matters already noticed, there had been various developments in Natal and Zululand. The state of affairs among the European settlers, through lack of effective control, was rapidly

---

[1] This, of course, refers to the author of this Diary.—*Editor.*

becoming chaotic and even suicidal. Something of this is reflected in an outspoken denunciatory letter addressed by no fewer than 14 of them on 27th November, 1836, to the *Grahamstown Journal*, from which the following extracts are taken. " On the return of the Commando which volunteered in consequence of Dingane calling the whites to his assistance,[1] Mr. Blanckenberg remained at the King's palace on the pretext of having important affairs with His Majesty. He shortly afterwards returned to Natal with 30 to 40 head of cattle when it transpired that the greater part of these were the produce of a sale effected by him to Dingane of a new elephant gun. In a few days after his arrival he forwarded to the King a supply of powder and lead, with a boy to cast the balls at the King's residence. The great price obtained for the gun induced Messrs. Lake and Isaacs to follow his example. They have since sold to Dingane four elephant guns, with a proportionate supply of ammunition. Mr. R. Biggar (clerk here for Messrs. Maynard and Norden), on a late journey to the King's also sold a double-barrelled percussion elephant gun for six elephants' teeth. Mr. P. Kew, who has been tailoring for Dingane, has also, according to his own accounts, made Dingane a present of two guns. And there are reports of one or two Hottentots following his example, and of another Hottentot, John Brouwer, being on the road to Natal to repair six guns belonging to Dingane. Mr. C. Blanckenberg asserted he was, in a measure, compelled to let the King have his gun, but Dingane complains that the gun was in a way forced upon him. Mr. R. Biggar states that the gun was not his own, but he introduced the gun to Dingane and explained its superiority over the other guns. On Dingane asking the price, he replied it was not his but another man's, who wanted six elephants' teeth for it. This man was his younger brother. The gun remains with Dingane, and Mr. R. Biggar has received the elephants' teeth.

Previous to late events, confidence of security was increasing from the number of guns amongst us, say from 200 to 300 stand of arms, but, at present, the minds of the natives are completely alienated, who observe that if the whites will supply

---

[1] Referring no doubt to the expedition against Sobuza of Swaziland, about August–September, 1836.—*Editor*.

their inveterate enemy with guns, etc., for a few pounds of ivory, or a few head of cattle, how can they be assured that their lives may not as readily be bartered away.

Dingane has recently taken by force from Mr. D. Steller and party six guns. On being applied to for their return, he complained that the party, in defiance of repeated orders, persisted in hunting on his reserve elephant ground, adding: ' I have given the whites from the Imslatense[1] River to the Umzimvoobo to shoot in, which is surely large enough, but if they come and kill all my elephants, where shall I procure ivory to purchase things of them ? ' He therefore detains the guns till the arrival of Captain Gardiner.

Owing to the escape of some fugitives, a man and a woman, he has again interdicted trading and shooting, and has sent orders to the American missionaries, who are forming a station on the other side of the Thukela River,[2] not on any account to harbour or shelter, on any pretext, the people of Natal. The man who escaped was apprehended by Mr. John Stubbs, but effected his escape from one of Mr. Cane's villages, so that, to exonerate themselves, there is little doubt of the messengers[3] endeavouring to impute it to the whites. . . .

Dingane seems to place every hope on the arrival of Captain Gardiner. Should that gentleman be unfortunately delayed in England, which we begin to fear is the case, and this letter meet the eye of the Colonial Government, we do fervently hope that they will feel convinced of the imperious necessity of speedily sending some authority here, invested with power to preserve order and restore confidence till Captain Gardiner's arrival, and thereby avert that crisis which such conduct, if persisted in, cannot, in our opinion, fail speedily to produce."[4]

Further light is thrown on the traffic in firearms by the following piece: " The traders trading with Dingane in guns and powder are becoming rich—but they have hit on a happy expedient of cheating the Chief, who has at last discovered the roguery. They sell him guns, but before delivering them

---

[1] By this probably Mhlathuze is meant.—*Editor.*
[2] That is, Nginani.—*Editor.*
[3] That is, Dingane's—to whom the refugee had been handed over.—*Editor.*
[4] The signatories hereto were : John Cane, Henry Ogle, L. Carden, W. Bottomly, Thomas Lidnell, Charles Adams, Henry Batt, Richard Wood, J. D. Steller, G. White, Robert Russel, C. J. Pickman, Joseph Brown, F. Halstead.—*Editor.*

they take either the mainspring out of the lock, or some screw, which renders the gun useless."[1]

In the meantime Dingane continued to rule his own people with inveterate and despotic severity, resorting to the foulest forms of treachery as often as it appeared that other devices were unlikely to succeed. A remarkable illustration of his iniquitous practice is afforded by the case of Duɓe, chief of the Qadi tribe, an account of which has never been published, so far as we are aware. This case is not as well known by Europeans as it deserves to be, if only because it shows that the despot could behave as villainously towards his own people as he subsequently did to foreigners, viz. Piet Retief and his party. Indeed, in trying to appreciate the mysterious enormity of wrong done to Retief and his men, we cannot do better than study what was done to others on previous as well as subsequent occasions. For it is not isolated but habitual conduct that shows the man.

In a district of Zululand, lying along the left bank of the Thukela and opposite to the well-known mountain Ntunjambili (or Kranskop), there lived a large tribe called Qadi, an offshoot of still older and more famous tribes called Nyuswa and Ngcoɓo. The Qadi at the moment in question were living quietly under their chief Duɓe, the son of Lilwane. For some reason or other Manqondo, an aristocrat of the Magwaza tribe, offshoot of Langeni—the one Shaka's mother belonged to, went, presumably with followers, to occupy ground between Duɓe's area and the River Thukela, thereby making it impossible for Duɓe or his people to reach the river, except by traversing Manqondo's holding. Now, it so happened that the Thukela was the boundary between Dingane's country and that of the white people—Natal. " Why," said Duɓe, " does Manqondo go and live below me in this fashion ? Should any of my children at any time be said to have befouled themselves, how may they manage to escape ? " As soon as Manqondo got to hear of this he went and told Dingane. " Is that what Duɓe says," asked the King. " Father, that is indeed what he says. Whatever's to be done ? " " Then," said Dingane, " as often as Duɓe comes along here, he is on the alert, wondering

---

[1] *South African Commercial Advertiser*, 21st January, 1837.
The above statement is by a Natal trader called Lake.—*Editor.*

where children that befoul themselves can find a convenient exit ? Nay, befoul themselves they shall and this very day."

The great indunas Ndlela and Dambuza, who were present, at once pointed out that the Qadis, being numerous, would certainly kill many of the King's men. " The best plan is not to attack them at all. Rather let the King issue an order for poles to be cut and brought here." The advice was acted on. Many of the Qadis accordingly carried poles to Mgungundlovu. " No ! This won't do at all," they were told on arrival. " You are not all here. Go back and fetch the rest. Every soul must bring a pole, even old women who complain of bad knees." Again the poles were brought, this time so many carriers coming, men and women, as to include even the bad-kneed old women. As they walked one behind the other in the usual single file, they are said to have covered a distance of two or three miles.

They all then entered the great cattle enclosure, and, proceeding slowly to the upper end, one by one, deposited their burdens. No sooner had all entered than Dingane directed that the warriors, till then concealed in the huts, were to come forth and block every exit. And no sooner was this done than the fatal word, " babambeni ! " (lay hold of them) was uttered. The troops then poured into the enclosure itself and forthwith attacked every soul, battering them mercilessly to death with short stout cudgels, just as was done ten months later to Piet Retief and his followers. But, of the latter there were only 100 all told, whereas of the Qadis massacred at Mgungundlovu alone there must have been three, four, and five times that number.

A member of Dube's tribe, who for some reason had not entered the kraal, happened to be spectator of the massacre. As soon as he realised what was taking place he ran home as fast as he could and gave the alarm to his chief. By the time Dube quitted his kraal, the force sent from headquarters had already invaded the district. He succeeded in entering Nongoxi forest near Middle Drift but, being seen, was followed up, surrounded and put to death.

Large numbers of those who, for various reasons, had not gone to the capital were now ruthlessly and indiscriminately massacred, exactly as was done to the Boers at Doornkop, Blaauwkrantz, Moord Spruit and other places in Natal, the only difference being that the Boer women and children were slaughtered 11 days after the catastrophe at Mgungundlovu, whereas the Qadi women and children were exterminated probably within 24 hours of the massacre of the unfortunate pole-carriers at Mgungundlovu, a place notorious for its "blood-covered sticks." There was, however, yet another difference; of the Boers, including Hottentots and coloured servants, some 631 were slain, whereas of the Qadi there were at least half as many again.

The survivors, including the child-heir to the chieftainship, Mqhawe, and afterwards father of Mandlakayise, the late chief of the tribe, immediately crossed over into Natal to seek the protection of the British at the port. They were located a few miles from the coast in the neihgbourhood of the Inanda and Mdlothi Rivers.

Now the massacre occurred probably in the month of April, 1837. Another exodus from Zululand, also on a large scale, seems to have occurred about the same time, namely of the Phisi tribe, the fugitives once more placing themselves under the British settlers.

The sudden inrush of large numbers of men, women and children, all fugitives from Zululand, at once became in the eyes of the settlers a most formidable problem and one demanding immediate, resolute and united action. The treaty, of course, required that the whole of the deserters should be arrested and returned to Dingane, a duty that had to be carried out regardless of the means at the disposal of the settlers. On the other hand, to refrain from taking action was almost tantamount to a declaration of war against Dingane.

The settlers, when face to face with the difficulty, did not hesitate a minute. "We all agreed to reject the treaty," they said, "as most cruel and utterly impracticable, and to protect the people; and though we by no means wished to come into collision with Dingane, yet if he molested us, to offer resistance." Such a message was sent to Dingane; and though, before that, he had stopped the trade and even taken guns from one of the hunters . . . "yet, we had no sooner assumed this firm attitude than he immediately declared the trade open, and expressed a wish to be on closer terms of friendship and alliance with us, than ever."[1]

The situation now became so critical, particularly when rumours began to circulate that Dingane was about to attack the settlement, that the settlers took steps to defend themselves to the utmost of their strength and capacity. Alexander Biggar, father of R. and G. Biggar, was appointed Commandant for the time being. On a proclamation issued by him on the 4th of May he says: " Whereas in consequence of the recent distresses, the Qadi and Phisi tribes have fled for protection from the Zulus to Natal, serious apprehensions are entertained that it may afford a pretext to the Zulu Chief, Dingane, to carry into execution his long and often threatened intention of invading and attacking this Settlement—it became the duty of the white inhabitants to assemble and consult, as to what measures should be adopted on this alarming occasion; and whereas, an alarm-post, as a place of defence and assembly, has long been considered as absolutely necessary, in the event of any sudden attack, they, therefore, after attentively examining several places, have fixed upon Point St. Michael's as a proper place to erect a fortification for the protection of themselves and property. . . ." The proclamation, after deeming it proper that all this coloured population should be enrolled and embodied as a militia force and be officered by their British chiefs, ends by calling on all to yield a ready and cheerful obedience to any orders that may be issued.

In general orders it was laid down that " beacons of alarm be prepared on the different commanding heights (as pointed out) to be fired when the enemy is perceived." Fortifications were erected at Point St. Michael's, six captains and ten lieutenants were appointed, patrols were sent out and various other steps were taken for the proper organization of the men available. Dr. Adams, superintendent of the mission station, having offered his services in a medical capacity, was appointed " Surgeon to the Forces " and requested also to act as " Chaplain to the Troops."

---

[1] In a letter to the *Grahamstown Journal*, written subsequently to Gardiner's arrival (24th May) and most probably in July, 1837. The signatories were eight in number including R. Biggar and D. C. Toohey.—*Editor*. See also Bird's *Annals of Natal*, I, 322.

Dingane soon began to receive exaggerated reports of what was afoot at the port. He sent two messengers to ascertain the truth. These were well treated and sent back with assurances that the settlers' intentions were pacific and the measures they were taking of a purely defensive nature. On the 25th May a further message arrived from the King to say, on oath—he swore first by the God in Heaven, the white man's oath; then by the bones of his father, the most solemn oath of the Zulus—that he never had the slightest intention of attacking or destroying the settlement, and that he would never kill a white man. He, moreover, desired all at the port to leave the bush, i.e. resume their ordinary avocations.

It was just at this moment that Gardiner returned to Natal, after an absence of 19 months. In the meantime, as will have been inferred from what has gone before, the relations between Dingane and the settlers had considerably altered, whilst a spirit of independence was fast developing among the latter. Although King William IV disclaimed, in the most direct terms, all right of sovereignty in Natal and all intention of extending his dominions in that quarter, seemingly, and this on the grounds of expense, the Governor of the Cape was instructed to appoint Gardiner " Justice of the Peace " under the Act of Parliament of 5th and 6th William IV, chap. 57, which in truth, though it vested him with a legal right to do certain acts of subordinate police, gave no power either in means or money, or any sort of machinery, to execute them. Gardiner saw at once that such office would be illusory. However, he said he was " willing to attempt, by a mere moral influence, for the credit of my countrymen and for the benefit of the missionaries about to be established . . . . to palliate what I am not permitted to remedy."[1] He accordingly appointed Charles Pickman as Clerk of the Peace, and two other persons as constables, but, not having been authorized to assign any pecuniary stipend to the posts, found himself obliged to remunerate them from his own private means or " leave the duties entrusted to me wholly unfulfilled."[2] The next step was to explain his commission to the settlers. This was done at a public meeting held at Port Natal on 1st June. A few days

---
[1] Bird, *Annals of Natal*, I, 317.
[2] Ibid., 318.

later seven of his principal settlers, including A. Biggar, Cane and Ogle, drew up and sent to him a protest against his being appointed to exercise jurisdiction over them. They claimed that Natal was not an acknowledged part of the British dominions, but a free settlement; that it was granted by Shaka to the resident inhabitants, the grant being subsequently confirmed by Dingane; they complained that the power vested in Gardiner extended to British subjects only, not empowering him to punish acts of aggression by natives, or by Europeans on British residents of Natal; that he was not empowered to adjudicate in civil cases; that as criminal cases must be decided by the nearest magistrate in the Cape Colony, on depositions taken by Gardiner, hardship and oppression must result to offenders; that no redress was provided for in the event of Gardiner himself or his agent committing any act of oppression on the inhabitants; and that, before leaving for England, Gardiner had materially injured the inhabitants by advising the Zulu King to prohibit their trading with his people; in conclusion, they trusted that Her Majesty's Government would recognise Natal and appoint magistrates to afford them substantial protection and encouragement.

In forwarding this document by overland express, Gardiner pointed out that his office was virtually at an end as, though a Clerk of the Peace had been appointed, "not a single individual is willing to perform the duties of constable, neither have any tenders been received for the erection of the Magistrate's office or the gaol." As to the grant made by Shaka, he observed that it had reference merely to the "right of hunting." He denied that he had persuaded Dingane to stop the trade *in toto*; he had recommended him merely to prohibit such Europeans as had wantonly offended against the laws of his country, instead of sending an armed party to Natal to punish them.

George Cyrus, Gardiner's interpreter, in a letter to the *Commercial Advertiser*, June, 1837, in reply to Gardiner being accused in the protest of stopping the trade, declared, on the strength of notes made at the time, that Gardiner " advised Dingane to appoint special messengers, and that if any white man wished to trade in the Zulu country, that person, on receiving permission, should be furnished with a messenger, whose business would be to see that the trader was not insulted and also that he did not secrete Dingane's subjects." Thus

Gardiner's defence was a good deal stronger than he himself had made it out to be.

After this protest, Gardiner, finding himself unable to perform the duties of his commission, withdrew from the port to the mouth of the Thongathi River, to await further instructions. Here he erected another mission station, called Hambanathi (go with us), and for the time being devoted his energies to the education and improvement of the natives.

" The rising ground on which the village stands was about a mile from the sea and looked down on the river, winding among the hills and forest wood. Beautiful glens invited retirement. Trees stood out in individual beauty, forming a great contrast to the ornamental woods beyond. The steep wooded banks of the Thongathi occasionally hid from view the course of the stream. Imagine all possible combinations of rich and varied scenery and tints of all colours; the brightest sunlight and the deepest shade; remember the unpretending house on the hill, with Indian corn waving in all directions, and an open sea view on the eastern side and you can form some idea of the beautiful Hambanathi. In a northerly direction a very steep hill arose immediately above the shore from which the whole line of coast was visible as far as Port Natal, the point of which appeared to be exactly opposite, stretching far out into the sea."[1]

In answer to the protest from the settlers, the Secretary of State pointed out, on 29th October, 1837, that they had not ceased to be subjects of the Queen, to be responsible to Her Majesty's courts and officers; " that the pretension which they make to constitute a free and independent state is so extravagant " that it assuredly will not be admitted by Her Majesty's Government nor by any other foreign civilised state, and that he " disclaimed any right or wish . . . to impose on Captain Gardiner the discharge of the duties in his commission should he find that no good practical result can follow from his continuing to hold it; or should he . . . desire to be divested of it."[2]

The missionary, the Rev. F. Owen, who had accompanied Gardiner from England arrived in Natal at the beginning of August. His first interview with Dingane took place at Noɓa-

---
[1] Marsh, J. W., *Memoir of Allen F. Gardiner*, 110.
[2] Bird, *Annals of Natal*, I, 327.

mba, some five miles from the capital Mgungundlovu, on 19th August. On the following day (Sunday) " I sent word to Dingane in the morning," says Owen, " to ask his permission, as it was Sunday to preach God's Word to his people in the cattle fold, a large open space in the centre of the town, or to teach in the *isigodlo*, as the King pleased. He sent word that I was to come directly to the *isigodlo*. Accordingly, accompanied by Captain Gardiner, I went. He was seated, as the day before, in a chair. His women came in and sat on the ground. When they were all assembled he told me to begin." [1]

A lengthy sermon (most probably the first ever preached before a Zulu King) now followed, in the course of which Dingane asked several questions. Hearing, for instance, that Hell was a place of everlasting fire, he interrupted the preacher by asking where Hell was. " I was proceeding to speak of it in Scripture language as a place, 'where the fire was not quenched,' when he again interrupted me, *where* Hell was ? I said the Word of God did not tell us where Hell was, but only that there was such a place. . . . He asked who were they that should rise up—whether we, pointing to his women, shall rise again—what bodies we shall come with—whether the same bodies that we have now—whether we should see one another and know one another again. Some of these questions he repeated; and I gave such answers as the Scriptures furnished me with. He seemed to think it incredible that the dead should be raised again, not knowing the power of God. Finally he said, ' Why do not the dead get up now, that we may see them ? ' To which I replied that God had appointed the day . . . The next day, Monday, he sent for us early and looked at my presents, with which he was much pleased, though he said little."[2]

Mr. Owen was then desired to address the people now assembled, in the words he had used the previous day. The same attention, however, was not paid, but just as in England, a smart bonnet or a shabby coat sometimes attracts the attention which ought rather to be given to the prayers or the sermon, so in the Zulu country, a poor blind man who was

---

[1] The first religious instruction to Dingane appears to have been given on 22nd January, 1836, at Mgungundlovu by the American missionaries Champion, Grout and Adams, apart from Gardiner's various conversations in 1835.—*Editor.*

[2] Which included some fireworks.—*Editor.*

present excited the ridicule and occupied the attention of Mr. Owen's audience.[1]

" He then gave me leave to look out for a site for a mission station at Khangela. We left Nobamba on Monday afternoon, and walked to Mgungundlovu. The King sent a man with us, to show us the hut he is building for me. It is not in the place Captain Gardiner had previously chosen. He has built the hut on the top of a high hill[2] where there is not a tree or a twig near, exposed to every blast of wind, in as wild and dreary a place as can well be conceived . . . "

Adverting to the preaching of the American missionaries to Dingane, the following account taken from Bird's *Annals of Natal* is of interest: " A Testament, they say, was shown as a part of God's Word. Dingane wished to know how many leaves it contained, and was surprised to hear us tell without counting them. He asked to hear some of it read. He then inquired about the creation. A short account of the Saviour was given. They all seemed interested. One asked if God was not displeased with the treatment of His Son, and what he did to the people. We were asked if men knew anything about God before Christ came. One query was, if God was so powerful why not pray to take away all disease and misery ? . . . . In speaking of God to any of the people, they have usually stared about the heavens in wonder, or listened to our words as an unmeaning story, and perhaps have interrupted us by asking for something that caught their eye."[3]

Gardiner and Owen now returned to Hambanathi via Khangela. The latter thereupon prepared to take up his residence permanently at Mgungundlovu. This he did on 10th October, being accompanied by Mrs. and Miss Owen and a youth of about 16 called William Wood, a Zulu interpreter.

The expedition to Sobuza, in June, 1836, soon completed what it had been sent to do. Dingane organised another in the following winter (June, 1837) to attack once more his old foe Mzilikazi. As has already been stated, the army that went to Sobuza was accompanied by a number of the settlers. None of these, however, took part in the later campaign, presumably

---

[1] Marsh, J. W., *Memoir of Allen F. Gardiner*, 100.
[2] Nearly two miles from the town, says Gardiner.—Marsh, J. W., *Memoir of Allen F. Gardiner*, 101.
[3] Bird, *Annals of Natal*, I, 207.

because Mzilikazi occupied high veld territory and therefore devoid of fastnesses inaccessible to Zulu warriors.

And so the story of the Settlement at Port Natal is brought up to the end of 1837. In the following year the Voortrekkers, led by Piet Retief, came down the passes of the Drakensberg from the Free State, and opened up communication with Dingane direct.

The arrival of the Voortrekkers changed the character of Natal from that of a Port Settlement to a Colony, and increased its importance in the eyes of the British Government. What took place thereafter does not belong to this book, but the events which followed are recorded in other books to which the reader is referred.

ADDITIONAL NOTES ON HISTORY AND CUSTOMS

Origin and Language

THE Zulus have no idea of creation, but each tribe imagines their forefathers were the original from whence the others sprung, the original stock being supposed to have sprung from *Umhlanga Omkhulu*, or large reed, and are termed *Imvelangqangi*, or first comers. Beyond this they have no ideas. The few traditionary accounts being of a late period, most likely any that might have existed worth notice, has been lost in consequence of the continual series of wars which during the last century the whole race of Kaffirs have been continually involved. So far as appearances have allowed me to observe in tracing the different tribes which occupied the country before the destructive overthrow was begun by Shaka I have been led to the following conclusion by tracing the definition of the dialects spoken by each tribe which my knowledge of the language enabled me correctly to observe.

The various tribes inhabiting Kaffraria can only include those between the Colony and the environs of Delagoa Bay, extending from the sea to the chain ridge of mountains called Ingale or " Snow " which extends through the country from the Colony as far as the country has been examined beyond Delagoa. As they are evidently one people using only one language, and although they are divided into many petty tribes, their manners and customs only differ in a provincial degree, and having originated from one cause the uninformed and unenlightened state of their minds, the result of ages of the grossest ignorance and feeling conscious of existing superior powers endeavour to supply that deficiency by invention from their own limited ideas.

In the map of the country I have, in consequence of my conclusions, laid down the positions each tribe inhabited previous to the disturbances which removed many tribes to their present abode, and laid the country of the many slain in battle waste and depopulated as will be seen in the map.

In the above space of country they afterwards became divided into three from whence the many tribes lately destroyed and those still in existence became subdivided. The tribes eastward of the Thukela to Delagoa speak one language which is spoken smoothly, clearly and copiously and in a precisely grammatical manner, being much more soft and expressive than any of the other tribes.

From a general opinion throughout Kaffraria of their being the only cunning people, and the evidence I have acquired of most of the tribes at present forming the frontier of the Colony having originally come from that direction, I conclude that the tribes east of the Thukela were the original tribe from whence the others descended, and removed westward in consequence of the unsettled state that the country has been in. As far as memory can trace those tribes which inhabited the land between the Thukela and the Umzimkhulu doubtless originated from one speaking the same language, differing from the Zulus by various letters being omitted, and the others used in their place, and attended with an uncouth manner of delivery, apparently forcing their words suddenly and using many gutturals, dentals and clicks, which the Zulus have used only in a small degree.

The time that many of these tribes came from the eastward of the Thukela is traced only to a late period during the disturbances of that country, where it is more than likely they were induced to follow their relatives who had left long before them, and had become separate tribes. The language of the frontier tribes is neither so expressive nor clear or soft as that spoken by the Zulus, containing more gutturals than that country. It invariably happens that things are called after different names which I account for from the following cause. Children when born are named by their parents as fancy guides them, frequently derived from public occurrences which have taken place previously or at the time of birth. The friends of chiefs so named consider it disrespectful to make such common use of the name, so the thing's name is then changed. So many similar occurrences appear to make almost an entire change in the language. Similar instances are in the life of Shaka.

The ceremony of circumcision, a custom so common among the Kaffir tribes, the necessity for which they assert is made obligatory, because their forefathers did it before them, was always attended to among the tribes east of the Thukela till the reigns of the latter kings Dingiswayo and Shaka, so that

Gudu's Kraal at the Thukela, Women making Beer
From the painting by George French Angus in *Kaffirs Illustrated*

only the oldest men among the Zulus, of which there are but a few, remain circumcised. Dingiswayo had omitted or deferred the custom till he should have completed his wars, which day never arrived. Shaka from the same motives also omitted it. The ideas they conceive of circumcision when performed proclaiming them as having arrived at manhood, till which they are only considered as boys, have induced me to attribute the real cause of the omission to the wishes of Shaka to appear as young as possible. He was always disgusted at old age, of which the reader may in some way judge from his anxiety to possess the Macassar oil to eradicate the few grey hairs which appeared on his chin. Futhermore, his massacre of old men shows the same trait.

Home Utensils

All pottery is made by the women, consisting of large and small pots for various uses. Those for milk or beer are glazed previous to baking them by rubbing them with glossy stones. Those used for cooking are of various sizes. Several used by Shaka's mother for boiling beer would contain 60 gallons each.

Mats are made by the females of almost every family, but baskets are the work of the men, and are of neat workmanship.

There are a few Zulus and Mthethwas who understand the carving of wood, which was introduced by Dingiswayo, and the use of them is only with the Zulu King.

The only articles so manufactured are milk bowls, headrests, pillows which are carved from solid blocks, having ornaments projecting, being carved in lines or marks which are burned with red hot irons, which chars them, making them handsome and durable.

Spoons and milk-pails are in common use. They are of neat workmanship, and not so difficult to make as the former. They use no other tool than an axe which they reverse in the handle by which it becomes an adze and an assegai crake at its mouth.

Beer

They make beer from four sorts of grain, a small part of which is first malted. The remainder is ground with water between stones. It is then put in boilers, with a proportionate quantity of water and allowed to simmer, when it is put into coolers, and when cold the malted 'corn is ground dry, and mixed with it. In eight hours it ferments. It is then sifted through a sieve, made from wild date leaf plaited like leghorn hats, after which it remains an hour, by which time it regains its fermentation. The grains used for the purpose are Indian corn, Guinea corn, millet, and *luphoko*. The two latter are the best, being a most pleasant and wholesome beverage. Neither is fit to drink after two days by a European, but the natives will use it as long as the name beer may be applied to it.

BLACKSMITHS

The occupation of blacksmith is so general in every tribe of this part of Africa that he is as necessary to the kraal as our European smiths are to a small village, and before the country was destroyed by Shaka there was generally one to every three or four kraals.

At the present they are scarce, and as poor as others who have no employment, but that of mere subsistence, whereas the former smiths were men of opulence. The unsettled state that the country has been in, during the whole of Shaka's reign and since, has made them careless as to what they earn, their profits from industry never being safe from superior force.

The articles manufactured by them are but few, viz., hoes, assegais, choppers, razors and needles. The business of coppersmith is combined with that of the blacksmith in making brass beads as large as plums and brass rings for the neck and arms. The iron, which is now seldom or ever worked from the ore, is brought to the smith by the person wanting work done. It has been taken from the enemy or picked up at the old habitations, and only the work is paid for at an average of a heifer for ten hoes, two strings of beads that will encompass the waist for an assegai, and a string as long as a man's arms for a needle or a razor, which is generally combined.

The working of brass is at an average of 50 or 60 balls or beads for a cow, and four strings of beads for a brass collar for the neck. The brass, as well as the iron, has been for the most part taken at different times from the enemy, but immense quantities are brought from Delagoa Bay by the natives. They purchase it from the Portuguese for ivory and slaves, but how the brass originally found its way among these tribes is not known by the oldest men living. It may, however, be concluded that it was procured from a number of wrecks on the coast, as we find that at the wreck of the *Grosvenor* the blacksmith remained on the spot, working iron and copper for the natives. The forge whereon he worked is as he left it, formed of heavy iron ballast laid on the ground, consisting of 13 pigs.

It would appear, by the superior quality of the brass found in use, that some more valuable metal than zinc was used as an alloy with the copper. The country being so much depopulated put it out of the power of an enquirer to find out. It has thrown so much iron and brass among the few remaining people that they are not necessitated either to work iron from the ore or, if there was an alloy used with their copper, ever now to have occasion for its use. It would appear strange that men of 50 or 60 years of age, of whom Shaka has left a few, can give no information with respect to the mixing of any metal with the copper as an alloy. We seldom find any inquisitive enough to care for knowledge which does not appear for their benefit, although to a European at first sight they appear anxious to be improved.

On my first arrival in this country I was so much surprised at the superiority of some of their rings that I purchased some quantities under the idea of their being gold. Mr. Farewell, under the same opinion, had it tried and it proved to be brass. Yet it induced us to believe that it was of a superior kind. In crossing several of the rivers, small particles of metal were to be seen amongst the sand as also amongst the mountains, of both of which Mr. Farewell procured several samples which he took with him to the Colony, the result of which is not publicly known. In one instance I purchased a milk pot of clay which had so much of this metal that it appeared more like a pot bronzed intentionally, than accidentally.

In another instance I purchased from a man residing on the Umzimkhulu River, two arm bangles of solid silver, for the value of four pence in beads, one of which I still have by me and the other Mr. Farewell took with him to the Cape, both proving to be the best silver. My inquiries from whence they came met with no further result than that they had been taken from a nation whom they had defeated three years back, inland from the Bloody River. Shaka, seeing one of them in my possession, took it from me and kept it for six weeks. With great difficulty I recovered it and by him I was informed that it was procured from a glittering white clay called *usebanga* which they used to besmear their faces on great days of dancing. Neither from him nor any other source have I been able to find out more concerning this metal.

But to return to the blacksmiths. It will only be necessary to explain how they made their tools and of what they consist, viz., for an anvil they use a stone and in cases of another smith not being near at hand from whence they can get a hammer so as to manufacture other tools they want, they proceed first to make a hammer weighing 2 lbs., using in its place a round stone. Instead of pincers the bark of a thorn tree, and instead of a punch the head of a chopper, being pointed, makes a hole for the hammer handle. The forge is formed by digging a hole in the ground and as a protector to the mouths of the bellows they form a tender of tempered clay.

The bellows is plainly two square bags made of old worn-out karosses of bullock's hide. A hole at the extreme corner of each, wherein is fastened a bullock's horn, forms the mouth. The upper parts of the bag are left open, with a stick sewn on each side, between which the forefinger of each hand in the separate bellows is played. The thumb and middle finger withhold the bellows which is worked by opening the mouth of each as they are drawn upwards from the ground and shutting them as they are pressed alternately down. Being smartly used, this throws out a sufficiently strong force of wind for welding iron, which they do moderately well. They have no idea of hardening iron, although it is generally very good. Their pincers are made after the same manner as our own only roughly, as also their cold chisels which are not steeled (used for jaggering assegais and cutting iron).

The process of smelting the ore is, that when a sufficient quantity is collected, a ditch is dug one foot wide and three long, wherein it is thrown with the charcoal. The charcoal is usually found by the owner of the iron. Two pairs of bellows are used, one pair at each end, several men taking their turns at the bellows. When the iron melts into cakes it is beaten out by means of large stones into more convenient pieces, as the work it is intended for may require. In the working of brass, they use sandstone crucibles, which are easily worked and attain a strong heat to form the beads or balls. Cowdung is

Scene in a Zulu Kraal, with Huts and Screens
From the painting by George French Angus in *Kaffirs Illustrated*

placed in a circle on an aloe leaf, in the centre of which is placed a splinter of wood to form the hole by which the beads are threaded. The melted brass is then poured in, which leaves them in a very rough state, but they are afterwards beaten with a hammer and brought to form.

The rings are formed also by casting narrow pigs into cowdung and the anvil stone being of a soft gritty nature, there are carved half-circles for the balls to be beaten into, and channels to the shape required for the neck rings when beaten out, and they are rubbed on the stones instead of being filed and are polished by the use of cowdung. But the balls are not smoothed or polished, the owners liking the marks of the hammer to appear on them, that everyone who takes notice of them may see they are newly made articles. Thirty of a large size will procure a cow. The neck rings are in no demand, being used only by the ladies of the seraglio or such chiefs as the King may give them to. The arm bangles in the like manner are only used by the old dowager queens or great ladies of appointment.

On forming any new forge the gall of cattle is poured round it. Lacking the gall, the juice of the aloe leaf is used, under the superstitious idea that success would fail their endeavours if not thus sprinkled. In welding, iron roots are placed on the iron with clay made from ant heaps. Without this, they suppose the iron could not possibly be welded.

Tanning and Dressing Hides

The manufacturing of hides for the various purposes for which they are used is performed by the men. They are dressed in the following manner; two forked sticks are driven into the ground, three feet high, on which is placed a ridge pole whereon the hide is placed, and pinned down with pegs on each side. Water being thrown on it, the man proceeds with an axe taken from its handle and scrapes from the flesh side till it is sufficiently thin for use. The hair is then shaved dry from the outward side. A quantity of sour butter milk is then laid on the hide, with which it is rolled up and remains till nearly dry, being then rubbed by the hands till soft. Leaves of the prickly aloe are then used like a curry comb on the inside which produces a shag-like felt. It is then greased and rubbed over with the ashes of burnt grass and cut into petticoats (those for full dress having a tail hanging from each side three feet long and one foot broad). These last one or two years and sometimes more. The grease and ashes are frequently renewed and although they are filthy to the touch, their appearance is neat and handsome. Some are used by the men like cloaks, in which case the hair is not taken from the hide nor are they blackened as the petticoats.

Another article of dress which is worn by the newly married woman, or in cases of pregnancy over the breasts, is the skin of the riet buck. It is differently dressed as the particles shaved off are from the hair side, leaving the hair three inches broad on the two sides. The two hind feet being used to tie it up behind the two fore feet hang down below the knees, ornamented, as also is the neck, with large brass balls. The fragments of the petticoat are used for the *umutsha*, either of men or girls.

The payment for dressing a hide is from eight to ten strings of beads of about a yard, but there is no regular price either on articles or work. The prices differ according to the circumstances. The tribes bordering on the frontiers of the Cape Colony always preserve the shavings from the hide which they beat on stones with water till it is of a consistency like paste, then forming articles according to fancy in the shape of bottles, elephants, hippopotami, etc. Forming these with soft clay, they lay the paste over them, when dry it rises, and the inside being taken out leaves the paste, which becomes a durable snuff box, for which purpose they are generally used.

Izinyanga Zokubula (Diviners)

In attempting to give an account of the *inyangas* or soothsayers is even more than I could presume to accomplish, being in itself so mysterious a profession and therefore shall only attempt to state such facts as come within my knowledge. This species of witchcraft is professed by men and women which appears not to be a choice, nor could it be accomplished by choice, but as they state, commences with a fit of sickness in which case, as is general with all sick, they kill a cow, praying a recovery from the spirits of their forefathers. They are then attacked with a delirium during which they dream dreams and run wild in the river or woods during which time the spirits appear to them with a song composed for his or her use which is the one sung by them on all occasions when called on.

He or she then plucks some plants from the riverside, part of which is eaten and the rest tied about the neck when he recovers from the trance which with the first sickness has been brought on him by the spirits of his forefathers with the intention that he should follow the profession of *inyanga*. (Perhaps the meaning of the word means a person qualified. It certainly means skill above the ordinary, so that there are men of skill or *inyangas* in every occupation. If a person is employed by reason of his skill he is called an *inyanga*.)

His neighbours, having quietly observed the past, have, during his absence from the kraal, hidden something unknown to him. On his return he is addressed with the same respect as is given to a chief, being **Letha Mngane** (we want your information). Having previously prepared his dress for the event, he then puts it on, differing in persons as fancy may dictate. Some, the blown entrails of a bullock tied round the neck and breast, on others immense numbers of gall bladders blown. Others, pieces of hides about their necks, in fact almost each have their various dresses, as also songs. Being dressed, he proceeds by telling them to *Vuma* (agree with him) and continues in the following manner, a cow, bead or brass being first paid in proportion to the importance of the case:

A song is sung in which the *inyanga* alone dances to the tune, the party sitting in a half circle singing with him such as:

Maye ! bayathakatha bona
Bayavungama, eshe
Eshiya, eshe, eshe, eshe, eshiya.

This is repeated often. The interpretation is:

Oh ! they are evil doers, they
They growl, saying
Eshiya, eshe eshe eshe eshiya.

the latter line only being composed as a finish to the music.

The *inyanga* then proceeds in imitation of the following harangue, during which he puts himself into such a ridiculous attitude as to strike a stranger with astonishment, such as imitating death in its last gasps.

Inyanga: You are come to know who is sick ?

Party: (Clapping their hands to all he says or beating with a stick on the ground, answers) *Siyavuma.*
Inyanga: No, you have lost beads.
Party: Agree.
Inyanga: You've come to ask news?
Party: Agree.
Inyanga: No, you are not come to ask news.
Party: Agree.
Inyanga: You are come to ask news?
Party: Agree.
Inyanga: You are come to ask after someone missing?
Party: Agree.
Inyanga: No, you are not.
Party: Agree.
Inyanga: You are come to ask who uses poisonous roots?
Party: Agree.
Inyanga: No, you want to know who has stolen your cow?
Party: Agree.
Inyanga: No, you want to know who has caused the sickness? Now on the person sick?
Party: Agree, agree.
Inyanga: The person you apply for is poisoned. No, he is sick?
Party: Agree.
Inyanga: There is a person who has put poison in his food, and it remains in his breast?
Party: Agree.
Inyanga: No, the man's sickness is caused by his forefathers who are angry with him for allowing his sister to wed without sufficient cattle being paid for her, and requests you will kill (such a) cow out of your flock, having such marks as a white tail and a white spot on the back.

The party then leaves to inform the sick person of the *inyanga's* decision. The cow is then brought before the house of the sick, and one of the oldest men in the kraal, or nearest relations (the kaross being worn always on this occasion) proceeds to pray to the spirits of the forefathers for the recovery of the patient, as example: " We salute you. Here is meat. You ask for food. We are not aware what should so cause your anger as to bring such sickness upon us. Here is meat. Eat it and let your patient recover."

The cow or ox is then stabbed which frequently causes a bellow, this being considered a good omen produces general applause from the bystanders. Immediately the beast has fallen, it is so placed that the head points to the house wherein the sick person lies, in which position it is slaughtered. Each piece being carried into the house is wrapped up in the hide and left till the following day when it is then boiled and when cooked everyone present partakes of it. The bones, being collected together, are burnt to a cinder and the fore part of the skull with horns is placed above the door of the sick patient. Such a proceeding I can affirm from experience to have cured persons when despaired of by their friends and without the least aid of medicine. A plan I have practised repeatedly myself on persons violently attacked with dysentery, which convinced me of the truth of the old adage, that " conceit can kill and conceit can cure."

But to return to the *inyangas*. They are applied to on most occasions of doubt, the fee being always first paid and their decisions generally relied on, although out of four cases if properly examined one only would be satisfactory. And this they might either guess or deduce from information received as to the person suspected. In cases of trial the party concerned puts so strong an emphasis on anything the *inyanga* says that to them appears alluding to the case on which he is being consulted, that he is able by repeating every general occurrence that he can collect from his brain, and by observing where the emphasis is laid, to arrive at a correct solution.

But what still holds their credit good is that there is no appeal by a person accused of a criminal act by an *inyanga*, his decision being final. The person accused is killed immediately and leaves no doubt as to guilt, and from the number cured by killing of cattle, induces the superstitious multitude to put faith in their decisions; nevertheless they are not respected in the light they might be supposed to be from their power, profit being their only gain. In a political view they are of service as they would not presume to attack the strong side, and generally only such as in their opinion displease the chief, with whom they reside and by whom they are paid.

Izinyanga Zokwelapha (Medical Doctors)

The doctors of medicine are generally accompanied by their students who are taught the art gratis, their services being thought equivalent to what they learn. The greatest annoyance occasioned with the doctors is that almost every kind of sickness has its separate doctor which occasions great delay, it seldom happening even when applied properly, that they trouble themselves to move before it is quite convenient. The different forms they have of giving medicine is purging, vomiting, clysters, cupping and smelling. Were the above all that was used, it would perhaps be better for the patient, but the ignorance of the doctors induces them to keep their art in the dark as much as possible, and in consequence they mix with their good medicines a number of unnecessary roots to cause mystery and which can never do the patient much good. The unnecessary addition of these roots, so frequently used and in such irregular manner, would at once convince the sick of the imposition were they to observe it. In consequence, the sick, who might recover with those medicines properly applied, are retarded by unnecessary additions.

As I have before mentioned the *izinyanga* are applied to in all cases of doubt. It will be necessary to explain such circumstances, as, from the superstitions of the natives, they are led to put belief in. As a dream or parable requires an interpretation, so numerous are their superstitions that few of them are aware as to what they really are. The most serious crime that is committed, in their idea, is that of keeping a cat for the purpose of destroying or causing sickness among their neighbours. This cat (which is the red wild cat of Africa, and is well known among the Dutch farmers) is supposed to be kept closely confined in secret by persons wilfully inclined.

Merely by ordering it to cause sickness, to kill individuals or cattle, is sure to be effected by the cat being taken to the house. It will scratch the person it is sent to. In two or three instances I have seen a bald place on people's heads not larger than a sixpence, apparently shaved, which is said to be the cat's doings, taking away the hair to its proprietor who mixes it with roots, after which nothing, in their opinion, can save the life of the scratched person. Leopards are also supposed to be kept in like manner and for the same purpose.

During my residence in this country I have seen several of the cats and leopards caught, which by their account must belong to someone, as there are marks put on by their respective owners which appear plain enough, some having notches in the ears or tail. But the real fact, when argued with them by a European, has no effect, for they will not believe that such marks could be produced by fighting with others of their species. Owls in like manner, when found screeching on the fence of the kraal are considered as messengers sent by some malicious person for their destruction. Dogs will also sometimes climb on the top of their straw huts and although it may perhaps belong to the owner of the hut still it must, in their opinion, have been induced to climb by malicious persons. Too numerous are such occurrences to relate. They are attended with the consequences of a visit to the *inyanga*, who is sure to point out some object for death. And although the person pointed out may be under the jurisdiction of the chief or applicant, yet he is generally given up to prevent slander, which would be the case were he not given up.

In case of sickness, application is always made to the *inyanga*, who has various ways of deciding, but it is very seldom that he tells the real truth by merely saying it is sickness. Such an answer would make his abilities look too simple. He, therefore, to make himself more important, tells them to kill a cow as an offering to their forefathers, the gall of which is to be sprinkled over the patient's body and the gall bladder being slit at the end, is drawn on the arm, lined inside with the caul of the bullock. Various good omens there are also which require the *inyanga's* interference, such as swarm of bees flying over the kraal; a long green snake remaining for several days on the kraal fence; dreams being decided good or bad omens, as the *inyanga* may think fit.

A partridge rising in front of the army is a good omen, and a comet appearing about the time of any intended attack on an enemy, decides their movements. Should the comet, on its disappearing, point from the enemy to the attacking party, they will not attempt to fight, but should the comet take a contrary course, their fate will be favourably decided.

The son or daughter of an *inyanga* or soothsayer cannot follow the profession of its sire or mother, but the grandchild may and it is strange that this is not only observed by the Kaffirs, but I have seen it in general. The son of an *inyanga* has some deformity as squinting, shaking of the head, etc. In cases of sickness, when the application is made to the *inyanga*, he recommends them to the medical *inyanga*; every complaint being a separate profession. The applicant then proceeds with his string of beads or a small brass ring which he gives him only to call his attendance, in which they are very dilatory. For, although the case may require his immediate attendance, he will perhaps not stir till the next day, and never visits the patient for two or three hours after he is called, as he requires that time to collect his roots, which are picked fresh every visit. He then digs such roots as the nature of the case requires, and, accompanied by his student, he attends the patient.

Worms, which are very common in the country, both with young and old, they have a most excellent medicine for, called *inkomankoma*, one dose of which will extirpate the tapeworm and a second dose entirely clear the stomach from any of their remains. Every European that has lived in Natal has been troubled with them and has experienced the good effects of *inkomankoma*. The worm called tenes or the long round worm, although not so common as the tapeworm, attacks the patient in such a violent manner as to cause a stoppage of speech for several hours and to cause an appearance almost of death. For such worms a different root is used with equally good effect.

The form of an emetic is such that, to a European stomach, one could dispense with the emetic itself, since what is done at the end would be sufficient to produce the desired effect. The roots, being bruised on a stone, are boiled in two quarts of water and drunk lukewarm, the patient being directed to put his two fingers or a long feather as far down his throat as possible. I have seen Shaka, who had emetics almost as frequently as his meals, throw up as much slime, day after day, as would fill a quart pot, and immediately afterwards eat a good dinner of beef with as good an appetite as if he had taken no emetic.

The quantity of slime has so surprised me, and happened so repeatedly, that I have thought it must have been the emetic itself passing through some change in the body. For to me it appeared impossible that such foul property could live in the body of a man in perfect health. It was not taken from necessity of sickness, but with the idea of throwing up any poisonous properties remaining in his breast, which from his situation, he was hourly impressed with the idea would be given to him.

In fever or headache the patient is made to smell burnt roots while they are smoking, in some cases a powder is used like snuff which so sets the patient asneezing that an antidote is always at hand to stop it. Their plan of cupping is by means of a bullock horn tip, about four inches long, open at each end. The larger end is placed on the spot, which is lanced with one of their razors. The *inyanga* then draws with his mouth till he has taken a sufficient quantity. Cupping is used in cases of rheumatism, swellings or local pains. From the state the country has been in for this last 12 years there are few either men or women who have not scars on their heads, some of a surprising size where the skull has been much fractured, leaving after its cure a cavity sufficient to hold a gill of water. It sometimes happens that such wounds occasion pain in the head years after the wound is healed, which in their opinion is from the remaining matter under the wound, in which case the wound is opened to the bone crossways with an assegai. In opening a vein the skin is cut across the vein, a hooked thorn is then used to hold up the vein which they cut with their razor, bleeding a swelling or local pain.

Another case where I have known them to make a perfect cure is that of rupture in the testicles. They open them with the point of the assegai, the patient being seated in a running stream, the parts alternately pressed which draws out quantities of green foul matter. A plant whose properties are that of collecting foul matter into a moss, is then put into the incision and remains for two days, during which it is constantly running, and the former operation is repeated in the water, which takes the swelling down and I have known it produce a perfect cure.

The most prevalent sickness in the country is the dysentery which comes on with the hot easterly winds in the months of August and September. Rheumatic pains are very common, occasioned by excessive exercise in dancing accompanied with singing. The least cold striking their persons during the perspiration, leaves them with rheumatic pains and sometimes causes fevers. The climate in itself is equal, if not superior to that of any other part of this coast as far as Natal is concerned.

Doctors to Kings are of two kinds, both different professions to those who attend on the community, the one professing to provide antidotes against all sickness or poisonous attempts on the person of His Majesty, while the other professes to prevent any enemy subduing him or his nation. The former attends the King every morning about ten or eleven o'clock, when he provides him with a solution or wash which by having a stick slit at the one end turned smartly by the hand produces a soap lather with which the King washes himself.

The doctors also provide him with an antidote which the King places on his tongue before each meal and by the doctors' account prevents poison taking effect. The doctor professing to prevent any enemy subduing him or his nation attends on any intended attack and with many superstitious proceedings gives numerous roots. One in particular is chewed and, pointing with the finger, the remains are thrown out in the direction the enemy is. However these particulars being kept in secret, prevents my giving a fuller account of the proceedings. Only the party subdued allows the subduer to possess a doctor with better medicines than himself.

It would appear that their doctors as well as the soothsayers were men of wisdom in the opinion of the nation, yet they are not in any way more respected or thought of than the commoners.

There are other doctors who attend on the King for the purpose of dispelling thunder or causing rain, and the wonderful tales they tell of torrential rain being produced by these *inyangas* are sufficient to make illiterate persons believe it as a fact, although, as I have said before, the people in general are more enlightened than formerly from experience (not from connections with Europeans, as they have seen but few) and do not put so much faith as formerly in the *inyanga's* fabrications.

Izinyanga Zemvula (Rain Doctors)

Among the pretenders to superior skill and power are those termed *izinyanga zemvula* or Rain Doctors, who are employed only by Kings. They are supposed to possess the power of producing rain to any extent or preventing it and of controlling thunder and lightning as it may please the King to command. This gift is hereditary, being communicated from father to son.

During a dry season the King, anxious for rain, sends to the *inyanga*, who names the kind of animal necessary to be sacrificed on that occasion to the spirit, with prayer for what is desired. A cow with a black belly and white belly and a brown face, as their invention may dictate, being produced after a long search, is killed and eaten. Should this fail in producing rain, the spirit has appeared in the interval and demanded a sheep with a black face, and should this also fail, an animal of a different colour is required, or perhaps similar to the first, turning his head when killed to the gate of the kraal instead of the upper end, which possibly caused the failure. During the time consumed by the ceremonies it perhaps rains, which is ascribed to their powers.

Dingane a short time back had ordered rain to be made, but in vain. After producing the various descriptions of cattle and animals required till his patience was exhausted, another application was made for an ox which he supplied, but on second thoughts retained, asking the chiefs if it would not be better that the *inyangas* should attend, and in consequence of the seriously dry season assist the offering by singing the war song by which the sacrifice would be of a more solemn kind. This agreed to, the *inyangas* came, to whom the ox was given. While in the act of offering, the King joined them in the soldierly singing of the war whoop, at the end of which he made the signal for their deaths, desiring them to go and ask the spirit why no attention was paid to his orders. Those present were all killed.

Shaka placed little or no belief in them, but dreaded thunder, in which case he was surrounded and covered by his girls till the storm was over.

The Military System

Villages or, as they are termed, kraals are of two kinds, those of the King being used as barracks for the several regiments, at which the nation collects on requisite occasions.

Each regiment is divided into battalions, each having two or three captains, over which there is a general who has the entire management. He is responsible for the cattle and the conduct of the soldiers committed to his charge, receiving his orders from the King, who is despotic. Nevertheless the generals, on most important occasions are collected together to discuss the joint questions. Such meetings are merely nominal, as no chief would dare to propose anything in opposition to the King, as such conduct would be detrimental to his future safety. To each of these kraals are attached three or more matrons or dowager queens, who have equal power with the general in taking away the lives of those under them. The people under their immediate care are the females of the King's seraglio, they being formed into regiments in the same way as the men, only not for the same purpose.

Each kraal is supported by the King's cattle, these being in the same manner formed into regiments, assorted to each regiment agreeing with the colour of the shields worn by them. When the cattle arrive from an enemy, they are assorted and sent to their respective regiments. At such a time each individual drives away one or two, or as many as he can in the general scramble. This entitles him to their milk which is for his support while he remains with the regiment. Sometimes they are allowed to take these cattle to their private kraals. In such case they may be called together at a moment's notice to be given to individuals or to be slaughtered without the knowledge of the possessor, the milk being the only remuneration for their services during their lives. The whole of the cattle taken in war are the sole property of the King, who gives away tens, fifties or hundreds to chiefs, favourites and private servants. The common soldiers have little or no expectations of such favours.

Their war trappings are mostly provided by the King, each regiment being differently accoutred, the lightest coloured shields belonging to the men and the darkest to the young lads. The dress worn by the men is a turban of otter skin round the forehead, stuffed with bull-rush seed or dry cowdung. In front stands a feather nearly three feet in length, which is obtained from the gigantic Kaffir crane. From the turban, hanging down the cheeks, are two pieces of monkey skin, and in the upper parts, are bunches of feathers, having been stripped of the quills, which makes them light, neat and airy. Round the neck is hung a necklace of pieces of wood which are worn as medals of bravery. One is added for every one they kill in battle till there is no room left.

Round the arms and legs are ox and cow's tails; across the breast are two cords to which is suspended the skin of the genet and monkey cut into strips about six inches long and half an inch broad, which are so neatly twisted that a stranger without untwisting it would be assured that they were the tails as cut from the body, merely the bone having been taken out. The *umcubulu* or dress worn round the waist, is made in the same manner, only so long as to reach within an inch of the knee. They generally contain from 15 to 20 skins in a dress, sometimes 50 or 60, putting an astonishing value on them, which, if it is ever offered, will not induce one to part with it. The warlike appearance of a man in his full dress, certainly exceeds anything of the kind that any savage tribes wear in South Eastern Africa. On Shaka coming to the throne, he compelled the old superannuated chiefs to wear a petticoat similar in shape to those worn by women, only that they were made of monkey skins with the fur left on. The shields are cut nearly in an oval shape, strips of a contrary colour being laced up and down, which makes a finish to the shield. There are a handle and a vacancy for the shield stick, at the top of which is the tail of a genet neatly sewn round. One ox-hide only produces two shields, as they are supposed to reach from the feet to the chin in length and nearly twice the body's breadth. One of the regiments of boys wear hats which Shaka introduced from seeing me wear a Malay hat. Their shields are black, and round the waist is a band of hide behind, as Mr. Thompson says, the girdle of hunger, for the purpose of slackening or tightening as hunger may require, to which is attached a piece of hide as ornament. Various are the dresses, some having their heads covered with feathers, others with pieces of ox-hide, all being inferior to the above full dress.

Their manner of attack, in which they generally follow the track of the spies, is to take the enemy by surprise if possible. A regiment being, previous to leaving home, pointed out for attack volleys down, spear in hand, on the enemy, shielding off the showers of thrown assegais from the enemy as well as they can. Always they come to close quarters, which prevents the enemy from making use of their weapons, not being acquainted with any other method than that of throwing. From so repeatedly conquering in their attacks, they have become daring, though not brave, as I firmly believe that one repulse would so completely throw them back as to dispossess them of their remaining courage.

Private kraals belong to individuals who, having sufficient cattle, are sure of getting sufficient people to establish a kraal either from the regiment or stragglers in distress. Those belonging to regiments are obliged to attend, whenever called on, to their respective divisions. Every chief of a kraal possesses despotic power in his kraal, only that he must not presume to imitate the King in any plans he may adopt, under pain of death. In fact the people in his kraals are slaves at his command whom he can drive away or kill as his caprice may lead him. Although on important occasions the people are collected to give their voice, it is, as with the King and chiefs, merely nominal, as their whole welfare depends on him with whom they reside.

They are supported by the loan of his cattle to milk, only planting their own fields of corn. The cattle are herded by one or more boys as the number may require, which they take to grass at daylight, bringing them home to milk about ten or eleven o'clock. When milked they return to grass and are brought home an hour before sunset, when they are again milked. The cattle altogether are quiet and tractable, more particularly so than those of the Cape Colony, and are never tied up to milk. In cases of their being wild, a hole is bored through the nose in which a cord is put through and fastened round the horns, and while being milked a stick is put in the cord which by twisting round holds the cow on the spot.

The calves frequently die. They have a plan of skinning the dead calf, through which they place a three- or four-pronged stick, stuffing it up with straw, forming the most rude shape of a calf imaginable, but they succeed with it very well, as immediately the cow sees the stuffed skin, which it will lick, it gives down its milk. The calves, till they leave their mothers, are kept in the house with the men.

Taboos Regarding Milk

Various superstitions have arisen from time to time from the death of calves and in consequence laws have been established to save them but all without effect. Young married women are not allowed to pass either through the cattle or in the circumference where the cattle stand till they have, by public consent of the men, sprinkled certain roots over the cattle. Neither are they allowed to eat of the milk perhaps for six, nine, or 12 months after marriage. Females, young and old, during their monthly evacuations are not allowed to eat milk for seven days. Young girls, after the first evacuation, not for three or four months. Women whose husbands or children have died are prohibited for 12 months. Instead of deriving pity for the loss of his offspring, a man has a slight stain on his character. In a quarrel he will be reminded of it, and were he to be known to have connection with a female during her evacuation it would cause a blast on his character. Men who have killed the enemy in battle cannot eat of milk or any other food till first having eaten roots which they must obtain from the doctors at their own expense. Neither can a man be connected with his own wives after killing criminals or enemies till he has had connection with some strange female, otherwise his wives would take sick.

Males having sweethearts are not allowed to eat milk in the kraal to which the female belongs, and a case is seldom ever known of those laws being broken. Sweet milk is never drunk by children. The milk being poured into calabashes is left till the whey separates from the curds. The whey is given to young boys or girls and the curds mixed with crumbled bread is eaten by people grown up. They always prefer to go without several days rather than touch the milk before the whey is separated or the calabash is full.

Method of Slaughtering Cattle

The manner of killing cattle is by sticking them in the left side with an assegai about three inches from the shoulder and four from the back. It is generally dexterously done and proves instant death, but it sometimes happens that they require to be stabbed three or four times before the operation takes effect. The assegai must not be used in eating the beef as it will cause pains in the stomach. The hide is then skinned off. The *izinso-nyama*, as they call them, are the meat taken off the ribs from the loins to the shoulder, and from three inches of the brisket to the backbone. Then the shoulders are taken off, the legs being taken off at the joint. The brisket with the belly is next carved, then the entrails are taken out and the blood collected in pots. The ribs are next chopped off, then the hip bones, and lastly the head and neck. The *izinsonyama* of the cow, if belonging to a commoner, are sent to the chief. In failure to do so he loses his whole drove and perhaps his life. He is liable too if it is smaller than it ought to be. If the cow belongs to a chief or anybody, after the *izinsonyama* are taken away, the heart and lights are the perquisite of the herd. The head (if the cow is given to a stranger to kill or to a visitor) is the perquisite of the people of the kraal wherefrom the cow is given. The backbone is the perquisite of the slaughterer. The gall blader is placed on the arm of the proprietor of the cow, whereon it remains till it is rotten. The small stomach is eaten raw by the women. The white entrails containing the chyle is a dainty which (without washing as that would spoil it) is generally eaten by the proprietor with any other part that may suit his palate. The remainder is generally boiled the following day and eaten by all present. The harder meat from the loins is chopped up fine and boiled with a quantity of suet, which when done, the soup is taken from it and the blood is thrown in and boiled with the meat, which forms one of their most dainty dishes. The fundamental entrail is generally included in this mixture. After they have eaten, some having been given to the women, they stand up and return thanks to the chief, if the cow was killed by him, otherwise no thanks are returned.

Their manner of cooking is stewing and roasting. The meat is stewed in clay pots, some will contain 15 gallons. Each pot is always covered with another. Very little water being used and a splash of cowdung is smeared round the pot to prevent the steam escaping. They sometimes roast their meat on sticks over the fire, but most generally cut the meat into about yard lengths and an inch thick which they roast on the coals, using as a general dish a mat which is called *isithebe*, being used for meat only. There is a separate one used to receive the corn as it falls from the stone when ground. Pots as well as other house utensils are cleaned either by the dog's tongue or by cockroaches. As to the latter, scullions may laugh if they will, but experience has shown me that no common cleansing would

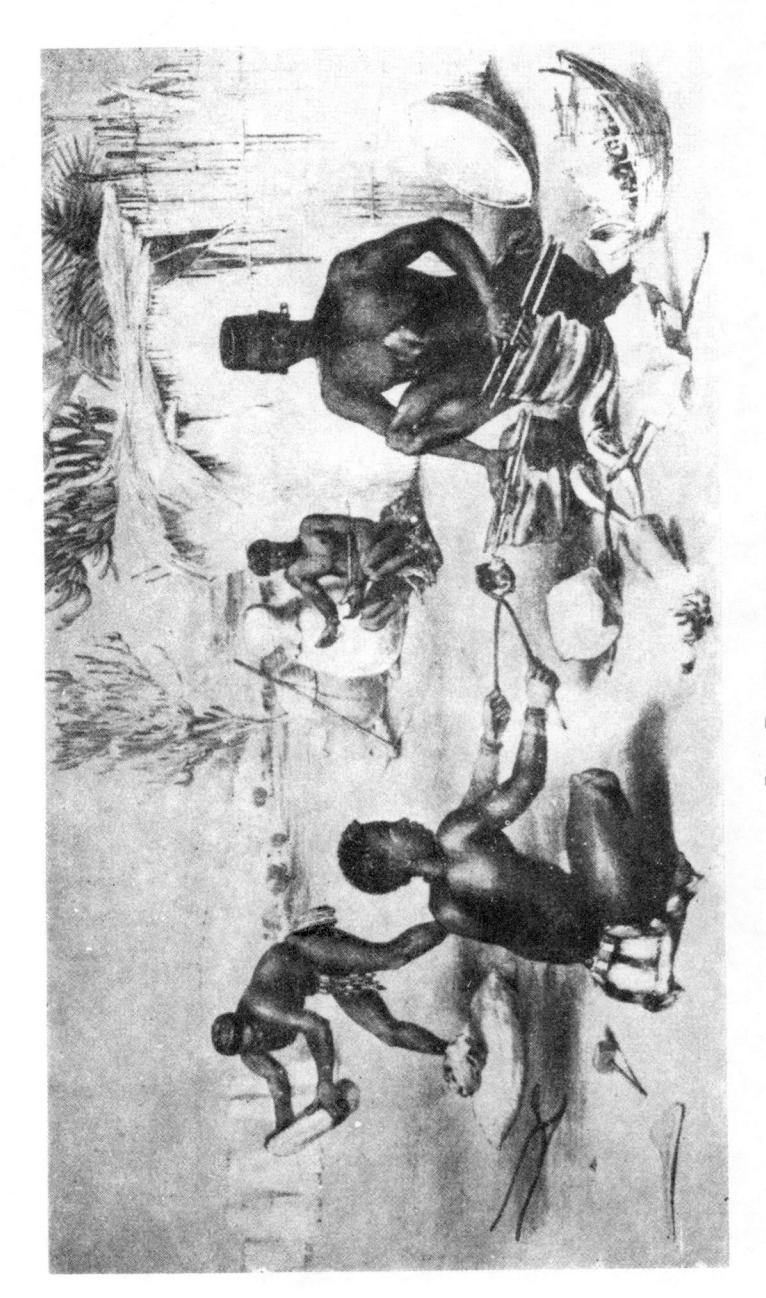

ZULU BLACKSMITHS AT WORK

From the painting by George French Angus in *Kaffirs Illustrated*

be sufficient to clean such utensils. They are obliged to invent from necessity, as well as the cockroaches, which scour every particle of dirt remaining on them. In fact I have known cockroaches to be collected in a calabash and carried to kraals in want of them, as scullions. They are not above a fourth the size of the common cockroach.

Organization of Kraals

Kraals contain from ten to 100 houses according to the quality of the proprietor. Some having from ten to 20 kraals to each, in which they appoint a captain, who is responsible for seeing the order obeyed from the chief, whose work, such as building the kraal or house, is done by people. Once a year people are collected together for the purpose of digging a field of corn for the chief. The kraals are built circular, being formed by two fences, one circle within the other. The inner one is for the cattle and the outer one encloses the huts which surround the cattle kraal and defend the cattle from being plundered without the knowledge of their proprietors. In one case, however, it is attended with dangerous consequences, as it enables the party who may attack them to surround the kraal and prevent the inhabitants' escape, the gateways being also stopped up. Such cases frequently happen, not from enemies but parties sent from the King.

A chief having erred, the whole kraal of men, women and children are put to death, but if it be an individual the chief is ordered by the King to put him to death. Whenever a chief is attacked it is generally at break of day, for which the attacking party is always eagerly waiting, as the property plundered becomes theirs, excepting cattle. Sometimes they spare the young girls, but the principal wife is always looked after, she being supposed to be privy to all her husband's conduct and, with the people of the kraal, ought to have objected to his faults. But such an idea, if it is an idea, can never be attended with the required result, as informers obtain little or no encouragement.

Hut Building

The kraals, as I have before described, are one circle within another, the inner one protecting the cattle; the outer one the huts. The common way of making their kraals is merely bushes piled up to form two circles, but there is another plan of a superior sort which forms a most excellent fence and lasts three or four years.

The manner of building huts, which are circular and about 12 or 18 feet in diameter, is as follows: They are formed of long thin stakes, pointed at one end, and fixed in the ground forming a circle, the other ends being bent over form an arch and are tied together with rushes. Cross poles are then tied together with rushes. Cross poles are then tied to the top inside; two pillars of wood then placed along the centre line of the hut, which by being put under the cross pieces, support the otherwise weak roof. The thatch is never more than two feet high above this, and over it is laid a thin coat of grass, gathered into a top knot at the centre, resembling that worn by the women. Small twigs of about a foot long, pointed at each end, are bowed into the thatch in regular circles about four inches apart; each circle is so formed as to appear like a twisted rope of twigs.

Huts thus built are secure from the severest weather and have a remarkably neat appearance, resembling as much as possible the bee hives used in Europe, the door being in the same proportion. The principal people in the nation pride themselves in the closeness of the laying of the sticks, so that the handles of their spoons will not pass through them. When thus finished they form a most neat piece of basket work.

The ground being levelled inside, the earth from ant heaps is collected and ground down with cowdung, which is damped and laid an inch thick on the levelled earth. The women, each with a mat (the same as they eat their meat on) in the one hand and a stone in the other, proceed to beat it down. About a foot from each pillar, the centre pointing exactly towards the door, is formed a fireplace, by raising the earth about four inches into an oval of three or four feet, which when beaten is as sound as a brick.

Such being the fireplace without a chimney, the smoke rises, leaving only a foot of clear air, in which its inhabitants lie down and breathe. Huts are better ventilated than one might imagine, air entering and passing out through the door and also quite easily through the thatch.

The earthen floor, after becoming dry, is rubbed hard with smooth stones, and frequently washed with cowdung and water, which keeps the house remarkably cool and far from being unpleasant in smell. Some huts, after washing with cowdung, are greased with suet, which, being rubbed in with a stone, polishes it like a looking glass, and causes the floor to be of a shiny black.

The doors are made of wickerwork slats, which are slipped in between two small posts about two inches from the doorway and fastened above by a stick in the framework. On the right-hand side, going into the hut, is tied up the firewood. A calabash of water, several calabashes of milk, a milk pail, several milk pots, beer pots, spoons and baskets, mats to eat off, stones for grinding corn, stones for grinding snuff, with a few mats and pillows, are the whole furniture of a native hut.

Milk pails are solid pieces of wood about 18 inches long and four inches in diameter, which is scooped out with no other tools than an axe and a crooked assegai. Although the entrance at the mouth is so small as not to admit a man's hand, by means of the crooked assegai they scoop it out clean to within three inches of the bottom, and it is finished off in a workmanlike form.

When milking, a man sits on his hams, holding the pail between his knees, and when full, pours the milk into a calabash. There are always separate small calabashes for the children.

Dress and Personal Habits

There is perhaps, in the whole world, no people who are more capable by custom to bodily cleanliness than the Zulus. They have aversion to anything that will in any way harbour filth, which makes them avert also anything incumbersome [*sic*]. This may be easily imagined by their almost nudity of person. In stature they are of middle size, there being none over tall and none remarkably short. Their men are of a warlike kind, perhaps owing to the peculiar fashion in which they ornament their heads, the hair of which is never allowed to grow above a quarter of an inch and seldom if ever half an inch, exclusive of the King's, which is allowed to grow to one inch, when a new head ring is always sewn on. No man throughout the Zulu nation is excluded from this national fashion of the head ring, the deficiency of which would be disgraceful to the person. It is generally oval or according to the shape of the head, originating from the front above the forehead to the crown, being about three inches long and four broad.

The hair being only a quarter of an inch long, through which the ring is sewn by men who hold it as a profession and for which they receive a trifle in payment.

It is performed by seven or eight long strips of the sennet leaf about an eighth of an inch broad, tied into a circle, the head being cleanly shaved, leaving the hair only on which the ring is to be sewn. A thread is then twisted of the sinews of an ox, with which the circle of sennet is bound round, drawing the threads close together. It is then placed on the head with an iron, horn or bone needle, which is threaded, taking every other thread which has encircled the sennet, and stitching it with the clove knot, drawing the flesh up in regular puckers, which a stranger would be induced to believe was occasioned from some strange fracture or deformity. It wears off in a day or so. Some beeswax or a similar production, formed by insects, and which they obtain from a tree, is drawn out (having first been blackened with charcoal) and encompasses the ring, giving it a neat finish. On this last addition is a soft kind of wax. The sun has the effect of destroying it. Such being the composition of the ring, it only requires smoothing every day or two, the head being shaved every three or four.

About this ring are worn feathers of birds taken from the quill and tied in neat bunches, having a very pretty effect. The hair is not only shaved from their heads, but it would appear that they have a particular aversion to it in any way, as from under the armpits and the lower part of the stomach they pick it out, as it appears, by the roots with their fingers. Till the hair on the head requires shaving (it being rarely that they do not wash in the river daily) they wash the head with clay, which when washed off leaves ridges, the clay having entangled the hair together, that being considered the height of fashion. Generally before washing in the river, meat is pounded on a stone, or milk or bread or clay is first used to rub the clay off.

A most remarkable feature of the Zulus is the ears, which are cut about the age of 10 or 13 to admit earrings of carved wood of an inch in diameter. In several instances, but one in particular, there was a man belonging to a nation westward of Natal, who always wore larger ones than those to the eastward, whose ears touched his shoulders. It would admit into the earhole a quart pot with the greatest of ease, from constantly stretching with larger earrings. This man has not long since entered my service, and in consequence of being laughed at, as the fashion is not so extended here, he has the greater part cut away and the two remaining ends joined together.

Round the neck they wear a few beads, and on days of dancing two large necklaces across the breast from the shoulders to below the knee and a thick quantity round the waist. On their penis is worn a small cap which is made of prepared oxhide. They measure by the thickness of their thumb. To a waist belt is attached several strips of fur or prepared skins, which being brought up to the lower part of the stomach is attached to a cord, encompassing the waist, whereto is fastened either furs or dressed parts.

It frequently does not cover one part of the buttocks, but as long as anything in the name of *umutsha* is worn on the buttocks and the cap remains in place they are in full dress. But should the latter be off it is considered as the extreme of indecency, and would be scouted as much by their countrymen as a woman in London without her shift. So much does custom determine matters that a man thus dressed, washed and slightly greased is in full dress. As to greasing, it is as necessary to a naked person as washing is to one that dresses. It keeps the skin pliant in opposition to a hot sun and sharp winds, and without it a Zulu looks as if he had been rolled in wood ashes. Dressed hides are sometimes worn by old men, but seldom or ever by the young and healthy, although they like European cloth as blankets.

Women differ widely from the men in their headdress, by shaving all except a top knot of an oval shape on the crown of the head, about four inches long and three broad, the length of the oval crossing the head. This is greased and clotted with red ochre clay, being trim and in the form of peppercorns. The ears of the women are cut the same as the men and beads worn in the same manner except that the women wear a few round the forehead, ankles and arms. Round from the hips they wear a petticoat, as before described, only reaching to the knees. They are equally particular with the men in washing and cleaning their heads with clay as also in shaving and plucking hair from all parts of the body where it appears, failure of such being disgusting to the husband. The only difference between grown-up people and young is that boys and girls only differ in their headdress, by not shaving, but merely greasing their heads and shaping the knots to peppercorns. They use scents of an agreeable smell, much like the Tonquin bean, to scatter on the top. The boys' dress is the same as the men. The girls wear a fringe round the middle, seldom deeper than three inches and frequently not so much. Custom teaches them to be as modest as this trifling shelter will allow them, as an unobserved curiosity could seldom be satisfied.

It is the custom of Zulus which originated from the Qwaɓes to tattoo the body. The operation is performed by the use of a Kaffir needle, the point being covered for the purpose, by which the skin is held up while it is cut moderately deep with a razor, having been first marked with red clay, representing the figure as fancy dictates. The number of cuts is from 200 to 300, which cause an effusion of blood, which they bear with a surprising degree of patience. On its healing, it is perceptible by its having risen above the other parts.

To speak of the character of the females in general, I could not say they were immodest. Readers may say I either contradict myself or do not know the meaning of the word, but, in their ideas of modesty the Zulus exceed all Europeans could imagine. It seldom or ever happens, I believe, that uncivilised nations will not prostitute themselves for gain, but here is seldom or ever such a thing known. Notwithstanding the great plurality of women which fall to the lot of man, his happiness is seldom or ever troubled by his mat being defiled. The crime of adultery is seldom heard of. This is no doubt occasioned from custom and from fear of death, as neither man nor woman would escape if found out. The probability is in favour of the husband. Even suspicion is sufficient to authorise the husband to punish with death. Jealousy, therefore, never troubles their brain.

External Intercourse (Ukuhlobonga)

Another species of connection which is known in this country, and I believe in no other, which goes by the name of *ukuhlobonga*, is very common. There being no house of ill fame throughout the nation, and no possibility of satisfying such claims, some course of satisfaction must follow which is that of *ukuhlobonga*. Unmarried girls are considered nearly in the same light with Europeans. If found pregnant before marriage they are, in general, discarded by their parents.

For the same reason the Zulu can no longer demand payment for his daughter which proves she is not virtuous. The custom, which can only account for strange things, is that a party of girls without distinction are always waiting for sweethearts. They may come from all parts of the country, from different kraals, and wherever they arrive ask permission from the chief of the kraal to *hlobonga*, which is generally granted. The girls being informed of their arrival, collect together, and stand at the upper end of the kraal, planting a post opposite them. Then the men by turns dance singly towards the post, and if agreeable to any girl she dances out to meet him. Failure of a girl to dance out shows he is objected to, which produces laughter on the man. This plan is repeated as often as strangers make their appearance, so that one girl may have 100 sweethearts, as also a man the same. The man then gives a string of beads to his sweetheart, and courtship commences, but in a kind of understood browbeating from both parties with hot arguments; all however, properly understood. With night coming on the language is not so violent. According to custom only *ukuhlobonga* is allowed. It is merely satisfying the ideas by following the act of cohabitation on the outward parts of the girl between the limbs. Anything beyond is not only dangerous to the girl's reputation, but the man will consider her as a designing wench who wishes to credit him with some other man's child or, under the shadow of love, to marry him. Should, however, the man commit rape, the father may always demand a cow from such intercourse.

Marriage Ceremonies

Marriages are frequently arranged. It sometimes happens otherwise by girls falling in love and running away from their parents, on which they follow and demand cattle. It sometimes happens that the match is made up by the intended husband and the father of the girl. In either case, the girl, accompanied by her female companions, proceeds to the kraal where they stand at the upper end, waiting the invitation of the intended husband's mother or principal wife. She gives beads to the bride, conducting her into the house, where a mat is placed for them to sit on, beads being again given a third time before they will eat. A day is then appointed for the wedding, until when the bride and her party remain under a bush at a distance from the kraal, to which she comes only to sleep. According to the situation of the husband, so are the neighbours invited by numbers. When the wedding day arrives, the friends invited arrive generally driving oxen before them as part of the ceremony. A half-circle is formed by the men, the women standing opposite. Dancing and singing commences of different kinds to the tune and meaning of the songs. So are the attitudes with feet and hands of the men, which they perform in a surprisingly able manner. The songs are of two kinds, the one being a dancing song. The girls merely follow the attitudes of the men, keeping the same time in music. The others are in two parts when the women only, clap their hands to the time sung by the men. When the women sing their parts the men pass through the attitudes in mime for each separate song, seldom exceeding one verse, sometimes two, always being sung on the principle of a coach wheel, which is by going round. One performer commences and at each repetition another joins in, till the singers are ten in number.

During the singing, the bride and her attendants are trimming themselves off to the best advantage. When ready to enter the kraal, the men and women make way for them and they dance by themselves. The mother or principal wife of the intended husband, walking to the bride while singing, cautions her on her conduct, and telling her what immense work such as digging, etc., they shall now expect by this new addition in their fields. The bride, dancing in the middle of her companions, takes very little notice of the advice, treating it as a mere matter of course. Now and then she dances out from the rest of the bridesmaids holding out beads for the relations of the intended husband whom she baulks repeatedly by turning back. At length, however, the bride dances towards the principal relation of the bridegroom to whom she throws down some beads, and then returns to fetch more from the bridesmaids which she gives the next nearest relation, and so on, including the wives of her intended husband, and even the servants, if the bride is to be the chief wife. At times they cry out and abuse the bridegroom with all the abusive language that the bride is capable of; but this is no more than custom, all being meant in good part. At other times again, the bridegroom's party addresses the bridesmaids who are requested to listen to the bride's cases of infidelity which generally satisfies the husband that if she does err it will not be for want of knowing better. During this part the men are gathered in clusters drinking beer and talking over the cattle or the nuptials. Then the cattle for slaughter are brought in, either one or two or more, according to the quality of the husband (seldom, however, more than one) unless the man takes two wives in one day, which frequently happens. Immediately the cow or ox is fallen, the bridesmaids throw some beads on the wound where the animal was stabbed, which any man takes who gets them. The beast is then slaughtered by the friends of the girl who have accompanied her, and is disposed of by the bride's attendants, half being given to the kraal where the bride is to be married, the other half being given to her friends. The hide is generally preserved for a petticoat for the bride, the dress which she then wears having been given new from her parents, with a dress of beads. The girl is then taken to her husband's house, where she remains a week or a month as the husband thinks proper. Then she is put on the same footing as other wives and takes her turn with the next in his favours. The day after the ceremony the bride's relatives, with a small staff and assegais, come to the kraal, where they stand some time in silence and then demand cattle. One or two are given according to the ability of the husband. Should he be a man of property, an ox is sent to him from the girl's parents, in which case many cattle are expected in return. It is at the option of the husband to accept or return the ox, which he frequently returns.

For should he accept it there is no end to the demands. It is strange that although these marriages are nothing more than a barter in women for cattle no bargains were ever made before or after marriage as to the number of cattle to be paid. But an exact bargain is never known among them nor the consent to such if proposed. Formerly, before Shaka destroyed so many nations, marriages were the only traffic[1] in cattle. This was well seen from there being such an abundance of cattle, the precious value they put on women. I cannot be sure, but conclude that the lowest rate that women were parted from their parents was five cows, and the average was 15, but in many cases I have known 40 or 50 to be paid for a woman and beyond that. For the daughter of a chief 100 cattle would only be considered reasonable; but since the dissolution of so many nations the Zulus only pay a few head, 15 being considered sufficient for a chief's daughter.

The reader, from the above, may be induced to think it a species of slavery, and a man may make his offers as he would for a slave, but it is far from that nature, the whole being a custom which they would not break in any of its parts, and the idea of slavery is as disgusting to them as it is to an Englishman.

Shaka has, in a great measure, prevented marriages under the idea of single men only being fit for warriors. To each regiment of warriors was attached a regiment of girls, who resided in the *isigodlo* of each barracks. An instance of communication or young men entering the *isigodlo*, under any pretence, has, in several instances, been the cause of the destruction of such a regiment.

The Zulu Kings had the practice of sending their sisters in marriage to chiefs whom they considered capable of paying a suitable price. They were accompanied by a large number of bridesmaids, and two oxen, as his mouth, to the chief.

However displeasing such an arrival may be, he is necessitated to appear pleased, and to acknowledge in the strongest terms how much he feels the honour, and to express the fears he entertains of the whole of his cattle not being sufficient to

---

[1] Should a girl die after marriage or on a visit to her parents or by running from an enemy be killed, the cattle must be returned or her sister sent in her place and if no other girl can be provided, one at the breast is bespoken and delivered when of a proper age.—*Editor.*

satisfy his King. He proceeds to pay by 50's and 100's, in some cases nearly impoverishing himself.

The least insinuation of the bridegroom not being willing to accept such an honour would be punished with death.

It was formerly the custom not to allow intermarriages in one kraal and to avoid, if possible, marriages in the neighbourhood, thus encouraging the intermarriage of foreign tribes. In the present intermixed state of the Zulus, owing to tribal upheavals, marriages in the same kraal are common, but if any relationship can be traced between the parties marriage is strictly forbidden.

Two sisters may marry one man. A man may marry the wife of his elder brother, not the reverse. The mother of the married girl always hides her face from her daughter's husband. In like manner the girl must avoid as much as possible the company or conversation of her husband's relations; not calling them by their names, but using the terms father and mother, and being generally modest.

Contempt for Slavery

A Portuguese is, in consequence of their dealing in slaves at Delagoa Bay, treated by the Zulus with the most wilful contempt. A slave vessel, only in the month of October, 1829, was wrecked at Natal, and had it not been for my brother, Mr. W. Fynn, accompanying them through the Zulu country to the King's residence, it is doubtful whether they would have got through. Many liberties were taken with them which would never have been inflicted upon an Englishman when travelling alone. The King treated them in the light of Delagonians, asking them many questions as to their manners and concerning slaves in irons. Had it not been for my brother begging so hard, they would have been necessitated to travel to Delagoa without a guide.

Polygamy

Polygamy is universal among the Zulu, although Shaka and Dingane, the late and present King, have not taken wives. The number of concubines of Shaka was not less than 5,000, those of Dingane being about 500, by whom they are not supposed to beget children, although one instance of such appears in Shaka's reign. During his reign the elder chiefs only were allowed to have wives, the young and vigorous being permitted to have concubines, any one of which producing a child would have caused the death of that chief, unless, as was sometimes the case, he had previously sent oxen requesting permission to marry them. This was sometimes granted. The soldiers were almost excluded from speaking with women, only those who had been married before Shaka's reign being permitted to retain their wives. This custom extended to every tributary tribe that joined the Zulus, from whence the single men of each were enlisted to join a Zulu regiment, so that a few of the former Zulus and those of the tributary tribes formed the whole of the married men in the country. Some of the married chiefs had as many as 50 wives and the men from one to 20.

The first wife of a commoner is the principal one, but not so with kings and chiefs. They, after having taken many wives, choose the daughters of other kings or chiefs for their queens who will produce their heirs, although the former wives may have sons at that time grown up. The name of *Inkosikazi*, i.e. Queen, is the term by which all principal wives are known, even by the meanest subject. She has much respect paid to her by other wives and is called by them " mother," and to her is reported all the domestic affairs which she regulates. In the absence of her husband, if a chief, she consults with the chief of the kraal even in public affairs. Their mutual consent empowers them to have any person killed in the kraal, messengers being sent to report the death to the *umnumzane*, i.e. head. It is the duty of the wife to dig the ground, plant, stack and thresh the corn, make the floors of the houses and keep them clean, collect firewood and water and make clay pots for cooking and drinking vessels. Also collecting grass for thatching their huts, according to the numbers of his houses, or of chiefs, the numbers of kraals, each hut having from one to four in it. A man possessing only one wife and only one cow, the wife would rather he would part with it for another wife than live by herself, the husband being no company for the wife, seldom taking notice of her in public, and, although he may have come from war or a long journey, no compliment passes between them, the husband only asking for a pinch of snuff.

The wives of one house live generally on most affectionate terms, those of different huts or kraals endeavouring by their attention to monopolise as much as possible of the husband's favours. During his visit, the wife visited supplies him with food, a mat and a pillow and a box of snuff, but on no account will a woman allow her husband the use of the mat when he visits another wife. The *Inkosikazi* is bound to see the *umlobokazi* or young married woman has enough to eat, and leaves her house for a month during the honeymoon. This she is also necessitated to do when any of her husband's sweethearts arrive, cleaning the house and laying the mat.

There are many circumstances which prevent the husband from cohabitation; seven days abstention during menses. Any person in the kraal severely wounded by assegai, stick or bite of any animal or the death of a relation, each three days' abstention. A man having wounded or killed another in battle must first be connected with a woman of a strange kraal before he connects with his wife. After the birth of a child, the husband refrains from his wife till the child is weaned.

Pregnancy and Childbirth

During pregnancy the woman wears an *isidinga* over her breast, but in no form is she allowed to have any brass about her person. She is supplied with *isihlambezo*, a medicine which she puts into a calabash and carries always with her, of which she drinks as inclined, for the purpose of supporting the child in the womb until delivery, then it is given to the child until it has gained strength. Twins at birth are rare, but five children have been produced at birth. The women are laid on a bed of straw, not permitted to use a mat. On these occasions they are attended by the old women of the kraal and during delivery, if fearful, cords are passed round the ankles and passed through the sides of the hut and held outside. This seldom is necessary.

The child produced, it is washed in cold water, the navel string is then cut with a split reed or stem of grass, the part left on the infant being two inches long. This is washed repeatedly with a mixture of juice of the small aloe leaf, milk from the mother's breast, and wood ashes, till it falls off. A fire of charcoal is made and mixed with roots, over the smoke of which the child is frequently drawn. The custom of the tribe to which her husband belongs is then followed.

In cases of five children or twins or where the mother is deficient in milk, the children are given to the grandmother or some old woman to suckle, whose breasts will in general produce milk sufficient after two days suckling. On a child being weaned, the breast is milked into the cavity of a hoe handle, cowdung being placed at the bottom to receive it, and when filled covered with the same, this is placed above the fireplace and allowed to remain till, by moving the kraal or by chance, it should be lost. An omission of any of these customs would be considered dangerous to the child's health throughout life.

Till children are able to walk, they are carried on their mother's back, a soft calf or goat skin being used to tie them. Boys from infancy are brought up to herd cattle and from the highest to the lowest families it is considered a necessary qualification to manhood.

Girls are brought up to fetching water, firewood, carrying corn on their heads and digging in the fields. Queens and princesses labour with as much pains as the poorest women.

Puberty Rites

A girl on first having her menses reports it to her parents, who give her a cow to kill for the occasion. She is then placed behind a screen of mats where she remains for a month to six as the parents may think fit. On her going out of the hut on necessary occasions, she is covered with a kaross to hide her from the sight of men. During her confinement she is never left alone, and the girls in the neighbourhood collect every evening singing the most lewd songs imaginable, without the least shame, it being that at any other time an indelicate word is never known to escape their lips. Any stranger entering the hut is kept in till he forfeits beads. If obstinacy is shown, the girls make a large fire surrounding him, and singing their indelicate songs, cause the man so much surprise that he soon pays their demand. The beads so collected are divided between the girls at the end of the confinement. She at this time sends a few beads to her sweetheart, who sends others in return.

There is a custom named *eMhosheni* when the girls of each tribe collect together, leaving their dresses at home. They dress

ZULU WOMAN RETURNING FROM WORK IN THE FIELDS
From the drawing by George French Angus in *Kaffirs Illustrated*

themselves with leaves and sing in different parts of the country, sleeping in the bushes for three nights, during which their food is left at a distance from the kraals. On their return home the oldest woman of the kraal has cooked victuals for them which she hands them from behind her.

They will not converse with men, who, if they do, will attack and rob them of their beads. On the fourth day they go to the extreme end of the country, wash themselves in the river and from them the next tribe take it up, so passing it on. The custom originates from an idea of there having been a princess, half her body being of the common form and the other of grass. Her hinder parts were red, and as she used to leave the hut she desired the girls not to look at her hinder parts. The custom is kept up out of respect to the princess, who would afflict them with sickness if neglected.

Planting, Reaping and Storing

It is the business of the men to cut such bushes or wood as obstruct the women in the fields. These they leave to the women, who merely scratch the grass up at the roots, having previously cast the seed. The roots are left on the fields till the corn is fit for hoeing, first to protect the young plant from the wind, and secondly to prevent the seed being picked out by the birds. When the corn is nearly ripe a man is placed there to protect it from the pigs, which are very destructive. They are frequently hunted during the winter months, the bushes being clear, at the time, to allow a passage through them. If they are found in the garden during the night, the party enter the fields rustling the corn, and at intervals standing motionless, making sounds in imitation of the pigs, which take them for a drove of their own species, by which means the party are able to come upon them by surprise.

When the corn is ripe it is plucked and stacked into a reed basket work, some being six feet high and 15 feet in diameter, from whence it is threshed at the beginning of winter, some being put into baskets for immediate use. A few bunches of cobs are preserved for seeds. The remainder are put into cellars in the cattle kraals. These are dug into a conical shape, the entrance being only large enough to admit a young lad. Round the sides and bottom it is covered with wild plantain leaves, the top being covered with stalks crossed, which is filled up with earth. It seldom remains long in the ground before the urine of the cattle, soaking through the dung, has filled the cellars, by which it has become to them a most delicate feast, particularly to women in pregnancy, whom I have known to go 50 miles for a treat of it.

Crops Grown by the Zulus

As the manner of planting does not differ in any of their productions, I shall only mention the different kinds of grain. Millet, called by the natives *imbela*, is grown only in small quantities by the Zulus, but it is the principal food of the tributary tribes. It grows from six to 12 feet in height, producing sometimes five to six heads to a stalk. They commence planting in June and it is ripe in the beginning of September. By September they have a second crop and in March they have a third, some years having green corn all the year through.

The King is supplied with corn by every regiment and their families planting every year. So are the owners of kraals provided by the people of each, exclusive of what is planted by their own families, but the community are only dependent on the exertions of their wives.

According to the number a man has in each hut, they dig the fields of the mistress of that hut, but they are generally late before they commence planting in consequence of a law preventing their using the fruits of their labour till the King should first have eaten of the fruits of that year. The non-observance of the custom never fails of being punished with death to the whole kraal of people to which the culprit belongs. Their cattle go to the King, who generally defers it till late in the season and the early crops are spoilt in the fields. Picking a fallen corn is as bad as eating it. When the King intends eating the first fruits of the season, all the people and families attached to the regiments are called to his residence. The men appear in their war-dresses and a feast is given on the occasion and a national dance takes place at that time and no other, when the names of their enemies are shouted as a degradation. Any chief's tributary not appearing is considered as an enemy and killed in consequence. This annual meeting, by which they are enabled to count the years of any King's reign, lasts three or four days and defines Kings from chiefs, who dare not presume to such a privilege. Dancing, singing and showing of oxen are the amusements. The King does not allow this opportunity to pass without killing many of them to convince them of his power and cause himself to be feared. On the last grand day the King enters the circle of his soldiers, with his seraglio grandly decorated. His favourite concubines stoop while entering, and during the intervals of singing are surrounded by others who stand up, secreting them from the eyes of the soldiers as much as possible. The amusements of singing ended, a calabash is held by the King, surrounded by a number of young boys, when he runs about with it, pretending to throw it, but frequently baulks them and at length throws it, the boys scrambling after it. During the meeting the King informs them of his intention to attack some foreign power, which takes place early in the winter months, the rivers being only passable at that time. On their leaving, instructions are given them early as to the time and they proceed home to eat their corn and stack it, but from the unsettled state of the country they generally have but two crops. They use no artificial means to promote the growth, only leaving it unsown for one year after five years' work.

Amabele or Guinea corn is the principal crop of the Zulus and requires longer time in coming to maturity then the former, only one crop being produced during the season.

Luphoko, a grain produced from a ...... grows about one foot in length, is six months coming to perfection, is grown principally for making beer, which is a most pleasant beverage, and often intoxicates the drinker.

Beans are of two kinds, the one, *izindumba*, is a running bean and is similar to the French bean. The other kind, *izindlubu*, is produced from underground, with one bean in each pod, leaves similar to trefoil attached to the stem without stalks.

Amazambane grow underground, something of the flavour of a potato but a little bitter. The stem is 18 inches high, from which a leaf like sage arises parallel from two sides, the stem being square.

Amadumbe is a plant, the leaf and growth being similar to the water lily but the flower different in shape and of a pinkish blue colour. The food is like the potato underground, and is something like that vegetable, but has a glutinous matter on it. These are as large as the largest size potato.

Inqalothi is a grain, in length and appearance, in stem and seed similar to the bull-rush, and is very apt to be destroyed by birds. It is principally used for making beer which is stronger than the *luphoko*. It is frequently ground with water and eaten raw. A piece of this raw, the size of a penny roll, will prevent the pain of hunger for several days during a journey.

There are four kinds of sugar cane, *uMoba*. One is the West Indian kind and is planted in pieces underground in low damp soil and is very prolific. It is only used to eat. A winter stock is sometimes preserved by burying it underground.

Pumpkins of a small and inferior kind were used but the *amaselwa* pumpkin, introduced on our arrival, is in more general use.

Melons, similar to water melons in appearance, they use to make soup. Gourds are universally planted, and while young and tender form a principal part of their diet. When they become hard they are scooped out and used for beer, milk and water vessels. I have seen three which hold 18 gallons. When they become broken they are usually stitched with thread, being watertight.

Tobacco is planted from the plants of fallen seeds, not having an idea it would rise from seeds sown. They only produce sufficient for their consumption in snuff, which they take in immense quantities, never being satisfied till, by a pressure with the thumb and finger, over the eyes, tears are produced. It appears to give them much relief. The tears are traced by finger-nail each side of the nose and water is ejected from the mouth. It is pungent from the manner of making it, it being ground by a small round stone on a large flat one by the constant rolling it backwards and forwards. When nearly brought to a powder, it is mixed with an equal quantity of ash from dried aloe leaves, in want of which, wood ashes are used. Persons seldom meet without one asking the other for a pinch of snuff. It is never offered without being asked for, and then reluctantly given from a fear of their readiness to attribute any sickness attacking the partaker of it to the giver who is suspected of having bewitched it.

Making of Fire

The manner of producing fire is done with facility by means of two pieces of dry wood, eight or nine inches long, containing a pith on the one which is to lay on the ground. A notch is cut. The other is sharpened to an obtuse point which is put into the notch of the other, is turned swiftly between both hands which are shifted repeatedly, increasing the pressure as much as possible, the dust powdered having caught fire falls over the sides of the notch on to the dry grass.

Remedy for Weak Eyes

Cuttle fish bone is used in powder for weak eyes with success. It is supposed to be the excrements of the moon which it passes in rising and floats to the shore.

Men's and Women's Complaints

They assert, and it is generally believed among them, that a complaint exists of beetles being seated in the stomach and when driven from it by medicine it is necessary to kill them with sticks. Another complaint is supposed to be caused from detached particles of blood under the skin, which is extracted with a razor. A complaint called *uMdiyasi* is very common. They believe it arises from the medicine drunk by the warriors after battle, being a decoction of roots in which an axe, red heated, is put and bears the name of *izembe* or axe. The person who receives the complaint from this decoction is not afflicted nor his wives, but whoever should connect with them after the husband's death is attacked, falling off to a skeleton, in which state he remains without any particular pain, lingering, as in a decline. The woman becomes pregnant and being delivered, he dies. I have had sufficient proofs that such a complaint exists and have no doubt of its being communicated by coition, the woman having no pain or appearance of disease, yet every man who cohabits with her falls off in a decline and dies, the woman remaining in apparent perfect health. This disease is well understood by the doctors, which they cure on payment of a cow.

Aphrodisiacs. Stimulants to submit to the wishes of the men were used in common among the natives, but now only partially so by the tributary tribes. Shaka had forbidden the use of any medicinal preparation more than necessary to cure sickness.

Relief from barrenness is practised with success.

An ingredient is sometimes used as a stimulant to cause the girls to love the giver, which is mixed and taken as snuff.

Instances of insanity are few, but are in general relieved by the native doctors.

The Ghost of Mbiya

Mbiya was a Zulu chief of the tribe of Mthethwas, taken into favour by Shaka from the intimacy which had existed between them while Shaka was under the protection of Dingiswayo. He died in 1827, Shaka regretting much his loss. A few months after his decease, a report was current that the spirit of Mbiya had appeared at his own kraal, intending to visit Shaka, who, in consequence, sent chiefs repeatedly to see him, always taking with them oxen, which were stabbed in his kraal as offerings to him. The truth of his presence was confirmed by all who went to his place, with whom he entered into conversation on topics of a political nature, ever praising Shaka as a superior power, assuring them of Shaka's being much favoured by the spirits from whom he had been sent on the present mission. They did not omit asking for snuff, when he directed them to a spot where a box was placed. So satisfied were they of the spirit being there that they confirmed it to Shaka, who appointed a day for his appearance; in the meantime he had a handsome kaross in which he was to appear, sent to him on the day appointed.

Shaka and his chiefs were ready to receive him when, to the astonishment of all, an old woman, pretending to be the spirit, commenced delivering her mission, which Shaka soon put a stop to, ordering her away as an impostor, giving his opinion that she had been ordered undoubtedly by Mbiya, who did not wish to appear.

Crocodiles

Crocodiles abound in all the principal rivers east of Mkhomazi. Some have been seen in the rivers west, but seldom, and never west of the Mthamvuna. During the summer months they are to be seen in numbers, appearing like floating logs on the water, or basking in the sun on a sandy bank, where they lie like a log of dry timber till an animal may get within 30 yards of them. Should anyone approach, it stretches itself from the coiled position in which it is apt to lie, and like a boat being launched appears to slide into the water. The direction of its course may be followed for a considerable time by small bubbles following it. During the summer months they are much to be dreaded, when the rivers are risen from the heavy rains. Their manner of attack is, when they have got sufficiently close to their prey, to seize it by the parts under the water. At the same moment it throws itself over, dragging its prey to the deepest water, and when dead drags it to the reeds of the river side to devour it. The Mkhomazi, Mngeni, Mhlali and Thukela are the rivers where they are most ferocious, often attacking people and cattle. The latter, excepting calves . . . . they are only able to bite. They are stabbed and killed by the natives, who assert that for the spear to have effect the blade must be held in a position that it may enter parallel with the animal, which plan alone will admit the spear on the sides and belly of the animal, into the apparently impenetrable shell. From the difference in their size and ferocious habits between those of the eastern and western, although it has to be proved, they would appear to be of two kinds. Their eggs are often to be found, but I have in two instances picked up young ones, when not a foot in length, and although I bestowed some care in keeping them alive, they died after a few days. The natives hold them much in dread. Those living on the banks of rivers are less fearful of them and pretend to have an antidote as a preventive to their being seized. This is no more than the hard scales of that animal, which in appearance resemble the bark of trees. Pieces of this are given to persons when crossing the river, who eat it, rubbing some of it over their body. In deficiency of that article, strong-smelling plants such as wormwood are rubbed over the body, from an idea that such smell is disagreeable to them.

During the winter months they are not destructive, which the natives believe to be occasioned by either of two causes. First that they lose their teeth, secondly that they are prevented from lack of water to be able to steal on their prey unperceived; but it is doubtless owing to the partially torpid state they are in. Natives in the crossing, seeing the crocodiles, sometimes throw a calabash in the water, which is generally pawed by the animals and from its lightness keeps turning over, they following it down, which keeps them at play till the persons have passed.

SNAKES

Boa constrictors, called by the Zulus *umonya* or *izinhlwathi*, are frequently to be found in the Natal country, but they are more numerous east of the Thukela, inland and along the coast west of the Mthamvuna where game of the antelope kind are plentiful. They prey on numerous animals, such as goats, antelope, dogs and even leopards, sometimes taking men and women. The manner of seizing their prey is raising their head two or three feet erect, sometimes being previously coiled round, they then entwine round the middle of their prey, placing the fork of its tongue in the nostrils of the prey, tightening themselves round till their prey is strangled. They then lick the body with a slimy substance and proceed to suck the body in, commencing at the head. In performing this they are sometimes three or four days, the head being apparently swelled and the jaws extended to a surprising size. As their prey enters the stomach, it may be seen to rise gradually till swallowed, when it lies from that time in a torpid state and, although attacked, becomes helpless for 18 to 20 days.

They frequently exceed 18 feet in length, spanning 2 feet 6 inches round the belly. It is asserted by the natives as a fact that a man of the Mthwani tribe on the Mzimkhulu, in argument with others of the strength of the *nhlwathi*, declared he would overcome that animal. To effect his purpose, he went to the hole in the absence of the serpent and lay down, apparently dead, on his face, to prevent the snake stopping his nostrils extending his arms erect before his head. The serpent attempted to enclose his arms and elbows, when the man by extending them kept freedom of movement for them and succeeded in overcoming it.

Indlondlo is a serpent above 12 feet in length. It remains constantly in the woods, always near a river, to which it has always a road made by its repeated visits. From the crown of the head rises a crest much imitating a feather, about four inches in length. It makes a noise similar to a pheasant and attacks various birds near it, on which it preys. The bite of that serpent is of the most dangerous kind; persons living but a few hours should they not be able to obtain the valuable remedy *isibiba*. The bites of snakes are very expeditiously cured by a composition of the poison taken from every snake they can collect, which is dried up into a powder. An emetic is first given and then a small pinch of the powder. A little is then put into the place bitten, which is opened with an assegai to admit it. If application is made within four hours after the bite, there is no doubt of the cure, of which I have seen sufficient proof.

Forerunners of the Voortrekkers

Natal was a *terra incognita* to the Dutch inhabitants of the Cape until Messrs. Petersen and Hoffman, co-partners to Lieutenant Farewell, proceeded by sea to Port Natal. These gentlemen's knowledge of Natal on their return to the Cape was not circulated beyond Cape Town, hence had nothing to do with the movements of the Boers from the Cape frontier districts.

On Doctor Smith's arrival at Natal he had in his service a Dutch Boer William Berg. His father was an Englishman, and had married a Boer woman. He had adopted all the domestic Boer habits in which his children were brought up. The doctor's trip along the coast, after passing through the country of Kaffirs as far as St. John's River, brought him into the country which had been depopulated by Shaka.

After their arrival in Natal, while the doctor was residing with me, William Berg on several occasions spoke in raptures of the rich country he had passed through, and how certain he felt that if the Boers in the Cape Colony knew that such a country was uninhabited they would rush to its occupation.

On William Berg's return to the Cape Colony with Doctor Smith it is most probable he communicated this knowledge to the Dutch in his vicinity.

Piet Uys, an influential Dutch farmer in Uitenhage, would have heard of the advantages this country afforded him. I have therefore considered that William Berg was the first Boer who came to this country, and instigated the subsequent emigration of the Boers to Natal.

There came also about that time overland a Boer called Vanvega, who, after a few months' elephant shooting, returned to the Somerset district in the Cape Colony. From him the Dutch of that locality will have derived much information. It was not, however, till 1834, when the Emancipation of Slavery occurred which produced great discontent among the Boers of the Cape Colony, that they savoured the idea of emancipating themselves from the British Government by meeting beyond the boundary of the Cape Colony. Hans Lange was the first Boer who attempted to escape beyond the boundary with his slaves, and he located himself on the Swart Vlei River below the junction of the Kloof Plaats and Klaas. The Cape Government on learning the locality he was occupying beyond the frontier border despatched Colonel A. B. Armstrong with a troop of the Cape Corps to proceed and demand from Lange the slaves he had taken with him.

Colonel Armstrong's long experience and influence with the Dutch Boers at the Cape Frontier enabled him to perform that duty satisfactorily without using force. This duty was performed in the latter end of December, 1834, Lange having crossed the boundary in October or November of that year. Therefore, unless we may suppose that the rumours of a Kaffir invasion existed in November, it could not have been the invasion of the 25th December, 1834, which led the Boers first to contemplate migrating from the Cape Colony, though there is no doubt that the invasion increased the desire and brought on the crisis. It would appear the communications that were made from one frontier district to another annoyed the leading Boers, for simultaneously we find Piet Uys, wealthy and generally respected, leading the migration from Uitenhage district; from the Somerset district we find Maritz leading; while from Grahamstown and Albany, Piet Retief, who had associated much with the English of that locality a leader of the Boers from thence. From the commencement of this migration in 1834 until 1848 I was on the Cape frontier and in a position to know the movements and the objects of the migrating Boers.

Piet Retief, aware of my knowledge, my influence and experience, urged me to leave the Government Service, and join them in their contemplated migration, tempting me with the offer of giving me one of the highest appointments and a handsome salary. I felt assured that no one was so competent as myself to save them from the dangers in which they were certain of being involved with the native tribes, especially the Zulu nation. My attachment to Natal and having no desire to live in any other country was a strong motive for my accepting his proposals, though I felt assured that from whatever difficulties I might save them in reference to the native tribes, my services would not be appreciated. Had I accepted Retief's proposals, I certainly should not have consented to his proceeding to Dingane, as may be well imagined from my previous escapes from that chief. The non-appreciation of such services as I might have given had I joined Retief did not weigh with me in my determination. I should have been content with returning to Natal to occupy my farm on the Isipingo and having the protection of the Boers from any attack of the Zulu nation, my influence being sufficient to increase the native force of Natal and with the aid of the Boers to defy the Zulu nation. I believed then as I do now that the migrating Boers did not contemplate warring against the Cape Government and fighting with British troops. The acts of Sir Benjamin d'Urban, under whom I had served with much pleasure, were disapproved of by the Colonial Minister, which made me little desirous of continuing longer in the service. In this state of indecision I asked by letter the friendly advice of a military officer of rank with whom I had seen some service in the field, and who had encouraged me on all occasions to appeal to him for friendship and advice. To him I stated the matter fully and freely. His reply, with the advice of Sir Richard England, then commanding on the frontier, led me to decide on remaining in the service. The reply I received from my friend was as laconic as some of the Duke of Wellington's.

  My dear Fynn,
    You be d . . . . d.
      Yours truly
        G.H.S.

The leaders of the migrating Boers from the several frontier districts led their families, cattle, sheep and horses with a long train of bullock waggons across the boundary beyond the village of Colesberg. The three persons named were in the position of Field Commandants, forming separate encampments a few miles from each other. I believe their intent then was there to await other Boers who might be led to join them from the Cape Colony, and not at once to proceed to Natal. Retief had drawn out a set of rules to be observed by the emigrants for the future conduct which were signed by some of his followers. Uys, hearing of these rules, sent to the followers of Retief urging them not to sign any rules for their Government until the whole party of Boers should unite to elect the leader and establish rules for their Government.

This appears to have irritated Retief and he may have been led to conceive the chieftainship to be his personal right. It is therefore likely that he thought the best way of attaining that position was by his proceeding to the Zulu chief Dingane and inducing him to cede the country of Natal to him and emigrant Boers, the result of which is so clearly described in the Honourable Cloete's lectures.

Retief may have considered that in his dealings with the Zulu chief a plain, honest representation of his case would meet a corresponding honest dealing from Dingane. Little did he know the wily chief. He informed him that the Boers had left the Cape Colony a numerous body of men and were desirous of becoming his peaceful neighbours in brotherhood and aiding each other in difficulties, if Dingane would cede to him the country of Natal for their occupation. Had Retief been acquainted with the history of the Zulu nation he would have known that one of the principal objects of Shaka, who had made the Zulus a great nation, was totally to depopulate the surrounding country as far as his soldiers could penetrate, that his followers over whom he held such despotic sway might have no asylum or refuge if they attempted to escape his murderous power. Few European diplomatists could have planned a more perfect mode of destroying an enemy than that conceived by Dingane. The very idea of so powerfully an armed force anticipating the occupation of so close a neighbourhood at once alarmed him. He therefore assented to cede the country to the Boers on the condition that they would attack and retake cattle which had been taken from his country by the roving chief Siqonyela. This service Retief accomplished and anticipated the reward of his service. Dingane had attached to Retief's force some of his own followers, and, knowing the Zulu chief as I do, I conclude his object was that his followers were sent to observe the Boers' mode of fighting and the result, in which it might be possible the Boers might be defeated, thus saving him the necessity of their destruction, or, on the other hand, enable him to judge how he might defeat them himself. It is, however, certain that he adopted the same mode of treachery as Retief had done when he enticed Siqonyela into Mr. Allison's garden and, making him a prisoner, put him in irons until he refunded the cattle. Dingane could, without the possibility of failure, have defeated the tribe under Siqonyela without the aid of the Boers.

On Retief's arrival at Port Natal two of the earliest followers of Lieut. Farewell were at Natal, and from 15 to 20 who were with him in three previous years travelled overland from the Cape Colony. Retief and his party might have obtained much valuable information from these persons, but unfortunately the Boers had publicly expressed the old saw " Might is right. You few Englishmen here must submit to us the more powerful." The local knowledge and experience of these English, few as they were, made them a valuable ally. Union with the Boers would have produced a very different result in the subsequent battle which took place in the Zulu country. These few English had suffered much by Dingane's hostility and oppression. They had sufficient to revenge and they took this opportunity of doing so. After the death of Retief and party and the attack on the Boers' encampments, the Boers proceeded in force and entered the Zulu country. John Cane, the most experienced of the English, planned a party with some 800 natives and made an attack on one of Dingane's encamped regiments. The slaughter was great. The English fought as Englishmen sometimes do and not one of them that day disgraced his country. Much has been said by Natal colonists in admiration of the order in which the natives of Natal were kept by the Boers and the subjection they continued in until Natal became a British Colony. From 1824, when the first natives were brought by myself and subsequently by others from hundreds of miles to occupy the country of Natal from which they had been driven, up to the period when I left Natal, no people of any country could have been under more protection, could have been more honest and faithful than the natives who looked up to the several white men as their protectors and chiefs. In thus lauding their character it was not attributable to the wisdom or good judgment of the white inhabitants but to the circumstances in which the natives were placed. The power had been given us to protect; without that protection the natives of Natal knew that destruction was their lot. In the attack made by Cane and his party only two white men escaped. The natives on this occasion fought most desperately, fulfilling the assertion they frequently make use of " that they will die round the body of their chief." This was literally the case. Where a white man fell they rushed to cover his body, where they were killed in heaps. This has been related to me both by the natives of Natal and the Zulus themselves. That the natives of Natal since it became an English settlement can no longer be spoken of in such high terms is our misfortune and theirs.

Burial of Kings

Kings are interred after various ways. Some are interred standing, some sitting, others lying down, a hut built over them and people placed to live on the spot to take care of them and guard them.

Those left in the care of Shaka having, after 12 months' confinement, consumed the cattle, grain, etc., given them for their subsistence and not having planted, relying on an additional supply, were without provisions, and yet not daring to leave this sacred spot, stole several head of cattle from the neighbouring kraals. Being detected, a detachment was sent for the purpose of destroying them all. The principal of them was a well-known warrior under Shaka, and in this instance again his bravery was rekindled and shone forth anew. He killed several on the spot, driving others into the burial ground, where they must have remained had it become known to the King. At length, finding himself closely pressed by the detachment, who by this time had slain all his companions, he resorted to the only plan that could save his life. He sprang on the hut that had been newly erected over the grave of Shaka and sang the national war song. This was instantly attributed to the interference of the spirit of Shaka on his behalf, and he was left without further molestation. He now flew to me for protection in Natal. Knowing the risk I should run by allowing him into my kraal, I sent people to conduct him to the elephant hunters, where he might have remained in safety till the King should decide his fate, but, suspicious that the people I had sent with him would kill him, he ran away and joined Mr. Collis, a trader, who was going to the Colony, and with whom he returned. On his return to the King, he was received at the gate of the King's residence by Dingane and two regiments, the King being painted from head to foot in compliment to him as a friend from the spirit of Shaka.

Omens

The Omens which are considered to decide the fate of war are numerous:

Elephants met by the army, a snake passing through their centre, eagles flying in a line, are auspicious omens.

On Shaka's preparing to attack the Ndwandwes, a meteor appeared which detained him some time from proceeding till perceiving it throwing its meteoric sparks in that direction announced a favourable issue, it being a sign that the enemy would be entirely defeated, which was verified as before related.

The birds known in the Colony as Haw-di-das rousing their voice on the approach of the army, a red buck called *Umkhumbi* passing through them, a dog watering on a shield, are omens of misfortune.

Dogs or calves climbing to the tops of the houses, a cow lying down while milking or sucking one another, the stopper of a milk calabash flying out, denote someone guilty of witchcraft in the kraal.

A snake called *iMamba* is considered as the protector of the hut in which it is found, and although its bite is venomous it is allowed to remain unmolested and a cow killed as an offering to the spirit in consequence of its visit.

A small snake the size of a lizard appearing in a kraal is a sign of its destruction and a cow is killed as an offering to the spirit for its removal.

A ground toad hissing as any person is passing it informs that person of the death of a relation.

A screech owl is considered as the harbinger of death occasioned by witchcraft of some evilly disposed person.

A wild red cat called *Impaka* and also leopards are supposed to be in possession of and under the control of evilly disposed persons who command them to inflict sickness on those they wish to destroy. On the appearance of either of these inauspicious omens the *inyangas* are visited and someone falls a victim to their false denunciations.

AmaNgwane

The tribes of amaNgwane, under their chief Matiwane, being known by their irruption among the frontier tribes may render the following account of them necessary.

They distinguished themselves in laying waste part of the now inhabited country situate above those destroyed by Shaka coastwise. The amaNgwane lived above the confluence of the Black and White Umfolozi Rivers, and was, during the chieftainship of Malusi, Matiwane's grandfather, the most considerable tribe of eastern Kaffirland. On his death a dispute arose between the two sons of Malusi, Mathumela and Masumpa, which divided the tribe. Mathumela proceeded inland, calling his tribe Phembeni. Masumpa remained and was the father of Matiwane.

He was attacked by Dingiswayo, to whom he became tributary. On the death of that chief by Zwide, he offered to be tributary to him, sending his daughter, with oxen, to marry Zwide, but Zwide accused him of sending his daughter to bewitch him, and attacked him, taking his cattle. He in return took those of Mthimkhulu, son of Bungane, whom Dingiswayo had protected, but, from the fear of Shaka, determined to invade other tribes, following the system of Shaka.

His first attempt having been so successful, and his fear of Shaka continuing, induced him to continue his exertions, remaining no longer in one place than to consume the corn of those he had destroyed. For the space of ten years he was roving about destroying all he could overtake and avoiding the attacks of Shaka and Zwide. In one instance, having left his cattle with the old men and women, he attacked Dinsela, a Bechuana tribe on the Khahlamba mountains, whom he succeeded in defeating, but during his absence Mzilikazi succeeded in taking most of those he had left behind with many women. He lost no time in following them up, when an engagement took place in which Matiwane's tribe fled. On their return, to their surprise, they found all they had left with these taken from Dinsela had in their absence been taken by the Zulus. Although thus stripped of all his cattle and many women, the loss was but little felt, as they had but to follow the same course as before, and to gain a new stock by fresh invasions. This they soon effected, and increased their stock much above the quantity lost. They now determined to leave the eastern countries where the Zulus were their masters and cross the Khahlamba mountains. During this long route Matiwane had destroyed 65 tribes of considerable magnitude, besides numerous small ones, whose names were not generally known. He never omitted, if the principal chiefs were taken, to drink of their gall by which he might gain a superiority of power over his future enemies. He had spared none but those who were willing to join him and by his liberal and fatherly conduct had increased his people to a considerable number. On his crossing the Khahlamba mountains, he sent a part of his people to travel far into the country and ascertain what hopes there were of continuing their attacks, with orders to attack any they might meet with in order to form some idea of what sort of people they would in future have to contend with.

This division were those who attacked Madikane when Mr. Thompson was there (Madikane was killed 20th December, 1824), but their purpose was defeated, not capturing the cattle.

During the absence of this division, Matiwane was attacked by a party of the Bastards who were beaten off. Shortly after this, four Europeans, or perhaps Bastards, on horseback entered his tribe. They were immediately killed and their horses, being considered a new species of cattle, were eaten.

Owing to their failure with Madikane, they returned to the eastward and were joined by a tribe of Bechuanas, when they were again attacked by the Zulus, who took from them immense droves of cattle, which all died from the change of country.

They then moved towards the frontier tribes, having been informed of their weakness and of the large droves of cattle they possessed and, for that purpose, proceeded to reside above the Mtata River, when they were attacked and defeated by the Colonists, as before related. Matiwane then, with many of his tribe retraced his steps towards the Zulus, passing through the remains of a tribe under Mahlaphahlapha whose cattle Matiwane having formerly taken, had become cannibals. They did not let this opportunity pass of cutting off numbers of his people to feast on, so that he arrived at the Zulus with only a small number compared with those with which he had escaped. He was received by Dingane with every mark of respect and kindness and was permitted to proceed to his original country with his people, great numbers of whom, having travelled coastwise, there again joined him. Dingane's first present to him was 300 head of cattle, which was much increased by repeated gifts. By such kindness Matiwane had nothing to suspect, but on a visit to Dingane he had not been long seated before two regiments were collected for an attack on Sobuza, an enemy who was in the neighbourhood stealing cattle, which they were immediately to follow. Dingane asked Matiwane's opinion of the route they had better take. He agreed with Dingane that it would be better to pass through his kraals. They then departed, the commander receiving his private orders as usual, Matiwane little dreaming of his fate, they having been collected for no other purpose than the destruction of his own people. No sooner had they left than Dingane entered into pleasant conversation with him and on moving towards the seraglio gave him an ox for his consumption, during the slaughter of which a party was sent who seized and killed him.

Four other tribes under their separate chiefs, Madikane, Ndinga, Nxumalo, and Ngoza were driven by Matiwane and Shaka at various times, when they adopted the same mode of warfare as those chiefs pillaging the country, especially of those tribes left by them. The quick movements they were obliged to make to attack the other tribes and avoid their superior enemies, who were often in search of them, induced them to destroy their children when born, which procedure was generally adopted, except where the affections of the mother exceeded the fatigue of carrying them. It was by a combination of these chiefs who attacked several of the large tribes west of the Umzimkhulu, being more desirous for cattle than for the destruction of people, that so many of those tribes escaped who passed forward to the frontiers and now form the principal part of those tribes by whom they are held in much subjection and are termed " Fingoes," a name of degradation. The chief of most of them, who are termed Xolos and who resided on the Umzimkhulu, was taken from a bush by a Zulu chief from whom I purchased his freedom. He, with a number of his people, have been with me about six years. They are generally an honest and industrious set of people.

The country east of St. John's River being entirely depopulated by various marauders, Ngoza attacked the amaMpondos, by whom he was killed.

The other three by wars among themselves were much diminished. Madikane attacked the people of Wolf Kaross, by whom he was killed. Soinyanga, the next brother, succeeded him.

When Mbazo proposed attacking him and induced three traders from the Colony, Kew and Conway and Malie, to assist him, they surrounded the kraal at break of day and burned Soinyanga in his hut, but the tribe, learning his fate, collected and attacked their enemy, who immediately retreated, leaving Peter Malie, of the traders, in their hands. He was killed.

Ncaphayi, the next brother in succession, became chief till the son of Soinyanga should arrive at maturity. Tired of marauding, they have joined the amaMpondos, but both live in distrust of each other's intentions, and Ncaphayi in dread of the Zulus, who are likely to attack him to recover the cattle formerly taken from Nqetho.

The Story of Zimuzimu

The native stories of old to those conversant with the manners and language of the people are very amusing, but to those ignorant of either, I am afraid, will appear very insipid. I shall, however, transcribe one, leaving it to your revisal and disposal.

Zimuzimu was a noted canibal who used frequently to purchase from his neighbours straggling people whom he always devoured. In one of his predatory excursions he was eating some spinach near a kraal when he was seen by a woman far gone in pregnancy who longed for the spinach which he refused her till she promised if he would remain behind the kraal at night she would send one of two orphan boys which she had, to fetch firewood from the back of the house, whom he might seize. On this agreement he gave her the spinach and the woman, true to her word, sent the boy for wood, when his brother advised him to take a stone with him in case cannibals might be about. On taking hold of the wood the boy, seeing something near him, threw the stone which hitting Zimuzimu caused him to cry out and made the boy run back to the house.

The next day Zimuzimu met the woman again who expressed her regret at his disappointment, but assured him to convince him of her sincerity she would send the lad at night to a neighbour for a pinch of snuff. The boy was accordingly sent, but seeing something that alarmed him threw a stone which again hit Zimuzimu, and made him again cry out and the boy escaped as before.

The next day Zimuzimu and the woman met again when they agreed for the future to live as man and wife. The woman's husband cared little for her, but it was felt that the cannibal had better publicly pass off as her relation in which character he was introduced to the neighbours who did not know Zimuzimu personally.

After a short residence he proposed that the elder boy should accompany him to his friends at a distant tribe, which was agreed on. On the road Zimuzimu pointed to a hill which he called "Find Spears," when they found two. Coming to another he called it "Find Spoons," of which they also found two. The next hill he called "Throw Away Spears." On this they threw them away. The next hill was "Throw Away Spoons," which was also done. But Zimuzimu concealed his, letting only the boy really do what he pretended. At length they arrived at Zimuzimu's friends, who, not aware of his cannibalism, gave him beef, milk and bread, when he desired the boy to produce his spear and spoon, to which he replied he had thrown them away as directed. Zimuzimu observed "From poverty I get rich," and ate the food alone. At night when all slept, Zimuzimu got up, entered the cattle kraal and killed a cow, taking some of the blood and dung, with which he besmeared the boy's feet while he slept and then laid himself down. The people rising at daybreak and finding a cow killed and one entering the hut of Zimuzimu and seeing the boy besmeared with blood and dung killed him as the guilty person. Zimuzimu agreed that their suspicions were no doubt right as to the boy's guilt and proposed returning home directly. However after leaving the kraal he remained in an adjacent bush till he had devoured the boy, when he returned to his house.

The younger brother eagerly inquired for his elder, but Zimuzimu in answer told him that such large quantities of beer, beef and bread, milk and beans were given by his friends that he could not persuade the boy to return. The boy hearing this, begged he might be allowed to go with him the next journey, which took place in a few days.

He passed the same hills as on the previous journey, finding assegais and spoons as before, but which this lad took the precaution to keep instead of throwing away as his brother had done. On arriving at his friends' house the same fare was set before them, and on Zimuzimu asking for the spear and spoon the lad, to Zimuzimu's surprise, produced his and heartily partook of the provisions.

On nearing the kraal the boy had picked up a bone of his brother out of which, supposing it to belong to some animal, he had made a mouth organ. Zimuzimu, as before, when all were sleeping, went to the kraal and killed a cow, but during his absence the bone call awoke the boy, crying out to him in his brother's voice: "Zimuzimu wants to smear you with the blood of a cow he has been killing, when you will be killed as I, your brother, was." Hearing this, the boy was determined not to sleep any more, and shortly after Zimuzimu entered the hut with the blood. The boy asked what he intended doing with that. He received no other answer but that he was going to the river to wash. Instead he hid himself in a dunghill, from whence his hair only appeared. A girl, throwing out ashes, took hold of it, on which Zimuzimu cried out: " Don't hurt me, I am your relation." She, alarmed, immediately called the people of the kraal, who told her to pull the hair again, when Zimuzimu again cried out, on which they dragged him out, and desired him to leave as they were now satisfied they had killed the boy before who was innocent, but his being a relation by marriage they spared his life. Zimuzimu and the boy then left the kraal, when meeting on the road two cows they drove them into the bush, and killed them, each taking one for himself. When they were skinned Zimuzimu, seeing the boy's cow the fatter, sent him to collect firewood. In his absence he cut some of the fat off the lad's cow which the boy perceiving, took a stick, and beating a hollow tree cried out " It was not me who stole the cattle, it was Zimuzimu, who is now eating it." Zimuzimu, alarmed, made the best of his way home and the boy remained several days eating the beef by himself. When he returned home Zimuzimu, seeing him so fat, asked him how he got so very fat. The boy replied that he should not mock him after leaving him to be killed, and seeing his body now swelled as it was with the severe beating. When Zimuzimu asked him if beating would make him so fat the boy assured him it would be the case. He then laid himself down for that purpose, on which the boy, striking him with a club on the head, killed him at once.

When the woman asked him why he had killed him, he replied it was for having killed his elder brother. She in consequence drove him away, and he was taken into the house of a neighbour, who sent him to wash some entrails in a spring. So soon had the lad imbibed the ideas of Zimuzimu, which tells how much we should avoid wicked men, that he ate them, returning and saying that as he was washing them toads had snatched them out of his hands. But the man, knowing from his appearance it was false, had him immediately killed.

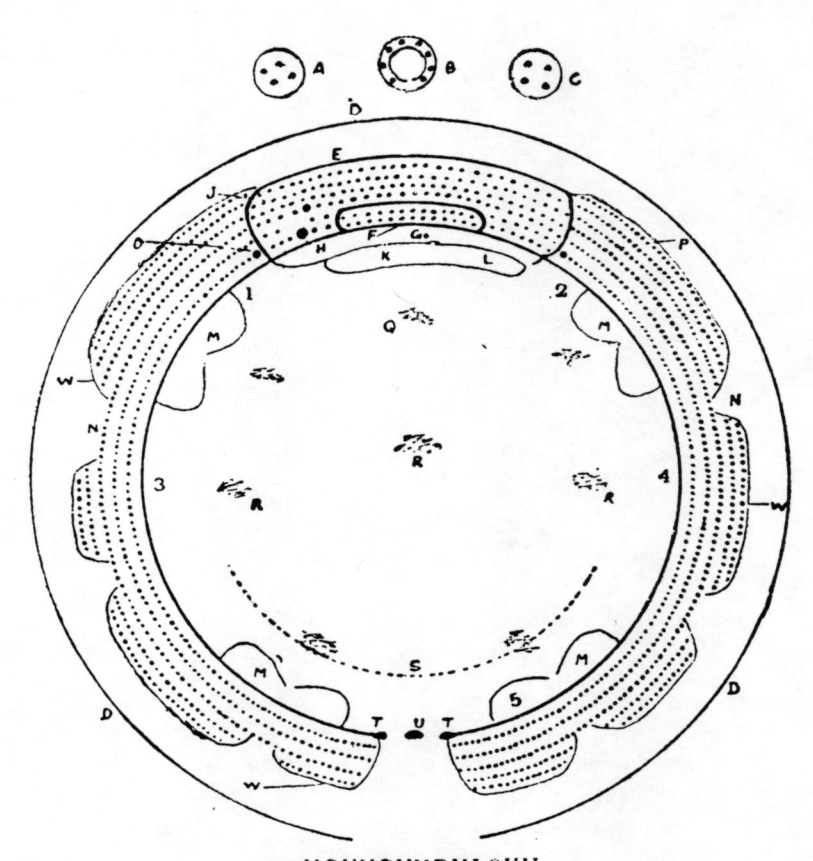

uMGUNGUNDHLOVU.

Dingane's Kraal
Plan drawn by James Stuart

UMGUNGUNDLOVU

This diagram, taken from James Stuart's book *uKulumetule*, is circular for reasons of space, and in order to be more easily handled for details. The kraal was, in fact, elliptical in shape.

Explanation

A.	uMvazana—the little outside left kraal.
B.	uBeje—the little outside centre kraal.
C.	KwaMbeceni—the little outside right kraal.
D.	Outer fence of the big Royal Kraal.
E.	Fence of the white seraglio.
F.	Fence of the black seraglio.
G.	Barracks of the guards of the seraglio.
H.	House of the King.
J.	House of Mpikase, mother of Dingane.
K, L.	Kraal in which the cattle for slaughter (the cattle for the mouth) were kept, and in which the King washed.
M.	Kraal for the cattle of the community.
N.	Regimental barracks.
O.	House of Commander-in-Chief, Ndlela.
P.	House of the Commander, Nzoɓo.
Q.	Abattoir enclosure.
R.	Milking enclosures.
S.	Enclosure in which soldiers danced at milking time.
T.	Gate posts.
U.	Central dividing gate post.
W.	Fences of soldiers' barracks.
1 & 2.	Where the pillows, i.e., headrests, are.
3.	All the space right down to the gate is the side of the kraal.
4.	Great cattle kraal.
5.	Large cattle kraal of the amaWombe regiment.

There were many entrances on all sides, and many wind-screens in front of doors, and grain huts and storehouses for shields, but they are not shown on this paper for they are too small.

The soldiers at Mgungundlovu filled the whole place. At the headrest on the left side of the kraal there was the Nqoɓolondo regiment ; then followed the Mankamane (imiKhulutshane) ; at the stomach of the kraal were the Ziɓolela and Fasimba regiments ; and when you went towards the gate there was the Tshoyisa. Near the large cattle kraal on the right at the headrest (near seraglio) was the Zimpohlo ; then followed the Mankentshane (imiKhulutshane) and the Dukuza regiments ; then towards the gate was the large cattle kraal and amaWombe.

In the white seraglio stay the 1,500 girls who have been sent as tribute to the King. The *iNdlunkulu* and *iKhohlo* and *iNqadi* of every kraal of importance in Zululand were required to present to the King at least one grown-up girl. This girl was sent to one or other of the King's numerous kraals, and lived there with the other girls in a similar position. She belonged to the King and he could either marry her himself or marry her to someone else, in which case he received the *loɓolo* cattle for her. The matron who was in charge there was Bibi, daughter of Nkoɓe (or Sompisi), the sister of Ndlela, the Commander-in-Chief.

In the black seraglio, where no one enters (only a boy servant who has not reached the age of puberty works), stay the King only with his concubines, together with the part of the seraglio responsible for his food. The matron in charge at first was Langazana, daughter of Guɓashe. Then, when she was transferred to Khangela, the matron was Mjanisi, the wife of Lenzangakhova. The food and beer and calabashes were kept in the huts of the girls. They do not stay in the house of the matron.

In the seraglios there were slave girls and widows who did the work of the place.

Note—
James Stuart's information concerning Mgungundlovu, Dingane's Kraal, was taken from his Zulu book *uKulumetule*, as told by the Zulus, Tununu, son of Nonjiya of the Qwaɓe clan, Ngidi (or Magambukazi), son of Mcikaziswa of the Langa clan, Lunguza, son of Mpukane of the Thembu clan, Sivivi, son of Maqungo, son of Malunga of the Hluɓi clan, during his investigations on Zulu History from 1889 onwards.

INDEX

Adams, C., 236, 256.
Adams, Dr. Newton, 246, 248, 260, 264.
Adultery, 129, 294.
Agriculture (Native), 24, 47, 230, 286, 289.
Albany, 35, 312.
Algoa Bay, 35, 52, 53, 94, 118, 129, 142, 154, 155, 181, 182, 185, 235, 246, 254.
Alligators, 137.
Allison, Mr., 315.
Aloes, 273, 301, 306.
Ambergris, 48, 52.
Ammunition, 31, 91, 122, 193, 228, 255, 256.
Amusements (Native), 30, 50, 67, 78, 80, 305.
Ancestral Spirits, 6, 17, 86, 134, 136, 139, 154, 157, 162, 171, 217, 248, 274-6, 283, 308, 317.
Andries (Hottentot), 204.
Animals, Domestic, Cats, 77.
    Dogs, 8, 77, 104, 288.
    Goats, 33, 34, 310.
    Horses, 5, 68-70, 74, 94, 95, 98, 101, 105, 108, 109, 129, 176, 180, 181, 192, 202, 206, 247, 254, 258, 265, 289, 317, 319.
    Pigs, 39, 77, 78, 303.
    Sheep, 35, 74, 314.
  Wild, Buck, 99, 124, 147, 222, 223, 274, 310, 317.
    Buffalo, 120.
    Cats, 201, 279, 318.
    Dogs, 310.
    Elephants, 61, 66, 100, 104, 119-21, 129-31, 141-3, 198, 213, 222, 230, 255, 256, 312, 317.
    Genets, 48.
    Leopards, 22, 68, 96, 97, 279, 310, 318.
    Lions, 3, 4, 33, 209, 210.
    Monkeys, 14, 48, 284.
    Ratels, 151.
    Rhinoceros, 124.
    Wolves, 22, 29, 59, 60, 64, 68, 109.
Anthropology (Native), 267, 268.
Armstrong, Commander, 53, 54.
    Colonel A. B., 312.
Aspeling, Mrs., 129.

Babies (Native), 29, 232, 268, 300-2, 320.
Bandla (Native), 32.
Bannister, S., 234.
Bar, The (Bay of Natal), 55, 58, 119, 178.
Barracks (Native), 25, 75, 132, 136, 246, 249, 283, 298.
Barrenness (Native women), 308.
Barter, 7, 10, 36, 40-2, 47, 48, 50, 52-7, 61, 96, 103, 110, 111, 116, 117, 131, 142, 175, 177, 178, 181, 185, 189, 194, 214-7, 220, 221, 225-9, 234, 243, 255, 256, 259, 262.
Bathing (Native methods), 28, 127, 139, 149, 282, 291-4.
Bathurst, Earl, 52, 54.
Batt, H., 256.
Bay, The (Natal), 55, 177, 216, 229, 230, 238.
Beads, 4, 5, 7, 10, 16, 28, 39, 41, 45, 47-9, 60, 62, 63, 71, 73, 77, 96, 107, 133, 142, 147, 157, 164, 172, 177, 192, 201, 230, 270-5, 280, 293, 294, 296, 297, 302, 303.

Beer (Native), 27, 31, 71, 74, 123, 128, 134, 269, 270, 291, 297, 305, 306.
Beliefs, 32-4, 267, 319.
Berea Mission, 238, 254.
Berg, W., 311, 312.
Berkin, F., 243.
Bible (Zulu), 254, 265.
Biggar, A., 255, 260, 262.
       G., 260.
       R., 260.
Bird's *Annals of Natal*, 51, 54, 58, 73, 75, 86, 88, 174, 183, 216, 224, 230, 233, 234, 246, 249, 260, 261, 265.
Birds, 29, 70, 72, 74, 77, 89, 99, 120, 124, 134, 156, 226, 279, 284, 303, 306, 311, 317.
Blaauwkrantz, 258.
Blacksmiths (Native), 90, 270, 272. See also Mbethi.
Blanckenberg, C., 236, 255.
Blood River, 31.
Bluff, The, 60, 61, 63, 191.
Boats, 37, 40-2, 46, 48, 53, 54, 58, 60, 75, 110, 112, 116, 119, 177, 183, 185.
Boers, 31, 35, 48, 56, 57, 68, 91, 113, 167, 180, 183, 202, 230, 235, 244, 249, 258, 259, 266, 278, 311-5.
Boschberg Ridge Mountains, 35.
Boteler (Author), 182.
Bottomley, W., 256.
Boyce, Revd., 207, 219, 220.
Brass, 2, 4, 28, 48, 49, 71, 73, 77, 85, 109, 112, 147, 157, 164, 195, 231, 232, 270-2, 274, 275, 280, 301.
Bravery (Native), 127, 188, 234, 316.
Brouwer, J., 255.
Brown, J., 256.
"Bubulongo" (Port Natal), 87.
Building methods, 42, 242, 247, 289-91.
Bulawayo (Giɓixhegu) (Shaka's residence), 30, 88, 131, 132, 187.
Bulwer, 245.
Buntingville mission, 206, 207, 219, 244-6.

Calabashes, 108, 134, 287, 289, 291, 301, 305, 306, 310, 317.
Callaway, Revd., 81.
Cane, J., 130, 131, 155, 168-70, 188-97, 203, 204, 207, 211, 213, 214, 217, 219, 223-5, 230, 234, 236, 243, 250, 251, 256, 262, 315, 316.
Cannibals, 22, 320 (In Folk-lore, 321-4).
Cape Colony, 24, 35, 44, 67, 103, 111, 113, 116, 118, 141, 143, 144, 147-9, 155, 158, 168, 169, 175, 180, 184, 188, 193, 203, 208, 217, 219, 220, 227, 241, 244, 262, 315.
Cape of Good Hope, 51, 53, 69, 91, 131, 154, 187, 237, 311.
Cape Town, 5, 35, 40, 51, 52, 55, 56, 77, 129, 180, 181, 234, 237, 244, 246, 249, 254, 311.
Captains (Native), 9, 65, 79, 170, 200, 203, 218, 219, 226, 289.
Carden, T., 250, 256.
Cato's Creek, 60.
Cattle, Kraal making, 289.
       Show, 75, 78, 80.
       Slaughter methods, 287-9.
       Umlomo, 26.
Caves, 100, 102, 105, 125, 150, 153, 195, 193, 250, 266.
Cawood, Messrs., 213-20, 224, 225, 229.
Cellars (Grain stores), 167, 303, 304.
Ceding of Natal, 314.
       Tembe, 40, 44.
Champion, Revd., 246-8.
Chase, J. C., 51.
Cheeseman (Author), 40.

INDEX 329

Chiefs, Beje, 21, 128, 130, 131.
    Benziwa, 89.
    Bungane (Pangane), 3, 4, 5, 318.
    Dinsela (Bechuana), 318, 319.
    Duɓe, 236, 257, 258.
    Gendeyana, 13.
    Hawana, 125.
    Hintza, 114, 144, 244.
    Hlomendlini, 192, 202.
    Ingnasconca, 157.
    Joɓe, 1, 2, 4, 6, 47, 91, 92, 94, 109.
    Khokhela, 191, 192.
    Krcli (Xosa), 244.
    Lilwane, 257.
    Lynx, 181.
    Madikane, 18, 116, 319, 321.
    Magaye, 34, 70, 166, 167, 209, 210, 220, 221, 241.
    Mahlaphahlapha, 320.
    Majuɓana, 112.
    Makhasane (Delagoa), 7, 37, 41, 45-7.
    Makome, 235.
    Malusi, 318.
    Mandlakayise, 259.
    Mangcuku, 95-8, 106, 108.
    Manqondo, 257.
    Mantshongwe, 29.
    Manyaɓa, 104.
    Mapitha, 144.
    Masumpa, 318.
    Mathumela, 318.
    Matiwane, 17-9, 148, 149, 169, 218, 318-20.
    Mawewe, 1, 4-8.
    Mbalawa, 111.
    Mbalijala, 95, 96, 99, 106-8.
    Mbazo, 321.
    Mbengi (Makidama), 13.
    Mbikwana, 64-72, 78, 79, 88, 89, 186, 187.
    Mbiya, 31, 32 (ghost of, 308).
    Mɓopha, 156-60.
    Mdlaka, 144, 145, 162, 163, 184, 221, 241.
    Mfokazi, 13, 140.
    Mgabi, 13.
    Mgoduka, 221, 227.
    Mhala, 235.
    Mahlungwana, 13, 17, 156, 158, 160, 161, 221.
    Mhlophe, 65-7, 88.
    Mkhonto, 175, 209.
    Mlotshwa, 21, 128, 129, 149, 150.
    Mondisa, 15.
    Mpangazitha, 78.
    Mphezulu, 221.
    Mqhawe, 259.
    Mqomboli, 13.
    Msika, 67, 88 (uMsega, 201, 202).
    Msoka, 29.
    Mthimkhulu, 318.
    Mtoɓela, 191-3, 197, 199-204.
    Mayetha, 37, 43, 44, 46, 48.
    Mzakali, 198.
    Mzilikazi, 20, 21, 173, 174, 218, 219, 226, 241, 246, 249, 265, 266, 318.
    Mzoɓoshi, 95-9, 106, 108, 109, 191, 194, 195, 204.

Chiefs—*continued*
    Ncaphayi, 23, 172-4, 218, 220, 221, 227, 229, 245, 321.
    Ncumbatha, 191.
    Ndapha, 112.
    Ndinga, 320.
    Ndlambe, 180.
    Ndlela, 163, 238, 250, 258.
    Ngathane, 114.
    Ngcoɓo, 257.
    Ngendeyana, 13, 140, 158.
    Ngomane, 13, 136-8, 140, 147-9, 157.
    Ngoza, 249, 320, 321.
    Ngwadi, 13, 14, 140, 156, 158-61, 221, 241.
    Njanduna, 192.
    Nkantolo, 153.
    Nkoɓe (Sompisi), 13.
    Nomxamama, 157.
    Nqetho, 17, 165-76, 220, 221, 227, 241, 245, 321.
    Nxumalo, 320.
    Nyuswa, 257.
    Osiyana, 100, 101, 104-6.
    Phakathwayo, 5, 7, 16, 17, 80, 170.
    Phungwa, 149, 150.
    Senzangakhona, 12, 13, 123, 139, 140.
    Sigujana, 13, 14, 122.
    Sikhunyana, 18, 118, 126-8, 141, 142.
    Sikonyela, 315.
    Sindane, 153.
    Sithayi, 156.
    Siyingila, 63, 64, 69, 70.
    Sobageli, 204, 205.
    Sobuza, 153, 249-51, 255, 265, 320.
    Soinyanga, 321.
    Somaphunga, 122.
    Sompisi, 13.
    Soshangana, 20, 153, 161, 163.
    Sotoɓe, 141, 154, 184, 187, 207, 209.
    Sumbiti, 73.
    Tyali, 235.
    Vadama, 236.
    Vezi, 149.
    Wolf Kaross, 321.
    Zatshuke, 249.
    Zihlandlo, 221, 241.
    Zikode, 20.
    Zuede, 122.
    Zwide, 9, 11, 15, 17, 19-21, 47, 85, 91, 118, 128, 150, 318.
Christian Observer, 251, 253.
Church (Native's idea of), 217, 264.
Clambamaruze (Interpreter), 88.
Clay (Face and Head), 80, 112, 292-4.
Cloete, Major, 154, 184, 230, 314.
Cloth (Calico, dungaree), 39, 48, 49, 142, 193, 195, 206.
Colenso, Bishop, 81, 139, 248, 249.
Colesberg, 314.
Coliat (Interpreter), 88.
Collins, W., 36, 37, 39.
Collis, Mr., 196, 207, 209-14, 216, 218, 219, 223, 225, 230, 232, 236, 245, 317.
Coloureds, 50, 198, 259, 260.
Conway, Mr., 321.
Cooking (Native), 21, 27, 48, 125, 145, 222, 288.

"Coolies," 46.
Copper, 47, 77, 99, 270, 271.
Corn, 17, 21, 35, 47, 99, 107, 123, 143, 146, 166, 192, 201, 203, 263, 270, 286, 288, 289, 291, 305.
Counting (Native method), 80, 81.
Cowan, Dr., 4, 5, 8, 170.
Cowie and Green, Messrs., 175-7.
Cows, 9, 10, 63, 66, 97-9, 105, 136, 152, 156, 195, 219, 288.
    Dung uses, 272, 273, 284, 290, 291, 302, 304.
Crafts, Baskets, 26, 48, 50, 74, 269, 290, 291, 303.
    Boats, 49.
    Furniture, 10, 11, 27, 76, 101, 113, 264, 269.
    Karosses, 2, 10, 32, 156, 276, 302, 308.
    Mats, 27, 43, 48, 107, 123, 135, 157, 173, 269, 288, 290, 291, 294, 296, 301.
    Metal, 50, 113, 195, 269-73.
    Pillows, 269, 291, 301.
    Pottery, 269, 273, 274.
    Rope, 49.
    Sandals, 124.
    Sieves, 40, 270.
    Sjamboks, 181.
    Tanning, 273, 274.
    Thatching, 290, 291, 300.
    Utensils, under "U"
Crime Criminals, 82, 129, 130, 163, 232, 277, 278, 287, 289, 295.
Crocodiles, 61, 309, 310.
Cruelties, 8, 18, 19, 29, 30, 78, 136, 140, 152, 224, 226, 227.
Cultivation (Native), 47, 50, 54, 55, 64, 136, 302-6.
Culula Mission, 246, 254.
Customs, Aged people, 30.
    Aphrodisiacs, 308.
    Assegais, 16.
    Attacks by night, 8.
    Body incisions, 5.
    Burial, 135, 136, 139, 157, 158, 316, 317.
    Cattle, 3, 23, 26, 73, 156, 219, 274, 276, 277, 286-8, 297.
    Childbirth, 301, 302.
    Circumcision, 12, 115, 140, 268, 269.
    Cleanliness, 70, 86, 291, 294.
    Cohabiting, 139, 140, 147, 287, 295, 301, 307.
    Concubines, 29, 299, 300, 305.
    Death, 30, 133-5, 157.
    Divining, 146, 274-7.
    Dress, 276, 293, 294.
    First Fruits, 1, 232, 237, 304.
    Food, 145.
    Forges, 273.
    Gall, 11, 273, 319.
    King's, 11, 282.
    Marriage, 165, 232, 287, 295-9, 301.
    Medicine, 82, 89, 278.
    Milk, 286, 287.
    eMosheni, 302, 303.
    Mourning, 32, 86, 121, 133-40.
    Ornaments, 86, 133.
    Pregnancy, 301.
    Presents, 41, 143, 144, 176, 237.
    Puberty, 302, 303.
    "Pulling ears" (To impress), 186, 200, 202, 209.
    Purification, 28, 127, 138, 139, 155.

Customs—*continued*
- Rain, 282, 283.
- Regiments, Royal, 28, 72, 136.
- Shaving, 86, 87, 292, 294.
- Shields, 11, 123.
- Sickness, 274-82.
- Soldiers, 127, 144, 149, 219, 300.
- Soma, 139, 140.
- Spies, 221.
- Tattooing, 294.
- Ukuhloɓonga, 295.
- War, 89, 122, 159, 219.

Cyrus, G., 243, 245, 262.

Dances, 2, 25, 26, 50, 73-5, 80, 83, 95, 103, 115, 120, 139, 164, 174, 182, 272, 275, 295, 296, 304, 305.
Davis, Mr. 88, 90, 94, 98, 105-7, 109.
Dawa (English lady), 112.
Decher, Lt., 44.
Delagoa Bay, 1, 8, 10, 11, 16, 19, 20, 27, 36-40, 43-6, 52, 56, 57, 66, 77, 87, 93, 131, 153, 161, 175-9, 182, 198, 230, 231, 267, 268, 299.
Delagonians, 7, 47, 48, 56, 182, 299.
De Lange, H. and J., 230.
Deneis (Portuguese Governor), 231.
Dhlomo, R., 161.
Diɓinhlanga (Shaka's residence), 131, 142.
Dictionaries, 81, 139.
Dingane, 13, 15-7, 21, 31, 140, 156-8, 160, 161, 164, 167-75, 194, 197, 201-11, 215-9, 221, 225, 226, 228, 230-4, 236, 237, 244, 246-50, 257, 261, 262, 264, 283, 299, 313-5, 317.
- Character, 162-4, 175, 178, 219, 228, 233, 236, 257, 314, 320.
- Kraals, 178, 179, 195, 196.
- Treaty, 239-42, 251-53, 259.
- White people, *re*, 188, 189, 226, 230, 232, 239, 240.

Dingiswayo (Godongwana), 1-18, 20, 21, 24, 30, 31, 47, 136, 140, 268, 269, 308, 318.
Doctors, European, 5, 66, 76, 77, 84, 117.
- Medical, Native, 42, 66, 76, 77, 89, 132, 139, 196, 278-82.
- Rain, 4, 282-3.
- War, 89, 127, 144, 149.
- Witch-, Diviners, Soothsayers, 4, 28, 29, 70, 146, 155, 274-7, 318.

Doornkop, 258.
Drakensberg (Khahlamba Mts.), 68, 221, 245, 266, 318, 319.
Dreams (Native), 31, 70, 146, 154, 156, 171, 214, 274, 279.
Dress, Female, 26, 49, 73, 112, 141, 164, 274, 291-4.
- Male, 30, 74, 75, 77, 237, 238, 291-4.
- War, 2, 9, 14, 61, 71, 89, 90, 96, 127, 133, 137, 138, 144, 226, 284, 285, 304.
- Witchdoctors, 34, 70, 89, 275.

Dukuza (Shaka's), 131, 137, 138, 152, 153, 156, 159.
D'Urban, Sir Benjamin, 235, 242, 253, 313.
Durban, 46, 60, 61, 242-5, 248.
Dutch East India Co., 57.

Edie, Lt., 214, 215.
Ekukhanyeni mission, 249.
Elephant Island, 37.
England, Sir R., 313.
Entumeni forest, 7, 17.
Europeans (Natives' idea of), 5, 81, 96, 97, 129, 145, 171, 173, 180, 185, 189, 196, 200, 201, 205, 210, 211, 217, 218, 240, 246.
"Evil-doers," 70, 275, 318.

Faces, marked, 80, 86, 133, 272, 317.
Faku, 64, 67, 103, 104, 110-4, 146, 167, 168, 171, 172, 175, 206, 207, 213, 220, 221, 224, 229, 235-7, 240, 245.
Farewell, G. F., 36, 51-8, 66-79, 85-8, 90, 91, 110, 116-9, 123, 124, 128-31, 141-3, 155, 168-75, 180, 182, 183, 185-7, 195, 196, 215, 220, 230, 233, 234, 271, 311, 315.
Fire (Interpreter), 103, 106, 107, 109, 110, 182, 185.
Fire-arms, 4, 6, 7, 39, 59, 74, 81, 82, 91, 97, 101, 119-21, 123, 126, 130, 169, 173, 181, 187, 190-2, 194, 195, 198, 206, 213, 222, 223, 225, 238, 242, 249-51, 255, 256, 259, 260.
Fish, 39, 40, 54, 94. (Shellfish, 92, 100-2, 105, 109, 113.)
Fleck, Mr., 113.
Folk-lore, 303, 321-4.
Food, 31, 35, 91, 94-8, 114, 123, 125, 145, 161, 177, 188.
    Grain, 23, 24, 47, 54, 64, 167, 269, 270, 304-6, 316.
    Honey, 98, 99, 102, 150, 151.
    Meat, 26, 27, 63-5, 70, 98, 108, 109, 125, 127, 128, 222, 223, 276.
    Milk, 71, 77, 96, 97, 103, 107, 108, 136, 145, 284, 293, 317.
    Potatoes, 27, 305.
    Roots, 21, 92, 95, 100, 109, 110, 127, 287.
    Rice, 39, 47, 65, 94, 95, 98, 177.
    Vegetables, 47, 305, 306.
Forts, 37, 39, 44, 46, 47, 196, 231, 260.
Fotheringham, Capt., 36, 37.
Francis, J., 236.
Frazer, Major, 181.
Frederick (Interpreter), 58, 60, 61, 63, 68, 80, 88, 125.
Fruits, 50, 94, 95, 303, 306.
Fynn, Frank (Pobana), 192, 194, 204-6, 236.
Fynn, William, 36, 189-94, 199, 204, 205, 234, 236, 299.

Gardiner, Capt., 81, 224, 226, 227, 231, 232, 236-48, 251-4, 262, 263, 265.
Gold, 40, 50, 52, 54, 68, 69.
Government (Native), 8, 21-3, 46, 48, 50, 162, 186, 195, 212, 214, 215, 226, 233, 236, 257.
Governor (Cape), 35, 88, 183, 203, 230, 233, 235, 236, 240, 243, 244, 248, 253, 261.
Gowagnewkos, land, 87.
Grahamstown, 35, 181, 196, 215, 229, 233, 237, 245, 246, 312.
Grahamstown Journal, 208, 209, 212, 214, 216-20, 222-5, 227-30, 232, 234, 236, 255, 260.
Graves (Native), 135, 136, 139, 157, 158.
Gray, Bishop, 248.
Green, Messrs. Cowie and, 175-7.
Griffith, Mr., 60.
Grout, Revd., 81, 246, 248, 249, 264.

Habits, Native, 182, 291-5, 299.
Hair, Native, 27, 49, 86, 124, 151, 269, 278, 292.
Halstead, Mr., 190, 236, 243, 250, 256.
Hambanathi mission, 263, 265.
Hart, R., 35.
Hawes, Lt., 118.
Head, Dress, 30, 73, 74, 141.
    Rings, 27, 74, 292.
Heredity, 280, 283.
Hewetson, Revd. H., 254.
Hides, 215, 216, 220, 297.
Hippopotamus (Sea-cows), 40-2, 54, 58, 61, 64, 68, 82, 105, 120, 129, 172, 222.
Hlomendlini district, 240, 246, 249, 253, 254.
Hlomula (Servant), 184.
Hoad, Mr., 45.

INDEX

Hochenberg, K., 167.
Hoffman, Mr., 56-8, 68, 93, 311.
Hood, Admiral, 51.
Horns, 215, 216, 272.
Hoste, Capt., 51.
Huts, 8, 19, 21, 25-8, 46, 48, 63-5, 70, 89, 92, 96, 103, 107-9, 290, 300-2.
Hutton (ship-master), 119, 155, 158, 234.

Indians, 46.
Ingoma Forest, 130.
Inhambane (place), 161.
Insanity, 21, 308.
Insects, 38, 134, 288, 289.
Isaacs, N., 119, 130, 131, 142, 155, 158, 173, 175, 185, 189-94, 196, 200, 203, 204, 215, 216, 234 ("Dambuza," 196, 202, 238, 239, 258).
    Travels, 73, 86, 116, 119, 122, 130, 174, 179, 181, 182, 184, 188, 191, 195, 242.
Ivory, 5, 7, 10, 40-2, 48, 52, 56, 64, 66, 67, 69, 72, 80, 103, 104, 118, 119, 121, 131, 141-3, 146, 155, 181, 187, 189, 190, 193, 196, 216, 230, 256.
Izigodlo (Royal), 24-8, 78, 183, 264, 298.

Jacob (Interpreter—also Hlambamanzi and Soembitchi), 52, 53, 73-6, 78, 83, 88, 121, 123, 125, 126, 141, 154, 175-7, 179-90, 196-8, 201, 208, 212, 216-8, 247.
Jandoona (place), 223.
Jantyi (Fynn's servant), 61-3, 65.
Jeffrey (Native), 113.
Joɓe's Rocks (place), 91, 94.
Joe (servant), 94, 106, 109, 110.
John (Hottentot), 69, 129, 191, 193.
Jukujela (Native), 114.

Kaffraria, 22, 267, 268.
Kelly, W., 44.
Kew, Mr., 250, 255, 321.
Khangela Mission, 58, 60, 239, 265.
Kieviet (Hottentot), 222-5, 228.
King George, 76, 80, 90, 91, 97, 141-3, 155, 159, 178, 184, 233.
King William IV, 216, 261.
King, Lt. J. S., 36, 51-6, 115, 118, 119, 122, 129-32, 141-3, 154, 155, 158, 175, 181, 184, 187, 196, 230, 233, 234, 242.
King, Richard, 245, 250.
Klaas, 99, 100, 108.
Klaas's Flat, 92, 94.
Kloof Plaats, 312.
Kobus, A., 223.
Konier, Mr., 113.
Kraals, Organisation of, 289.
    Royal, 25, 110, 119, 131, 175, 209, 215, 250, 255.
Kranskop Mts., 257.

Lake, Messrs. Isaacs and, 255, 257.
Landman, K., 230.
Lange, H., 312.
Lapoot, J., 113.
Law, 122, 130, 181, 262.
    Native, 23, 50, 79, 129, 163, 165.
Lidnell, T., 256.
Lighting Lamps, etc., 83, 84, 192.
Lindley, Revd. D., 249.
Locusts, 136, 161.
Lovedale, R., 250.
Lukulimba (Kelimba) (Fynn's Native), 192, 197, 198, 201-5.

Macassar Oil, 131, 142, 143, 155, 269.
Mackeurtan, G., 230.
Madagascar, 182.
Mahamba (Fynn's boy), 61-3, 65.
Malabar, 113.
Malie, P. (trader), 321.
Manners (Native), 46, 48, 93, 114, 163, 164, 257, 267, 306.
Maps (sketches, plans, charts), 55, 242, 267.
Maritz, S., 230, 249, 312.
Marriage (Native), 10, 13, 16, 25, 50, 112, 113, 115, 139, 165, 204, 232, 287, 295, 296, 298-300.
Marsh, J., 237, 247, 263, 265.
Mattoll country, 37.
Mauritius, 51, 52, 182.
Maynard, H., 36, 37, 42.
            Messrs., and Norden, 255.
Mbangwa (Fynn's), 192.
Mbethi (Blacksmith), 99, 101, 111-3, 271.
Mbozamboza, 141, 154, 187.
Medical, 2, 78, 82, 85, 89, 106, 139, 278, 280, 301, 307, 308.
Medicine, 66, 76-9, 82, 85, 131, 132.
            Native, 43, 84, 143, 301, 307, 308, 311.
Meteor (Comet), 317.
Mgungundlovu (Residence), 190, 191, 201, 246, 249, 251, 254, 258, 259, 264, 265.
Mica, 68.
Michael (Hottentot Interpreter), 80, 125, 129.
Middle Drift, 258.
Military, Systems, 8, 9, 18, 126, 283-6, 320.
            Tactics, 171, 172, 190, 221, 285.
Missions, Missionaries, 40, 43, 45, 81, 181, 196, 206, 217, 220, 236-8, 244-9, 253, 254, 260, 261, 263-5.
Mining, 50, 87.
Moolman, J., 230.
Mornegal, 113.
Mosiga Valley, 249.
Mozambique, 178, 182.
Mpande, 13, 202, 214, 234.
Mtata, 22, 319.
Murray, John (Ship Chandlers), 36.
Music, 26, 49, 50, 75, 275, 296.

Namaqualand, 45.
Nandi, 12, 13, 17, 29, 124, 132,˙136, 137, 139, 140, 142, 153, 158, 257, 269.
Nel, S., 223.
Newburg, Governor (Portuguese), 231.
Nginani Mission, 246, 249, 256.
Noɓamba (Residence), 185, 263, 265.
Nogandaya (Hero), 188.
Nohadu, 127.
Nongoxi Forest, 258.
Norden, B., 219 (Messrs. Maynard and, 255).
Nourse & Co., 35, 36, 38, 39; 52.
Noziphongo (Isaacs' servant), 173.
Ntombazi (Zwide's wife), 149.
Nyakomuɓi (Shaka's residence), 156.

Oaths (Swearing), 19, 30, 152, 159, 261.
Offerings (Sacrifices), 17, 32, 34, 86, 134, 136, 137, 139, 156, 157, 279, 283, 317
Ogle, Mr., 58-60, 68, 131, 174, 195, 197, 198, 208, 209, 211, 213, 219, 223-5, 227, 229, 230, 236, 243, 245, 256, 262.

INDEX

Omens, 277-9, 317, 318.
Orange Free State, 266.
Ornaments, 10, 11, 73, 133, 195, 285, 294.
    Bangles, 49, 50, 232, 271.
    Ear, 74, 293.
    Head, 292.
    Necklaces, 99, 109, 112, 127, 270-3, 284, 293.
Owen, Revd. F., 254, 263-5.
    Lt., 38, 39, 45, 73, 182.
    Capt. W. F. W., 38-40, 44, 45, 52, 73, 118, 181-3.

Page, Capt., 175.
Peter (Native), 113, 114.
Petersen, Mr., 51, 56-8, 68-71, 75, 77-9, 91, 93, 94, 311.
Philip, Revd. Dr., 246.
Philology, 267, 268.
Phondwane Mountain, 128.
Phongolo Mountains, 250.
Physiognomy (Native), 124, 293, 294.
Physique (Native), 124, 227, 291.
Plants, 49, 50, 89, 275, 281, 305, 309.
Point St. Michael's (Fort), 260.
Poison, 21, 70, 93, 114, 177, 232, 281, 282, 311.
Polygamy, 297, 299-301.
Pondoland, 116, 122, 206, 209, 219, 220, 223, 240.
Port Elizabeth, 54, 119.
Port Natal, 22, 23, 53, 54, 56, 68, 87, 90, 91, 109, 110, 118, 141, 175, 194, 208, 216, 217, 221, 223, 228, 233, 261, 262.
Ports, 53, 182.
Portuguese, 7, 10, 27, 37-9, 42-8, 52, 56, 77, 176-9, 230, 231.
Potgieter, 249.
Praises (Speeches), 14, 18, 19, 26, 28-30, 32, 64-6, 72, 112, 123, 138, 152, 248, 275, 308.
Pregnancy, 136, 140, 274, 295, 301, 307.
Pretorius, W. J., 230.
Prophecies, 31.
Psychology (Native), 200, 221.

Queens (Native), 13, 25, 136, 140, 273, 284, 300.
Quilimane, 38, 40.

Regiments (Native), 9, 30, 75, 120, 123-5, 129, 161, 172.
    "Bees," 153, 159.
    Cape Corps, 35, 312.
    Coloured, 260.
    Dingane's, 226, 232, 315, 317.
    Girls, 25, 30, 71, 73, 80, 298.
    Izimpohlo, 127.
    Mbelebele, 152.
    Mkhindi, 139, 144, 149.
    Motha, 129.
    Shaka's, 16, 17, 27, 123-5, 128, 138, **144**, **161**.
    Umzimvuɓu, 169, 170.
    Young, 19, 135, 285.
Retief, P., 200, 202, 235, 257, 258, 266, 313-5.
Richmond, 245.
"Rights," Hunting, 262.
    Land, 87.
Rivers, Amatigulu, 240.
    Avon (Umbilo), 242.
    Bashee, 244.

Rivers—*continued*
    Bloody. Under Umzimkhulu, 271.
    Buffalo, 242.
    Bushman's, 180.
    Embokodweni, 166.
    English (St. George's) (Imbulze), 37, 46-8, 177.
    Farewell's, 87.
    Fish, 35, 181, 244.
    Ilovu, 191, 193, 195.
    Imbizane, 106.
    Inanda, 259.
    Kat, 222.
    Kei, 245.
    Maputha, 37, 40, 41, 43, 45, 46, 177.
    Mbilanhlola, 205.
    Mbogintwini, 166.
    Mdlothi (Umhloti), 204, 259.
    Mhlali, 191, 309.
    Mkhomazi, 309.
    Moord Spruit, 258.
    Msunduze, 246.
    Mthamvuma, 100, 309, 310.
    Olifant's, 218.
    Phongolo, 250.
    St. John's (Umzimvuбu), 19, 20, 68, 111, 116, 117, 171, 196, 207, 213, 215, 219, 222, 231, 235, 236, 244, 245, 321.
    Swart Vlei, 312.
    Thongati, 63, 69, 184, 263.
    Thukela, 1, 5, 7, 111, 137, 191, 226, 232, 240, 243, 246, 256, 257, 268, 309, 310.
    Tugela, 231.
    Umbilo, 242.
    Umfolozi, 71, 318.
    Umgazi, 111.
    Umhlathuze, 7, 29, 30, 71, 131, 139, 249, 256.
    Umlalazi, 131.
    Umlazi, 243.
    Umngeni, 54, 61, 64, 68, 309.
    Umphenjathi, 106.
    Umsikaba, 100, 105, 144, 219.
    Umtata, 105, 112, 114, 116, 145, 148, 222, 244.
    Umthentu, 100, 105.
    Umvoti, 137.
    Umzimkhulu, 98, 99, 105, 106, 108, 112, 130, 143, 151, 158, 167, 175, 222, 229, 230, 243, 268, 271, 310, 320, 321.
    Umzimvooboo. See St. John's.
    Witte, 222.
    Zwart, 222.
Robben Island, 73, 82, 181, 182.
Ross, John, 131.
Rudolph, G., 230.
Russel, R., 250, 256.

St. Jago, 44.
St. Lucia, 20, 36, 37, 45, 52-6, 73, 75, 182, 183.
St. Stephen's Point, 101.
Saldanha Bay, 58.
Salisbury Island, 242.
Salt, 111.
Scents (Native), 294.
Schools, 243, 246, 248, 249, 253, 254, 263.
Schroeder, Revd., 81.

INDEX

Seraglios, 12, 13, 24-8, 50, 73, 83, 84, 119, 124, 140, 156, 157, 164, 165, 198, 273, 299, 305, 320.
Servants (Domestic), 3, 11, 23, 28, 71, 74, 76, 80, 118, 146, 153, 168, 169, 198, 259.
Settlers, 35, 51, 57, 76, 115, 117, 174, 189, 196, 207, 216, 227-30, 233, 234, 236, 238, 239, 241, 243, 244, 250, 254, 259-61, 266, 311.
Shaka, 1, 8, 9, 13-6, 21, 22, 31, 42, 58, 60-8, 79, 85-8, 90, 91, 93, 103, 110, 113, 115, 116, 118-21, 126, 129, 131, 133-9, 155-7, 162, 168, 170, 183-8, 211-3, 218, 233, 234, 262, 267, 280, 298, 308, 314, 318.
    Assassination, 31, 83-6, 137, 139, 156-9, 162, 174, 175, 188, 214, 221.
    Burial, 316, 317.
    Character, 18, 19, 29, 30, 121, 136, 145, 162, 174, 185, 212, 233, 268, 269.
    Europeans, *re*, 27, 31, 80, 145, 189.
    Fynn, 72-4, 76-8, 130, 144, 189.
    Names, 12, 13, 16, 140, 268.
    Residences, 25, 27, 30, 61, 70, 71, 88, 122, 131, 132, 142, 183.
    Song by, 153, 154.
Shepstone, T., 248.
Shields. See under Weapons.
Shipping, Ships, 48, 51, 123, 177, 182, 196, 242.
    American, 37, 175.
        Building, 54, 55, 119, 131.
            Wrecks, 37, 50, 51, 53, 99, 113, 118, 131, 178, 187, 299.
Ships, Names of—
    African Adventure (Portuguese), 178.
    Andromache, 38, 39.
    Anne, 129.
    Antelope, 57, 58, 67, 68.
    Barracouta, 37, 38.
    Cockburn, 38.
    Dauntless, 237.
    Dove, 246.
    Elizabeth Susan ("Shaka"), 131, 142, 143, 155, 158.
    Ellen, 67.
    Ganymede, 237.
    Grosvenor, 99-101, 111, 112, 271.
    Helicon, 122, 154.
    Jane, 36, 56.
    Julia, 52, 53, 55-8, 67, 91, 94, 118, 182.
    Leven, 37, 38, 40, 45, 52, 73, 118, 181, 186.
    Levert, 35.
    Liverpool, 245.
    Mary, 36, 37, 40, 53, 56, 118, 119, 130, 131.
    Orange Grove, 52.
    Palmyra, 254.
    Princess Charlotte, 51.
    St. Michael, 194.
    Salisbury, 51-3, 55, 56, 118, 181, 182, 185.
    Saucy Jack (Whaler), 37, 44.
Si6u6ulungu Country, 244.
Sickness, 32, 38, 42, 43, 45, 47, 66, 78, 79, 117, 121, 132, 140, 159, 161, 176, 209, 280, 281, 306, 318.
Simon's Bay, 36, 38, 39.
Siphezi (Shaka's Kraal), 160.
Slaves, 39, 40, 43, 47, 48, 113, 177-9, 286, 298, 299, 312.
Smidt, Miss E. (Farewell's wife), 129.
Smith, Dr. A., 164, 210, 213, 215, 216, 230, 311, 312.
Snakes, 32, 279, 310, 311, 317.
Snelder (Trader), 243.
Snow Mountains (Ingale), 267.
Snuff, 10, 28, 32, 107, 151, 195, 274, 281, 301, 306, 308.

Somerset East, 35, 312.
    Farm, 35.
    Lord Charles, 35, 51, 54.
Songomela, 99, 100, 107, 109.
Songs and Singing (Native), 5, 6, 26, 30, 33, 50, 73, 75, 88, 96, 121, 134, 149-53, 157, 162, 164, 217, 248, 275, 281, 283, 296, 302, 303, 316.
South African Commercial Advertiser, 53, 115, 195, 196, 200, 204, 207, 252, 257, 262.
Spirits. See Beliefs.
Stanger, 131.
Steedman (Author), 216.
Steller, D., 243, 256.
Sticks, Native. See under Weapons.
Stubbs, J., 256.
Sugar-cane, 27, 46, 74, 306.
Superstitions, 11, 135, 146, 171, 172, 214, 215, 217, 273, 274-82, 286, 287, 306, 317, 318.
Surveys, 38, 45, 52, 55, 73, 118, 131, 181.
Swaziland, 251, 255.

Tainton, Revd., 236.
Thackwray, Mr. (Calamaish), 116, 168, 173, 220.
Theal, G. M., 36, 52, 55, 58, 236.
Themba Mission, 249.
Theopolis Mission, 181.
Thompson, G., 35, 52, 53, 182, 183, 185, 285, 319.
Threlfall, Revd. W., 40, 43, 44, 177.
Tobacco, 48, 106, 123, 222, 306.
Toohey, D. C., 230, 260.
Tools (Native), Anvils, 272, 273.
        Axes, 269, 272, 273, 291, 307.
        Bellows, 272.
        Hammers, 90, 272.
        Hoes, 270, 302, 303.
        Needles, 270, 294.
        Spades, 223, 224.
        Stones (Grinding and Polishing), 10, 89, 269, 270, 272, 273, 291.
Townshend, Lord James, 55.
Trees, 27, 29, 49, 50, 55, 71, 90, 100, 125, 135, 137, 263, 272, 292.
Tr als, 111, 163, 217, 277.
Tribes, AmaBele, 13.
    AmaGushara, 167.
    AmaJayi, 149, 150.
    AmaNhlwenga, 46.
    AmaPhisi, 259, 260.
    AmaMpondo, 24, 91-3, 95, 98, 100-2, 106-8, 110, 116-8, 143, 149-51, 156, 158, 167, 168, 171, 172, 196, 205, 206, 216, 218, 220, 221, 224, 225, 235, 236, 321.
    AmaThonga, 37.
    AmaNtusi, 104, 110, 111, 114, 116.
    AmaXesiβe, 167.
    AmaXolo, 112, 113, 321.
    AmaZiligazi, 20.
    Bastards, 218, 319.
    Bathwas, 149, 150.
    Bechuana, 124, 156, 318, 319.
    Bomvana, 111.
    Bushmen, 45, 230.
    Buthelezi, 9.

INDEX

Tribes—*continued*
    Cele, 32, 70, 209, 210, 212.
    Fingoes (Fengus), 22-4, 192, 321.
    Hlongwe, 192.
    Hlubi, 124.
    Hottentots, 35, 42, 45, 58, 61, 68, 69, 80, 82, 91, 92, 94, 124, 125, 129, 130, 143, 167-70, 176, 181, 204, 207, 213, 222-4, 226, 228, 229, 242, 255, 259.
    Inhlangwini, 254.
    Iziyendane, 124.
    Jayis, 149, 150.
    Khondlo, 10.
    Kuyiwane, 9.
    Langeni, 2, 9, 12, 13, 17, 139, 140, 257.
    uMacingwane, 14.
    Magwaza, 257.
    Matabele, 249.
    Mlotha, 3.
    Mthethwa, 1, 2, 5-8, 10, 15, 31, 47, 139, 140, 150, 269, 308.
    Mthimkhulu, 3.
    Mthwani, 310.
    Ndwandwe, 9, 11, 17, 18, 30, 47, 48, 85, 118, 122, 150, 317.
    Ngwane, 1, 17, 18, 318-21.
    Nhlungwini, 18.
    Ntshali, 9.
    Ntuli, 13.
    Phembeni, 318.
    Qadi, 9, 236, 257-60.
    Qwaɓe, 2, 5, 7, 9, 13, 16, 17, 80, 165-7, 169-73, 220, 294.
    Swazi, 9, 149, 150, 249, 251.
    Tambookies, 23.
    Tembe, 46.
    Thembu, 9, 235, 236.
    Xhosas, 9, 235, 236, 240, 244.
Tudor, Mr., 45.

Uitenhage, 113, 230, 312.
Umbalijala (Native), 106.
Umhlanga Omkhulu (uMvelinqangi) (Creator), 81, 267.
Umlazi school, 243.
Utensils (Native), 10, 11, 27, 50, 108, 145, 195, 222, 269, 271, 289, 291, 300, 306.
Uys, P., 230, 312, 314.

Vanvega (a Boer), 312.
Venable, Revd. H. J., 249.
Vidal, Capt., 38.

Walker, Mr., 168, 173, 220.
War, Accoutrements, 284.
    Cry, 6, 165, 217, 283.
    Kaffir, 23, 24, 231, 234, 237, 267, 312.
    Native, 8, 9, 21, 48, 64, 67, 122, 126, 139, 159, 173-5, 235, 267, 321.
Wax, 49, 52, 292.
Weapons, Assegais, 2, 16, 55, 70, 75, 84, 89-91, 95, 97, 99, 104, 105, 108, 112, 115, 120, 127, 152, 156, 159, 160, 174, 177, 182, 207, 222, 223, 225, 270, 272, 281, 287, 291, 297, 301, 311.
    Knobkerries, 13, 29, 78, 89, 90, 135, 222, 258.
    Shields, 9, 11, 13, 27, 70, 74, 75, 81, 82, 89-91, 95, 103, 123, 125, 127, 133, 141, 142, 174, 222, 225, 226, 250, 284, 285, 317.
    Spears, 21, 285, 309.

Weapons—*continued*
    Sticks, 71-3, 78, 86, 89, 136, 147, 156, 159, 174, 258, 259, 272, 276, 285, 286, 301.
Weenen, 202.
White, G., 256.
Wilson, Revd. A. E., 249.
Wine, 44, 64.
Winterberg, 235.
Witchcraft, 4, 6, 16, 28, 29, 31-3, 70, 155, 196, 210, 214, 232, 275-8, 318.
Wolf's Head Hill, 109.
Wolhuter, F. M., 129.
Wood, R., 236, 250, 256.
    W., 249, 251, 265.
Wyngart, Mr., 245.

Zinc metal, 271.

© 2022 Giulio Einaudi editore s.p.a., Torino
www.einaudi.it

ISBN 978-88-06-25747-7

Maria Grazia Calandrone

Dove non mi hai portata

Mia madre, un caso di cronaca

Einaudi

Le conoscenze espresse nel testo sono ricavate dalle innumerevoli testimonianze raccolte dall'autrice.
Sebbene si tratti di un'opera principalmente in prosa, alcuni paragrafi presentano a capo e spaziature inconsuete: la scelta è intenzionale.

Dove non mi hai portata

Ogni cosa che ho visto di te,
te la restituisco amata

La materia prima

Si chiamava Lucia

Di mia madre, ho soltanto due foto in bianco e nero.
Oltre, naturalmente, alla mia stessa vita e a qualche memoria biologica, che non sono certa di saper distinguere dalla suggestione e dal mito.
Scrivo questo libro perché mia madre diventi reale.
Scrivo questo libro per strappare alla terra l'odore di mia madre. Esploro un metodo per chi ha perduto la sua origine, un sistema matematico di sentimento e pensiero, cosí intero da rianimare un corpo, caldo come la terra d'estate, e altrettanto coerente.

Comincio da quello che ho, le due fotografie che la ritraggono, nell'ordine in cui sono apparse nella mia vita. La prima
è stata scattata nel giorno del suo matrimonio, sabato 17 gennaio 1959. Lucia ha ventidue anni, veste in bianco integrale e non sorride.

Un giorno, guardando questa foto fino a far scomparire le immagini e apparire la realtà dietro le cose che chiamo poesia, ho appuntato su un ritaglio di giornale quattro frasi, che diventeranno chiare scrivendo questo libro: «Si chiamava Lucia. Pochi avevano a cuore la sua vita. Oggi è il giorno del suo matrimonio. Qualcosa di lei non esiste piú».

La seconda fotografia è il rettangolo di pochi centimetri incollato sulla carta d'identità, trovata nel giugno 1965 in una borsetta abbandonata in Roma. Mostra una giovane donna piuttosto bella e persuasa di sé, vestita con maglia e giacca nera, orecchini e collana d'oro. Un'eleganza semplice. Lo sguardo è sincero, aperto, e remoto. Nonostante Lucia sorrida appena, il labbro inferiore un po' sporgente dà all'intero viso un'espressione infantile, lievemente imbronciata. Ricorda Claudia Cardinale nella *Ragazza con la valigia* di Valerio Zurlini. Non so quanti anni abbia in questa foto.

Nello scatto dove Lucia veste in nero l'espressione «fotografia», scrittura di luce, scrittura con la luce, appare corretta.

Nella fotografia in bianco, lo sguardo della sposa risucchia l'intera scena in una vitrea assenza di vita. Lucia fa gli occhi lisci della preda che finge di non esserci, arretra in uno sguardo impenetrabile, dove il mondo è un paesaggio di bestie aguzze e senza sogni, addormentate fuori dalla natura. E su quegli occhi aperti il mondo scivola, non posa piú.

Lei che non è venuta dalle stelle (l'indesiderata)

Lucia viene alla luce in piena notte.

O all'inizio del giorno, data la ragionevole aspettativa – ancora, nel 2022 – del sorgere dell'alba al termine di ogni notte.

Viene espulsa dal corpo della madre all'una e cinque minuti di domenica 16 febbraio 1936. È una fase di luna calante, solo la luce bianca e primitiva di Sirio, apice sfavillante della costellazione Cane Maggiore, proietta sulla calce della parete opposta alla finestra l'ombra dei corpi appena separati, senza troppo clamore.

Prendere vita è muoversi da soli e poi durare. Il corpo di Lucia è una fra le miriadi di forme nelle quali si esprimono l'indipendenza e la volontà di persistere della materia. I suoi capelli puntano tutte le direzioni.

I genitori, Amelia Greco e Luigi Galante, agricoltori, hanno già tre figlie: Anita, Ersilia e Gemma. La quarta femmina è indesiderata, suscita addirittura un filo di rancore, insieme all'umiliante ipotesi di un seme paterno poco vigoroso e di un cognome che non si tramanda. Sei anni piú tardi, chi sa se dopo una serie di gravidanze finite nella demenza del nulla, a Lucia segue Rocco dalla bocca che ride: un avvento di radiosa sostanza muscolare al quale – dopo la prima prova di energia, espressa in un pianto dirotto – viene attribuito il nome d'arte Ercolino, che sostituirà con effetto immediato il nome di battesimo, nei registri dell'anagrafe famigliare.

L'azienda agricola di famiglia è un solido a due piani: poggia, massiccio e bianco, nella disordinata campagna di Palata, provincia di Campobasso, ai tempi ancora inclusa nella regione Abruzzi e Molise. Il Molise si staccherà dalla regione madre solo nel 1963, come un neonato millenario caduto in un rovescio di mandorle e grano. La masseria Galante insiste su una contrada tuttora assente da quasi tutte le mappe.

Per accedere alle due stanze e cucina che costituiscono l'abitazione, bisogna inerpicarsi per una scala di gradini fuori misura: in campagna, al livello del terreno, è indispensabile lasciare grandi spazi per la stalla e la rimessa degli attrezzi agricoli.

Al piano terra si apre dunque il pezzo forte della fattoria: la stalla delle vacche coi loro vitelli. «Stella stellina, la notte si avvicina...» Davanti alla masseria c'è un maestoso albero di fichi, che sormonta il pollaio e la conigliera. L'erbaggio fresco che promana dall'albero dentro l'aria scricchiante del mattino d'inverno, misto all'affumicato della legna che brucia nel camino e al sentore dell'erba cisposa, è odore di casa, per Lucia. Sarà l'odore del quale avrà piú nostalgia, quando la vita la spingerà lontano e lei sarà perduta. Ma padrona del proprio scomparire.

Di giorno, dietro la masseria, tenuti con le corde a certi solidi anelli fissati al muro esterno, o alle giovani querce, stanno capre e maiali e la mucchia dei covoni risplende, sotto il tetto in lamiera del fienile. Piú oltre, i campi arati, messi a grano. Dalla camera da letto si apprezza tutta la tenuta. La vasta, l'ampia pace del possesso.

Di notte, la casa si satura dell'odore dei corpi addormentati. All'alba, tutto è immediatamente movimento, d'uomini e altri animali. Gran parte del lavoro con le bestie si svolge alle prime luci: portare il fieno a mucche e conigli, qualche volta carote zuccherine o piccoli fasci di rughetta pizzicosa; spargere orzo, grano e granturco per le oche, i tacchini e le galline; rovesciare i freddi, sapidi resti della cena umana nel truogolo dei maiali; mungere vacche e pecore – e poi la solitaria, la riottosa capra. Intorno è tutto un rianimarsi di gatti e *cacciún* (cani), una complessa orchestrazione di notifiche del risveglio, composta da crescenti pigolare, abbaiare, muggire, chiocciare, miagolare, grugnire, starnazzare – e belare, per il momento invano: pecore e capre vanno al pascolo dopo la colazione delle donne.

Per Lucia, l'odore del mattino d'inverno è di latte e farina di grano: una fetta spessa di pane duro, ammollato nel latte appena munto e portato a ebollizione, per eliminare i batteri. I dolci sono un lusso inaccessibile. Alla sera, nei vicoli del paese, i bambini corrono dietro gli asini, per strappare alle fascine legate al dorso degli animali la *sulla*, una pianta foraggera profumata, dai fiori rossi che hanno un'ariosa e intima esalazione di miele.

Il paese è una strada principale, via San Rocco, un paio di piazze, qualche diramazione intersecante e due chiese. Tutta pietra, posizione collinare, aria mite e, a lampi, vista sulla tavola azzurra dell'Adriatico, un castone di pace che barbaglia nei vuoti tra le case, arroccate a corona lungo i belvedere perimetrali. E lontano lontano all'orizzonte c'è l'impulso scosceso di un fantasma, il macigno di monte Amaro, che svetta tra i nevai della Maiella. Si dice che il profilo della massicciata sia il profilo del corpo abbandonato della ninfa Maia, primogenita delle Pleiadi, che si è stesa a morire di dolore sotto l'insulto del cielo, dopo avere sepolto il figlio Ermes tra le erbe aromatiche del Gran Sasso. Il corpo supino della madre è corso da un'allerta di camosci, caprioli e cinghiali, quando nei boschi frusciano gli orsi marsicani dal compatto sembiante o, allo scoperto, filano a branchi i lupi a coda bassa, truppe mute dagli occhi fluorescenti dentro l'azzurro elettrico dei fiordalisi. In quegli anni, Palata conta poco piú di tremila abitanti e non dispone di rete fognaria. «P' la Majell!» è l'imprecazione del posto, cambia senso a seconda del tono.

Quando non lavorano alla masseria, i Galante vivono in una casa con affaccio a balcone sulla via principale. Sono una formazione quadrata, uno schieramento a testuggine: una famiglia normale.

Terra di Lucia vista dal futuro

Calcare e girasoli, andando verso il paese. Sterpa e colline dolci. Ho scritto «sterpa» per dire sterpaglie e steppa insieme, un colore desertico, il bruciaticcio del fuoco che è passato e alcune cime di rogo.

È il 14 agosto 2021. Il 16 febbraio (mi accorgerò della stupefacente coincidenza solo molti mesi piú tardi) di quest'anno la sindaca di Palata mi ha sentita nominare il paese durante un'intervista televisiva di Serena Bortone sul libro dedicato a Consolazione, la mia eccentrica mamma adottiva, e mi ha subito invitata a parlarne nella terra – a me semisconosciuta – di Lucia, mia semisconosciuta mamma biologica. Una casualità, travestita da conseguenza logica, alla quale, al solito, non mi oppongo: seguo curiosa il flusso degli eventi, mi osservo dall'esterno. Giusto il dolore bruto mi confina nella mia unica vita, perimetrata e sola. Altrimenti, mi sento vita di tutti.
Manco da questa terra da quarant'anni: Consolazione e io siamo scese dalla corriera nella piazza petrosa di Palata nel 1980. La mia professoressa del ginnasio, Paola Moretti, aveva lavorato per allacciare al tronco delle generazioni di sangue i getti di una persona (io) che, come la maggior parte degli adolescenti, ramificava a caso e sembrava a disagio nella circoscrizione del possibile che chiamiamo realtà. Agli adulti dovevo parere una pianticella idiota, che protende germogli verso zone presunte di mistero, senza comprendere che il mistero piú imperscrutabile è, appun-

to, la realtà. La quale, purtroppo, viene spesso sottostimata e presenta il difetto di bastare soltanto ai felici. La mia storia pregressa forniva la speranza di una giustificazione al mio confusionario slancio creativo, e quelle due signore piene d'affetto (mamma e professoressa) hanno intuito fosse indispensabile aumentare la mia vita includendo in essa l'icona metafisica della madre perduta. E la poesia. Due regali impossibili da ricambiare, che forse sono uno.

Oggi sono alla guida della mia Panda. Accanto a me, mia figlia Anna, di tredici anni. Anna ha deciso di starmi vicina e accompagna il nostro viaggio all'origine con una colonna sonora scelta da lei, dolce e allegra. Le sono grata per questo. Ogni tanto, cantiamo. Sono disponibile ad assorbire il paesaggio che hanno visto gli occhi di mia madre.

Scrivo solo su quaderni a spirale coi fogli vuoti, senza righe o quadretti. Comincio ad appuntare frasi impressionistiche sui luoghi, che, col passare dei giorni e dei mesi, diventeranno appunti sulla vita di mia madre, interviste, esame di fascicoli d'archivio. Infine, una vera e propria investigazione su Lucia e tutto ciò che la riguarda.

A cominciare dal nome del suo paese, Palata, che scopro provenire da una lingua fluviale: la *palata* è uno sbarramento di funi e catene che, avvinte a un fascio di pali, impediscono il passaggio per acqua. Una dogana. Se la borsa non basta, il prezzo sia la vita. Per acqua, nel fiume. Ma *palata* può anche significare sostegno, una svelta sequenza di tronchi infissi in verticale nel terreno, legati con traverse e controventi in filo d'acciaio, che rinforzano al mezzo ponti e passaggi. Ostacolo o sostegno. Come tutto.

Passano infatti i mesi e l'iniziale grandinata di memorie si dirada, negli occhi di molti appare il lampo cieco dell'amnesia. Il ronzare incessante delle mie domande re-ca dolore, pochi mantengono l'ostinato amore necessario a districare il bagliore della vita di Lucia dall'ingroviglio di vergogna, omertà e colpa che l'ha sepolta. Devo affondare le mani nella cecità del tempo, senza sapere cosa troverò: laggiú, nella terra dove il silenzio lascia cadere i non amati. Poi guardare che corpo viene in luce.

Col passare dei giorni, dal nulla che abitava emerge una figura tridimensionale, eretta nella storia del suo tempo. Una figura con la faccia pulita.

Senti questa creatura come ride

Quando mamma Amelia frigge la pasta cresciuta col lievito, Lucia ride e corre intorno al tavolo della cucina, battendo le manine.
«Sent chest criatur comm rir».
Il dialetto si mangia le vocali. Altrimenti, Amelia a mezzogiorno presenta in tavola la solita solfa di pasta con le verdure o coi legumi: sagne con le cicerchie o coi *fasciuàl*, i borlotti nel coccio. Tanto Lucia ha sempre fame, si mangia pure lo zuppone di farro coi broccoli, ma preferisce l'asciutto, i cavatelli soprattutto, l'impasto fatto a mano con l'incavo al centro, dove la salsa di pomodoro si raccoglie in concentrati di sapore. Quando è Natale, al cuore della festa bolle lento il ragú di spuntature. E le fettuccine tirate a mano sulla spiana di legno infarinata, le patate cotte sotto la brace, le noci. La carne solamente alla domenica, e sempre bianca: pollo, piú raramente coniglio. Le vacche, servono vive. Quando d'inverno si ammazza il maiale, è festa grande. Ci vogliono almeno cinque uomini, che cominciano subito dopo l'alba. Però il maiale strilla forte, povera anima, e Lucia si copre le orecchie con le mani.

Dopo, nella cucina col camino grande, appare una popolazione di salsicce, capocolli compatti e ventricina, che al taglio sporca le dita col rosso del peperoncino diavolillo «Mamma, comm còce!» e profuma di finocchietto selvatico. Periodicamente, ai salumi si aggiungono le scamorze, appese insieme ai grappoli di pomodori invernali che

stanno ad asciugare sulle canne. Sotto, le donne mettono in fila sulla panca caci e caprini, le ricotte che ancora colano siero, le salsicce di fegato sott'olio:
«Lucí, passm a buatt».
Nel camino c'è sempre il fuoco acceso, per il caldo e per l'affumicatura. Tutto quel bendidio, fa bene a guardarlo, quando d'inverno a tavola si riunisce la famiglia intera: le cinque femmine (quattro sorelle e madre) lungo i due lati, Luigi a capotavola, indiscusso padrone. Luigi è burbero e severo, diritto e solido come un soldato, mamma Amelia è dolcezza e rassegnazione, si alza di continuo per servire lo sposo, a volte neanche siede, mangia in piedi, si strofina le mani sul grembiule.

Quando masticano, nessuno parla, si sente solo il suono delle scucchiaiate e il croccare del cibo fra i denti: tutti sono impegnati nel sacro rito del nutrimento, che costa fatica e del quale si apprezza ogni briciola, perché *chi magne* combatte *c'a morte*. Il vino è solo per Luigi, è un rosso giovane, fresco e sincero, impregnato di fumo di legna.

Piano piano che cresce, a Lucia, che è la piccola di casa, sono affidati i compiti piú chiari: al mattino, raccogliere le uova nel pollaio, scegliere zucchine e pomodori maturi nelle file dell'orto. A primavera, mamma la manda negli incolti dietro casa a fare mazzetti di asparagi selvatici per le frittate e a spostare le foglie col bastone per scoprire qualche fungo d'abete.
Quando è un poco piú alta e a fine agosto Amelia, dalla finestra aperta, può vedere la testina arruffata di Lucia come si muove nella lontananza, le permette di spingersi fino quasi alla strada, per raccogliere cesti di more di rovo e poi aiutarla a bollire le pile della marmellata e a macinare con le pietre il granturco per la polenta e la pizza di granone.

Lucia ha il suo amico cane, Topolino, un bastardino biondo e intelligente, che chi sa da che pancia di divina iro-

nia è stato rovesciato sul verde prato della vita, con quelle zampe storte da bassotto e la coda ritta di bracco sbruffone. Quando c'è il sole, gioca con lei a rincorrersi sull'aia, e insieme fanno scappare i tacchini, si divertono a sentirli gridare, *alluccare* e spennacchiare:
«Glu! Glu! Glu!»
Ride, Lucia e, dopo che le ha spolpate, astuta e svelta come una volpe, si ficca in tasca le ossa lunghe del pollo. Furta ai maiali, per il suo Topolino. Oppure, gioca a nascondersi con l'ultima sorella nata prima di lei. Le altre due sono troppo noiose, guardale là che già fanno pensieri di donna.

Quando Lucia se ne andrà, Topolino metterà radici in una disperazione tranquilla, in cui ama se stesso ma disprezza la propria mala sorte.

Color guerra. Ferro naturale

«Il problema razziale è per me una conquista importantissima, ed è importantissimo averlo introdotto nella storia d'Italia [...] ci eravamo convinti che noi non siamo un popolo, ma un miscuglio di razze [...] Bisogna mettersi in mente che noi non siamo camiti, che non siamo semiti, che non siamo mongoli [...] siamo ariani di tipo mediterraneo, puri».

Cosí un ormai crepuscolare Benito Mussolini, il 25 ottobre 1938, espone la sua allucinazione di seconda mano: l'orgoglio razziale. E la impone, per quanto possibile, all'indisciplinato popolo italiano, il quale non si mostra particolarmente reattivo a questa iniezione di veleno, che insinua delazione e disgrazia tra consanguinei e amici.

Il tritacarne però lavora, impassibile: dopo la progressiva espulsione degli ebrei da scuole e pubblici impieghi, nel 1940 il governo fascista individua alcuni comuni dell'Italia centromeridionale, lontani da zone d'interesse militare e per ciò idonei all'internamento coatto di «stranieri et italiani che est necessario allontanare loro residenze».

Uno di questi luoghi di coercizione è l'allora provincia abruzzese di Campobasso: in palazzi, ex conventi, aziende e abitazioni requisite a privati cittadini (di Agnone, Bojano, Casacalenda, Isernia e Vinchiaturo), tra il 1940 e i tre anni successivi vengono rinchiusi dapprima ebrei, rom e sinti, poi soprattutto slavi, rastrellati durante la brutale aggressione nazifascista del 1941 in Jugoslavia.

Le condizioni dei prigionieri non sono propriamente

quelle dei lager del Nord Europa, qui gli internati godono di alcuni diritti elementari, ma sono reclusi a causa del proprio pensiero o, peggio, della sola etnia. Almeno fin che i cancelli dei campi vengono spalancati dall'intervento alleato, incardinando un debito morale non ancora estinto.

È quasi l'alba del 3 ottobre 1943 e il temporale sferza schiene e volti dei soldati dell'Ottava armata britannica, che sbarcano a sorpresa sulle rive di Termoli, in quel momento occupata dalla Prima divisione paracadutisti tedeschi. A guidare l'Ottava è il cinquantaseienne Bernard Law Montgomery, che l'anno precedente ha sconfitto Erwin Rommel a el-Alamein e il 5 ottobre già telegrafa entusiasta al primo ministro inglese Winston Churchill: «Siamo avanzati d'un lungo tratto e molto rapidamente».

Montgomery è un comandante esperto e intuitivo, memorabile per la sua freddezza, temperata dal bel giaccone con cappuccio e alamari, che diventa una moda giovanile.

Il generale tedesco Albert Kesselring reagisce all'attacco inatteso dividendo le truppe per linee parallele lungo i tre fiumi molisani (Biferno, Trigno e Sangro) e schierando una quarta linea fluviale temporanea lungo il Volturno.

Ai tedeschi già insediati in Palata da fine settembre, il 10 ottobre si aggiungono quelli ricacciati da Termoli verso l'interno, che rifugiano nel paese sotto raffiche dure di mitraglia e andirivieni di voli dell'Aeronautica a bassissima quota, in atterraggio e decollo dalle piste provvisorie costruite sul Biferno dagli Alleati con lucenti lingue d'acciaio perforato che chiamano grelle.

Palata diviene dunque, suo malgrado, fronte di guerra e bersaglio di bombardamenti profondi. I soldati trasportano in paese la gran parte del materiale bellico, lasciando aperte nelle piazze le bocche di fuoco di migliaia di armi. Lucia ha sette anni, il fratellino è nato l'anno prima. Lo scontro, che ha lasciato molte vite a spegnersi fra i girasoli di tutta la provincia, a Palata conta due morti, molte macerie e interi corredi di biancheria depredati, insieme a viveri e patrimonio animale.

Mentre infuriano i bombardamenti, i civili riparano in ricoveri estemporanei e cantine ma, per lo piú, le famiglie vivono arroccate in regime di parziale autarchia nelle case di campagna, nutrendosi coi frutti di terra e animali sopravvissuti al passaggio della razzia: i tedeschi, installati nella residenza del signorotto locale, si sfamano dove e quando vogliono, sequestrando mangiare vivo e morto nelle tenute attorno. Ai Galante prendono piú volte bestiame e pagnotte di pane, il cibo che sarebbe bastato alla famiglia per una settimana.

Intanto, al generale Mark Wayne Clark viene l'idea che decide la vittoria della Quinta armata americana sul Volturno: attacco simultaneo lungo tutto il corso del fiume.

Il 12 ottobre gli Alleati confondono l'acqua esplodendo granate fumogene e, oltre che contro i tedeschi, lottano pure contro gli esiti di piogge fragorose, che hanno reso gli argini sdrucciolevoli e impetuose le correnti. Le radici degli alberi, affondate in un fango fiabesco, non reggono le funi, ma gli americani riescono a passare la linea tedesca, lasciando fra l'acqua turbolenta del Volturno il piú ingente volume di sangue sprecato nell'autunno 1943 in Italia meridionale.

In poco tempo, il Molise è liberato. Nelle campagne di Palata la guerra non si è sofferta molto, né troppo a lungo. Qualche restrizione, qualche minaccia di rappresaglie, certo terrore e i due uccisi: Angelo, un sedicenne che cammina verso la sua campagna per andare ad accudire il bestiame e reagisce all'«Alt!» intimato dai soldati tedeschi mettendosi istintivamente a correre verso una salita. I tedeschi gli sparano. Il ragazzo non muore. Lo raggiungono e lo finiscono all'arma bianca tra le braccia del padre. La versione ufficiale è che il ragazzo avesse tagliato i cavi telefonici, forse per confezionare staffili per le bestie: affronto che, nella logica militare nazista, va evidentemente lavato col sangue. La seconda vittima cade sotto uno dei molti bombardamenti alleati, che durano fino all'alba del 24 ottobre, quando le truppe indiane e nepalesi riconsegnano Palata ai palatesi.

La chiesa del patrono di Palata, san Rocco, che ha subito qualche danno, nel 1945, è già stata restaurata. Non cosí la memoria dei civili.

«Erano gente brutta. Uno ce ne avevamo, di vitello. Ce l'hanno preso e ce l'hanno ammazzato davanti agli occhi. L'hanno lasciato lí, ad agonizzare. Per sfregio. E avevamo quaranta vicci [*tacchini*]. Li hanno ammazzati tutti, uno per uno, e ne hanno mangiato neanche un terzo. Glieli ha dovuti cuocere mamma, con la pistola alla tempia».

Cosí il fratello di Lucia, al telefono. Lui ancora vive nella masseria dove è stato bambino con Lucia bambina.

Sempre la guerra avanza incurante delle giovinezze che spergera, ma si aggiungono pure le morti per autentico scialo, dovute alla bile ottusa dei vinti. I nazisti in ritirata lasciano spesso a terra stragi di civili, a volte compiute con la complicità dei fascisti locali, come avverrà a Sant'Anna di Stazzema, ma non nei due eccidi precedenti che qui prendo a campione, in memoria di tutti: il 13 ottobre sono i soli tedeschi a incendiare e saccheggiare la casertana Caiazzo, lasciando foschi ammassi di pietrame e corpi, ventidue civili straziati e dati alle fiamme. Ideatori maligni dello scempio il sottotenente ventunenne Wolfgang Lehnigk-Emden e il sergente Kurt Schuster, rimasti impuniti grazie alla complicità del governo tedesco, che non concede l'estradizione. Emden vivrà poi indisturbato altri sessant'anni a Coblenza, organizzando feste per bambini.

Il 21 novembre, nel bosco abruzzese di Limmari, i tedeschi trucidano centoventotto persone, fra le quali trentaquattro bambini che non hanno ancora festeggiato i dieci anni.

La morte per il piacere della morte. L'odore del sangue, che ubriaca, è l'odore del potere di decidere se risparmiare o uccidere tutto quello che ancora vive e respira, libero. Nonostante la bollita mediocrità dei tiranni.

E salutava sempre

Una colazione rapida, fatta in piedi quando è ancora buio, mentre il cielo sta per accadere sopra la vastità della campagna. Poi, come tanti, Lucia percorre tutti i giorni quasi un'ora a piedi verso la scuola, dalla campagna passa per le contrade, entra in paese dopo chilometri di provinciale tra i campi messi a grano o girasoli, con le colline azzurre all'orizzonte.
Utilizzando le mappe disponibili in rete e incrociando dati satellitari e lineari, sono infine riuscita a individuare la copertura in ondulina di lamiera del locale adibito a fienile in masseria Galante e ho rifatto il percorso virtualmente, piú volte. Da dicembre a febbraio, sono quattro chilometri abbondanti di sterrato glaciale, fra l'erba appuntita e crespa dell'inverno e salite e discese sulla via scivolosa, o sulle crete molli di concime e pioggia. Ogni tanto, passando, Lucia stacca dal ramo una mela zitella, soda come un biscotto. Oppure, gira il viso al bel sole di marzo, quando a tutto presiede la primavera imminente e le foglie verdissime erompono dalla bituminosa
   scorza invernale dei rami, cristallizzati dalle sublimazioni del vapore in brina. Mimose e mandorli sono i primi a fiorire, posano sulla sonnolenza del paesaggio macchie di giallo e rosa come un canone inverso, un contrappunto raggiante dentro il quale, tra poco, i nidi si animeranno di ghiandaie e cinciarelle che svolacchiano lievi. All'imbocco del paese, qualche struggente siepe di pitosforo. In contrada Cupariello, Lucia saluta sempre. È bella e garbata, ha tanti riccioli neri.

Lucia inizia la prima elementare nell'autunno 1946, a dieci anni e mezzo, quando la marea di sangue sparso dalla Seconda guerra mondiale si sta lentamente prosciugando, torna a gocciare nelle profondità della terra e ogni tanto risbocca come un animale in agguato, come il male.

Lucia frequenta il primo anno in paese, nella piazza del Popolo, e il secondo in una delle tre abitazioni private in pietra bianca messe a disposizione della scuola, che si trovano poco distanti dalla comunale Fontanella. La sua maestra è Agnese Spetrino. Attenta, essenziale, occhi generosi e capelli lunghi, innamorata dei suoi bambini, quaranta alunni per classe.

La maestra si accorge subito quando Lucia al mattino si è svegliata tardi, perché ha dovuto prendere la scorciatoia per lo mezzo dei campi invernali e arriva in classe con le scarpe tutte infangate. A nulla vale sfregarle sugli spigoli degli scalini, Spetrino ci vede benissimo. I suoi occhi gentili dicono tutto.

Nell'edificio scolastico principale, appena salite le scale, c'è la classe così detta «differenziale», una di quelle riserve per bambini perturbanti che verranno abolite solo nell'agosto 1977, su iniziativa della senatrice Franca Falcucci. I «normodotati» di tutte le età vengono invece messi in un'unica classe.

In paese e in campagna non c'è acqua, per ciò a scuola non ci sono i bagni: a ricreazione viene presentato ai bambini un gran secchio di latta, dove essi, uno dopo l'altro, vuotano i visceri e il secchio viene a sua volta svuotato nei canali di scolo a bordo strada.

Riesco a rintracciare le pagelle di Lucia. I suoi voti sono tutti buoni, la materia in cui eccelle è Educazione morale, nella quale allo scrutinio finale si guadagna un bel nove. Visto com'è poi andata la sua vita, la scoperta fa sorridere amaro.

«La maestra diceva sempre a nostro padre: "Falla studiare, questa figlia, falla studiare!" Ma non c'erano soldi...»
Questa ancora la voce di zio Rocco, tanti anni dopo, quando, per tutti noi, il caso è già diventato destino.

Siccome Lucia è una ragazzina sveglia, a metà della terza elementare viene inviata alla Scuola popolare, dove potrà guadagnarsi il certificato di «studi elementari superiori» (dalla terza alla quinta).

La Scuola popolare nasce da un esperimento compiuto nelle scuole di Roma nell'anno scolastico 1946-47 e subito formalizzato dal Provveditorato agli studi, con l'intento immediato di recuperare i giovani che si sono allontanati dallo studio a causa della guerra e con quello, a piú lento rilascio, di «combattere l'analfabetismo, completare l'istruzione elementare e orientare all'istruzione media o professionale» gli studenti piú promettenti. Nella Scuola popolare è infatti prevista la fornitura gratuita di libri e oggetti di cancelleria sotto forma di premi, per non scalfire in alcun modo la dignità degli alunni bisognosi.

Il nome di Lucia non appare però nei registri. Quelle scolastiche sono ore sottratte al lavoro e le autorità devono intervenire spesso, per imporre ai genitori di mandare a scuola le figlie femmine, pena il pagamento di una multa. Cosí dev'essere andata, per Lucia: onorato il minimo indispensabile, la ragazzina è stata ritirata dalla scuola ed è tornata ad attendere alla faccenda domestica.

Poiché il corso inferiore di studi elementari, che coincide coi primi due anni di studio, prevede insegnamento religioso, lettura, scrittura, aritmetica, principî della lingua italiana e nozioni base del sistema metrico, quando è costretta ad abbandonare la scuola Lucia sa certamente leggere e scrivere, sa fare conti semplici, anche se la matematica è il suo risultato peggiore.

Non ha però studiato geografia e storia nazionale, né le

«cognizioni di scienze fisiche e naturali applicabili principalmente agli usi ordinarii della vita» e neppure calligrafia, né le regole della composizione.

Ciò nonostante, come vedremo, scriverà.

Faccio mesi di ricerche, per avere la gioia di vedere la faccetta di Lucia bambina, esamino la moltitudine di foto dell'epoca e del luogo disponibili in rete, finché l'archivista scolastica mi fornisce due dati essenziali (anni di frequenza e nome della maestra) e, il 28 gennaio, la riconosco. È un colpo. Non c'è ombra di dubbio: la somiglianza con mia figlia è miracolosa. A catena, la rintraccio nelle altre due foto.

In tutte e tre, Lucia è in piedi nell'ultima fila. I tratti distintivi sono la massa di capelli ricci, raccolti da un fiocco a scoprire la fronte e le orecchie, le sopracciglia ad ala di gabbiano e l'aria resistente, già mitigata dalla brezza di un sorriso, che trasforma la sua riservatezza in qualcosa di leggero. E lo sguardo frontale, dritto nell'obiettivo.

Nella prima fotografia (10 giugno 1947), la maestra le tiene la mano sulla spalla e la bambina sembra nutrire un torvo desiderio di sparire dietro le teste delle compagne. Probabilmente è la prima fotografia della sua vita. Ma lo sguardo non cede, è spaventosamente fermo. Altre compagne sono piú disinvolte, ma le espressioni di tutte oscillano tra sorpresa e terrore, nessuna sorride.

La seconda foto è del giugno successivo, 1948, Lucia ha compiuto dodici anni da quattro mesi e appare eretta, lieve e luminosa, ha una dolcezza onesta e disarmante. In quell'anno è successo qualcosa. Dalle braccia conserte sporge l'osso del polso sinistro, la sua mano è nascosta sotto il braccio destro. Questa è l'unica traccia delle mani di mia madre.

L'ultima foto è il fossile di un'adolescenza sviluppata in altezza, aggraziata, informata di sé, col sole in faccia.

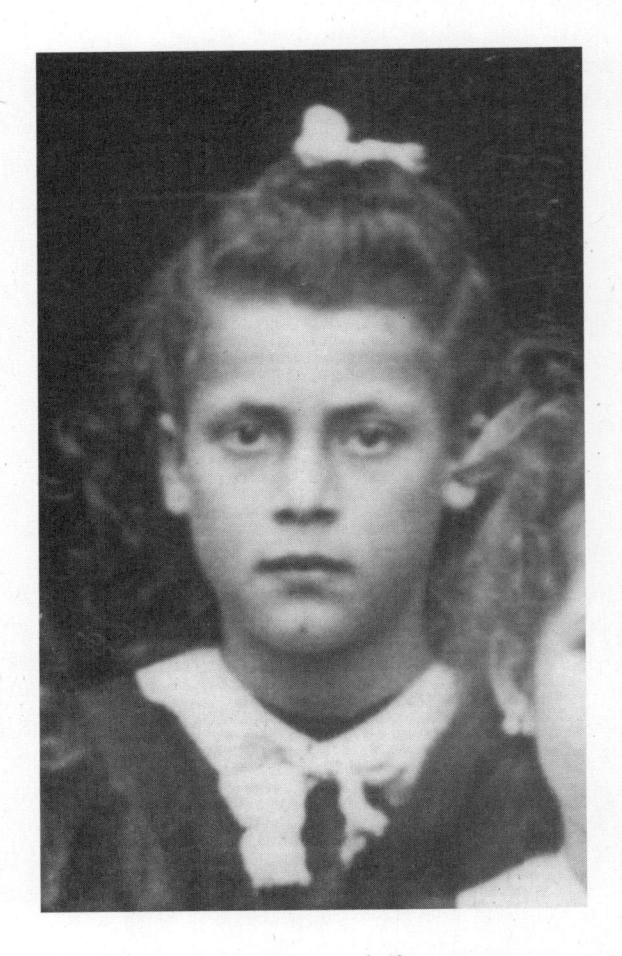

Lucia Galante, giugno 1948, seconda elementare.

Tonino

1947. La gioia oggettiva

Poco dopo che il ferro della guerra ha impazzato e incrudito sui mortali, nell'estate 1947 la famiglia abruzzese De Grandis si trasferisce nell'azienda agricola del notaio di Palata, a cinquecento metri dalla masseria Galante.

I De Grandis sono mezzadri, coltivano le terre d'altri. Fra loro c'è il piccolo Antonio, Tonino, nato il 27 marzo 1936, un ragazzino bruno con gli occhi spiritosi, il ciuffone alla moda e la bocca disegnata. Nell'azienda Galante abita la piccola Lucia, anche lei di neanche dodici anni.

Fuori scuola, Lucia porta i capelli sempre sciolti. Mossi, abbondanti, lunghi fino alle spalle. Come ho scritto, ha un viso dall'espressione lievemente ritrosa. Nello sguardo, però, brilla una luce ironica, aperta. Il contrasto fa effetto, è un invito che nega se stesso.

«Facevo chilometri, per vedere Lucia. D'inverno, d'estate, sotto la neve e con l'acqua. Chilometri, per mandarle un bacetto da lontano.
Quando portavamo le mucche e le capre ad abbeverarsi, ci scambiavamo un salutino alla fontana.
Io, per quella ragazza, prendevo la cavalla pure se c'era la neve alta un metro...»

Tonino gironzola a cavallo intorno alla fattoria di Lucia. Impettito, giovane giovane, sorridente, ha gli occhi che brillano e il ciuffo nero che spiove sulle ciglia e sobbalza a ogni passo della bestia. Fa la sua gran figura, la parata a cavallo per Lucia. Lucia stravede, il padre s'imbestialisce.

Gonnellina sotto il ginocchio, cuore che batte forte, Lucia va a pascolare le pecore o le mucche e ogni giorno i suoi animali ritengono che l'erba che cresce davanti alla masseria dove abita Tonino sia la piú fresca e abbondante, la piú dolce di tutte le erbe.

Certe sere di festa, lucide e rare come la fortuna, viene Gino che suona l'organetto. D'inverno, si balla la *zumbarella* dentro casa. D'estate, sull'aia. Eccoli che si sguardano attraverso, Lucia e Tonino, quasi quasi si sfiorano le mani, quasi quasi bambini. Fanno le giravolte, il cuore sale a trottola, a spirale, mira al cielo. Potenza schietta. Mani sui fianchi, e come le si muovono i capelli, lei fa la ruota con la gonna, pavoncella rossastra o smeraldina con le vesti tessute al telaio e lui, mani dietro la schiena, ha i calzoni col cintolo di bronzo che gli luccica al lume delle stelle.

Per sei estati Lucia e Tonino si spiano, nascosti dai covoni del grano.
Per sei inverni, nascosti dal calesse. Non si rivolgono mai la parola. Solo mezzo sorriso, un saluto con gli occhi. Lucia ha la pelle chiara, quando lui osa un bacio da lontano arrossisce tutta. Le parole non servono a niente.
La figura di lei che si sfila dal calore dei campi e gli casca in braccio. Questo il sogno di tutte le notti di Tonino, pure se sgronda e scroscia la pioggia nera di gennaio.
La spiegazione del suo amore è semplice e, per ciò, spiega tutto: Lucia è bellissima.

Le cose confabulano amabilmente tra loro, mentre il corpo di una ragazza esiste, occupa uno spazio semplice e vero, che odora di paglia e polvere di terra alzata dal vento, mira il suo sommo bene tra corti di fieno e torna a casa come illuminata dall'interno. In tasca, ha qualcosa che scotta: un filo d'erba, un sasso, un rametto di salvia, un pugnetto di fave prese in ostaggio all'orto di Tonino. È tutto un rapimento, una melassa, un raccogliere indizi. Lucia si fida
        degli altri, parla sempre di lui, delle tracce di lui nella vibrazione dell'alba, dei dettagli di lui dentro la consistenza del reale. Insopportabile, come tutti gli innamorati. E quante volte in chiesa s'è voltato, e hai visto la *giacchètt*, e chissà se gli piaccio con la treccia...
Nelle notti d'estate, Lucia si butta sul fieno con la sua compagna coetanea Maria. A sinistra, il vascone delle aromatiche, una realtà dove le cose sembrano esaurirsi pro-

fumando. E lei, sotto la luminaria delle stelle, intona per l'amica la canzona infinita di Tonino.

Nei fatti, Tonino dà ininterrotte prove di gradimento, lo sa tutto il paese che ogni giorno trova una scusa per svolacchiare intorno alla sua bella dal nome che splende: Lucia-chiaro-dell'alba, Lucia che ha il nome inciso sulla fonte con la scheggia di pietra. Lucia non nega niente, guarda in alto a destra, come fa sempre, e sorride, arruffata come una rosa canina. Il suo ragazzo è un vivo, un entusiasta. È l'annuncio di una vita felice.

Come molte coppie di senzaterra, Lucia e Tonino saleranno col sudore i poderi di altri; ma insieme. Non lo devono dire: gli occhi di lui che ridono, gli occhi di lei che dopo un po' si abbassano, scrivono nell'aria e nel sangue ogni promessa. Del corpo, che sa tutto quanto serve. Pertanto, quando lui compie diciassette anni, in omaggio all'usanza del luogo, manda ai genitori di Lucia un ambasciatore di matrimonio in calze rosse, per chiedere la mano della figlia. La risposta è:
«No».

Il pretendente è povero, non ha terreni, non è all'altezza di Lucia. Una mannaia.

Poi il padre lega Lucia all'abbeveratoio delle vacche e – col fucile dritto in mezzo al petto della figlia, dice Se ti rivedo con Tonino tutteddue v'ammazzo. E lei appaura, del piombo e della padronanza brutta, di quella faccia dura come il mare che rampa dal vuoto delle campagne.

Lucia non fa come Maria le dice, non va via. Rimane.

Colpito al cuore e nell'orgoglio, Tonino si accartoccia e ripiega sul mare da dov'è venuto, a Torino di Sangro, in Abruzzo. Siamo nel 1953.

Senza quel rifiuto lontano, non sarei nata, e ciò mi avrebbe – credo – danneggiata. Ma la vita di Lucia sarebbe stata semplice e contenta.

1955

Caldo anomalo. Quest'anno le rondini si fermano in paese fino a settembre inoltrato.

E Tonino, al telefono, nel 2021, è un uomo simpatico e affettuoso, con una buffa cantatina del Nord che si mescola ai bassi terrestri:
«L'ultima volta l'ho vista dietro un mucchio di paglia e la madre è arrivata col bastone.
Quando ho sentito che l'avevano fatta fidanzare a quel buono a nulla di Centolire mi sono sposato con una brava ragazza di qui, anche perché, nel 1957, chi si sposava veniva esonerato dal servizio militare. Mi sono sposato in fretta e furia, senza neanche la festa.
La festa di nozze l'abbiamo fatta l'anno dopo a Palata, perché il prete di Torino di Sangro si è rifiutato di far entrare in chiesa la sposa con l'abito bianco, dopo un anno di matrimonio...»
Lo interrompo, cattiva:
«E Lucia, l'hai invitata alla festa?»
Un attimo di silenzio. Gli ho causato dolore.
«... È una battuta, vero?
Siamo rimasti a vivere a Palata, a pochi passi da Lucia. Nel 1958 ci è nata subito una bambina e nel gennaio del 1961 ci siamo trasferiti a Lissone, in provincia di Monza. Viviamo ancora qui, da qui non me ne sono piú andato.
Però quella ragazza è nel mio cuore finché vivo, era bellissima.
Dovevo insistere, portarmela via...»

Mi pento di averlo ferito. Tonino è un uomo buono, all'epoca era un ragazzino di diciassette anni, e il suo rimpianto è vivo come allora. Naturalmente Lucia sa della festa di matrimonio di Tonino. Naturalmente non va mai a trovarlo, ma sa che gli è nata una figlia. Dopo tre anni, perde le tracce di lui, sente dire che è partito con la famiglia per il Nord. Dieci anni piú tardi andrà a cercarlo, invano, forse in memoria del solo amore semplice e sincero ricevuto in vita.

1958. Un quadernetto sotto il materasso

Quasi nessuno tra i molisani si distingue per altezza, ma hanno gambe solide, buone a scalare il loro impervio e bellissimo territorio, macchiato da esplosioni di girasoli e rocce semisommerse, che sembrano dadi appena sparsi dalla mano di un gigante che abbia lasciato a mezzo una partita, per ironia estetica e volontà di somigliare questa terra a un'allegria, ma lunare e introversa.

Il lavoro nei campi si fa ancora quasi tutto a mano e i contadini del vicinato si aiutano l'un l'altro. A inizio novembre fanno i solchi guidando l'aratro legato all'asino, che s'impunta spesso, com'è vizio degli asini. Meglio i bovini da traino legati a coppie, le belle vacche bianche dagli occhi dolci e i fianchi di madonna, che di rado finiscono nei piatti. Poi, si semina il grano. Tra la fine di giugno e metà luglio, quando è tempo di mietere o trebbiare, lavorano in gruppo: prima un campo, poi l'altro. Corpi simili ai chicchi del grano. Corpi arsi. Ma seri, spesso allegri. Lucia falcia con gli altri.

Stoccata la mucchia dei mannelli al sole vivo, con le cime voltate tutte da un verso, le donne stendono all'ombra della quercia la tovaglia con pane, cacio e tagli sugosi di pollo.
«Brav femmn, quant grazieddío!»
Falcetto nella tasca posteriore dei calzoni, uomini di tutte le età, dai bambini agli anziani, si passano la boccia del rosso.

Quando il grano è asciutto, viene quello che ha la trebbiatrice, a separare i chicchi dalla pula: da pochi anni non si batte piú il raccolto a mano.

Se il campo da lavorare si stende vicino alla masseria, quando il sole d'estate che sfiamma rende la terra impossibile da camminare e gli scuri si accostano nella controra, ciascuno custodendo il suo segreto, Lucia si butta sul letto a pancia sotto. Dice che ha mal di stomaco. Invece, allunga la mano sotto il materasso, sfila qualcosa che crede di sapere solo lei e va via a volo radente, da quel lettuccio di vedova bianca: ha un quadernetto e una penna, gomiti per appoggiarsi e le poche parole in italiano che ha imparato nei due anni di scuola. Dicono scriva poesie. Ci credo, perché Lucia entra nella giovinezza ristretta in una solitudine che modifica il suo istintivo abbandono alle circostanze. Entrambi i testimoni della sua adolescenza, pure senza volerlo, l'hanno tradita: Maria, l'amica del cuore, nel 1958 si è sposata ed è emigrata in Svizzera. Tonino, amore ragazzino che le fa ancora girare la testa, quando disgraziatamente ci si mette a pensare, vive a un passo da lei, con un'altra. Lucia si irrigidisce nella circoscrizione del suo silenzio, ora sente il bisogno di indagare il mistero e accostare il suo corpo a tutto ciò che fugge. Quello che ha provato per Tonino sarà la guida per il tempo futuro: la sua ormai innominabile presenza, il cuore che tempesta, non li dimentica piú; ma ora, su quel letto di ragazza, sono solo malinconia. E invisibile.

La penombra che argina la vampa del sole nei dopopranzi estivi le somiglia. Come tutti, Lucia si muove dentro la sua vita con una direzione apparente e una segreta, spesso sconosciuta a lei stessa. È sola nel suo corpo, come tutti. Dentro la sua gioia, dentro la sua fatica. In una delusione che non merita, che sa di vento fermo.

TONINO

Il piccolo Ercolino è il ristoro del cuore di Lucia. Con lui, si sente libera, le piace tanto quando vanno insieme a sminuzzare il terreno dell'orto con le zappe a mano – l'odore della terra, le radici, e il silenzio grande della campagna che scende piano dentro le persone e si fa spazio – o quando, a primavera, tutta la terra profuma di nuovo e lei è avanti a seminare, con il grembiule pieno, butta nei solchi i semini di fave, ceci, granturco e il fratellino dietro, a coprire la terra col concime. La schiena di Lucia vista dal basso, l'ombra della sorella che canticchia

Vola, vola, palummella vola.
Vola, vola,
dimme l'amore addò sta...

Quando Lucia ha vent'anni, zio Rocco ne ha quattordici.

Luigi

Fuori luogo e triste

Quando la fanno fidanzare, Lucia scappa. Il promesso sposo è lo *sciaccò*, il buffone del paese, lo chiamano Centolire per via della canzone, perché sogna l'America come un bambino ed è arrivato a trentun anni scapolo, perso nei suoi mondi di dentro. Chissà che altrove sogna Luigi, che vita qui inimmaginabile... Certo non ha interesse per le donne, i ragazzini del paese gli ridono dietro:
«Non sei un uomo!»
Però ha il pezzo di terra che confina con quello dei Galante. Lungo lungo, ché quando sta sull'asino i piedi gli strofinano per terra, bell'uomo dal viso affilato e la mascella forte, Gino ha la terza elementare e dicono sia succube di madre e sorella. Le donne di casa sua hanno finalmente trovato qualcuno che se lo prende, quel bietolone, umorale e inetto, che tutte le mattine appena sveglio già accompagna il caffè col cognacchino. Indolente per natura, Luigi spesso è intontito dall'alcol. In tutte le fotografie, gli occhi neri all'ombra delle belle ciglia, rimandano lo sguardo di un assente. Luigi è un infelice e un obbediente. Non si oppone al suo stesso matrimonio, perché non crede di poter sanare la sua congenita infelicità.

Lucia, invece, fa i numeri del circo e il padre ritira lo schioppo giú dal muro e la insegue col ferro imbracciato lungo il corso principale del paese. Altri genitori legano le ribelli a un albero coperto di formiche e le lasciano lí tutta la notte, per piegare la loro volontà a matrimoni indesiderati. *Miserere mei, Deus, secundum magnam misericordiam tuam.* Pietà di me, Dio, secondo la tua misericordia, grande.

Sabato 17 gennaio 1959. La sposa

La sposa ha il labbro spaccato.
La sposa continua a non volere. È costretta a ceffoni, ma la sua volontà non è piegata. Contro la sua determinazione, il contratto è comunque siglato: utilizzo della considerevole forza lavoro e riproduttiva di una giovane femmina, in cambio dell'aumento delle proprietà. Oltre al terreno confinante, i Greco hanno parecchie terre, anche qualche casetta in campagna. Corpo di vergine insorta in cambio di terreni. Si profilano nubi. Ma ovunque usa cosí. E si capisce: è la solidarietà degli affamati, la logica nella quale ogni singolo corpo, ogni singola vita, è affluente di un unico fiume: la scalata sociale della famiglia. Senza attacchi di nervi, concentràti a durare. Gettano ancora la loro ombra spettrale sul presente, i tempi nei quali a fine pasto si raccolgono le briciole di pane dalle tovaglie, per impastarle di nuovo, e le ragazzine di campagna devono vendere i propri capelli alle cittadine che possono permettersi una parrucca. Appena usciti dall'orrido della miseria, occorre consolidare un possesso durevole, una superficie economica liscia, piana, per camminare sereni verso la vecchiaia. Ogni singola azione della famiglia è un ponte strategico verso la meta.

Oggi è la festa di Sant'Antonio Abate, protettore dei maiali e di tutte le bestie, con figura del santo in processione accompagnato da animali domestici, falò e canti. Lo sposalizio muto di Lucia è circondato dal mugghio musicale delle celebrazioni. Forse, per risparmiare, profittano della festa grande del paese.

Nell'unica foto del matrimonio, la sposa è serrata fra padre e marito. Una fila compatta, un esercito contro l'angoscia. Padre poco piú alto di lei e roccioso alle spalle, la faccia come un pane di terra petrosa solcata da rivoli di sole asciutto. La figura del padre, in abito nero e cravatta, è una crepa di vento fermo, stirato come un'ombra della storia sopra la spalla destra di Lucia. Lucia ha la mano sinistra incastrata sotto il braccio destro dello sposo. Lo sposo, in doppiopetto grigio, posa la mano sinistra sulla spalla sinistra della suocera. Delicato, in punta di dita. La madre di Lucia è la figura piú avanzata verso l'obiettivo, eppure è marginale. Volto perplesso, sopracciglia alzate. Un digradare lento della forza, nel suo vestito nero col colletto tondo rifilato in merletto bianco e i bottoncini chiusi fino al collo. Un mese prima del ventitreesimo compleanno di Lucia, nessuno tocca Lucia. Nessuno prova a simulare gioia. La chiesa è quella del paese, che tornerà fra queste pagine alla fine.

Lucia indossa un abito di tulle avvitato: gonna coi veli e corpetto a manica lunga. Sotto, le scarpe *décolleté* bianche, col tacco alto. Per alto, s'intendano cinque centimetri. Le scarpe me le hanno raccontate, perché la foto s'interrompe poco sotto l'inguine, è un piano americano.

La sposa non ha un filo di trucco sul viso. Purtuttavia, ella è simile in tutto a un clown bianco dentro schiera animale. In quel momento perde l'equilibrio, non indovina.

Bianco su bianco

A occhio nudo non si percepisce la posizione della mano destra, perché è guantata di bianco e ha come fondo il bianco del vestito nuziale. Contrastando la foto, emerge la verità: Lucia si tiene con forza all'eccessivo mazzo di fiori. Per sopravvivere
      l'albero, invece, lascia cadere i fiori. Poi, le foglie.

I guanti da sposa di Lucia mi sono stati consegnati nel 1980, dentro la sua borsetta nera a bauletto. Sono piccoli, adatti alla mano di una ragazzina. Li ho qui, davanti a me.
Sono magra, ho le mani sottili, ma questi guanti mi entrano a fatica. Odorano ancora di crema Nivea per le mani.
Asperges me, Domine, hyssopo, et mundabor;
   lavabis me, et super nivem dealbabor. Aspergimi, Signore, con aromi di piante medicinali e io sarò
     lavata, bianca piú della neve. In paese
   non ci sono ristoranti, al pranzo di nozze pensa la sposa. Si consuma in casa.

La casa coniugale

La casa coniugale di Lucia e Luigi è la casa da scapolo di Luigi, un garage con stalla interna in via Amodio Ricciardi 8, che in paese chiamano «la buca».

La visito il 14 agosto 2021. Il piano sotto è un vano seminterrato a volta, intonacato in bianco e adibito a cucina. In fondo a sinistra c'è una piccola stalla, anch'essa a volta, con una griglia di luce al livello stradale, in alto a destra.

Il tavolo, verniciato in verde acqua, è accostato al muro di sinistra della cucina e una stecca laccata di bianco è inchiodata a secco al muro destro. Alla stecca è avvitata una fila di ganci, ai quali è appesa una stoviglieria in ferro che, nel 2021, si presenta arrugginita e con lo smalto scheggiato: tre padelle a due manici in scala crescente (la piú grande ha la vernice dei manici completamente saltata, per l'uso), una pentola rossa da spaghetti, un bricco in smalto bianco e una brocca verde da un quarto. Alcune tovaglie bianche, spoglia mortale e sindone della dote di Lucia, e le posate buone del matrimonio, legate con lo spago, stanno in fondo a una piccola cassapanca. Non c'è corrente elettrica. Non c'è acqua. Non ci sono finestre. Nel 2021 l'intonaco del soffitto, sollevato in bolle dall'umidità, è caduto per terra a grandi scaglie.

A destra: il cassone del grano a tre ante orizzontali e una ripidissima scala, a chiocciola stretta, che sale da metà stanza. Per non rubare spazio allo spazio già limitato delle due camere sovrapposte, chi ha costruito la scala ha dovuto mettere uno sull'altro nove gradini quasi impraticabili.

Al piano sopra, ecco la camera degli sposi, anch'essa in calce bianca. Giusto lo spazio per un letto e una cassettiera di legno scuro a quattro cassetti, dalla quale è stato rimosso il piano di marmo. L'8 febbraio 2022 saprò che questo comò, che sto aprendo cassetto per cassetto, è lo stesso che apriva Lucia. Esso, oggi, contiene solo polvere.

L'armadio è un rettangolo senza porta, scavato nel muro che dà sulla strada. Tra parete e parete della rientranza è fissata una stecca, gemella di quella che regge le pentole.

Quando salgo, appesa al centro della stecca, sta una gruccia di legno marrone da cappotto. Sul fondo dell'armadio, una coperta color senape.

La stanza è senza finestre. L'unica apertura è in cima alla scala, una finestrella a due ante di legno scuro, che affaccia sulla piccola strada.

Nel gennaio 1958, una settimana o due prima del matrimonio, qui è tutto un pullulare: la gente del paese si arrampica al piano di sopra per vedere il letto degli sposi. La dote della sposa è esposta su un tavolo in cucina. E Lucia stessa, esposta in cucina, offre i dolci fatti con le sue mani. Gli ospiti posano sul tavolo soldi e regali. La tenaglia si chiude. *Et secundum multitudinem miserationum tuarum, dele iniquitatem meam.* E date le tue innumerevoli compassioni, lavami dal peccato.

Lucia e Luigi vivono tre anni tra la buca e la casa di campagna dei suoceri. Senza luce, senz'acqua, senza corrente elettrica. È tutto.

Sch sch sfrusc sfrusc. Condizionali

Il materasso degli sposi è *'u saccone d' frusce*, il grande sacco riempito di foglie di granturco sul quale dormono i poveri; i ricchi preferendo quello imbottito in lana. Il *saccone* è un rettangolo con due larghe asole lungo i lati maggiori, nelle quali Lucia al mattino potrebbe infilare le mani, per spianare gli ammassi di foglie che il peso notturno dei corpi, addormentati insieme al centro del letto, ha formato lungo i due lati esterni, rimasti vuoti. Al mattino Lucia potrebbe spingere le foglie verso il centro, ripensando a cos'abbia causato quel disordine, l'avvallamento centrale. Potrebbe sorridere, sentirsi confortata e solidale, sostenuta dall'intelligenza di un affetto, se non proprio felice. Il titolo di questo breve paragrafo è l'onomatopea con la quale in paese si canzona il rumore del sesso.

Invece, quando dorme in paese, la ricordano di mattina presto, affacciata ad appendere il materasso a cavallo dell'unico davanzale, per smuovere le foglie con la forcina in legno a doppia punta, simile alla forca di metallo che si usa per rivoltare il fieno e che presto le verrà puntata contro. Il materasso di Lucia e Luigi ogni mattina presenta un demoralizzante cordolo nel mezzo, se lei e lo sposo dormono cosí, disuniti e soli. Lucia arieggia la delusione dell'ennesima notte bianca ai pochi refoli della via stretta dove affaccia la casa e lei riposa, inutilmente sola col marito. Il materasso di Lucia è muto. Canta solo quando lo smuove lei, affacciata alla finestra.

Le resta il grande amore per i bambini: Lucia tiene accanto alla porta un piatto pieno di caramelle, da regalare ai ragazzini che passano. Come tutte le donne sposate, dovrebbe portare i capelli decorosamente legati. E invece.

La casa di campagna

Intanto che si svolgono i lavori di ammodernamento della casa nuova nella via principale, gli sposi fanno mostra di abitare qui, nella casa da scapolo di Gino Centolire. In realtà, appena sposati stanno piú spesso in campagna che in paese.

Il giorno di Ferragosto 2021 entro in quello che resta della minuscola masseria, affacciata sull'orlo di una valle interna. Mi colpisce immediatamente la somiglianza tra questo luogo e un rudere che visitavo spesso tanti anni fa, al ciglio di una valle in tutto simile a questa. Oh, le cose lavorano dentro di noi, che non sappiamo niente.

Qui, in venti metri quadri, dormono in quattro. Stanno come i piccioni nei loculi. Sotto loro, due vacche. D'inverno, il fiato delle bestie li riscalda. A sinistra della porta d'ingresso c'è il camino. Due passi avanti alla porta d'ingresso, il letto coniugale. Il letto coniugale è diviso da quello dei suoceri con una tenda di cotone bianca come un sudario, appesa al trave del soffitto. L'imbarazzo basterebbe, forse, ad abolire ogni contatto fra gli sposi. Ma, ovviamente, c'è di piú. C'è che a Luigi va bene cosí. A Lucia, no.

Com'è finita qui, dove mai avrebbe voluto essere? Testa a testa coi suoceri, in una rappresentazione involontaria dell'invisibile che la domina, Lucia si addormenta nell'infelicità. Quando la fame non la tiene sveglia.

Come un diorama

Lucia guarda la valle ancora livida. È l'alba. Quale disegno del demonio l'ha collocata qui, su questa piccola sporgenza di terra e, sotto, ettari di lavoro da fare a braccia per un tozzo di pane e nessuna carezza. Luigi la tocca solo col forcone, la spinge avanti come coi maiali.

Ogni tanto, però, ha delle accensioni, la massacra di calci e pugni in testa.
«Tutti sapevano che la picchiava, nessuno faceva niente. Quando Lucia se n'è andata, alcune donne del paese hanno detto "Almeno non prende piú botte!" All'epoca le donne venivano picchiate quasi tutte, anche dalle suocere. Per un nonnulla, sí, ma lí era troppo...»

Il promontorio dove poggia la casa, la striscia azzurro metafisico dell'erba sotto. Lucia guarda. Guarda la vigna, l'ombra verde follia dei primi pampini. Di tutto, la colpisce l'eccedenza, il troppo esistere delle cose, cosí persuase di essere proprio quello che sono, mentre lei vorrebbe sparire, morire qui e rinascere davvero, ricominciare tutto dall'inizio, questa volta sul serio.

Forse questa è una prova, un errore, chiede alle alture circostanti, chiede al rosso dei rami e alla Madonna: Santa Madre, fai che questa sia solo la copia – sbagliata – della vita mia.

Fa sera

Grazie all'aiuto del vigile del paese, mia figlia e io siamo ospiti per la notte nel b&b di una donna generosa, che ha ristrutturato la vecchia casa accanto a quella coniugale di mia madre come un pezzo d'Inghilterra e ce la lascia per una cifra simbolica.

Pezzi di terra verde galleggiante nell'arido, la strada resa liquida dalla luce incidente del tramonto. Quante volte ho descritto la terra. Ogni volta che questa mi ha parlato. E la voce veniva dall'erba, dal grano, o dai corpi che l'hanno coltivato. Seminagioni, sfalci, trebbiature. Silos di sementi e serbatoi d'acqua, materie prime stipate.

Il vento cade nella sera lunare. Il celeste assoluto prima della notte sulla conca soave della valle. E i corpi si preparano al sonno, pieni di violenza.

Affacciata alla finestra, fumo la mia unica sigaretta di ogni giorno. Guardo le pietre. Vorrei esistere dentro la sera tiepida come un albero, essere solo vuoto che raccoglie la voce degli altri e dei pianeti. Invece, ho ancora tanti sentimenti.

Bellezza che è veleno

Lucia guarda
la macina del sole sopra il grano, che ruota
gialla sul giallo. Sotto il sole imperiale di luglio
il mondo pare fatto di pura luce
e nei mattini limpidi si vede il mare sbrilluccicare al fondo della terra

La distanza tra la masseria e la fonte
aumenta nella vampa come un grande inciampo. Lucia guarda
gromme di resina
dove l'arteria madre del ciliegio
si divarica in rami pieni di senno
e sostanze, che grondano fuori. Dovrei dargli
il veleno che mi scivola lento dal cuore, perché è veleno pure
la vita mia

Lucia passa con l'asino
lungo la mulattiera, va alla fonte dell'acqua pulita, proprio accanto all'abbeveratoio dove Tonino

Lucia guarda
la fluorescente aragosta del tramonto
a capofitto nel mistero
dietro le colline, guarda l'ombra sul grano e la pralinatura dei granelli d'incenso delle olive immature sul-

l'ostenso dei rami, fra le gole
gonfie di canto dei cardilli. Madonna mia
fammi la grazia, fammi
morire. Invece, come se li indossa bene gli anni, questa giovane donna di luce, questa povera polvere che sa di fieno

Confidenze di Lucia (del furore e del pianto)

Ogni tanto Lucia torna dalla campagna col somaro. Smonta davanti casa e scende gli scalini traendosi dietro la bestia, attraversa la cucina, mette l'animale a riposo nella stalla in fondo alla cucina, poi attraversa la strada e va a prendere il caffè da un'amica che abita di fronte.

I primi tempi, brucia di umiliazione:
«Meglio le mazzate che stare con quello! Magari fosse cattivo, magari mi picchiasse!»
Vuole essere presa in considerazione, inclusa in una forma di rapporto, in qualunque modo a Luigi riesca di farlo, pure a manate in faccia. Ignorata, Lucia sospira:
«Vuje parlate, ma li sacc ije i guai miei...»

Spesso a Lucia salgono le lacrime agli occhi. Le trattiene, ma ha gli occhi trasparenti, si vede tutto. Dice che Gino e i suoi genitori sono «cattivi e stupidi». Quando esce con la suocera, quella allarga le gambe in mezzo alla strada e fa pipí dove si trova. Lucia si muore di vergogna.

Dice che lei va a caricare l'acqua e Gino dorme, lei sbatacchia le piante di ulivo e Gino dorme, lei falcia, semina, pasce le bestie, affetta le patate, sforna, lava, ricuce, zappa la vigna – e Gino dorme. In quest'ultimo caso, sotto gli ulivi. Dice che, pure se fa la serva a tutta la famiglia, la lasciano senza mangiare, anche due o tre giorni:
«Pure le uova mi nascondono!»

Quando le danno cibo, spesso è pane e cipolla e niente piú. La puniscono senza ragione, Lucia vive in allarme, senza pace, in una brutta fatica. Anche la raccolta delle olive le fanno fare a mano: con la rete, la pertica e i cestelli, ché lei ci sgobba dieci volte tanto. Quei piccoli proprietari terrieri non le perdonano l'onta del rifiuto. Cercano di sfiancarla come una mula, forse sono semplicemente avari. Lucia annega nella piccineria di quei pensieri.

Tutto il paese conosce l'infelicità di Lucia. Tutto il paese sa che Lucia chiede ogni giorno ai genitori di riprenderla in casa:

«Io stavo a casa mia a fare la signora, ora sto qui a fare la serva! Fatemi tornare. Come faccio la serva a loro, la faccio a voi...»

«Moglie e marito come li trovi te li devi tenere», risponde il padre. Ma la vita, come usa fare, stringe a cappio i suoi nodi non sciolti. La madre, consapevole che le nozze di Lucia neanche sono state consumate e che adesso sí, l'inerte Gino saltuariamente sfascia di mazzate la sposa, si batte come può per «far sfasciare – invece – il matrimmonio». Ma sono gli uomini ad avere il potere di decidere. O meglio, il loro pregiudizio sul giudizio degli altri:

«Mo la gente c' dic?»

«Certo la sua famiglia era proprio una zappa. Faceva male».

«"Io credo che questa povera ragazza a sofferto tantissimo. E che le sue sofferenze sono servite ha darti tanto Onore a te". Queste sono le parole di un'anziana donna del paese».

Sette anni. Passano sette anni e gli errori precipitano a valanga, la convivenza con la parentela di Luigi si fa aspra e feroce. La famiglia di Gino non la sopporta piú, *chest femmn* che non si rassegna. Certi giorni, Lucia bussa piangendo alla porta di un'amica. La vediamo che mendica, umiliata.

«Mi ha detto che non mangiava da due giorni. Ha detto che stavano in campagna, con Gino e la suocera, lei ha protestato che aveva fame, nella lite ha alzato la voce, loro le sono andati contro con le forche. Lei ha avuto tanta paura, è scappata via per le campagne...»

La voce fuori campo, che sono io che scrivo, interrompe il racconto per segnare il dato con l'evidenziatore: Lucia ha tanta paura di morire.

«Io le ho fatto un panino e se n'è andata subito, non voleva che la trovassero qui, non voleva compromettermi...»

La forca è un attrezzo che serve a muovere e caricare il fieno, ha un manico di legno e una forcella in ferro a due punte di circa trenta centimetri. Questa, adesso, è la vita di Lucia. La vita di una figlia abbandonata da genitori vivi.

Racconta la vigna

La bambina è andata via, al suo posto c'è una ragazza bruna che zappa la vigna
    sotto gli ulivi, dove la luce dell'inverno fa una croce bianca.
Quando smuove la terra, Lucia indossa le *centrelle*, le scarpe da lavoro coi chiodi a testa quadra piantati a ferro di cavallo tutt'intorno alla suola. Scarpe che pesano, fanno rumore e fanno scivolare sui pavimenti, ma la suola cosí non si consuma e le scarpe attraversano indenni piú di una vita, decumani di fanga, col latrato dei venti sulla schiena.

Aria a raffiche ferme. Ventilazione tesa, improvvisi rovesci sui rilievi. Il vento sorge alle sue spalle, mentre lei libera i canali dalle foglie che ostruiscono il flusso dell'acqua. L'acqua scansa gli ostacoli. Lei no.

Vento accanito, assoluto. Spianate di vento. Vento sociale. E lei, in mezzo, vestita di nero mentre zappa la terra. È battuta dal vento. Lo sguardo è sovraccarico
    e minerale, quello di un sasso, di una bestia da soma.

Nel cuore di fantasma di gennaio, Lucia sgrana a mano le zolle come un rosario, per mettere a dimora il ciliegio regina. Guarda le radici, che vogliono stare nel nutrimento. Sente in faccia la polvere della sua terra, sente la nebbia che le circonda le spalle. Come un ramo, Lucia sta nelle cose della terra. È tutta vuota.

Corpi marinati dal sole di gennaio fra alberi di mele e trebbiatrici, che arrugginiscono nella solitudine della zona nord del paesaggio. Sono materia inerte.

Lucia guarda la vita muoversi sotto la forma infinitesimale di una mosca
   sul tronco, dove i secoli sono sovrapposti in anelli che partono dal centro. Sopra, la patina lamellare delle cortecce, la pellicola occidua
   del tempo. Lucia guarda la brace che si spegne, sente il tempo
   che passa. Un altro giorno inutile
   finito. Lucia
   respira. Inciso in una strana fissità, l'avorio delle betulle somiglia il mondo a una foresta d'ossa. Un paradigma.

Qui dove crescono
   le proverbiali rose, Lucia respira
   le note alte dell'odore di foglie invelenite. Il marcio inverno. Piogge scure cadute nei millenni. L'umido
   penetra l'osso. E le mormorazioni degli stormi.

Da quando se n'è andata, non lo vuole nessuno, quel pezzo di terra. Il terreno sul quale Lucia ha *ittat lu sanghe* è rimasto incolto. Quella è una terra che d'inverno scivola, terra senza gradoni, lasciata a se stessa e alle radici del grano.
Le radici del grano non tengono ferma la terra, le radici del grano sono sottili. Fanno massa, però. Tutte insieme tengono la zolla. Ma la zolla scivola a valle. E trascina il lavoro di Lucia.

Lucia è rimasta lí, dove il mondo finisce e l'impressione della valle è il suono di un respirare immenso.

Vengo a prenderti, adesso che ho il doppio dei tuoi anni e ti guardo, da una vita che forse hai immaginato per me.
Adesso vengo a prenderti e ti porto via.
Lucia, dammi la mano.

Le voci allegre. Sai dirmi se l'hai mai sentita ridere

Poi ci sono le voci allegre delle amiche di Lucia e delle bambine di allora. Una, in particolare: Maria, che Lucia chiama *la bambina dalla faccia rosa*, per via del colorito acceso. Dice che lei le sorrideva sempre:
«Quel giorno che ti ho vista in televisione (rimarco, per chi non avesse memorizzato la singolare sincronicità, che era martedí 16 febbraio 2021, giorno del compleanno postumo di Lucia) c'era qualcosa di strano. In genere ascolto senza guardare. Quel giorno, invece, non so... era come se qualcuno guidasse la mia mente e mi dicesse "Guarda!"... Quando sei entrata, mi sono dovuta sedere, sennò svenivo. Sono tornata indietro di sessant'anni, ho rivisto l'immagine di tua madre!»

Mi raccontano quello che ricordano. Bevo ogni informazione come acqua nel deserto di un'assenza della quale comincio a intravedere i confini, con un lieve sconcerto.

Mi dicono Lucia come si veste quando va in paese: un cappotto nero sciallato, di astrakan; una gonna di lana scozzese verde e beige a tubino e, sopra, il coordinato di lana: maglia a manica corta e giacchino verde. Ha scarpe nere di vernice lucida col mezzo tacco.
Ha un portamento elegante, pure quando accompagna i suoceri con l'asino. Ci tiene: pure se sono false, mette il filo di perle.

Lucia aspira a qualcosa di meglio di quella miseria, non vuole stare in quell'oltraggio continuo; lei vuole emergere, guardare avanti. E davanti c'è l'estero, le coppie giovani sciamano quasi tutte verso il Nord Europa: chi in Germania, chi in Belgio, chi in Francia.
Mille volte gli dice *Partiamo*.
Mille volte lui dice *Macché. Stiamo bene qui.*

Quando non c'è la fatica nei campi Lucia si annoia, è inquieta. Spreca la vita, forza e giovinezza a lavorare ai ferri con la lana sfilata, poi la sfila di nuovo e la rilavora, per non restare con le mani in mano. E cosí, passa il tempo.

C'è una quercia, che adesso non c'è piú. Sotto la quercia c'è una ragazza bruna, che fa e disfa
      una formella di lana di pecora, che non c'è piú.

La casa nuova. Vista con elementi mobili

1962. Finalmente la casa nuova è pronta. La casa nuova ha il bagno, subito a sinistra del portoncino d'ingresso: uno scavo di un metro per due di altezza, con sola tazza del gabinetto a piedistallo.

Di fronte all'ingresso ci sono le scale, che sboccano nella cucina al primo piano. In cucina c'è il tavolo con due sedie, il camino sulla parete in fondo. A sinistra del camino la bella madia verde acqua, coordinata al tavolo che ho sfiorato il 14 agosto 2021 e, lungo il muro perimetrale di destra, si apre una portafinestra col balcone. A sinistra della cucina, la camera da letto: letto matrimoniale e comodini sulla parete portante, armadio su quella davanti. Tutto di legno pieno, angoli stondati, maniglie lavorate. Una finestra illumina le cose da sinistra. Qui la casa finisce, ma c'è luce, un armadio. Lucia ha comprato un armadio, piccolo ma a due ante, con la specchiera interna a figura intera.

Di domenica, quando si mette a punto per la messa, Lucia scende le scale di traverso, con le scarpe bianche del matrimonio, la catenina d'oro e gli orecchini. Ha il naso sottile, il mento volitivo e la figura snella da ragazzina. Della sua imbronciatura infantile ho già scritto. Chiara di carnagione, i suoi occhi cambiano colore con gli umori e col sole. Talvolta, splende insieme alla stella del mattino. Se si emoziona, sono giallo tigre. Ha tanti capelli ricci e scuri, li porta ancora sciolti sulle spalle, nonostante da tre anni sia una maritata.

Lucia è devota: anche quando in campagna è tempo di lavoro, il sabato sera dorme in paese, non manca mai una messa. La domenica mattina è lavata e perfetta. Arriva in chiesa col vestito sfiancato a fiorellini, quello della domenica, ha un odore di biancheria pulita. Evidenzio anche questo vestito. Del profumo, a parte la ventata salina del detersivo a mano Ava, non sappiamo piú niente, solo un'aria lievissima, come di viole, come di lavanda, che risale dal buio del tempo come dal fondo di un cassetto chiuso da mille e una vita.

È cosí fina, Lucia, che può aggiustare l'abito da sposa per la prima comunione della nipote Laura, che ha nove anni.
«Stringo qua, stringo là, accorcio qui sotto...»
Lucia cuce e ricama. D'inverno, quando la campagna dorme, tesse al telaio le tovaglie pure e i teli a filo doppio da allungare a terra, per mettere ad asciugare il grano e le mandorle. Forse un ramo d'alloro, un sempreverde.

Lucia e il mare

Che impressione deve averle fatto il mare, e che impressione la città di Termoli, alta sul mare, con la sua scala in calcestruzzo armato per entrare nel borgo e i vicoletti, coi lenzuoli messi a sbandierare sulla calma di mare, interrotto
      da trabocchi fenici, palafitte che suonano sull'acqua come archi: moli agili di corde, tavole e pali nei frangenti di costa, strutture a zampe altissime, montate con l'estetica delle libellule, a sorvolo sull'acqua iridescente
      tra efflorescenze di muschio, bave di alghe e un altorilievo
      di gusci di bivalvi. Anche per te, Lucia, scelgo le rime chiare che il poeta Giorgio Caproni ha dedicato alla madre Anna, Anna Picchi. E tu, Lucia Galante: una rima elegante. Perturbante.

Quattro anni di matrimonio senza figli, la colpa deve per forza essere della donna. Una donna che non è buona a fare figli non vale niente, è materia morta:
«Vai a Termoli a farti curare!»
Per aumentare la fecondità, la mutua passa rapidi trattamenti di acque termali, le cui proprietà – per cosí dire – fertilizzanti sono state scoperte a inizio secolo, forse registrando un'improvvisa impennata di presenze nei nuclei familiari di coloro che vi si bagnassero. Negli anni Sessanta del Novecento si ripone tanta fiducia nell'azione dell'acqua mineralizzata che Sophia Loren si avvale apertamen-

te dei benefici di quella che sgorga in Salsomaggiore verso fine decennio.

Si tratta comunque di terapie dolci, non invasive: una settimana di insufflagioni di vapore, applicazioni di melma sul basso ventre, ivi spalmata in luogo di mutandina (fanghi pelvici) e immersioni in vasche di acque ricche di sali sulfurei o salsobromoiodici, che pare incoraggino la microcircolazione uterina e la funzionalità ovarica, oltre ad avere proprietà antinfiammatorie e riequilibranti dei valori ormonali. Ultima, la meccanica: una serie di irrigazioni profonde scolla aderenze e sblocca tube ipoteticamente occluse, attraverso l'azione della pura forza idraulica.

E Lucia parte, prende tre corriere e va a farsi infangare, spiccare l'umido delle membrane e investire da getti di condensa nelle piscine della riviera. Lucia compra un costume, per scivolare dentro l'acqua fossile, risalita dal buio sotto la terra. L'acqua attraversa le stratificazioni delle argille dov'è impressa la storia del pianeta ed emerge alla luce del sole, in questa storia minima di malmaritata. Viva come una bestia, l'acqua gira
    intorno al corpo vuoto di Lucia e alle rocce che portano il calco di felci preistoriche. Acqua chiara, ricuci la ferita banale e tragica del disamore. Acqua che tocca e acqua che guarisce dove tocca. La profezia di un'acqua che scioglie il male come un pugno di sale viperino. Lucia compra un costume da bagno. Questa ripetizione non è un errore, è una sottolineatura, che avrà senso alla fine, come molte cose.

Per adesso, alla semplice fine d'ogni giorno, poco prima di sera, Lucia scende a guardare, alla marina
    e mescola lo sguardo dei suoi occhi color bosco screziato da filacce di luce trasparente
  a un'acqua che non termina

con segni naturali. Da terra verso il tramonto, brezza orizzontale. L'incidenza della luce del sole sulla scena. Piatta, schiacciata al suolo. Tutto quel movimento, quella culla a perdita d'occhio. Madonna, dammi un figlio, qualcosa da abbracciare, una creatura viva
    che mi consoli. L'aperto della vita davanti
        all'aperto dell'acqua. Gli storni in formazioni prolisse, o brevi, sulla piazza del porto, la vista che dilaga dagli uccelli al mare. Com'è lampante il mare, come cosparso dal sole di macchine del tempo, di un acume eccessivo.
    Sei come le oleandre sul lungolago azzurre e generose
      come la festa delle luminarie
        e il nero che soccombe. Senti il cuore, Lucia, e i motori a scoppio, i tonfi a corpo morto delle ancore. Tra quei lenzuoli che non sono tuoi
      il tuo mondo scompare, ti addormenti nel battito del cuore tuo, finalmente solo.

Giuseppe

Entra in scena l'uomo

Giuseppe Di Pietro nasce il 5 luglio 1909 a Tagliacozzo e, all'incirca fino al 1960, fa base a Nettuno con la moglie Anita Scansani, una figlia femmina e quattro maschi, il piú piccolo ha dieci anni. Giuseppe evidentemente approva la vita e, partito manovale, riesce a mettere su una piccolissima impresa edile.

In giorno impreciso, come tanti altri, viene spedito in Africa.

Nessuno dei parenti ricorda le date di partecipazione di Giuseppe alla guerra d'Africa, ma il lungo intervallo infecondo fra la comparsa del terzo e del quarto figlio, riportato dalla cronaca di Roma dell'«Unità» del 29 giugno 1965, permette di formulare un'ipotesi semplice: se le nascite dei primi tre figli scandiscono gli anni, regolari come i cicli naturali – ma Riziero, il terzogenito, viene al mondo nel 1939 e il quarto figlio, Giovanni, addirittura dieci anni dopo (nel 1949) –, si può supporre che il padre non sia partito prima del 1938 e non sia tornato prima di un decennio, avendo quasi certamente – nel frattempo – subíto periodi di prigionia severa.

Le date di nascita dei figli fanno sfumare con verosimile approssimazione la terrorizzante ipotesi che Giuseppe Di Pietro abbia partecipato all'invasione coloniale italiana in Africa, quella durante la quale il ventiseienne Indro Montanelli, comandante di un plotoncino di ascari imberbi, ac-

quista regolarmente in sposa la dodicenne bilena Fatuma, o Destà, un'altra di troppo fra le troppe bambine vendute dai padri, agli invasori o ad altri;
    e quella della carneficina di Addis Abeba («Nuovo Fiore», in amarico) quando, in neanche tre giorni (19-21 febbraio 1937) gli italiani, ormai gonfiati come tacchini dalla farneticante convinzione mussoliniana della propria superiorità razziale, per eccesso di reazione al lancio di granate etiopi contro il gruppetto di autorità italiane riunite intorno al viceré Rodolfo Graziani, falcidiano con sbalorditiva determinazione una stima finale di diciannovemila innocenti: bruciandoli vivi, impiccandoli, ammazzando donne e bambini con pugni, calci e manganellate, fucilandoli a freddo, secondo la prassi ormai consolidata dello squadrismo fascista, qui incarognita dal convincimento di trovarsi di fronte a una popolazione subumana.

  Quasi certa, però, stando alla datazione deduttiva, la partecipazione del trentatreenne Giuseppe Di Pietro alle due cruciali battaglie nordafricane di el-Alamein, combattute lungo i bordi dell'enorme depressione paludosa di al-Qattara, diciottomila chilometri di fanghiglia salata, ciuffi di cannucce e altre erbacee perenni, sprofondati a centotrentatre metri sotto il livello del mare e perlustrati dagli occhi cristallini e ipnotici dei ghepardi.
  La guerra è anch'essa progettata da Mussolini, il quale, non sentendosi sufficientemente appagato dall'espansione italiana in Etiopia e Libia, sposa il sogno nazista di strappare l'Egitto agli inglesi, per aprirsi una via maestra verso i Paesi petroliferi del Medio Oriente. In realtà, l'Egitto non è che un tassello della fantasia di dominio planetario che gira come un cane infernale nella mente di Hitler e che il Führer realizzerà con ogni mezzo (vite umane, non altro), per cercare di stringere Unione Sovietica e Inghilterra in una morsa. Il noto binomio di potere e soldi, ordinariamente rimpannucciato dalla suggestiva messa in scena

dell'orgoglio nazionale, l'ininterrotto sciupio di vite umane sacrificate a un male ancora evidente, tridimensionale. Poi, la danza luciferina della finanza sostituirà quasi del tutto gli scontri novecenteschi, fatti di corpi, fino a ruotare sulle nostre teste una falce immateriale, mossa da fluttuazioni di mercato. A dare impulso al braccio del futuro oggi sono le trame e le risacche delle oscillazioni monetarie, e le vittime si accumulano ai lati della storia ufficiale, folgorate nel sonno.

Ma il 13 settembre 1940 il generale Graziani – frattanto decaduto dai recenti fasti della propria crudeltà – su prematuro ordine di Mussolini muove di nuovo la sua vita fisica alla conquista dell'Egitto e penetra per cento chilometri all'interno, senza incontrare resistenza. Tre mesi dopo, il 9 dicembre, l'armata italiana è annientata dalle truppe inglesi, le quali vengono però distratte verso la Grecia, attaccata da Mussolini a fine ottobre. Cosí, già negli ultimi giorni del febbraio 1941, Hitler cerca di riequilibrare le forze inviando in Egitto, a sostenere il sopraffatto complice fascista, il genio della tattica e delle guerre-lampo generale Erwin Rommel e le sue unità meccanizzate, gli Africa Korps.

Per un paio d'anni Rommel infligge agli inglesi una certa sequenza di sconfitte, grazie alla propria capacità di adattamento e a spericolate e fulminee manovre, che mettono i cingoli dei mezzi corazzati a rischio di spaccarsi sulle pietraie del deserto nordafricano; ma dimostra anche di non possedere l'ampio pensiero strategico del quale è invece dotato il glaciale britannico Bernard Law Montgomery, già apparso in queste pagine al comando di una successiva vittoria e qui subentrato alla guida dell'Ottava Armata.

Anche le battaglie di el-Alamein, la prima del luglio e la seconda dell'ottobre-novembre 1942, si concludono con la disfatta dell'esercito italo-tedesco, spossato da una perdurante mancanza di viveri, acqua, munizioni e carburante per mezzi d'aria e di terra, rifornimenti che sarebbero potuti passare attraverso Malta, se Hitler non avesse commesso l'errore di impedire a Rommel di contenderla agli inglesi, dopo la riconquista nazifascista di Tobruq nel giugno precedente. Gli inglesi sono perciò ancora ben equipaggiati, sono anzi provvisti dei piú moderni mezzi prodotti dall'industria bellica americana, ma pure loro devono impiegare la metà almeno delle forze psichiche nella lotta contro la natura sconosciuta e ostile del deserto e contro le astrazioni della terra vuota. Una guerra non è soltanto fatti, è catena di conseguenze umane.

I soldati italiani percorrono sabbia e pietrisco della soglia costiera nordafricana coi piedi laschi nelle scarpe da ginnastica del Regio Esercito, confezionate con la tomaia in tela e la suola di cartone pressato, mentre la dotazione regolamentare di stivaletti in cuoio viene venduta ai beduini di Tripoli. Accecati dal ghibli, il malefico vento sollevatore di giganti di sabbia, coperti da nugoli di mosche appiccicose, che impediscono quasi di mangiare il modestissimo rancio, già lievemente corrotto dallo stagno delle gavette, soffrono di miraggi e allucinazioni diurne per il calore cui non sono avvezzi e che raggiunge i cinquanta o sessanta gradi, utili però a cuocere uova sui radiatori dei carri armati: tegamini e padelle improvvisati sono infatti i punti dove il metallo rovente è rimasto scoperto, gli angoli ciechi dove non ricade l'ingegnoso rivestimento di sacchetti di sabbia allineati sulle corazzature per ammortizzare i colpi ben piú potenti dei *tanks* inglesi, che spesso sono anche preziosi depositi alimentari. La poca acqua distribuita agli italiani defluisce invece da fusti che hanno stoccato nafta, benzina o gasolio; in molti finiscono per bere direttamente dai serbatoi dei carri. Tanto vale... Il risultato è che tutti, incluso Rommel, soffrono di infiammazioni acute del tratto digerente e irrefrenabile dissenteria, che costringe a produrre piú volte al giorno muco e sangue, in assenza totale di carta igienica.

Di notte, poi, quando il freddo punge la spugnosa, la purtuttavia tenera midolla, sembra che i fanti siano costretti da ragioni igieniche a bruciare coi lanciafiamme i corpi dei caduti in quella vastità a perdita d'occhio.
Generalmente privi di metal detector leggero, recentissima invenzione polacca della quale sono invece forniti gli inglesi, e a corto di munizioni, soldati italiani appiedati sondano la sabbia coi pugnali in cerca di mine inglesi da riutilizzare contro chi le ha sepolte: se la mina trova l'uomo prima che l'uomo trovi la mina, il suo femore resta pulito come una preparazione anatomica. Impossibile rimuovere i feriti dai campi minati: quei ragazzi bruciano o si dissanguano dove sono caduti, implorando un aiuto che non può arrivare, straziando coi lamenti i commilitoni. Nonostante tutto, alcuni si sdraiano fra i cingoli dei carri armati britannici e incollano cariche esplosive sotto la pancia delle macchine in moto, per rotolare via prima dello scoppio.

Il mascelluto dux di Predappio ha mandato il suo popolo a combattere dentro un inferno di fuoco, fumo, polvere e sporcizia, tra cannonate, carri armati e incursioni di cacciabombardieri, mitraglie a bassa quota, truppe di terra che sganciano bombe a mano e bottiglie incendiarie, come documentano i filmati dell'Istituto Luce con stridentissimo sottofondo di marcette trionfali, cosí tronfio e retorico da far sorridere, di fronte a immagini per le quali andrebbero spese soltanto lacrime e malinconia, malinconia e lacrime: per quelle masse umane dilapidate, sperperate a strisciare, coi caschi marinati dal sudore, secondo un delirio strategico pianificato ai tavoli intorno ai quali – in questo caso – siedono uomini arrivati al comando utilizzando il ferro delle armi, la propaganda, l'azione capillare di delinquenti comuni e il consenso cordiale di un popolo che il dittatore stesso ritiene ingenuo o, peggio ancora: amorfo. Ogni tiranno domina un popolo che non stima, proprio perché è un popolo che ha avuto bisogno di un tiranno, una nazione fatta anche di gente che, spaventata dalle incombenze della libertà, ha formulato il sogno di un mondo infantile, affidato alla guida paterna di un despota dalla mano salda. L'obbedienza dei popoli, la loro spesso addirittura grata sottomissione, sorprende per primi gli obbediti.

Malgrado le promesse, inoltre, la partecipazione dei combattenti alla guerra d'Africa si rinnova di sei mesi in sei mesi, perché manca il ricambio dei soldati. Quelli che riusciranno a sopravvivere verranno a sapere tanto, dai compagni di prigionie francesi e inglesi, sparse chi nel deserto a spaccare le pietre per gettare le strade, nutrito di pane e rape bollite, chi trasvolato in altri continenti.

Probabilmente Giuseppe Di Pietro è un ignaro, un formiciforme individuo, chiamato a fare massa nel formicaio di ignari individui che i corrispondenti di regime descrivono come «indomabili fanti» e sono piuttosto uomini e ragazzi devastati dalla sete, che corrono dietro i carri chiedendo un dito d'acqua e a volte si nutrono di scatolette avanzate dal precedente conflitto mondiale, esseri umani che gettano la propria carne intrisa di cognac contro l'acciaio delle pallottole, delle schegge di mine e dei carri armati, fino al massiccio e fatale attacco inglese del 23 ottobre 1942, condotto da migliaia di pezzi d'artiglieria e incessante martellamento di granate. Sferrata sulla piana illuminata dal plenilunio, l'offensiva lascia corpi ridotti a travi di carbone, occhi di semivivi che implorano, dopo aver visto le proprie stesse viscere sparse nella sabbia. Gli inglesi hanno sfondato il fronte tedesco, ma non quello italiano: aggirano dunque la linea di trincea e prendono alle spalle gli italiani. Non ci sarebbe piú niente da aggiungere, è finita.

Rommel salverebbe infatti tante piú persone, se Hitler la sera del 2 novembre gli permettesse la ritirata che il generale chiede, ormai alla chiara luce della disfatta. «Resistere fino all'ultimo uomo! Vittoria o morte!», bercia invece il dispaccio del capo di Stato, come muovendo soldatini e non veri uomini, finiti in cenere. Per coprire il ripiegamento dei suoi, Hitler impegna le divisioni non motorizzate della fanteria italiana, a fermare letteralmente a braccia i carri armati inglesi, posando bombe in precario equilibrio sul retro dei carri in movimento e dando poi fuoco alle micce. Montgomery riporta una vittoria fredda, limpida e prevedibile. Il bilancio finale dei morti è 9000 tedeschi, 13 500 inglesi e 17 000 italiani.

Le ultime ventiquattr'ore di combattimento, strenuo e inutile, volute da Hitler, costano il dimezzamento delle vite in azione nel deserto. Senza cibo né acqua, senza sonno, trainando a braccia nella sabbia i 4732, cannoncini ormai privi di munizioni, i ragazzi della Folgore, corpo d'élite di paracadutisti qui impiegati come fanteria, affrontano un ripiegamento di quattro giorni a piedi nel deserto. L'ultimo giorno si dissetano con l'acqua di un provvidenziale temporale. Gli inglesi non sparano piú, rendono anzi l'onore delle armi a quei soldati abbandonati e soli nella propria sola vita.

La battaglia di el-Alamein cambia favorevolmente il destino del mondo e prepara la sconfitta nazista, poiché ridimensiona le ambizioni italo-tedesche sul Canale di Suez e consegna il Mediterraneo agli inglesi, aprendo il varco per lo sbarco alleato in Sicilia.

Vista la data ipotizzata per il ritorno a casa di Giuseppe, esiste la possibilità che sia stato ulteriormente coinvolto nella campagna di Tunisia, terminata il 13 maggio 1943 con la resa, richiesta dallo stesso Mussolini al generale Giovanni Messe.

In ogni caso, sia che sia stato rinchiuso in campo di concentramento inglese dopo la sconfitta di el-Alamein, sia che sia stato invece consegnato ai francesi dopo la resa di Tunisi (forse subendo un trattamento speculare a quello sopportato da mio padre adottivo, il comunista Giacomo Calandrone, picchiato e torturato dai *cagoulards* francesi dopo la propria partecipazione volontaria alla guerra civile antifranchista in Spagna), Giuseppe viene quasi certamente rimpatriato dopo i trattati di pace mondiale firmati a Parigi il 10 febbraio 1947, magari a bordo dell'incrociatore *Garibaldi*, in rotta verso le coste di Taranto, dove – chi sa con che animo – sbarcano molti superstiti italiani. I conti tornano.

E torna anche Giuseppe, devastato da una guerra che probabilmente neanche condivide, visto che piú avanti scopriremo che è anch'egli lettore di giornale comunista. Ma, per chi ha vissuto la guerra, da qualsiasi parte fosse durante i combattimenti, il dolore per lo spettacolo intollerabile del dolore arriva dopo, ineludibile e ineliminabile. Sul momento, agisci e basta, obbedisci e basta, secondo quanto la tua umanità ti permette, o impone, di fare.

Frammenti d'Algeria

In mancanza di testimonianze o memorie dirette dei vivi che lo hanno visto combattere o trascinarsi nella prigionia e riportare le ferite che, come vedremo, risulteranno cruciali, cerco cos'hanno visto gli occhi di Giuseppe avvalendomi dello sguardo di un poeta, che nel 1947 dà alle stampe il suo inconsumabile *Diario d'Algeria*: Vittorio Sereni, prigioniero, «morto alla guerra e alla pace» e accompagnato dalla musica delle tende che sbattono sui pali, a lui bastante. Cerco la storia nelle pagine della poesia, con totale fiducia, perché conosco che la poesia è sorpasso, addirittura inversione, di retorica e mitologia.

E tu mia vita salvati se puoi
serba te stessa al futuro

Ride una larva chiara
dov'era la sentinella

Tra gli ordini e i richiami
mancavo, morivo
sotto il peso delle armi.

Se passa la rombante distruzione
siamo appiattiti corpi,
volti protesi all'alto senza onore

I soldati dentro i fossi

mascherati dalle fronde
e come ridenti d'amore.

Ho visto uomini stravolti
nelle membra

il muso erto d'Europa, della cagna
che accucciata lí sta sulle zampe davanti

– e sbrindellato, scalzo
in groppa un ciuco, ma col casco
d'Africa ancora in capo
un prigioniero come me
presto fuori di vista di dietro la collina.
Quanto restava dell'impero...

Trafitture del mondo che uno porta su sé
e di cui fa racconto a Milano
tra i vetri azzurri a Natale di un inverno di sole

se quanto
prolifererò la nostra febbre d'allora
è solo eccidio tortura reclusione
o popolo che santamente uccide.

Qualunque cosa abbia visto, fatto e subíto in Africa, i familiari ricordano le parole di Anita, moglie di Giuseppe:
«Tornato dall'Africa, mio marito non era piú lui. La guerra l'ha cambiato. Era diventato inaffidabile, andava appresso a tutte le femmine».
Come tanti, Giuseppe ha scoperto la mortificante fragilità dell'essere. Oppure, è uscito di senno.

1962. Un simpatico forestiero

Tornato dunque a casa certamente turbato e psichicamente instabile, ma sempre buon lavoratore, dopo un imponente rovescio economico alla fine degli anni Cinquanta e qualche mese di disperazione, Giuseppe viene assunto a Roma, come capomastro, da una ditta che la moglie ricorda come Immobiliare Genovese e va a lavorare in uno degli innumerevoli cantieri della capitale. Da cosa nascendo, come sempre, cosa, trova un nuovo ingaggio: l'impresa *Tenaglia* sta costruendo un acquedotto in Molise. Un lavoro grosso: si tratta di edificare serbatoi idrici a San Giacomo degli Schiavoni e a Palata, la relativa ragna di tubazioni per la partizione delle acque e la rete fognaria. Giuseppe si getta nell'impresa. A casa, lascia il primogenito trentunenne Francesco gravemente compromesso nel fisico dalla nefrite. Il dovere di un uomo è lavorare, alla salute pensano le madri.

La ditta appaltatrice dei lavori fa tutto al meglio e fornisce agli operai tavole di legno nuove di zecca anche per le impalcature e il contenimento provvisorio delle fiancate degli scavi. Giuseppe, sempre con la qualifica di capomastro, dirige i lavori di costruzione del serbatoio di Palata. Il risultato sarà il bel cilindro esagonale, alto una trentina di metri, coi mattoni rossi posati a cortina verticale e le travature color tortora, completato alla fine del 1962 e oggi chiamato dai palatesi *sua altezza il serbatoio*.

Esiste una foto, fatta mentre durano gli scavi per la posa delle condotte idriche ed erroneamente tramandata agli atti della memoria da una didascalia scritta da mano ignota: «Ricordo del Cantiere rinboschimente». È una scena all'aperto, di terra rocciosa. Giuseppe è accanto al suo apprendista giovane, entrambi in piedi all'orlo di una grande buca rettangolare, nella quale sono inclusi otto lavoranti in camicia coi picconi abbassati per lo scatto. Maglioni e giacche dei lavoratori sono un mucchio riverso a faccia in giú su due pile di lastre in pietra nuda. Presumo sia l'inizio dell'autunno 1962, perché i lavori sono ormai avanzati in aperta campagna e le zone scoperte dei corpi trattengono la bella abbronzatura della piena estate. I due operai che indossano il cappello hanno una mezzaluna orizzontale sulla fronte, dove ricade l'ombra della visiera: una piccola area, rosea come dovette essere la loro prima pelle (emersione dello zero assoluto, della cera vergine dell'infanzia dal corpo adulto). La buca nella quale posano gli operai è fonda al ginocchio, e alcuni degli uomini in essa calati sono anziani. Facce severe e belle, prosciugate dal sole. Giuseppe è l'unico in giacca: scura, a doppio petto, su pantaloni ampi di colore piú chiaro. Ha in mano penna e quaderno, capelli neri a taglio corto, con le basette e la sfumatura alta degli uomini che hanno cura del proprio aspetto; è il solo a sorridere appena, la testa di tre quarti, ancora china sul taccuino aperto nella mano sinistra, e la destra posata sulle pagine. Giuseppe emana il soffio dell'allegria degli scampati.

Il 24 agosto 2021 sono a San Ginesio (Macerata), dove la mia cara Sonia ha aperto il suo palcoscenico a un dialogo con me intorno al libro su Consolazione. La signora Antonella ci raggiunge e mi consegna una lettera toccante, nella prima parte della quale esprime la gioia di aver saputo che sto bene, perché il fantasma di quella bambina abbandonata e rifiutata dai parenti (lo scopriremo), ha turbato da sempre i suoi pensieri, poi racconta l'episodio che qui trascrivo:

«Ero piccola, non andavo ancora alle elementari. Un giorno facevano gli scavi vicino casa, perché ci avrebbero portato l'acqua, dicevano! Ho strappato un foglio di quaderno di mio fratello, ho messo lo zucchero dentro, mi sono seduta davanti casa e leccavo questo zucchero, ostentando qualcosa di prezioso, un po' di zucchero in un foglio di carta! L'uomo della ruspa incrocia il mio sguardo, capisce che la bambina vuole mostrare di avere qualcosa di buono e le offre una BANANA!! Chi aveva mai visto e mangiato una BANANA!! Allora mamma lo invita a mangiare le melanzane ripiene: "Su povr uaglión po magné ngopp a la rusp! Vie' ecc, assiett c' nuj!"»

Durante le pause degli scavi Giuseppe, oltre a competere in dolcezza con le bambine e a scambiare banane con melanzane, si dedica a lavori di muratura in tutto il paese. Al contrario di Gino Centolire è vitale, gli piace lavorare e, quando è libero, scatena la propria fantasia. Eccessivo e generoso come chi è soddisfatto di sé, decora con rami di cemento a colori la scala esterna e il ballatoio di una villetta, ispirandosi all'albero della vita di Gustav Klimt, e ne dipinge la riproduzione sul muro perimetrale.

Infine, come gli esuberanti, ama la musica: poiché il lavoro all'aperto inizia al mattino presto per concludersi a mezzo pomeriggio, all'ora tarda dei feriali, o alla domenica, Giuseppe fa girare a tutto volume nel juke box del baretto in piazza lo struggente tango di Luciano Tajoli *Violino tzigano*, sempre quello.

Quella musica riempie le case intorno, entra dalle finestre, strapazza i cuori delle donne che pelano patate per la cena e dei maschi che, nella piccola circonferenza d'acqua delle tinozze, sciacquano la polvere e il grasso della giornata dalle mani e dal collo.

Anche Pier Paolo Pasolini mette in azione le note di *Violino tzigano*, per provocare la danza di Mamma Roma col figlio ritrovato, una giostrina di risate e commozione dissimulata dagli sberleffi:

«Ammazza che casché c'amo fatto!»

commenta il figlio Ettore dal pavimento. Per insegnare al figlio a ballare il tango, Anna Magnani ha poggiato sul piatto del giradischi la versione eseguita dalla voce infantile di Joselito: lievemente stonata, con marcata pronuncia spagnola, tanto piú suggestiva. Anche in quel film del 1962 *Violino tzigano* è la canzone che il padre, malfattore sentimentale, cantava sempre.

1963. La vita dopo gli scavi

Durante l'anno di lavoro al serbatoio, Giuseppe si è inserito cosí bene nel tessuto sociale del paese da ricevere l'onore di ben tre soprannomi: Mastro Giuseppe – descrittivo, mera didascalia lavorativa – e sor Peppe o «il romano», in omaggio alla sua provenienza laziale. È un gentiluomo, come ci ha dimostrato la foto veste sempre con pantalone, camicia e giacca, è simpatico e benvoluto da tutti, i ragazzi ai quali dà lavoro lo ricordano con affetto:
«Guarda questo balcone. Lo ha fatto il famoso Mastro Giuseppe, come lo chiamavano qui. Ci ha messo un mese a farlo! Mio papà ha lavorato come muratore per lui. Anche mio fratello se lo ricorda: avrà avuto nove o dieci anni e il sor Peppe tutti i giorni gli regalava cinquanta lire. Ma, se andava cosí d'accordo con mio papà, sarà stato un bel mascalzone pure lui!»

Conclusa la grande impresa del serbatoio, il sor Peppe si ferma nell'appartamento che ha preso in affitto a Palata. Prima fa il muratore per una piccola impresa locale che aggiusta le case, e presto riesce a mettersi in proprio, è lui a dare lavoro ai ragazzi del posto: in quegli anni a Palata c'è molto da fare, perché le famiglie hanno preso l'abitudine di murare gli spazi vuoti tra i corpi perimetrali delle abitazioni, per ricavarne piccoli garage, magazzini o rimesse. Inoltre, quelli che hanno scale da salire all'ingresso di casa, con cucina e camera da letto a monte delle scale e il servizio igienico al piano terra, decidono uno dopo l'altro di lasciare cieca la camera da letto e aggiungere, sul retro, allo stesso livello delle stanze, un secondo locale con piccolo balcone e bagno vero, completo di vasca, lavandino e bidet. Cosí dispongono anche Lucia e Luigi.

Giuseppe apre e ricostruisce il muro della camera da letto di Lucia.
Forse lei sale in casa a controllare i lavori, o a lasciare qualche materiale per la rifinitura. Una maniglia, una greca. Insieme ai materiali, uno sguardo che posso immaginare. Dritto, pulito. Stupito. Lo ha visto. Le cose del destino si sanno subito. Il resto è il superfluo, è psicologia.
Giuseppe ci sa fare, con le donne. Lo sguardo ironico, la testa malandrina di traverso, mezzo sorriso, maniche arrotolate, canottiera. Giuseppe somiglia in modo impressionante al padre di Lucia. Ma sorridente e vivo, ma gentile.
«Glielo faccio, un caffè?»
Lucia e Giuseppe nella cucina nuova, tirata a lucido. Mentre gli parla, Lucia coglie il riflesso del proprio volto nel vetro della madia e non si riconosce.
O gli versa un bicchiere del suo rosso novello, che sa di affumicato e va giú liscio e allegro come acqua. La volta dopo lui le porta un fiore, una pastarella, un'attenzione cui non è abituata, e lei fa il viso chiaro, da bambina. Sorride, con quello sguardo serio e trasparente. Quando succede, Giuseppe non sa niente della vita di Lucia, è solo un'altra bella femmina che cede, chissà se a lui, o all'aria zuccherina di settembre.

Cecità

«Se sapevo che era intatta non ci provavo!»
«Se sapevo che la trovavo signorina non l'avrei mai fatto».
Un amico dopo l'altro, con variegate sfumature, l'inconsulto e sconcertato Giuseppe sparge la novella per l'intero paese.

Ma Lucia è cieca, sorda e nuova. Quanta strada devi percorrere per tornare a casa, Lucia, con il corpo squassato dallo stupore come un ramo di pesco nel levante.

A parole e coi fatti, lei gli propone tutta la sua vita.
D'improvviso, Lucia ride sempre, è sempre distratta. Tutto il paese vede che ha i denti bianchi come l'agnello.

La ferocia

Risolini, battute, chiacchiere, ammiccamenti, il veleno che spira dalle porte socchiuse. E Luigi la picchia piú forte. Per una volta vuole fare l'uomo, vuole fare vedere chi comanda, a quella spudorata, e a tutti quelli che non stanno zitti. Questa volta la mano di Luigi è messa in moto dalla (pur veritiera) maldicenza. Il paese è spaccato: gli Indifferenti azzannano l'osso sugoso di quella storia di passione e corna, se lo litigano, l'una fauce lo strappa all'altra fauce.

Poi ci sono le dita dei Sensibili, che ogni giorno ricuciono il tessuto della verità lacerata e ribadiscono le cose come stanno: che quella tra Lucia e Luigi era la piú infelice combinazione.

La reazione dipende dalla tenuta della compassione e dalla trasparenza del pensiero. Molte donne, raccolte a corolla dietro i portoncini chiusi, spargono parole di dolcezza sul destino di Lucia, mentre sbucciano, affettano, impastano, trasformano in cibo i rari elementi sanguinanti e le materie asciutte, e i mariti nei campi sono erba del sole. I fiati filtrano dagli spiragli come profumi di minestra e incenso, che però non assolvono. Nessuno appoggia apertamente Lucia.

Nei dopocena, quando si trovano nel bar in piazza per vedere la televisione, il miracolo ambiguo che in quegli anni comincia a livellare costumi e lingua di tutti i piccoli centri, in molti si distraggono dal varietà per trasmettersi – in dialetto stretto – la diceria del giorno. Di domenica, tra i banchi della chiesa, Lucia sta dritta, pulita. La sua schiena resiste alle punte di freccia degli sguardi biliosi, o ai sorrisi di complicità o compatimento. Quelle davanti si voltano a guardarla, ridono nei guantini della comunione. La normalità è solo quello a cui siamo abituati.

«Che svergognata!»
«Quella non è mai stata al posto suo... E mo' l'ha fatto pure cornuto!»
Eppure, tutti sanno la verità: da sette anni i ragazzini ripetono ad alta voce quello che sentono bisbigliare in casa. Che Lucia quel Luigi proprio non lo voleva, che il padre l'ha dovuta inseguire col fucile, lei era uscita pazza per Tonino. E poi Luigi «non è manco un uomo», lo ripetono sempre.

Cosí comincia la violenza sociale, quell'assoluta assenza di pietà che, giorno sommandosi a giorno, e dolore e umiliazione a dolore e umiliazione, può portare una vita a esaurire la propria carica di energia naturale. E finire, finalmente finire.
La fiatella sociale imputridisce tutto quello che tocca. Spire di fiato acido escono dalle bocche e avvinghiano i denigrati del momento, se li mangiano a mozzichi e li lasciano a macerarsi nel verde atrabiliare dell'invidia di quelli che non osano. Oggi le prede sono una sposa infelice come una morta, che ha deciso di non restare lí, dov'è tutti i giorni calpestata dal dolore. E il povero Luigi, costretto dall'onore a perseguire una donna per la quale non prova interesse alcuno.

Il 30 marzo 1964 Luigi Greco, legittimo consorte di Lucia, presenta ai carabinieri di Palata una querela, nella quale descrive l'increscioso frangente nel quale, suo malgrado, si è venuto a trovare. La legge è totalmente dalla sua parte: i carabinieri devono accogliere l'istanza di

Luigi e sporgere denuncia penale contro Lucia per relazione adulterina.

Ipotizzo che la denuncia di Luigi ostacoli massivamente la vita nuova di Lucia e Giuseppe. Il 7 gennaio 2022 inoltro dunque ai carabinieri di Palata richiesta formale del fascicolo inerente Galante Lucia, per scoprire se la denuncia di Luigi Greco abbia o meno avuto corso legale e, dunque, abbia o meno gravato – e in che misura – sulle future circostanze emotive. Il primo febbraio il maresciallo dei carabinieri di Palata sostiene che agli atti non risulta alcuna denuncia contro Lucia Galante e mi consiglia di presentare istanza alla Procura di Larino.

Il male minore

Nei casi di infedeltà coniugale, il diritto italiano dell'epoca prevede una vistosa disparità di trattamento tra mogli o mariti. Secondo gli articoli 559 e 560 del codice penale, che disciplinano rispettivamente i reati di adulterio e concubinato, la moglie incorre nel reato anche se tradisce il marito un'unica volta. Il delitto è punibile a querela del marito e, con lei, è trascinato nella pena l'amante. Se il tradimento evolve in relazione stabile, dunque se fra i due attori del reato verosimilmente si installa Amore, il castigo aumenta.

Quando invece è il marito a tradire, l'infedeltà viene punita solo se l'uomo convive «nella casa coniugale o notoriamente altrove» con la sua «concubina».

La Corte costituzionale affronta ripetutamente la questione della palese disuguaglianza e ripetutamente la sottoscrive, adducendo la motivazione che «oggetto della tutela», nella norma dell'articolo 559 del codice penale, «non è esclusivamente il diritto del marito alla fedeltà della moglie, ma il preminente interesse dell'unità della famiglia, che dal comportamento infedele della moglie è leso e messo in pericolo in misura che non trova riscontro nelle conseguenze di un'isolata infedeltà del marito». Retropensiero, giusto un filo evoluto, della tradizione omerica Penelope-Ulisse. La donna è il collante del nucleo domestico.

Solo a fine dicembre 1968, sulla base dell'articolo 29, che stabilisce «l'eguaglianza morale e giuridica dei coniugi», la Corte dichiara finalmente incostituzionali i commi 1 e 2 dell'articolo 559 (reato dell'adulterio semplice compiuto dalla moglie), ma deve passare ancora un altro anno (sentenza del 3 dicembre 1969 n. 147) perché l'incostituzionalità venga estesa ai commi 3 e 4 degli articoli 559 (reato di relazione adulterina della sola moglie) e 560 (concubinato del marito). La legge arranca dietro i piani di evidenza della prassi e della giustizia, spesso ufficializzati con ritardi rischiosi per la vita.

Nel 1964 Lucia e il coimputato amante Giuseppe sono infatti due ricercati. La pena è due anni di galera, deterrente che vorrebbe arginare la piena di un amore che si è già tradotto nella costituzione di una nuova vita, con diritti naturali equivalenti. Come stringere chiunque nella vita che non vuole piú vivere, come obbligarlo alla convivenza in un disamore coniugale, ormai naturalmente concresciuto dal tradimento in delusione e ferocia?

Quasi certamente Lucia non ha notizia delle lotte femministe che in quegli anni cominciano a percuotere a colpi di reggiseno le fondamenta delle famiglie tradizionali, vorrebbe solo vivere una vita voluta, solo vivere in pace quel tratto di tempo corporale che pertiene alla fisica e chiamiamo vita. Nonostante il fascismo naturale che la investe in pieno viso.

Spinta oltre se stessa dalla necessità, Lucia combatte la sua guerra inconscia e solitaria contro la dittatura della normalità, contro il comune bisogno di espellere il perturbante, il disordine, tutto ciò che si scosta dal sordo imperio della maggioranza. L'imprevedibile, cioè, il vivo, l'ingovernabile che è la vita dei vivi. Pochi, purtroppo, hanno l'umiltà di perdere il controllo sull'esistenza (propria e altrui) e sorridere della propria definitiva ignoranza.

Ma Lucia ha scelto, ha aggiogato la mula imbizzarrita della sua vita al rumore del futuro, a certi movimenti attivi dentro il suo corpo che dai primi di maggio le fanno compagnia. Lucia adesso è piú grande di se stessa. Santa Madre, forse questo è un tuo segno. Lo *ricev ije*, che sono nel giusto. *Auditui meo dabis gaudium et laetitiam: et exsultabunt ossa humiliata*. Dammi gioia, per favore, Madre mia, lascia che le mie ossa umiliate provino gioia. Fammi diventare scema, *bambaliscimi* come chi è felice. Cosí sbocciano i fiori di campo. *Famm diventà pazz comm lu sciure ammiezz a la jerva*. Fammi diventare logica e pazza come il fiore nell'erba. Lucia non cede. I suoi comportamenti si alzano in coro per dircelo, oltre mezzo secolo dopo, e per sempre.

Soltanto i fatti dicono chi siamo, lo dicono per primi a noi stessi. Noi, che siamo la nostra sorpresa.

21 maggio 1964. Lucia agisce in piena luce

Nel 1964 non esistono test di gravidanza, le donne che hanno fretta di sapere combinano le proprie urine in modi fantasiosi: le rilasciano, secondo l'uso delle egizie, su cesti d'orzo e di grano, in attesa della rapida crescita dei germogli, rivelatori della presenza dell'ormone gonadotropina corionica; o le iniettano in una rana viva e cronometrano i tempi di deposizione delle uova: se l'anfibio depone entro ventiquattr'ore, anche l'umana gravidanza è certa. E altrettanto è sicura se il miscuglio di urina e candeggina ecco che frizza e si tinge di riflessi fiammanti, color rubino.

Il 13 aprile, ottenuta certezza piú razionale della gravidanza di Lucia dallo scadere del doppio ritardo mestruale di quella che ormai ritiene la sua nuova compagna, Giuseppe salda i propri operai e trasloca a trenta chilometri da Palata, nel paesino di Ururi, dove tenta di nuovo di mettersi in proprio come costruttore.

Lucia fa strani sogni da fanciulla in fiore. Non è scaltra, Lucia, non s'infilza nel ventre coi ferri da calza, non si ustiona la lingua coi decotti di prezzemolo, per sbarazzarsi del guaio che ha combinato. Anzi, il 20 maggio compie un gesto impensabile per il tempo e il luogo: raccoglie al volo le sue poche cose e si trasferisce a casa di Giuseppe. Alla luce del sole. Una donna sposata, incinta di tre mesi. Ovviamente certa che il bambino che aspetta sia di Giuseppe, Lucia va a vivere con la famiglia eletta come propria.

Ma nel 1963 non è stata ancora formalizzata dalla legge degli uomini una delle infinite ovvietà che appunto faticano a essere accettate e la normativa sul divorzio entrerà in vigore solo nel dicembre 1970. Lucia ha tutti contro, anche la legge: non solo, com'è giusto, non è permesso tradire, Lucia non può neanche separarsi.

L'amore, la magnifica follia che ci fa giganteggiare sopra la nostra vita, che trasloca il nostro piccolo esistere dentro il corpo totale del mondo, è qui ancora ridotta a miseria, concubinaggio.

E a rinfocolato rogo di pettegolezzo:

«Se n'è andata con quello che le faceva i lavori in casa!» vocifera il paese. Scandalizzato, sovreccitato, invidioso.

Festa di matrimonio

Anche lo smargiasso Giuseppe, nel frattempo, è stato colto da follia di lei, quella bruna e tenace ragazzina che pesa due etti e lui credeva di poter dominare. All'inizio dell'estate 1964, stando alle testimonianze rese a caldo (nel calor bianco dei fatti che accadranno l'anno dopo) dalla moglie Anita a «l'Unità» e «Paese Sera», Giuseppe vede per l'ultima volta la famiglia, alla festa di matrimonio della figlia Carolina, che ha la stessa età di Lucia. Giuseppe è ormai cosí coinvolto nella sua nuova vita da portare con sé, al matrimonio, il parroco di Palata e alcuni ragazzi del paese, che ha assunto come operai.

Anita, disperata, cerca di farlo ragionare, gli parla di un milione di lire in cambiali da pagare, lui promette che presto manderà i soldi, ma non lo fa. In quegli anni un Cremino gelato della Algida costa cinquanta lire, oggi un euro e cinquanta, cioè quasi tremila lire: una proporzione di uno a sessanta. Poi accadranno lo schianto della svalutazione e il vertiginoso aumento di prezzo degli immobili, ma nel 1964 con un milione si può acquistare un monolocale in città. A Palata, ci compri una villetta. Ma un milione di lire resta ancora una somma considerevole, oltre 11 000 euro odierni. I guadagni di Giuseppe sono purtroppo scarsi pure a Ururi e lui deve affrontare la spesa decisamente imprevista della composizione di una nuova famiglia.

Da quell'estate Giuseppe che, pur tradendolo ormai da vent'anni, è sempre legalmente rincasato nel nucleo familiare calamitato intorno alla figura della coniuge Anita, non dà piú notizie di sé.

Le condizioni di salute del figlio si sono intanto aggravate e l'anno successivo, Anita – misteriosamente ribattezzata Censa da tutti i giornali – confida sgomenta al «Corriere della Sera» di essere rimasta sola ad affrontare debiti e malattia, perché il marito «aveva perso la testa per quella donna. Non c'era modo di farlo ragionare».

Esperanto economico

Lucia è felice. Eccola. Tutta scapigliata, euforica, piena di energia. Senza pensiero e lieve come erba, sorride pure quando ha la nausea, sorride sempre, sorride piú che mai nella sua vita. Una foglia nell'alito del vento estivo. Ecco un uomo capace di sognare insieme a lei il sogno semplice del futuro. Uno come Giuseppe fa crescere la voglia di andarsene lontano, dentro una vita quasi materiale, quasi vera. Lucia è ormai troppo consapevole di sé, per privarsi della gioia d'essere ingenua.

Quell'anno, la canzone vincitrice della prima edizione del concorso «Un disco per l'estate» è *Sei diventata nera* dei Los Marcellos Ferial. A dire l'umore generale del Paese, scanzonato e allegro, l'invito a vivere, di un'epoca tutto sommato serena, che raggiunge Palata solo di riflesso. Sono gli anni del twist, i giovani hanno fretta: se il futuro non arriva qui, andiamocelo a prendere! La città luccica nell'immaginario.

Da un paio d'anni la terra promessa dei palatesi è Milano. Sono partiti in tanti, verso la metropoli della ricostruzione, che pompa a pieno ritmo di motori inossidabili, condensatori e gruppi elettrogeni dentro il miracolo economico. Se ne vanno ubriachi di speranza, con le stente valigie. Tra i vicoli sempre piú vuoti del paese, il toponimo aleggia come una morgana benigna e piena di lusinga: Milano...

Verso metà agosto, anche Lucia e Giuseppe si lasciano sedurre dalla marea collettiva. Sono già quasi entrambi fuori tempo massimo, ma hanno la pazzia fiera e feroce degli innamorati. Continuare a vivere a Ururi, poi, per loro è arrischiato: Lucia ha una denuncia penale pendente, che oscilla sulle teste di entrambi. Pure sulla mia, peraltro, per quanto ancora microscopica.

E ci sono gli artigli dei parenti che ogni notte graffiano alla porta, fanno voci d'agnello, suonano i flauti dell'ipocrisia:

«Torna a casa, che sistemiamo tutto...»

Per Centolire è una soluzione miracolosa: ha ingravidato la moglie senza sporcarsi le mani col corpo di lei. Oh, sangue del mio sangue. Chissà come lo cresce, poi, quel figlio che non è manco suo e sarò io, una femmina, e incontrollabile. *Inarginabile*, come mia madre.

Certo, il mondo cambia solo grazie a chi sogna un mondo nuovo.

Certo, l'identità dei vivi è una rettifica continua degli errori già fatti, anche da chi è stato vivo prima di noi. Lucia potrebbe rimanere lí, essere l'avanguardia di chi l'ha preceduta e lavorare alla modernità del suo paese. Aiutare, cioè, la sua piccola comunità a raggiungere quello stato di grazia sociale nel quale non è piú necessario protestare per difendere il proprio diritto alla vita. Lucia potrebbe incarnare il progresso, provare a rendere la sua bellissima terra un luogo dove abita l'utopia, addirittura farne un avamposto di libertà legislativa. Ora Lucia potrebbe dare l'esempio. Ma questo è troppo, qui la lotta è impari e, quasi certamente, lei nemmeno ci pensa a queste cose, la moralista bacchettona sono io, a quella donna giovane la nostalgia del fico e della legna arriveranno dopo, come un morso notturno alla nuca che posa su un cuscino imbottito in poliuretano espanso. Ora Lucia non vede l'ora di andarsene. Lei vuole finalmente la sua vita. E basta.

Negli ultimi due mesi l'energico Giuseppe organizza dunque il trasferimento a Milano. Lui è uomo di mondo: telefona, scrive lettere agli amici costruttori, cerca e trova lavoro. Eccoli che preparano i bagagli. Eccoli che sognano, come tutti, la Vita Nuova. Piú che a coprire i circa settecento chilometri che separano Palata da Milano, Lucia, Giuseppe e tutti gli emigranti, si preparano a un viaggio nel tempo. Tra Palata e Milano esiste un varco spaziotemporale. Sono pronti a passarlo.

Come dice Anna al marito nella *Vita agra* di Luciano Bianciardi, attraversando la *rinascente* Milano del 1962 (che l'anno successivo il regista Carlo Lizzani già filma, consegnando al futuro una doppia intelligenza – sua e di Bianciardi – della destabilizzante contemporaneità):
«Ma via, testone, quanta gente hai visto tu, per la strada, morta di fame? Di fame non è mai morto nessuno, specialmente quassú. Ce la faremo anche noi, vedrai. E poi, ci sono io che ti aiuto».

I treni e le speranze partono infatti da ovunque, in quegli anni, i contadini abbandonano le campagne di tutta Italia a flusso continuo, diretti, oltre che all'estero, verso le grandi città industriali a nord del Paese. Grazie alla forza lavoro che confluisce dai tanti mondi ai margini dell'impero, a Milano si edificano forme imperative (grattacieli, palazzi iperbolici), mentre da Roma Pier Paolo Pasolini lancia un grido che lacera l'aria della metà del Novecento, documentando i primi movimenti della globalizzazione come un delitto in atto, che il corpo di un poeta non arriva a fermare, e identificando il proprio pianto per l'accecante futuro con quello della scavatrice, che riorganizza il disordine fitto delle campagne secondo «un ordine ch'è spento dolore» o, peggio, in nome di «un decoro ch'è rancore».

Negli albori del frenetico *sviluppo* edilizio e dell'urbanizzazione, Pasolini intravede le ombre della deriva verso l'«isteria urbanistico architettonica» e la «cacofonia cementizia» che nel 2002 colpirà a morte un altro geniale e furioso scrittore, Vitaliano Trevisan, che organizza il male etico, cioè estetico, a lui contemporaneo in righe perfette come lamine di bronzo, sulle quali sbalza e cesella l'annuncio del proprio suicidio, portato a termine mentre scrivo questo libro, il 7 gennaio 2022.

Con cinquant'anni di anticipo sul testimone diretto Trevisan, Pasolini lancia con tutto il corpo la profezia del nostro presente (quest'evo informe e senza idee, nato dall'improvviso crollo del passato e subito appiattito dalla masticazione dell'indifferente e dell'omologante: il mercato), fino a confezionare la propria morte come la piú atroce fra le opere d'arte, quella di una Cassandra novecentesca.

Chi ha occhi cosí acuti per vedere, chi lascia che in sé viva il mondo prima della delusione, quello rapimentoso delle origini, creduto sano e santo, rischia la vita per la delusione. Lo ripeterò ancora.

Ma, in quegli anni, chi ha fame è felice e orgoglioso di far andare a tutta forza la benna della scavatrice dentro gli sterri, per spianare i pratoni con colate di asfalto e cemento. I problemi di economia planetaria posti da Pasolini si scontrano coi bisogni immediati e urgenti dei singoli individui, operai che devono sfamare le famiglie. Pure sottopagati. Pure a costo di devastare territorio e ambiente. E cosí è, cosí è, ancora. E poi, c'è l'entusiasmo per l'ingegno: qui e là nel tessuto residenziale urbano, sporgono opere di architettura razionalista come la magnifica casa a tre cilindri di Angelo Mangiarotti e Bruno Morassutti, un edificio residenziale in via Gavirate, quartiere San Siro, completata nel 1962 e divenuta, giustamente, simbolo della Milano del boom.

In viaggio

Da Palata parte una sola corriera, al mattino presto. Non ci sono autostrade, né treni.
Il viaggio fino a Milano è lungo e complesso: in automobile sono sette ore. Altrimenti, bisogna cambiare tre pullman per raggiungere Termoli, e solo da lí si continua su rotaia. Lucia è al sesto mese di gravidanza, forse prendono il treno della notte.
La piccola cosa composta da cellule differenziate, il primo abbozzo dell'io che diventerà la persona che sta scrivendo queste parole, sta dentro il corpo di Lucia. Niente è devastante abbastanza da staccarmi da lei. Nessun dolore, nessuna fatica, nessuna incertezza. Per quel tratto di tempo, mangio quello che mangia. Se, finalmente, mangia.

Adesso che un pochino la conosciamo, possiamo immaginare quell'elegante ventottenne bruna di campagna, seduta nello scompartimento di un treno, incinta di un uomo che ha l'età di suo padre e non è il legittimo marito.
Pochi bagagli, lo stretto indispensabile. Ha portato con sé solo cose a cui tiene, l'essenziale. Ha portato il vestito marrone a fiorellini, ha portato i guantini da sposa. La sua vita di prima, ridotta all'osso. Si muove all'orlo di un abisso, che può essere tragico o radioso.
Scendiamo insieme a lei in quella città, che insieme mette gioia e mette paura.

Milano

L'arrivo in Stazione Centrale

Lucia e Giuseppe alla Stazione Centrale di Milano.
È un allunaggio dentro una cattedrale, coi tralicci d'acciaio che reggono la volta e calate di gesso, travertino e granito su orizzonti di marmo. Giuseppe, trionfante, se la tiene di fianco come un padreamante, scende con lei la grande scala centrale.

Il modellino del bianco transatlantico *Michelangelo* in scala 1:50 sotto una grande teca di cristallo nella galleria di testa. L'altissima Torre Galfa, appena fuori dalla stazione. Lucia posa lo sguardo sull'universo alieno della metropoli. Taxi, autobus e tram, il Vicky Bar in piazza.

Per Lucia, tutto è enorme. Tutto è un'altra lingua. La gente parla e lei non li capisce. Il rumore di fondo della città, le luci.

La prima notte. La prima di trecento
 ultime notti.

Nella Milano dell'immigrazione

Probabilmente prima della partenza Giuseppe ha organizzato anche l'affitto dell'appartamento che figurerà come mia residenza al momento di un ricovero, nel marzo successivo. Immagino il filo incandescente dei suoi pensieri, immagino la prospettiva di un bilocale nella prima periferia operaia a nord, dove la città sta lentamente inglobando i paesi immediatamente posati lungo la sua cintura esterna. La parte periferica dell'urbe, ma pur sempre Milano. La città del lavoro, il lavoro che dà la libertà.

L'indirizzo è viale Monza, una zona popolare, probabilmente l'ultima disponibile all'immigrazione interna, vicina com'è alla zona industriale. Ecco le ciminiere in lontananza. Poco avanti, la mezza campagna, dove ancora si pescano i gamberi nelle rogge.

Viale Monza nasce in piazzale Loreto, la piazza tristemente nota perché il 10 agosto 1944 quindici partigiani vengono lasciati morti sul marciapiede da un corpo militare fascista milanese e il 29 aprile 1945 vi sono prima esposti, nel medesimo luogo dell'eccidio, poi appesi a testa in giú al distributore di benzina Esso, i corpi di Claretta Petacci, Benito Mussolini, Achille Starace e altri quattro gerarchi fascisti. Il viale, da quella grande piazza umiliata dal sangue, arriva fino a Monza. Per percorrerlo a piedi da un capo all'altro, ci vogliono oltre due ore e mezza. Teniamo a mente questa informazione.

Ma, soprattutto, da sette anni viale Monza è il luogo piú operoso dell'operosissima Milano, contiene un vero e proprio alveare, sotterraneo e affiorante: il cantiere magno dei lavori per la metropolitana, che da piazzale Loreto percorre al mezzo la carreggiata per dodici chilometri, fino a Sesto Marelli. Per cominciare, hanno abbattuto tutti gli alberi, dilatando lo spazio e la vista.

È probabile che Giuseppe sia riuscito a farsi assumere in quell'enorme e magnanima impresa e gli sia pure riuscito di trovare alloggio negli immediati dintorni. Tale è la suggestione di questa ipotesi che mi sembra di riconoscerlo nel breve video *Caleidoscopio Ciac* dell'Istituto Luce, girato una sera di ottobre 1964 in un self-service appena aperto in zona. Serio, elegante, in giacca e cravatta, taglio corto e basette, osserva la fila degli alimenti proposti per la cena con aria perplessa. Potrebbe essere uno dei nove giorni (tra il 15 e il 24 ottobre) che Lucia trascorre in ospedale, implicata nel mettermi al mondo.

Alle 10,30 del mattino del primo novembre 1964 una festa grande – alla presenza del sindaco socialista Pietro Bucalossi e di altre autorità politiche e religiose, inclusi i presidenti dei metrò di Londra, Parigi, Mosca, New York e Berlino – inaugura la prima partenza della metropolitana M1 dalla stazione in piazzale Loreto, che avviene solo undici minuti dopo. Efficienti pure nel gioire.

In un editoriale sull'evento, uscito sul «Corriere della Sera», Dino Buzzati elogia i cittadini milanesi, che si sono autotassati per pagare i lavori, senza ricevere «neanche un soldo dallo Stato» e tramanda a parole fino a noi quell'aria rarefatta da film di fantascienza, affascinato pure dai «biglietti stampati con inchiostro e sali di ferro per influenzare l'elettrocalamita di controllo».

Lucia è lí, dentro quell'aria cosmica, e per lei ogni cosa è ancora piú novissima: da otto giorni è uscita dall'ospedale dove ha partorito. Io non sono con lei. È un'ingiustizia grande, che documenterò.

Sente una gran dolcezza in mezzo al petto e una mancanza come mai niente e nessuno le ha fatto provare, un sentimento irreparabile, che si radica. Lucia trasfigura. Dietro i vetri della finestra, appare il volto di una fenice, è un baluginare della luce che la fa immortale. Rinascerai, Lucia, anche solo a parole. È tutto quello che posso. Intanto, affàcciati.

Dalla strada, le arriva la musica del concerto grosso delle bande rionali, a ogni fermata dei vagoni rossi sotterranei: Pasteur, Rovereto, Turro... È musica che passa e si allontana. Lucia s'incanta ad ascoltare, prova pace, strazio, allegria, una forza ansiosa e ruggente e una fitta di nostalgia arcaica, delle cellule, per la banda del paese, che a fine maggio sfila in processione in onore della Madonna di Santa Giusta. Il suono della banda finisce per coincidere col corpo di sua figlia, Maria Grazia. Le molecole piccole, fatte di suono.

Francesco!

Il treno che trasporta i terroni si chiama Fata Morgana. Negli anni Cinquanta gli emigranti che arrivano da Sud vengono sversati come scorie radioattive in discariche sociali ultraperiferiche, pullulanti di casette abusive e vagoni di treno adibiti a uso abitazione, o in quartieri di casermoni fabbricati in fretta nelle periferie delle città, intorno alle grandi fabbriche. Sono isole di fango e impalcature, aree non comunicanti col resto del tessuto urbano, città nelle città, cosí remote e diverse che andare a passeggiare in centro si dice «andare a Milano (o a Torino)» e lí venire individuati a colpo d'occhio, per abbigliamento e postura: i milanesi chiamano Coree quelle vaste paludi, a indicare lontanissime zone di guerra, naturalmente abitate dai «coreani».

Pasolini trasferisce in Cina le omologhe borgate romane: «internati in mezzo a una Shangai di orticelli, strade, reti metalliche, villaggetti di tuguri, spiazzi, cantieri, gruppi di palazzoni, marane», s'innamora della crudele dolcezza preindustriale di quella Cina capitolina e ne fa lo scenario di molti lungometraggi, fin dal magnifico *Accattone*, ambientato nella baraccopoli addossata a casermoni anonimi, ancora pseudourbani: «Via Fanfulla da Lodi, in mezzo al Pigneto, con le casupole basse, i muretti screpolati, era di una granulosa grandiosità, nella sua estrema piccolezza; una povera, umile, sconosciuta stradetta, perduta sotto il sole, in una Roma che non era Roma».

Il grido dell'indimenticata Anna Magnani in *Roma città aperta* di Roberto Rossellini già echeggiava tra i muri del Pigneto.

Lucia e la merce

> – l'organo genitale del denaro,
> ogni singola cosa e il tutto, e il processo –
>
> RAINER MARIA RILKE, *Elegie duinesi*

Televisore, frullatore, tostapane
bollitore, automobile, Vespa
frigorifero, ventilatore, aspirapolvere.

Le gite fuori porta, a bordo della Seicento verde acqua coi finestrini abbassati. Le cose. E le mille bolle blu.

In centro, pare ovunque Carnevale: le donne hanno capelli cotonati e minigonne insolenti, sgargianti camicette a stampe geometriche e optical, vestitini svasati, senza punto vita, tempestati da piogge di pois; ogni tanto si accendono una sigaretta. Alcune richiamano il taglio geometrico degli abiti nei capelli a caschetto, altre decidono per acconciature corte e spettinate, con la frangetta a schiaffo, obliqua sulla fronte. Le donne piú sottili marcano la magrezza con uno stile androgino e giocoso: sono le *gamines*, le donne ragazzino. Quasi tutte hanno occhi evidenziati con eye-liner e ombretti scuri e le ciglia (finte e raccolte in ciuffetti di nylon da cartone animato, oppure ridefinite, vellutate, allungate, lievitate sotto l'azione di scovolini di tutte le fogge emersi da glitterati stick di mascara) lasciano tracce di bagliori e profondità subacquee nella sera.

Lucia impara che a Milano scemo si dice *pirla*, anziché *fesse*. Lucia è intelligente, è donna che mette a frutto l'esperienza. A Milano, cambia. A Milano e con Giuseppe, che ha tanti anni piú di lei e possiede una pratica del mondo e uno stile solido e cosciente, d'uomo in giacca e cravatta, intramontato. Agli occhi dei passanti, Lucia è un'inconsapevole Dramatic con le curve: magra, senza trucco, lascia a vista gli spigoli vivi del volto e non rinuncia alla cascata di capelli lunghi. Da un po' veste a colori, con le scarpe bianche, o le nere stringate. Scarpe solide, col mezzo tacco, per avanzare comoda sugli sterrati. La sua eleganza concreta nel prodigo azzurro.

Lucia è sopraffatta dalle cose. Non ancora dal loro desiderio.

Il moto perpetuo dei quadri metropolitani le mette in corpo una bella euforia, un friccicore che sa di futuro, quando attraversa la rotatoria di piazzale Loreto e non decifra il senso di marcia delle automobili. I clacson le strombazzano contro risentiti, e lei si tiene ai manici della borsetta come a un tempo passato e conosciuto, come al ramo del fico dove si dondolava da bambina.

Milano è l'impero delle cose
   e chiassoso è il dominio della merce.

C'è «il magazzino della famiglia italiana» Standa, ci sono i supermercati Esselunga – catena varata proprio a Milano, nel 1957 – coi carrelli e polli stretti come salsicce nei budelli di plastica, all'angolo con la piazza c'è una gigantesca Coin in costruzione e, in piazza, il Loreto, cinemino di terza visione da mille posti, aperto dentro il palazzo dei magazzini.

Al Loreto, tra il 1964 e il 1965, proiettano tre film dei due rispettivi anni precedenti: nel 1964 *Il silenzio*, magnifico e austero lungometraggio di Ingmar Bergman sulla divina afasia contemporanea e, nel 1965, *Per un pugno di dollari* di Sergio Leone e *Crisantemi per un delitto* di René Clément.

In Italia non esiste la legge sui trapianti d'organi tra vivi, la donazione in vita. Mentre Anita supplica il governo attraverso i giornali per ottenere il permesso di travasare un proprio rene dentro il corpo del figlio Francesco e salvargli la pelle – ancora una volta il buonsenso amoroso contro i protocolli burocratici –, Giuseppe è ormai decisamente altrove: ha accettato di ricominciare il viaggio della vita dalla partenza e lavora come manovale, impasta ghiaia e sabbia che arrivano sui barconi dei Navigli.

Francesco, figlio maggiore di Anita e Giuseppe, morirà nel luglio 1966, a trentadue anni. La legge sulla donazione d'organi in vita verrà approvata il 26 giugno 1967. La norma macina e miete, soffia vite come pula di grano.

Giovedí 15 ottobre 1964. Astronave Madre

Mercoledí 14 ottobre 1964, presso il presidio ospedaliero Macedonio Melloni (o I.O.P.M., Istituto ospitaliero provinciale per la maternità), nella zona un tempo rigogliosa e opportunamente detta Acquabella, Lucia si sottopone all'esame per la «Profilassi e trattamento della Malattia emolitica del neonato», risultandone di gruppo sanguigno Rh positivo.

Il 21 gennaio 2022 ricevo la cartella clinica del parto. Alla citofonata del corriere che recapita la busta mi precipito giú per le scale. Lucia dunque è esistita, ha lasciato altre tracce, oltre me. La Signora
   Galante Lucia, di professione contadina, primipara, gentilizio indenne, alle 8 di mattina del 15 ottobre si ripresenta all'ospedale in travaglio, con «feto cefalico a termine e già tendente all'impegno». Siamo pronte. Lucia è costretta dalle circostanze a tenere nascosto il suo indirizzo e si dichiara residente a Palata, in via San Rocco. Non dice il civico, dunque non saprò mai se sta pensando alla casa dei genitori o alla nuova casa coniugale. Sbaglia la data del proprio matrimonio, anticipandola di un anno, forse perché quel tristo coniugio le pare essere durato piú a lungo di quanto in realtà.

Il distacco dal corpo di Lucia dura in tutto otto ore, la temperatura esterna dell'ambiente nel quale vengo rilasciata si aggira intorno ai 12 gradi. Parto spontaneo, tutto nei limiti di una sana ragionevolezza naturale. Penso alle immagini degli astronauti che si staccano dall'astronave madre, per galleggiare dentro il nero indifferenziato che, nel caso del nascere, è la luce abbagliante di un mondo privo di dettagli.

Il principio è materia vivente

In principio è la materia vivente.
Vita increata e autogenerata in lontananze incommensurabili dello spazio e del tempo.
Il mistero della vita increata s'incarna in forme pressoché infinite, siano esse infinitesime (*Adactylidium*) o gigantesche (*Balaenoptera musculus*). Il principio che muove acaro e balenottera azzurra è lo stesso: *il voler vivere*.
La vita replica se stessa producendo un numero a oggi incalcolato (poco sappiamo delle specie abitanti lo scintillante buio oceanico) di ingegnosi contenitori viventi di sé materia vivente, sparpagliata nell'immensa separazione che tutto tiene.

Perché ci sia vita, è necessaria la separazione.

Nei mesi precedenti la comparsa di quello che diciamo individuo, esiste solo la materia, mossa dalla volontà di aggregazione selettiva delle cellule. Materia incapsulata in una solitudine giusta, e che aspira alla propria durata.
Se esiste coscienza, dentro la cecità del tuttovivo, essa si esprime nell'aspirazione a durare.
In principio, di noi, c'è solo il sogno di durare della materia.
Al principio di noi troneggia
    la matrice, inclusa nel mistero d'essere viva.

Ma, perché ci sia vita, è necessaria la separazione.

Il primo e piú lungo dolore è separarsi.
Perlomeno, è un dolore condiviso. Nascere è un dolore condiviso.

Separarsi è il dolore, simultaneo e indispensabile, della matrice che espelle e dell'individuo che viene espulso, per entrare attivamente nella (sua, propria, singola) durata.

Sono istruzioni scritte nella materia vivente, sono il codice d'ogni futuro, legge che si ripeterà, per tutta la durata di una crescita, sotto forma di simboli o fatti. Scindersi dalla propria matrice diretta e poi
    vivere, soli come non siamo ancora stati.

Il 22 ottobre,

alle 9,20 del mattino «avanti dell'applicato scelto» Ettore Ronzoni dell'ufficio di Stato civile del Comune di Milano, compare il cinquantenne Felice Bonanomi di Mozzate, commesso in Milano, in qualità di ufficiale delegato dal direttore dell'i.o.p.m., l'ospedale Melloni. Bonanomi, insieme ad altri due impiegati piú anziani, Liberté Toffolo e Luigi Bernacchi, nativi rispettivamente di Porcia e Corsico, attestano la mia nascita e mi impongono il nome scelto da Lucia: Maria Grazia. Lucia è devota alla Madonna di Santa Giusta. Maria le ha fatto la grazia.

Il giorno precedente, 21 ottobre, sono stata battezzata nella cappella ospedaliera dedicata a Maria Santissima Bambina e Sant'Anna.
Il Servizio per la disciplina dei sacramenti della Curia arcivescovile di Milano (in base all'articolo 8 §5 del Decreto generale della conferenza episcopale italiana in materia di riservatezza, aggiornato al 24 maggio 2018) non è però autorizzato a rivelarmi l'identità dei miei padrino e madrina, né può dirmi se Lucia sia contumace anche nella circostanza religiosa. A nulla vale protestare che sono passati cinquantasette anni. L'articolo mi viene trascritto integralmente, a scoraggiare qualunque ipotesi di spionaggio: «L'interessato in ogni caso non ha diritto di ispezione dei dati del registro e dei dati sottratti alla sua conoscenza». La legge diocesana è inflessibile:
«Il diritto canonico è piú restrittivo del diritto civile»,

conclude l'avvocatura, con cortesia esangue e sovraccarica. Poiché i due nomi non mi paiono dati sostanziali, non insisto. Ma questa asettica e frugale imposizione del nome è un indizio che il futuro rovescia tra noi.

24 ottobre 1964. Mito dell'erosione della pace

A causa del frequente sviluppo di emorragie *postpartum*, negli anni Sessanta capita che le puerpere vengano tenute in osservazione.

Il 24 ottobre, a nove giorni dal parto, Lucia firma e si precipita fuori dall'ospedale, «contro il parere del curante», tutta ancora sbregata e rammendata com'è là sotto. Ma il nome di sua figlia, Greco Maria Grazia, di Luigi, è apparso nei registri del «Nuovo Brefotrofio» di Milano, l'I.P.P.A.I. (Istituto provinciale protezione e assistenza dell'infanzia) di viale Piceno 60.

Un corridoio sotterraneo collega l'I.O.P.M. all'I.P.P.A.I. Brefotrofio e ospedale sono cosí intimamente comunicanti perché, il 28 ottobre 1932, l'ospedale Melloni nasce come semplice distaccamento ostetrico-ginecologico del brefotrofio. L'evidenza ha reso necessario correre ai ripari, di fronte a tanta orfanità: dei figli e delle madri, orfane dei figli. La lama degli acronimi prova a rendere astratto il pianto dei bambini ricoverati nell'istituto a causa delle loro «condizioni scadenti di nascita», di una patologia perinatale, perché sono illegittimi o perché abbandonati. Tutto, qui, cerca di diventare immateriale, perché si tratta di materia inguaribile, di corpi maternoinfantili costernati, che durano fatica a separarsi, vite che non vogliono abbandonare la loro vicinanza irripetibile, per cadere in uno stato di orfanità, permanente e reciproca.

Ogni anno l'istituto ospita migliaia – io sono la numero 1068 – di piccole solitudini, quelle isolate singolarità, quasi senza ossa e dal futuro incognito, che, messe insieme, costituiscono il morbido corpo dell'infanzia abbandonata o bisognosa, accolta in cambio di non saprei quanto cospicua retta versata dall'O.N.M.I. (Opera nazionale maternità e infanzia) o dallo Stato. Oggi le case famiglia ricevono dal Comune di residenza tra i 1800 e i 2400 euro mensili per ciascun minore ospitato.

L'I.P.P.A.I. si presenta come luogo di solidarietà sociale e, nel maroso di quell'anno, vi veleggiano pure le suore di carità della Beata Capitanio, abbigliate in nero spinto. «La visita ai bambini nell'Istituto è permessa per due persone: *nei giorni retro indicati*».

La cartella clinica testimonia che non soffro di alcuna patologia ma, in quanto figlia riconosciuta dalla sola madre, per le leggi dell'epoca sono figlia illegittima. Dunque, in attesa di accertamenti, vengo sottratta pure alla madre e «lavorata» dai servizi sociali.

Ecco spiegata l'assenza di Lucia durante la pratica del mio riconoscimento: forzata a non comparire.

Ecco spiegata l'insistenza di Lucia, che pareva ingenua, a mettere ovunque nero su bianco, fin nel suo venturo testamento spirituale, che io sia figlia di Luigi. Cosí, all'alba del 29 dicembre, dopo la lunga telefonata del pomeriggio precedente con l'archivista dell'i.p.p.a.i., scrivo alla mia amica Sonia: «Adesso vado in radio, poi ho il colloquio finale per il visto si stampi del libro sulle poetesse e da domani posso dedicarmi totalmente a Lucia. Ovvero dedicarmi, come ti dicevo, a valicare gli ostacoli che per cento anni (cioè quando io avrò cento anni) mi impediscono l'accesso agli atti riguardanti Lucia e ai miei stessi "dati sensibili", in quanto figlia non riconosciuta da entrambi i genitori. Ma ti pare? Ora capisco l'ostinazione di Lucia a far scrivere ovunque il falso, cioè che fossi figlia del marito. Provava a proteggermi facendo lo slalom fra le leggi irrazionali e ridicole dell'epoca. Che sono però valide ancora oggi. Intanto a quest'ora cantano gli uccellini».

Ecco i comportamenti di Lucia baluginare a tratti nella camera oscura del passato: eccola che firma carte false, con la lingua fra i denti per l'impegno a districare sua figlia dalle leggi di una stagione di confine tra arretratezza ottusa e intelligenza morale.

Nonostante siano state ampiamente superate dalle normative vigenti, quelle leggi mi impedirebbero, ancora per i prossimi cinquant'anni, l'accesso integrale agli atti che mi riguardano: per i figli dichiarati illegittimi dalla vecchia legislazione, valgono nel presente le regole di allora. Per cento anni, cioè, non possiamo ricevere «informazioni sensibili» sulle nostre madri, né su noi stessi, ma solo dati relativi al parto.

Molti, esasperati dall'irrazionalità della norma, si sono rivolti alla Corte europea per i diritti dell'uomo, o si sono avvalsi della «volontaria giurisdizione».

Nel frangente della telefonata del 28 dicembre sopra descritta, sono ancora in attesa della cartella clinica del parto. Dopo i primi trenta giorni, un estenuante passaggio all'Ufficio legale e molta mia insistenza, sento me stessa protestare al telefono, opponendomi a ulteriori opposizioni:

«Mia madre so benissimo chi è, lei s'è ammazzata, mica mi ha abbandonata!»

Ci si riesce a vantare di qualsiasi cosa.

La realtà è un'opinione. Frequentemente sbagliata, perché di rado osserviamo le cose senza pregiudizio. Ma le cose esistono, e hanno una voce chiara. Per comprendere, basta osservare i fatti, senza sovrapporre ai fatti nessuna intelligenza umana. Lasciarsi attraversare dalle cose, fino a che esse esprimono quel che hanno da dire nonostante noi. Questo libro desidera essere opera di trascrizione e testimonianza dell'energia indelebile delle cose. La verità è nei fatti, emancipati dal nostro punto di vista.

L'osservazione della vita vera di Lucia dice che *mai* lei inoltra richiesta di privatezza, agisce anzi allo scoperto, vive quello che sente sotto gli occhi di tutti. Non incurante, ma risoluta e cosciente del proprio volere, e del diritto naturale del suo amore.

Cara Suora, dammi la testa della puttana e un Tir

A libro ormai chiuso, vengo a conoscenza della durata del mio internamento all'I.P.P.A.I. Benché dimessa «in buone condizioni» dal Melloni, non lascio l'ospedale, ma vengo subito inoltrata al reparto patologia pediatrica dell'istituto, per un «ricovero d'urgenza» della durata di un mese e mezzo in quanto «debile congenita», diagnosi mai prima intercettata dal mio stesso perplesso referente medico. Il fascicolo sanitario e quello sociale, però, sono entrambi assenti. Unica traccia, aver attraversato l'«Accettazione legittimi» con la qualifica di «normale».

Qual è il motivo del ricovero in brefotrofio di una neonata legittima e in buona salute?

«È la prima volta che vedo una pratica cosí...»

Durante una conversazione telefonica, vengo a sapere che Luigi Greco, il marito di mia madre, richiesto dalla direzione dell'istituto di versare le quattromila lire della retta del mio ricovero tramite Cassa mutua malattia per i coltivatori diretti – com'è prassi, e senza che Lucia ne abbia iniziale contezza –, reagisce con lunga e circostanziata lettera, nella quale nega la sua paternità e accusa Lucia.

«Lo comprendo, – dico, – certo, ha ragione...»

Il mio interlocutore non è convinto. Prima di inoltrarmi la lettera – la cui presenza all'interno del mio fascicoletto esclusivamente amministrativo rappresenta ulteriore anomalia –, sente lo scrupolo di telefonarmi ancora, per valutare la mia tempra umana:

«Guardi che in tanti anni non ho mai letto niente del genere...»

Lo persuado di poter sopportare la lettura.

  Voglio brondo risposta
  Cara Suora vengo Ascrivere alla Bambina Greco Maria Grazia è Ricoverato allo Spedale che sono il padre ma che lo scrivo ma non so se nutrito Con mio Sangue oppure con La mando che traeva mia Moglia Galande Lucia perché si a fatto incannare mia Moglia mi Avotato un po Lespalle Dal mese Di Dicembre Del 1963 poi sono Accorto che filava storta scropendo il mese di Aprile con il suo Cornuto che si affatto ingannare poi e Venuto tante store Di Case e ne Fuggito anche essa mia Moglia con il suo Amando Aveva annamorato puro lo perdonavo si stava con il suo padre e La sua madre pure Veniva lostesso La pace io stava ingampagnia essa Aveva lisciata La Casa con la sua Dodda se ne va via Dal 20 Maggio estato un mese con il suo Cornuto poi Lo va prendere La Madre sua e La sua zia poi Di nuovo se ne Ritorno con il suo Cornuto non a Voluto stare no con il suo padre e no con madre e non a Voluto tornare con me che era il Marito Avoluto Fare propria La puttana si e Allondanate Molte Dal suo paese Palata e Fuggito nella puglia Provincia Di Foggia e Stava con 3 persone Dopo Parecchi Tembi non si sapeva Dove Stava e Sta immane Alla Leggia che affatto tutte queste cose Asmmacherizato Tutto i parendi Cara suora Voglio Sapere Da Voi se sta Da Sole o Sta Con il suo Amando oppure Con La sua Sorella Cuggina Sua che Abbita lo stesso a Milano Cara suora Voglio Sapere se La Bambina Sta Ricoverato oppure e uscito Dal Ricovero se sta nel Ricovero le spese chi Lo paga io non Voglio niente Rispossabile Cara suora se mi Vengono Le spese Della Bambina Vengo a Milano Prende a mia Moglia Galande Lucia prima Le taglio La Testa poi Lo mette Sotto le Ruote Degli Autotreni prendete La Bambina consegniatela Alla Madre La Bambina e Venuto Al Mondo non cia Colpe Di nessuna Cosa ma La Matre ci merita sole di Essere Tagliate sole La Testa Le Cose Barbare che a Fatto nel suo paese Palata Da quanto Abbiamo Sposato non Abiamo Avuto Figli perche era Sembre Ammalate Mia Moglia poi o Fatto una Visita il Professore Del Nostro ospedale e addato Le Cure Di Medicine per fare i Figli Facendo queste Cure Avevamo

qualche Bambino ci addetto il Professore Adesso Accapitato con me chera il Marito a Dormiva e Con un Altra perssona si Affatto ingannare si e messo proprio il Diavolo mai si faceva queste Cure mai si Faceva ingannare.

Ma di tutta la scienza

Non posso (né voglio) negare che la mia tempra umana esca provata dalla lettura di queste parole: sono un ringhio salito dai fondali, una scarica chimica rettiliana, uno sbocco di fiele. Avevo tanta pena per Luigi. Però.
La compitazione delle parole di Luigi mi precipita dentro l'imbuto della *realtà* di Lucia, dentro il sentire piú segreto di mia madre. E, come lei, mi sento soffocare. E in lei io sento che non sente scampo. Questo è il fondo dell'immaginabile. Neanche coi maiali si fa cosí. Neanche i maiali vengono ripresi a forza da padre e madre, quando scappano urlando dal recinto e vogliono salvarsi dal beccaio. Le mani di sua madre la ributtano sotto la mannaia, nella circoscrizione dei condannati. Ma Lucia è nata con un'anima destinata a scorrere: garbata, trasparente, refrattaria. Eccola, l'ho trovata. È tutta vera. Questa donna, resa segreta dalla morte, mi ha lasciata entrare. Viva e reale come la midolla del pane, eccola che resiste pure alla violenza di chi l'ha messa al mondo. Lucia resiste, resiste ancora. *Non a Voluto, Non a Voluto, Non a Voluto*. Resiste anche a Milano. Non ha il cervello molle della preda. Si alza dal letto e firma per uscire. Pure la figlia mi prendono.

Gli operatori capiscono che qualcosa non va. Luigi si è premurato di sostenere la propria estraneità all'evento – ormai irreparabile – della mia nascita, spingendosi davvero troppo oltre. L'indomani vengo edotta di qualcosa che né io né chi legge questo libro può forse sapere: nella mente dei palatesi dell'epoca la provincia di Foggia è «il luogo delle prostitute». Il piano di Luigi risplende chiaro, nella sua ottusa ferocia. Chi non ha sentimenti e pensieri non solo non comprende sentimenti e pensieri di chi invece li pensa e sente, non arriva neanche a sospettarne l'esistenza; e tanto meno riesce a prevedere le conseguenze e gli echi delle proprie azioni nel sistema emotivo degli altri. Fiutata l'imponenza cupa della tempesta che si addensa sul corpo di Lucia mentre lei lentamente si richiude, disarmata, dopo essersi aperta come una variazione musicale del destino per lasciarmi andare, le Care Suore decidono di fermarsi a considerare la situazione e l'ignara persona che fui, al mezzo di esso flutto minaccioso, a quel mite scialo di sangue umano e presagi.

Ci vuole piú di un mese, per riavermi. Trascorso, per Lucia e me, come decido di non immaginare. L'abbiamo solo vista affacciarsi a una finestra di viale Monza, suggestionata da una voce che viene dal futuro – la mia – con il viso appoggiato fra le mani, dentro un respiro incontenibile e una furia grande, un caleidoscopio di luce e carattere che la trasforma.

Tra poco, sentiremo il bisogno di abbracciarla, perché la vedremo costretta a sporcarsi la bocca con una menzogna meschina: per amore di me, la vedremo piegarsi a rinnegare l'amore che l'ha emancipata da qualcosa che per lei è peggiore della morte. Ho sempre detestato novembre.

Non so a quali arti magiche o implorazioni sia ricorsa Lucia per ricondurmi a sé, in quel travagliato contesto di illegalità e brutalità, ma il primo dicembre la creatura che fui viene rilasciata e consegnata alla madre, «di passaggio a Milano presso lo zio Di Pietro Giuseppe».

Dimentichiamo la necessaria menzogna. Il primo dicembre 1964 è uno dei giorni piú felici della sua e mia (nostra, per un breve tratto) esistenza.

Vengo a sapere della nostra lunghissima separazione il 16 febbraio 2022, giorno nel quale Lucia compie ottantacinque anni in memoria.
Penso che, giusto in questa ricorrenza, Lucia voglia confidarmi il suo ultimo e piú grande dolore. Un dolore maturo, che lavora alla base la fermezza dell'essere: venire ritenuta indegna di essere madre.
Mamma, vieni con me. Ti scollo dal segreto della realtà. Metto a disposizione della tua figura tutto quello che so. Ma, di tutta la scienza, conta solo che sei venuta a prendermi. E adesso io prendo te
 e ti lascio libera, pure di abbandonarmi.
Penso questi pensieri nonostante le mie convinzioni, li penso anche se credo
 che di Lucia rimanga solo polvere. Ma questo amore grande.

Toccala solo con le mani pulite

Mi pare qui indispensabile ricordare un genio umiliato dal pregiudizio: Ignác Fülöp Semmelweis, il medico ungherese che, nel 1847, salva migliaia di madri grazie a un'intuizione che, però, gli costa il mancato rinnovo del contratto da parte dell'ospedale viennese nel quale lavora.

Dopo una lunga osservazione statistica, Semmelweis comprende empiricamente la causa delle febbri che portano a morte le puerpere e formula l'ipotesi, straordinaria per l'epoca, che la fatale malattia venga trasferita da corpo a corpo attraverso il contatto delle partorienti con medici e studenti appena usciti dalla sala anatomica delle dissezioni. Affinché la morte non contamini la vita, Semmelweis chiede allora ai colleghi di abituarsi a una pratica semplicissima: toccare le vive con le mani pulite:

«Prima di passare dalla sala anatomica a quella ostetrica, per favore, lavatevi le mani con una soluzione di cloruro di calce».

La comunità medica non tollera l'accusa di ammazzare chi vorrebbe assistere e Semmelweis, deriso e praticamente licenziato, si ammala di rabbia e frustrazione fino a essere ricoverato in manicomio.

L'inoppugnabile dimostrazione della giustezza della sua teoria, la contaminazione batterica da streptococco, viene formalizzata da Pasteur nel 1864, dopo diciassette anni e chissà quante altre morti e dolore piú che mai superflui. Semmelweis muore in manicomio l'anno successivo, a causa della setticemia dovuta alle ferite inflitte dalle guardie. A volte è cosí amara, l'ironia del vivere.

Nel 1924 il grande romanziere, nonché medico, Louis-Ferdinand Céline dedica a Semmelweis la propria tesi di laurea.

3-14 marzo 1965. Civico 24. L'incubatrice

A dicembre il termometro scende sottozero, è uno degli inverni piú freddi degli anni Sessanta, la temperatura rimane diaccia e umida fino a marzo inoltrato. In periferia, da ottobre a maggio piove quasi sempre e l'ombrello non basta, perché dal fango degli sterri si alza un nebbione che lambisce i corpi sotto la lana grossa dei cappotti. Ma il Natale a Milano è un'ubriacatura di insegne al neon Biancosarti, Cinzano, Facis, luci intermittenti e traffico, traffico di automobili e persone, ruminare a secco di acciaio su acciaio delle ruote di tram con le porte che soffiano, già descritte per sempre, nel 1956, dal poeta livornese Giorgio Caproni:

> Amore mio, nei vapori d'un bar
> all'alba, amore mio che inverno
> lungo e che brivido attenderti! Qua
> dove il marmo nel sangue è gelo, e sa
> di rifresco anche l'occhio, ora nell'ermo
> rumore oltre la brina io quale tram
> odo, che apre e richiude in eterno
> le deserte sue porte?...

mentre a Porta Ticinese le donne lavano tovaglie e lenzuola nell'acqua del Naviglio e gli industriali piú generosi, in quell'aria di euforica malinconia, raddoppiano il sussidio settimanale da destinare ai poveri.

Devota a Maria, per la messa di Natale Lucia va quasi certamente nella chiesa art déco lí vicina, dieci minuti a piedi, Santa Maria Beltrade, col bar dell'oratorio gestito dal «Picciotto», pure lui emigrante sempre in giacca e cravatta e, soprattutto, con una malinconica raffigurazione di Maria che si è fatta notare, portata in processione il 15 settembre per la festa patronale. La chiesa contiene infatti una magnifica cappella dedicata alla Beata Vergine Addolorata, con statua secentesca della Madonna dei sette dolori, una bella adolescente bruna dal viso ovale reclinato a destra, vestita di porpora e seduta in preghiera, recante sette vere spade di metallo infilzate nel petto. Da ventiquattro giorni Lucia ha riavuto la sua bambina, quella notte sente di avere anche lei una famiglia, tutta lí stretta nella galaverna. Se fossi lei (Lucia, certo, non la Madonna), stanotte proverei una vicinanza speciale con la dolcissima madre di tutte le madri, obbediente e incrollabile ragazzina dei cieli, lacuna terrestre nel cuore del figlio. Se fossi lei, stanotte sarei profondamente commossa e la mia vita mi parrebbe un nulla, che però brucia d'amore.

Martedí 16 febbraio 1965 Lucia compie i suoi ventinove anni per sempre.

Quel febbraio è il terzo piú freddo del ventesimo secolo, martedí 9 Roma viene sommersa dalla piú abbondante nevicata della sua storia: trenta centimetri di soffice bianco la ricoprono in meno di sette ore. Sul Paese si spande un'aria da fiaba nordica.

A Milano vento teso, nebbione e piovaschi producono alcuni effetti, tra i quali il mio benché insignificante ricovero all'Ospedale Maggiore Niguarda per bronchite acuta febbrile (40°), dal 3 marzo alle 10 del mattino fino alla successiva domenica 14.

Il ricovero tuttavia interessa perché, adesso che è responsabile di una vita altrui, Lucia fornisce finalmente – al dottor Russo, medico dell'ufficio accettazione dell'ospedale e indirettamente a sua figlia oggi, qui, nella storia dipoi – il primo riferimento concreto di residenza: viale Monza, numero 24.

Sulle mappe tridimensionali che immediatamente consulto, appare la facciata di un edificio a cinque piani con cortile interno. Sembra una di quelle case di ringhiera dove tutti si sta con tutti – e nelle quali avrei sempre amato abitare, per esprimere nei fatti la mia mitologia privata di famiglia comunitaria –, con ampio ingresso carrabile sormontato da balcone panciuto in ferro battuto verniciato bianco. Prenoto subito un b&b nel portone affianco, per la notte a cavallo tra febbraio e marzo 2022, circa quaranta giorni dopo il momento della prenotazione, quando prevedo che dovrò passare su questo libro l'ultima mano, quella della dolcezza e dell'addio.

La mattina del 28 febbraio 2022, entrando al civico 24, m'investe il soffio materiale di una vita di poche parole, fatta di gesti che hanno uno scopo. Non c'è spazio per la decorazione, qui la vita si attiene all'essenziale. La corte è un luogo della Milano segreta: oltrepassato l'ingresso, si aprono non uno ma due cortili interni, chiusi da due quadrilateri di palazzi bassi color mattone e collegati (l'uno all'altro ed entrambi al viale d'accesso) da una breve galleria passante sotto le abitazioni del primo piano. Sulla destra del primo cortile – fuori, nel cementato – è schierata una fila di cinque contenitori cilindrici a rete traspirante per immondizia: quelli che si aprono non già a pedale, come i moderni bidoni in plasticone verde, ma afferrando la maniglia fusa al coperchio che, quando ricade, fa il tonfo del metallo sul metallo, come quando qui c'erano il meccanico e il lattoniere. Immagino i colpi del battilamiera rimbalzare tra le pareti delle case, il sibilo tagliente della fiamma ossidrica che rifila le saldature, i goal dei ragazzini, contro i muri e le saracinesche e, insieme alle picchiate delle rondinelle, il grido delle madri che richiamano i figli per la cena.

Ecco il corpo del suono che raggiunge la vita di Lucia alla fine di agosto 1964, quando lei, incinta di sei mesi, varca il portone accanto al suo uomo. Qui è passata la vita di Lucia con la figlia in braccio, qui è stata sentita la speranza di una sistemazione, poi l'erosione della forza viva di una donna e di un uomo, nelle moltitudini. Questo è l'unico luogo del dispersivo spazio siderale dove ha vissuto l'insieme che un tempo mi concerneva, il microclima primario che sbozza la forma grossolana di un essere e la veste di strati di memoria, prima della proiezione nel freddo.

La tarda sera del 28 febbraio 2022 è spazzata da raffiche di vento barbaro, che raggiungono i 43 chilometri orari. Il termometro scende (di nuovo) sottozero. Sigillata in cappotto e cappuccio, esco a fumare sul ballatoio, richiudendo la portafinestra alle mie spalle, perché mia figlia non geli. La mia sigaretta della notte è un occhio di brace che assorbe la vita di Lucia dentro questa miniatura del suo villaggio. Chi lo sa a che piano abitavi, se pure tu vedevi la luminaria di finestre accese e le tremule stelle oltre i palazzi, quelle sagome umane che raccolgono il corpo per la notte. Rientrando in camera, mi colpisce la presenza fuori stagione di una mosca. Mi sbanda la ragione, sorrido all'insetto. Creatura con creatura.

Poi, i tre animali vivi in quell'interno si abbandonano al sonno e, nella camera sul nostro cortile d'allora, che ora galleggia dentro il cuore artico della notte, si materializza un caldo agostano, che costringe Anna e me a dormire svestite, fuori dalle coperte. Ci svegliamo nel primo mattino di marzo essendo state accompagnate in un nuovo mondo, dove le madri e le madri delle madri proteggono le figlie dal freddo tenendole sotto una cupola d'aria a temperatura corporea.

Il sole sorge alle spalle dei palazzi. Lucia adesso ha il colore dell'alba e di ogni luogo.

In nero

Nella cartella clinica del mio ricovero nel marzo 1965 esiste un altro dato che rileva: mamma viene registrata come «lavorante a ore non mutuata». Fantastico che il parroco dell'Addolorata, al quale Lucia si è certamente confessata, abbia trovato per lei qualche brava *sciura* che ha bisogno dell'aiuto di una gagliarda giovane di campagna per le cose di casa. Ma che è successo? Perché la madre di una bambina di quattro mesi, con un compagno finalmente attivo, fa le pulizie a ore nelle case?

Lo spiegherà ai giornali la signora Anita, moglie di Giuseppe, solo tre mesi dopo: Giuseppe, dopo la chiusura del cantiere – forse proprio quello della metro, dismesso a fine ottobre 1964 – rimane disoccupato: in quegli anni a Milano c'è sovrabbondanza di manodopera e Giuseppe è un uomo quasi anziano, che ha ricominciato da muratore come un garzoncello. A cinquantasei anni è piuttosto difficile reinventarsi la vita, specialmente se la propria offerta è lavoro manuale. Inoltre, negli anni Sessanta non esistono ancora gli antigelo per il calcestruzzo e cosí, da novembre ai primi tepori primaverili, la maggior parte dei cantieri chiude, specie quelli di Nord e regioni montane.

Quando Giuseppe incontra casualmente il fratello della moglie, impiegato postale a Milano, gli dice di essere in attesa di una somma dal Genio civile. Mente, per orgoglio. La sua Lucia, intanto, va a servizio. Naturalmente, in nero.

Martedí 27 aprile e 1 giugno 1965. Antipolio a Crescenzago

La terza somministrazione sarebbe dovuta avvenire a distanza di trenta giorni. Ma, trenta giorni dopo, Lucia non c'è piú. Né a Crescenzago, né a Milano, né altrove.

Ancora Bianciardi: «Lassú se caschi per terra nessuno ti raccatta e la forza che ho mi basta appena per non farmi mangiare dalle formiche e se riesco a campare credi pure che la vita è agra, lassú».
Lassú, nella Milano dei cantieri aperti.

Che ormai chiudono, uno dopo l'altro. Il miracolo economico è agli sgoccioli. E Giuseppe è un uomo maturo che forse, nonostante l'ottimismo naturale e il sovrappiú di energia con cui l'amore, quel malandrino refo di primavera, impavido lo sospinge, ha diritto di essere stanco, soprattutto quando si sente addosso pregiudizio ed emarginazione, stavolta non dovuti a moralismo – o non solo – ma perché quella coppia cosí strana è uno schizzo nell'onda gigantesca dell'offerta che risale la penisola, da Sud.

Lucia lo ama, lo ama certamente, o non avrebbe messo fieramente in moto la macchina dello scandalo che l'ha travolta, ma non ha fatto un buon investimento, scegliendo un uomo dalla forza contrattuale ormai usurata. Fortunatamente, chi ama non ragiona, si prende tutti i rischi dell'amore, tutte le conseguenze, anche giuridiche. Lucia sente di farcela: lavora lei, si espone, anche se non può essere assunta, né nella vecchia filanda, né nell'industria tessile locale, né altrove, perché sulla sua bella *capa* arruffata pende una denuncia penale, ed è quindi probabile che presti servizio (appunto in nero) in una delle ricche abitazioni lungo il naviglio Martesana. Negli anni Sessanta Crescenzago è detta «la Riviera di Milano»: immerse con balconate di fiori, pergole e ponti nella folta e cinguettante alberatura fluviale, vi insistono parecchie ville settecentesche, elette come luoghi di aristocratico riposo. Ma – penso – quanto può guadagnare una ragazza che deve vivere nascosta, all'erta, e senza nome? Esploro dunque la possibilità che io sia stata vaccinata a Crescenzago perché, quando Lucia ha dovuto *sostenere* (questa parola tornerà tra poco) da sola la nostra piccola famiglia, per risparmiare abbiamo traslocato da viale Monza al quartiere satellite dell'urbe. Le ricerche in Crescenzago non danno però risultato. Noi non abbiamo mai abitato qui.

«E allora che ci facevo, io, a sei mesi, a Crescenzago?»
Cosí vocifero, piú e meno interiormente, finché un bel giorno la buca delle lettere contiene la cartellina gialla che aspettavo e la semplice aggiunta della precisazione «servizio medico-scolastico» in testa al certificato vaccinale cartaceo, mette immediato ordine nell'ingarbuglio degli elementi: per poter lavorare, Lucia mi affida al nido comunale piú vicino al suo posto di lavoro, perché Giuseppe, a primavera e con le riaperture dei cantieri, si è certo rimesso in moto per cercare un impiego.

Vivere, in certi casi, può significare una progressiva rinuncia ai desideri dell'inizio. Per sopravvivere, Lucia rinuncia ai primi sogni, come un albero senz'acqua lascia cadere i fiori, poco a poco. Prende esempio dall'albero.

Ma non basta, non basta, non basta ancora. Giuseppe non trova. Niente. E l'asilo, a giugno: chiude. Una svolta in salita. Sono soli, lui e lei. Lucia e Giuseppe – e tutto il mondo altrove, oppure contro. Forse è lui, a trascinarla nella propria stanchezza: è la terza volta che fallisce, in una vita sola. Forse è troppo, forse ciondola vinto e avvilito, non si può piú permettere neanche una di quelle tossiche granite viola del dopolavoro, lo scioglimento sciropposo da due soldi che inchiostra la lingua e lo fa contento. O una fetta di carne per Lucia, che allatta. E Lucia condivide fino alla fine la sorte dell'uomo che ha voluto. Pazza, onesta, sfinita. E la sua vita è legno da tempesta.

«Mettendo la mia vita nelle sue mani, ero stato in grado di spingermi là dove, senza di lui, non mi sarei mai spinto», scrive Vitaliano Trevisan. Forse qualcuno li ricorda ancora. Quella madre bruna, col compagno che sembra suo padre e una neonata in braccio, fermi per sempre nel fluoro di un tramonto industriale.

La stessa persona

A Crescenzago c'è una casa di ringhiera chiamata la *curt de l'America*, forse perché, proprio dirimpetto, parte il tram per Stazione Centrale, dove si prende il treno verso Genova, e poi si salpa per il vivo, per il sogno a colori della Merica.

Negli anni Sessanta la corte è un microcosmo, un villaggio coi suoi negozi: spaccio alimentare, parrucchiere, ferramenta, panettiere. Il retro del palazzo affaccia sul metro d'acqua del Naviglio, che è insieme spiaggia privata e discarica, pure dei vasi detti «da notte», benché usati da tutti anche in orario diurno, visto che i gabinetti sono esterni, due per quattro famiglie di quattro o cinque persone ciascuna. Ma si vive anche bene, il cortile è di tutti, i ragazzini giocano a pallone fino a sera, le donne stendono i panni e commentano guai e soddisfazioni di quella comunità fondata sul bisogno; ogni tanto si litiga per una cipolla, poi ci si riappacifica e si mangia insieme.

Gli emigranti di allora come gli arabi oggi: stipati dentro case provvisorie piene di infiltrazioni, di spifferi e d'acqua, lavorano pochi giorni al mese e non possono programmare niente.

«Non è quello che avevamo sognato...»
Questo sospiro attraversa la storia, pronunciato in tutte le lingue e i dialetti del mondo con lo stesso dolore, la stessa rabbia, la stessa rassegnazione, come fossimo tutti la stessa persona.

Gesti e anima di Lucia Galante

I palatesi che vivono in Lombardia raramente hanno accesso alla metropoli, alloggiano quasi tutti nella cintura esterna di Milano, tra Monza, Bollate e Lissone. A Monza, dal 1962 vive un compaesano che è riuscito a sistemarsi bene, lavora nella fabbrica della Società elettrica nazionale e ha aiutato molti meridionali, affluiti negli anni, a trovare casa e inserirsi nell'organico della ditta, fornendo ai datori di lavoro le garanzie necessarie: assicurando, cioè, che i soggetti da lui medesimo proposti non soffrano dei vizi endemici che l'immaginazione attribuisce loro (tra i piú frequenti, scarso interesse nei confronti dell'attività lavorativa stessa).

Un giorno di primavera inoltrata, alla sua porta bussa Lucia. È sola e non va a chiedere lavoro, né per sé né per il suo Giuseppe. Come già calcolato e ripercorso, ha fatto oltre due ore e mezza di strada a piedi lungo viale Monza. O mezz'ora sui mezzi pubblici, un piccolo viaggio. Lucia è venuta a chiedere l'indirizzo del suo fidanzatino dell'adolescenza, Tonino De Grandis.

Sicuramente le è arrivata voce che il gruppo di amici e colleghi del suo paese s'incontra, alla domenica, per delle belle gite fuori porta alla cascina di Tonino, dove Lucia non è ovviamente invitata.

Sono undici minuti di macchina attraverso la velenosa Brianza, lungo viale Cesare Battisti, dal quale ci si immette nella statale 36 del lago di Como e dello Spluga – o, in alternativa, se si ha il tempo di allungare il viaggio di qualche minuto, si percorre via Boito, che diventa la verdeggiante provinciale 111. In quei tempi, è tutta campagna. Sopravvivono oggi gli ulivi.

Lucia non sa dove sia la cascina. Ma sa che Antonio non è piú il suo Tonino degli anni leggeri: ora è sposato, ha due figli, il secondo gli è nato nel 1963. Lucia lo sa.

E il compaesano non se la sente di portare turbamento nella vita ordinata dell'amico e rifiuta il favore a Lucia, ma informa Tonino di quella visita misteriosa: «La tua ragazzina di Palata è venuta a cercarti». A Tonino rimane tanto impressa la notizia da riferirmela, cinquantasei anni dopo.

Lucia, che cerchi? Cosa vorresti chiedere al tuo primo amore e, per la prima volta, con la tua voce?

Ci verrò io, da lui, e non varrà nulla. Ma Tonino sentirà il bisogno di abbracciare mia figlia, farle vedere la sua bicicletta e il banco di lavoro e quante cose sa fare e che brav'uomo è stato, in tutti questi anni. Ecco, la vedi, questa
 è la vita mia. Guardala, per favore.

Il regalo è il sorriso di Anna, che attraversa le generazioni e si posa
  su questa vita finalmente vista.

L'ultima porta

Martedí 1 giugno 1965: Lucia mi porta a Crescenzago per il richiamo dell'antipolio, seguendo scrupolosamente le istruzioni mediche. Pochi giorni dopo torna, sempre sola, alla masseria dei genitori con la sua piccola di sette mesi, e si ferma una notte. Il fratello è in servizio militare a Udine e la mamma sbriga le solite faccende con fare nuovo, va tutta rianimata verso l'orto, a cogliere primizie per la cena.

La scena si svolge al piano terra. Piú che una scena, l'istantanea di un crocevia. È pomeriggio, protagoniste sono cinque donne: una è Laura, la bambina che osserva e, cinquant'anni dopo, illumina con le parole questo frammento di vita, per me che trascrivo ogni dettaglio col metodo di una forsennata scienza. Una sono io: ancora inconsapevole di tutto, me ne sto sdraiata all'aria aperta, dentro una cesta di vimini appoggiata sull'aia. Poi c'è un piccolo crocchio formato da tre donne, due giovani e una anziana. Una delle due giovani è Lucia.

Topolino starebbe sdraiato come una coperta ai piedi di Lucia, ma può solo sentirla arrivare fin da sotto la terra dell'aiola, scodinzolare immobile per lei. Lucia lo sente, gira gli occhi a quel cespo di rose che trema
e lo sa, che non è per il vento.

Lucia indossa una camicetta bianca a maniche corte e una gonnellina nera pieghettata, che le arriva al ginocchio. Lucia adesso veste da città. Le sta bene ogni cosa che si mette, anche questo abitino da collegiale: è tornata magrissima, ha sempre la sua aria da bambina espansiva e sincera e parla a bassa voce con sorella e madre nello spiazzo davanti alla casa, con parole che cambiano il destino.

Il mattino dopo, Lucia non c'è piú. La madre piange, è disperata, a stento smozzica le frasi:
«Se n'è andata, perché non è rimasta? Io non so niente... Le ho detto rimani! Dice che non poteva rimanere. Con chi è andata via, non lo so... Non so niente...»

Lucia sapeva di non poter restare. Lucia rischia due anni di galera. O, peggio, di tornare dal marito. Dunque, che cerca? Perché va via con l'alba e la bambina, senza un saluto?

16 giugno 1965. Minore di una

Il 16 giugno 1965, primo giorno del mio nono mese di vita, Lucia va al Comune di Milano e richiede il mio certificato di nascita, nel quale, a completare il vuoto alla voce «Padre», figura il nome di Luigi. Lucia intende darmi un'identità. E, con essa, proteggermi dal rifiuto che subirò comunque, essendo ritenuta «figlia del peccato». Insisto a ripeterlo come lei – irrazionale, lucidissima – insisteva: Lucia spera che dichiararmi formalmente figlia del marito basti a darmi lo statuto legale di figlia legittima, benché il marito sappia di aver lasciato illibata la sposa. Ormai tutto, ogni gesto, va inserito in un quadro piú grande. Ormai tutto è pensato per un unico scopo, è parte di un piano. Calmo, severo, perché ormai irrevocabile.

Roma

Giovedí 24 giugno 1965, ore 15,30. Deposizione

Il sole splende su Roma nel primo pomeriggio d'estate.
È il sole generoso di giovedí 24 giugno 1965, sono quasi le quattro del pomeriggio. Presidente della Repubblica è Giuseppe Saragat, Aldo Moro è presidente del Consiglio, suo vicepresidente Pietro Nenni.
Tra un'ora i Beatles suoneranno al Velodromo Vigorelli di Milano e replicheranno in serata, suscitando insania, e incassando cinquantotto milioni in un giorno. Domani, a Roma, ricambieranno la tiepida accoglienza capitolina suonando giusto mezz'oretta.
Ma adesso il trentaquattrenne Ivo Micucci se ne va in sé tranquillo dentro il sole che illumina viale Giorgio Washington, la strada che percorre quotidianamente per andare al lavoro al C.N.E.L. (Consiglio nazionale dell'economia e del lavoro), organo di consulenza del governo, dal 1958 ospitato nella storica sede di Villa Lubin, edificata a inizio secolo alla sommità di un piccolo poggio.
Come mi racconterà lo stesso Micucci nel 1995, data della seconda tappa di avvicinamento all'inchiesta che questo libro conclude, l'attenzione dell'Ivo di allora viene attratta da un'anomalia, quasi muta e invisibile: una neonata seduta su una coperta parlotta tra sé, sul prato poco oltre gli imponenti propilei d'ingresso da piazzale Flaminio in Villa Borghese. La bambina sta sola sulla sua copertina in mezzo al prato poco oltre gli enormi portali. Non piange, ma è una strana apparizione. Tra il suo piccolo corpo, tra

le sue poche forze e l'esterno del mondo c'è una sproporzione eccessiva.

Il giovane è colpito, gli prende il desiderio di soccorrere. Si guarda intorno, non vede nessuno. La bambina, invece, intercetta il suo sguardo e gli tende le braccia. Dopo qualche indugio, Ivo si china a raccogliere la neonata e in quel momento registra, con la coda dell'occhio, la figura di una giovane donna che si allontana di corsa.

Il «patetico esserino che urla a squarciagola» («Paese Sera» del 25 giugno, peraltro poco oltre, nello stesso articolo, riferendo di suoi «vagiti flebili») e «coperto di stracci» (sempre «Paese Sera» il 30 giugno) o addirittura «nascosto in un mucchio di stracci» («Il Messaggero», 30 giugno), rinvenuto, piuttosto, intra l'erba di Villa Borghese, è Greco Maria Grazia. Io, Maria Grazia Calandrone, nascerò piú tardi.

Un guardamacchine di piazzale Flaminio conferma ai carabinieri di aver intravisto, intorno alle 15,30 o qualche minuto piú tardi, «una coppia poveramente vestita, quasi certamente contadini, che si aggirava con aria incerta, forse disperata, nel prato dove poco dopo veniva trovata la piccina» (ancora «Paese Sera», 25 giugno).
Nel medesimo giorno, «l'Unità» sostiene che gli indumenti della bambina confermino l'ipotesi che sia figlia di povera gente. La neonata che porta il mio antico nome è deposta su un plaid rosa a quadretti azzurri e indossa una maglietta color crema, una camicina bianca e un abitino chiaro con il ricamo di una testa d'asino. La temperatura esterna è di 37 gradi. Si potrebbe pensare che Lucia, come tutte le madri, abbia una paura irrazionale che la sua creatura prenda freddo. Ma Lucia ha ragione, lei lo sa, che Maria Grazia è sempre intirizzita. Mamma e io non abbiamo ancora mai passato insieme la bella estate, che sola mi emancipa dalla costrizione nei panni. Per il momento, è

rimasta svestita la mia bambola; ma adesso non è con me, è a mezz'ora di strada da me.

Ivo Micucci porta la neonata a bere un po' di latte nella caffetteria della propria sede di lavoro e l'insolita presenza rimane impressa nella sensibilità di molti dei conferenzieri presenti, tra i quali un dirigente del Partito comunista italiano, Giacomo Calandrone. Micucci consegna poi la bambina agli agenti di servizio al C.N.E.L., i quali mi traducono alla Stazione di tenenza Flaminia dei carabinieri, dove il tenente Antonio Varisco conduce le prime indagini.

Varisco, che dal 1966 sarà al comando del servizio scorte del Tribunale di Roma, verrà ucciso dalle Brigate Rosse con una scarica di fucile a canne mozze nella mattina del 13 luglio 1979, quattordici anni dopo essersi occupato di rintracciare ovunque i miei genitori. Nel 1982 Antonio Varisco viene insignito della medaglia d'oro al Valor Civile «alla memoria».

Dato che è vivo e ha sentimenti giusti, Varisco spera che i genitori vengano a chiedere della neonata. Non accade. Alle 18,45, dopo circa tre ore di vana attesa, il maresciallo Del Gaudio, della caserma dei carabinieri Flaminio, si risolve a consegnare l'«infante anonimo di sesso femminile» alle suore dell'I.P.A.I. (Istituto provinciale per l'assistenza all'infanzia) di Villa Doria Pamphili, che in quel momento ospita altri quattrocentoquarantuno figli di ignoti e novecentocinquanta ne ha già affidati, in quell'anno, a famiglie o altri istituti. Questa la cubatura, il tonnellaggio degli abbandoni neonatali, all'epoca.

La neonata viene contrassegnata con medaglia recante numero progressivo 65124. «La bambina è sveglia, balbetta parecchie parole. Nessun dente», si legge nella sua cartella clinica. Mangio di buon appetito e mi addormento «così profondamente che non è possibile svegliar*mi* per far*mi* altre fotografie» («Il Messaggero», 25 giugno). In effetti, è stata una delle giornate piú impegnative della mia vita. Scrivo «mia» pur non avendo autentica coscienza di essere quella bambina. Solo contatto, la descrizione del temperamento: allegra.

Ti chiamavo col pianto (tra i propilei neoclassici)

Luogo e momento dell'abbandono sono ovviamente significativi. A otto mesi, in un giardino d'estate.

Il luogo, come ho scritto, è a un passo dai propilei neoclassici del monumentale ingresso di Villa Borghese da piazzale Flaminio, realizzati nel 1827 da Luigi Canina su commissione del principe Camillo Borghese. Un luogo veramente molto strano dove lasciare una neonata. Il luogo è sproporzionato, dispersivo, enorme. Il piccolo corpo si sente perduto. O è la porta d'accesso a un altro mondo, sognato. Ma il piccolo corpo ha bisogno d'aiuto anche solo per muoversi. Tra poco, non piú dell'aiuto di chiunque.

Il tempo: tanto perfetto da sbalordire. Allo scadere del mio ottavo mese, Lucia richiede il mio certificato di nascita. Una settimana dopo è a Roma, per abbandonarmi.

A otto mesi il neonato comincia a variare la propria alimentazione. È finita la fase dello svezzamento. A otto mesi comincia a gattonare e a tenere gli oggetti adoperando il pollice opponibile. A otto mesi il neonato comincia a sospettare di essere un corpo diverso dal corpo materno e questo suscita nella sua biologia (in quel momento quasi completamente sovrapponibile alla sua psicologia) lo spavento di essere lasciato solo nella propria incompetenza a vivere, dentro un silenzio velenoso, radiante come cadmio. Siamo a un passo dall'ansia di separazione dalla madre, ma il neonato è ancora figlio di tutti.

Una scelta cosí incredibilmente indovinata può essere casuale? Ma non posso davvero immaginare che i miei genitori, col manuale di puericultura aperto sul tavolo in viale Monza, aspettino, per lasciarmi, il momento in cui comincio a diventare autonoma, ma non ancora abbastanza consapevole della realtà da rendere l'abbandono troppo doloroso e destabilizzante per la mia crescita psichica. Ammesso che il momento sia stato scelto con tanto criterio, ritengo piú probabile che Lucia e Giuseppe abbiano solo letto e interpretato i nuovi segnali emanati dalla creatura misteriosa che fui, i primi pianti di richiamo quando mamma si allontana da me. Come Semmelweis, ogni madre possiede la sua scienza empirica, fatta di osservazione e deduzione.

Per istinto infallibile, scienza o caso fortunato, vengo comunque lasciata prima che lasciarmi diventi impossibile, forse cristallizzandomi, cosí, nell'età in cui il neonato è appunto «ancora figlio di tutti».

La foto pubblicata da «Oggi Illustrato» dice che ormai, aggrappata alle sbarre del lettino, so stare in piedi da sola. Le altissime colonne dei propilei somigliano alle sbarre di un lettino neonatale. Per il neonato, la proporzione interiore è piú o meno la stessa.

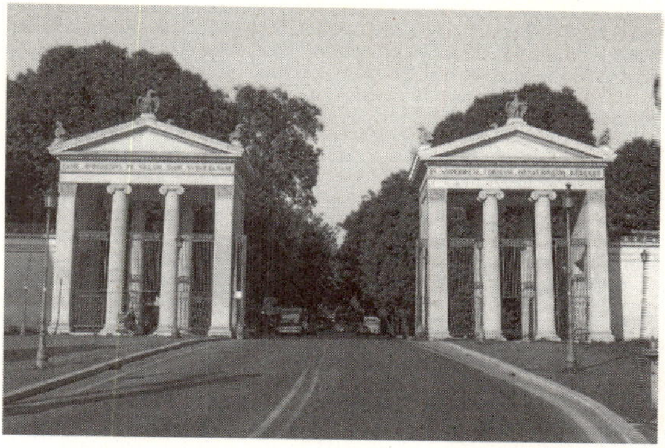

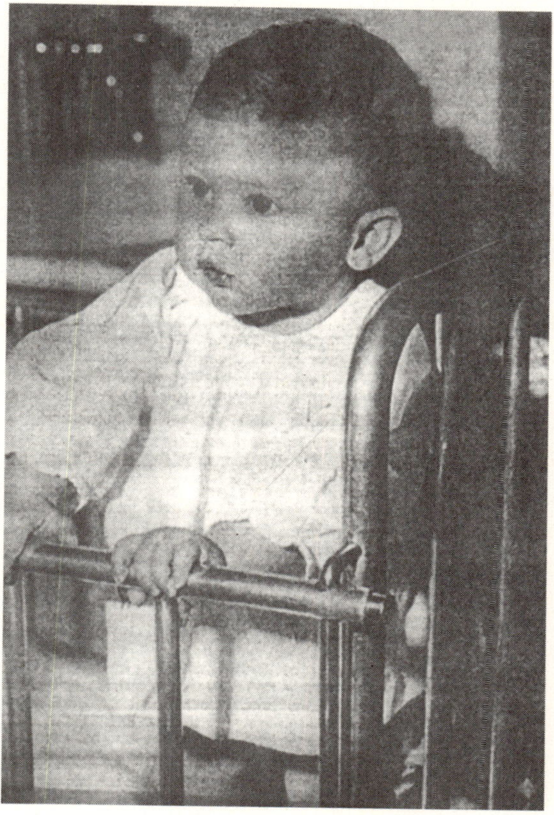

Sabato 26 giugno. La lettera

Nella mattina di sabato 26 giugno il primo giro di consegne postali recapita all'«Unità» una lettera recante il timbro di «Roma Ferrovia» e la data del 25 giugno 1965 – ore 10 del mattino:

> La bambina trovata a Villa Borghese si chiama Greco Maria Grazia. Nata a Milano il giorno 15 ottobre 1965 [*sic*]. L'ho abbandonata in Roma. Perché il mio amico non aveva possibilità finanziarie da sostenerla e mio marito cioè suo padre diceva che non era sua. Trovandomi in condizioni disperate, Non ho scelto altro che la strada di lasciare mia figlia alla compassione di tutti, ed io con il mio amico pagheremo con la vita ciò che abbiamo fatto, o, indovinato o, sbagliato
>
> Galante Lucia in Greco

Tunc acceptabis sacrificium iustitiae, oblationes, et holocausta: tunc imponent super altare tuum vitulos. Allora accetterai il sacrificio, le oblazioni e gli olocausti: ecco, sopra l'altare, il tuo vitello.

La spedizione documenta che almeno uno dei due, fino alle prime ore della mattina del 25 giugno è ancora in vita, strillano uno sull'altro i cronachisti di tutti i quotidiani, copiando uno dall'altro.

Secondo «l'Unità» di mercoledí 30 giugno, poi, nel pomeriggio di venerdí 25, Lucia e Giuseppe inviano altre poche parole alla direzione dell'istituto nel quale sanno, dai giornali, che sono ricoverata, confermando il mio nome e cognome e confermando di essere «nella determinazione di uccidersi». Nell'archivio dell'I.P.A.I., dentro il plico che mi riguarda, non è incluso alcun biglietto.

Nonostante il dispiegamento di fonogrammi e indagini messo in moto dal capo della Mobile dottor Nicola Scirè – il fascinoso, colto e temutissimo «Maigret del Lazio», che nel 1973 subirà una condanna dall'esito incerto per favoreggiamento di una bisca clandestina in via Flaminia Vecchia – non c'è traccia di Galante Lucia in Greco, né del suo «amico» ancora senza nome. I loro passaggi non sono registrati in alberghi o pensioni, né pare abbiano mai affittato posti letto, a Roma o nell'intera regione Lazio. Essi non sono stati. In nessun luogo.

Fiume. Guarda l'acqua come ride

Nel 1965 il Tevere è ancora protagonista della vita romana. Una strada come le altre, la gialla e popolosa strada d'acqua, percorsa in ogni direzione da bagnanti, ciclisti e *flâneur*. I romani lo chiamano Fiume, senza l'articolo, come un nome proprio. Temuto e amato, Fiume spesso si porta via la vita di qualche temerario, o accompagna a morire chi ha in sé troppo scontento per campare:
«Me vado a buttà a Fiume»,
è la soluzione, drastica e rapida, quando la vita presenta nodi che appaiono inestricabili, è il sogno di pace che nel 1961 aleggia sull'intera vita di Accattone, protagonista del primo film di Pasolini: giú da ponte a volo d'angelo e la mala vita finisce.
«Vai, che Fiume pija tutti!»
lo sbeffeggia il Moicano, un sodale della compagnia di perdigiorno. Prende, sí. E non è detto che restituisca.

Ogni tanto straripa, inonda Roma, si riprende lo spazio che i muraglioni contengono, e gli contendono. Tra il 1964 e il 1965 Fiume si gonfia e distende i suoi muscoli in tre piene monumentali (due nel dicembre 1964, la terza il 3 settembre 1965), si ripiglia in un *amen* la misura divina.
Il Tevere respira davanti alla riposante nullità dei mortali, i quali, d'estate, quando il sole rovescia calura sull'urbe, stazionano sui banchi sabbiosi delle sue rive, o si tuffano nella sua dorata frescura, per sfuggire allo sciame incalzante dei raggi. Dopo il tramonto, quando si allungano le om-

bre, si trasloca sui tavolati degli stabilimenti balneari e dei barconi, dove ci sono bar e ristoranti. Si mangia, si balla, ci si ubriaca. Qualche volta si scivola nell'acqua.

Dagli anni Venti del Novecento sulla riva sinistra del Tevere, appena oltre ponte Milvio, dove oggi corre Lungotevere Flaminio, c'è la spiaggia Polverini, cosí chiamata dal nome del traghettatore che porta i bagnanti verso Prato Falcone, sulla destra. È la spiaggia tra ponte Duca d'Aosta e ponte Risorgimento, una piazza di sabbia bianca e fina con la vista sul verde arruffo di Monte Mario. «Il Messaggero» scrive che, lí sotto, i bagnanti «profittano delle libertà di cui possono usufruire per la strada quasi deserta, si denudano e si bagnano rimanendo al sole, alcuni per l'intera giornata». Polverini è sorella in magnificenza alla riva inurbata della Renella in Trastevere, che ovviamente, però, non permette di spogliarsi, per non offrire la propria suggestiva nudità allo sguardo indiscreto dei passanti.

L'anno piú triste dei fiumaroli è il 1932, quando devono lasciare la Polverini alla colonia estiva dei marinaretti del Duce. *Er duce s'è bevuto puro Fiume*. La diaspora divide per la prima volta i fiumaroli per censo: i piú abbienti si possono permettere gli ampi spazi galleggianti di circoli privati e dopolavoro, i proletari affollano i barconi attrezzati a stabilimenti, come la chiatta di Luigi Rodolfo Benedetti, «er Ciriola de Sant'Angelo», che a Ferragosto è piú gremita di Ostia e viene pure eletta come set da qualche gigantesco cinematografaro di passaggio: nel 1953, William Wyler fa vivere su quella piattaforma acquatica un frammento galeotto delle *Vacanze romane* di Audrey Hepburn e Gregory Peck e, quattro anni piú tardi, Dino Risi scatena sul fondale del Ciriola i suoi *Poveri ma belli*, film nel quale, alla simpatia dei fustacchioni in braghe di tela, risponde l'astuta ritrosia di fanciullette formose. Infine, nel 1961 è su quelle tavole che Accattone vede ballare la sua amata Stella con un altro uomo.

Ciriola è l'anguilla, in dialetto. Er Ciriola è pescatore d'anguille, nonché salvatore di anfibi antropomorfi: la parte d'acqua recintata dai pali davanti al suo stabilimento si chiama «gallinaro», e frotte di bambini pigolanti sguazzano tutti i giorni entro quei limiti certi: al sicuro, specie nei pomeriggi di secca e d'arsura. Bella, la fiumana vociante dei bambini in mutande di cotone dentro l'acqua materna di Fiume, sotto l'occhio dorato del custode e il sole che si abbassa su di loro. Ma a quell'occhio tocca tené d'occhio anche tanti innamorati delusi, che compiono il «gesto estremo» giusto nei pressi del bagnino pluridecorato al valore civile per i suoi oltre duecento salvataggi. L'amore ha le sue leggi dell'onore. Ma pure la vita, pure *il voler vivere* è una legge.

Di lí a pochissimo, la crescita demografica e l'inurbamento inquinano le acque e diffondono il pericolo di leptospirosi e possibile sua complicazione in sindrome di Weil, dall'esito spesso letale. Ecco allora il divieto di balneazione, e Roma vedova del suo mare urbano.

Ma ogni tanto l'acqua ancora ride. Ridere è un termine antico, dice dell'acqua che scoppietta e saltella come di gioia, dice le schicchere delle piccole onde dove il fondale è basso, o incontra ostacoli.

Domenica 27 giugno. Il costume da bagno

Nella tarda mattinata di domenica 27 giugno la signora Dotti scorge tra le acque del fiume Tevere un corpo femminile affiorante.

Il corpo galleggia all'altezza del Lungotevere degli Inventori, poco oltre ponte Marconi, proprio dove la sindaca Virginia Raggi farà riabilitare la spiaggetta estiva. La signora Dotti informa immediatamente la vicina stazione di Polizia portuense.

La Polizia fluviale ripesca il corpo e lo trae a riva. Annota che la donna ha capelli sciolti, lunghi e neri, misura un'altezza di un metro e sessantacinque centimetri, è scalza e priva di documenti, ma porta la fede all'anulare sinistro. Indossa un abito marrone a fiorellini e una sottoveste color crema. Sotto i vestiti, ha un costume da bagno. Un gesto di pudore
            definitivo.

Oppure, una stranezza che insospettisce molti, perché in quell'anno il Tevere è appunto ancora balneabile.

Era lei. «Bellissima statua sommersa»

L'abbiamo capito subito, che si tratta di lei.
Chinarsi su quel corpo diventato sconosciuto e cominciare a ripulire il volto. Guardare la materia finché parla. Ascoltare ogni parola pronunciata dal corpo, dalla sua lontananza irrimediabile. Raccogliere il significato dal corpo abbandonato. A che scopo.
Lucia, voglio rimettere il sorriso morbido e infantile di quand'eri innamorata, al posto dello spasimo del *rictus* che, nel mattino domenicale, piega le tue labbra in una smorfia di delusione senza rimedio. Per te affronto il sarcasmo involontario dei suicidi sopra il deserto della vita che si lasciano dietro. Voglio fare fiorire la tua pietra.

Ispeziono dunque, per prima, la teoria di un bagno al fiume finito in tragedia.
Da qualche giorno i romani sono resi ancora piú indolenti da un'ondata di caldo improvviso e anomalo, che squaglia le strade cittadine e «Il Tempo» del 27 giugno arriva a definire «*blitz-krieg*, guerra lampo», cosí proseguendo: «i commandos dell'estate sono entrati in azione, con il lanciafiamme in pugno». Le magnificenti fontane di Roma sono prese d'assalto da chi cerca refrigerio, le sirene delle autobotti dei pompieri squarciano l'afa dei pomeriggi correndo a spegnere le combustioni spontanee delle boscaglie urbane, come quella nei pressi di via Cortina d'Ampezzo, che richiede l'impiego di ben quattro mezzi, risultati comunque insufficienti a evitare la distruzione quasi com-

pleta dell'area verde. In tutta Italia muoiono persone, per «paralisi cardiaca e insolazione» e molte aziende prendono la decisione di fare ponte fino a martedí 29, ricorrenza dei santi Pietro e Paolo, che nel 1965 è ancora nazionale e solo dal 1977 rimarrà festa patronale esclusivamente romana. Dalla serata di venerdí 25 giugno, dunque, il caldo e l'insperato ponte lungo lasciano le città arse e semivuote.

Proviamo a inserire in questo scenario apocalittico una coppia che giovedí 24 ha abbandonato la figlia neonata all'ingresso di un parco pubblico.

«Lucia, andiamo a prendere il sole sul greto».

Poi la ragazza scivola nel fiume, come la Marinella di De André. Cosa dovrebbe averne fatto, di te, Lucia, il tuo bel muratore senza corona?

Rifiuto categoricamente l'ipotesi, offensiva per la dignità e il dolore di Lucia e Giuseppe, che, uno o due giorni dopo essersi separati dalla sottoscritta, Lucia sia stata attratta da Giuseppe – o da chiunque altro – sulla spiaggia fluviale con la promessa di un bagno di sole e sia stata invece spinta in acqua, o vi sia incautamente slittata.

Come scopriremo tra poco, Lucia possiede alcuni capi di biancheria. Entro nella mente, allora raziocinante, di mia madre, entro nella sua anima pensante: Lucia considera che anche un vestitino scuro come quello che ha scelto per morire, una volta impregnato d'acqua, diventa trasparente, si solleva in maniere ormai incontrollabili e scomposte, o aderisce al corpo, sagomandone la forma come per nudità, e decide di serbare il proprio contegno infilando, in vece della propria biancheria, il costume comprato due anni prima per le sue cure di fertilità.

Dunque, indossare il costume da bagno, al contrario di quanto apparirebbe evidente, contraddice ogni proposito di balneazione in Lucia, e manifesta invece la sua precisa e autonoma determinazione a uccidersi per acqua.

Indossare il costume da bagno sotto il vestito è il gesto sacro di una donna che non vuole essere sconcia, neanche da morta. Indossare il costume da bagno sotto il vestito è l'ultimo gesto di rispetto per sé e per il proprio corpo, di chi pure lo sta accompagnando a morire. Ma con dignità. Provo un grande e commosso rispetto per la sua decisione.

Miserere

> *Madre*
> Come una ferita porto te
> sulla fronte, che non si rimargina.
> Non sempre fa male. E il cuore
> non se ne sbocca via fino a morire.
> Solo talvolta d'un tratto son cieco e sento
> sangue nella bocca
>
> GOTTFRIED BENN, *Morgue*

Il fatto che il corpo sia visibile da riva dimostra che è affiorato in superficie. Perché il corpo galleggia?

L'ipotesi piú semplice: al suo interno i batteri hanno già cominciato a produrre metano, anidride carbonica e idrogeno solforato. Secondo le tabelle di riaffioramento, nei mesi caldi tra giugno e agosto, ove non ostino altri impedimenti o agganciamenti subacquei, il corpo torna in superficie dopo almeno due giorni dal decesso. Non sembra dunque praticabile l'ipotesi che Lucia si sia gettata in acqua poche ore prima, cioè nella giornata di sabato 26, come riporta l'urna funeraria.

La piccola scatola di zinco che contiene le ossa di Lucia – fortunosamente recuperata dall'ossario comune, dopo un precoce disseppellimento del quale non sono stata informata – fornisce infatti dati quantomeno dubbi: sopra di essa sono scritte a pennarello nero la data di morte del 26 giugno 1965, che ho sempre creduto fosse stata trascritta dal referto del medico legale, e una data di nascita incorretta: 19 anziché 16 febbraio.

Se vogliamo provare a considerare valida la data di morte del 26 giugno, dunque un riaffioramento piuttosto precoce del corpo di Lucia il 27 mattina, dobbiamo prendere in considerazione due ipotesi, una straziante, l'altra agghiacciante.

La prima ipotesi è il laringospasmo: i polmoni di Lucia sono rimasti pieni d'aria a causa di una reazione disperata e involontaria del corpo che, nel dieci per cento dei casi, interviene a proteggere se stesso corpo, cosí bruttato dalla volontà di morte di chi lo abita. Il corpo ingaggia una lotta muta tra la propria volontà di vivere e la volontà di morire di chi lo muove, producendo violenti conati di vomito (per espellere il liquido penetrato nell'albero respiratorio), laringospasmo (chiusura della gola), seguito da edema polmonare (congestione dei polmoni). Attraverso lo spasmo della glottide, il corpo sigilla le vie respiratorie superiori e impedisce, all'estraneo liquido, ogni accesso alle vie aeree del sommerso. Naturalmente, si tratta di un desiderio tutto fisico di vita che può condurre a morte: se nel frattempo la volontà suicida decade, permettendo alla persona di guadagnare la superficie, tutto torna a respirare; se, viceversa, l'immersione dura piú a lungo della capacità individuale di apnea, la persona va via da questo mondo soffocando all'asciutto, pur trovandosi immersa dentro l'acqua. La fine è stata solo rimandata di qualche secondo.

In questo caso, si parla di «annegamento secco» e il corpo galleggia, tenuto in superficie dall'aria contenuta nei polmoni, anche se non è ancora trascorso abbastanza tempo dal momento del decesso perché, nell'organismo appena tradito, si instauri la produzione dei gas dovuti alla scissione cellulare: il corpo mantiene i polmoni leggeri, pieni di aria, non appesantiti e diluiti dall'acqua, come accade nell'annegamento per ingestione di liquido.

Se ha avuto un laringospasmo letale, Lucia potrebbe essersi gettata in acqua addirittura la mattina stessa e non piú il galleggiamento, ma lo studio di altri elementi, permetterebbero la datazione del suo gesto mortale. Contro se stessa?

Oppure – ecco infatti la seconda ipotesi – Lucia è colata a picco già morta o incosciente e, dunque, con le vie aeree superiori e i polmoni normalmente pieni d'aria inalata, ma ormai incapace di prodursi salvezza, né nuovi atti respiratori.

Gli accennati reperti

Mentre studio quello che mai avrei voluto studiare, il susseguirsi dei processi cadaverici, attraverso i quali meglio approssimare data e causa di morte della donna che mi ha dato vita, questa vita mia, vengo percossa dalla suggestiva bellezza di alcune parole, che affiorano dall'Enciclopedia Treccani, alla voce *Annegamento*: «Talora si hanno saponificazioni parziali, aspetto cretaceo per incrostazioni di sali calcarei, vegetazioni di muffe, d'alghe o di altri prodotti della fauna e della flora delle acque, non esclusa la produzione di microfiti pigmentati, che talora impartiscono al cadavere strani aspetti vellutati, colorati, erbacei».

Tutto, davvero tutto, può diventare poesia. *Morgue*, lo scarno (è il caso di dire) volumetto di versi, scritto intorno all'omonimo luogo dal geniale anatomopatologo Gottfried Benn, lo testimonia dal 1912. *Macello*, di Ivano Ferrari, lo conferma nel 2004. Versi di pena caustica, rabbiosa, affilata, stralunata, la commozione come una ferita aperta che continua a buttare sangue, finché la trascuriamo. Bisogna lasciar affiorare dalla ferita parole lucide fino allo spasimo. Mostruose, come queste.

Torno dunque alla domanda cruciale sul perché il corpo abbandonato da Lucia – quel tocco di pura materia detto cadavere, nel quale niente riconosciamo di colei che fu viva – sia ritornato a galla nell'afosa mattinata di domenica 27 giugno e la data di morte attribuita sia il 26.

Nel caso di annegamento per acqua, i gas si concentrano in torso e addome; nel caso di annegamento asciutto (per laringospasmo o morte precedente all'affondamento) l'aria rimane sigillata all'interno del solo torace.

Immagino che, nel primo caso, il corpo gonfiato dai gas affiori a faccia in giú, con testa e arti rivolti verso il fondo, nella posizione cosí detta «del lottatore», ed emerga francamente a galla l'intero dorso, come trainato verso il cielo; nel secondo caso, immagino che affiori il solo tronco, mentre il resto del corpo flotta semisommerso, dentro quell'acqua dolce come il male.

Nell'impossibilità forse cronologica, certamente morale, di perturbare la signora Dotti con domande circa la posizione del corpo rispetto alla superficie del fiume, sulla presenza o meno dell'indiziario *fungo schiumoso* sulle labbra, serrate o dischiuse, sul colore e l'aspetto delle povere, delle intraviste mani sotto il pelo dell'acqua: se bianche e grinzose (la *cute da lavandaia*, che in estate si sviluppa entro le dodici ore), se bianche e innaturalmente gonfie (a causa del parziale distacco cutaneo detto *cute a guanto*, che avviene dai tre giorni fino agli otto); nell'impossibilità di chiarire, avvalendomi di una visione altrui intervenuta quasi sessant'anni fa, se il corpo di Lucia presentasse lesioni da sola fauna marina (carpe, rovelle e anguille, ma pure specie marine, come il cefalo) o anche aerea e di terra (roditori), mi risolvo per il piú difficile dei passi, quello che fa fatica anche solo scrivere: cercare l'autopsia di mia madre.

Dove non mi hai portata

Il 30 dicembre telefono all'archivio della Procura della Repubblica di Roma. La gentilissima archivista mi spiega che, dopo quarant'anni, gli atti (anche quelli d'indagine) vengono mandati al macero, a meno che non si tratti di casi di rilevanza storica. Mi promette però di controllare se nei cosí detti *libroni* sia stato trascritto qualche dato, foss'anche il solo nome del medico che ha eseguito l'esame autoptico. Purtuttavia, mi segnala, i «reati contro se stessi» vengono conservati per tempi meno lunghi.

Realizzo che Lucia si è macchiata di tre reati: abbandono di minore e suicidio, delitti ai quali è stata in larga parte indotta dalla prima incriminazione, per adulterio.
Ovviamente, nei casi di suicidio con esito (per cosí dire) positivo, la portata dissuasiva del divieto penale, la cosí detta «funzione deterrente della pena» non ha piú alcuna ragionevolezza. Ma scoprirò ben presto in che modo la rea Lucia verrà punita per la sua scelta di porre fine a una vita che le è diventata insopportabile.

Inoltro intanto domanda all'Archivio centrale di Stato, per ottenere il permesso di verificare personalmente l'esistenza di un fascicolo a nome Lucia Galante, anno 1965. Mentre aspetto queste e molte altre risposte e fascicoli, con lo stato d'animo radioattivo di chi sente di compiere un dovere rimandato per decenni, vengo con te dove non mi hai portata: nella morte. Scendo a conoscere cos'hai sentito.

Nei caduti in acqua dolce, la vita cessa entro tre, massimo cinque minuti. Attraverso i capillari polmonari, l'acqua penetra nel torrente circolatorio, raddoppia il volume del sangue che ruota nel corpo e ne gonfia i globuli rossi, fino a farli esplodere. La carenza di ossigeno trasportato dall'emoglobina causa una fatale fibrillazione ventricolare.

Trascorsi i primi due minuti, nei quali si avvertono forte bruciore e peso al petto, la mancanza di ossigeno produce nell'animo di chi sta annegando un sentimento di pace, dovuto alla progressiva perdita di coscienza, che copre i tre o quattro minuti che separano dalla morte per arresto cardiocircolatorio.

Sembra che la morte per acqua sia la piú dolce.
Due minuti, ed è tutto oblio.
Due minuti e sotto il fiume ci sono le stelle della tua campagna
ci sono le mattine dell'infanzia, la Pasqua
e mamma che ti lascia dormire
col tuo cane,
ci sono io che dal futuro ti guardo
calarti piano in quello specchio atomico,
in quella fine del mondo, e ti guardo
e ti lascio
libera, ti lascio
cosí senza rimedio
e, per me, prendo solo da chiarire
la solitudine della tua materia
disabitata.
Siamo dentro una vasca di luce. Ogni passo che faccio verso di te fa un rumore subacqueo.

Spero che mentre te ne vai, Lucia, risenti le campane della festa, che fanno piovere larghezza e fiori sulla campagna ancora addormentata.
Spero che finalmente ti riposi.

Lunedí 28 giugno. Le cose lasciate sole

Alle ore 18 del pomeriggio Franco Mastrandrea, un portabagagli trentacinquenne della C.I.T. (Compagnia italiana turismo), avverte i carabinieri della presenza di «quattro colli» abbandonati da diversi giorni in Roma, sotto i portici di piazza Esedra, davanti alla sede della compagnia presso la quale lavora.

La pavimentazione dei portici di piazza Esedra sulla quale sono posati gli ingombri è a grandi scaglie di marmo policromo, singolarmente uguale a quello dell'ingresso del palazzo nel quale abiterò.

Certe creature con la divisa da poliziotti mettono le
nostre cose a contatto col tavolo della questura. Chissà
se ne hanno pietà, se le toccano
con amore, mentre le infilano nel sacchetto
dove vanno le cose dei morti. Chi lo sa quante volte
hanno già ricomposto le cose dei morti, questi corpi
in divisa, che devono difendersi dall'urlo di dolore che sale
dalle cose
che non sono piú altro che cose. Magari scherzano fra
loro, magari pensano alle loro madri, mentre aprono
quella borsetta abbandonata.

Elenco delle cose lasciate sole:

una valigia in similpelle verde, all'interno della quale sono ripiegati dei vestiti da uomo e da donna, il certificato di nascita di Maria Grazia Greco, rilasciato il 16 giugno dal Comune di Milano, e un braccialetto d'oro;

una cartella nera da uomo in pelle di foca contenente la patente di Giuseppe Di Pietro, una penna stilografica, alcune fotocopie di costruzioni edilizie e qualche lettera, alla fine neanche spedita, dove Giuseppe chiede disperatamente un lavoro qualsiasi a ex colleghi imprenditori edili;

una borsetta nera da donna, a bauletto, coi manici, contenente la carta d'identità di Lucia Galante, di professione coltivatrice, e alcuni altri oggetti, che vengono esposti in una foto pubblicata a pagina 5 dal «Messaggero» del 29 giugno:
la collana d'oro e i due orecchini con castone a raggera e pietra scura indossati da Lucia nella fotografia incollata alla carta d'identità, un ciondolo con la medesima lavorazione, una catenina d'oro 750 a 18 carati con crocefisso, un anello, un orologio in acciaio, due orecchini a pendaglio nella relativa scatola da gioielliere, un anello in metallo con pietra rossa e due chiavi sfuse;

una rete in nylon rossa, contenente pannolini e indumenti per neonato, insieme a una bambola di plastica alta almeno quaranta centimetri, riproduzione in scala quasi reale della mia figurina di allora, coi capelli corti e le orecchie a vista.

Lucia si è spogliata di tutti gli oggetti di valore tranne della fede.
Nessuno, per un numero imprecisato di giorni, ha toccato quella borsetta abbandonata al suolo.

I carabinieri hanno fotografato solo gli oggetti di valore, ma, nel 1980, insieme alla borsetta che li contiene, mi sono pervenuti: un portamonete nero in finta pelle di coccodrillo con 20 lire del 1958, un tubetto «campione gratuito non commerciabile» di dentifricio Colgate, una confezione trapezoidale in plastica trasparente azzurra, con tappo bianco, di collirio Stilla, nella quale il liquido è stato trasformato dagli anni in una pietrolina ovoidale azzurra di circa due millimetri, il bugiardino ripiegato con cura del collutorio Forhans, i due guantini bianchi del matrimonio, un salvacolletto in plastica per camicia da uomo, un ditale di bronzo recante una macchia d'inchiostro blu e una confezione rotonda di crema Nivea dentro la quale, come ho già scritto nel 2010, quando condussi un primo rapidissimo tentativo di questo resoconto, «la stagnola riporta una leggera piegatura anomala e conserva l'impronta di un indice destro e la relativa strisciata a semicerchio sulla latta del fondo. Tutte le donne prendono la crema per le mani con lo stesso gesto».

Ma c'è di piú, c'è un regalo che viene dal tempo e allora mi era sfuggito: il tubetto di pasta dentifricia conserva, sulle due facce opposte, il calco metafisico delle dita da bambina di Lucia, pollice e indice. Le mani di mia madre.

Ordinata e precisa, lo ha spremuto una volta sola, tenendo la superficie dov'è stampigliato in rosso il nome Colgate rivolta
   verso l'alto, dove ancora brillavano i suoi occhi.

Non riscontro, comunque, alcun segno d'indigenza terminale. Collirio, dentifricio e crema per le mani. Niente trucco, a Lucia piace stare pulita.

Ma quali porte aprono le due chiavi che Lucia ha lasciato sfuse nella borsa? A Roma, nonostante le affannose ricerche di carabinieri e polizia, Lucia e Giuseppe non risultano registrati in nessuna pensione, presso nessun affittacamere né ostello.

Sembrano arrivati fino a Roma solo per uccidersi.

Infine, nella foto degli oggetti rovesciati davanti agli obiettivi dei giornalisti dalla valigia aperta come una vongola lungo la cerniera perimetrale, si riconosce un reggiseno bianco. Esposto cosí, sui giornali. Le cose dopo di noi, le cose
   quando non siamo piú responsabili.
E la bambola nuda, di plastica. Una povera cosa che era tutto il possibile.
Nella foto, la bambola ha le gambine messe di traverso, a coprire la nudità interposta. Per caso, o per l'ammirevole pudore di un carabiniere.

Fra i bagagli abbandonati non è stata rinvenuta alcuna carrozzina, io stessa sono stata deposta su un plaid. Posso immaginare di aver fatto l'ultimo viaggio, da Milano a Roma, tra le braccia di Lucia, o in un marsupio leggero, poi abbandonato sulla sponda. Per esempio nel plaid, annodato a fascia trasversale alla spalla di lei, come io stessa ho portato i miei figli. Sempre addosso, al sicuro.

Martedí 29 giugno. Autopsia. Pianto della materia disabitata

Temperatura minima: 15 gradi. Temperatura massima: 37 gradi.
Roma in festa per san Pietro e Paolo, uffici chiusi, città paralizzata da una serrata amministrativa e percorsa dalle occhiate di panico dei pochi residenti rimasti, minacciati dall'imminente sciopero dei netturbini.

Nel pomeriggio, all'Istituto di medicina legale del policlinico viene trasferito il corpo di un uomo salito alla superficie del Tevere alle 10 del mattino «a monte di ponte Giuseppe Mazzini», fra i ponti Vittorio e Principe Amedeo. Il corpo sembra essere rimasto in acqua oltre quindici giorni, scrivono i giornali. Indossa solo un paio di pantaloni in gessato blu, in tasca ha un fazzoletto e tre cravatte, dimostra tra i cinquanta e i sessant'anni. «Il Messaggero» di giovedí primo luglio riferisce che la polizia ritiene di poter identificare il ripescato con l'uomo ritratto nella fotografia della patente intestata a Giuseppe Di Pietro.

I due corpi vengono dunque rinvenuti a circa cinque chilometri e mezzo di distanza uno dall'altro: come sappiamo, quello di Lucia emerge per primo, lontano dal centro, all'Eur, altezza Lungotevere degli Inventori.
I carabinieri (colonnello Filippi, capitano Aliberti, comandante della compagnia Urbana Prima, e il già noto tenente Varisco) che dirigono le indagini non possono ancora sovrapporre con certezza la fotografia del documento di

Lucia al corpo che «Il Messaggero» del 29 giugno definisce anch'esso «irriconoscibile».

Corpi scempiati dalla volontà di non essere. Essi corpi, sopraffatti dalla volontà di dissolversi di chi li abitava, sono diventati materia. Il maresciallo Del Gaudio si dichiara comunque convinto all'ottanta per cento della somiglianza tra la foto sulla carta d'identità di Lucia Galante e quella figura umana mescolata all'acqua di Fiume.

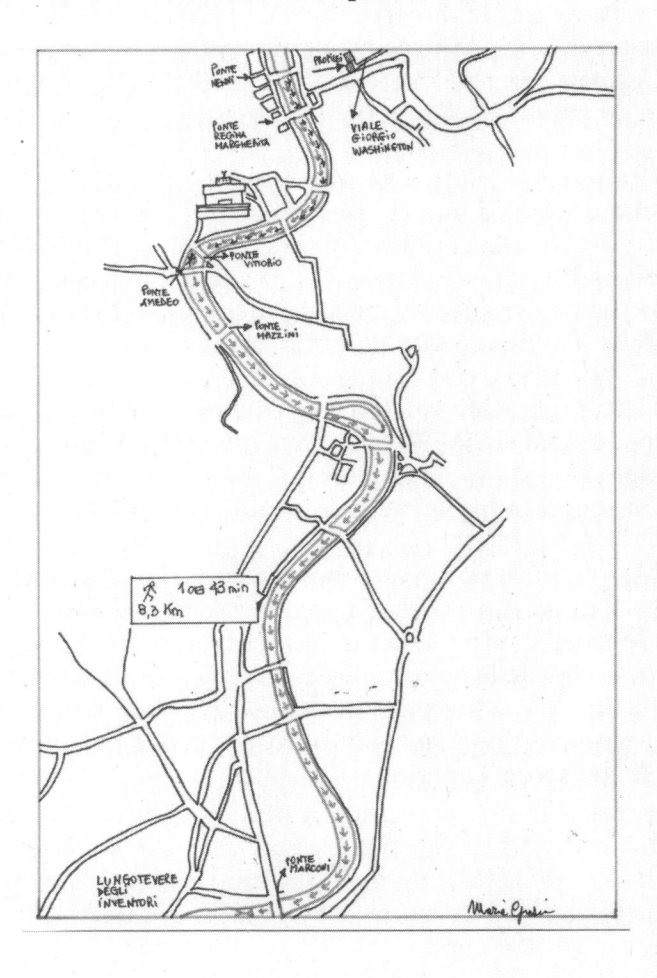

Supponendo si tratti di loro, e che Lucia e Giuseppe si siano lasciati scivolare dalle prossimità di ponte Pietro Nenni o Regina Margherita, cioè dai dintorni di Villa Borghese, il corpo di lui è avanzato per soli due chilometri. Rimasto poi incagliato sul posto e percosso dai flutti del fondo, è stato preda facile di animali, pesci e ratti, che lo hanno degradato in fretta, tanto da farlo apparire come immerso in acqua per un tempo piú lungo.

Se ha avuto un laringospasmo, Lucia ha invece flottato in superficie per circa otto chilometri ed è stata perciò sballottata, ma non morsicata, ha urtato solamente tronchi e sponde.

Per andare a morire, entrambi hanno indossato gli abiti della domenica, quelli che, secondo il guardamacchine, fanno di loro una coppia «quasi certamente *di* contadini». Quei due vestiti, scelti magari in un mattino di sole, prima dello sferragliare della Vita Nuova, contengono la solitudine della materia caduta nel disincanto, il pianto
      della materia disabitata.
Eccoli, gli Affiorati, ecco la fine di un amore sotto le lampade scialitiche. Non c'è piú niente da capire. Forse soltanto una stanchezza grande. E accostare silenzio a silenzio, lasciarli intatti nella Solitudine.

Ma i vivi indagano, non conoscendo pace passano anch'essi
      di tregua in tregua, risondano il sondato, hanno una febbre in corpo, una rapina. La magistratura ordina la misurazione della velocità delle acque del fiume, per stabilire se Lucia e Giuseppe si sono abbandonati nello stesso momento al grande abbraccio di Fiume che promette pace. A che serve, saperlo?

Mercoledí 30 giugno. Corpi e altre invenzioni

30 giugno, ore 9, Istituto di medicina legale di Roma: Luigi e Rocco Galante, rispettivamente padre e fratello di Lucia, riconoscono senza dubbio il corpo da lei abbandonato. Rocco è sceso da Udine.

Corpo verde come un ramo di giunco. Lucia ha perso le sue scarpe da sposa.

Luigi e Rocco firmano il verbale di riconoscimento ufficiale e si trattengono a Roma per organizzare il trasporto di quella cosa che Lucia animava. In quel frattempo, rifiutano di vedermi: «Quella è figlia del peccato e noi non la vogliamo», insistono a riferire «l'Unità» e «Paese Sera».
Zio Rocco ha ventun anni, è un bravo figlio, la sua voce interiore è sommersa da quella del padre, la cui determinazione è a sua volta deformata da quella che «l'Unità» definisce «paura di offendere un preteso "senso dell'onore", legato a miti e pregiudizi ben lontani dall'essere debellati». In piú, tutto è accaduto quando Rocco era a fare il militare, altrimenti
«La casa a mia sorella gliel'aggiustavo io e niente succedeva...»
Caro zio che finalmente lo dici e finalmente mi guardi come guardavi lei.

Giuseppe, invece, si presenta per l'ultima volta ai parenti a petto nudo: ha perso la camicia, probabilmente anche giacca e cravatta, visto che i pantaloni rimasti addosso al corpo sembrano la metà di un completo elegante. La moglie Anita e Remo, fresco marito della figlia Carolina, convenuti essi pure all'istituto, non riconoscono Giuseppe nel corpo rinvenuto presso ponte Mazzini, perché non rintracciano su quei maceri resti le ferite di guerra d'Affrica che contraddistinguono il loro congiunto.

È possibile che una sposa abbandonata e un genero, che non ritengo abbia mai avuto occasione di denudare il suocero, fissino lo sguardo cosí in profondità su un corpo in quelle condizioni da riconoscere cicatrici di guerra vecchie di almeno vent'anni, a meno che quei segni non siano profondissimi, deformanti, mutilanti?

È, piuttosto, possibile che la moglie, non desiderando ereditare gli ingenti debiti accumulati dal marito, peraltro in parte con un'altra donna, per la quale si è pure buttato nel fiume, abbia – consciamente o inconsciamente – perso la memoria. E, una volta negato nel caldo dei fatti, con gli anni le sia diventato sempre piú arduo confessare ai figli di aver lasciato il padre privo di sepoltura per questioni economiche e di pur condivisibile gelosia.

Su «Paese Sera» del 29 giugno, in un'intervista rilasciata il giorno prima che il corpo venga ritrovato (l'intervista pubblicata il 29 essendo ovviamente del giorno precedente), Anita «ritiene che, se il marito ha scritto quella lettera, si è certamente ucciso». Ancora piú esplicita la dichiarazione resa dalla moglie alla polizia il pomeriggio precedente e riportata il 30 giugno dal «Corriere della Sera», in un articolo a firma M.B., paragrafo *La relazione fatale*:

«Quando la polizia ieri pomeriggio ha parlato con Censa [*sic!*] Scanzani [*sic*], la donna ha detto che si aspettava da un momento all'altro una brutta notizia: "Giuseppe aveva perso la testa per quella donna. Non c'era modo di farlo ragionare e so bene che non avrebbe esitato a morire, pur di non perderla. Abbiamo fatto il possibile tutti noi, ma non siamo riusciti a niente"».

L'uso dell'imperfetto parla da solo: Anita arriva in obitorio dando per ovvio che il corpo che le verrà esibito sarà quello di Giuseppe. Invece, non lo riconosce.

Ma ecco la dinamica dei fatti completa, nella successione esposta dai giornali:

giovedí 24 giugno intorno alle ore 15,30 Lucia e Giuseppe lasciano la figlia;
venerdí 25 giugno alle 10 del mattino spediscono la lettera nella quale rivelano la mia identità formale e dichiarano il proposito di uccidersi;
la lettera arriva a destinazione il giorno successivo, sabato 26 giugno, e viene resa pubblica domenica 27;
venerdí 25 giugno pomeriggio Lucia e Giuseppe inviano un biglietto alla direzione del brefotrofio nel quale hanno letto, sui giornali del mattino, che sono stata ricoverata. Il biglietto non risulta però nell'archivio del brefotrofio;
domenica 27 viene trovato il corpo di Lucia, sulla cassetta delle cui ossa è scritta a pennarello nero la data del giorno precedente, 26 giugno;
lunedí 28 vengono rinvenuti i bagagli contenenti i documenti con le fotografie dei due presunti suicidi;
martedí 29 viene ripescato un corpo, non riconosciuto dai parenti come quello appartenuto a Giuseppe.

Una sequenza psichedelica. Perché Lucia e Giuseppe avrebbero inscenato questo mosaico, le cui tessere paiono sparse apposta, nell'acqua e sul rovente suolo romano, perché si impazzisca, per farle combaciare? Perché informare della mia identità attraverso una lettera spedita a un giornale e non con un biglietto accanto, o addosso, alla mia pur esigua persona? Sarebbe stato certo piú lineare appuntarmi sul vestitino (con apposita spilla di sicurezza, detta da balia, perché non avessi a pungermi), un biglietto con nome e data di nascita, anziché affidare alle poste la scoperta dell'identità di una neonata, lasciata fino a quel momento anonima. Se quella lettera (senza neanche indirizzo postale del quotidiano) non fosse arrivata all'«Unità», nessuno sarebbe mai venuto a cercarmi per dirmi da dove venivo.

Questo fatto, reale ed empirico, sembra bastante a dichiarare che Lucia e Giuseppe non vogliono essere immediatamente rintracciati. Chi ha deciso di non mettere il mio nome accanto a me, forse ha bisogno di tempo. Per cosa?

Il disperante caos degli elementi, insieme al mancato riconoscimento del corpo di Giuseppe in quello dell'annegato venuto a galla il 29, da parte della donna di dolori, la moglie abbandonata, getta un'ombra lunga cinquantasette anni sulla figura di lui, apre nella mente di molti un ventaglio di convinzioni maligne, sul momento e negli anni. È il momento di affrontarle.

Teoria dell'omicidio

Se, anziché spedirla a un quotidiano, la lettera contenente anche solo il mio nome e il mio luogo di nascita fosse stata lasciata accanto a me, gli inquirenti sarebbero potuti risalire nel pomeriggio stesso al nome di mia madre, legato al mio negli archivi degli ospedali milanesi.

Lasciare che questo legame venga scoperto in breve, anche solo trascorsa l'oretta impiegata a diramare fonogrammi a tutti gli ospedali milanesi, per Lucia non cambierebbe nulla: a morire per acqua, l'abbiamo studiato, ci vogliono circa cinque minuti. E, se anche sapessero il suo nome, il nome non basterebbe certo a riconoscere la figura fisica di Lucia, dunque a fermarla.

Forse, allora, confondere le acque è interesse di Giuseppe.

Il nome di Giuseppe Di Pietro non risulta però associato a quello di Lucia Galante in alcun documento ufficiale, neanche nella denuncia di Luigi Greco a Palata, luogo al quale gli investigatori non possono risalire senza aver prima identificato Lucia, per poi eventualmente affidarsi a indagini da svolgere in paese, per conoscerne il concubino.

Dunque, se anche Lucia e Giuseppe lasciassero accanto a me la lettera contenente, oltre al mio nome, quello di Lucia, Giuseppe correrebbe un rischio davvero minimo di venire rintracciato prima di sparire: dati i mezzi dell'epoca, infatti, nonostante «l'Unità» trasmetta immediatamente ai carabinieri la lettera ricevuta al mattino di sabato 26 e contenente i nomi di Lucia e mio, solo il ritrovamento delle due carte d'identità nel successivo pomeriggio di lunedí 28 permette alle forze dell'ordine di collegare il nome di Giuseppe Di Pietro alla bambina abbandonata.

A meno di credere che Lucia e Giuseppe vogliano avere il tempo per valutare come si sentano dopo avermi abbandonata, se possano o meno sopportare la vita, durante i due giorni del mio anonimato e i presunti quattro del loro.

Sfidiamo comunque, con tutti i corollari, l'ipotesi piú frequentata da chi negli anni ha esaminato la storia, cioè: che io sia figlia di un assassino.

Ipotesi piú blanda: induzione al suicidio.
Ho già escluso l'ipotesi che Giuseppe spinga nel fiume Lucia fingendo di portarla a prendere il sole dopo avermi abbandonata, poiché diamo per ovvio che poche donne, tra le quali senz'altro non figura Lucia, accettino di andare a fare i bagni di sole dopo aver abbandonato la propria creatura.

Rimane però possibile che l'uomo si voglia sbarazzare di Lucia e si impegni per mesi a manipolarla psicologicamente, tanto da persuaderla ad abbandonare la propria figlia e uccidersi, per essere poi libero di darsi alla fuga. Uno sforzo comunque immotivato, poiché basterebbe separarsi, o abbandonare una famiglia indesiderata, come peraltro Giuseppe ha già mostrato di saper fare, senza spingersi a faticare tanto.

Ma c'è di piú: come convincere Lucia a lasciare la sua creatura, anonima, su un prato, a disposizione di tutti?

«Lucia non ti avrebbe lasciata sola in mezzo alla strada, in balía di qualsiasi delinquente! Anche se era disperata, anche se non capiva piú niente, anche se ha aspettato che ti trovassero. Non poteva sapere chi fosse l'uomo che ti ha presa! No, Lucia ti avrebbe portata in una chiesa, dalle suore, in un posto che secondo lei era sicuro...»

Lucia è irragionevole, fa storie. Si rende dunque necessario eliminare prima la madre e, solo successivamente, lasciare la figlia, in quelle incaute e strampalate condizioni. Ecco dunque affacciarsi l'ipotesi efferata: l'omicidio effettuato di propria mano. Non potendo trascurare il fatto che Lucia indossi un costume, dobbiamo collocare l'eventuale bagno di sole prima del mio abbandono.

«Ma se l'ha uccisa, perché lei aveva il costume?» oppongo, infatti. La replica:

«Magari Lucia pensava veramente di andare a prendere il sole con te, non aveva nessuna intenzione di lasciarti e la lettera l'ha scritta lui, dopo che l'ha buttata nel fiume. Altrimenti, che senso aveva non mettere la lettera accanto a te? Mandarla a un giornale. Lasciare i bagagli da un'altra parte. Non vedi che è tutto strano? Cosí agisce una persona che vuole far perdere tempo ai carabinieri».

Verifichiamo questa ipotesi.

Esasperato dalla convivenza con Lucia, divenuta ingombrante e addirittura riprodottasi in piccola copia urlante, o insonne, lo sfibrato Giuseppe pianifica di uccidere Lucia, dunque le fa firmare in calce un foglio in bianco, sopra la firma di lei scrive la lettera di suicidio (da cui la composizione della lettera integralmente di pugno di lui, siglata dalla sola firma di Lucia) e poi depista gli investigatori, per avere il tempo di darsi alla fuga.

Intanto, ha predisposto che un paio di giorni dopo, quando lui è ormai al sicuro in un altro paese, il caso venga sciolto dall'arrivo della lettera chiarificatrice. Fine di ogni indagine ulteriore, archiviazione definitiva come suicidio. Giuseppe conta sul fatto, purtroppo verosimile, che a nessuno interessi scandagliare ulteriormente la morte di una contadina, disperata e ripudiata da tutti.

Perseveriamo in questa narrazione. Lucia e Giuseppe lasciano i bagagli in una compiacente pensioncina romana, una di quelle dove nessuno chiede i documenti. Ma, per avere addosso il costume, Lucia deve sapere dove stanno andando:
«Senti che caldo! Portiamo la bambina al fiume a prendere un po' di fresco...»
le fa lui, pensando già a spingerla nell'acqua, oppure no.
Lucia acconsente, si spoglia dei suoi ori tranne la fede, li mette in borsa e indossa il costume. Mettere orologio e catenina battesimale nella borsetta è un gesto strano, se si dispone di camera d'albergo. Ma sorvoliamo, perché lei può averli sentiti piú al sicuro dentro la sua borsetta, o può averli raccolti lo stesso Giuseppe. Dopo, a cose fatte.
Qui segnalo pure che il corpo del presunto Giuseppe non indossa il costume. Ma diciamo che, allora come oggi, agli uomini è permesso bagnarsi in mutande e proseguiamo.
I due arrivano al fiume, con me in braccio. Lei si schernisce. Lui, in mutande, la invita, diabolico:
«Vieni, l'acqua è bellissima, non avere paura, ti tengo io!»
Macché. La ragazza è ostinata, non si spoglia.
«Dài, Lucia, bagnati almeno i piedi!»
Lei si leva le scarpe, sguazza coi piedi in acqua. È il momento! Adesso è necessario che molli la neonata, per spingere la madre dentro il fiume, lasciarla andare dentro la corrente. Poi abbandonare altrove la creatura, ma senza nome, per far ruotare a vuoto gli inquirenti. Intanto, fuggire.

Per ora non rispondo, raccolgo altre voci:
«Giuseppe ha avuto un raptus, è impazzito, ha ucciso e abbandonato e ha costruito il caso a posteriori».
«Per me c'entrano i debiti di Giuseppe, forse lui a Milano era entrato in un brutto giro, o aveva chiesto i soldi a qualcuno pericoloso. A chi aveva firmato quelle cambiali? Magari lei aveva paura, per questo era andata a cercare il

suo fidanzatino di quand'era piccola, cercava protezione per voi due...»

«Voleva denunciarlo e lui ha dovuto eliminarla, era diventata pericolosa...»

«La odiava, non la sopportava piú. Capita, nelle coppie...»

«Secondo me Lucia aveva deciso di lasciarlo e lui è andato fuori di testa per il dolore. O mia o di nessuno! Uno dei tanti femminicidi. Sai, il senso di possesso...»

Naturalmente improbabile che, in orario diurno, pure nascosti da un pilone o un'ansa («Vieni, Lucia, stiamocene un po' soli»), lungo la riva piatta si consumi un delitto, il quale si suppone susciti nella vittima una legittima opposizione, qual che ne sia il motivo. Schizzi, grida. O è stata una botta in testa e via, giú a picco nell'acqua. Un colpo, cosí forte da stordire, ma che non lascia segni.

L'uccisione andrebbe allora, piú verosimilmente, inclusa nella tragica notte, dunque ore e ore dopo l'abbandono, che Lucia trascorrerebbe viva senza motivo e, se non è stata lei ad aver disposto di morire per acqua, senza motivo indossando un costume da bagno sulla riva del fiume, data l'incoerenza naturale di abbronzarsi al sole nella notte.

Poi, al mattino, Giuseppe rincasa, sempre senza motivo lascia i bagagli sul marciapiede e spedisce la lettera da solo, all'ovvio scopo di sciogliere l'enigma della morte di Lucia tramite la dichiarazione di suicidio contenuta e firmata in quelle poche righe, e tosto far chiudere il caso.

Replico la medesima obiezione immediata a tutte le ipotesi, di induzione piú e meno estemporanea al suicidio e piú e meno rapsodico omicidio: per Giuseppe la morte di Lucia è superflua, pericolosa e anche estremamente impegnativa. Basterebbe sparire, come comunque Giuseppe avrebbe fatto, visto che da quel giorno si perdono le sue tracce, per sempre.

Resta inoltre l'enigma dei bagagli abbandonati in piazza. Ipotizziamo che Giuseppe, dopo aver assistito o procurato la morte di Lucia e aver abbandonato la propria (sesta) figlia, senza motivo abbia voluto abbandonare anche i bagagli, invece di precipitarsi su un treno per destinazione sconosciuta.

Dimentichiamo che i nomi di Giuseppe e Lucia non risultano da nessuna parte: per favorire l'ipotesi, ho immaginato un'oscura pensioncina di anonimi. Accettiamo tutto.

Ma non possiamo dimenticare che i bagagli contengono parecchi oggetti di discreto valore. Perché Giuseppe non porta via l'oro, l'orologio, la stilografica? Nessuno può sapere quali siano, in quei giorni, le proprietà in possesso di Lucia, nessuno mai si accorgerebbe del furto. E perché prendersi la briga di tornare in albergo, prelevare i bagagli e gettarli in strada?

Ma abbiamo la testa dura e insistiamo allo stremo, anche oltre la ragionevolezza. Supponiamo che Giuseppe dichiari nella lettera il proprio proposito di morte per essere dato per deceduto e non venire piú cercato. Supponiamo che anche abbandonare i bagagli in mezzo alla strada e lasciarvi all'interno gli oggetti di valore sia il parto di un pensiero criminale, che voglia cosí sottolineare l'ipotesi dell'impulso suicidario, cioè una sovrana indifferenza verso le cose, che ai morti non servono laicamente piú.

Ma perché lasciare accanto alla carta d'identità di Lucia i propri oggetti e, soprattutto, la propria patente, via primaria per venire associato alla ragazza trovata morta, e, dunque, immediatamente: ricercato? Se volesse sparire, Giuseppe distruggerebbe il proprio documento, quel compromettente pezzo di carta rosa, o seco lo recherebbe.

Opposizione ulteriore:
«Una volta trovato il corpo di Lucia, presto o tardi le indagini avrebbero condotto gli inquirenti al nome di Giu-

seppe. Allora, lui ha lasciato tutte le sue cose vicino a quelle di Lucia proprio per essere dato per morto insieme a lei».

Questa confutazione assume consistenza solo nel caso in cui Giuseppe abbia premeditato di uccidere Lucia, progetto tuttavia – ripeto al mio appassionato interlocutore – complesso da realizzare con la connivenza di un fiume come il Tevere, cittadino e meridiano. La generosità indifferente del reale presenta una selezione pressoché infinita di alternative altitudini (vette, dirupi, promontori marini), solidi (rocce, graniti, spigoli piú e meno acuti), veleni e fiumiciattoli riposti, certamente piú disponibili all'impiego per scopi omicidiari. Inoltre, come già chiarito, uccidere Lucia per liberarsi di lei è, per Giuseppe, perfettamente inutile.

La presenza superflua e, anzi, pericolosa, del documento d'identità di Giuseppe Di Pietro all'interno della cartella abbandonata in piazza Esedra, mette dunque a tacere tutte le voci e fa sfumare l'ampio corollario delle ipotesi preterintenzionali: dal bagno al fiume finito in *raptus* (uno spintone), alla casuale tragedia (una scivolata irrimediabile), e tutto quello che la generosa e partecipe fantasia umana può produrre, nonché lo scenario di qualsiasi altra immaginabile e inimmaginabile sventura della quale Giuseppe sia stato spettatore o, peggio, responsabile.

Niente di tutto questo. Né paura, né odio, né *raptus*. Illimpidita meticolosamente la scena, resta solo l'ipotesi piú umana: il ripensamento, sola teoria accettabile, per spiegare la permanenza in vita di Giuseppe (dato peraltro dubbio, ricavato – come ho scritto – esclusivamente dal mancato riconoscimento del corpo dell'annegato da parte della moglie Anita).

Giuseppe è sempre stato vittima della propria «disperata vitalità». A cose fatte, e senza averlo predisposto, Giuseppe sorprende anche se stesso, non ce la fa, proprio non vuole trapassare, la sua forma di vita è piú egoista e tenace di quella di Lucia e la lascia morire da sola, all'ultimo momento lui non salta – nell'improbabile caso lei si getti da un ponte – o non si lascia scivolare con lei – nel caso in cui Lucia entri in acqua da bordo fiume – oppure, alla fine, pur immersosi insieme alla sua donna, in lui prevale la volontà di vivere (che sempre, fin che dura, ci tiene al mondo) e Giuseppe si trae affannosamente in salvo dalle acque del fiume. Infine, fra il rovello dei debiti accumulati nella prima famiglia e il disastro della seconda, ubriaco di fallimento e dolore, decide di far perdere le proprie tracce, espatriando o arruolandosi nella legione straniera, come ad alcuni detta il malpensiero. Giuseppe cambia nome, riprende un treno e va a rifarsi una vita chi sa dove. Fine.

Scopriremo tra poco perché, nell'eventualità del ripensamento, il 28 giugno i bagagli si trovino dove in effetti si trovano.

Voi due e la notte

Escluso l'omicidio, resta comunque arduo immaginare che due adulti scivolino e anneghino fra i bagnanti nel fiume in pieno giorno, e nel pieno centro di Roma. Chi lo sa se hanno atteso la notte. E con che cuore mai.

Senza che nulla cambi (se non la durata dello strazio al quale Lucia e Giuseppe si sottopongono), il suicidio può essere spostato al tardo pomeriggio del 24, poco prima dell'ora di cena, tra le diciannove e trenta e le venti, quando i bagnanti iniziano a rincasare e non è ancora cominciata la luminaria della dolcevita notturna a bordo fiume.

O possiamo incunearlo nella notte, mentre io dormo altrove un inconscio sonno di pietra, quel vostro scivolamento silenzioso nella solitudine finalmente larga e nera di un fiume contemplato per ore, fermi sul posto, inebetiti dal dolore, visto che il corpo di Giuseppe viene ritrovato proprio lí, a neanche due chilometri e quattro ponti oltre i due adiacenti piazzale Flaminio. Ma certamente il passo dentro l'acqua lo avete mosso entrambi, almeno nelle intenzioni, vi siete inoltrati insieme nella vostra premeditata pazzia, e dev'esservi parsa sollievo, e mancare alla vita dev'esservi sembrato l'epilogo spontaneo della storia perché, prima che in acqua, siete stati immersi in una bolla logica, la lucida demenza degli amanti, tutti.

Ci caschiamo tutti, mi ci sono incastrata pure io. Nei pregiudizi, dico. Ma, scavando nei fatti con la massima razionalità e onestà possibili, i fatti stessi hanno espresso la totale innocenza di Giuseppe, anch'egli vittima, come Lucia, di pregiudizi: pensavamo forse a Lucia come a un'amabile sempliciotta di campagna, e ha mostrato di essere tutt'altro. E pensavamo a Giuseppe come a un dongiovanni navigato e cinico talmente da architettare contro la sua donna un piano da angoscia hitchcockiana. Ma ho appena scansato da queste pagine la teoria della mattanza. Sono state le pagine piú faticose.

Cronologia di un amore

I puri fatti

La sequenza degli spostamenti romani della coppia riportata dai giornali è incoerente, caotica e sensazionalistica, conduce francamente fuori strada. I giornalisti seguono la successione casuale dei ritrovamenti, nei quali pare impossibile rintracciare una logica, né topografica, né psicologica. La confusione crea mostri. I mostri sono il sonno, o l'eccesso, della ragione.

Stando ai quotidiani, Lucia e Giuseppe avrebbero architettato un piano suicidario contorto e schizofrenico, fatto di immotivati andirivieni – o motivati dal desiderio di far perdere le proprie tracce – ma, soprattutto, estremamente freddo: lunghe ore trascorse a girare a piedi per Roma senza documenti, senza denaro né ripensamenti, confermando il proposito abbandonico e suicidario per tutto il resto della loro vita, cioè una somma di istanti equivalente addirittura a giorni.

Mi dico: inietta il sangue vivo del tuo pensiero dentro il circuito delle loro menti, ripensa tutto quello che loro hanno pensato prima di te. Tutto quello che arrivo a pensare io, è già stato pensato da loro. È matematica. E così, si riattiva il pensiero degli Scomparsi, il congegno geometrico della separazione e della perdita, ovvero l'incrocio delle due coordinate (spazio e tempo) alla modalità dell'abbandono. E così si decifrano logica e senso di una sequenza di gesti rimasti incomprensibili per sessant'anni.

Grazie a un'analisi minuziosa delle tracce, viene alla luce una trama chiara e coerente, cosí chiara, coerente e determinata da essere quasi bella:
>quella di Lucia e Giuseppe è una progressiva spoliazione.

Logica, pulita, estetica. Si spogliano di tutto, come alberi, in progressione fatale.

Prima abbandonano le cose che costituiscono il loro tesoretto e la loro identità ufficiale, normata, poi
>depongono la figlia, si accertano che sia al sicuro
>e si spogliano infine

della propria stessa vita.

Credo di poter dire che lo abbiano fatto insieme.
Io sono il loro tronco messo a nudo. L'essenziale.

Mi spiego, tenendomi ai fatti:
nel 1965, in piazza Esedra, proprio sotto la c.i.t. (Compagnia italiana turismo), cioè il luogo dove vengono rinvenuti borse e bagagli, ci sono le fermate degli autoservizi c.i.a.t. (Compagnia italiana autoservizi turistici).

Quando scendono dalla corriera, dunque, e non dal treno, Lucia e Giuseppe sanno cosa sono venuti a fare, hanno deciso da tanto. Il loro piano è semplice e lineare: disfarsi di tutto, fino a disfarsi della propria vita. Lasciar andare tutto. Credo, anzi, che vogliano fare tutto bene, ma presto.

Ripercorro la cronologia dei loro passi e controllo se i tempi coincidono.

È verosimile che Lucia e Giuseppe, avendo ormai stabilito di uccidersi, spendano tutti i soldi che hanno, per concedersi l'ultimo viaggio su un autobus di gran turismo: è un periodo di generale entusiasmo per gli autoservizi, perché i treni vengono piuttosto associati all'indelebile Morgana degli emigranti; ed è verosimile che, appena scesi a Roma, nel primissimo pomeriggio del 24 giugno, Lucia e

Giuseppe si liberino dei bagagli che verranno rinvenuti sul posto qualche giorno piú tardi. Che tra i bagagli non figuri un passeggino dice che non hanno intenzione di organizzarsi per vivere.

Il percorso tra piazza Esedra e viale Washington (dove verrò trovata poco dopo le 15,30) è di un'ora scarsa. Se non si fermano a passeggiare e tanto meno a pranzo – come mi pare ovvio, in quello stato d'animo e come, anima a parte, è reso verosimile dal fatto che abbiano abbandonato soldi e bagagli appena scesi dalla corriera – il loro arrivo potrebbe essere avvenuto intorno alle 13,30 o 14,00, orario perfettamente congruente con le tabelle delle corriere del 1965.

Se poniamo l'arrivo nella capitale fra le 13,30 e le 14,00 e la durata del viaggio in autobus tra Milano e Roma copre: nello spazio, circa seicento chilometri, dunque – nel tempo – circa sei ore, la partenza si colloca in un lasso di tempo assolutamente ragionevole: tra le 7 e le 8 del mattino.

Ora sciogliamo l'ingroviglio vistoso della lettera «*imbucata* venerdí 25 e *timbrata* da Roma Ferrovia, dove viene smistata tutta la posta *imbucata* al centro» («l'Unità», 27 giugno, a firma N.C.) e arrivata in redazione con il primo giro. All'errore di N.C. fa eco «Paese Sera» del 27 giugno: «Dalla busta poco da rilevare: solo che è stata *spedita* da Roma Ferrovia il 25 giugno, cioè l'altro ieri alle 10 di mattina». E ancora, su «Paese Sera» del 28: «La lettera risulta essere stata *impostata* venerdí nella zona del Centro». Infine, sempre N.C., ormai confitto (o confitta) nella sua fantasia, qui lievemente modificata, per «l'Unità» del 29 giugno:

> «Lucia Galante e il suo amante hanno scritto la lettera al nostro giornale *dopo* aver abbandonato la piccola Maria Grazia sul prato di viale Giorgio Washington: l'hanno *impostata* solo nelle prime ore della mattina successiva, venerdí, ad una buca postale o della stazione o del centro. Avevano passato tutta la notte girando, a piedi, da un capo all'altro della città, senza una meta, ormai decisi a uccidersi: poche ore prima avevano lasciato i bagagli [...]»

Caro (o cara) N.C., per cominciare lascerei sfumare l'ipotesi che Lucia e Giuseppe vogliano porre fine alle loro esistenze a causa del senso di colpa per il mio abbandono, come suggerisce lo spiritello acidulo che vagamente aleggia tra le sue parole, perché a essa colpevolezza potrebbero rimediare all'istante, esigendomi giusto le caserme o al brefotrofio stesso: alle 10 di venerdí 25 tutti i quotidiani hanno già diffuso la notizia del mio ritrovamento, riferendo anche il luogo presso il quale sono stata tradotta.

Superato l'inciampo, veniamo dunque al sodo: secondo lei due genitori che – come lei stesso (stessa) rileva – hanno già determinato di uccidersi e hanno previdentemente messo in salvo da se stessi la figlia, una madre che ha appena aperto le sue braccia per lasciar cadere sua figlia di nuovo nell'indifferenziato della nascita, in un anonimato che chi sa quanto durerà, se nessuno la prenderà a cuore, prolungano un dolore e un sentimento di colpa che posso immaginare insopportabili per fare del turismo, o ruzzare traverso la metropoli, artigliandosi le capigliature con le dita grondanti di pianto? Compiuto quel gesto, mi creda, avrei posto fine al piú presto alla mia insostenibile nausea di esistere.

Imbucata, impostata, spedita. La realtà è che la lettera è stata *timbrata* alle 10 della mattina del 25 giugno.

Ragioniamo su quel timbro. Anzi, su quei due timbri: uno a doppio cerchio, del quale è stampigliata solo una porzione, restando il resto fuori dalla busta, e contenente, fra le due circonferenze concentriche, solo quattro lettere: LA AN, forse un logo commemorativo o pubblicitario – magari dell'autotrasporto, che all'epoca funge pure da raccoglitore postale – e l'annullo a cerchio semplice, con sei onde che inchiostrano regolarmente il francobollo, recante data e luogo della timbratura: ROMA FERR. CORRISP. 25.6.65 - 10.

Pur considerando il volume certamente inferiore della corrispondenza dell'epoca, non è detto – rifletto – che una lettera venga timbrata dall'ufficio di distribuzione (in questo caso addirittura il centralissimo Roma Ferrovia) appena il postino rovescia il suo sacco sul piano delle lavorazioni, o nella tramoggia di alimentazione delle bollatrici.

Roberto Monticini, direttore della rivista di cultura filatelica e storico postale «il Postalista», conferma: «Dato per certo che la data del timbro sia il 25.6.65 - 10, occorre tener presente che la lettera è stata ritirata in un giro che riguarda la levatura anche in molte altre cassette. La posta deve poi essere suddivisa per quartieri e data al postino competente. Tutto questo in un giorno? Ne dubito, non sarebbe successo neppure in una piccola città». È pragmaticamente impossibile che la lettera sia stata imbucata il 25 mattina.

Lucia e Giuseppe devono dunque aver messo in buca la loro ultima lettera entro l'orario di ritiro pomeridiano o serale del 24, perché i postini degli uffici di Roma Ferrovia abbiano avuto il tempo materiale di smistarla e timbrarla alle 10 della mattina successiva. Sono, anzi, quasi certa che salgano in corriera con la lettera in busta e già affrancata, anche perché, una volta abbandonati i bagagli, non hanno piú carta e penna, e neanche gli spicci per la busta e il francobollo da 30 lire – serie michelangiolesca – che, nella foto diffusa il 27 giugno dall'«Unità», vi risulta applicato.

Obiezione a me stessa: se la lettera fosse stata però portata allo sportello di Roma Ferrovia la mattina del 25, l'impiegato avrebbe potuto timbrare la busta contestualmente all'atto della consegna (magari suggerendo ai suoi confusi clienti di aggiungere l'indirizzo del giornale), ma Lucia e Giuseppe dovrebbero essersi recati di persona all'ufficio postale. Dopo aver abbandonato la figlia e poco prima di uccidersi. Tesi emotivamente insostenibile, ma non posso scartarla: da sola, l'argomentazione emotiva mi è insufficiente, devo sentire il suono dell'osso del reale. Come escludere con certezza – insisto tra me, in uno sfarzo estremo d'ostinazione – che la lettera sia stata consegnata e timbrata il 25 mattina in un ufficio postale?

Monticini mi usa allora l'ulteriore cortesia di girare la foto della busta ad Alcide Sortino, uno dei maggiori esperti italiani di bollature e macchine bollatrici, il quale scioglie definitivamente ogni dubbio: si tratta di «una impronta della bollatrice-raddrizzatrice SEL Lorentz, macchinone alto due metri in servizio solamente nelle grandi città. Non si tratta certo di macchina da sportello e viene usata per la posta ritirata nelle cassette postali, nonché da altre provenienze (grandi utenti, posta in blocco consegnata alle succursali, ecc.) Quindi la lettera è stata messa in buca e non portata allo sportello. Anche una prima levata fatta al mattino dalla buca delle lettere, non avrebbe permesso che giungesse a Roma Ferrovia per essere annullata alle ore 10 del 25 giugno, per cui è stata messa in buca il giorno precedente».

Sebbene dedotta al negativo (poiché non agiscono, non sono piú vivi), emerge – accompagnata da un tripudio di invettive e da un'allegrezza idiota che urge riferire – la data di morte di Lucia e Giuseppe: 24 giugno 1965. I puri fatti dicono che Lucia e Giuseppe, se non l'hanno già consegnato a bordo del pullman, infilano il loro scarno testamento in una cassetta postale (o lo affidano al Sale e tabacchi di via Nazionale o di piazza Esedra, a pochi metri dalla fermata della C.I.A.T.) giovedí 24, prima dell'ultimo giro di svuotamento delle buche. Il mattino dopo né Lucia, ma neppure l'indiziato Giuseppe, agiscono piú. Questo dato scagiona per la seconda volta Giuseppe dalla seconda accusa (dalla quale l'abbiamo qui in parte già prosciolto) che i giornali e le menti dell'epoca direttamente e indirettamente gli addossano: aver premeditato di sopravvivere alla sua Lucia. Se è rimasto vivo, viceversa, non ne aveva pregressa l'intenzione. Vale solo l'ipotesi già fatta, dell'umano ripensamento.

Neanche lo spostamento del suicidio alla notte, o al primo schiararsi dell'alba, è dunque compatibile con l'orario di spedizione del testamento. Avevo inteso bene: Lucia e Giuseppe imbucano la loro lettera entro lo stesso pomeriggio-sera del mio abbandono.

Pazzi, completamente pazzi (come ho scritto) perché ancora insieme, raccolti in un circuito dove la sacra insania dell'uno alimenta la sacra insania dell'altra. Sono fissati nella loro idea, due forme umane spinte dal di dentro. È un'infatuazione puntata, un magnetismo immobile, di tendini e coronarie, uguale all'inerzia apparente della materia, tenuta invece insieme dalla rotazione incessante e ordinata delle molecole. Il piano si consuma in poche ore, dopo la sua lunghissima preparazione, come una forma di sollievo, una faccia del poliedro della libertà, quella controfigura della nostra vita, quell'utopia parallela alla vita, che cambia volto col mutare di noi. Mi accorgo, mentre le scrivo, che le parole appena pensate per descrivere la libertà sono valide pure per rappresentare la morte: controfigura e utopia dei vivi.

Ecco stagliarsi contro il grande abbaglio del fiume le due figure – innamorate, perdute – nell'infuocato e ruvido pomeriggio del 24 giugno 1965, entrambi vivi poco oltre il solstizio, nella crepuscolare onestà di un proposito condiviso.
Li vedo, sono loro. Mi ostino. Fino a quando? Fino a quando siete rimasti vivi? Conoscere l'orario dell'ultimo ritiro postale mi permetterà di conoscere fino a che ora i cuori di Lucia e Giuseppe hanno senz'altro seguitato a battere, la fascia oraria entro la quale entrambe le figure, dalla riva, scorrono giú, a confondersi con l'acqua. Piano, addirittura con amore. Adesso che mi sono spinta insieme a voi senza piú argini su questa sponda, mi è permesso sapere che la vostra morte si è consumata con definitivo amore. Non vi posso fermare. Non allora, non ora. Mi siedo qui e vi guardo. Sento il suono che fate. Anche il suono dell'acqua
          somiglia all'ultima preghiera che esce dalla bocca di Lucia. A lei, pensaci tu. Madonna mia. È innocente.

L'ultimo giro

La notizia conferma lo splendore feroce della fine: nel 1965 l'ultimo giro di prelievo dalle buche postali avviene alle ore 17. La spedizione è avvenuta fra le quattordici (probabile orario dell'arrivo a Roma) e le diciassette di giovedí 24 giugno.

Dunque, è cosí: ve ne siete andati subito, in pieno giorno, come arti fantasma di un mondo, con voi cosí efferato e indifferente; stanchi di una stanchezza che attraversa il tempo e arriva qui, alla superficie di questa scrivania di vetro azzurro, che vorrei fosse quella di Fiume, per spaccarla a manate, trarvi a riva e lasciarvi qui, vivi e sconvolti dall'acqua, disperati e vivi, avere cura di voi piú che a parole, nel clamore sottile dei gabbiani e di tutta la da voi rinunciata ruota del vivere.

Eppure. Dall'appurata chiarità dei fatti traspare ancora la brillante filigrana caratteriale e morale, la fiducia davvero incrollabile – ancora, nonostante tutto – di Lucia e Giuseppe nell'intelligenza, nella curiosità e nel buon cuore altrui, nonché nell'interesse che il progressivo svelamento del vero avrebbe suscitato nella stampa.

Sembrano, anzi, voler agire in collaborazione con la stampa. O meglio, con la stampa di sinistra, che hanno scelto come destinataria della loro confessione testamentaria.

Prima di dilatare questo stupore etico, un ultimo ultimo giro: ingrandendo e contrastando la foto degli oggetti apparsa sul «Messaggero» del 29 giugno, si può apprezzare l'orario al quale l'orologio di Lucia si è fermato per sempre: le dodici meno venti.

Si tratta, con ogni probabilità, di orologio meccanico a carica manuale, che Lucia attiva tutte le mattine al risveglio, e la cui autonomia dura poco piú di ventiquattr'ore. Lucia ruota la corona del suo orologio la mattina presto, come sempre. La sua ultima mattina presto. Poi, il meccanismo va avanti da solo, nel tempo, fin che ce la fa, fino alla tarda mattinata del giorno successivo alla morte della proprietaria, che finalmente so quand'è avvenuta.

Questo dato non aggiunge elementi all'indagine, solo quel tanto di malinconia che fanno le cose abbandonate dopo di noi, a quell'ultimo giro di lancette.

Ricostruzione di una retta

Nella notte tra il 23 e il 24 giugno Lucia e Giuseppe liberano l'appartamento di Milano, del quale forse non riescono a pagare la pigione da mesi, e mettono in valigia le poche cose che possiedono. Partono tra le sette e le otto del mattino, premeditando di gettarsi nel grande fiume romano, che in quegli anni accoglie molte giovani vite.

Lucia parte col costume da bagno sotto il vestito. Sceglie con cura l'abitino a fiori col quale sa che verrà poi trovata, è quello che indossa per la messa domenicale.

Giuseppe parte col suo miglior gessato e, nella tasca dell'abito, ha già pronta la lettera, in busta chiusa e affrancata.

Appena scesi a Roma dalla corriera, intorno alle quattordici, abbandonano a terra tutti i bagagli, tengono solo me.

Se non hanno già imbucato il testamento in autobus, lo infilano nella prima cassetta stradale.

Imboccano via Nazionale o, meno probabilmente, la salita di via Bissolati, per raggiungere, verso le ore 15,30, il luogo dove lasciarmi.

Accertatisi che io sia stata prelevata da persona adulta, si dirigono al fiume e si lasciano scivolare nell'acqua. Li immagino in silenzio.

Il corpo di lui rimane incagliato sul fondo dopo appena due chilometri e riemerge dopo cinque giorni trascorsi a bagno in acqua con quasi quaranta gradi esterni: mezzo spogliato, contuso, strattonato dalle correnti, certamente sbocconcellato dalla fauna acquatica e poi da quella d'aria e di terra.

Il corpo di lei flotta invece per circa otto chilometri, piú dolcemente, sale regolarmente in superficie al terzo giorno, quasi completamente vestito, avendo perso solo le scarpe.

È tutto. Tutto chiaro. Un disegno coerente, tragicamente bello. Ma rimangono ancora da spiegare alcuni dettagli. Primo fra tutti, perché Lucia e Giuseppe non hanno messo accanto a me perlomeno il biglietto col mio nome.

Vivo in un sogno sottoproletario

Il 30 dicembre 2021 è una gloriosa giornata di sole. Mia figlia Anna e io siamo andate in centro a goderci le corolle di luce della festa, la bellezza dei corpi degli altri, i luccicori di vetrine oceaniche con la merce esposta come un magnifico anatema. Ho la testa ancora piena di domande, ma ho imparato a chiudere e aprire i cassetti mentali, o verrei risucchiata dall'indagine. Camminiamo dunque serene da oltre un'ora e, all'altezza di piazza di Spagna, mi viene un'idea che smentisce quanto appena affermato:

«Che dici, andiamo a vedere dove mamma è stata abbandonata?»

Anna approva. Mi giustifico:

«Cosí poi lo racconti agli amici...»

Con dolcezza, Anna finge di credermi. Ridiamo di me.

Il luogo è bellissimo, monumentale. Nell'ampio viale alberato ci sono la generosità della natura e l'imponenza di Roma.

«È un posto molto bello, – dice mia figlia, – lo hanno scelto, non ti hanno lasciata qui per caso».

«Non capisco, sai Anna? Non lo capisco. Come dev'essere il momento in cui una madre si stacca dalla figlia neonata... Il gesto che fa. Come apre le mani. Come la posa, come si allontana...»

Ripercorriamo la strada che ha fatto Ivo Micucci con me neonata in braccio e saliamo fino al C.N.E.L. La vista è mozzafiato. Ampia, boschiva, storica. Arcaica. Ha ragione mia figlia, è un luogo troppo speciale, pur nella straordinaria bellezza di Roma, per essere casuale.

In quegli anni, è il parco pubblico piú antico di Roma. E l'ingresso accanto al quale mi hanno deposta è il piú maestoso fra i molti accessi alla villa.

Scendiamo verso viale Washington. Racconto ad Anna:
«Poi sono andati dall'altra parte della strada, vedi, dove c'è il parcheggio? Ecco perché hanno scritto che li ha visti un guardamacchine! E hanno aspettato che venissi presa...»
Poi mamma e papà (mi accorgo mentre lo dico, che sto dicendo mamma e papà) hanno imboccato piazzale Flaminio. Vedi quel palazzo? Il fiume è proprio lí dietro, sette otto minuti a piedi... Chissà come si sono sentiti... Pensa che i giornalisti hanno scritto che se ne sono andati a spasso fino al mattino dopo... Ma ci pensi? Chissà che prova una donna, dopo aver abbandonato una figlia...

In quel preciso momento vengo assalita da una nausea violentissima, che dura circa otto minuti.

Percorrendo via del Babuino per tornare verso casa dico a me stessa, piú che a mia figlia:
«Chissà perché hanno scelto Roma, non lo sapremo mai...»
«Volevano lasciarti nella capitale!»
risponde Anna, col tono di chi mostra la luna allo sciocco che guarda il dito che la indica.
«Loro due erano poveri, – prosegue, – guarda la cosa dal loro punto di vista: forse per loro vivere a Roma era una meta, volevano darti il meglio che potevano. Eri il frutto del loro amore. Pensavano che a Roma avresti avuto piú possibilità di avere una vita almeno decorosa. Se non c'erano riusciti loro, magari tu...»

Rimango a bocca aperta. Netta. Semplice, chiara. Una ragazzina di tredici anni arriva oltre il punto nel quale si sono arenati tanti giornalisti. Mi fido della sua intuizione.

Anna non può inoltre sapere che in quegli anni, a Milano e Torino, vengono esposti ovunque cartelli recanti la dicitura «Non si affitta ai meridionali», Anna non può sapere che le condizioni di vita degli emigranti interni sono cosí difficili e complesse che Goffredo Fofi ha dedicato loro un libro intero, *L'immigrazione meridionale a Torino*. Lucia e Giuseppe avrebbero dovuto lasciarmi priva di identità. Altrimenti, in che vita sarebbe precipitata, l'orfana di due emigranti? Sarei cresciuta in un orfanotrofio, l'I.P.P.A.I., dal quale Lucia mi aveva strappata a fatica, sarei stata ovunque un *corpo estraneo*.

Lucia voleva partire, andare all'estero. Roma, per lei, è l'estero piú raggiungibile. Un crocevia. Eccomi dunque dentro un miraggio cosmopolita, eccomi, viva, dentro il sogno dei miei genitori.

Cosa avrebbero potuto immaginare, di piú efficace, alla loro portata?

Allora, un'idea irrefrenabile. Comincio a fare ricerche negli archivi dei lavori pubblici. Dal 1958 al 1960 il ministro dei Lavori pubblici è il democratico cristiano Giuseppe Togni, al quale succede Benigno Zaccagnini, l'onesto e fragile Zac. Durante i suoi quattro mandati, Togni realizza uno stupefacente programma di opere pubbliche, dall'Autostrada del Sole alle imponenti opere infrastrutturali destinate a ospitare le Olimpiadi di Roma 1960, molte delle quali erette intorno alla zona della mia deposizione: Palazzo e Palazzetto dello Sport, Villaggio Olimpico, Viadotto Flaminio, via Olimpica, e i sottopassi dei Lungotevere.

Anche il limitrofo Stadio nazionale viene demolito nel luglio 1957, per realizzare al suo posto, entro i successivi due anni, l'attuale Stadio Flaminio, inaugurato il 19 marzo 1959 e destinato a ospitare gli incontri del torneo olimpico di calcio del 1960. La ditta aggiudicataria dei lavori è la Nervi & Bartoli.

Ma ancora: nel 1959, Villa Lubin viene restaurata ed ampliata dall'architetto Clemente Busiri Vici, ma non riesco a scoprire quale impresa abbia ottenuto l'appalto per i lavori. Mi permetto di immaginare che Giuseppe, nel suo periodo romano, sia impiegato in una di queste imprese e che, dall'esperienza, tragga la fantasia decorativa che tre anni piú tardi impiegherà in Palata.

Suggestioni, certo, solo suggestioni. Ma potenti.

Giuseppe, se coinvolto in quelle costruzioni e ricostruzioni, conosce piuttosto bene la zona. Di certo, comunque, va e viene dalla casa coniugale utilizzando quasi certamente le autolinee S.I.T.A. (Società italiana trasporti automobilistici), che in quegli anni coprono la tratta fino a Nettuno, e sa perciò orientarsi a Roma, tra via Gaeta, strada nei pressi della Stazione Termini dove un tempo fermavano le regionali, e il posto di lavoro, ovunque sia.

O, piú semplicemente: oltre la stazione della Roma Nord, nei pressi di viale Washington ci sono le fermate delle corriere che s'inoltrano nel profumo di menta e rosmarino dell'Agro romano.

Certamente, dunque, Lucia e Giuseppe mi hanno immersa in qualcosa che sognavano, coi desideri semplici, bellissimi e chiari della povera gente. Roma, da sempre, è una destinazione. Forse, a Roma, Giuseppe era stato felice.

Corpo, nome, storia

La lucida intuizione di Anna chiarifica, a catena, molti passaggi della macchinosa architettura del mio abbandono, che finalmente diventa quello che è: un progetto intelligente.

I gesti di Lucia e Giuseppe appaiono infatti indecifrabili se li paragoniamo ai gesti consueti dell'abbandono, alla sequenza, cioè, di azioni necessarie alla chirurgia del distacco: taglio netto, meno male possibile per tutti.

Se, viceversa, li spostiamo in blocco nel contesto emotivo della cura (che prevede una strana permanenza, un fantasmatico aleggiare intorno alla persona dell'abbandonato, pur nell'assenza), ecco che sotto i nostri occhi, riga dopo riga, si srotola il cartiglio del pensiero che ha preceduto e determinato la scelta del luogo:

   poiché Lucia e Giuseppe sanno che lasceranno una neonata senza nome e spediranno una lettera con nome e storia della bambina a un quotidiano (consapevoli del fatto che il giornale sarà in grado di pubblicare la notizia solo due giorni dopo il ritrovamento dell'«infante anonimo»), il luogo dell'abbandono non può essere un luogo comune, uno di quelli che solitamente si scelgono in quei casi infelici, come il portone d'accesso di un ospedale o di un orfanotrofio, o i gradini di una chiesa, col rischio che la neonata senza nome venga confusa con un'altra. Il luogo dell'abbandono dev'essere unico e molto riconoscibile, un posto chiaro del mondo, al quale fare riferimento nella lettera, senza che nella mente di chi la leggerà si formi l'ombra dell'ombra di un dubbio.

Scelgono, dunque, uno spazio spettacolare, paradossalmente quasi trionfale, per loro forse simbolico, o – meglio – affettivo.

«D'accordo. Fin qui ci siamo, – ragiono ad alta voce, – ma perché ritardare la scoperta della mia identità?»
Qual è il senso segreto dell'enigma? Perché montare un piano di sospensione, rischiando inoltre che la lettera – peraltro priva di indirizzo stradale – non venga mai recapitata?

Perché separare il corpo dal suo nome? O, meglio, dalla sua identità legale? Per sottolineare il valore primario del corpo, il quale basta a se stesso e domanda salvezza, qualunque nome gli sia stato imposto?
O a sottolineare l'importanza del nome, al quale è legata una storia biografica, unica e irripetibile, come unica e irripetibile è la storia biografica di tutti?

Mentre affollo la sera romana e la testa castana di mia figlia di siffatte astrazioni, ora sfilando senza neanche accorgermene lungo le appetibili e ignorate vetrine di via Appia Nuova, la pazientissima Anna, che ha il dono (evidentemente non ereditario) di non perdere mai di vista la geometria del reale, consegna un'altra volta la soluzione. Rapida, pragmatica, semplicissima:
«Perché vogliono fare scalpore».

Lucia e Giuseppe vogliono che la loro bambina, insieme alla storia che ha condotto al suo abbandono, venga notata. Non vogliono che la loro tragica storia venga confusa con altre pur tragiche, paragonabili storie.

Il mio piccolo oracolo ha ancora una volta ragione.
In quegli anni, come abbiamo scoperto a Milano insieme a Lucia, è frequente che povertà, carenze di legge o pregiudizi altrui spingano i genitori ad abbandonare i

figli neonati: all'I.P.P.A.I. Lucia ha visto coi suoi occhi la pur meritoria catena di montaggio neonatale, la schiera di bambini lavati da mani troppo esperte, del tutto prive delle goffaggini e degli indugi materni che formano un destino irripetibile, ha visto lattanti piú e meno amorevolmente cullati da un'equivalente schiera di balie, che affolla gli stanzoni coi pavimenti a rombi. Tutti uguali. Tutti soli.

Colpiti al cuore da quella brulicante solitudine infantile, Lucia e Giuseppe, che a loro volta hanno abitato esilio e solitudine, non desiderano quel destino anche per Maria Grazia, non vogliono che la figlia cresca cosí, schiacciata dal bruciante volume degli abbandoni: non a Milano, ma neanche a Roma. Allora, pensano.

Consapevoli che il rilascio di neonati innanzi ai brefotrofi o sui gradini delle chiese è purtroppo un numero in carne e ossa che va a sommarsi a un lungo elenco di numeri in carne e ossa, Lucia e Giuseppe stabiliscono di mettere in salvo il loro unico futuro possibile tramite una successione di azioni comprensibili solo alla luce di un'uguale mania: simulando, fino ad assumerlo provvisoriamente, lo stato alterato di coscienza, la cupola di senso maniacale, l'altra logica (troppo stabile, contronaturale) di chi si prepara a morire. Spingiamoci con loro, un passo oltre la soglia del tirannico *voler vivere* d'ogni nostra cellula.

Febbricitanti a freddo, ultracorpi allucinati dal controsenso, Lucia e Giuseppe escogitano un gesto pazzo e forte, che attragga l'attenzione sulla bambina
   e la loro bambina non rovini nella loro rovina. Maria Grazia è serena, spontaneamente allegra, abituata a tutti. Maria Grazia abbraccia tutti.

La vita degli adulti, responsabili, sia il prezzo. Ma non sacrificare la pura vita. Cosí è deciso.

Lo scritto

Forse Lucia e Giuseppe non si aspettano che anche la notizia della neonata trovata a Villa Borghese riempia le pagine dei giornali. Forse la storia ha piú risonanza di quanta Lucia e Giuseppe abbiano immaginato, ma le cose sono comunque andate come la concatenazione di eventi messa in moto dalle loro vive e ultime volontà lascia immaginare che desiderassero.

Lucia e Giuseppe non volevano dare l'impressione di essersi disfatti della figlia e, insieme, volevano pronunciare pubblicamente le proprie ragioni, legarle al tribunale del futuro. Chi sa, se hanno pensato che io pure avrei letto le loro parole. Chi sa, se le hanno scritte anche perché echeggiassero nella mia vita.

Adesso che li conosciamo meglio, mettiamo la nostra sensibilità al servizio delle poche frasi espresse nel testamento pubblico di Lucia e Giuseppe:

> La bambina trovata a Villa Borghese si chiama Greco Maria Grazia. Nata a Milano il giorno 15 ottobre 1965 [*sic*]. L'ho abbandonata in Roma. Perché il mio amico non aveva possibilità finanziarie da sostenerla e mio marito cioè suo padre diceva che non era sua. Trovandomi in condizioni disperate, Non ho scelto altro che la strada di lasciare mia figlia alla compassione di tutti, ed io con il mio amico pagheremo con la vita ciò che abbiamo fatto, o, indovinato o, sbagliato
>
> Galante Lucia in Greco

Lo scritto comincia con le parole «La bambina» e la telegrafica narrazione si svolge tutta in relazione alla mia persona, nominata una seconda volta dalla firmataria Lucia come «mia figlia». Quel possessivo.

Quel possessivo singolare: siccome vogliono regolarizzare la mia esistenza in vita, Lucia e Giuseppe non possono scrivere «nostra». Giuseppe è obbligato a disconoscermi, attribuendo di suo pugno la paternità della mia persona a un altro, loro benché legittimo persecutore. Mio padre mi ripudia però all'imperfetto, istruendo una rinuncia che già pertiene ai bilanci della memoria («non aveva», «diceva»). Cosí agisce la psiche di chi ha ormai deciso che l'intera sua vita sia passato, e il passato un ingombro da lasciare cadere, come una rima di colatura del superfluo dalla distruzione del vivere. Tu, vita, prenditi quello che credi perduto e lasciami ciò che è mio.

Nel singulto dei tempi verbali, trasale l'animo di chi li impiega: quella coppia già avvolta in una radiazione siderale, che mette al presente soltanto il nome della propria figlia. Solo il mio falso nome è il presente (il reale), nel bianco immateriale che li assorbe. Sono medianici, riversati nell'identità dell'altro, sono materia che decifra l'immateriale. E se ne va. Divinità. Divino. Cosí nascono mito e religioni, da questa irrimediabile assenza basale. Anche di sé: da sorella morte.

Tanto piú evanescente è lui, Giuseppe, fermo dietro le quinte, innominato e anonimo: per due volte è «l'amico» di Lucia.

La maggior parte della breve lettera viene utilizzata per spiegare il motivo di quello che dagli stessi Lucia e Giuseppe viene detto abbandono. Solo l'ultimo periodo è dedicato a se stessi, e rivolge alle loro due vite l'unica frase fatta, dal tono duro, noncurante e determinato: «pagheremo con la vita». Senza ombra di patetismo, senza dramma. Essi estranei a se stessi. Il suicidio viene prospettato come conseguenza doverosa della situazione nella quale versano. Essi guardano alle loro due vite ed emettono una condanna morale e mortale sulle loro due vite. In quegli anni non si dà comunque alla propria esistenza l'esagerata importanza di oggi: per quanto si desideri la gioia, si ha la ferma coscienza di essere un'irrisoria particella del gran corpo sociale.

La causa del suicidio non è solo la miseria, la causa del suicidio è anche una sentenza, emanata contro se stessi da Lucia e Giuseppe, che si ergono a voce del giudizio con la voce di un altro, con una formula preconfezionata: «pagheremo con la vita».

Lucia e Giuseppe si condannano a morte con la voce di altri, ormai alieni a se stessi. Sembrano il popolo chiamato a giudicare, che si rivolta contro se stesso. Sembrano due ventriloqui, hanno introiettato la censura sociale. A quel punto la decisione è presa, con fermezza: noi pagheremo «ciò che abbiamo fatto, o, indovinato o, sbagliato». L'ultima parola prima della firma, la seconda fra le due possibilità, è *sbagliato*. Poi, la lettera finisce senza punto.

Ma a cosa riferiscono l'espressione «ciò che abbiamo fatto»? All'intera vicenda, dalla peccaminosa scaturigine, definita dalla stessa stampa – tranne, come vedremo, a onore della loro scelta, dall'«Unità» – «adulterio», «peccato», «amore sbagliato», «concubinaggio»? O si riferiscono esclusivamente al gesto dell'abbandono, cioè al pagare (con la vita) il gesto di avermi abbandonata? Ma il gesto dell'abbandono è stato il penultimo – il suicidio rappresentando l'ultimo – anello di una catena di azioni alle quali Lucia e Giuseppe sono stati indotti e costretti.

Lucia e Giuseppe intendono pagare l'orgoglio di essersi amati che, data la convenzione sociale di quegli anni, ha come conseguenza l'impossibilità di «sostenere» una figlia. Le due cose sono – è il caso di dire – una figlia dell'altra: se non si fossero amati, non avrebbero nessuno da abbandonare.

Chi sa se Lucia e Giuseppe non conoscono la parola *sostentare* o se vogliono deliberatamente attribuire una sfumatura psicologica al carico rappresentato da una neonata, appunto, da *sostenere*, come Atlante sostiene l'intero globo terracqueo. Un neonato ha bisogno di tutto. La sua esistenza sottopone gli adulti a uno sforzo, psicologico ed economico che, forse, a Giuseppe dev'essere sembrato insostenibile. Il testamento contiene infatti un lapsus: la mia data di nascita è spostata a un giorno che, al momento della composizione della lettera, deve ancora venire: il 15 ottobre 1965.
Chissà quante richieste di lavoro ha già scritto Giuseppe, mettendo data e firma dell'anno in corso. Oppure, semplicemente, mentre scrive le sue ultime, definitive parole, preferirebbe che io non fossi nata. Lo capisco. Una scheggia insolente di futuro che deflagra nel loro diseredato presente.

La vita come prezzo, dunque. Ma lasciando comunque serpeggiare il dubbio finale che *quello che hanno fatto* possa essere stato «indovinato». Senza rivendicare la legittimità delle proprie azioni. Ma senza neanche discolparsi per il proprio amore, lasciano agli altri l'onere di giudicarli. Soppesateci voi, a noi adesso non importa piú sapere se abbiamo o meno avuto ragione di agire come abbiamo agito. Il solo verbo coniugato al futuro è «pagheremo»: l'avvenire di Lucia e Giuseppe si restringe al pagamento che resta loro da onorare.

In quel momento Lucia e Giuseppe sono liberi di scrivere tutto quello che vogliono, hanno la possibilità di difendere la propria scelta e scagliarsi contro chi li ha rifiutati e giudicati e li ha fatti talmente soffrire da indurli prima all'esilio e infine al suicidio. Eppure, la lettera mantiene un tono mite. Le parole si tengono ai fatti: pulite, esplicative, descrittive. La loro è una lingua di prassi, che aderisce alle cose.

Anche quando rendono conto di una disperazione tale da indurre chi scrive al suicidio, lo fanno con ammirevole dignità. Sbaglio. Lo fanno forse ormai con distacco. Col distacco da sé che immagino preluda all'abbandono della propria vita, quando l'analisi delle proprie emozioni ha perduto il calor bianco della tragedia e resta l'esoscheletro, la spoglia ninfale del resoconto di un dolore insopportabile, al quale il disperato sta finalmente per sottrarsi, morendo.

Ma, anche in questo caso, sono le «condizioni» a venire descritte come disperate: chi scrive non riferisce la disperazione alla propria persona. Si intuisce che, posta in contesto favorevole (immaginiamola legittimamente divorziata e accolta da una comunità benigna), la persona che nella breve lettera dice «io», continuerebbe di buon grado a vivere. Ha ventinove anni, è innamorata, ha una figlia neonata. Se solo non trovasse davanti a sé soltanto strade chiuse, Lucia vivrebbe, forse ancora, la sua vita arriverebbe forse a lambire questo 15 gennaio 2022, ovunque pieno di sole

e su questa panchina di un parco periferico della nostra bella Roma

oggi non scriverei della sua morte.

Tutta la lettera, tranne la firma, è scritta dalla mano di Giuseppe, che però non firma la dichiarazione di suicidio.

La grafia di Giuseppe è chiara e ferma, ordinata. Traspare tutto: non è una pagina vergata sotto l'impulso di un'onda emotiva al tavolino di un bar o su un muricciolo.

È la notte del 23 giugno, Lucia e Giuseppe sono seduti al tavolo della cucina che stanno per abbandonare, ci sono io che dormo accanto a loro, sulla tavola c'è qualcosa di rosso (un pomodoro, una mela) e c'è la pagina bianca. Giuseppe impugna la sua stilografica:

«Dobbiamo dire chi è, dove la troveranno...»

«La bambina»... La superficie liscia delle cose regge, Giuseppe comincia a scrivere stendendo l'inchiostro delle parole con la massima calma che il contenuto rende possibile, si prende pure il tempo di essere elegante, svirgolare dal testo con qualche svolazzo. «L'ho abbandonata in Roma». Punto.

Poi, la scrittura cambia, sembra procedere alla cieca, non è piú un documento ufficiale, le parole si piegano in fondo al foglio, che non le può contenere. Non le può contenere. Lucia incalza:

«Metti perché... Lo devono sapere...»

Di chi è la voce che aggiunge

«Io, lo devo sapere...»

E di chi sono gli occhi che mi guardano. Poco dopo, un indizio: le parole «strada» e «figlia» sono acquerellate da qualcosa di liquido. Dopo avere composto la frase «Trovandomi in condizioni disperate», chi scrive non riesce piú a mantenere un contegno. Conclude la condanna, fino all'ultima goccia, a lettere sempre piú piccole e affrettate. La lettera è divisa in tre parti. Tre organi di senso, tre brandelli. Le tre persone lí presenti, ancora.

«Firma, Lucia...»

Strano che il tavolo non si sia aperto in due. Le cose, come sono indifferenti. La firma di Lucia è a bordo foglio, e tira al basso come un tralcio di vite che si stia per spezzare. La grafia è piú esperta e piú svelta, rispetto alla stenta sigla sulla carta d'identità che, nel comporre la parola «Galante», riprendeva la «enne» lasciando, tra la «enne» e la «a» che la precede, un infantile tratto d'incertezza, e attaccava la «elle» di Lucia con due arzigogoli fiduciosi e lenti. Lucia adesso apre la «G» iniziale del cognome e la «elle» del nome svetta, nervosa e decisa. Lucia ha perso la sua pacatezza. «Greco», patronimico del suo carceriere, è l'ultima parola che è costretta a scrivere da viva. Oh, se aveva sperato di sfuggirgli! Ma non era finita la tua pagina, Lucia, e adesso scrivi, con le mani mie, la vita che hai già scritto col tuo sangue in me.

Di certo, tra la prima e l'ultima firma della sua esistenza, Lucia Galante ha pianto molte lacrime: lo testimoniano in molti, è una ragazza espansiva e una donna che piange. Certo si è fatta forza, forse si è indurita, sicuramente contro se stessa. Quella che lascia non è ormai piú una lettera sentimentale, è uno scritto deciso, di cose, nel quale Lucia e Giuseppe intendono spiegare due gesti spaventosi (abbandonare una figlia e poi uccidersi) senza nessun ornamento, senza accusare, prendendo su di sé la piena responsabilità delle proprie azioni di adulti.

E, da adulti, danno la propria pubblica, ultima e definitiva versione dei fatti. Loro, costretti alla fuga e all'esilio, obbligati a nascondersi come criminali, probabilmente fino a non riuscire a trovare lavoro in una società che comunque ancora abbonda di offerte, vogliono pronunciare a voce alta la propria verità. E, per farlo, selezionano un «pubblico» che sperano riceva le loro parole con *compassione*, prefigurandomi – come vedremo – un destino: le parole di Lucia e Giuseppe sono destinate ai lettori di un quotidiano che porta in prima pagina la dicitura esplicita «Organo del Partito comunista italiano».

Ogni abbandono ha la sua logica interna. Questa dunque la logica del mio, emersa dall'analisi di due menti pensanti, riesumate dal fondo del tempo: condotto in modo da fare notizia, e col sostegno di un giornale letto da operai come loro, e da intellettuali di sinistra.

Costruito l'evento a loro postumo, Lucia e Giuseppe possono verosimilmente assicurare alle proprie coscienze che la figlia superstite, quando loro non saranno piú in grado di proteggerla attivamente, finirà nelle mani di persone perbene. E ci finirà presto, potrà divincolarsi quasi subito dalla pania di tanta solitudine.

Nella prevedibile ipotesi che Luigi non ne voglia sapere della sottoscritta, come in effetti avviene, Lucia e Giuseppe ritengono che la loro storia possa essere meglio compresa dai lettori di quel giornale, e io abbia immediata speranza di venire adottata da una famiglia sensibile e *studiata*. Una famiglia che legge «l'Unità». Come in effetti avviene.

E avviene pure che «l'Unità» sia il solo quotidiano a riportare due approfondimenti sociali sul caso, entrambi a firma D.N.:

Una tragedia da ricordare, del 29 giugno, dove chi scrive sembra convalidare a caldo la scelta del suicidio, mostrando di comprendere, con amarezza arrabbiata, che il futuro di Lucia e Giuseppe sarebbe stato la «stabile prospettiva di una vita illegale e densa di costante miseria», dovuta alle «ferree e ipocrite leggi del moralismo borghese»;

e *Il rifiuto non basta*, trafiletto del giorno successivo, nel quale D.N. ha avuto tempo per riflettere, ha ripensato le sue stesse parole, e l'indomani, quando la sua emotività è tornata a depositarsi al fondo della morale (o delle direttive della testata giornalistica), coglie l'occasione di quei due corpi rinunciati per impartire ai lettori una breve lezione di politica, rimproverando i suicidi di aver sferrato, con la loro morte, «una sfida soltanto romantica» alla società, piuttosto che essersi impegnati a combattere, giorno dopo giorno, nella lotta collettiva che vuole cambiare «un mondo ancora fondamentalmente primitivo».

Scritto col sangue sull'acqua

Lucia e Giuseppe hanno dunque scelto con criterio: «l'Unità» ha dato voce politica alla loro motivazione umana, mentre su altri quotidiani i fatti vengono riportati con termini irrispettosi, quando non umilianti o disturbanti, come il titolo dato da «Oggi Illustrato» del 15 luglio 1965 al doppio paginone a firma Stefano Giordani: *Maria Grazia non sa che la sua mamma si è uccisa per lei.*

Eccomi, faccia a faccia col gruppo cruciale: che la mia vita sia costata la vita quanto meno di mia madre, la bella Lucia.
Bisturi.
Incisione, estrazione, dissezione del glommo di materia reattiva. Il bolo ruminato, l'indigesto. La mina alla radice della vita. Facciamola brillare.

La nascita di una bambina complica l'esistenza di Lucia e Giuseppe, per un numero congruo di ragioni che è superfluo spiegare. La notizia della gravidanza dell'amante, nella *Vita agra*, viene accolta da Luciano (interpretato dal naturalistico Ugo Tognazzi) con queste parole: «Ci sei rimasta!», accompagnate da corollario di relative considerazioni sul «pasticcio in cui ci si viene a trovare».

Ipotizziamo che l'andarsene volontario di Lucia (il solo accertato) sia stato il piú amoroso, generoso e pieno di ambigua grazia dei gesti: allontanarsi, nella speranza di offrire all'abbandonato una vita piú degna di quella che vivrebbe in nostra compagnia.

Cosí pensando, abbiamo rovesciato il tavolo dell'abbandono, trasformando la feroce rinuncia in gesto d'amore. Questo valga per i molti compagni dell'I.P.P.A.I. di Milano, dell'I.P.A.I. di Roma e per tutti i neonati lasciati soli. Questo passaggio è chiaro, è emotivamente comprensibile.

Lucia non si limita però a privarci del reciproco amore, per farmi crescere in una casa all'altezza dei sogni di una madre. Lucia va via pure dalla sua vita.

Il suicidio è un eccesso di abbandono, è il superfluo, il ricamo di sangue sul male. Ipotizziamo che sia stato per questo, che davvero *la mia mamma si sia uccisa per me*: si tratta di andarsene, ma già sapendo di non poter sopravvivere al dolore e alla colpa di aver respinto una figlia. Gettando però, cosí, sulle spalle della figlia il proprio addio, come un mantello pesante, dal quale ella (io) si deve una volta per tutte divincolare.

Ho sempre rifiutato il fardello di questo eccesso di sacrificio, che peraltro mi colloca in una centralità sproporzionata dentro la vita di Lucia, che certo aveva altri sentimenti, altri legami, altri impegni, oltre al suo incommensurato amore per me, sua figlia.

Lucia ha dimostrato, piú di una volta, di sapersene andare. Lucia fa i fatti. E i fatti dicono che non improvvisa, che organizza – anzi – il proprio sacrificio sull'altare del fiume con lucidità e calma, portando prima a compimento ogni proprio dovere, ogni congedo. È dunque possibile che quel titolo perturbante riassuma in parte correttamente lo stato d'animo di Lucia Galante, mia madre, nel senso complesso appena analizzato, col massimo equilibrio del quale oggi dispongo.

La verità dedotta appare migliore e peggiore di quella espressa nel titolo: mia madre non si è uccisa *per me* (migliore), bensí anche *a causa mia* (peggiore). La mia nascita ha contribuito a far esplodere l'ordigno già innescato di una congiuntura esistenziale di abbandoni e rifiuti, di fiatella sociale alla nuca.

Finalità del suo morirsene non ero dunque io (*per me*), ma abbandonare il soma per abbandonare sulla riva del fiume la soma intollerabile dell'esistenza. Non sono stata io, però, a rendere intollerabile la sua esistenza. Anzi, direi: tutt'altro.

Qui mi permetto di allargare brevemente la zona di autocoscienza dello scritto, esponendo l'ovvio dentro un piccolo corpo di otto righe: quando una figura primaria decide di scollarsi dal paesaggio della vita di un figlio, può verosimilmente immaginare di lasciare, in luogo di sé, la forma ustoria di un'assenza che, chi rimane, passerà la vita (o parte di essa) a cercare di ridimensionare, ripiegandola come un origami, per rendere tascabile il metafisico: coi suoi mezzi, inutili e mortali come quelli di tutti, e che passano pure di moda. Rovesci di parole, nel caso mio. Aria modulata. Inno al nulla. O prodigio.

Dal passato, dall'orlo di quel fiume dove vuole senz'altro riposare, Lucia collabora coi miei intenti futuri: cerca, con tutte le sue forze, di dominare il tragico e arrecare il minore dei mali

L'articolo continua infatti con una lunga intervista al vicedirettore dell'istituto di Villa Pamphili, professor Stefano Moschini, che manifesta sotto i nostri occhi l'istantanea di un miracolo. Il neuropsichiatra afferma che Maria Grazia «è una bambina molto bella. Sorride a tutti, non ha mai pianto, non ha rivelato traumi per il cambiamento d'ambiente al quale è stata bruscamente sottoposta. Prima ancora che la lettera della madre ci indicasse la sua data di nascita, avevamo già stabilito, da diversi fattori, che doveva avere intorno agli otto mesi; ma da un punto di vista psichico direi che dimostra dieci mesi, un anno. È vivace, intelligente. Denota di essere vissuta in un ambiente familiare sereno, si capisce che la madre ha fatto l'impossibile perché la bambina non fosse toccata dal dramma che stava sconvolgendo la sua vita, e che avrebbe avuto la sua tragica conclusione con il suicidio nel Tevere. E c'è riuscita, per uno di quei miracoli che soltanto le madri sanno compiere. Nella lettera che la donna ha scritto prima di morire, c'è anche un accenno al fatto che né lei né il suo amico potevano piú provvedere ai bisogni della bimba, ma fino all'ultimo alla piccola non è mancato niente: è in perfette condizioni di salute, sana e ben nutrita. È una bambina intorno alla quale c'è sempre stato un grande affetto, è stata coccolata, insomma: lo si comprende dal fatto che spesso vuole essere presa in braccio. Non lo fa per capriccio, ma per un desiderio divenuto naturale per l'abitudine».

Ecco dunque che penso di nuovo l'impensabile, cioè che i miei genitori rimandino volontariamente il momento di uccidersi fin che io sia autonoma abbastanza, ma ancora inconsapevole di quanto accade. Un pensiero quasi impossibile da pensare, ma forse è andata cosí. Di certo, mia madre mi ha insegnato a fidarmi del mondo nonostante tutto, a fidarmi di tutti. Una lezione fatta solo coi gesti: esemplare, preverbale, cosí profonda da diventare natura.

Intelletto d'amore

L'amore di Lucia *per me*, a me in persona sicuramente e semplicemente destinato, sta nel non avermi portata con sé nella morte, sta nel *dove non mi ha portata* e nel suo avermi riconsegnata alla vita. Alla vita di tutti. Facendo, della mia vita, fin dalle sue origini, vita che torna a tutti.

Infine, nell'aver sopportato, per quel suo pur brevissimo tratto di sopravvivenza, lo strazio di andarsene lasciandomi nel rischio al quale mi esponeva, abbandonandomi.

In quegli anni, però, si accorda piú fiducia ai bambini, e alla vita tutta. La vita fa una musica diversa, basso profondo con piccoli trilli di risate. Chi ha sopportato la guerra, riposa nella giusta convinzione che chi ha voglia di vivere sopravviva a quasi tutto. Che non esista vita senza ferita. Nessuno resta integro, se vive.

Malgrado questa diffusa saggezza, le ultime volontà di Lucia e Giuseppe sono, comunque, mettere al riparo la vita della figlia, nel miglior modo a loro disposizione e nel miglior mondo da loro immaginabile e, soprattutto, raggiungibile, attraverso un moto interiore che possiamo definire con una sequenza di espressioni d'uso ordinario, tutte improvvisamente vivificate e chiare: «forza della disperazione», «ingegno dei poveri», «arte di arrangiarsi».

Ma, sopra tutte, splende e riluce un faro: la definitiva formula alchemica dantesca «intelletto d'amore», quel sentire dell'intelligenza che permette a una contadina e un muratore di montare pezzo a pezzo un caso di cronaca, per salvare il salvabile, cioè me, vita lasciata vivere e che deve scampare allo sfacelo.

Una volta e per sempre, Dante ha trovato il nome dell'amore immortale dei mortali.

Lucia s'è fatta il segno della croce, prima di immergersi. Anche se nei due anni con Giuseppe si è risolta a votare P.C.I., la sua fede politica ha certo convissuto col valore simbolico di un gesto che proviene dall'infanzia e lega al sacro della terra e dei cieli.

Poi, s'è affidata all'acqua, senza violenza. Sono certa – per quanto possibile – che sia andata cosí: un suicidio come questo non è un tuffo dal ponte, d'impulso, è un lasciarsi andare all'acqua, a un elemento simile alla vita prima della vita, simile al destino.

Alla compassione di tutti

A oggi, non esistono modi migliori, per fermare il tempo della nostra vita, se non morire. Non esistono modi per fermare il dolore del tempo se non il dolore definitivo di andarsene dal tempo, abbandonare i corpi degli altri al loro destino di stare immersi nel tempo. Anche il corpo di una figlia. Abbandonare il corpo di una figlia dentro il tempo e andarsene dal tempo. Un disarmo totale.

Lo stesso che arrese Marina Cvetaeva, sensitiva e polimorfa personalità della poesia. Riporto qui alcune parole che ho scritto intorno al suicidio di Marina Cvetaeva, avvenuto per impiccagione il 31 agosto 1941 a Elabuga, in Tataria, dove Marina non trova piú lavoro neanche come lavapiatti:

«Cvetaeva, che perdonerebbe e comprenderebbe tutto, non perdona se stessa di non perdonare la storia, di trovare la storia cosí imperdonabilmente diversa da come dovrebbe essere. È per questo stridore insostenibile tra realtà e giustizia che un poeta si uccide. O si fa uccidere, come Pasolini. A queste profondità, poco importa, importa solo che la vita che dovrebbe essere ci ha irrimediabilmente abbandonati, importa l'inguaribile esilio interiore, che un'anima cosí non si rassegna a cantare. Dunque, meglio restare eternamente muti e parlanti, come i morti sono muti e parlanti».

Alla vita dei morti possiamo invero aggiungere quel che vogliamo. Essi non sono ostili alle novità, e quasi mai sono definitivi.

Eccomi infatti a far parlare i miei morti. Lucia e Giuseppe, visti da cosí vicino da sentirne il respiro e da sentirli finalmente ridere, non paiono arresi alla totalità del disarmo. La dignità degli adulti sta nel senso di realtà. Soprattutto, è sapere di non sapere, accettare il mistero. A volte, significa riconoscere la propria nullità, di individui e di specie, e intuire quando arriva il momento di fermarsi, andarsene.

Quei due, però, non parlano soltanto coi comportamenti, scrivono anche parole che, prima o poi nella vita sperata, possono immaginare che avrei letto e, in quella loro cruda e acuminata insonnia di cinquantasette anni fa, inventano una formula bellissima, derivandola forse dai messali della misericordia mariana che Lucia compitava: «alla compassione di tutti».

Indosso quella formula come un diadema. Di piú: come un amuleto.

Quella frase reagente, che mescola una figlia al dominio del caso e alla fluida vita, di tutti, indica una strada che può diventare destino: affidarmi sorridendo in mani umane, alle mani di tutti, con la stessa fiducia che può avere un campo di malerba di venire lasciato a vegetare lí, nella svolta del paesaggio dove a filacce sfilano le nuvole sopra i rami del noce.

Questa mia vita, con il gratuito e a volte immeritato bene che incontra, aderisce ogni giorno alla disperata speranza di Lucia e Giuseppe. Ci vuole un gran coraggio, per sperare. La storia dice che Lucia e Giuseppe sono morti sperando. Il mio bene, almeno, se non piú il proprio. E loro due, mettiamoli tra quelli che hanno vinto l'invincibile solitudine del morire, morendo insieme.

Pellegrinaggio. Ipotesi uno

La luce dei fatti è retroattiva. L'analisi degli ultimi sviluppi schiara i due viaggi di Lucia nel caldo giugno di quell'anno, sola, mentre vive a Milano con Giuseppe: poiché a giugno entrambi hanno già deciso della propria vita, si aprono due ipotesi, che potrebbero richiedere l'inversione dell'ordine dei viaggi, avvenuti in una successione rimasta imprecisata.

La prima ipotesi è che Lucia e Giuseppe vogliano lasciarmi in mani sicure. Com'è ovvio, Lucia chiede per prima alla madre se può tenermi per qualche tempo (certo senza rivelarle le proprie intenzioni definitive). La madre vuole che Lucia rimanga, le chiede di tornare dal marito. Nonostante i dieci mesi di assenza di Lucia, la situazione lí non è cambiata. Lucia informa Giuseppe:

«Mamma se io non resto non la tiene. Andiamo via».

E se ne va, di notte, con l'identica dignità mantenuta nell'ipotesi precedente.

Se Lucia è venuta per questo, la conferma della rinuncia dei suoi familiari a tenermi è nei fatti: perché io possa essere adottata, nessuno degli aventi diritto legale a crescermi si è fatto avanti, né Amelia e Luigi, genitori di Lucia, né altri parenti di linea materna.

Incassato il rifiuto dei congiunti, Lucia pensa di cercare la sola altra persona della cui bontà d'animo si fida: Tonino, il ricordo piú semplice e dolce della sua vita. Ma fallisce di nuovo, non ottiene l'indirizzo.

Non avendo dunque nessuno cui affidare la figlia, non resta che consegnarla alle mani generose del mondo. L'inserimento della formula appena onorata («alla compassione di tutti») nel corpo della loro ultima lettera, mostra che Lucia e Giuseppe sono consapevoli del fatto che il recapito testamentario della mia persona al padre formale Luigi Greco non avrà effetto. Ciò nonostante, logorati dall'ansia della legge, mettono nero su bianco la pervicace menzogna. La quale, in quel mio frangente di passaggio dentro la neutra Terra di Nessuno, mi espone al pericolo di crescere con marito e suoceri di Lucia.

Ma il mio padre legale (comprensibilmente, benché negli inaccettabili termini riportati) non si presenta a esigermi, con ciò guadagnandomi definitivamente lo statuto di adottabile e con ciò guadagnandosi l'appellativo di Mostro. In paese, nessuno passa piú davanti alla sua porta.

Malgrado la propria stessa esperienza, Lucia e Giuseppe hanno ragione di confidare, ancora, nella solidarietà umana. In soli tre giorni le richieste di adozione sfiorano infatti l'inusitato numero di cinquanta, arrivano anche dall'estero: Germania, Austria, Stati Uniti d'America. La storia di Lucia, Giuseppe e Maria Grazia ha commosso tutti.

Il primo luglio vengo affidata all'ennesimo servizio sociale, l'U.A.I.R. (Ufficio assistenza infanzia riconosciuta), e si registra, dunque, un mio secondo ingresso ufficiale nell'I.P.A.I., stavolta decorata da numero 65 076 bis, dove il «bis» sta a significare che non sono piú ignota e i quarantotto numeri di differenza rispetto alla precedente numerazione indicano quarantotto bambini in meno, tra i riconosciuti, rispetto ai cosí detti figli di *Nomen Nescio*. Ma affogo comunque fra sigle e veli monacali, insieme ai circa quattrocentocinquanta miei piccoli compagni. Noi abbandonati nella capitale ci confermiamo innumeri.

L'ammontare della somma, dall'apertura dell'I.P.A.I., nel 1894, fino a quel momento, è 130 199 bambini in 71 anni: 65 124 + 65 076 - 1, perché io sono stata registrata due volte. A Roma, ogni anno, vengono abbandonati piú di 1800 neonati, in media cinquecento in piú che a Milano.

Poiché nessun consanguineo – o preteso tale – assume l'onere della mia crescita, l'8 luglio il giudice tutelare Luigi Reibaldi, con provvedimento urgente di efficacia immediata, mi affida in via temporanea alla famiglia ritenuta giusta per me, i coniugi Consolazione Nicastro e Giacomo Calandrone.

Le firme dei miei nuovi genitori sono: ferma, chiara ed equilibrata come l'acqua limpida quella di lui, disastrosa e convulsa quella di lei, inconsulta e ansiosa, leggibile solo a chi l'ha molto conosciuta e amata, la grafia di chi si stia freneticamente disfacendo di una noia insopportabile e ingiustificata, quando la meta è avermi fra le braccia. E cosí è, cosí sono Consolazione e Giacomo. Limpido e disastrosa. Due giganti.

Le cose sono andate come desideravano Lucia e Giuseppe.

Auguro ai miei compagni, uno per uno, la stessa buona sorte, lo stesso ristoro.

Ipotesi due. L'addio

La seconda ipotesi è la piú semplice: l'addio. A motivare il pellegrinaggio breve di Lucia nel giugno 1965.

Lucia vorrebbe solo dire addio all'amore venuto prima della catastrofe, ascoltare la voce della sua vita mancata, che le è rimasta accanto come un sogno insistente. Prima della dissoluzione nella quale ha deciso di procedere, Lucia vorrebbe far sentire a Tonino il suono della sua voce, dire al protagonista della sua storia immaginaria, di ragazzina invece sacrificata al denaro:
«Tonino, guarda cosa mi è successo»,
consistere un'ultima volta nei suoi occhi, scaldarsi all'energia di quelle belle mani da lavoro che da sessant'anni, ogni 16 febbraio, accendono una piccola candela rossa su un altarino domestico tempestato di conchiglie di mare. I gusci e i tuberocoli madreperlacei incastrati nel cemento a Lissone, vengono dalle rive di un azzurro lontano moto perpetuo, che illumina la terra nativa di Lucia con un andirivieni di bagliori e squame, e d'inverno trascina sui litorali una poltiglia di felci submarine e legni di deriva.

Eccolo, il distillato, il filo d'incandescenza
         che illumina una vita. Sono davanti alla quintessenza della vita di Lucia e Tonino, esposta all'angolo di un giardinetto che Lucia non ha raggiunto e Anna e io abbiamo visto per lei. Vita umana riassunta in concrezioni di mare e cera rossa rapprese su una tavola di pietra organica.

Lentamente, tra i vuoti delle inferriate, si allunga l'ombra di un tramonto boreale.

Cosí Lucia, un passo dopo l'altro scomparendo, un giorno dopo l'altro abbandonando la vita e il suo teorema, imperfetto e struggente, va a dare il proprio addio alla madre ignara. E se ne va con l'alba, senza salutare, perché non reggerebbe la separazione, l'insistenza, le lacrime. Un gesto di assoluta dignità.

E poi abbandona la sua vita già quasi trasparente in me. Perla. Calco. Matrice. Sovrabbondanza.

Messa in gloria

Non sappiamo che fine abbia fatto il corpo dell'annegato rimasto anonimo, che forse era Giuseppe. Non sappiamo dove siano i resti di Giuseppe, ovunque e comunque egli sia ormai morto.

Intanto, a Palata, la notizia del suicidio di Lucia passa di bocca in bocca. La banda dei ragazzini del paese la intercetta. Quando capiscono che è accaduto l'irrimediabile, i ragazzini esplodono contro Luigi, con la sintesi semplice e crudele dell'infanzia:
«Assassino! L'hai ammazzata tu!»
«Sei tu che l'hai fatta scappare!»
«Se n'è andata perché non sei normale!»
Luigi li insegue con le pietre in mano. Da quel momento, per tutti, Luigi diventa l'Orco.

L'Orco, il Mostro. Dopo i fatti, Gino Centolire, che sognava l'America e non è mai partito, continua a vivere come un eremita, in casa non allaccia la corrente elettrica, neanche i parenti vanno piú a trovarlo e lui si corica col primo buio, si alza all'alba e se ne va a dormire sotto gli alberi delle sue campagne, sempre piú solo. La vita l'ha schiantato in un'ubriacatura permanente.

Per il 27 luglio 1965 il direttore dell'I.P.A.I. di Roma dispone una santa messa in suffragio «della mamma» Lucia Galante, scomparsa «il 25 o 26 giugno». Sarà la sola messa in sua memoria. A parte questa posa di parole come fiori per sempre.

Il suo fantasma, adesso, siede qui, dentro il ruminare delle macchine della lavanderia che sganciano le molle dei portelloni. Le piacerebbe. Mi siedo qui perché le piacerebbe. La meccanica, il senso delle cose come sono dentro. Lucia ama capire.

Il 22 gennaio 2022, arrivata a scrivere la centoventitreesima pagina di questo libro cominciato il primo gennaio, mi sveglio da un grande sogno, che dispone financo di un titolo: *Domenica di pioggia a Crescenzago*. Una pioggia cosí imponente da rovesciare il cielo sulle strade. Il viale che sto percorrendo diventa un fiume sotto le ruote del mio fuoristrada. Ma non ho paura, ormai sono capace di guidare dentro questo fiume. Anzi, guardo le cose dall'alto, vedo che tutto è bello, come appena rinato. Sono venuta a prenderti, Lucia. Qui dovevo arrivare. Anzi, tornare. A pagina 123 del mio dattiloscritto posso finalmente accarezzare il volto di mia madre, e il suo corpo di luce e di niente. E abbandonare il pregiudizio che solo la cultura ci permetta di capire le cose e conoscere il mondo fuori e dentro noi. Lucia aveva la seconda elementare, ma era libera. Perché aveva cuore. Quello che ancora splende, irreparabile.

Portami a casa

Sorge il carro, lentissimo, dal fondo della campagna. È la prima mezzanotte di luglio, il corpo di Lucia viene da Roma, ha attraversato un'altra volta l'ombra e le montagne, ha sfiorato i paesi dei dintorni, è risalito dalla provinciale fino alla soglia di casa. Ma non la fanno entrare, neanche morta: metà degli abitanti del paese è radunata al bivio in fondo alla via principale, appena fuori dall'abitato. Anche il parroco è sceso alle porte del paese, per consegnare a un Padre benigno la vita breve di Lucia Galante, senza aprire le porte della chiesa alla cassa coi resti. Aspettano. Da quando hanno saputo, a Palata non si parla d'altro. Stanotte anche i piú piccoli sono svegli, s'intrufolano tra le gambe dei genitori, sentono il capannello mormorare:
«È la ragazza che s'è buttata...»
Molti adulti sono caratteristi, tristi ruminatori di disgrazie, alcuni invece sono davvero qui, a fare notte per dare l'ultimo saluto alla figlia di questa terra. I ragazzini grandi, contagiati dal turbamento degli adulti, corrono avanti e indietro:
«Sta arrivando, sta arrivando!»

Il carro ferma al bivio dove c'è la gente. Asperso il legno della bara con acqua benedetta, chiuso il portellone sulla riconfermata solitudine del proprio corpo, Lucia passa sola lungo la strada dove andava a scuola, s'inoltra nella notte senza luna. Prima di andarsene, Lucia mi ha insegnato la parola mamma. Per stanotte, la lasciano nella stanzetta del cimitero, in attesa di orario di lavoro per la sepoltura.

L'indomani, la mettono in silenzio dentro la sua terra, a occhi bassi e in furia per la vergogna. Senza messa e senza funerale. Perché Lucia, che ha voluto a ogni costo scegliere la vita, ha infine rinunciato al dono della vita, come ultima libertà possibile.

Quarantasette anni dopo, la rimuovono dalla terra, per locarla in ossario comune, perché a qualcuno serve di passare dove lei dorme senza disturbare. Ecco il sole di un sabato di maggio toccare gentile
        la tua poca materia. Che la musica sia con te, figlia mia.

Grazie

Ho cominciato a scrivere questo libro il primo gennaio 2022. Il 12 febbraio ho finito. Quarantaquattro giorni fuori dal mio tempo.

L'ho concluso di nuovo il 4 marzo, avendo aggiunto le pagine relative a scoperte e accadimenti successivi alla data del 12 febbraio.

Grazie prima di tutto a mia figlia Anna, che mi ha accompagnata in Molise, nelle peregrinazioni a piedi attraverso Roma e infine a Milano, Lissone e Crescenzago, regalandomi le sue preziosissime intuizioni e la colonna sonora che mi ha tenuto compagnia nei momenti piú severi delle indagini e della scrittura. Grazie a mio figlio Arturo, che spesso si è strappato ai suoi studi storici, travolto dal mio entusiasmo per ogni nuova scoperta, testimonianza o ritrovamento, durante le ricerche e lo studio delle fotografie e dei fascicoli d'archivio.

Grazie alla generosità di Costanza Rizzacasa d'Orsogna, che ha tenuto a battesimo la mia storia e grazie all'accoglienza intelligente e partecipe di Serena Bortone e della redazione di *Oggi è un altro giorno*, nelle persone di Giovanna Bonardi e Alessandra Di Pietro: questo libro è nato – nella realtà, prima che sulla pagina – quel 16 febbraio 2021, dai racconti dei telespettatori che mi hanno scritto attraverso la rete per rievocare, spesso con amore grande, i loro incontri con Lucia.

Grazie a mia cugina Laura Sappracone che, con molta pazienza, mi ha raccontato ripetutamente le avventure di «zia Lucia».

Grazie all'archivista di Palata Maria Teresa Vitulli che, oltre a fornirmi le pagelle di Lucia, si è appassionata alla storia e mi ha scritto un augurio memorabile: «Spero che tu possa vivere tua mamma e godere di un abbraccio lungo che va dal momento del distacco ad oggi».

Grazie alla sindaca Maria Di Lena per l'invito a tornare nel paese e per la toccante presentazione, curata con la giornalista Elena Berchicci.

Grazie ad Antonella De Angelis, alla quale sono grata per la ricerca degli originali delle foto e per la bellissima lettera che cito nel corpo del libro; a Rosetta Sacchi e a Gabriella Di Vito, che si è appassionata con il cuore alla storia di Lucia Galante e ne ha seguito con intelligenza i rovelli e le tappe.

Grazie a Gabriella Cavedo per la ricerca delle foto e a Rossana Bottinelli per le testimonianze sull'immigrazione interna in Lombardia.

Per alcune informazioni storiche e topografiche mi sono affidata alla memoria della guardia comunale e vigile di Palata Maurizio Marchetti.

Grazie per le preziose direttive tecniche all'amico avvocato e poeta Nicola Bultrini, grazie all'amico medico legale e scrittore Gino Saladini per le conferme anatomopatologiche e al regista Francesco Cannito per le notizie su Crescenzago.

Grazie a Sonia Bergamasco, Maria du Bessé, Patricia Peterle, Federica De Paolis e Franco Buffoni, per tutto tutto quello che sanno.

Grazie, infine e per sempre, alle mie due mamme: Consolazione, che mi ha dato le parole per dire di Lucia e una casa dove scriverle; e grazie a Lucia, per avere voluto, difeso e immaginato questa mia vita.

M.G.C.

Note

I versi in epigrafe sono tratti da Maria Grazia Calandrone, *Giardino della gioia* © 2019 Mondadori Libri S.p.A., Milano.

Le parole di Benito Mussolini citate a p. 17 fanno parte del discorso pronunciato il 25 ottobre 1938 al Consiglio nazionale del P.N.F.

L'estratto dal telegramma citato a p. 18, inviato a Churchill da parte del generale Montgomery, è contenuto in Winston Churchill, *La seconda guerra mondiale*, a cura di Aldo Chiaruttini, traduzione di Arturo Barone, © 2022 Mondadori Libri S.p.A., Milano.

Informazioni su Wolfgang Lenhing-Emden – cui si fa riferimento nel capitolo «Color guerra. Ferro naturale» – si trovano nell'intervista realizzata da Maria Cuffaro nel 1993 per la trasmissione *Il rosso e il nero* di Michele Santoro, poi trascritta nel «Corriere Matese» dell'11 ottobre 2011.

Immagine di p. 30: scritto memoriale di Antonio De Grandis, 18 agosto 2021.

I versi in latino che fanno da controcanto alla narrazione da p. 42 a p. 156 sono tratti dal Salmo 51, *Miserere*. Musicato, fra gli altri, da Gregorio Allegri intorno al 1630, recava indicazioni del compositore di eseguirlo a luci spente nella Cappella Sistina durante il mattutino, come parte dell'ufficio delle Tenebre della Settimana Santa. Le traduzioni dell'autrice sono, com'è evidente, liberissime, talvolta esclusivamente sonore.

I versi citati alle pp. 79-80 sono tratti da Vittorio Sereni, *Diario d'Algeria*, © 1998 Giulio Einaudi editore S.p.A., Torino.

La data della querela di Greco Luigi contro Galante Lucia citata a p. 89 si ricava dal «Messaggero» del 29 giugno 1965.

Le citazioni da Luciano Bianciardi a p. 100 e a p. 137 sono tratte da *La vita agra*, © Giangiacomo Feltrinelli Editore, Milano. Prima edizione nell'«Universale Economica» maggio 2013.

Le citazioni da Pier Paolo Pasolini a p. 100 sono tratte da *Poesia in forma di rosa*, 2021, Garzanti, Milano.

Le citazioni da Vitaliano Trevisan a p. 101 e a p. 139 sono tratte da *I quindicimila passi*, © 2002 Giulio Einaudi editore S.p.A., Torino e da *Il ponte*, © 2007 Giulio Einaudi editore S.p.A., Torino.

La prima citazione da Pier Paolo Pasolini a p. 109 è tratta da *Ragazzi di vita*, 2022, Garzanti, Milano.

L'epigrafe a p. 111 è tratta da Rainer Maria Rilke, *Elegie duinesi*, © Giangiacomo Feltrinelli Editore, Milano. Prima edizione nell'«Universale Economica» – I Classici, novembre 2006.

Immagine di p. 113: Milano, viale Monza e piazzale Loreto come apparivano in una cartolina del 1965.

Immagine di p. 120: modulo di accesso di Greco Maria Grazia all'I.P.P.A.I. di Milano, 24 ottobre 1964.

Immagine di p. 126: stralcio della lettera inviata da Greco Luigi all'I.P.P.A.I. di Milano, 24 gennaio 1964 [*sic!*].

I versi citati a p. 132 sono tratti da Giorgio Caproni, *Il «terzo libro» e altre cose*, © 2016 Giulio Einaudi editore S.p.A., Torino.

La dichiarazione «Non è quello che avevamo sognato...» a p. 140 fa riferimento a *La curt de l'America*, film-documentario del 2011 di Lemnaouer Ahmine e Francesco Cannito.

Immagini di p. 155, in alto: Roma, ingresso di Villa Borghese. (Foto Blackca / Wikimedia Commons); in basso: foto di Maria Grazia Greco tratta da «Oggi Illustrato» del 15 luglio 1965.

Il verso «Bellissima statua sommersa», contenuto nel titolo del ca-

NOTE

pitolo a p. 162, è tratto dalla canzone dei Matia Bazar *Ti sento*, testo di Aldo S. Stellita – musica di Sergio Cossu e Carlo Marrale, © 1985 Universal Music Publishing Ricordi Srl / BMG Rights Management (Italy) Srl. Tutti i diritti riservati per tutti i Paesi. Riprodotto su autorizzazione di Hal Leonard Europe BV (Italy).

L'epigrafe a p. 165 è tratta da Gottfried Benn, *Morgue*, © 1997 Giulio Einaudi editore S.p.A., Torino.

La citazione a p. 175 è tratta da Maria Grazia Calandrone, *Atto di vita nascente*, © 2010 LietoColle Editore – LietoColle è un marchio di Ronzani Editore, Dueville (VI).

Immagine di p. 178: mappa del percorso dei corpi di Giuseppe Di Pietro e Lucia Galante nelle acque del fiume Tevere. Disegno di Maria Grazia Calandrone.

Immagine di p. 199: Roma, piazza Esedra nel 1965 tratta da www.romaierioggi.it

La citazione a p. 231 è tratta da Maria Grazia Calandrone, *Versi di libertà. Trenta poetesse da tutto il mondo*, © 2022 Mondadori Libri S.p.A., Milano.

Il titolo dell'ultimo capitolo, «Portami a casa», nasce da una suggestione legata alla canzone *Runaway*, di Aurora.

Indice

LA MATERIA PRIMA
p. 5 Si chiamava Lucia
7 Lei che non è venuta dalle stelle (l'indesiderata)
11 Terra di Lucia vista dal futuro
14 Senti questa creatura come ride
17 Color guerra. Ferro naturale
22 E salutava sempre

TONINO
29 1947. La gioia oggettiva
33 1955
35 1958. Un quadernetto sotto il materasso

LUIGI
41 Fuori luogo e triste
43 Sabato 17 gennaio 1959. La sposa
45 Bianco su bianco
46 La casa coniugale
48 *Sch sch sfrusc sfrusc.* Condizionali
50 La casa di campagna
51 Come un diorama
52 Fa sera
53 Bellezza che è veleno
55 Confidenze di Lucia (del furore e del pianto)
58 Racconta la vigna
61 Le voci allegre. Sai dirmi se l'hai mai sentita ridere

p. 63 La casa nuova. Vista con elementi mobili
65 Lucia e il mare

GIUSEPPE

71 Entra in scena l'uomo
79 Frammenti d'Algeria
81 1962. Un simpatico forestiero
85 1963. La vita dopo gli scavi
87 Cecità
88 La ferocia
91 Il male minore
94 21 maggio 1964. Lucia agisce in piena luce
96 Festa di matrimonio
98 Esperanto economico
102 In viaggio

MILANO

105 L'arrivo in Stazione Centrale
106 Nella Milano dell'immigrazione
109 Francesco!
111 Lucia e la merce
114 Giovedí 15 ottobre 1964. Astronave Madre
116 Il principio è materia vivente
118 Il 22 ottobre,
120 24 ottobre 1964. Mito dell'erosione della pace
124 Cara Suora, dammi la testa della puttana e un Tir
127 Ma di tutta la scienza
130 Toccala solo con le mani pulite
132 3-14 marzo 1965. Civico 24. L'incubatrice
136 In nero
137 Martedí 27 aprile e 1 giugno 1965. Antipolio a Crescenzago
140 La stessa persona
141 Gesti e anima di Lucia Galante
143 L'ultima porta
145 16 giugno 1965. Minore di una

ROMA

p. 149	Giovedí 24 giugno 1965, ore 15,30. Deposizione
153	Ti chiamavo col pianto (tra i propilei neoclassici)
156	Sabato 26 giugno. La lettera
158	Fiume. Guarda l'acqua come ride
161	Domenica 27 giugno. Il costume da bagno
162	Era lei. «Bellissima statua sommersa»
165	*Miserere*
168	Gli accennati reperti
170	Dove non mi hai portata
173	Lunedí 28 giugno. Le cose lasciate sole
177	Martedí 29 giugno. Autopsia. Pianto della materia disabitata
180	Mercoledí 30 giugno. Corpi e altre invenzioni
184	Teoria dell'omicidio
192	Voi due e la notte

CRONOLOGIA DI UN AMORE

197	I puri fatti
205	L'ultimo giro
207	Ricostruzione di una retta
209	Vivo in un sogno sottoproletario
213	Corpo, nome, storia
216	Lo scritto
224	Scritto col sangue sull'acqua
227	il minore dei mali
229	Intelletto d'amore
231	Alla compassione di tutti
233	Pellegrinaggio. Ipotesi uno
236	Ipotesi due. L'addio
238	Messa in gloria
240	Portami a casa

243	*Grazie*
245	*Note*

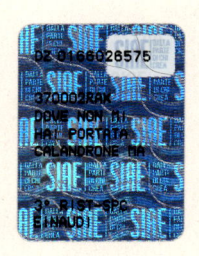

Stampato per conto della Casa editrice Einaudi
presso ELCOGRAF S.p.A. - Stabilimento di Cles (Tn)

C.L. 25747

Ristampa   Anno

        3   4   5   2023 2024 2025